# BARON WENCKHEIM'S HOMECOMING

# WARNING

He took an apple out of the basket, rubbed it, raised it to the light to examine it, made sure it was shining everywhere, and raised it to his mouth as if he wanted to bite into it, he didn't bite into it though, instead he drew the apple away from his mouth and he began to turn it around in his palm, while his gaze ranged over the people standing around, assembled before him; then the hand that was holding the apple dropped into his lap, he sighed deeply, leaned back a bit, and after a long silence which, in the whole heaven-sent world, meant nothing at all, he said: speak to me, say whatever you want, although he would actually recommend that no one say anything at all, because the person could say this or that, and it wouldn't have any meaning anyway, because he wouldn't feel himself in any way, shape, or form to have been addressed—you, he said in a metallic voice, will simply never be able to address me at all, because you don't know how to, it's more than enough for me if you somehow handle your instruments, because that's what's needed now, for all of you to somehow handle your instruments, because you have to make them ring, make them speak—he raised his voice—in other words make them *depict*, he explained, and there was this: he already knew everything, and, he added, he wouldn't mention at this point that he was already, of course, in the most complete possession of knowledge about everything, and this pertained to the matter that they—he raised the apple in his hand, and while he held it firmly in his palm with four fingers, he extended his index finger, and pointed at them—that they, music-making gentlemen, should inform him concerning all matters immediately, before me there can be no secrets, this is the main thing, I want to know about everything and in due time, regardless of the fact that—I reiterate—everything that could be possibly known is *already known* to me in the greatest possible detail, before me you must not be silent about anything, even the most insignificant detail must be reported to me, namely you are obliged, from this point on, to give to me unstinting accounts, namely, I am requesting your trust; and he began to explain what this meant, saying that something—in this particular case, the trust between them—needed to be unbounded as possible, without this trust they would never get anywhere, and now, at the beginning, he would like to chisel this forcefully into their brains; I want to know, he said, how and why you lift your instruments from their cases, and now, he explained, the word "instrument" should be understood, for simplicity's sake, in a general sense, namely he wouldn't start bothering with the details as to who was playing the violin, the piano, or who plays the bandoneon, the bass, or the guitar, as all of these were uniformly and appropriately designated by the term "instrument"—because the main thing, he said, is that I want to know what kind of strings the string players are using, how they tune them and why they tune them in that exact way, I want to know how many spare strings they keep in their case before the performance, I want to know—the metallic tone in his voice grew stronger—how much the pianists and the bandoneon players practice before the performance, how many minutes, hours, days, weeks, and years, I want to know what they ate today and what they're going to eat tomorrow, I want to know if they prefer spring or winter, the sun or the shade, I want to know ... everything, you understand, I want to see the exact image of the chair they practice on, and the music stand, I want to know exactly what angle it is set at, and I want to know what kind of resin is used, especially by the violinists, and where they buy it, and why exactly from there, I want to know even their most idiotic thoughts concerning the falling resin dust, or how often they trim their nails, and why exactly then; in addition, he also wished to enjoin them—he leaned back in his chair—that when he said he wanted to know—and they really shouldn't gape at him with such fear in their eyes —that also meant that he wanted to know the most insignificant details as well, and in the meantime they needed to realize for themselves, that he—whom essentially they could refer to as a kind of impresario, if somebody were to inquire—that he was going to observe their every step, their minutest of quivers, all the while knowing precisely in advance all about that possibly minutest of quivers, and they, all the while, would be obliged to make detailed reports about these matters: accordingly, they now found themselves between two fires—to sum up, on the one hand, there was, between them, this unconditional, unbounded trust, as well as the obligation to report everything; on the other hand, there was the undeniable, but for them endlessly disturbing, indeed unsolvable, paradox—don't try to comprehend this, he suggested—of his knowing in advance everything they were obliged to report, and in much more detail than they did; so their contractual agreement would, from this point on, proceed between these two fires, about which—and this is something that he would add, he added—they should be aware that this also implied an exclusively unconditional dependency, naturally unidirectional and one-sided; what they were going to tell him, he continued—and once again he began to turn the apple that was radiant in the resplendent light slowly in his palm—what they told him could never be shared with anyone else, take note, and for all eternity, he said, that what you are bound to tell me must only be told to me, and to no one else; and parallel to this, never expect that, under any circumstances, that I—he pointed to himself with the apple in his hand —following this present and (for you) fateful discussion, will say anything again, will explain or explicate or repeat anything—moreover, it would be even better if you listened to my words as if (and here I'm joking now), as if you were listening to the Almighty himself, who simply expects you to know what to do in any given situation, in other words, figure it out for yourselves, this is how things stand, there can be no mistakes, that metallic voice quivered more ominously than before, there would be no mistakes, because there *could be no mistakes*, everyone here, he opined, was capable of accepting this; of course he wouldn't claim that their cooperation henceforth—he was explaining what this entailed only once, namely right now, clearly, and in detail—would be a source of great joy for them, because it wouldn't bring them any joy, and it would be better if now, from this moment onward, they would regard it as suffering, as they would get along much better if now, at the very beginning, they would conceive it not as a joy, but as suffering, a kind of hard labor, because in reality what awaited them now was suffering, bitter, exhausting, and torturous work, when shortly (as the one single accomplishment of their cooperation, albeit an involuntary one), they would *insert* into Creation that for which they had been summoned; in brief, there was no room for mistakes here, just as there were to be no rehearsals, no preparation, no "well, let's take it from the top," and suchlike, they weren't just playing some *milonga* here, they had to know straightaway what they had to do, and these words, he said, no matter how misleading *in their essence*, or, if they were understanding him only on a superficial level —which was the case here—would never smooth away the aforementioned sweat and lack of joy, because that was their fate, through their activities no pleasure would ever be extended to them, for taken as individuals, what were they?—a band of music-making gentlemen, he thundered at them, just a troop of scrapers, a ragtag crew flailing away helter-skelter at their instruments, who could never take credit for the whole; by which, in their case, he meant the production before them, namely, in no way could they trace back to their own individual selves what they were to signify as a whole; so, he told them, they should realize this whole thing had nothing to do with them; if they took it upon themselves in full measure to honor their contract it would *somehow emerge*—who the hell knew how—but it *would emerge* somehow, and right now he could never repeat enough that he knew that this is how it would be, because this is how it had to be, it would be much better for them to resign themselves and not make any inquiries: as, for example, if in each particular case, the ineptitude was really so great, then how could the end result, created together, be so different—he wasn't willing to answer questions like this, he said with weary arrogance, no, as this was none of their business, they could rest assured that as a matter of fact, none of them were contributing anything, each with his own ineptitude, the mere thought should never enter their minds, but enough about that already, because just the mere thought of him having to think again and again—of the bow being scraped across that string *in that way*, or the keys being banged on *in that way*—filled him with dread; and all the while they would never understand anything of the whole, because the whole went so far beyond them, he was filled with horror, he stated with complete sincerity, considering the deplorable contingency of being badgered with questions, when he thought of how, just how much this aforementioned whole surpassed them as individuals ... but enough about that, he shook his head, if, nonetheless, the fact—not even sad, but rather laughable— was clear to him of whom he had to work with here, in the end it *would emerge*, indeed, already at the beginning he would speak as, according to expectations, he was compelled to—and as for rebellion—his voice suddenly became very subdued—if anyone even contemplates a plan against me, or if the desire would be manifest, even in a suggestion, that anything should be executed any differently than how I want it to be—well, do not even let this appear in your dreams, cast it out from your minds, or at least try to cast it out, because if you make any attempts, the ending will be woeful, and this is a warning, although not a benevolent one, because there's only one method of performance here which can be executed in only one way, and the harmonization of those two elements will be decided by me—he once again pointed to himself with the apple in his palm—and only by myself; you, gentlemen, you will play according to my tune, and believe me, I speak from experience, there is no point trying to oppose me, no sense at all; you can fantasize (only if I know about it), you can dream (if you confess it to me) that one day things will be otherwise, that they will be different, but it won't be otherwise, and it won't be different, it will be and it will be like this for as long as I am the—ah, if we're coming to this already—*impresario* of this production, as long as I'm directing what's going on here, and this "as long as" is something like eternity, because altogether I am contracting all of you for one single production, which is at the same time, for all of you in this role, the one single, possible performance; any such other performances are automatically excluded; there is no after, just as accordingly there is no before, and apart from your admittedly modest compensation there is no reward whatsoever, of course, accordingly, no joy, no consolation, when we're finished with it, we'll be finished, and that's all—but I must disclose to you now, he disclosed, and it was as if that metallic voice had softened just a bit for the very last time, that it will be none of those things for myself either, there will be no joy, no consolation, and it's not that I could care less whether there will be joy or consolation, or about what you'll all be thinking and feeling following this agreement that we have established, and not in the least about how you will explain the piteous quality of your participation here later on, namely what kfind of lies you'll be telling yourselves, I'm not talking about that, but about the fact that there is no joy for me in this whole thing, and my own fee is hardly tenable in view of what we are calling a production here—it shall come to pass, he said, because *it will be*, and that is all, I don't love and I don't hate you, as far as I'm concerned you can all go to hell, if one falls down, then another will take his place, I see in advance what will be, I hear in advance what will be, and it shall be sans joy and sans solace, so that nothing like this will ever come about ever again, so when I step onto the stage with you, musical gentleman, I won't be happy in the least, if this commission, predicated upon a possibility, comes to fruition—and I now wish to say this to you as a way of bidding farewell: I don't like music, namely I don't like at all what we are about to bring together here now, I confess, because I'm the one who is supervising everything here, I am the one—not creating anything—but who is simply present before every sound, because I am the one who, by the truth of God, is simply waiting for all of this to be over.

ALSO BY LÁSZLÓ KRASZNAHORKAI

*Animalinside*

*The Last Wolf* and *Herman*

*The Melancholy of Resistance*

*Satantango*

*Seiobo There Below*

*War & War*

*The World Goes On*

# BARON WENCKHEIM'S HOMECOMING

László Krasznahorkai

Tuskar Rock Press

First published in Great Britain in 2019 by
Tuskar Rock Press,
an imprint of Profile Books Ltd
29 Cloth Fair
London
EC1A 7JQ
*www.serpentstail.com*

First published in the United States of America in 2019 by New Directions

Originally published in Hungarian as *Báró Wenckheim hazatér*



The translator would like to acknowledge the kind support of the Hungarian Translators' House in Balatonfüred, Hungary, where the first draft of this translation was largely completed, as well as the kind assistance of the author in answering her queries.

Design by Erik Rieselbach

The quotation from the poem 'Consciousness' by Attila József is taken from the English translation by Michael Beevor at *www.babelmatrix.org.*



1 3 5 7 9 10 8 6 4 2

Printed and bound in Great Britain by Clays Ltd, Elcograf S.p.A.



A CIP catalogue record for this book is available from the British Library.

ISBN 978 1 78125 891 0
eISBN 978 1 78283 374 1

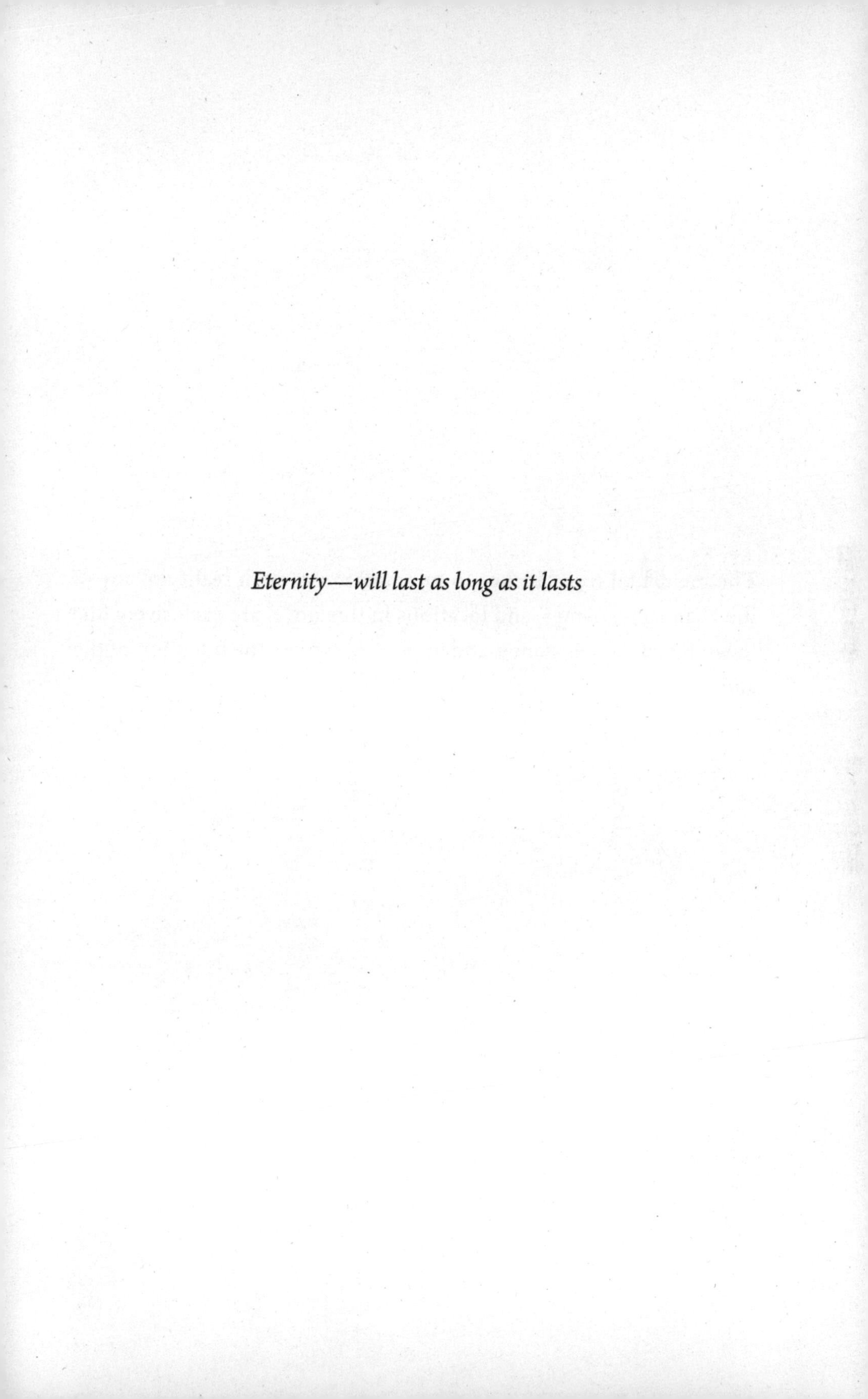

*Eternity—will last as long as it lasts*

The incidental resemblance to or concurrence with reality of any of the characters, names, and locations in this novel are exclusively due to wretched happenstance, and in no way express the intention of the author.

# DANCE CARD

*TRRR . . .*

# I'LL CUT YOU DOWN, BIG SHOT

He didn't want to go over to the window, he just watched from a respectable distance, as if those few steps he'd taken from there would offer protection, but of course he looked anyway, or more precisely, he was incapable of taking his eyes off it, because he tried to strain out, from the so-called clamor filtering in, just what was going on out there, but unfortunately at that moment no clamor filtered in, so altogether he would be able to state that there was silence, and as far as that went, there'd been silence for quite a while now, and yet after everything that he'd been forced to endure ever since yesterday, he really had no need to go over there, remove the Hungarocell polystyrene insulation panel, and peer out through the gap thus liberated, because even so it wasn't so difficult to extrapolate events, namely that from behind the security proffered by the Hungarocell panel, concealing the events taking place outside, he still knew with dead certainty that his daughter hadn't cleared off, she was still standing around there in front of his hut, accordingly approximately twenty-five or thirty steps away, so in a word he said to himself "I'm not going over there again, and I'm not going to look out there," and that's where things stood for a time, really, he stood, at a safe distance from the window, and he tried to listen, withdrawing, as it were, behind the protection of the Hungarocell panel, and in this state of protection—he repeated to himself, not only inside his brain, but aloud— there was no point in removing the Hungarocell panel yet again when he'd only be greeted with the same sight as before, no point, he shook his head, but like someone who knew that he was on the verge of removing it again anyway, well, what could he do, he was flustered, already yesterday evening at 5:03, accordingly after twilight, he'd believed it was all over already, and that didn't happen, because night came, morning came, and ever since then, every single time he pried the Hungarocell panel away, already even while he was moving his hands, he had absolutely no doubt that as soon as he shifted that panel and gazed out through the crack, he would see exactly what he'd seen before, just as his daughter out there would notice that in his so-called "window" the Hungarocell panel had been moved, namely that she would get a glimpse of her father, purse her mouth contemptuously, and *immediately* raise that rotten sign toward his head, a smile appearing on her face that would send chills down his back, because this smile told him that he was going to lose—so he concentrated as much as he could for a bit, from his secure bunker, on everything that was happening outside, but then he couldn't take it anymore, and because no sounds were filtering in now, he once again removed the Hungarocell panel from its opening, and then he put the panel back again, because of course he had sized up the situation in a single second, and because of this—and not for the first time ever since this whole circus started up—his hand began to shake so much from nervousness that, as he tried to stuff the Hungarocell panel back into the crack, small bits and pieces began crumbling off of it, but he couldn't stop his hand from shaking, he just looked at his own hand as it trembled and that caused him to be filled with suddenrage, which made him even more nervous, because he was certain that he wouldn't be able to make any good decisions with this suddenrage, and he had to be able to make good decisions, he began to repeat to himself again in a subdued voice: "calm down, calm down now already," and this even worked to a certain degree but the nervousness was still there (and this equipped him with a kind of fortitude): the nervousness remained, but not the suddenrage, so that in this state he now returned to the question of *why* what was happening outside was happening, because as to *what* was happening, he was able to grasp that naturally, once again it was nothing new, he however was less and less able to control himself, and he felt the suddenrage was about to overwhelm him again, and he would have been very happy to scream at them to get lost before it was too late, so that the local TV team, accompanied by the local journalists—whom his daughter had succeeded in luring here—would quit this whole thing, and get lost while they could, but he didn't scream out to them, and of course they didn't quit, they didn't get lost, and especially not her, not this girl who did not for a single moment leave off her "position," as opposed to the journalists who nonetheless stole away now and then to take a leak or warm up and finally—or so he believed—to get some sleep at night so they could return the next day at dawn, albeit reduced in number, not this girl, though, she just stayed there, or at least it seemed to him that her entire being—as she planted herself onto one spot where she had an excellent view if anything even as much as stirred in the window of the hut—suggested she would not leave this place until she got what he, this "skunk," had owed her from the moment she'd been born, as she'd stated in the first interview she'd given there, which of course, from the Professor's point of view was pure absurdity, because what could he owe anyone, especially this spoiled, misbegotten child,there in front of his whose conception, coming into and then remaining in this world, in addition to being a cheap evil trick, he could only attribute to his own irresponsibility, carelessness, unforgivable naivete, endless egoism, and boundless vanity, namely his own innate boorishness, the consequence of which he had never seen either in a photograph or with his own eyes—in addition he hardly could recall (indeed expressing the essence of the thing a little more sincerely, he expressed to himself more sincerely), he could hardly even remember that he had a daughter at all, who, as people tended to put it, was "from the wrong side of the blanket," he'd forgotten about her, or, to put it more precisely, he'd learned not to think about her, at least when he was able to do so, there were periods —even if transitory—when he was left in peace, sometimes even for years, just as now, he'd been left unperturbed "from that direction," he'd washed his hands of the entire matter, as in general he did with his entire past, he'd washed it away, and as for a good few years now nobody had been pestering him, he'd already reached the conclusion that he was free of all this, free, that is, until yesterday afternoon when out of the blue, unexpectedly, this daughter had just suddenly shown up here, and grabbing a megaphone, yelled out to him "I'm your daughter, you basest of skunks," and then "now you'll pay," then she raised a sign, and there could be no doubt that this "little monster" attacking him so unexpectedly out of the blue had planned everything quite well in advance, because she had acquired (or had she always had one?!) a kind of bullhorn-type thing, she had cobbled together a sign, she had gotten the local press to come with her, and she had arrived here with them, so that it seemed that she really knew what she was doing, and this, at the beginning, was already frightening to him, because it obliged him to assume that he had forgotten something else as well, something else he should have known that he didn't know, because he hadn't thought of it, because without that supposition, none of this made any sense, because what the hell did she want here after so many years, that is to say after nineteen entire years, he tried to remember but he couldn't, as he'd already advanced greatly in his hitherto completed exercises and he wasn't capable of remembering, particularly something so far back in the past, and this now appeared to be dangerous, because if he couldn't remember what he was supposed to remember, then he wouldn't be able to protect himself, he tried convulsively to piece together what it was, everything here was so senseless, because nothing was happening as could be expected, for example "this daughter" did not proceed simply by knocking on his door and directly telling him what her problem was, but she "immediately took aim," she had arrived, having prepared everything in advance, namely she had started off here with the biggest hoopla possible, namely she was staging a protest, in order to make sure that scribbling riffraff came along, because of course, what was a demonstration without this scribbling riffraff, nothing, looking at it from the girl's point of view, the entire event was accordingly calculated, deliberate, and planned—her entire program, its progress, its choreography—whereas from his point of view, it was troubling from the very beginning, from yesterday at 12:27, and it was still troubling to him now, here in the midst of events, because on the one side there was his bewilderment and incomprehension, and of course his suddenrage, on the other side, however, there was someone he didn't even know, someone with a clearly planned strategy, and only now had the existence of this strategy been disclosed to him, i.e., the fact that she had one, and that she had arrived with it, namely with her strategy in tow, because it was as if the whole thing were being realized only through these smaller steps building upon each other in a hierarchical manner, and this was, directly, that certain beginning she'd planned in advance, yesterday at 12:27: to surround him with the journalists and two television crews as soon as they located him in the Thorn Bush, as the locals called the terrain—completely feral, impenetrable, and abandoned to its own fate—that lay to the north of the city; it was clear that she wanted immediate witnesses, witnesses who would write and record what she was about to yell into her bullhorn or whatever it was, namely "come out you skunk"; the "skunk," however, didn't even understand what was wanted from him, at the beginning he understood nothing at all, he didn't even know who she was, who these people were, what they were yelling, or what they wanted with him, only later did it began to dawn on him who she was and who these people were, and that this daughter wanted something very much, which made him think and consider for the first time: well, so what can she want, the same as always, if not in the form of a personal request but a legal demand, namely—money, because in addition, she spoke about this in her interview the next day, but very indirectly, she made allusions; the only problem was that the whole thing seemed too serious, too far-reaching, and the resolve with which she attacked him was too troubling—because that's what was going on here, he was being attacked, there was no other way to put it, as the Professor put it to himself, he'd been taken by surprise and he was being struck down, he was the victim; he now began to suspect that maybe on this occasion, in an alarming fashion, it wasn't even money that was behind all of this; he, in his hut, didn't get the sense, from this entire circus, that it was yet again about the "the extortion of accumulated maintenance payments amounting to tens of thousands," as had been demanded of him during her entire nineteen years until this point, and which he wouldn't be able to fulfill now either, and she, his daughter, had to know this, if she were to inquire just even a bit as to his situation, as clearly she had inquired, because otherwise how could she have known where to find him, in a word: nooo, in the past few hours he had shaken his head many times when he tried to tackle this question, no, something else was going on here, the girl seemed ready for anything, and it was obvious that at the very least she had been cut from the same wood as her mother: the evocation, even for a mere moment, of whose figure and features, detested a thousand times over, caused him, the Professor, decisive physical pain, so that for years now he had not evoked it, only now when he was forced to do so, and to determine that although he saw his daughter for only a brief moment, only now and then for a brief Hungarocell moment, he could see that "she really resembled her"—indeed she resembled her so much he stared with his eyes wide open in horror—that as a matter of fact she was exactly like her, and with this "exactly like her" he quickly came to the fundamental aspect of this question: yes, this girl in the most decisive way possible was exactly like her mother, but even worse, so much worse, in any event she didn't even clear off at evening, namely yesterday at exactly the fall of dusk, it was 5:03, and she didn't leave the spot along with the journalists, so that when they were suddenly swept away to pursue some newer sensation (about which he could hardly guess, as he had thought that they had cleared off to get some sleep), yes, it was entirely likely that she'd stayed there all night, this is the conclusion he reached, but he hadn't gone any further than this, because after dark it had been futile to try to shift the Hungarocell panel upward, it had been futile to try to see in the darkness if she was still there, the darkness had been so dense that he didn't see anything, he didn't dare go outside, so as not to become an object of attack, not to mention the fact that he had built up his hut in such a way that the door could only be opened from the inside after some serious labor, and from the outside—due to considerations of defense—it was impossible to tell where the door was, in a word it really seemed that two people had slept poorly the preceding night: he here inside, and the girl there outside, he was able to fall asleep only for a few minutes at a time, always startling awake in fright, and clearly the same thing could have happened with the daughter too, but he couldn't figure out how she did it, he couldn't make it out, in any event from the first light of dawn he was on his guard, when he, from the inside, took down the Hungarocell panel and he looked out, he saw the girl standing in exactly the same place where she'd been standing the night before, he didn't know how she did it, how she was able to withstand the cold and in general how she could have found something to lie down on in this spot which was clearly unbearably unpleasant to her, the entire thing was a mystery, this little whimpering cosseted child and the Thorn Bush, he couldn't wrap his head around it, so he was at the point of recognizing that he himself could have hardly made a better job of it, which made this daughter even more frightening in his eyes, clearly she had planned this scenario in advance in order to be able to "keep him under continuous fire," and clearly she'd brought some provisions with her to withstand the cold, otherwise how could what had happened have happened: namely, that she stood there the next morning just as fresh and battle-ready, her gaze fixed upon him, as when she had arrived, standing there as if she hadn't budged a millimeter, exactly in the same pose, and she wasn't moving, and because of that nobody else was moving either, and it was already the second day, it was already 3:01 in the afternoon, he muttered to himself pacing back and forth in his hut, and no and no, this can't go on like this anymore, the blood rushed to his head, he didn't need to look at his watch—although he looked at it—in order to know that he was *already* late, that *already* more than one minute had passed since it had been time for him to commence his mandatory thought-immunization exercises, no wonder this was making him nervous, how could it not make him so, well if he thought about it—and of course he thought about it continuously—this was already the second day that had been ruined like this, and what was going on out there wasn't simply an attack, but the threat of an attack, and nothing made him more nervous than a threat, a punitive measure announced in advance, an intimidation inserted into the murky immediate future, he pressed his ear to the Hungarocell panel, but outside nobody was saying anything to anyone, the girl was obviously standing there in the circle of journalists in her heroic pose, leaning forward a bit, like Nike of Samothrace, but she wasn't speaking, so that it seemed that between her and the journalists there wasn't any communication, although there hadn't been too much of that anyway so far, only the first brief interview last night, and this morning—as opposed to the sensation of last night, as they were just kind of monitoring the situation to see how it would develop, having arrived separately by car—this morning there had been a second interview, an even shorter one; the Professor had clearly heard the approach of the car across the rags and bars of his hut, but that was it, after that he heard nothing, they kept asking the girl questions to no avail, she behaved as if she neither saw nor heard the journalists standing around her, so that at the most they could amuse—for now—the residents of the city with progress reports, because nothing was happening, they telephoned their editors every ten minutes: the girl is standing here facing the Professor's hut, and the Professor is looking out, she is holding up the sign with the same writing on it, that was all that the journalists could report ever since that morning, and it wasn't too much, indeed it was almost nothing, because there was nothing new, because there was always that part of the public who demanded new information concerning the breaking scandal—while the rest, as the editors termed it, were distracted by other news items—so that in the two television stations and the two editorial offices the editors were yelling out for so-called "background material," but where the hell were they supposed to get it, the journalists retorted in rage, here they were standing outside in the freezing wind, right in the middle of the Thorn Bush, where the girl was no longer uttering a word beyond what she had communicated to the public this morning, so there really was no news, there was only how she stood there, rooted to the spot, at times contemptuously pursing her "marvelous lips burning poppy red" while raising the sign, and always exactly at that moment when the Hungarocell panel was dislodged in the Professor's hut, so the journalists—as every now and then the voice in their cell phones grew more peremptory—reported on "her coat, judging from which the young lady attires herself exclusively according to the elegant fashions of the great cities of London or Paris," or "her shawl, a thick Scottish plaid, clearly woven from the finest of materials," in the latter case, they reported on the several wide arcs of this scarf, placed "above that thick fur, presumably not prepared from animal pelts, and around that neck, equally presumably, yet manifestly, dainty"—and they didn't report on anything else, because they had already said everything there was to say about the sign yesterday, and this had been reported in both the evening news and the morning news bulletins: the sign, the text of which unceasingly informed its intended recipient—the Professor, taken prisoner in his own hut—that he bore "an original sin," as the girl had explained in her first interview, the sign's enigmatic text namely two words visible on a piece of cardboard pasted onto a pinewood beam, "Justice" and "Reckoning"—and who (that is to say the girl), the journalists added in their first reports, otherwise seemed to be like anyone else of her kind from the capital city, who from time to time roamed around here in God's little acre so as to speak out against something, most often against the "unacceptable provincialism, unspeakable corruption, and the exploiters of misery," slogans which down here, far away from the capital city, no one really understood, so no one took them seriously, because these little excursions down here always ended the same way: they raised their voices and raised their signs, until sooner or later the Local Force showed up, gave them a good thrashing, took them to the train, and sent them back to where they'd come from, so they'd lose all taste for this kind of bedlam; which was obviously what was going to happen in this case too, or that's at least what the journalists out there were hoping, as well as the Professor here inside, and there even was a chance of that happening, because while no one knew too much about the aforementioned Local Force, everyone knew that they didn't favor any event disruptive to peaceful tranquility, and that—as was stressed by one of the newspapers, the one that was a little edgier in its opposition—"was about to occur here," because until this morning, until the next sensational news item—which, as the chief editors liked to say, "would sweep everything away"— came along and exploded, this was the number one topic of conversation in the entire city, namely what was going on here, what was happening here in the so-called Thorn Bush between the Professor (at one-time renowned, but for a while now he'd completely lost his mind) and his daughter, "paying him a visit here, absolutely without precedent, from the capital city"—there was no doubt that everyone had already been informed about this by the local press, the two competing newspapers and the two competing television stations in the city, although nobody was conveying any clear information as to what was really going on, because apart from the girl herself nobody understood why she had chosen this form for her demands, and, in general, what this demand even consisted of, so that the only thing that was clear was that there was a commotion, as well as an even newer one concerning the Professor, because, "well, *based on this*, it seems he has a daughter," and this daughter, *based on this*, "wasn't getting enough," but that was everything, because the essence of the matter—namely "who was this exquisite young lady who had arrived here, with her blond tresses, almost enchanting with her blue eyes, and her opulent mouth colored with poppy-red lipstick," as well as the question of what was lurking in the past of this renowned individual of their city, who until recently had enjoyed the greatest public prestige, but who, as opposed to what news reports claimed, had lost his mind not seven, but nine months ago—what was this "black stain," from the obscurity of which there had suddenly now—if you please!—leapt out a piece of the Professor's past hitherto suppressed, and which was not clear to anyone in the least.

He was wearing three different coats: a brown woolen coat with a velvet collar, which was the only item from his old wardrobe, apart from his watch, that he was attached to, and two shorter coats; below that were two sweaters, and below that were other shirts and a T-shirt that had almost grown onto his skin; on his legs were two pairs of trousers, one pair which was very snug and another that protected his legs from the wind; there was a Russian fur cap on his head, and a black scarf tied around his neck, namely nearly all these items had come from the van that regularly supplied provisions for the homeless; it had appeared eight months ago, earlier that year toward the end of March, on the edge of the Thorn Bush, so that its volunteers could ask the single resident of this place if he needed anything, which was a brave act considering these two volunteers could have no idea what to expect, as they too were of course aware of the famous departure—namely that the Professor had become unhinged—but before they came along, nobody had spoken with him, or more precisely with one exception, no one had dared approach him, because shortly after his scandalous withdrawal he had sent a message "to the city" via his one confidant, a peasant who lived on a nearby farmstead and who duly supplied him with water and provisions, that if anyone should come along and pester him, let all and sundry be warned that whomever dared to approach his hut in the Thorn Bush would be shot immediately and without warning.

He decided he wasn't going to shoot his daughter, when under the pressure of a newer wave of suddenrage he walked to the rear of his hut, and began to throw to one side the pile of clothes stacked (as camouflage) above the secret ditch, not even if she were just a ghost, a shadow from the past, a shadow that he couldn't even remember, but if the others—these good-for-nothing scribblers—didn't clear off, he murmured to himself, then pretty soon everything would be helter-skelter, I'd bet my life on that, he muttered, but for now I'll just watch and wait and give them a bit of time to withdraw, and with that he took up his place to the left of the window opening, leaving one hand free to act immediately if the time should come, although outside the journalists still didn't suspect anything, they were describing this momentary state as an "impasse" to their bosses, and they were preparing to spend—just as they had done yesterday for most of the afternoon until late at night, even if in greatly reduced numbers—the entire day here, because they were generally convinced that nothing would happen anyway, not here, they shook their heads, so that anyone who still didn't have enough layers to keep warm went back to his car for a warm blanket, and anyone who already had enough layers wrapped them around himself even more tightly in the growing cold of the afternoon, because as one of the journalists put it, this was going to last again until late evening, but it was more likely, noted another to the reporter standing next to him, as he offered him a cigarette, that this will die out nicely in an hour or so, and we can all go home; in short, that game of patience was created with its well-known and tedious order, which reporters like this on the job were very used to; whoever was sitting got up in order to stretch his limbs; whoever had been pacing around for a while and had gotten tired of pacing sat back down on the stump of a tree or some twigs and leaves cobbled together for that purpose; the thermoses of tea were slowly emptied, and they began to mention that it certainly would be good if these thermoses got filled up again, and if somebody could go do that, for example you over there—they pointed at the youngest one, a lanky, pimply assistant—your legs are long—when suddenly shots thundered from the direction of the hut, but to such an extent that the reporters flew off in their alarm just like the frightened sparrows, in those first moments it was even hard to discern what was going on, after they had first scattered, they stood there rooted to the spot as if their legs had grown roots into the ground, when they realized what was going on—their eyes weren't deceiving them, they weren't hallucinating, but someone really was shooting at them from the direction of the hut—they crouched and they threw themselves on the ground, they began to shout and point and flail, in the blink of an eye there were cell phones in their hands, and at first they just shouted disjointed words to the person on the other end of the line, then came sentences, broken and tormented, that namely there were shots being fired from the hut, yes, they yelled for a second time and a third time, it's the Professor, yes, it's not a mistake, the Professor, can't you hear me?! he's shooting even now, yes, no warning, no threat, no prior notice, yes, well, do you understand?! he-is-shoot-ing, they yelled it out syllable by syllable as they jumped up, and began to flee helter-skelter into the prickly bushes, yes, and he was shooting, and they knew it was unbelievable, but he was shooting, they explained to the clearly flabbergasted editors on the other end of the line, and their voices became hoarse from shouting amid all the noise; the TV crew, jumping back and forth among the prickly bushes, quickly turned on their cameras, and fleeing while half turned around, just like the Huns of old, they vehemently began to transmit images of the trees in the bushes, because there was nothing else they could do in this rush, from this spot nothing could be seen at all of the hut, they only heard the detonations, and these detonations simply wouldn't stop, so that ever more horrified and ever more stupefied, they tried to get away, and they couldn't decide what was more appalling, the fact that he was shooting at all, or what he was shooting with, because each individual shot was so loud that it almost made them deaf; there was a huge explosion, then at the same time a huge echo, then came another explosion and another echo, but to such a degree that the ground itself trembled, the air trembled, keep going, keep going, one of them cried when they realized that "the Professor had seriously cracked up," let's get the hell out of here, he urged the others, but there was no need to urge anyone, because even without that they set off as fast as they could, topsy-turvy on top of each other and out of the Thorn Bush, onto the pitched road toward the parked cars, while from the hut, with just a few seconds between each round, there came shooting and shooting, but of course nobody realized that it was only into the air, because for as long as his magazines held out—the prisoner in the hut rasped to himself, replacing the magazine, and he shot into the air, up into the lead-colored clouds—*for as long as he still had ammunition,* he shouted ... then he shouted that he had told them all of this, had declared it would end like this, and he raged in fury, he trampled all over the Hungarocell panel flung onto the floor, he told everyone in advance that this would happen, he choked on his breath, exactly this, until all of his cartridges ran out.

If she has a strategy, he hissed, his brain darkened over, then I have my rifle, and not only do I not give a fuck about her big strategy, but I'm going to blow it to pieces, and still he waited a few moments, but only so he could look over all of the magazines he'd prepared, and double-check the cartridges which he then put back into the weapon with a single confident movement, still though that didn't take more than a moment, with one rash gesture he tore away the Hungarocell panel, glanced at his watch, and it was 3:35—and without further thought he pulled on the trigger and just fired, but in such quick succession as if it were a submachine gun, and from time to time he screamed out exultantly "get lost, you stinking cunts," then when the first, the second, the third, the fourth, and finally half of the fifth magazines were emptied, then he let go of the trigger, and like a victorious commander looked around at the muddled, chaotic clearing in front of his hut, but now he was obliged to realize that he couldn't speak of victory, because if the journalists had been routed, the girl still stood there, leaning forward, those two illuminating blue eyes glittering in their resolve, and they were looking exactly into his two eyes, the same light blue color, which made his brain go even darker, and he yelled at her "so you think this bullet won't hit you?!" and he lowered the barrel of the gun, which until now he had been aiming high, he lowered it so as to just try a round in front of her feet, even if he wouldn't exactly shoot her down, but this never came to be, because as the girl heard what her father was yelling from the window of the hut, and seeing at the same time the gun's lowered barrel, she herself no longer held out, but flung away her sign, and shrieking, beat a quick retreat, back through the bushes, and that was the end, it was all over, there were no other sounds, just the Professor's vehement gasping for breath, and there was nothing else to see, just the empty clearing and a few random paths which this troop had made for themselves from the outside leading toward his hut, and now back to the outside world again—he only saw the twigs leaning down, the clambering weave of the weedy bushes' wild diffusion, as a branch here or there slowly still swung, indicating the trace of those who had just fled.

Well, which one would yer be needin' now, he'd been asked on the nearby farmstead, cos you just go ahead and choose the one that be right for yer—the wound next to the peasant's wide mouth distorted as he smiled—cos there always be enough, this one 'ere—he raised it into the flashlight's beam—is a PPD-40, you see it, look, an' it has seventy pieces of live ammunition, in th' cartridge, well what do ye say, he looked at him grimacing, but the Professor didn't say a word, he just looked at the weapons laid out on the old soldier's cloak which had been spread and smoothed out on the ground, he looked at one after the other and didn't ask anything, and ultimately he didn't even answer the peasant's question as to well, which one; he lifted up an assault rifle, and the peasant immediately broke in with some incomprehensible grimace that it was a Sturmgewehr, a German piece wi' an intermediate cartridge, but he didn't say anything else, because this strange person—well, this city gentleman, as the peasant referred to him in his regular haunt, the bar known only by its old registration number, 47—while he showed *not at all* if he was *at all* interested in this thing, his gaze showed nothin', as for himself, though, he could tell those whom he could bring out here to the shed—and open up before them, here beneath the corn stalks, what he called, almost jokingly, his Aladdin's box, because that's what he called his valuable collection at the base of the shed, not with two *d*'s, but directly with three—*Aladddin*—

although it was impossible to know how many shots of brandy led to the two *d*'s and how many shots to the three *d*'s, in any event now he said it with three, he said: well, come along now, I'll show ye what there is, when th' gentleman all of a sudden popped up in the afternoon at his place, an' the sheepdog almost tore him to shreds, the gentleman only asked if there was anythin' from his collection he wanted to sell, or did he just keep it for himself, and himself said: of course there would be, where did th' gentleman think he got th' money for the spaur parts for his motorcycle, could anyone imagine *at all* how hard it is t'day to fin' anythin'— an' them folk should know what he was sayin', anything!— for a real Csepel motorcycle, cos to be frank, he told th' whole world about it, but nobody was interested in how he did love his Csepel, cos if he ever had also loved those weapons which 'is grandfather collected after th' war an' hid there outside under th' ground—he loved them, how could he not, he oiled them, cleaned them, took care ay them, rubbed 'em 'til they gleamed, everything 'at was needed—but what *he* felt about his Csepel was more than love, cos as for these Csepel motorcycles, he just worshipped them, frankly speaking he could even die for them, if life wanted 'at, God help him, cos when he hears that tu-tu-tu sound, how those pistons give off such a heavenly sound as his hands touch th' rubber covering of the handlebars, how he feels when every once in a while he sits down on his Csepel, that tremblin' beneath his haunches, he couldn't compare 'at to anythin' else—well, fine, said the gentleman from the city, when he moved over here, you know where, here into th' Thorn Bush, an' he was just headin' homeward pushing his bike along an' the two of them met, an' they started to gab, an' of course the end was that he couldn't put a lock on his own mouth, an' right after he had offered some of his plum brandy, crystal clear like a brook, but to no avail, the gab turned to his special collection in th' shed, well, fine, 'en th' city gentleman said to him, he would come over one day an' have a look to see what he had, to see if he could use something, an' that was just what happened, not even three days went by—the peasant related in his regular haunt, the "47" stand-up bar on Csókos Road, but no one was listening to him—just like that, cos he came to my place, an' th' sheepdog nearly ate him up, an' he looked, an' he was a particular kind of body, he just kept looking an' looking, at the one and the other one, not saying a word until th' end—when suddenly he pointed at one and asked if this one was the loudest, it was an AMD-65 from the Hungarian Weapon and Machine Company—a wee patched together, and seventy-five cartridge shots also went into th' deal, well, he said, so how much you want for it, well, he said to him, that one here is a special favorite, cos it's a one-off, one of the Keserű make, and he told him th' price, and that gentleman didn't e'en make a peep, he just got out his money, counted it, an' bought all th' cartridges to go with it too, an' he said to him: isn't that a bit much, what do you need so much ammunition fur, but th' gentleman just hemmed an' hawed, an' he bought some machine oil too, well, he gave it to him for five hundred, and he just took a few rags and a gun-cleaning rod, so he said, for cleanin', and then he was gone, an' he never even saw him since, cos he himself never went to th' Thorn Bush, what for, just to be torn apart by th' cursed bushes, he would only go there—of course he would go—if wee gypsy kids started falling from th' sky, only then, but even so, it was more than enough, he had sold him that assault rifle, he'd be happy to take it back, cos he knew what would happen if th' gentleman did anything with it, then he'd be asked where all this money came from—and who would get in trouble, he would, for example, everybody said about him that he was on th' bottle and everythin', but he couldn't do anything about it, he had his wee collection and that was the truth, he didn't deny it, he never had, and with that the matter was closed, cos ye could tell that gentleman was up to something, an' even today he was like that, cos he made him take a message to the city folk to never dare come close to him, cos then it would be th' end, what was th' point of saying things like that to folks, he wanted to ask, here in Csókos Road, he himself was someone who would never e'en hurt a fly, could anyone here tell him, had anyone here ever known as gentle a body as himself, cos th' only reason he had those weapons was cos they were so beautiful, and for no other reason, not to speak aboot th' Csepel, cos th' Csepel, that was somethin' else altogether.

He found the Hungarocell panels there inside the thicket, and that's what made him decide on the location of his settlement, it wasn't as if he could have found even a trace of a clearing there, no, where the Hungarocell panels had been piled up, where they'd clearly been forgotten by someone, there was no clearing at all, nor any kind of shanty or farmer's hut, simply, there had never really been a clearing here, there couldn't have been one; in all likelihood things had happened differently, no clearing had been formed in the midst of these thickets, and these panels had been hidden for some unknown reason, but instead they had first been stacked and then forgotten here, someone had left them here to their own devices in this dreary, uncultivated, flat land, and the weeds came *afterward*, the thickets of thorn bushes and acacia had grown over everything here *afterward*, namely the notorious Thorn Bush had risen precisely around these few piles of Hungarocell panels; whoever had brought them here clearly had had some kind of purpose in doing so, and what was certain was that something might have happened with that purpose, so that after some time it became pointless for that same person to come back and take them away; the main thing is that when they ended up here—and the Professor came to this conclusion as he was preparing to move out here, he examined the territory just as much as he could, namely, there had been nothing else here, only these few towerlike structures made out of stacked-up Hungarocell panels—that is maybe what happened, he reasoned to himself at that time, the Hungarocell panels were brought out here to this marsh or meadow or gnarled thicket or desert, it doesn't matter what you call it, the panels were dumped here and then forgotten, the surfaces hardened, and then no one needed even a single panel anymore, the tower of panels just tottered to the left and to the right, just like the peasant on the nearby farmstead as he tried to make his way home on his weather-beaten bicycle, and the wind couldn't blow them away, because they were strapped together, it could only knock them over, and it knocked over almost all of them, and so they remained, and then the thorn and the acacia bushes and a thousand kinds of weeds grew over them, and the Thorn Bush came into being—that's what the residents of the city called it—as if it were some kind of proper neighborhood or something, as for all intents and purposes it was, and that was what could have happened: first the Hungarocell panels, then the weeds, completely, just like the one-time Magyar Conquest, the Professor looked around, no, it couldn't have happened any other way, so that it was the Hungarocell panels he had to thank for the present location—the one, he realized, where he wanted to live from now on—and, already because of the mere name, if he ever had to write down that entire word—due to the densely abundant, infinitely exact, and repulsive agglomeration of meaning associated with "Hungaro"—he would write it only in capital letters; so there was nothing left to decide, he would build his hut where they were, precisely among them, more precisely *in between them*, because altogether he found five huge piles of Hungarocell panels, of which one still stood, and the four remaining were either half or wholly collapsed in the thicket, and so he decided that it would be best to proceed in the spirit of the place, and build his homestead in their proximity, and so he began to build his shanty here, leaning the back of the hut against the one Hungarocell tower still standing: namely the three Hungarocell towers that were still at palletheight formed the starting point, and this is where he began the work of building, which—not in small part thanks to his above-mentioned and deeply symbolic interpretation of the Hungarocell panels—he truly designated as the Magyar Conquest, and it went much more smoothly than he expected, because as his decision was formed, and he began to come out here, as he made the choice of this place, and took a more thorough look at the wider area to see what he could use for building materials, he came upon riches, a treasure house, which was comprised —everything amassed from the surrounding area—of wooden planks, strewn car tires, the remains of abandoned farmstead buildings, upturned stakes that had been used as baulk markers, tar paper rolls, knocked-over and rotting hunters' blinds, scarecrows, rusty plowshares, harrows and well covers, former drinking troughs and broken well poles, roadside shrines collapsed onto the grass, battered tin Christs, old refrigerator doors and television screens brought here secretly and tipped over, wrecked cars, and thousands of worn-out, cast-off articles of clothing, and all of the usable materials therein—comprised, in a word, of the timeless elements of dispersed garbage; accordingly, the same garbage—the Professor noted to himself while working—that we are too.

It was not a good question at all, but he had tried in vain to beat it out of his head, he wasn't able to do so now, so that when everything had quieted down outside, namely that whoever was supposed to clear off had cleared off, he too went outside, so that he could be persuaded of it with his own eyes, and he just kept brooding over *why*; he somehow had to arrive at the intention, the cause, and the goal that had brought her here, because he was certain that if he didn't do this then she would really start pestering him, gaining the upper hand, and upsetting that relative order which he'd been able to create for a while, and the maintenance of which was much more difficult than he'd originally thought; to find out why, this was his task now, he stooped down here and there around the clearing, but he saw no trace of anyone, that riffraff had completely dispersed, had finally departed through the dense meshwork—difficult as well for him to traverse—of bushes, trees, creeping vines, branches, and moss clumps— moss clumps which, at one time, had been the object of his admiration—probably as far as the roadway; he decided that later he would go out some two hundred or three hundred meters, which was the distance, according to the peasant, that the weapon could shoot, to see if he might find some of the shells, because it was beginning to grow dark already, especially here in the exact center of the Thorn Bush, here you could hardly see anything, so the police would probably not be coming for him immediately, only tomorrow after daybreak, he could count on them, of course, but not today, and today he still had time to go over the entire story, so he went back into his hut, he reassembled the complicated door mechanism, he turned on the flashlight, he took off his outer coat, and sat down on the battered kitchen chair with armrests—he had thoroughly stuffed it with plaid blankets and newspapers—this was a chair which he had found in the early days on one of the old farmsteads, and since then it had taken pride of place in the interior of his hut, facing the blind window opening; he sat down among the wool blankets, and wrapped them around himself along with the newspapers, he turned off the flashlight, and in the sudden darkness he evoked the daughter's mother, he evoked her, and he trembled, because in that moment as he evoked her, as the form of that woman appeared before him, as in this evocation again that woman's face appeared before him, and he saw her eyes, he immediately knew that she was behind this, that she had stage-managed the entire thing, she was stage-managing everything right now, the girl was clearly back in the city by now, and informing the mother on the telephone as to the latest developments, he saw the woman's gaze as she listened to the account, and he saw that she was already racking her brain, grimacing in the meantime, pursing her mouth—she was able to purse her mouth in such an infinitely repulsive way whenever she listened with completely unjustified superiority to some account unfavorable to her— at such times, while she smiled, the rage boiled within her, but this smile actually meant that the instigator of this bad news was soon to reach his end, she would eliminate him, and she already knew how, she had a frightening ability to see through any person whom she happened to encounter, and immediately find this person's weak point, namely the assembled possible lines of advance for wounding the enemy, and that was why this haughty smile appeared on her face, a smile which had made him shiver with cold ever since the time of their acquaintance—brief, yet for all that even more ominous—that smile that indicated that she knew just how she would take care of the next victim to turn up in her path, which this time was him, once again him, because to his misfortune he had called this fate down upon himself; he hadn't been aware of it at first, but he had called it down upon himself for an entire lifetime, and at that time, realizing just what kind of trap he had fallen into with this woman, he felt compelled to flee, of course it was hard to say how he had exactly called this fate down upon himself, maybe it would be best if he saw it as beginning that moment when the woman looked him up and down thoroughly in a bar in the capital city, where, due to the boredom of the embassy reception, he had drunkenly—and desiring further drunkenness—set foot one evening, most likely it was this first thoroughgoing scrutiny which had determined his fate, and moreover for an entire lifetime, because then, when he escaped from her she had let him know fairly quickly that he would never be able to truly escape, that she, this woman, would forever—to the end of his days—be after him, torturing him for all eternity, she would be after him in the form of financial claims, and in this form of financial claims she would torture him, and this torture would be rendered all the more vivid through abusive missives that wounded him all the more because it was humiliating to him to have to read such squalid letters, these letters dragged him down into a world for which he felt only repulsion, letters, accordingly, in which only the most foul words sounded, about what, but really what a mangy figure he was, the Professor, to leave a child to its fate, a child who was his, but whom he denied, well it was obvious before all the concerned parties that it was not the child he was escaping from but this woman, but this was all in vain, and he sensed this now too, sitting here hunched over in the kitchen chair with the armrests, staring determinedly in the pitch dark at the blind window, the Hungarocell panel, as he tried to figure out just what she was plotting now, and how this woman was planning to do away with him.

At that time, he had thought a great deal about the problem of the door, but in no way did it occasion as much mental exertion as that of the window, because at the beginning he was of the opinion that he didn't even need a window for a hovel like this, a lair, a shed, a shanty—for a while he called it all these things, and it was only toward the middle of the second month at 4:14 a.m. when he finalized its designation—for the wall of a *hut* like this it would be a mistake to create a window, this was his opinion, because in the winter it would be decidedly illogical, he reasoned, and in the summer it wouldn't be of help against the heat, he turned the matter over this way and that, but he only dared acknowledge to himself slowly that the basic problem with a window wasn't a question of this or that practical advantage or disadvantage, but it was the *principle* of the window that troubled him greatly, and namely not because a window could be gazed into, but because that window could always be gazed out of—and he hadn't planned the kind of lifestyle which he'd chosen for himself here in the Thorn Bush in order to gaze and gawk out the window, to continuously peek out at a world which he repudiated in its entirety—that's how things stood at the beginning; but still there ended up being a window, and this was thanks to the fact that he realized that from the protective standpoint it was truly necessary for him to be able to look out at any given time, namely that he should be able to see the space in front of the hut, the one direction, the one section, from where, and through which, his hut could be approached, he therefore accepted the reasoning of that inner voice that argued that if there was a window, then there would be protection, moreover only in this case would there be protection, because the essence of protection is to create the possibility of preparation, namely, without a window, without being able to look out unrestrictedly, anyone could approach or arrive at his hut with him unprepared, and he had to avoid this by all means, he wanted to feel secure, so he ended up with the window; he was able to create it fairly easily with the use of reinforcements, taking into account the natural characteristics of the site, and he realized that if he bought a used saw from the peasant and fit a Hungarocell panel trimmed to the correct size into the window opening, then this window, constructed in this manner, would meet his needs in every respect, in winter, and summer, and finally it would mean that somebody would only be able to look in if he so permitted, namely if he took the Hungarocell panel out of the opening, and similarly in any given moment if he might need, he could do the same himself, namely he would be able to look out and survey what was happening there outside.

The Thorn Bush was, at the beginning, the object of derisive commentary, only becoming notorious later on; but even then its reputation was enhanced not by the spice of juicy murders or sexual violence, but rather by being a no-man's-land in the city, completely left to its own fate, an ownerless piece of land, needed by no one, and about which no one even debated who might need it and how it might be used; it was, accordingly, completely left to itself, and because of this, public opinion concerning this plot of land was determined only by its suitability for potentially criminal acts and its lack of supervision, the fact that it had become a place where anything could happen, although nothing so truly frightening ever happened there, the residents of the town, if they even knew about the northern outlying district, tended to be bored by it, because these entire northern outskirts—namely all of the territory that lay beyond Csókos Road—simply never turned up on the living map of the consciousness of the town residents, only onto its desiccated perimeter, or at times, word spread that some homeless person had skulked over there and been detained because he had stolen a decrepit generator from one of the courtyards of the nearby Waterworks, or a Gypsy family from Romania had come along, clearing out a small parcel for themselves and pitching a tent, well, for a few days it was a topic of conversation, kick them out immediately, the town residents demanded at such times, and like a well-practiced chorus, they grumbled in indignation that well, not that now, we can't be having it, just to let some horde of gypsies set up camp here, what are the police for, and in general why haven't they done something already with that whole accursed place, you could almost hear them as they repeated the words, pronouncing every syllable, *ex-pel-them-now*, out with these marauders, because if they don't do something immediately in one week "all those stinking gypsies" will be coming here from the Romanian border, well, nooo, you can't leave it like that, please do something already, get rid of them, these words were heard during the gatherings of the town residents next to tea and pastries, wipe them out, that's the only solution, they kept repeating, and they were influenced by their own agitated words, the excitement of which evaporated just as quickly as it had come into being during the afternoon teas, and with the expulsion of the Gypsy family, the question of what to do about the Thorn Bush vanished from the town's "agenda," once again floating out to the perimeter of consciousness, because in reality nobody, but really nobody was interested in this, nobody was interested in the fact that there was this "wasteland" of some hundred acres, as they kept repeating while daintily raising their teacups, although they weren't aware of the true sense of the word, that because of the high groundwater the land there was fallow, bordered to the west by the industrial plant for state consignments, and in the direction toward the town by Csókos Road, well, it had always been there since the beginning of time, the teacups were lowered, it's "always been left like that," maybe because of the River Körös, and the floods, they looked at each other a little foolishly, because no one had any idea about the past, and so they took another little piece of pastry from the plate.

Her arrival had gone well, she glanced into the mirror in the bathroom, and when she noticed that the train had pulled into the station, she glanced one more time at herself, and she was satisfied, the lipstick, a burning red color, which she'd applied to her lips, decisively burned poppy red, and this was what she wanted, precisely this, for that red to burn like poppies on her lips, there was still a bit of a shadow beneath her eyes, but it had mostly faded away, as always her opulent blonde hair, pulled back, emphasized her light blue eyes, the scarf looked good, the coat looked good, her stockings looked good, the boots were perfectly fine, so she'd said to herself that the time had come for her to take care of this, and it was as if she had stepped onto a stage, she sprang into action: she got off the train, and people were noticing her even as she arrived in front of the station, which of course she was aware of, she was capable of immediately noticing all the gazes trained on her, and of course she'd learned this from her mother; she also noticed the ones that were not trained on her, because the question remained, of course, how was that possible, and who were these people, and why weren't they interested in her, she with all her innate qualities, but now she didn't bother with them, she realized what the number of these gazes during this morning hour signified: they had noticed that she'd arrived, the taxis began to roll toward her almost of their own accord—I swear, one of the drivers related that night in the warming stand, I didn't even step on the gas, my car started moving toward her by itself, she was so hot, and she proceeded like that, a hot number, according to her plans arranged in advance; she went across the square in front of the train station toward the head of Peace Boulevard and from the many taxis gathered there, she let one turn in front of her, she got in, and said quickly, contemptuously: to the editorial office, and the taxi driver didn't even ask which one, he immediately knew that she wanted the opposition newspaper, and he released the clutch carefully, as if he were transporting a frail butterfly, the young lady, however, was anything but a frail butterfly, she was fairly well-built, a few women's gazes established, as they looked her up and down, already in the town center where she paid the taxi driver's fee, and set off by foot in the direction he'd suggested, a strong frame, wide hips, and wide shoulders, with slightly pudgy features; I know—her own gaze signaled back sharply at these other gazes—I'm aware, those blue eyes flashed, of who I am, whereas the lot of you know fuck all, you bunch of dried-out, cowardly, provincial sluts . . . that's what those two neon eyes and her face said, as she cut her way through them, because this was her habit, just like her mother, she always walked ahead at full speed, her mother had tried to get her out of this habit a hundred times, a thousand times, but it wasn't so easy, she had an explosive nature, as if something were always driving her on, and so the vehement pace remained, at least, she thought now, she would get there more quickly, and so it was, she found the place within minutes according to the taxi driver's directions, and she buzzed at the door of a building, and from this point on there were no obstacles, they looked at her stockinged legs, just at the surface, but the male glances traversed the elevations of the coat up and down, crept up to the gorgeous opulent mouth and its scarlet red, right up to those blue eyes, which immediately cast a spell on them, and the doors opened of their own accord, they came forward, they showed her inside, this way, they indicated to her, and everywhere there were faces with smiles of recognition—oily, self-satisfied country hicks, she smiled back at them—and she said thank you in soft tones, finally she was shown into a room, which clearly could only have been the Chief Editor's lair, coffee? a cautious woman's voice, a little offended, asked behind her back, yes, she mumbled back, without even turning around, and she just sat in the armchair that had been pulled in front of the enormous desk, and from time to time she crossed those stockinged legs, and she told him why she was there, she confessed, in all sincerity: she was so inexperienced in such matters that she really didn't know if it was a good idea to come here, at first, well, but of course it was, of course it was, a pulsating person said from the other side of the desk, the very best possible idea that could ever be imagined, namely this affair, inasmuch as he—this someone who pointed at himself from behind the writing desk—could judge, was of such gravity, that as a media representative—and, he could confidently state, as a representative of the media with the largest possible readership, that he was more than happy to extend his helping hand; well, the young lady, who had just arrived from the capital city, answered, she thanked him very kindly, but altogether what she needed most was for her own modest cause to receive a little publicity, as without that, she felt herself to be so weak—this matter was so difficult and complicated for her, precisely due to its personal nature, so enervating, and well: there was a degrading task to be completed, it had to be be carried out, and left completely to her own devices, she felt she would never be able to manage, at which point the pulsating someone sitting across from her jumped up, and going around the enormous desk, which this time was in his way, stood in front of his guest, leaned over close to her, and told her: she could trust him—himself, personally—and this was sufficient for the guest, because she had already risen from the armchair, and daintily placed the coffee cup with the remains of a wretched espresso on the table, she was already headed out the door, moreover, she was already outside on the street, and she was asking the journalists jumping all around her if well, could they tell her exactly where she could find—and here she held a pregnant pause, so pregnant, that she stood still for a moment, as did the others—her father, where was he hiding, because as she had just heard now, he had moved to new premises, to which the journalists, as if acknowledging the young lady's wondrous sense of humor, broke out in shrill laughter, and interrupting each other they explained that, well, how to explain it, but really what had happened is that the Professor—whom they all held in great esteem—well, something had happened with him, and she, his daughter, needed to know, it was no use that she hadn't seen him for a while now, as she had said, indeed, they told her, she should know it was as if the highly respected Professor had lost all taste for his previous life, and because of that he had moved house to—well, how could they put it—the northern part of town, and here, they added that it was pretty difficult to use the words "moved house," but later on she'd see what they meant, because they would be more than happy to show her the way, for without them she would never find it, even though it wasn't far from here, we'll go there—the most enthusiastic of the journalists made tiny, mincing steps beside her—and we'll be there in a jiffy.

So you say in a jiffy, the girl turned toward the journalist, but—she suddenly stood still on the sidewalk—she didn't need to be there in a jiffy, because before this "jiffy," she had something to attend to, at which the enthusiastic journalists immediately rooted themselves to the spot as well, surrounding her, and when they understood what she needed, immediately recommended their own services, if the young lady would promise that inasmuch as her affairs here reached a satisfactory conclusion, she would unconditionally consume with them one, just one single cup of espresso—or whatever else she might want, the eldest of the troop added, winking at her—in the town's very best confectioner, at which the young lady raised her beauteous eyebrows, and turning toward the elder journalist, asked him what did he mean by saying *inasmuch as*—and her voice became completely subdued as she smiled at the journalists standing around her, and they reassured her: she'd misunderstood, because they had only been thinking that if she were to complete what she had come here to do, then in the confectioners' she could, with all of them together, or one by one, enjoy an excellent espresso, because this assistance was no skin off their backs, for if they had understood well, altogether the young lady needed a sign, as well as a few other odds and ends, and of course a megaphone, the kind used in processions or demonstrations, which in particular around here, journalists called a squawk box; he—they pointed at the youngest one among them, who was leaping up already—nothing would be simpler than getting hold of a sign and a squawk box and the other odds and ends, added to which the young lady said she had brought a felt marker—and really the boy had already run off, and they had hardly gone a few blocks and turned by the colossal building of the Courthouse, and the quick-witted boy was already pulling up to them in a car, and in great confusion, with burning ears, he reported that "I've got everything."

He tried to chase away that idiotic compulsion to ask himself why again and again, and yet he allowed the question to come up, because nothing was ever perfect, as he couldn't cast aspersions on his own intellectual exertions, just as he could't condemn them as meaningless, he was truly well on the way to accomplishing one of his main goals; in certain situations, however, the functional results of these intellectual exertions were still limited; and he still wasn't able to completely put the brakes on the sick compulsion of thought—as he termed it—just as now, when he had been sitting futilely, hunched over in the kitchen chair for at least two hours already, while outside the darkness grew thicker and thicker, and he just kept on sitting in that same spot, where he'd been sitting for the past two hours, chewing the same thing over and over: why had she come, what did she want, and why exactly now, and so on, and he was getting so worked up, as he was getting nowhere with these questions, that he decided to embark upon a task that had at least some practical use, so once again he turned on his flashlight and gathered up all the cartridge shells from the ground into a large woven synthetic shopping bag, counting each one precisely as he tossed them into the bag, and when he had counted 207 shells from the total of 225 that he had, according to his own calculations, used, he tossed in the empty magazines as well, then he took apart the door again, got out his flashlight, and went out behind his hut to the Hungarocell columns, concealing the entire lot in a hidden cavity, so that later on, at the appropriate time, he could finally dispose of them—and of course this would also include the hidden weapon, it was concealed, along with other items, beneath a large pile of clothes at one end of the interior of the hut—then he walked around to the clearing in front, and headed into the thicket, and went along one of the—unfortunately—by now fairly well trodden paths about three hundred meters away, where he thought the other cartridge cases might have landed, and he began to search on the ground, but he just stopped when finally his head had cleared a bit, and he realized the senselessness of this activity, because in this pitch black darkness, in the dancing light of the flashlight, the chances of him finding even one cartridge were truly trifling, 1:2,500,000, so he decided to go back, and when he had once again reached the clearing in front of the hut, he didn't go inside right away, he just wandered slowly around, and as he wandered, he strolled a bit this way and that, when, roughly, on that place where the girl had stood for the entire day—more precisely, three or four meters from that spot—he glimpsed her signboard lying on the ground, which he hadn't even noticed until now, the sign which the girl had been continually holding up when she saw him: it was a pinewood contraption attached to a stick, including a frame with a few crossbars, and on the thick piece of cardboard attached to it were inscribed, with a felt pen, the words "Justice" and "Reckoning," well, now this too, he said angrily, and he turned it over, looking at it, but he didn't find anything in particular, nothing that could have told him anything new, so that he was just about to toss it to one side, and stamp it into the ground in rage, when he noticed that there were a few more pieces of that same kind of paper on the ground, a kind of thick carton paper, the same kind that had been pasted onto the pinewood sign, he picked them up, there were smaller ones and one larger one, and on the smaller ones there was also some kind of writing, but in the dark with the flashlight's beam he couldn't make them out, and as these pieces of paper held out some promise of revealing more of the girl's intentions then he had been able to glean until now, he gathered them up and went back into the hut, and then he began to evaluate them, examining them—once he had finished putting the door back in place—and he sat down in the kitchen chair, he palpated them, he turned them over, he sniffed them, but it wasn't easy to figure out what they were for, one of them, he estimated, the thicker and bigger piece of cardboard, could be about the size of the sign itself, so that perhaps, he reflected, she was planning to paste this onto another sign at some later point, or something like that, but then what the hell is this, he raised the cardboard closer to his eyes, and pointed the flashlight directly at it, what were these cracks here, and then here, and he realized that what he was holding in his hands was a specially prepared piece of cardboard that functioned so that the words on the small pieces of paper could be inserted individually into the vertical bands attached to the cardboard's surface, so that this sign—he held it away from himself, somewhat in shock—was a professional job, the kind used by professional demonstrators, professionals, he stared at it in fright, and he threw the thick cardboard onto the floor, then he bent over it, he picked it up, and he began to examine it again, pushing aside with his foot the smaller pieces of paper that he had brought in from the clearing, then he held them up one by one, and on each one there was a different word, he tried to insert one into the strip on the large piece of cardboard, and for sure he had figured this out well, because it went in easily, then he slid in another—so that's how it worked, he sighed, how depravedly resourceful this girl was, and here he was, as once before, under the influence of the events, he was prone to grant her some recognition for her inventiveness, and just as he was amusedly shuffling around and exchanging the paper slips in the large piece of cardboard, suddenly his heart nearly stopped, because as he was shuffling and exchanging the little paper slips, what emerged was:

YOU ARE MY PAPA

and then he quickly exchanged the first and second slip of paper, and he read the following:

ARE YOU MY PAPA

and the question marks were added by himself in that heart that had stopped for a moment, that heart which was his, and which he believed had grown cold a long, long time ago, and it had no other job than to keep pumping the blood through his organs—he had put one word in the place of the other, and then he put the other back in the place of the first, but he couldn't decide which version the girl had intended, and as he struggled there in the hut, out there in the clearing in the darkness were still five important slips of paper, although he didn't find these, and perhaps they would have been useful, because if he put them into the right order, he would have deciphered this: "I'll cut you down, big shot!"

The next morning at dawn he was already at his sentry post behind the Hungarocell panel, listening to what was going on out there, but there was no noise, nothing, nothing that would have indicated that they'd come back, although he was convinced that they were going to come back, how could he not be convinced of this, in part because, due to the events of yesterday, the police were now sure to put in an appearance, in part because it was now clear that as far as the girl was concerned, this was by no means at an end; he sat behind the Hungarocell panel, as if in a situation of a reversed hunt, when the hunted waits lying low in his hideout for the hunters to come, but, well, he waited in vain, because the hunters of this prey simply didn't want to arrive, 6:10 passed, then 6:50, then 7:20, and finally 8:20 passed as well, outside it had grown completely light, and he still sat there trying to listen in vain, there was no one out there, because he had long ago been able to sense any unaccustomed sound that didn't belong there, even the quietest sound; today, however, he heard nothing of the sort, well this is just impossible, he shook his head incredulously, it's not possible for them not to come, the possibility that they weren't coming here had to be absolutely excluded, but that's how it was, they weren't here, they hadn't come, and they still weren't there and it was 9:20, and not only out in the clearing, but also in the entire Thorn Bush, the silence was complete, not counting the rustling of the rising wind, but that only shook the dry branches and the bushes' bare thorny stems, there was only the ice-cold wind sweeping across the useless acres of the Thorn Bush, and eleven o'clock had already gone by, then 11:09, when he couldn't stand it anymore, and very cautiously, with the slowest possible movements, he lifted up the new Hungarocell panel —which he had prepared after having stamped the old one to bits yesterday—he lifted it from the window, because he wanted to see now with his own eyes if he hadn't been paying close enough attention, and maybe they were all there, waiting as mutely as possible, and looking at him, looking at his new Hungarocell panel, waiting to see when it would move, but he was mistaken, because when he had finally freed up the window and leaned out through the crack, he saw no one in the clearing, and among the surrounding bushes he also saw no one, he didn't perceive, with his x-ray vision, as much as the blink of an eye in the thickets beyond the clearing, he waited for a moment, he observed, not budging an inch, but nothing, so he put back the Hungarocell panel, and he sat down for a moment in the chair so as to think over what had happened, when suddenly his ear was struck by the sound of branches cracking and simultaneously the rumble of motorcycle engines—arriving from many directions at once, he determined—the sound of motors grew stronger, then he was able to tell that they were already in the clearing, a few of them still revved up their engines, as one or another rider pulled on the handlebars, and finally, one by one, they shut down their engines, and for a while there were just unidentifiable noises, then suddenly, there was the sound of dead leaves and branches cracking beneath thick heavy boots, so here they are, he determined, and he stood closer to the door, so, well, he asked himself, what was he going to do, block the door, or what—it's hopeless, he bowed his head in the Russian fur cap, if they want to come in here, then there's no point in resisting, and he had already begun taking apart the door, when from directly nearby a deep bass thundered out, saying "it's us," and then after a moment, "open up, Professor, sir, we mean no harm," and the Professor stopped in the middle of his movement, because somehow it didn't seem as if these people were policemen, and even less so that gang of journalists from yesterday—he extracted the rags, the wooden boards, more rags, the iron sheet, the newspapers, the wooden planks, the Hungarocell panel, and yet more rags, and suddenly he glimpsed a person in the doorway, so huge that he only saw his chest: this person was wearing huge boots, black studded leather trousers, and a black studded leather jacket, and already he was stooping down, and this enormous figure leaned into the doorway, a bearded man at least fifty years old, balding in front, his hair gathered into a pigtail in back, the dark motorcycle goggles pushed up onto his forehead, with a helmet in one hand, while he supported himself with the other in the doorway; he leaned down, and in that deep resonant voice he bellowed in a friendly manner: "a good friend has come, have no fear."

It's not entirely clear—she noted to the news editor of the local opposition television station while seated on the couch, pressing her knees together as tightly as she could, slowly placing a glass of water back on the low table in front of her—if it wouldn't be better to get some kind of legal assistance here, or try to arrange for that back at home, in this moment she really had no idea at all, but she had truly not counted on such a turn of events—they all could understand—her father simply had left her with no option other than to direct the matter along the customary legal route, because she had to do something; yes, the news editor nodded in deep agreement, his gaze somewhat mushy from sympathy, he more than understood this, in his view it was a very good idea, namely to take matters in hand here, in other words, the young lady would never find more competent legal services anywhere else, and as far as he was concerned, he perhaps could recommend someone who, in his own modest opinion, was beyond question the best in his profession, Géza, who could truly not be accused of being under the influence of the Professor's—the TV news editor leaned in across the table a little closer to the young lady—namely, of your father's undeniable reputation, when he, namely the Professor, had won over the complete admiration of much of the town with his own—why mince matters—renown, people are easily confused, aren't they, the news editor smiled uninterruptedly, and people try to manipulate them in so many ways that it's just laughable; morals, young lady—the tone of the news editor's voice suddenly changed—morals, that's nothing more than a word now, and I can claim without exaggeration that we are its last bastion, you know, to take up such a cause as your own is not only a humanitarian obligation, but this, this, this is simply—and now the young lady will surely be surprised—this is *our job*, and here the TV news editor paused meaningfully, while, inasmuch as he could, he gazed searchingly into his guest's wide-open, innocent eyes, so that he—he pointed at himself following this brief pause—in addition to supporting her in full measure (and she knew it was a matter of just one telephone call), in this struggle for justice the young lady would in no way find herself left alone, namely, in her search for sufficient legal support, he would find it most fortuitous if he could be of assistance, and here he paused again, he didn't take his eyes off the young lady, because, he said, he was thinking about creating a kind of communicative sphere, yes, so that when the trial began, the "ground"—to put it like this—would "already be laid" for the court to fully and deeply comprehend her feelings, the feelings—let's say, he said, leaning back in his armchair —of an innocent suffering child, because this, in his opinion, was the case here, this was an emotional matter, young miss, was it not? he asked her, now livening up again, if I understand well, yes, you do, she answered indifferently, and pushed the glass of water a little farther away from herself on the table's glass surface, you understand perfectly well, this is in fact a powerfully emotional matter, and I am genuinely grateful for the assistance you have offered, but could you explain a little more specifically what you have in mind when you speak of creating a communicative sphere, well, so, this is dead simple, the television editor was delighted, what this meant was, the starting point for him and his splendid colleagues here at the Körös 1 TV station was that in such decisive matters as these, they held it to be their extraordinary obligation to ensure that every judicial ruling be founded upon a shared civic certitude, namely that a sense of justice should be evident in every clause of the law, if he could phrase it that way, the television news editor phrased it, namely, it was simply the obligation of a public broadcaster with its foundation based upon prevailing public morals to shape this shared civic certitude, ah,

I see, the girl nodded with a brief smile, you're thinking of giving me an interview, but this time with your TV station, well, to put it more succinctly, you could say that, the news editor burst out laughing, you, young lady, grabbed the matter by the balls, and at the words "by the balls," his laughter suddenly became a sharp yelp-like guffawing, well, yes, young lady—the news editor, seeing his guest's cool gaze, suddenly stopped guffawing—I had something like that in mind, if you would agree, we've prepared everything in advance, studio number one just happens to be empty now, and if it suits you, we can go right in. Fine, let's go, the girl said, she jumped up, straightening out her skirt, put her coat on her arm, and not even waiting for the news editor to step out with her, she strode quickly out of the office. What an idiotic hick, she hissed between her teeth.

He didn't wish to introduce his friends right now, if the Professor would excuse him, because they didn't really like their names to be given, they'd decided there would be no names at that time when a common pain and a common interest had driven them together, if he could put it in such a beautiful, poetic way, of course he could say his own name if it mattered, and maybe that would be appropriate, because in civilian life his name was Jóska, but enough about that, if the Professor would permit him, the Professor could hardly be surprised by the fact that of course they knew him, that was to be expected, no surprise, everyone knew who the Professor was and respected him, and they wanted to be the first ones to say that, and that's why they were here, so that if somebody didn't grant the Professor the respect he deserved, they would bash his head into an electric pole, there'll be a little "accident," isn't that right, Little Star—this man spoke in a questioning tone to one of his companions who'd also squeezed into the hut behind him, a figure approximately the same height as he, but much fatter, who at this moment for some reason or another was kicking the pieces of the dismantled door apart in rage, right, Little Star, isn't that so, Little Star, he thundered at him once again, because he didn't hear any reply, yep, right, Little Star somehow forced himself to answer, and he continued to kick apart the pieces of the door with his heavy black boots, venting his rage in particular on an iron sheet, it was impossible to know why, and finally the man in the black leather jacket had to yell at him: stop it, Little Star, we can't hear what anyone is saying, at which point he stopped, but from the slack grimace on his face it was evident that he would start up again as soon he could, because these pieces here, especially this iron sheet, really made him mad—in a word, this man continued, we know who you are, and we really hope that you, Professor, know who we are, because we've already done a lot for this town, of course not as much as you, it would never occur to us to compare ourselves to you, the Professor, but we've always done our best and continue to do so, isn't that right, Little Star, and once again he was addressing that person behind him, but now he looked back, too, because this Little Star had not only not calmed down, but had begun to kick something apart again, but this time in a sneaky way, for the most part the iron sheet again, because it visibly seemed to greatly enrage him for some reason, but then he stopped, and snorting, blew out air from his nostrils, turned on his heels, trampled on all the bits and pieces of the door, bent down, clutched at the posts serving as a door frame with his two hands, and somehow, with great effort, squeezed his enormous body out through the doorway, and now he only answered from farther outside the hut, muttering that the whole thing should be lit up anyway, but at that point the other man—who now sat facing the Professor, his legs sprawled open in the Professor's armchair, and who now in all likelihood the Professor could judge to be the leader of some kind of group which he knew about only through hearsay—of course, he did not react, let him go, let him do what he wants, because if he has to set this place on fire, then he has to, and that's it, that was in this man's grimace as he realized Little Star had not calmed down, and he was not being obedient now, he looked at the other figure standing next to him, a mere pipsqueak of a boy with a pimply face, but he didn't say anything to him, he just signaled that he shouldn't be getting worked up about this—you had to let him, he was still a child—this was in his gaze, and the pimply pipsqueak boy understood, indeed, he clearly seemed to agree, because at one point he nodded a few more times than he probably should have, and his boss looked at him sternly once again, indicating that he wasn't pleased with this last nod, but then he once again turned to the Professor, asking him where he had left off, oh yes, now he remembered, well, they were talking about how important respect was to their group, and that they would do everything in their power to ensure that nobody would ever forget the Professor, and he repeated himself, saying yes, yes, and that's as a matter of fact why they were here, because they had heard about what had happened here sometime around yesterday afternoon, and he drew out the word "sometime," and he didn't want to make it sound as if they intended to supplant anyone else, that they had come there instead of anyone else, they had nothing to do with that, what mattered to them most was independence—along with respect, of course—they were indebted to no one and to nothing, faithful only to their own selves and their ideals, and in this world this was the rarest of values, am I not right, like a diamond, isn't that so, Professor, would you not agree with me? he asked the Professor, leaning forward a little bit in the chair, but the Professor just nodded uncertainly once, like someone who isn't quite certain of what he is nodding at, while the face of the leader, whose face reminded him of nothing so much as King Kong, clearly was satisfied with this, and after a brief pause—the purpose of which might have been so that he could gaze deeply into his face, as if he were searching deeply for his true gaze—he said that all of them here were searching for an honorable man, and that this was the one path, and once again he was silent, and again he continued with his examination of the Professor's face, like someone who suspected that his sincerity might be laughed at or mocked, because he was sincere, and he said this too, namely: I am sincere, before the Professor now there was nothing but this sincerity, so that he, who considered the greatest human value, next to sincerity, to be that of directness, would ask directly for what he wanted, with no equivocation, no hemming or hawing, he would say directly why they were here, because as he had mentioned already before, they'd heard about yesterday afternoon, but he had to immediately add that not only had they heard about yesterday afternoon, but they had heard about everything, and that was why there was so much respect in them, and for him personally too, because they knew more or less about everything, and what they knew did not please them very much, they knew they held the same values as the Professor, but until yesterday afternoon they could not be completely sure if their ideals were the same—but ever since yesterday afternoon they were certain that they were the same, and this was the basis of their respect, and from this moment on they would expect anyone who stepped foot into this town, as well as all people who considered themselves to be residents here, to surround the Professor with an even greater respect than he had enjoyed before, because the Professor was someone who lived according to his ideals 110 percent, and very few people could say this about themselves, in short, he wanted now to respectfully request, as—well, let's say as the spokesperson of this protective association—if the Professor wouldn't have any objections, if this anonymous posse, as they had often previously been called, if their association, formed in the interest of protecting the town, which nonetheless always avoided operating under a specific name, as he had mentioned before, would now nonetheless take up a name, so that underneath that banner they might continue to fulfill their duties, those duties which they must, as an obligation to the town—our town—fulfill day after day, night after night—because don't you worry your head for a single moment, Professor, because of what happened yesterday afternoon, it's all been arranged, no one is going to set foot here and bother you or even ask you any questions, because they had already explained everything this morning in the relevant locations, the most important details that the legal and official—and here he emphasized the word *official*—entities needed to know, of course only the most important parts they had explained to the town's guardians of order, and so everything was arranged, as he said, the case was closed, the Professor had no need to worry that anyone would bother him here anymore in his quiet solitude—if he could allow himself this poetic expression again—because this quiet solitude, he again looked deeply into the Professor's eyes, meant a great deal to them, because at long last they would be able to write upon their banner a name—of course just in imagination, just this imaginary name—and only if the Professor would agree to this, and then the path before them would finally be clear, the path upon which they searched for an honorable man, clearly, because they all felt here—for just look at them—that with his name on their banner they would be able to find this man very soon.

A motor revved up outside, then another and yet another, some were revving their engines for a while, others immediately switched into high gear, and he listened to the sounds outside, as one motorcycle started up, then another, and yet another, and yet another, changing into second or third gear, then back into second, then they began to move away, and after a few minutes the motorcycles roared in the distance, and they nearly roared simultaneously as if they had all just gotten onto the paved road at the end of the Thorn Bush, just as they had come from there, from several directions, like an army with its own outflanking troop formation, only now they left in the other direction, they departed from his kingdom on the same paths on which they had come, and from that point on, it was no longer what it had been, this occurred to him for the first time: when he realized he was still standing in his own hut, facing his own chair, so then how did they know—if there were no regular paths around here at all—not only to use the paths that had been trodden down during the brouhaha of the past two days, but even more than that, they'd clearly been able to use new paths to get to him, when did they do that? he posed the fairly disquieting question, then he waved it away, saying that he had more important things to do than to chew on this, but still it wouldn't leave him in peace, and he began to feel tormented again: if there had never been paths leading to his hut in the Thorn Bush before this, how did they suddenly appear all at once, just like that, uniformly, meaning that evidently last evening starting around midnight, presumably in the second half of the night, when he couldn't take it anymore and let himself fall asleep for a few hours, this posse had clearly turned up and had cut away these paths while he was asleep, but even then, if this was the case, how was it possible that he hadn't woken up, they must have been using some kind of jungle-cutting saber, it flashed across his brain, characters like this obviously love such things, yes, that was it, they came in the night and used some kind of machete, or something like that, and he sighed deeply, outside the silence was complete, only the wind kept blowing, he turned back toward the window, then reverted to his usual position in his chair, he adjusted the plaid blankets and the newspapers in it, and sat back down, or rather sank back down in order to think things through, what was going on here, who were these people, and what the hell was this King Kong babbling on about, no, it wasn't as if he didn't know who these people were, because he still remembered that once, maybe a year ago, when somebody back there in town had begun cursing them during a conversation, he had somehow come to their defense, saying that now, when the central government in the capital city was nothing more than a mere formality, when every locality in this unhappy country, sunk into destitution, was completely left to its own devices —when they had all been left to the mercy of frauds, robbers, plunderers, and murderers—then the formation and activities of such a group should instead be welcomed, that's exactly what he deigned to say, and by now he had regretted it exactly seven times, but afterward there was nothing he could do, indeed, he had to bear it when the news of his words quickly spread, and to his greatest surprise one day later in front of his house at the time, there in the old German Quarter, somebody had placed a gift parcel in front of his door, a gift parcel which was for him the most useless, senseless, and confused gift that could ever have existed, because in it all jumbled together were a bottle of men's shampoo, chocolate, a map of Greater Hungry, smuggled cognac, a cheap quartz watch, a bundle of matches, and a few old newspapers from 1944 with certain sentences underlined in red, as well as one single rose placed at the top of the package, he remembered this very precisely, but at that time he didn't think that they would somehow be relying on him, that *they* would be keeping an eye on *him*, and be treating him as some kind of intellectual reference point, moreover, because of yesterday's events they were now celebrating him as a kind of hero, because from the confused words of this hick King Kong it appeared that these certain events, namely, his own role in these events yesterday, in a harebrained fashion, had made him a noble figure in their eyes and no matter how he tried to approach this, he couldn't explain it by any other means, only by the fact that they were lunatics, a public danger, and there was no point in trying to hypothesize any rational or logical motives for their activities, because this posse—the Professor stared at the Hungarocell panel with rounded eyes—were simply sick psychopaths, and vile to such a degree that only the worst could be expected from them, just as he only expected the worst, and precisely because of this he had to do something, because this role which accordingly they had attributed to him could easily turn fatal, a role which he—he leapt up from the chair—had to impede somehow, but by then he was already outside of his hut, he stopped dead in his tracks for a moment, wondering what to do with the door, then he decided that this time he wouldn't bother with it, because he had to leave, he had to discuss this matter, get to the end of it, so he left the door as it was, and set off.

She was leaving town, she said, opening her eyes completely wide, and the spectators watching TV in the Biker Bar gaped with bated breath at these two wide-open eyes, she was leaving, she said, not to the reporter, but directly to the camera, because from now on this wasn't a private affair, but a matter for the official bodies, she had made her report, with which she hoped that her part in this affair had come to an end, at least insofar as her official obligations were concerned, nonetheless she would all the same like one more time to repeat her first words: that she had come here so that a private affair could once and for all be resolved in the presence of the public, and she did not wish to leave without arranging this, and so—here, sternly pursing her lips, she held a meaningful pause, then turned toward the camera, but she did not continue her sentence, and following this brief and effective pause she said, her mellow tones a moment before becoming as hard and sharp as possible—that she was a betrayed, abandoned child who had come here in order to uncover the truth, to inform the public not to believe appearances, because he to whom everyone in this town referred with the greatest devotion as an internationally renowned and learned professor for his so-called international, moreover, world-famous investigations into mosses, and whom she herself, despite everything, had, until yesterday, thought of as her own father, was not deserving—her lips convulsed—of the public's devotion, or the privilege of calling himself her father, I confess—and those clear blue neon eyes, already well-known from earlier television broadcasts, nearly set off sparks; I have come here today, to this marvelous television station, in order to announce, and particularly to announce to this town, which sees in him such a magnificent figure, that this person is no longer my father, and that's why I'm here, so that I may announce to the public that I now deny this person who denied me for twenty years, and I no longer recognize him as my father, and I'm no longer willing to bear his name, I declare that from this point on he has no longer any right to refer to me at any time or in any connection as his child, this common armed criminal, a sanctimonious swindler unjustifiably basking in his own renown, a petty moss forager, the girl whispered to the camera, and it could be seen that on the faces of the spectators in the Biker Bar that they were beside themselves from her beauty, the foam stood on the top of the beer, the pint glasses stood still in their hands, their hands stood still in the air, so intense was the attention with which they watched this girl, the television set was placed high up in the corner next to the entrance, mounted on an iron bar at the juncture of the ceiling and the walls, and their necks had grown stiff, but these necks hadn't moved for ten minutes now, because they all sensed there was something of great significance in the air, and namely whenever a matter of great significance came along, it always ended up involving them, so they paid as close attention as they could, but they were already very fatigued by such intense attention, and they just tried to make out the most essential parts of what the girl was saying, that for example she sought exemplary retribution for everything that he had committed, and she was never going to visit him in prison, where he obviously was going to end up, and she would like nothing more than for him to rot away there where he deserved to be, and that she hoped that there in his squalid cell he would wilt away on that stinking prison bunk, and that *finally he would be overgrown by moss*, and at this the intense observation suddenly broke down like water over the floodgates, this last point simply broke their attention down, namely, the guffaws broke out, they simply couldn't stand the tension anymore, and they all roared with laughter, they banged their pint glasses down on the bar, and they doubled over, because they had to laugh so much, and only the Leader remained silent among them, leaning on the bar with his right elbow, and there was nothing on his face except for a kind of gloomy concentration, and while his companions were still gasping for air in their great mirth, he fixed his gaze rigidly on the television set mounted up there, like someone who didn't understand, someone who really didn't grasp what he'd heard, or as if he were turning the words over in his head with which he would, in a moment, inform the others that although everything was still not completely clear, they'd been gravely mistaken, there was more to it than what they had just heard, they were not being confronted with the truth here, but the opposite, there had occurred here the most inexcusable defamation, which they, as a collective, were obliged to respond to as a unit, as was their wont.

A pure heart and a straight back, if this is within you—the solemn recruiting speech sounded on the opened website—then you may join us, moreover, then you are one of us, because whoever's heart is like that, whoever's spine is like that must directly feel the obligation to join us, it doesn't matter what kind of a motorcycle you have, you can come to us with an MZ, or even an old Berva moped, we don't care how old your Kawasaki is, how old your Honda is, because for us only one thing matters: honesty and ideals, if you feel both of these things within yourself—a motorcycle horn sounded—then you will find your place with us, come among us, come with a Kawasaki or come with a Berva, it doesn't matter—and of course it did matter, it mattered very much, because almost everyone came with a Kawasaki or a Honda or a Kawasaki or a Yamaha or a Suzuki or a Kawasaki or a Honda, the most frequent and the most popular was the Kawasaki 636 from eight or ten years ago, and the T2R from Yamaha, from about the same time, and quite a few Honda Varaderos turned up and of course the Suzuki GSF Bandit, and the Hayabusa, but that doesn't mean, the Leader—as they called him—explained, that you can only come with these, we will help you to get these, because we have a shop, but for members only, where you can find everything from leather gear to kidney belts, from Sixgear and DiFi Viking gloves to Forma Ice boots, and you don't have to pay right away, of course members can buy on credit, although it really is credit, meaning that you have to pay it back, little by little if you want, but you do have to pay it back, because if you don't then you'll be kicked out, and whoever is no longer part of the collective but still owes money has to pay a heavy price, this has to be stated right at the beginning, because belonging here comes with a sense of obligation, and I can't repeat enough that this sense of obligation must come from within, and it's better if you're aware right from the beginning that this is no amusement park and this is no nursery, this is a collective that requires strength, namely, if you understand, you must show strength, that means you understand, and you have to understand well, because this isn't just some club for weekend motorcyclists, for us to just form in procession and turn to the left and to the right like baby geese, no, there are tasks here, because to reach our goal we have to clear the path upon which we are searching for pure humanity and honor, because we are searching for an *honorable man*, and we are searching for the path, so you would do well to think over if you want to join us or not, because afterward there's no what-was-that-again; and while you're thinking it over, you should practice our anthem, because whoever joins us has an anthem, namely this one, so you should learn the text, even if you can't carry a tune, just learn the text, beat it into your head—because otherwise we'll beat it into your head for you, and that will hurt—so memorize:

*All pistons are rumblin' beneath me,*
*My heart rumbles in two broken parts.*
*The distance is shinin', every star sparklin',*
*I leave them Benzos far behind.*

*I don't know where I'm even headed.*
*I only know the pain is huge.*
*Life promises neither good nor bad,*
*And every mofo I'm leavin' behind!*

*The wheels are spinnin', my Bowden's torn.*
*There ain't no curve I ain't ridden on.*
*The Idea of Purity, it's leadin' me on,*
*'Cause I'm its fuckin' honor guard!*

He explained to him that this was a dangerous device, what's more he was sitting in his chair again, and when he came back this time, he was wearing a long leather coat, he came into his hut and immediately moved the kitchen chair with the armrests away from the blind window, and sat down on it, so once again he had to stand in front of him and listen, as he said: just have a look, here it is, Professor, imagine the entire thing, you can see that here is the body of the device, I wouldn't touch it myself, he added smilingly—although it would have been better if he hadn't been smiling—straight to it, we'll call the thing by its name, if you get me—well, to get to the point, here in the middle, you see—although you must know this already, because you were handling it pretty skillfully—do you see it? and he took out the imaginary magazine, and from the magazine, with his thumbs, he flicked an imaginary cartridge into his other palm, you see, here's the cartridge, he extended it toward him so he could see it clearly, here it is, you're very familiar with that, well, but do you know as well that below the cartridge there's a little bit of gunpowder which has two functions, one of which—he turned it over and he showed him this bottom part—is so the shot will be thrust out of the barrel with a lot of energy, but as for the other, just a bit of energy is needed to extract the next cartridge from the magazine, you understand, well, of course you do, and now it's clear you see that this isn't some new kind of Pacific Ocean moss discovered by yourself, but a dangerous weapon, and a dangerous weapon like this—an AMD 65—can't stay here, because my buddies might come visit you here, it would be much better for us to arrange this in a different way, it has all been taken care of, and he asked him now, he asked, while sitting in the Professor's kitchen chair and scratching his beard, for the Professor to note well his every word, because everything had to proceed according to the plan he laid out: when they came and asked about the weapon, then you are going to take out a pellet gun and show that to them, and you tell them that you were just shooting aimlessly with that and nothing else, because you can't help it if those scribbling hacks got scared so easily, well, you say that's what the pistol is here for, just to scare someone like those hacks off, but it can't do any more damage than that, and you need no permit to own it, is that clear, the guest asked patiently, then from an inner pocket in his long leather coat—because that's what he was wearing this time—from somewhere in the lower part of the coat, he took out something that looked like a pistol, and he said, here you go, here's your gas pistol, just pull the trigger and it's ready, it works, then he stood up, but of course only hunched over, because the ceiling of the hut was too low for him, and hunched over like that, he asked: so where did you put the AMD 65, and there was no protest, the Professor saw clearly that this character wasn't going to ask again, whether he was a figure of respect to them or not, it seemed advisable to move backward to the clothes piled up in the back of the hut without any discussion, take out the weapon, and hand it over to him with the remaining magazines and cartridges—these immediately disappeared beneath the long leather coat—and it also seemed advisable not to wait on the question of what happened to the empty shells or magazines, but to motion for him wordlessly to follow as they both went outside to the back, to the column of Hungarocell panels, where he lifted up the large woven plastic shopping bag from the hiding place;

the other man took it, carried it out front to his motorcycle, and threw it into the box attached above the back wheel, then he stood next to the motorcycle for a bit, and with a piercing look that he sank into the Professor's gaze—which had chilled the Professor the last time, or it should have made his blood run cold in his veins—he cleared his throat, extended his hand, and said they'd be seeing each other again very soon, because since the last time they had spoken, great changes had occurred in the town, because people were saying that somebody was arriving, someone for whom they had been waiting a long time, and that everything had changed, everything today was different than it had been yesterday, so that everyone was staking everything on tomorrow, he said, and with that he strapped on his helmet, threw his leg across the seat, straightened the long leather coat out around himself with the AMD 65 tucked beneath it, nonchalantly started up the Kawasaki, and already he was backing out, and while backing out he shifted into high gear, and already he was gone, disappeared as if he had never been there at all, and he slid away amid the thorn bushes so skillfully that it was as if the branches hardly even trembled.

He could tie up that old sheepdog of his, he mumbled to himself as he struggled with the huge dog, but as always, when he came here, this beast was interested in the visitor only for a bit, after a while ceasing the tugging and growling, and, as if grown weary of the task, it left the visitor alone—it being him this time—alone, it sneaked away, the old, sick dog, its fur fallen out, blind in one eye, it left everything there and lay back down in its doghole; he went in along the path haphazardly paved with broken pieces of cement up to the farmstead's entrance, and he rang the bell once, he rang the bell twice, and he rang the bell three times, but he waited in vain for the peasant to come out, he didn't come out, so once again he banged on the door, now with full strength, and he yelled in saying what's going on, are you asleep, open the door already, but the door didn't open, and then accidentally he just pushed down the handle, and it turned out the door was open, which was pretty strange, as ever since he had known this peasant, he had never known him to leave his door open even if he was totally drunk, he didn't understand what was going on, maybe he's gone mad in all this chaos, who knows, he asked, as if he were speaking to him, telling him that he was already here in the kitchen, but nobody answered, because there was not a soul to be found in the kitchen, and the entire situation was really pretty unusual, because the Professor knew that early in the morning like this, at 7:18, he was usually still in the house—for a very long time he hadn't kept any animals that had to be fed, he never repaired any tools, never bothered with the house, and in addition he never went to the town bar, because why wouldn't he have enough to drink at home, for as he told everyone, he only drank his own, and if he had some at home, he didn't need anyone else's swill—so what's going on here, the Professor asked again, and he just cleared his throat, and he kept calling out Halloo, where are you, come out already, but nothing, he opened the door to the sitting room, nothing, he opened up the larder, nothing, namely, when he was just about to close the door, he heard a kind of moaning, he went in again, but nothing, when, however, he was about to close the larder door this time, it was as if he heard that whimpering sound, and so he went back, and he came upon a small door which had been cut into the wall at the end of the larder, it was hidden behind some planks at least three meters long, propped up against the wall, and when he opened that door, there was the peasant lying on the earthen floor, lying in blood, his head smashed in, he couldn't see his eyes or his nose, his mouth drooped down, and this entire person was completely curved like a fetus, and he whimpered because there still seemed to be some life in him, but that was the only sign that he still lived, that whimpering, the Professor knelt down beside him in the pool of blood, and he tried to place his head in a upright position, because it was pushed to one side, and the mouth was touching another pool of blood, and the Professor tried to straighten his head so the peasant wouldn't choke, but he really couldn't bring himself to handle him, he was afraid to hold him, and then when he held him anyway, he was afraid to turn the head, lest it hurt him even more, well, then he stood up—what should he do?—there was nothing he could do, he went into the kitchen and quickly found a washbasin, he filled it with water from the canister, he grabbed a rag, and hurried back to the larder, which at some point could have been a kind of smokehouse, when there was still some meat to cure, very cautiously he began to wash the peasant's head, and was successful in that his eyes and nose were already visible, he washed off his ear and his hair carefully, and then he tried again to turn the head around, and if this wasn't entirely successful, at least he was able to move him so that his mouth no longer reached into the blood, what should he do, what should he do, he wasn't in despair, in difficult situations like this he always remained composed, but he just didn't have any other ideas, and at that point the peasant moved once, it wasn't much, but at least it was something, namely he blinked once, then he blinked again, well, then he got the idea of cleaning the blood away from around the body, maybe that would help, but maybe he was just playing for time because he was hoping that somehow the peasant would come to, and somehow that's what happened, first there was just that blinking, then his mouth moved, as if he were trying to say something, then his hand moved—first one hand, and the other hand, and so on—and the Professor just waited, completely impotently, because he couldn't think of what to do, he didn't even know where the wounds were, and if these were even wounds at all, because the peasant's face was so disfigured that it looked as if it had been smashed in, as if his head had become indented from one side, it was a horrifying sight, but then suddenly the peasant said a word, so softly, that the Professor knelt down beside him and bent in closer, the peasant said: drink, at which point the not entirely appropriate thought flashed through the Professor's brain: even in this state, this is the first thing he thinks of?! it boggles my mind, but then he suddenly realized that wasn't what he meant, and he ran into the kitchen again, and he brought a glass of water, he helped him to drink, but it was difficult, because it was as if his throat was also shattered as he tried to take a sip of water, immediately he retched it up, but this retching somehow was good for him, because it meant that his body was becoming more capable, and so slowly, step by step, movement by movement, at least after ten, twenty, or maybe even thirty minutes ... he simply had no sense of time, maybe because of the shock, which—regardless of his self-control—was affecting him, he didn't remember what the time had been when he came here, water, said the peasant, and again he gave him water, and this time he was able to keep some of it down, that was possible, and so it went until he could get the peasant to lie on one side—he realized that the blood somewhere in his mouth could choke him, so it would be better if he was lying on his side, and this really did help the peasant somewhat—what happened, asked the Professor, and only at that point was he capable at all of thinking: what had happened here?! although this would have been the first question for any normal person, it flashed across him, he'd been here for half an hour already, but it hadn't occurred to him to ask this, of course he didn't get an answer, the peasant couldn't talk, at least not at this point, he would only be capable of that after another quarter hour or so, and now he was already sitting up, you're made of iron, the Professor said to him, he leaned the peasant up against the wall, and tried once again to straighten his head, of course very cautiously, *only very cautiously*, a voice rumbled inside of him, then he was able to do it, the head was positioned upright, the body was sitting, or at least seemed to be sitting, I should call an ambulance, thought the Professor, but by the time it gets here it'll be over for this one, over, don't call an ambulance, the peasant said in a completely weak voice, as if he were following exactly the Professor's thoughts, no ambulance, he mumbled, and the Professor realized only at that point that the peasant had absolutely no teeth in front, he asked for water again, and this time he was able to swallow it down, he was able to open up one eye, and with that one eye he looked at the Professor as he stood or knelt down beside him again, and the Professor didn't know what to do, don't do anything, the peasant said—or rather stammered between his missing teeth—and now it was really haunting, because it was as if he really could follow what exactly was going on inside him, in his thoughts, fine, no problem, I won't call an ambulance, I won't do anything, but tell me, if you can, what happened, but at this the peasant just closed his eyes like someone who was completely exhausted, then he opened them again, and asked for a sip of water, and then in a barely comprehensible voice, hemming and hawing, and forming his words only very slowly, he began to talk, and in the Professor's mind, as he heard, the picture slowly came together, because, the peasant stammered, they had said to him that he could choose, either they would smash the Csepel into tiny pieces, or they would smash him into tiny pieces—you poor thing, they really beat you up, didn't they—and it was because I sold you what was theirs, but I needed it for the Csepel, I needed a new battery, plus a new piston replacement, and a new clutch shaft—what did you sell me? the Professor interrupted him, dumbfounded, but maybe the peasant didn't hear him, because he only said: this was no collection here, he didn't even know who his grandfather had been, he'd ne'er even known his own father, let alone his grandfather, an' nobody was collecting any kind of weapons here during th' war, this was just whit th' bikers told him to say to explain why he had all these weapons, cos this here was their weapons stash, cos this was th' agreement and 'at he had to keep saying this in th' bar on Csókos Rood, an' elsewhere too, and all over the place, cos nobody ever believed a word he said: cos they liked their security, an' if the bikers got in trouble with the law, then only he would get nabbed, and he'd go into the slammer, but only for concealing a few weapons, and them bikers promised they would take care of him: give him money, a wee something to drink, everything that a body needs, an' they would stand th' bill for him in th' standing-only bar on Csókos Rood every month—as long as he had enough for th' Csepel, and this Csepel, he said to th' living God, this Csepel was his everything, an' they promised him, an' it was fine for a while, but yesterday at midnight they beat down th' door and went completely mad, they broke down the door, how dare he sell that AMD 65, and first they started to beat his head wi' the water canister, and Wee Star beat him wi' a wood plank, cos he was the roughest, he couldn't an' he didn't want to stop, they told him that they were gonna beat him to death, an' maybe they thought that they had beaten him to death, cos he already wasn't conscious; and he just only knew that he, the grand gentleman, was here, an' he was trying to splash some water in his mouth—well, this somehow was what he was able to get out of him, and he left him there as he was already able to move somewhat, the peasant just cried, and he said to him as he cried: everythin' would be fine, no and no, he should leave from here, in case they might come back an' find him haur, he should go in case they find him, cos these ones, said the peasant, aren't people, they're animals. The Professor nodded, he went out, turned back toward the stash, he opened up the Aladdin, pulled out the first weapon that he saw and the attached cartridge bag (the very first one that turned up in his hand, from the very top of the pile) then hardly even shoving it under his coat, just letting it hang from his hand, with the strap dangling as he stepped, he left the farmstead, and headed off toward the Thorn Bush.

We're here to help you, they answered, after the girl had called back for the second time, asking what they wanted, they were there to make sure everything went smoothly, they said, or, if the young lady wished to know more specifically, to make sure there would be no insults to the young lady while she made her way to the station if she chose to go there by foot on this bitingly cold morning, there won't be any harassment, the girl said back to them out of the corner of her mouth, but there will be, they said to her behind her back, and they all proceeded toward the station on Peace Boulevard in silence for a while, the girl do could nothing else than put up with this uninvited retinue, and she kept glancing behind to see if by any chance an available taxi was coming along, but there was no taxi, not even by chance, and now somehow nothing was going as smoothly as when she got here, these were hefty fellows, all decked out in leather, that's as much as she had gathered when she saw them for the first time, there could have been five or six of them, in other words a whole little troop, she didn't understand what was going on here, who sent them?—or somehow it seemed to her that nobody had sent them, they'd just shown up of their own accord, as happened so often in the countryside in this ruin of a country, she knew their kind very well, they were called, or they called themselves, the Local Force, in this absolute chaos, when nothing worked anymore even in the capital city—the parliament, the courtrooms, the police stations, and in the offices—nothing worked anywhere in this country anymore, because everything everywhere had rotted away; she had therefore decided that she would join SMBD, that is, Something Must Be Done, namely, she became a member, moreover everyone had thought at the beginning that she had organized SMBD, as ever since she had joined it she had taken on a clear leading role, and they began to travel all over the country, they boldly traversed the country, so she was well acquainted with these kinds of characters, and she was repelled by them, she wasn't afraid of them, she noted to herself, if it came to that, and suddenly her gaze became blade-sharp, no, instead she was repelled by them, and she felt that now too, with them right at her back, but she didn't know what they wanted, maybe they wanted to beat or rape her, it wasn't as if that hadn't happened before, because these days attacks like that were an everyday occurrence, and in many places not even punished—if it could even be called a punishment when an investigation was launched after "suspects" whose identities were well known to all, including the police, well, that's how things went here, and that's why she thought that in contrast to all that gutless crap—as she designated the citizens of this country—she was Doing Something, and not just watching what was going on here passively, and this time, too, she was thinking how she would defend herself if some atrocity occurred, but nothing occurred, instead they just accompanied her, really, maybe so she could leave the city safely, and tell us again, not to offend you—one of them suddenly spoke behind her back as they stepped along in their enormous leather hobnail boots and in their motorcycle boots right behind her—tell us why you came here, and what did you want, and of course she didn't answer anything, just after a few steps, she said, what does that matter to you, well, it doesn't matter to us, or actually it does, because to trouble the Professor, that's not a proper thing around here, you know, my dear, I'm not your dear, the girl answered contemptuously, and she strode on farther, and while she sped up a bit, she was thinking, oh, my father sent them after me, may he rot in hell, well, he's really a mafioso, so, she heard from behind her back, tell us already, you won't lose anything by it, we won't tell anyone, and suddenly she turned around to them, and flung the words into their faces—lest they think her a coward, and especially her—so you want me to tell you?! I'll tell you! I want to make his life unbearable and I want to make the place that he's living in unbearable for him, you tell him that, she shouted at them, she kept on going, and they followed after her, and then she heard as one spoke to the other, saying: did you understand what she said, no, the other answered, do you get it, I don't get it, she heard that kind of dialogue, so that once again she was filled with rage, and she turned around again, and she flung in their faces that they should tell their rotten honorable commander that she couldn't care less if he was shut up in a lunatic asylum or if he rotted away in prison, and tell him to get ready, because that was what was going to happen, one or the other, either a lunatic asylum, with his arms tied up behind his back, or a prison, where he would rot away in a bunk bed, tell him, will you tell him?!—we'll tell him, the members of the retinue nodded, as if they been given a good dressing down, and as if there were some kind of compunction in their voices, or so it seemed, thought the girl, and she set off once again, lest her father had ordered them to beat her up, and she just strode onward and onward, and when she got to the station, she didn't even stop at the ticket desk, what was the point when there wouldn't even be a conductor on the train, on the other hand she was decidedly happy when she saw a carriage on the tracks, because that meant at least there would be some kind of train service, train schedules hadn't been in use for a very long time now, so she would clearly have to wait for hours, but at least there was a train, she thought, and the train cars seemed to confirm this, because they were almost completely empty, she looked in through the windows from outside, deciding which one to get onto, when suddenly the entire train jolted once, and slowly began to move, then there was no time to waste, she had to jump onto the steps of the nearest rail carriage, and she was able to, and she closed the door behind herself, and when she had flopped down onto one of the swamp-green seats and looked out the window, she saw the repulsive troop standing there on the platform, watching the train, and that concluded everything for her, that was the end of it, she was only sorry that when she jumped onto the steps of the train the lipstick had fallen out of one of the side pockets of her handbag, exactly that lipstick, and down between the train tracks, that poppy red lipstick, and she was really sorry, because this lipstick was her favorite, and now she was really sorry.

He didn't like anyone and no one liked him, and he was very happy with this state of affairs; respect, that was something else, that came of its own, unfortunately, on its own from human imbecility, in the face of which he was helpless, not that he bothered with it too much, he really didn't, if he did, however, find himself confronted with it, then he could really suffer, and namely this was what led him to his first decision, although when he left behind science, the mechanisms of science, and its so-called scientific investigations, he couldn't really term this a decision: it was instead a natural consequence of the fact that he had lost his interest in mosses—mosses, which had been his preoccupation his entire life, and thanks to which his name was renowned throughout the world—the day came when he was looking out the window, he was looking at the Penny Market sign across the street, as a long line snaked in front of it right before opening, clearly because today clustered tomatoes or half-liter bottles of Coca-Cola were on sale, he saw this, and his taste for all further scientific research left him, and suddenly he thought about how what he knew about mosses—and he was the only one in the whole wide world who knew what he knew—was completely superfluous, why the hell had he bothered with these mosses, and especially during his entire life, and in general why the hell did he bother with anything at all, because what interest was it to him that—as *Nature* magazine had stated—he was one of the three most important moss experts in the entire world, fuck that, he said, with his well-known profanity, fuck it and fuck it, he repeated violently, because fuck the whole thing, and I'm never even going to look at another piece of moss ever again, or perhaps I'm supposed to look at these clumps of moss because of *Nature* magazine, or so that in this wretched place, in this rotten city, these empty-headed, self-satisfied knuckleheads raise their hats if they see me, or should I be looking at these mosses because of the mosses themselves, the mosses couldn't care less if I look at them or not, or what I know about them, or what I think about them, mosses just *are*, and I too just *am*, and that's enough—that's how it began, but still it wasn't a decision, it was a state that he somehow slid into, so that maybe if clustered tomatoes or half-liter bottles of Coca-Cola hadn't been on sale at Penny Market that day, everything might have turned out differently, but both of them were on sale, and he saw the line winding in front of the Penny Market, and so his life couldn't have turned out any other way than how it did, because then one day he realized the app he had downloaded onto his iPhone, which caused a man's voice, every hour, to announce the correct time *while weeping*, wasn't going to help him, and he was fed up with his house being as immaculate as a virus laboratory, so that he would lose his mind if something wasn't in its place, he was fed up with wanting to stay on top of everything, meaning that he was tired of dealing not only with mosses, but with everything; his iPhone—with Twitter, Facebook, his email, and of course LinkedIn—was there lurking in his pocket at all times, he had a radio in the bathroom as well as in the toilet, three television sets, and apart from the specialist journals, he was capable of perusing four separate Hungarian dailies, and he thought about how he was always listening to, looking at, and reading the news reports, namely, what they were saying was always there in the background, when they reported on this or that, when a bus blew up, when a mother was beaten to death, where a new epidemic had broken out, and where a new Gregor Schneider exhibit was opening, so that one day, the time of the first decision really came, and he went through every room in his house, first he turned off all the radios and televisions and threw them into the foyer, then he tossed all of the newspapers, books, letters, and everything that he could find (along with his iPhone) on top of them, then he spoke to his cleaning lady on the still-functioning landlne, explaining the situation to her, and finally he threw this telephone onto the top of the heap, and he carried all of it outside, well, when this first decision happened, he already knew that there would be a second and a third one, and so on, because it was very difficult to liberate himself all at once from these circumstances and that helplessness from which he had suddenly began to suffer so much, he wished he could have liberated himself all at once, with one single gesture, as he liked these "once and for all" gestures, to be able to say:

well, no more for this, or: well, that's the end of that; for it to really come to an end—it was just that there was never enough of an end, there remained a full obstacle course, a thousand little details standing in his way, so he liquidated his entire circle of acquaintances; that wasn't as easy as with the newspapers, the radios, and the other things, to throw them out, because these acquaintances, no matter how much he drove them away, kept coming back, as if they hadn't heard enough already that they should just get the fuck out of there, as he (encountering rather frequent incomprehension) expressed it in his own way, and these were only just the acquaintances, because after that there were still the nonacquaintances, his admirers, the hat-raisers, the birthday besiegers, and the politicians and journalists and the national, the nonnational, and the local and even more local television stations, and other scurrilous editors from which he had to liberate himself, and this went only slowly and tortuously, making him ever more impatient, and all the while he became ever more violent and ever more crude, so that this violent, crude figure could set about terminating his bank accounts, changing all of his assets into hard cash, namely—although he kept a small amount in forints—converting it to euros, and now he was not only violent and crude, but frankly savage, when he liquidated every possible contractual agreement except for the water, heating, and the gas, entrusting these to his cleaning lady, so that she would take care of them, but only strictly when necessary, that is from month to month, and strictly only in cash, so that he succeeded in reaching a point where he only sat in an empty room all day long and didn't do anything, and nobody came to see him, because nobody dared to knock on his door, people only dared—if they dared at all—to raise their caps from a good distance away, and there he sat sans objects, news, information, sans any kind of personal or official obligations—*almost,* he added nervously, taking his present situation into account—and at such times the cleaning lady, Auntie Ibolyka, kept coming into his mind, and he immediately chased it away, it was just that it wasn't so easy to chase Auntie Ibolyka away, because he needed her, he needed this fat, wide-hipped, good-natured, slow-moving, plump, simple soul, he couldn't deny this, he and Auntie Ibolyka, that was all there was left of the world after a couple of months, or to put it more precisely, after a couple of years, when those three people smuggled themselves in somehow—but Auntie Ibolyka had to be in on it somehow, no matter how she denied it later on, and for months on end—one afternoon, just as he was concluding his thought-immunization exercises, they stood there before him, in the doorway of the living room, and for a while they didn't dare to make the slightest sound, with their hats rolled up in their hands, they stood shifting their weight from one foot to another; he was speechless from surprise, and by the time he came to himself and was ready to protest and kick them out of the house, they had already begun saying to him that they were eternally sorry for breaking into his house this way, for which they all assumed the responsibility as one, but this was a matter of such enormous significance, requiring sacrifice from them, they had to speak with him, they said, their mouths nearly contorted in weeping, Professor, it is simply necessary, because our town, the place of your birth, is this year celebrating the two hundredth anniversary of its founding, and they had been entrusted, on the occasion of this indescribably great event, with communicating a message to the Professor, a message according to which the town wished to commemorate him as an honorary citizen, honorary citizen?! he asked in shock, as the flabbergasted houseowner had just now became able to speak, but he was so beside himself that he wasn't able to say anything else, and the three standing there in the doorway used this opportunity to continue, saying that as a matter of fact, the festivity (due to the successful performances of the local folk-dance troupe) would of course begin with the world-famous—as it could be termed—Satantango, followed by an opening address from the Mayor, in which he would first and foremost salute him in the name of the town; so, the Professor then yelled, because it had taken him that long to collect all the oxygen that was needed for the manifestation of his first indignation, you'll be opening with the Satantango, the Satantango, and now he was roaring, which frightened the three emissaries so much that they slowly took a step backward, in case they had to clear out of there quickly, say it once again, Satantango, the Professor rattled hoarsely in a frightening voice, and they didn't dare to speak, because they saw that the time for escape had come, he however—as he heard them tumbling down the steps, and opening up the door below, then running helter-skelter along the street, as if they were afraid that some heavier object might come flying after them from the window—as he watched all of this, he suddenly realized that there would never be a secure refuge from all of this; finally anyone, he shook his head bitterly, would be able to break in here at any time and start telling me about the Satantango, well, no, he shook his head again, there will be no Satantango here, that cannot be, he took his coat, and he stormed over to Auntie Ibolyka, and there he sat in her kitchen all the while declining plates filled with pastries that she kept pushing over to him, and he said it once, then he said it again, and then he was about to explain for the third time to Auntie Ibolyka, who was staring at him with an uncomprehending expression from the other end of the table, what she had to do, when suddenly she answered completely rationally, of course, no need to explain, Professor, I understand, you want to sell your house, you want to leave here, and I'll take care of everything, that's what you want, yes? he nodded, and Auntie Ibolyka—he had to acknowledge this, the Professor acknowledged to himself—commanded everything magnificently, the house was sold on the day it was advertised, paid for in euros, except for 1.5 million forints, just as his thus far murky plans had dictated, for the lucky buyer was able out of the blue to purchase a two-story house in good condition with a balcony in the most central part of the city for the best possible price, and he finally could set off, on the morning of March 22, with just his coat, and as for bags, indeed, he left without even a single bundle, strictly instructing Auntie Ibolyka not to betray to anyone where he was going, in a word he set off, and he set off on the great Magyar Conquest out there in no-man's-land, in the middle of the notorious Thorn Bush, which he had come upon in the previous months during his extensive excursions, finding it to be an ideal hiding place after he'd discarded the idea of the huge concrete Water Tower on the outskirts of the city by Dobozi Road—a locale which had at first been in the foreground of his attention; there had been various reasons for this decision, but primarily it was because the extraordinary number of steps had to be climbed for a person to reach the top, where an astronomical observatory had once been located. Well, here, thought the Professor, when he arrived in the Thorn Bush, there will be no problems, and I will never be of any interest to anyone ever again.

My Linzer torte, she answered, if they asked—and they did ask—which pastry she was the most proud of, and well, the Linzer torte, there's no question, it was well known, not even in her building, but without exaggeration, Auntie Ibolyka exaggerated, in the entire street, indeed, in the entire town they all knew about Auntie Ibolyka's Linzer torte—if they asked, and they did ask, Auntie Ibolyka always smiled at this point; what was the secret, and she would say immediately, there is no secret, my dear girl, no secret at all, and I'll tell you, she said, there is no easier pastry to make than this, and I know quite a few easy-to-make pastries, because just look now, she explained, and she gestured to show what had to be paid attention to, you take this much and this much flour, you knead it with this much butter, just these few ounces, and as for how much of what, don't ask me, my dear girl, because with me it's just by looking, in a word, you knead it after adding the butter, you put a bit of chopped walnuts in there, it could be almonds too if you have some, then of course the eggs, the baking powder, and the powdered sugar, and you knead all of this up nicely, properly as it should be, but by hand, my dear, because you can only knead properly by hand, then you divide it up by one-third and two-thirds, and you put two-thirds of the dough onto a large cutting board, then you take a nice rolling pin, not some Chinese piece of junk, I'm telling you, a proper rolling pin, well, the kind you can get at any one of the big markets, but also at the weekday markets too, you roll it out nicely on the big cutting board, and you make sure that it's nice and golden, but you have to feel it, you know what kind of golden color it should be, you know when it is good enough, and when it's not, when it isn't good at all, you have to feel it, my pet, well, the main thing is that the dough should be nice and golden, and then you lay it down nicely in the baking pan all across and set it aside nicely for half an hour, and then, well, you knead that one-third of the dough just a bit, and make little balls out of it, and then you should roll these out by hand, by hand, my dear girl, make sure you roll them out by hand, and you get these little dough strips, just as many as you need, oh my God, I forgot to say that when a half hour's up, you should spread some preserves on the larger piece of dough, nothing too sweet, it could be raspberry, or blackcurrant, or plum, or something like that, it doesn't matter, it just shouldn't be too sweet, because it's good if the taste is just a little bit tart, well, and then you place the strips of dough parallel to each other, and then you put them going crosswise, which makes a nice grill pattern, and then you put the whole thing into the oven, and that's it, you see how simple it is, I tell you but no one ever believes me, and even today I'm baking one, Auntie Ibolyka was explaining just at that moment to her female neighbor, but she could never betray whom it was for, because she hadn't baked it for herself, but well . . . for someone, and she wasn't allowed to talk about that, she said quietly, leaning in toward her neighbor's ear, not a word, because that unhappy person is of no interest to me, but I'm not going to let him die of hunger, without even just a tiny bit of pastry, because this Linzer torte was always his favorite, and that's why she was taking it to him, three baking pans' worth, but of course she wasn't allowed to talk about this, she looked at her neighbor mischievously, then she sat next to her oven for a half hour, took out the baking pans, letting them cool off a bit, then she cut them very nicely into little slices just as it should be, and she packed it all up into a basket, covering it with a gingham cloth, and she was already taking it, a cold wind blew outside, and she wasn't going to let the gentleman not know the great news, and as she hadn't brought him anything for a whole week already, the time had certainly come, she wasn't going to let him chase her away like last time, he had such an unaccountable nature, but what could she do, she just couldn't leave things like this, and she was already walking on Csókos Road and had already turned into the Thorn Bush, and with surprise she saw that on the edge of the Thorn Bush there had been a lot of movement—tire tracks, very deep and crisscrossing everywhere, what could have happened here—then she immediately found a path leading in which certainly hadn't been there before, and Auntie Ibolyka was very happy to see this, because she was in no state to keep ripping herself apart to get to him, well, how easy, this path was so nicely trodden, and she went, she went with the basket on her arm, and the Linzer torte was nicely covered with the gingham cloth, and when she was already well inside, who should come out but—the Professor himself, no, not coming, but storming along as only he did if something was making him nervous, because he had that kind of nervous nature, he was just that sort of sensitive type, but well, that's how it is, and she said to him: God bless you, Professor, I thought I'd bring you a little Linzer torte, I can't let you starve out here, and well, there is great news, and I really hurried out here so that you would know—because I heard what happened here, but I don't believe what they're saying, that you were supposedly shooting and everything, shooting at your daughter and at the TV crews, they told me in vain, I just waved them away, saying really, but what nonsense are they talking about, and about the Professor too—it's still warm, she lifted up the basket, and turning back the little gingham teacloth, she showed it to her former employer, who still looked a little bit like that—and she said to him that she would never leave him, because that's how things were in her family, because if somebody served somebody else it was for a lifetime, but never mind, that wasn't why she'd come out now, but rather to say that the Professor shouldn't go around shooting people, he should leave off this life and all this shooting, because great things were happening here, that's what they were saying, because the news is going round that the Baron, you know the Baron—he is supposedly coming home, just imagine it, the Baron from America, I knew the old Baron, and I knew the entire Wenckheim family—nearly everyone in my family served them at that time, she said, but those were good times, when the old Wenckheims . . . but anyway, now, Professor, the important thing is for you to come home, and to leave behind this entire life here in this Thicket, come home, nobody has signed the papers on the house yet because everyone is talking about how, from now on, life is going to change because the Baron is coming home, and everyone is saying how everything will be different when the Baron gets here, and supposedly he's on the train already, and they're saying that they saw him in Pest or somewhere, and that he's surely on the train, the Baron, life-size, Professor, are you paying attention?! the Baron is coming home, he's coming home, and he's going to take back the Chateau, his property and everything, do you understand what I'm saying, Professor? but well, where are you going, she yelled after him, because he suddenly turned his back on her and went the other way, back into his hut, Auntie Ibolyka related to her neighbors all that evening, he just picked himself up and turned around, and went back into that tottering contraption, and of all people, he, the Professor, who used to give me a dressing-down if I didn't wipe off the top of the electric light switch properly, I said to him though, I just kept saying and saying as he left that at least he should take the basket, and he should forget about this place already, he should forget about it, he's really like a naughty child . . . well, doesn't he understand the Baron is coming home?

He didn't realize that someone was approaching the hut, and although the trials of the past few days could have been enough to explain why—but it wasn't that, but rather the shock, which was still exercising a nearly total effect on him, so that he needed some time, and still yet a little bit more, in order to somehow calm himself down and be able to concentrate, to clearly survey the situation so as to decide what to do, but he was incapable of doing anything at all with a clear head, he sat collapsed in the kitchen chair, he was so exhausted that when he got back he had only readjusted the door in an improvised way, so when the door was kicked in with one powerful kick, on the one hand he had only himself to thank, and yet on the other hand the kick was so strong that in all likelihood even if the door had been put back properly it wouldn't have been able to prevent anything, only slow it down somewhat, but it didn't even matter, because then came the following kick, it really didn't matter, because whatever was facing him now, if it wanted to come inside, then inside it went, he was able to size this up immediately as this entity plowed through the debris, then pressed its colossally thick body through the door opening—and suddenly it stood there in the hut, right there in front of him, and the Professor didn't have enough time to jump, it wasn't possible from that position of collapse to suddenly just jump up to his feet and do something, and all the while he knew—but this was merely an instant—that there was no time here for thought, something had to be done, but his body wouldn't move, as if he were pinned to the chair, and in front of him that form rose higher and higher, and it didn't even say a word, it just looked at him, namely it looked down to where he could have been, but somehow these eyes weren't exactly focusing on him, they weren't really focusing at all in general, namely they weren't merely troubled, but it was as if they were rolling down and trying to find the right place again, but they couldn't, and somehow they had got stuck up there in the space of the eye sockets, and were now looking down, and there was the usual leather gear, and the same thick-soled military training boots which he'd been wearing on the first occasion, but now these training boots weren't kicking anything, they just stood—motionless for now, and he was breathing with difficulty, and only his right arm was trembling, namely the Professor noticed this at the beginning, that his right arm trembled, and in the gloved hand there was nothing, but this hand was clenched in a fist, the entire arm was really trembling, and moreover, as far as that was concerned, his entire body was shaking, as if dreadful forces were struggling within, and it was only then that the Professor noticed that the glove was bloody, so the blood is still there, he thought, and he spoke quickly: there's something here that might be of interest to you—at which point the flesh-tower seemed as if it were about to tip over, as if it might lose its balance, it had wanted to do something else, but gotten thrown off by the sentence, and really it tipped over, the head jerked back, then it turned once again to him, and the vexed eyeballs tried to focus on him, they couldn't, they still couldn't, or rather they could even less, they just swam here and there in those eye sockets, but above, so that they got stuck in the upper right corner—I think, the Professor said again in a calm voice, you'll be interested in this, I found it on the peasant's farmstead, he added, but it's not the one that I bought from him, it's another one, and I don't know what it is, you'll know more about it, would you like to see it? and the Professor looked up at him: he had clearly fairly confused the intruder, because it now seemed very obvious that when he showed up that he had not intended to speak, this was not the time for talk, because he wanted to do something, and that is why he was confused now, namely he was tipping over, and his mouth opened a little bit, and formulating the words with difficulty, he said: I am Little Star, but I'm not going to talk, because the light's going out for you, buddy, and this could have been some kind of old payoff line which had won him some kind of favor when he'd pronounced it for the first time among his pals, and ever since then he'd gotten in the habit of firing it off, but now it only remained mechanical and came out like a can of Coca-Cola from a vending machine, or a bullet, and what's more it really seemed that he wasn't even aware of this, he's completely wasted, it flashed through the Professor's head, but he's a total drunkard, he realized, and only then did the repulsively reeking breath hit him, the breath that was exhaled with the words that he spoke—to cut a long story short, the Professor said, I'll show it to you if you like, and maybe you should take it with you, too, I've got no idea what to do with it, okay? I'll get up and give it to you, oh, there it is, there you go, the Professor pointed toward the back corner of his hut, where the light from the pocket flashlight didn't reach, and he didn't wait for a sign of agreement, but stood up immediately, and he stepped next to the behemoth, who was visibly completely confused, as his brain worked much too slowly for him to understand what was going on, because he'd come here to beat someone up, that was obvious, and not to have a little chat—an activity of which he didn't seem particularly capable—and now this character with his heavy blankets wanted to give him something, but all of this proceeded across his brain pressing down like lead weights, the Professor was already there in the back, in the dark corner, and in vain did he start at the sound, in vain did he hear the clattering of the safety lock, and in vain a clear picture of what was going on returned to his brain, he wasn't quick enough, not in the least bit quick enough, because he couldn't stop this character from turning around to him, taking a step forward, and now he only saw the backfire, and the smoke, and then there was nothing more to do, his legs wouldn't allow him to step to the side as he wanted, his muscles didn't work anymore, he just looked at this character, and then in the last minute, the eyeballs somehow rolled back into place, and once again he saw another backfire with the smoke darting upward, and he heard this character, all the while not taking his finger off the trigger, yelling, well, you see it now, this is a PPD-40, you animal.

He completely blew the wall apart, because for a long time he didn't dare to take his finger off the trigger, not until he was certain that these bullets would traverse that lard-mountain as if it were a normal body, but finally he released the weapon and threw it down, or rather let it fall out of his hand, because he didn't dare move, because he felt that something horrific awaited him now, although he'd just gotten through a horrific thing, he had caused it, and here was the victim lying in front of him on the ground, inconceivable, but there was no time—no time again—for thinking, or even for understanding what he'd done, he held his hands out in front of him, and he staggered out of the hut, and only later did he think about how carelessly he'd done this, but he really couldn't concentrate, he stumbled here and there because he didn't know where to go, namely there was nowhere he could go, his instincts whispered this to him while he was still stumbling around the clearing, and finally he set off, at first only slowly, in one direction, it didn't matter which, it only seemed essential that he not go toward the town, nor toward the farmstead, not that he believed there was a direction that would turn out to be the right one, but in no case should he go toward the town and in no case should he go toward the farmstead, a voice within him kept rattling, don't go to the town and don't go to the farmstead, anywhere but there or there, and he went along ever more horrified, and in the meantime rain began to fall, it was more like wet snow, and the wind kept blowing, so that there couldn't have been anything more merciless, he leaned into this snowy icy wind, walking straight into it, he couldn't think, he could only go, and only one sentence began to form in his brain, just one thought, from this point on, he turned it over and it swirled within him, unstoppable: Nazi pigs—you'll never get me, you will never ever get me.

Let's take care of everything before the train comes, he said, and let's go before the Baron with a clean slate, and not leave any loose threads, we'll not leave a pile of manure here, everything has to be in order, because it is our responsibility to maintain order; so, brothers—the Leader raised his pint glass in the Biker Bar—we must clean up this dirt, because in this town, in our town there's no dirt, and this is a pile of garbage here, not only is this a huge disappointment from someone in whom we believed, but it's like when you completely clean up the street, but you left some garbage in front of one door, that can't be, the Leader raised his voice, so it's time to clean it up the old fashioned way, we'll split up into three groups, Joe Child, J.T., Totó—yes, you three go in front, just as you did before, there's no room here for feelings, this isn't the place or time, I'm telling you, now we must be ready to get rid of that garbage, we must be disciplined, and prepare to wipe that piece of filth out—carve it up and crush it like a bug, then let it go up in smoke, you understand don't you, and I hope everyone agrees with me; then when the train comes we'll be there, and if somebody has to be standing there when the Baron arrives, then it's us, and only after, you understand, after we've done what we have to do at the station, namely when the time comes, I will tell you when, then we can open our hearts and make room for our feelings, because we will weep; have no fear, we will have the chance for an honorable farewell, because not only was Little Star my little brother, but he was your brother, too, so all of us—like a family that sticks together—we'll have a chance to say goodbye, don't worry, that will come, because if anyone deserves it, it is he, because he did everything, he gave his life in order for us to follow the pure path, he is our hero, our martyr, and we never forget our heroes and or martyrs, he was our brother, we'll bid him farewell, just wait until I tell you, and we'll say goodbye. We just have a few things to take care of first.

# *TRUM*

# PALE, MUCH TOO PALE

An extraordinarily elegant gentleman came over to him as he stood next to the steps, this gentleman was so elegant, never had he seen such elegance in his entire life, and he especially wasn't expecting anything like that here, in the Westbahnhof, in any kind of connection with the ET-463 Jenő Huszka Intercity Express going East, he'd been working for the rail company for thirty-one years now, and then suddenly, after thirty-one years, there steps over to him such an elegant gentleman, if somebody had told him this morning that something like this was going to happen, he wouldn't have believed it, because why would he believe that on the morning international express there would be such a traveler, whose manservant was so, but so elegant, that he couldn't even tell what kind of material his greatcoat was made out of, for example, as if it were made out of silk, or, let's say, he said, out of merino wool, but it didn't matter what it was made out of, because not only was the material unspeakably elegant, but the tailoring too, it was a long coat, reaching down to the ground, he demonstrated in the railworkers' rest station, the manservant's coat reached down to the ground, what am I saying, the coat was a greatcoat, he said, it reached all the way down to the ground, I'm telling you seriously, he told them seriously, it brushed against the ground, and he wasn't playing with words, he wasn't exaggerating, it really reached down to the ground, and it flapped against the ground, and all of this in the Westbahnhof, and this was just the coat, because his shoes were also so fine, not only had he never even seen such shoes, he couldn't imagine them made from such leather, and with such sewing, and such particular tips and heels, moreover sometimes they glimmered—sometimes one, sometimes the other—as that coat that reached down to the ground brushed up against them, they understood what he was saying, didn't they? well, and then that panache, colleagues—he shook his head almost rapturously in the railworkers' rest station—as he waited for the train going back on the other side of the border, really, he would say that as the young man first stepped over to him, and the flaps of that greatcoat slowly began to lose their momentum, and then slowly subsided, and once again those two wondrously refined shoes were covered by that coat ... he'd nearly broken down when he'd noticed his assignment and taken up his duties at such and such a time yet again on the Jenő Huszka 463 Intercity Express, he didn't know how the others felt about it, but he hated this route so much that he couldn't even say how much, during all of these thirty-one years, and because—his gaze ranged over the four people in the railworkers' rest station who were listening to him rather superficially, yet listening nonetheless—these thirty-one years, these ... thirty-one years, he asked them to consider: even after all that time he still couldn't get used to it, because it wasn't possible to, always just these lumpen Eastern types, that's the kind of route it was, this Eastern Jenő Huszka, and no one was expecting any surprises here, although of course anything could turn up, because after those thirty-one years after all ... well, he really couldn't have expected anything like this, and he wasn't expecting anything like it when he began his shift, he shook hands with the other conductors and took up his place next to the steps of railway carriage number nine; for as a conductor with these thirty-one years behind him, he still couldn't be prepared for the fact that one day, out of the crowd, leather suitcase in hand, there would suddenly step out a person like this, and with all unexpectedness there suddenly stepped out of this crowd a, a, a ... he didn't know how else to put it—that *elegance*, well, one word is worth a hundred, the main thing was he wanted to recommend his relative to my attention, he was saying this seriously, the conductor now said seriously, he said it exactly like this: "I wish to bring my relative to your attention," and the conductor would now quietly note, he quietly noted, that although he was clearly a foreigner—he, the conductor, was able to judge this —he spoke perfect German, well, all I can say, he said, is that my dentures almost fell out of my mouth, because suddenly I was thunderstruck, I really thought I wasn't hearing properly, because that coat and those shoes had distracted me a bit, so I asked: could you repeat that, please?, and that gentleman didn't repeat his words loudly, he just leaned a little closer in toward me, and in a voice that was just a shade quieter—get that, it was quieter!—he said he wished to bring his relative to my attention, and by that he meant that I'd have to practically watch over him, because he rarely traveled alone, more precisely he'd never traveled by himself at all, which suddenly made me think, the conductor now said, that the person they were talking about was a child, so he even asked politely: how old is the little traveler?—at which the manservant—because that's what he must have been, he certainly couldn't be a relative, because as this person led his "relative" into the train car, as he practically guided him in the corridor so he wouldn't bump into anything, as he sat him down, took the suitcase from him, and put it onto the luggage rack, and tried to make the great gentleman (for this was a great gentleman) more comfortable in his seat by pushing the armrests up and then pushing them back down—well, from all of this he could clearly establish that this gentleman was no relative, but unequivocally his master; in a word the manservant smiled, and he answered that he was a person of a certain age, well, I was thinking, he said, this must be some old bag of bones who's being put on the train one more time between the age of ninety and death, but as all of this was running across my brain, I grew tired of it, namely,

I didn't want to think of the old gentleman in this way, it's hard to explain, you know this manservant had a kind of effect, a demeanor; and now the conductor would say, he said, if his colleagues wouldn't burst out laughing, he had a kind of emanation which made him feel that something truly important was going on here—well, enough of this hot air, how much did you get, one of the colleagues interrupted in the railway-workers' rest station, smirking at the others, but the conductor just screwed up his mouth, like someone who didn't want to get into the practical side of this matter, because it wasn't about that, he'd decided to tell them the whole story—and the point of the whole thing wasn't how much, he looked all around, it was just like them to narrow it down to that—but this was about something much more elevated, even if they laughed at that word, but that was the only word he could use to describe it, the conductor had stood there, he allowed, fairly moved by the scene presented by this manservant, the conductor stood next to the stairs of railway carriage number nine, and all he could do was ask if the reservation was for this carriage, the manservant nodded, he gave him the ticket, handed over the suitcase, and slowly stepped to one side, so that the arriving passenger could board the train and mount the steps between them, the manservant stood there, looking out in the direction from where the traveler in question was supposed to arrive, and so they waited there: the manservant, the stairs, too, and finally the conductor, although really in that order, and they waited, and they looked, and finally the conductor was able to make out from among the people drawing near who it was.

From this point on you shall have to travel alone, milord—the young relative leaned in toward him, after he'd arranged everything in the compartment, and he said to him: trust me, there will be no cause for concern, I've spoken just now with the conductor, and he'll be at your service to the end of the journey, more precisely—the young man now switched from slightly broken Spanish to German—until Straß-

Sommerein, namely until Hegyeshalom, because that's where the Hungarian and Austrian conductors change places, namely the Austrian conductors disembark, returning with another train to Vienna, and the Hungarian conductors get on and take over the train, so until you reach the capital city, there will be with you, sir, a conductor who has been consigned to perform all duties in connection with yourself by the Austrian conductor, I've spoken with him, and he will inform his Hungarian colleague of everything, namely, he will request his Hungarian counterpart to assist you with boarding your next train, trust me, there will be no problems, he stood in the compartment doorway, observing his distant relative with a fair amount of concern, because this distant relative looked at him with so much fear in his eyes that he didn't dare quit the compartment, sir, there will be no problem at all with the transfer, please believe me, he repeated, and he took a breath before yet again launching into an explanation of why, unfortunately, he couldn't accompany him, as he unconditionally had to be present at the funeral of the last member of the Algerian branch of the family, precisely as the representative of this family's distant relatives, i.e., the baronial branch—for surely he himself, the gentleman sitting here, had insisted upon it; however, he explained, he couldn't satisfy these two—in his view, both equally justified—demands at once, namely he couldn't at the same time travel with him to his birthplace, and be present at this family funeral, as well as at the festivities to follow in the deceased family member's honor, but he couldn't even really get started on his explanation, because the face of the traveler to whom he had extended his assistance had become so indecisive, and from this point on it attempted to convey, with this eloquent indecision, how he felt, but at the same time he tried to convey that his younger companion really must go now, he had to leave the train: please hurry, I beg you, he said to him, and disembark from the train, because in a moment we shall leave, but this "in a moment we shall leave" was pronounced from his mouth so sharply, in such a manner so unaccustomed from him, like someone who has resigned himself to his doom, but at the same time he was shuddering at the thought of the plural that was in that phrase—"in a moment we shall leave"—he truly shuddered, his attention, however, was increasingly narrowed in this shuddering, and suddenly one single object aroused his interest, and that was the possibility that the train might set off, and he repeated that now truly and in good conscience the young man should leave him to himself to avoid an even bigger problem, namely what would happen if the young companion were to remain on the train, and as he was hardly capable of hiding how disconcerted he felt by the fact that this wasn't going to happen, he just gazed at the young man with troubled eyes, and these eyes begged his companion to go—and they also begged his companion to stay, however when the companion in question had had enough of this, he bowed, stepping out of the compartment, closing the door, and waving goodbye, clearly taking great care to make sure the other wouldn't have any time to intervene in this course of events, walked with quick steps to the end of the car door and left the train; and the gentleman remained alone, not even moving in his seat, his coat had unpleasantly bunched up beneath him as he'd sat down when he first got there, but he hadn't even straightened it out, hadn't even taken off his hat, not even unbuttoned his buttons, not even unwrapped his scarf from around his neck, he just turned his head toward the window, and he looked at the people standing around on the platform through the not exactly clean window, and every face was very strange to him, and on no face was he able to make out anything reassuring, because in every single face he saw either tension, or some kind of grim determination that whoever had to leave with this train should just leave already—they, thank God, were staying put—as if this train were setting off for some dark and baleful place; and there weren't even so many of them, indeed excepting the innumerable homeless-looking people lying around along the base of the wall, it seemed to him there were surprisingly few people—mainly women, children, young men—standing around on the platform, but it was even more of an uneasy feeling when that platform began to move, and he realized that the train had set off, and that no one, nobody else had gotten on, apart from him there wasn't a single traveler on this train, or at least there wasn't anybody in this carriage, so it was just one more reason for his mood to worsen, namely, he was alone, really and completely alone, and from this point on he would be embarking upon this adventure without any help whatsoever, even if that had been his own wish; the question hadn't yet emerged in his mind—only now, in these moments: what would happen if his decision became real, and everything actually happened, he hadn't thought about that when he had been persuaded (due to the unfortunate turn of events) to leave South America, and he decided that since he had to fly to Europe anyway, due to the demise of one of the last branches of the family, he would utilize this opportunity not to take part in the funeral, as this had only been a kind of pretext for his exit, but rather—and he'd been racking his brains about this for a long time now—he would leave Buenos Aires at the end of his life because he had no business there anymore, and return back to where he'd come from, to return back where everything had begun, where everything had always seemed so beautiful to him, but where, since that time, everything had turned out so terribly, but so terribly wrong.

They found out he was in trouble—namely in really big trouble—completely by accident, because in the residence they never read the tabloids, as they called the *Kronen Zeitung* or the *Kurier*, such items never turned up in the house, and of course not even in the kitchen or the staff lodgings, it was strictly forbidden, so that it was directly a miracle that nonetheless one had turned up, and an even bigger miracle that one of the servant girls had come across an article which talked about the renowned Argentinian aristocrat, who, due to his irrecoverable gambling debts, was threatened either with the retaliation of the local Casino, or with prison; the story completely captured the attention of the servant girl, because the figure of whom the article spoke was pleasing to her, namely his clothes were so nice, she explained later on, when she showed the article with the photograph to the chambermaid, and she also skimmed over it; she spoke about it later on to her employers, the family, too, and she already knew why, it was because the name had struck her, and set her thinking: just how many Wenckheims could there still be in this world who weren't related to this family, and when this struck her and set her wondering, she was already en route to her lady, and from that point on the news became an important matter in the residence, and the personnel weren't able to follow any further developments, it wasn't their business, well, of course when the gardener and the manservant, the cook and the chauffeur, were among themselves, they just occasionally whispered to each other that a rescue plan had been formed, and that the gentleman in question—as they knew from the *Kronen Zeitung* and the *Kurier*—was already en route to Europe, and the young count and his friends had already gone to pick him up from the airport, but no matter how cleverly they tried to plan it, not even one of the personnel was able to get a glimpse of that individual who, from this point, was referred to only as a distant relative, the gossip, however, swirled around unceasingly, about how this distant relative was just a lowlife card player, then, how he was a swindler, belonging to the panoptic of the degenerated family members, and at last there was the final version: he wasn't a slacker, or an imposter, but genuinely an idiot, just another idiot in the family, the gardener, known for his maliciousness, murmured insinuatingly, so what, he shrugged his shoulders, we'll survive this one too, we've had more than our share of cretins like that, what's one more, this is Austria—and that was the sum total of information that reached the estate personnel, and with that the gardener considered the matter as settled, he turned back to his flower boxes, and accurately pressed down the soil around the roots of the begonias planted in a row.

The knock on the door was so faint, just as faint as a knock on a door could be, but he noticed it immediately, and he pulled himself up on the seat; then whoever was knocking knocked again, then that person knocked a third time, but by then he could already see that the strange handle on the door was turning, somebody was pulling it back and stepping in to the compartment; he quickly shrank back, and—like someone completely absorbed by the view—he turned his head toward the landscape slipping by on the other side of the window, and he only looked up when it was no longer possible to ignore any further the slight cough cordially intended to alert him of the presence of another person, he looked up, but for a while he didn't understand at all what was being said to him, because his ears began to ring, and it was very hard for him to calm down and believe that this person was indeed the conductor, who had begun to pronounce something who knows how many times already, pronouncing the words very slowly, because he didn't know how much the traveler understood the language he was speaking, telling him that his ticket was perfectly in order, and that he, the conductor, would stay by his side, then hand him over to his Hungarian colleague who'd be taking charge of the train on the other side of the border, so the gentleman should have no worries about this, and the gentleman should have no worries about anything, because the train was on schedule, so that this much was certain: they would reach the border, moreover the town, where the aforementioned change of conductors would take place well in time; and as for after that—the conductor raised his voice with a joking half smile, and leaned forward a little—well, he couldn't really guarantee anything, but in recent times no serious complaints had been made concerning this route, and for a while now "even they"—he pointed somewhere in the direction of where the train was going—had been trying to conform to European standards, so the gentleman really had no cause for concern, and he, the conductor, had only dared disturb him now as he hadn't yet asked him if he could possibly be of some service to the gentlemen, if he perchance was thinking of some refreshments or coffee, or if he was hungry, perhaps if he desired a sandwich, he —the conductor pointed readily at his uniform—would be able to arrange it within minutes, the dining car was quite close, there were no other travelers in this carriage, so he really didn't have very much to do, he just happened to have the time right now to fulfill such a little task as this, for which as well he felt a great inclination, so that now he only waited for the gentleman to convey any possible wish and off he would go, oh, no—the traveler interrupted him in a weak voice: he thanked him, but he didn't need anything, and he turned his head back toward the window, the conductor stood there crushed, as clearly he had prepared for a longer conversation than this, indeed he'd counted on exchanging a few words with the gentleman and discussing what he could bring to help him calm down, if he was really of such an unquiet nature, but now it was as if he had lost his equilibrium, and without bothering to hide his disappointment, he just nodded, turned around, stepped out to the corridor, then looked back to see if the gentleman had changed his mind (he hadn't, he determined), and so he remained alone, somewhat relieved that he had gotten past these first difficulties, relief which however didn't last very long, because his rattled brain soon returned to those sentences which had been circling here and there within it for quite a while now, that this train was going much too quickly, its speed was too great, it was nearly sweeping along the tracks, as if it weren't even running on the tracks but in the air, it never jolted, never slowed down, there was only this pursuit, this rush, this mad dash toward the East. They were approaching the border.

It was difficult, the Casino didn't want to hear anything about letting the good relative off the hook in exchange for any kind of deposit, so the family ended up needing not only money, but also influence to get the desired result: namely there was no way they were going to handle this in a laissez-faire fashion when the owner of the Casino informed them of this via a lawyer, because the sad end of it all would be either jail or a psychiatric institution, no, the family council decided that no mud could be allowed to smear the name of Wenckheim—at the very most a little speck of beer foam, joked the head of the family—that's why, he stated before the horrified relatives (precisely because of the amount of money, which could be described as extraordinary), the Baron must be saved, because, as he put it, if we haven't held his hand throughout his entire life, we must hold it now in his dotage, so gritting their teeth, they paid out the entire liability, and they arranged—thanks to their excellent Argentinian connections, nurtured ever since 1944—for the official complaint raised by the Casino to disappear from the files of the judges' offices in Buenos Aires, and finally, with the help of an intermediary, they managed to put the Baron on the first plane headed for Madrid, from where he was sent further on to Vienna, but in Vienna no one knew the least thing about him, only his scandalous passion was known, the scandalous passion which led him here; namely they knew nothing at all about who he really was, what kind of person, this person who bore their name as the last living member of the baronial branch, they knew nothing about all of that, they didn't even know what he looked like, so that the unpleasant surmise that perhaps all was not right with their guest only began to arise in the arrivals hall in Schwechat Airport, as they were waiting for him to show up among the other passengers, they just waited and waited, and he didn't come and he didn't come, and the arrivals hall was beginning to empty out, when they suddenly noticed a person, standing around in a yellow shirt and yellow trousers, in a wide-brimmed hat, conspicuously tall and looking around completely lost, a gray-haired person, and that was him, but he looked so troubled, and they, the family welcoming committee, were as well, namely the few young members of that family were so confused, that the welcome came off fairly badly, they didn't even shake hands, let alone hug each other, because the guest reacted so uncertainly when they walked over to him and they asked if he was Baron Wenckheim, that "yes" that came in reply was so subdued, and in Spanish too, so that they only dared ask him where his suitcases were after the usual questions as to whether he had had a good trip, and so on, and then they didn't dare to ask about hardly anything at all, mainly because there were no suitcases as it turned out—no one among the younger family members wanted to believe this, but then thinking it over they decided that he must have sent them on already, and had them forwarded with some transport service, so they didn't press the matter anymore, just as they didn't press him by asking why he he had no coat, they only pointed in the direction of the car, he walked very uncertainly, as if he were dizzy, they didn't dare, however, to suggest that someone take his arm, although the two relatives who walked on either side of him drifted a little closer to him, at this, however, the Baron reacted almost in horror, so that both of them quickly drew back, he can't stand having people close to him, they noted afterward when they arrived at the residence, and they took him up to his room; later on they all sat down to dinner, waiting for him to come down, and of course they spoke about him, his inexplicably incomplete attire, the yellow hat and shirt and the yellow trousers, and his confusion, his sensitivity, and how he was nearly frightened by the fact that they wanted to take his arm while walking, and so on, and the young people allowed themselves one or two more witticisms, but the older relatives just waited with bent heads for the first course to be served, they said nothing, and after a while the young people ran out of things to say, dinner commenced, but without him, because although they had agreed on it, he didn't turn up even after half an hour, so for a long time only the clatter of the soup spoons was heard, or from time to time a glass was put down a little more forcefully back onto the table, until the oldest among them, cousin Christiane, who was a kind of tolerated resident of the house, suddenly in her own shrill voice, and with complete candor, noted: I wouldn't say that he's not an attractive person, but his face, well, it's somehow pale, much too pale for my taste.

He didn't wish to begin dissecting the question as to what had happened to his clothes, namely the question as to why this relative only had that single yellow shirt, a single pair of yellow trousers, a single pair of yellow shoes, and that strange hat, just as he wasn't in the least curious as to what had happened to his luggage, if he'd had any at all in the first place, he summoned his secretary, ordered him to continue keeping the journalists away from the house, and he entrusted him with making the Baron look presentable, the secretary understood what he had to do, and immediately he discussed the matter with the head valet, who was already picking up the telephone and calling the Hotel Sacher to see when they were expecting the delegates of the tailors of Savile Row, and when the valet found out that a mere month ago they'd given up on Vienna, he immediately contacted the secretary, who immediately got in touch with Savile Row itself, where, yielding to a "special connection," and exceptionally resigning themselves to the absurd request of completing the order with only one fitting, two days later assistant tailor Mr. Darren Beaman arrived, and with that the torture began, because he had to make the Baron understand that his cooperation was required in this affair, without which no results would be gained, whereas the Baron—completely incomprehensibly to those involved in this matter—in his own yellow shirt and his yellow trousers, having previously brushed aside the garments offered in exchange for his own, vehemently rejected the project of some kind of "measurements being taken," he made it impossible from the beginning, for example, when, downstairs in the smoking room next to the salon, in the midst of newer and newer attempts to persuade him, he suddenly asked to be excused, hurried away, and barred himself in his room, letting no one in when they came to get him, and the dialogue proceeded through the tightly closed door, but even when after a while the secretary informed him that he would have to conduct himself in a serious manner, and told him once again, as mildly as he could, what was going on here—because from the Baron's conduct, it was evident that his resistance was not only vehement, but persistent in nature, so they just circled around him—the secretary, the head manservant, and the tailor from London—and cast a fairly strange gaze upon him, because they couldn't grasp what was behind his resistance, and they didn't even really want to, because they were confident that, while respecting his peculiar sensitivities, they would still be able to persuade him that his cooperation would merely consist of him, the Baron, not making it completely impossible for them to take, with a tailors' tape measure, the measurement of his height, his skull, his collar size, his shoulders, his chest, his waist, his hip, his torso below the arms, and so on downward, it's just a few days, said the Irish tailor—maybe just even a couple of hours, the secretary quickly added when he saw the Baron's face, and that he had immediately sunk into the nearest armchair, like someone who's just been told he is going to be tortured but he won't feel a thing—the tailor tried to reassure him, but the Baron wouldn't cooperate, and from that point on he wouldn't even let the tailor come close to him, he had to stand in the doorway, and after a while the tailor just shook his head, saying that he couldn't do anything else, they should have a talk with the Baron, and he'd wait somewhere, and he disappeared from sight, and then the secretary motioned to the head manservant, and remaining alone with the Baron, he explained to him that all that was going on here was that henceforth they *saw it as necessary* for him to change his clothes, because he was here in Austria now, and as for where he wanted to go, he couldn't travel there in just a shirt and trousers, especially there, did he understand, it's winter there, not summer, like in Buenos Aires, winter, with cold, icy winds and frosts, he pronounced every single word, forcefully uttering every single syllable, at which the Baron in his own colorless voice asked only if all of this was truly unavoidable, the secretary nodded slowly, the Baron wrung his hands for a little bit, then he sighed, and he only said: well, as a matter of course, if it's unavoidable, then he understood, and he was endlessly sorry that he was causing such trouble to everyone here, and this was exactly what he did not want to do, that is, cause trouble to them, let them call back the tailor, he bowed his head; he asked only one thing, however: that when they took his measurements, the tailor should in no way touch him, he knew that this would make things more difficult, but, well, he just couldn't stand any kind of touch unfortunately, he'd never been able to, not even in childhood, and certainly not now, when already . . . fine, the secretary answered, smiling, he would speak with Mr. O'Donoghue, and he would discuss with him how to take the measurements, this is absolutely impossible, the tailor yelled out in anger when later on they began, and already when he was trying to take the first back measurement, he mistakenly touched the nape of the Baron's neck, this isn't going to work, please try to put up with it, I simply don't know how to take measurements without touching you, this is just a little measuring tape, a completely harmless tailors' measuring tape, and he showed him just how harmless it was, oh, as a matter of course, the Baron answered, his face even paler than usual, please complete your work in peace, so the tailor began again, and he sensed from that point on how the Baron bore this only with great difficulty, as he trembled now and then when his skin was touched, the tailor loudly announced the result at the end of each measurement, but the

Baron tried to steel himself, his face convulsing while the tape measure was at work, he remained disciplined, but he shuddered at every touch, the sweat was pouring off the tailor's forehead, his face turned completely scarlet, so enervated was he from the continuous agony, and finally when it grew dark outside, and many measurements for the suit were lined up in a notebook, they put off everything else 'til tomorrow, because the secretary had judged that the Baron had reached the end of his patience, he thanked Mr. O'Donoghue for the day's work, then, showing him the way out, led the Baron to his room, where the Baron closed the door, lay down on the bed, and didn't move until the next morning, and then wordlessly, with an empty gaze, he followed one of the manservants, who took him down once again to the smoking room next to the salon, the tailor arrived, and after cordial greetings the whole thing began all over, once again he had to endure the repeated attacks of the ice-cold tips of the tape measure; in the notebook of the tailor, however all the numbers that would subsequently be needed for the workshops of Savile Row to complete the order began to be filled out, because what was required was everything, and the firm—with a view to its relationships with its clients, formed over long decades—did not simply undertake to complete this work, but also ensured—in addition to the two double-breasted dark-navy-blue pinstripe wool suits, the two three-breasted suits in Donegal tweed, waistcoats to go with them, as well as the cashmere coat—that there would be delivered, simultaneously with the order (thanks to the excellent connections of Savile Row), and afforded extraordinary priority, twelve silk ties, twelve pocket squares, twelve shirts with cuff links, pocket handkerchiefs, socks, hats, three dressing gowns, gloves, as well as a smoking jacket, but at the same time they also had to ensure that the various footwear, prepared according to foot measurements gained amid unspeakable torture, would be ready in time from Schnieder of London, including that pair of crocodile leather shoes which now tried to clutch somehow at the sticky floor of the train compartment, but they slid, and that's how it was with everything, but especially with the chesterfield coat, which he now didn't even dare to unbutton sitting in the seat upholstered with fake leather, of course, for all this time was needed, because Savile Row hadn't given them a definite delivery date, that wasn't their custom and that wasn't how they did things, in consequence of which this distant relative spent several weeks in the residence, it's true he wasn't stirring things up too much, because he usually never even left his room, claiming he had his letter-writing obligations, and he never appeared at even one family meal, consuming his lunches and dinners up there, and only leaving the house (for a quick half hour, and in a borrowed coat) when cousin Christiane hauled him outside, ordering him to take a little stroll in the park attached to the residence, and so the days and weeks went by, until one Monday, when a conversation with the head of the family—the Baron's first and last conversation with him—having gone on for over an hour, was just coming to an end in the smoking room, from where namely—as related by cousin Christiane, who'd been obliged to accidentally pass by the closed door more than once—only the forceful voice of the paterfamilias could be heard from within: in short, the moment of redemption had come at last, and a special delivery arrived directly from Savile Row with the last items, and the Baron's wardrobe was complete; well, after that, events sped up, the secretary studied the train schedules, purchased tickets, and after the yellow shirt, the yellow trousers, and yellow shoes quietly vanished (it was impossible to get rid of the hat, as for some reason or other the Baron clung to it tooth and nail), it fell upon them to garb him in the clothes selected for travel, the rest was carefully packed away in suitcases purchased especially for the trip, and as they were packing they told him what each specific piece of clothing was, what material it was made of, on what occasions it should be worn, and of course how to put it on, fasten it, tie it, pull it up and once again tie it, but he said nothing at all, never betraying if he realized what each individual item was, of what material it was made, on what occasion it should be worn, and if he knew how to put it on, fasten it, tie it, pull it up, and once again tie it, it was clear to him that they treated him as if he were a child, but he saw this as unbounded goodwill, he didn't want to avail himself of excuses, he was infinitely grateful for the incalculable beneficence that the family was showing him, the solicitude and attention of which he was the beneficiary, and he thanked each of them individually for this, then he thanked them separately for the suits, for the hats, and then for the chesterfield coat, he thanked them for the silk ties, the handkerchiefs, the socks, the dressing gowns, the smoking jacket, the gloves and the shoes, he only requested one thing: that they would permit him to wear his own original hat, to which of course everyone immediately consented, and afterward they listened as he briefly mentioned all of the various gifts yet again, depicting at length all the beauty and gentility he'd been witness to, but especially that of the relatives, all those whom he must now thank, so that at the end of his stay here of more than two months, as—excepting one suitcase, which he was taking himself, the other suitcases having started their journey toward their end goal in the care of a trustworthy delivery service—the time of farewell had come, he pronounced all of this and the family received his words, which they interpreted as the manifestation of impeccable manners, with truly gratified surprise, so much so that the head of the family almost felt touched, and almost stepped over to the Baron to tap him on the shoulder, but then he realized in time what might happen were he to actually perform such a gesture, so that he just nodded and wished the Baron a good trip; then one of the members of the family who had arrived for the Algerian relative's funeral—he was one of the more entrepreneurially minded of them—drove the Baron and a manservant to Westbahnhof, and when he returned back from his mission, he related the details to the other members of the family of his own age amid great guffaws, all the while never suspecting that the Baron, as he looked out the window, frightened, as the train approached the border, was thinking of them, thinking of all of them there in the residence with affection and with gratitude, and in the knowledge that he would never see them again.

He was going to speak with him directly, man-to-man, even if it was hard to decide if there was any point to this, namely if the person sitting in front of him was capable of understanding what he was about to say, but now, before the Baron was to leave the protection extended to him, it had become necessary to speak openly, as—once he left this house—there were certain conditions that must be fulfilled, and with that they would be letting go of his hand, said the head of the family, trying in his own way to be humorous; they were in the innermost room, which they called the library, although on the bookshelves, instead of books, there'd been lined up trophies of various sizes for quite a while now, which the generations of the family, in its renowned entrepreneurship of recent times, had obtained as the fruit of their labors, namely—as one of the younger siblings had once pithily noted—they were won in ruthless brewery competitions, and the head of the family had sat him down here in a kind of armchair in which he could only crouch, then, sitting, he leaned with both his hands onto the gigantic writing desk, he leaned toward him, and he continued: he didn't want anything in return, let there be no misunderstanding about that, just as there should be no illusions either, in other words they hadn't rescued him from Argentina because they felt sorry for him, but because it wouldn't have been good for the family if the situation over there in South America hadn't been resolved somehow, but never mind, said the head of the family in his thundering voice, enough about that, they had done whatever they could, and now they wanted to let him go in accordance with his wishes, but first a few things had to be cleared up, namely before anything else: he didn't care where he was going and why, but he had to promise that wherever he went and for whatever reason he went there, he would never bring shame down on their heads ever again, and he asked him now to not just sit there nodding, but to really understand what they wanted from him, in other words what they wanted was for there to be no more scandals ever again, let him go with the blessing of God wherever he wanted to go, but he never wanted to see the name of Wenckheim in any kind of newspaper again, namely, the family here also carried this name, and never again did he want to see it besmirched, he hadn't lifted barrels as a young man, he hadn't knocked out the wooden plugs from the kegs, if he could put it that way, and he hadn't tended the name and the noble memory of this family—as he was going to do until the end of time—only to see an aging adolescent like you, Béla (here the head of the family leaned in closer to him, across the desk) drag it into the stinking muck of the tabloids and the sewer, you must promise me this, he thundered at him in the severest of tones, and now, he leaned back in the chair, just don't sit there nodding, but understand what we want from you, at which point his interlocutor—who could only crouch in this chair because of the high armrests—couldn't hold out any longer, and with full enthusiasm conveyed to the head of the family: he was perfectly aware that he was an idiot, but even so he could understand what was being said to him, so how could he not understand this warning, especially from those to whom he owed his life, or, to put it more succinctly, a more dignified death, because he would never be able to ever show enough gratitude for the fact that they hadn't allowed him be shut away in El Bordo, because that had been the threat: well it's El Bordo for you, that's what the state prosecutor, the police, and the lawyers who showed up in his cell had said to him, he would have ended up in El Bordo, the Baron said, sitting in the armchair; in the past few years, he had dreamed of the kind of end to his days that everyone dreamt of, but for him—thanks to this heavenly grace extended by his very own family—it was now possible, so how could he not understand all of this, how could he not be capable not only of making a mere promise, but also of keeping it, and that's why—he said to all of the members of the family now, with a particular regard to cousin Christiane, who had been extremely kind to him—he now wished to depart from this wondrous palace in such a way that they'd never hear anything about him ever again, for surely they knew that he'd requested only a one-way ticket, only the ticket going there, and in particular he would wish to call cousin Christiane's attention to the fact that in no circumstance had he asked for a return ticket, he wasn't able to thank the family for everything they had done for him in words, but he would confirm with his deeds how much they would be able to count on him, and even if he . . . and he acknowledged this, because when still in his forties the doctors had told him that this would happen, that he would become an idiot . . . well, and so he had become like an idiot, but thanks be to God, he understood everything they were saying to him, and mainly and as a matter of course, he understood what he was hearing now from the other side of the writing desk, and they could all count on him, he would do everything to make sure it turned out that way—well, then, so be it, the head of the family raised his voice with a more cheerful expression, and with that he considered the conversation closed, and when he accompanied the Baron out of the library, he almost gave in to his natural instinct of putting his arm around him while seeing him out, because from the very first moments, he had felt a decided sympathy for him, and he almost did too, he'd already raised his arm, but halfway there he came to his senses, and pulled it back, and that's why it was so surprising, when in the open doorway, the Baron, bidding him farewell, with a sudden movement pulled his hand toward himself and kissed it, then confusedly hurried away toward the staircase.

He didn't notice when they had crossed the border, because nothing happened, the carriage glided along the tracks until that moment when the train began to brake, then losing speed, it only jolted along, as if at a certain point the tracks had disappeared and the train was having to make its way over some kind of rougher ground, it was the moment when an international express train suddenly and evidently turns into a local train; then they arrived at the first place where the train came to a halt, but it stopped in such a way as if the train had stopped definitively, for all time, in front of an almost completely empty railway station, where a few people in uniform were loitering, but they immediately headed toward the train and got on, whereas the others—clearly the Austrian rail staff in their uniforms—got off, compartment doors opened and closed with a huge racket, the tramping of feet was heard, some of the men in uniform stomped up and down the corridor, this must be Hungary, he thought, quickly looking for his own hat, and exchanging it for the one he'd been given, his stomach wrenched in convulsions, with trembling hands he looked for his passport, but then he just kept clutching his passport, because for a while no one appeared at the door of the compartment, he only heard the thumping steps as the compartment doors were opened and shut closed, then the thumping sounds approached, and finally the door to his compartment was opened as well, a man in uniform looked him up and down, then up at the luggage rack, he propped the door open with one leg, because in the meantime the train had started again, and the motion of the train kept making the door slide shut, he propped it open with his foot, and even leaned his back against it, and he asked: *Deutsch?* no, the passenger swallowed, I'm Hungarian, and he said all of this in Hungarian, at which point the customs officer—as the Baron thought that was what he could have been—cast a visibly surprised glance upon him, so, Hungarian, he turned the word over, at which the Baron would have been more than happy to withdraw this statement, but it was too late, the customs officer wiped his greasy shining brow, and turned over the pages of the Baron's passport, more precisely, he didn't turn over the pages, but he began to flip through them with one hand, he wasn't, however, even looking at the passport because he was looking at him, at the clearly nervous Baron sitting in his coat, with his strange wide-brimmed hat, and the suitcase above his head, well, but this isn't a Hungarian passport, he said, well no, as a matter of course, the Baron answered, barely audibly, I can't hear what you're saying, the customs officer yelled at him, well, as a matter of course, no, because I happen to be a citizen of Argentina, the Baron said just slightly more audibly, oh, as *a matter of course* Argentina, said the customs officer sarcastically, and began to look at the passport again, turning over the pages some more, he found the page that clearly contained the visa, thus requiring some attention on his part, he looked it over, now inspecting the document from various angles, holding his head to one side, then he took out a large stamp from the bag hanging around his neck, smiled at the passenger, smoothed down one of the sides of his bag, and forcefully slammed down the stamp on the passport, well then—the customs officer slapped the passport closed again, and he began to beat it against his other palm, well then, he repeated, but for a while he didn't continue his thought, he just looked at him, and suddenly his gums were shining, so now perhaps you'll be that famous person I read about today in *Blikk*, aren't you? he suddenly switched from official tones to a civilian conviviality, you'll be that count now, won't you, who gambled away an entire little empire, or what, he cackled, and slapped his palm with the passport, then still smiling he just shook his head for a while, all the while his gaze—with a little impish light in his eyes—rested on the traveler, he slowly extended to him the passport, then wished him a pleasant homecoming, and added that he hoped that here—and he described a wide half circle with his arm in the direction that the train was traveling—he wouldn't lose everything playing cards, then he stepped out into the corridor, and closed behind him that door that kept trying to slide shut, then by means of farewell he playfully wagged his index finger at him through the glass, but now there was neither suspicion nor curiosity on that greasy face, but rather the sign of a complicit recognition shone there, and the light of the weak sunlight was cast onto the corridor for yet a moment more, which made it seem like a kind of little star was shining on his forehead, as clearly there his skin was the greasiest.

He wouldn't let me help him, I even went in and asked him, but he refused to let me bring something from the dining car, moreover he was visibly afraid of something, so I was a little bothered I couldn't do anything to help him calm down, I would have been happy to go get him something, in the end a person wants to do what's expected of him, and in this instance namely the expectations were great, what am I saying, great, gigantic, because, the conductor said: the manservant had forced him to take such a big tip—exceeding by far the sum total of all the other tips he'd recently received—but well, it wasn't just because of the money, he would have done everything from a sense of obligation, it was just that the passenger wouldn't let him, he passed a few times in front of his compartment—slowly, so that he'd have time to think about it and motion to him—but nothing, the gentleman didn't even move, and as far as that went, it just came to mind—the Austrian conductor continued to his colleagues, as their attention flagged—how he didn't move at all, all the way from Vienna to Hegyeshalom, he stayed exactly the same as when he had crammed himself into the seat when he got on, sitting in his coat, all buttoned up, with that wide-brimmed, red-ribboned hat on his head, and his legs pressed against each other, he looked out the window, but as he looked out, the Baron didn't see anything particular at all, because the landscape never changed, it was always exactly the same ploughed fields below low heavy cloud cover, those same dirt roads and strips of forest, but those appeared only for a moment or two, in a word he saw nothing, maybe he was observing himself in the reflection of the train window—he couldn't tell, he didn't have enough time to examine him closely, as he slowly walked up and down in front of the compartment, altogether he relied only on fleeting impressions, as he evoked them right now, but one thing was certain, he announced, stressing these words now in the railworkers' rest station: this person just couldn't be anyone, and the only thing that bothered him was that there hadn't been anyone, just as there was no one now, whom he could ask who it could have been—but then, from among his not very attentive audience, one of his colleagues, a young, hulking, peasantlike South Tyrolian, who'd been observing him with some irritation for a while now, remarked a little indignantly—he clearly didn't think much of this account or of the person who was giving it, but now, for some reason, he was filled with rage—he said he suspected who this could be, because just look, he grabbed his own thumb and shook it, indicating that what he had to say would be expressed in several points: there was the companion and there was the appearance of the traveler—and now he grabbed his index finger—then the fact that such a fine-looking gentleman was traveling on the Jenő Huszka toward the East, and now he was onto his middle finger, and finally there was how strange he was, his eccentricities, and then he raised his voice and began to shake his little finger so as to get the attention of those who at this point were beginning to doze off a little, an eccentric, and he leaned toward the conductor with a meaningful glance; well, isn't it beginning to dawn on you, what should be dawning on me? the conductor asked, nothing, the young South Tyrolian shook his head incredulously, and he finally released his little finger, it's obvious you don't read newspapers, because if you'd read one, you'd know that this can be none other than that Peruvian aristocrat, I can't think of the name right now, whose family, the Ottakringers, rescued him from the claws of the local cocaine mafia, because he was going to be put in jail, and they did put him in jail, because they wanted to do away with him, and they almost did away with him, because, as the newspaper said, they got him mixed up in card-gambling debts so they could get rid of him because it seemed he knew something—that's what they wrote—he knew something he shouldn't have known, well, so *that* was your eccentric on the Jenő Huszka, you smart-ass, but as for those hundred euros, he said, full of rage toward the conductor, I don't believe it for a minute.

He didn't have anything smaller, only a fifty and a ten euro note, and this vexed him, because from the very beginning he was brooding about how to distribute the one hundred euros that the manservant had entrusted to him at Westbahnhof, which, apart from his own tip of one hundred euros, he was supposed to give to the Hungarian conductor, well, he wouldn't give him the entire amount, even fifty euros seemed like too much, and ten seemed too little; what should he do, he went quickly to the dining car at least three times to see if the employees there could give him change, but they couldn't, there was hardly anyone on the train, no customers, my man, the Hungarian dining-car attendant said to him bitterly in broken German when he approached him for the third time; well he'd have to hand over that fifty-euro note all the same, and that's how the tip of the decade came together, because one hundred and fifty euros is one hundred and fifty euros, no matter how you cut it, he reassured himself, and right then it flashed through his mind: what would happen if he didn't give anything to his Hungarian colleague, maybe it would be enough if his interest were sparked—and this pleased him, "if his interest were sparked"—yes, he decided, that would be enough: so when the train stopped at the desolate Hegyeshalom station, and he met up with the conductor who among other things was responsible for railway carriage number nine, he told him he wished to draw his attention to a particular passenger who'd been entrusted to him at the Westbahnhof station, as it had been impressed upon him inasmuch as possible to convey the importance to him, i.e., his Hungarian colleague, of meeting all of this passenger's needs until they reached the capital city, including helping him to his connecting train in Keleti Station, then he could count on a sizable reward, and justifiably so, the Austrian colleague explained to his Hungarian counterpart, who displayed serious interest in the small amount of time they had at their disposal, then he handed him the passenger's ticket, left him there, retreated from the cold with the others into the railworkers' rest station to wait for the train going back to Vienna, and if for a while he was able to keep this event to himself, the two hundred euros made him so happy that he nearly jumped out of his skin, and almost right away he couldn't stop himself from telling his story, cleverly avoiding any telltale signs of joy, although he came very close two times to mentioning exactly how much money had been pressed into his palm—and this was just because he was so clever.

He knew exactly what was going on here, the news that the card-playing Baron was on his way home from Hawaii, traveling through Vienna by train, had been in the tabloid *Blikk* for days now, he'd even seen a photograph of him, so that nobody had to tell him twice what he had to do, he just passed in front of his compartment in railway carriage number nine, cast a glance at the passenger sitting inside, and he already knew who he was, he knew he'd get something out of it, namely he trusted in that, because of course he couldn't have known for sure that the Baron would be traveling on this route exactly during his shift, oh, great heaven, there is a God—he raised his eyes silently to heaven when the Austrian colleague told him about the situation, there is and there is and there is a God, and already he went to the dining car, and he said to the attendant, his acquaintance: that'll be a cheese sandwich and a salami sandwich, a little bottle of red wine, and a bottle of Coca-Cola, and coffee, well, wait a second, what else do you have; of course, he pondered—what desserts do you have?—well, the dining-car attendant pursed his lips like someone who would never touch a slice of his own wares because he had no idea how long ago the sell-by date had passed, there's Balaton Slice chocolate bars, Balaton Slice Extras, and walnut-rum cherry bonbons, which will it be, give me one of each, the conductor answered enthusiastically, put the whole thing on a tray, and I'll be right back to pay, at which point the hand of the dining-car attendant, which was already reaching for the second sandwich, stopped in midair, what did you say, he looked at him questioningly, look here—the conductor motioned the dining-car attendant closer—it's *for him*, in other words, *for him*, the dining-car attendant nodded in resignation and he stared deeply into the other's eyes, but then that hand progressed further in its journey toward the sandwich, because in the space of an instant he had decided to trust this fellow, he knew him as well as a bad penny, and he wasn't going to shoo him away because of this one customer, okay, but you be right back here with the money, of course, I'll be quick, the conductor explained, and already he was tottering off with the tray toward the compartment in railway carriage number nine, he knocked once, he knocked twice, he knocked a third time, and as he didn't hear anything—maybe because the train was right then rattling across some switches—he slid the door open with one movement, and as he lurched into the compartment with the tray, he said: a warm welcome to you, sir, to the old country, at which the passenger trembled just as much as he could in the coat tightly stretched across him, all the while edging away in the other direction on the seat, toward the window, and with rounded eyes he stared at this unknown person, who was preparing to crown his ceremonial greeting by patting the gentleman on his back with his free hand, but those eyes made him uncertain, so he also moved toward the window, wrenched open the table with one jolt, and skillfully —the Coca-Cola only clinked a bit against the bottle of red wine—placed the tray down, and he said, well, bon appetit, sir, enjoy these domestic delicacies, and (he spoke from the doorway now) don't let the coffee get cold, and then he was gone, I'll be back in a second, was all he said, but it was possible that the passenger didn't even hear it.

He guaranteed that nobody would disturb him, after he returned a good twenty minutes later, and with an "oh my God!" he flopped down on the seat across from him, untangled himself from his conductor's bag, and began to massage his legs above the knees, all the while not taking his eyes off the passenger, and he repeated that there was no cause for concern whatsoever, this train was the "ocean of tranquility" itself, and just imagine, sir, he said, in this whole carriage there's nobody apart from you, unfortunately that's how it is, he said, spreading his hands apart, with these weekday morning routes, and then he slowly blew out air, which caused a moderate smell of garlic sausage to strike the passenger sitting across from him, it's always like this on a weekday, you know, or if it's not some big holiday like Christmas or Easter, when everyone is rushing to Vienna to buy what they can't get at home—of course you, sir, will be thinking of luxury items—because people are capable of going there for even some eau de cologne, or a nightgown; he—the conductor pointed to himself—didn't understand such people, what was all this accumulation for, if there was this sale or that sale, what the hell was it all for, he said to him; for him, the conductor, what he had was enough, it wasn't much, but it was enough, he was able to get by, his children had all flown the nest, he was able to survive quite well with the old lady on what they had, she didn't need any kind of eau de cologne, or any kind of ridiculous tchotchkes, or whatever the new craze was, or the I-don't-even-know-what-kind-of iFon, or whatever it's called, well, he never could keep track of these names, in short she was happy with some kind of nice addition to the living room, for example, this year her Christmas present would be a new coat rack, they had already decided, because thank God the old lady wasn't the acquisitive type, they needed the coat rack, they'd decided, and so that would be her present, they'd looked it over, they almost had enough money for it, so there would be a coat rack, Christmas would be lovely, the gentleman should believe him when he said that they were happy, they had everything they needed: a nice TV set, furniture, everything, four and a half years to retirement, and well, then he'd be happy to say: thank you very much, that was enough now, he was done, no more of the stress that went with this job, because there was always something popping up here and there, and recently too, just last Tuesday, exactly on this route, only going to Vienna, some kind of Albanian gang got into a fight, it was a right proper dust-up, and he was hardly able to hide out in the dining car up there until they managed to stop the train and the police got on, there was always something, so that when a man went home, he was just a bundle of nerves—and for him too, when he finished his shift and was finally able to sit down in his armchair in front of the TV, he could feel the muscles in his legs trembling, up here, look—he pointed at his thighs—seriously, the stress, the nerves, it all came out when he sat in the armchair, but he had only four and a half years to go, and that would be the end, then would come, as they said, the tranquility of old age, and he was more than ready for it, because a person could never be at peace, even now, here's this nearly empty train, hardly anyone on it, but you'll see, once we get to Keleti, how they rush around like madmen, because the refugees will descend on that place, lugging whatever they can: plastic bottles, food bags, little bottles, big bottles, they're carrying everything, who even knows, they're like beggars, with neither country nor even, so they say, a roof over their head, and for years now they've just been coming and coming, and they're just lying around everywhere—he didn't say that he wasn't sorry for them, he was sorry for them, but just from a distance, because if he went up close to them, well, sir, you wouldn't even be able to imagine the stink, because they don't even wash, they're mangy, and that urine smell, you could really vomit out your guts, and the whole city is full of them, especially the train stations, and especially the underpasses, and especially Keleti Station, he couldn't imagine how so many could come week after week, there was nothing like this under János Kádár, although under Kádár . . . well but back then, Kádar gave everyone a job, an apartment, bread, he wouldn't say those times should come back or anything, but you had to recognize that back then there was everything, even if there was just a little of it, but there was enough, there wasn't all this big technology, there wasn't anything in the stores, but you could get by, and there wasn't such a big difference between one person and another, you know, the poverty that's mainly in the northern and eastern regions, well, and all those gypsies, the gentleman can't even imagine it, because that is the biggest problem in this country, let them all go to hell, those gypsies, because they don't work, but believe me, they grew up like that too, to them work stinks, because it's only stealing and robbing that they like, they spend half of their lives in the slammer, and when they get out, then it's back to stealing and robbing, then it's right back in the slammer again, and if they get on here, onto a train, it's doesn't matter where, people just hide away wherever they can, because nothing is sacred to them, how many times had he been beaten up just because of a ticket, but well that's how it was, everywhere there were just complaints and wretchedness and dissatisfaction, and of course those fat cats at the top only care about themselves; now one big boss got into a fight with another, they fought over some red Lammorgini, oh he certainly wasn't pronouncing it right, but just imagine, they keep fighting with each other over who'll get that Lammorgini, and then, of course, there goes the country, because nobody wants any of these refugees here, they just toss them on like a hot potato, from one to the other, the gentleman will see for himself, in the end everything is going to go up in flames here, well, whatever, he didn't really wish to make him sad, that's not why he'd said all this, but time passes more pleasantly if two people can chat together, isn't that so, he asked, then he bent above the tray, he took the plastic cup in his hands, he shook his head, and he said, this coffee really got cold, I'll take it back to the dining car if you don't mind, and they'll heat it up for you, sir, properly.

He sat closer to the window, pressing his forehead against the glass, and in that way he observed what was passing by outside, and as for what was passing by outside, he'd pretty much seen it when they'd gone across the border, but now everything was different, it was the same, but different, maybe because of the conductor's words just now, this endless dreary farmland; and in this plowed land, deep in the distance—as now and then a ruined farmstead leapt into view, sometimes a solitary tree, sometimes, not too far away from the tracks, a pack of scrawny rabbits as they flattened themselves down in the furrows at the sound of the passing train, and all this was making his heart beat so fast—nothing had changed, this heart throbbed, everything was the same as it had been before, it was only the sky that surprised him, because a few strips of this enormous, dark, heavy, and interconnected mass had broken open, so that the light broke through here and there across a few narrow bands, and the rays of light reached down from the heavens to the earth, innumerable thick shimmering rays of light gently spreading out—like an intricate aureole, he thought, just like in those cheap holy pictures in the Mataderos market near the church of San Pantaleon, he pressed his forehead against the cold glass, and he just watched as the streaks of light played across the landscape, he just watched, and he couldn't get enough of this sight, he was happy that he could see what he had never dared hope to see again, he was happy that he could be happy again, he stared and he wondered, his eyes filled with tears, and he thought that indeed now he had come home. And perhaps the tears were the reason he didn't notice the absence of Saint Pantaleon, and because what he was seeing right now was so spectral and beautiful—why would it even have occurred to him: he to whom this halo belonged was nowhere on this earth.

In railway carriage number ten, there was an old lady who didn't have a seat reservation, and then there were four people who didn't even have tickets, so that maybe three-quarters of an hour had gone by before he decided what to do—he didn't know how to tell him, but the buffet-car attendants weren't willing to put it off any longer, they said to him that they weren't going to heat up the coffee, that he had to pay now, so he went back to the compartment, he sat down across from him again, and although he still avoided the matter for some time, at last he mentioned that he had to take back the tray, although he understood very well that the Baron, as he had said, wasn't hungry or thirsty, if, however, he were to take the tray back, some money would also be needed, because the sandwiches and the drinks had to be paid for, to which the Baron only said that as a matter of course he would pay for these "exceptionally tasty domestic delicacies," he pulled out a brand-new wallet, and he showed the conductor two two-hundred-euro bills, asking if this would be enough, at which the conductor quickly shook his head, quickly chasing away the thought that immediately popped into it—no, no, less, less, he stammered, when the passenger put back one of the notes and showed him the other one, that's still too much, still too much, he gestured vehemently, well, this hundred, that'll be good, definitely that will be fine, the conductor nodded, everything is included—but your services, the passenger interrupted him—that's covered, there's more than enough for that, the conductor said, reddening, and he quickly took the money, then excusing himself, ran back to the dining car and paid the bill with his own money; before he got back to the compartment, he looked at the banknote the traveler had given him one more time, but he really didn't believe his eyes, because even when he looked at it a second time it was still a real, genuine hundred-euro note; he tucked it away in his inner pocket, then pulled his hand out of the pocket very carefully, so that he wouldn't pull it out again by mistake with some nervous movement, and while standing there, smoothing out his uniform two or three times, he could only bear to think: "that's the coat rack sorted," then he went back into the compartment, and he had no idea that this passenger really didn't wish him to be there, although he didn't show it, he would have liked to remain alone and keep on watching everything that was transpiring out there with the sky and the earth, but, well, it never occurred to the conductor—not this time, nor thereafter—to consider whether the gentleman was in the mood for him to show up here and amuse him, and with yet another deep sigh of "oh, my God" to throw himself down onto the seat across from the traveler, that thought never occurred to him, he thought only about how he could fulfill the task before him now, but nothing came into his mind, he searched for something, he wrinkled his forehead in deep concentration, but nothing and nothing—although visibly in the midst of a great endeavor, he was incapable of stammering out a single sentence, because he couldn't stop thinking about that inner pocket—so nothing and nothing, not even for the love of God, and for a long time he uttered not a single word, although he felt the expectations of the passenger sitting across from him to be justified, and he didn't want to be obsessing about his inner pocket right now—he wanted to be equal to the expectations placed upon him—but just that rotten inner pocket and just that, then the coatrack, those two things circled around in his head, he was bereft of any idea as to how he could break the silence, so the silence grew and grew, for which, however, the passenger sitting across from him cast a grateful glance more than once, because right now he was in great need of this silence, if the conductor was clearly already of the opinion that the right thing to do was not to leave him by himself, it was necessary for him to be able to gaze out the window undisturbed, the conductor's confusion just grew and grew, because he saw, in this turn of events, the sign of resentment, a justified resentment—briefly put, the misunderstanding in the compartment was complete, and it only reached an end when the train suddenly began to brake, and then with a jolting movement came to a halt, I'll see what's going on, sir, said the conductor, relieved, and he quickly disappeared from the compartment, the Baron, however, turned back again toward the window, pressing his forehead to the cold glass, and he was grateful, he was truly grateful to the conductor for behaving so tactfully, as he believed that everything had been a sign of how he understood; the silence had been good, but what he really needed right now was *to be alone* in the silence.

He had no idea why he'd said "I'll see what's going on," he knew exactly the cause of it, because they'd arrived in the outskirts of the city, and they were waiting for the signals that would let them onto that rail track, which, traversing the city, would direct the train to its temporary goal, Keleti Station; the train stopped and waited for the signal to proceed, and he stopped too, in between the railway carriages number nine and ten, trying to decide what to do now, but his brain wouldn't function, nothing was coming to mind, then suddenly he recalled what his Austrian colleague had said to him—he had to help the passenger make his next connection—well of course, his thinking suddenly became clear, carry I'll carry the suitcase for him, I'll carry it, how the hell could I not, and I'll put it on the connecting train for him, yes, that's the solution, which—as he considered—was necessary, because in truth he feared, every single moment, that just as this truly peculiar gentleman had paid for the dining-car bill so heedlessly, he could, just as heedlessly, demand the money back, but no, *not that*, his heart beat frighteningly within him, there was the coatrack and already it was his, and he wasn't going to renounce what he had just acquired in such a lucky fashion, no, that coatrack was necessary, he shook his head, like someone objecting to an intervention made by someone else inside of him, but of course nobody was interjecting anything within him, he stood there firm as a rock between the railway carriages number nine and number ten, his legs slightly spread apart, because in the meantime the train had slowly started up again, swaying back and forth across the switches, and he stayed there, his muscles nervous and taut, until he realized—from the noise of the train—where they were, then he finally emerged from the space between the railcars, and into railway carriage number nine, and knocked on the door of the compartment to let the gentleman know that he could now prepare for the arrival at Keleti Station, but don't be alarmed, he said to him nervously, just remain calm, and he tried somehow to calm down the jittery muscles in his legs, he—and he pointed to himself—would help him, he would take his suitcase, and he even took it down from the luggage rack, he would take it now, he said to him, and of course he would help him with the transfer to the next train, here's your ticket, and your reservation, from Keleti Station to the final stop, it would be better now for you to have it, hold on to it well and don't lose it, and just follow me, sir, and from that point on, he pronounced the sentence at least three times every minute—to follow him, follow him, follow him—because the gentleman could only get out of the train with much ado, and only with much ado was he able to keep up with the conductor, so that every step that they made together, the conductor only kept thinking about how he couldn't rely on this gentleman too much as everything having to do with him was so unpredictable, and, well, he went along so circumstantially, the whole thing was so muddled, although it's possible that he himself was rushing things a bit, it's possible that perhaps he was moving ahead with the suitcase a little too quickly, but what could he have done other than try to press forward in the crowd, which for the most part wasn't comprised of passengers making their way to the trains, but the usual gangs among the usual refugees, all preparing for a running assault, well, and he had to forge his way somehow through this chaos, and he did so, he made his way, suitcase in hand, as best he could, and he would explain later on why he had suddenly disappeared from the train, when he was supposed to hand it over to the next conductor, later on he'd explain everything, but the task at hand was more important now, because now before anything else he wanted to be free of him, be free, to be liberated from the burden, which this strange, lanky, scrawny old man presented to him, up until the final moment of his mere presence here, with his truly overly elaborate and complicated presence, this old man, however, was so overcome by the huge beggar-like crowd of human beings preparing to siege the train, by the stench that prevailed in the railway station, the cacophony, the slow, echoing nightmarish male voice of the loudspeaker as it bellowed out information about the trains, and the electronic musical tones that preceded every new announcement, that he straggled along after the conductor quite obediently, indeed he would have been very happy to cling to him and be carried along, because here below, on the station's asphalt, everything seemed much too wild, it was as if they were crossing a jungle, he gawked at everything but really didn't see anything, although he held himself to his own promise that as a matter of course he wasn't going to gape, he wasn't going to keep looking around, because he knew and understood that he didn't have much time to make his next train, so he tried, and he followed the conductor, with all his strength he tried to stop looking around, and yet he still sometimes had to look over at one point or another at this unknown world swirling around him, he had, however, understood, or rather he had grasped, the final instructions of the conductor right before they got off the train, that first and foremost he had to follow him, and only follow, not stop, and only follow him, not lag behind, and so on, as in this swirling unknown there was some kind of danger, but they had already reached the first car of the train on one of the outer platforms, and the conductor asked for his reservation number, he examined it to see which carriage and which seat, then he gave it back to him, and they went as far as the head of the train, then suddenly it was over: the Baron was led up some steps and found himself in a completely different kind of train than the one he'd just gotten off, and he sat down in a completely different kind of seat than the one he'd been sitting in 'til now, and the conductor, accompanying him, said: don't let go of your suitcase, sir, it would be best if you wrapped your arms around it, and the conductor showed him how, and so he wrapped his arms around his suitcase, he embraced it, and he couldn't even wave, only signal with his eyes, when the conductor closed the door and looked back at him to disappear forever from his life, because one of his hands was clasping the suitcase so tightly it wasn't free, and the other hand clutched at the little table as tightly as he could—the little table that stuck out from beneath the window sill, and was edged with a thick strip of aluminum, a frame which could have been conceived as a kind of decoration if it hadn't been obvious that no: this aluminum band had been designed to protect this small table from people breaking off its edge, if it couldn't prevent anyone already from sitting down there and trying to snap off whole thing from beneath the window just for the hell of it.

The woman was wearing leather trousers, a leather jacket, and her lips were pierced, because she wanted to show that she belonged to the old school, she held the child's hand firmly with her left hand, so she wouldn't lose him in the swirling chaos; they emerged from the terminal and walked alongside the train on the platform, because she—who knew every nook and corner of this train station and always worked by instinct—was looking for a place where she could take the picture undisturbed, and from this point the first signal lights were already visible, the poles dispersed randomly among the tracks, and above it all the horrifying chaos of the electrical lines dangling in the air, she was observing the length of the platform next to the train, and they went as far out along it as they could, and when they couldn't go any farther she spoke to the child who was an absolute dear, because he wasn't whining or softly crying for his caretakers, nor was he whining that he had to drink or eat or pee or poop, nothing, this child was an angel, you're a wee little angel, she said to him, when they stopped on a narrower part of the platform, and she knelt down and explained to him that now she was going to take a couple of pictures of him, and all he had to do was stand there and not do anything, just stand there and look at her, look into the camera, and that would be everything; okay, said the child seriously; he'd followed the young woman obediently, he was serious, much too serious, the woman had seen already when she was picking him out that no, no, this child wasn't simply serious, this child was *von Haus aus*, as they say, and this made him stand out immediately from the others in the Institute kindergarten where the selection had taken place, this child with this sadness in his two huge black eyes immediately jumped out at her, because in general, it really wasn't right for a four-year-old boy to stand around there so sadly among the others, all the other children were either playing or trying to play, in vain did the caretakers try to make them form one little group to make it easier for her to select one, but it wasn't really possible to keep these children in a little group, they were supposed to stand still and they weren't in the mood for that, hardly any of the children had any patience for this, only he, the one whom she quickly chose, who didn't want to immediately go running back to some plastic bowling pins or building blocks, he just stood there like someone with no desire to start debating with the caretakers, it didn't matter to him, his two eyes suggested, it didn't matter to him at all where he had to stand, and why, and with that the woman decided he would be the one whom she would borrow from the Institute's kindergarten, which had helped her out many times before when she needed a child for this or that photo shoot, and as she took his hand, leading him out to the street, and he got onto the tram with her, then the metro, and she took him to Keleti Station, she was more and more appalled at the indifference of this little child as to what was happening to him, he just came along with her, with a complete stranger, his face displaying no emotion whatsoever, he obediently took her hand, and he didn't ask why they were going or where, he just went wherever the woman led him, he took her hand because the woman told him: take my hand, and so they arrived into the early afternoon chaos of Keleti Station, they cut across the crowd of refugees and passengers, and they'd arrived at this outer platform, and when she had him stand in a spot where a ray of sunlight had just broken through a crack in the clouds, he looked at her with those same huge, sad, unmoving eyes as he had in the first moments in the Institute, a sad pair of eyes looked out at her from this four-year-old boy, and it didn't matter what he was wearing—the ragged little brown jacket, the brown knitted tasseled cap on his head—nothing else mattered, only those two eyes as they gazed at her, into the camera, and with which, as she now gazed back into them, she was somehow having problems: she couldn't focus properly, the lens cap fell out of her hand, then the strap got caught in her scarf wrapped around her short-cropped hair, in other words she botched one thing after the other, and moreover, once she had finally managed to get the camera ready, that strip of sunlight into which she had placed the child suddenly died out, so she had to look for a new spot.

There was no more fire in her pictures, that's what people had been saying about her work for the past few years, and for a while it didn't bother her, but still after a certain point such superficial and ill-intentioned statements (to the effect that somehow there was no more fire in her pictures) began to get on her nerves, that's what people were saying, and what's more, these statements were pronounced at this or that exhibit within her earshot, until at one point when some critic took it bravely upon himself to describe her as a kind of celebrated female artist who'd lost her touch, she said to herself, well, so let's put some fire in it, and she went to the Orphanage in the seventeenth district, where one of her acquaintances worked as a caretaker, to pick out a child, she was thinking of a three- or four-year-old, and so there was the child, and he was very sweet, and there were those two eyes which she needed very much, and there was the light, into which she had placed the child, and behind him were the tracks as they ran along into an expanding, squalid, open space, above them the vast sprawl of electrical wires, moreover even a bit of the dispatcher's station was in the frame, so maybe this would be good, the woman picked up the camera, but just then the sun disappeared, the child was covered in shadows, so she went over to him and looked around, and as she saw not a single train, either departing from the terminal or coming in, she crept along with the child to a spot in between the tracks where there was still a bit of sunlight—a ray was breaking through a crack in the clouds, now dispersing above them, she placed the child there, and in the meantime though she was careful, continually watching to see if some train was departing from the terminal building or coming in to the terminal, but no train arrived, she raised the camera, she looked into it, very good, she said to the child, stay like that, look into the camera, you're very clever, but right then and there the sunlight disappeared once again, well, never mind, she said to him, wait a second, let's look for another place, and they scrambled back up where they had climbed down, onto the platform next to the unmoving train, she craned her neck to see, well, where will the sun shine now, the problem was that the clouds up there were moving, obviously because a strong wind had arisen, which on the one hand was good because the clouds were now breaking up above them, meaning the sun could shine down on them here below, on the other hand these spots of sunlight flared up very quickly and then just as quickly disappeared, it was impossible to figure out where one of these sunlit spots would emerge and when it would vanish again, she placed the child here, then she placed the child there, and after a while she got exasperated because there wasn't enough time for the exposure, there were problems either with the shutter speed, the diaphragm, or the depth of field, and just when everything seemed right, the child once again stood covered in shadow—and he just sat there inside, behind the locomotive, for the time being alone in the first-class carriage, with one hand squeezing his suitcase, and with the other clutching at the little table, and he just watched them, a woman and a little child, as they clambered here and there, because the woman clearly wanted to take a picture of the child, and for that it was necessary for him to stand in a spot where the sun was shining, only that this sun kept playing a trick on them and continually moved around, a patch of sun would appear, but by the time the camera was ready the child was standing in shadow, then the pair went to another patch of sunlight which had just appeared, but the sunlight disappeared before they could complete the task—the Baron simply couldn't take his eyes off of them, he watched the child who obediently followed the woman to this spot and that spot, sometimes he was led between the tracks, he was made to stand in a patch of sunlight, but the sunlight continuously died out above him; then suddenly the train gave a great big jolt, it didn't start moving though, it just stood there, as if this great big jolt was indicating that there had been some kind of technical error, although it hadn't been a technical error because after a minute—with a great clattering and rattling and creaking and grinding—the train very slowly began to demonstrate that it was capable of movement, and he let go of the suitcase, and he stopped clutching at the little table too, because he continually had to turn around if he wanted to see them, and he did want to see them, until the last possible moment, that little child with the woman, but in vain had he stopped clutching, in vain had he turned around, because he quickly lost them from sight, although he wouldn't have seen too much anyway, because his eyes had become full of tears, but when the train passed by the sooty dispatcher's station he wiped the tears from his eyes, and once again he clutched at the suitcase and the little table, even if he wasn't squeezing them with as much strength as before, and he didn't look out the window, because he was staring into space, he was looking at the filthy oily floor, the two crocodile leather shoes on his feet, as they tried somehow to hold on down there.

The woman and the child had completely occupied his attention as he stared from the window of the slowly moving train, so he didn't realize exactly when he'd become aware that an army of people were running next to this slowly moving train, a troop of men and women, who with despairing attempts were trying to look into the windows of the compartments, jumping up in order to see better, and it was obvious that they were looking for someone, and whomever they were looking for, they weren't finding him, so they just ran from one carriage to the other, from one window to the next, until they reached the front of the train, and in part they were lucky, because the train was going slowly enough for them to do this, as, for quite a while, the train didn't even speed up, it just jolted along at its own peasant's tempo, so they were able to keep up, but, on the other hand, they weren't finding the person they were looking for, only in the very last moment, because he was sitting in the last, that is to say the first, rail carriage, the more fortunate and nimble turned up there, and they were successful in getting a glimpse of the person they were looking for in his hat, with its wide brim and red ribbon, by now a trademark, with his opulent gray hair flowing down on both sides, we've got him, he's there, they yelled back, he's on it, and by that they meant he was on this train, and all the while the Baron was wiping the tears from his eyes, not noticing any of this, and even if he had noticed, the only thing that might have come into his mind was that they were passengers who'd missed the train, and now they were trying to jump onto it, but without success, but things didn't get that far, the front of the train had already pulled away into that great chaos of the intricate construction of railway switches, detours, and intersections, loop lines and wyes, switch plates, distance signals, waiting bays, and overhead lines—the platform on which those people could have followed the train was no more, and in particular they weren't lucky, because they found him in the last, that is to say the first carriage, just as, in their moment of discovery, the train pulled away from the last few meters of the platform, so they couldn't do much more than take some pictures of the train itself: there would be documentation that the train was here, he was on it, exactly as the Austrian news agency had stated in its report this morning, namely he was en route to his primary destination, and they ran back with the news and their worthless photographs, and then the editors at *Blikk* and the *Evening Post* and *Metro*—after they had thrown these lousy photographers out of their offices—could only report that the filthy rich Baron from South America had left the capital city, and was on his way to the region of his birth, albeit one day later than he had planned, and once again they transmitted an exact description of his appearance, obliging them once again to make use of the information and pictures they'd gotten from the Austrian newswires, and they repeated that the Baron was returning home, because at the end of his life he wished to make an exceptional donation from his enormous wealth—accumulated from Colombian copper mines—to the place of his origin: he was a true patriot, they wrote, authentically exemplary, because everything being frantically scribbled in those greedy tabloids was comprised of lies, villainous lies: the story of his having gambled away all his wealth, the Mafia connections, the jail time, and everyone could be aware now (especially due to their own rolling news coverage) of the "factual truth," which was that he had returned, like a true Hungarian, to make a bequest, because, as he had stated publicly during his time in Vienna, he wished to show his gratitude to that land from which he had sprung, in order to be its true son, and so that the news of this land could resound across the entire world; indeed, the editors of *Blikk* wrote in their editorial, there are such people, namely those who when abroad do not disparage their homeland, but bring glory upon it; he is a true patriot, that's the right expression, they wrote in the front-page article along with the photograph taken in Vienna, or at least originally published there, for he could not only be compared to Count István Széchenyi, the great Hungarian benefactor, who—as was well known to their readership—left everything he owned to his beloved nation... and this was the point where the writer of the article felt compelled to put down his pen, so powerless was he before the depths of feeling that welled up in him, he was just on the point of finishing the article, and these feelings welled up, he was almost finished, and feelings welled up, which—and in *Blikk*!—were so hard to put into words.

We're not animals here, may God strike you down, this isn't some seedy rabble crowd, but people, well, really, stop pushing already, an older woman in a black headscarf screeched, losing her patience, as she squeezed herself into the crowd laying siege to one of the second-class carriages, she squeezed herself in, and that meant that she had had to force her way forward, either by deploying the basket in her left hand, or shifting her body weight at exactly the right moment, it was a serious battle until she got to the stairs leading up to the carriage, so her many years of accumulated experience were necessary here, only that as a rule these experiences had accumulated for other people too, and here and there a basket, a suitcase, or a cheap woven synthetic bag made their appearance, and a little shift of body weight, but never mind; she made it as far as the steps, however it was only there that her difficulties began, because there arrived at that spot—according to the nature of the thing— from various directions, various forces struggling to reach that first step, and they piled up there, they squeezed forward from this side and they pressed forward from that side, but she was tenacious, holding her ground with a strength that belied her age, and all the while just saying and saying: well now, what is it with all you people, well, why do you act this way, as if we weren't ev'n people, but really jist sum kind ay mangy rabble, but by then she was already standing with her left leg on the first step—only that right at that moment she was hit by a wave of people from the same direction, and was nearly swept across to the other side, almost losing her position—her only bit of luck was that in the meantime she had managed to grab on to the train-door handle with her free hand, so she was somehow able to navigate herself back into position and restore her balance, and then she regathered her strength, and ruthlessly gained a position for her right leg on that same first step, and this already meant victory, as from this point on it was only necessary for her to withstand the pressure from both sides, and she withstood it, and then she was already on the second—that is to say, the penultimate—step, and she was able, with her posterior, to push back a corpulent man wearing a fur cap, who—fairly dangerously—had stepped right behind her onto the first step, and finally there came that last moment where the throng of the crowd was the greatest, right there in the carriage door, here, of course, it was just a matter of perseverance, and that perseverance was in her (what would have become of her if it hadn't been for this perseverance?), so then she was inside, inside the train, she knew exactly—she sized up the situation with one x-ray glance—*which seat would be hers,* and so it was, and so she plopped herself down in that seat, overtaking two others who were competing for the same spot, she sat like someone sitting in her own place, and not someone else's, and, with the basket now taken into her lap, she still battled for those few extra millimeters with the person sitting next to her, although more from habit than anything else, and she even noted—as she raised her toothless, sunken mouth in her face again and again, adjusting the headscarf's knot beneath her chin—that this 2:10 train wasn't her cup of tea, because it's always like this, how people here pushed, nearly trampling each other down, how well now, they were really like animals being driven to the stable, well, couldn't they just get on the train nicely one by one, one after the other, that would be better for everyone, that's what she said.

It wasn't really causing him discomfort, but from this point on there was a passenger in every seat in the compartment, they weren't talking, however, his direct companions in this sixth compartment of the first-class car were either turning over the pages of some glossy magazine or—for the most part—busy with their smartphones, every head bent down, as if every passenger were sitting in some kind of impenetrable sphere, so he had no difficulty (apart from those few restless moments as the new passengers got on the train and found a place to sit down) in returning to his pastime on the previous train, namely looking out at the landscape, and this landscape was radically different than what he had seen when traveling toward the capital city: here ruined farmsteads appeared amid the plowed fields stretching out to infinity, then sped away, one after the other, solitary acacia trees and rabbits hiding in the plowed ditches at the sound of the train, roe deer escaping in fright, and if some obscure childhood memory remained of this in him, then these infinite plowed fields had been infinite in a different way, the farmsteads had been ruined in a different way, and the solitary acacia trees and the crouching rabbits and the deer escaping in fright had been ruined in a different way, solitary and crouching and escaping in a different way, this is the Great Hungarian Plain, he thought, here the sky is lower, the land is bleaker—the plowed ditches, the farmsteads, the rabbits and the roe deer, the winding dirt tracks, and in all this, Nothingness itself seemed so much more forsaken than in his obscure childhood memories, and yet—despite all this—this forsakenness, this infinite paralysis everywhere, was sweet to him, everything came back, all of his memories of this landscape, the fissured memories of childhood journeys, the familiarity of the summer heat waves and the winter snows, he clung to the glass of the train window as if by magnetic attraction, and he gaped at the desolate view out there because it was dear to him and touching, and as the train went forward, deeper and deeper into this bleak, cold, desolate nothing, he said to himself, good Lord, I'm here again—here on the way to what was informally known as the "Stormland," in Békés County, on the way home—where behold, everything was just the same as it had been in the old days, because here, essentially, nothing had changed.

I had absolutely no idea who the fellow was sitting across from me by the window, he cut a pretty strange figure, I could see that, he related later on at home when his favorite dish was placed before him—a bowl of steaming sour-potato soup with bay leaves—but who the hell would have thought that it'd be the famous Baron—and it didn't seem like anyone else had recognized him, and so we screwed up our big chance, to put it bluntly, he was such an elongated kind of guy—he responded to the questions at the table—he had brutally long arms, a long body, long legs, even his neck was long, and his head too, like it was somehow reaching upward, thin, starting from the chin and leaping up into the heights, well, I've never seen such a high forehead as that, although I have seen one or two gawky types in my day, but I'm saying that, in the meantime, he was so gaunt, like an old run-down nag pulling a gypsy cart, a real string bean, yes, but of course in the finest of clothes that you could ever imagine, and maybe between eighty-something and death, but looking good, his eyes were black, his eyebrows were thick, he had a good long nose, a narrow chin, and so much thick opulent hair up there above, which I, getting onto fifty now, could only dream of, but completely gray, well, never mind, let's say he was a long-legged geezer, but on the other hand, children, he was a complete spaz, because you could also see that his gaze just kept wandering around, you understand, he was looking, but not really looking anywhere, exactly like some spasmodic, even though I wasn't particularly watching him over there, it's just that my memory is good, you see, and I only needed a couple of moments to take note of all of this, it's my profession after all, that's how I make my living, and that's how I support you as well, in other words, nothing, you understand, nothing came into my mind concerning him, I would have identified him, but somehow—only the good Lord knows why—I never even thought of the Baron coming home, and this figure sitting there by the window, he never took his eyes away from the window, and it could have been interesting, I was sitting there diagonally across from him, I could have spoken to him, you understand, I could have chatted with him a little bit, and maybe he would have had some interest in security technology—and why? because for someone who has so much wealth, it's not entirely inconceivable that he might want to know something about a new alarm system or two—and I even had my tool bag with me, I could have shown him a few prototypes, well, never mind, that chance is blown, children, don't you worry about it, he finally concluded his thoughts, it will work out somehow even without that, and turn down the volume, because the news is over, and here's this delicious potato soup, let's eat it up, children, eat it up, because if we don't, the whole thing will get cold.

In his memories, the train station at Szolnok had been just one among many of the Alföld stations, he didn't recall exactly what it had looked like, like anywhere else here it had been a two-story building painted yellow, with the stationmaster's apartment on the second floor, and the ticket counter, transport office, and waiting room on the ground floor, and two or three beautiful old chestnut trees in front, but now he was really surprised, when, after a long delay, the train finally rolled into the station; there was a gigantic train station where the old one had been, an inhumanly cold, ferro-concrete monstrosity; even more alarming than this was the system of tracks, sprawling with unaccustomed breadth, in front of the building, what could have happened for Szolnok to become such an important place, the Baron kept looking around out the window, and he began to count the number of tracks, but he stopped at twenty, because at that point his attention was drawn by the approach of a few passengers who were getting on the train, then, as one of them opened the door, and, pushing his lined hood back, he cast a glance at the one seat left empty by someone who'd just gotten off, and stepping in, he flopped down with an "oh my God," across from him, then groaning, like someone who had already been exhausted by the wait, he began to massage his limbs, oh, it's nice and warm in here, he remarked cheerfully, and he took off his fur ushanka, his voice resounded deeply, and it was so strong that everyone stopped what they had been doing, and as they couldn't decide at first whether to be afraid or amused by him, they were obliged to look and see who he was, and then decide if they would be afraid or amused, well, yes, the newcomer immediately perceived the attention directed toward him, all of you obviously are used to this cold, but I come from elsewhere, here—by which I mean, out there—you can't even imagine—because Pest is Pest—but here there's such a rotten dank cold, which is only possible in Szolnok, these are the accursed regions of the globe, because listen up here—and now all eyes were fixed upon him, as it was already quite clear that the new passenger was the sort who, when turning up in a new place, required no transition, but simply picked up and continued where he had left off, namely, the sort whom one took for who he was, namely, the kind of person who likes to be the center of attention, and there was no question about it, he genuinely and gladly amused himself by amusing others, as he himself noted later in a half-uttered sentence, because they would never find a November like this anywhere else, he continued with strident serenity, as if he weren't even the bearer of bad tidings, but of good, because such miserable weather as this—he shook his shaggy head—could only be had here, this so-called "Szolnok November," you won't get that anywhere else, he looked at the person sitting across from him with an impish expression, all day long there's something *dripping* down, and I'm not saying—please take note—that it's raining, but that something is drip-ping, tri-ckl-ing down, with every syllable he tapped his right index finger onto the palm of his left hand—it sinks right into the marrow of a person's bones, in any event I can't stand it, I've tried everything, this kind of coat, that kind of scarf, this kind of glove, that sort of boot, and now I've entrusted the matter to this ushanka—he showed his hat to the person sitting across from him—so at least my ears will be protected, because the wind has been blowing since noon, but you know—he looked around at his audience, which still wasn't completely certain whether to be afraid of him or amused by him—it's the kind of wind that pierces you in a moment, and then you remember it for a whole week, it makes you numb with cold, and sitting down in a nice warm train is of no use, well, never mind, how do you like it, he asked the schoolgirl sitting next to him, who was trying to bury herself in her notebook, and he put the hat in her hand; just what the doctor ordered, huh? he smirked at her, I think it's good, just feel it, it's real rabbit fur, just put it on, don't be so shy, and he pulled it onto the girl's head; she instantly turned red, and in her own way tried to resist, well, don't stand on ceremony, I know how good it feels on a person's head, it's not fake you see, not Chinese, not Bulgarian, not Romanian, don't be afraid, just feel it with your hands, well, don't be afraid now, feel it, and the girl had no choice, she had to palpate it in her hands, and then with a feeble "well, really," she handed it back, well, that's what it's like, the new passenger tucked the hat in between his thighs, if a person has a real ushanka— because as you know in these parts we refer to it as an ushanka—which isn't fake, just tell me, and he turned again to the schoolgirl, could you tell it wasn't fake?—of course, of course, the schoolgirl nodded, smiling through her torture, and once again she buried herself in her notes, I could feel it; well, you heard for yourselves, the newcomer turned once again toward the others, that's the proof, because if this is the opinion of a pretty young lady like this one sitting here, then there's no point in debating it further, it's holy writ; and with that the matter of the ushanka was concluded, he leaned back, and sighed contentedly, followed then by a pause of several minutes—a pause no one had dared hope for after this theatrical entrance—the train lurched from side to side, and the passengers lurched along with it, and this lurching train, bearing its load of passengers, tried, with its speed of roughly sixty kilometers an hour, to live up to its designation, as it, traveling along this route (between Budapest and the "Stormland" region in southeastern Hungary), was classified as an "Intercity express" train—but it tried in vain: the only valid part of this designation was that it really did travel between those two localities; the train itself was incapable of attaining the speed characteristic of the "Intercity" routes, not for a single moment, and not even by mistake, as it simply couldn't, due to complicated technical reasons which never came to light, so that the passengers regularly traveling here never mentioned it anymore, and never even joked about it, they just accepted it, like everything else in this country, because especially in these parts, in the southeastern corner of this country, people were inclined to interpret events by saying that something was just like this or that, it was just the situation, or just one of those things that happened, who knows what kind of complicated circumstances had led to this, it was better not to investigate the whys and the wherefores, because all the same it was November, and already the wind was blowing so strongly, and the rain smote down, and every village and city froze into icy cold, and the switches began to move only with difficulty, so that who would feel like finding fault in weather like that, just making everything worse with meaningless questions.

I'm exactly thirty-four years old, and with this curly, abundant black hair, I can get every girl I want, with my dark, heavy eyebrows and my eagle eyes I can see the tiniest miscalculation in any tax return, my nose is large and wide, and with this nose of mine, my sense of smell is like a hunting dog's, my wide mouth is like that of an opera singer, and I have a strong chin, and with this chin of mine there's such a KO as only I can give, in addition, I'll show you, look, I've got twenty-nine good teeth, and three crowns here below, I'm roughly five foot four, and I weigh 190 pounds, but if you want, I'll lose weight, although I'd like this big haystack here in my head to remain as it is, because I don't like combing my hair, and if that's not enough, then I'll tell you, he told him, that I used to be involved with oil-refining activities, but I was also a soccer referee, a language exam proctor, and the manager of a brick factory, presently I'm a slot-machine operator based in Arad, but my plans include expansion all the way up to the River Tisza—just like the Romanians wanted in times past—and everything up to the Tisza will be mine, this is my plan, but all you have to do say the word, and I'll give everything up, just say the word—he entreated the Baron—and I'll grow my mustache, I'll lose forty pounds, and I'll learn Spanish in two weeks, just say it, I ask you, he implored him, hardly even noticing that the other passengers in the compartment who'd been inclined more to fear him could only laugh at him now, but silently, because now he was kneeling on the floor of the train compartment, and in this upright kneeling position he was desperately trying to convince the old man to hire him in any capacity whatsoever, I'll be your stable boy, I'll be your secretary, your bookkeeper, I'll carry the chamber pot after you, I'll dust off the chair that you want to sit on, you can dictate to me your official and private correspondence from even eighty feet away, I'll do everything for you, Your Lordship, if you just say yes; all I have to do is look at someone and I already know what that person needs, and I looked at you, and I immediately saw that you have everything—with the exception of myself—because it's abundantly clear to me that *I'm necessary* for you, without me you could end up in trouble, indeed as I've heard, you're already in trouble; you need support, a shadow, an invisible right hand that will always be of help, that you'll always be able to rely on, and that's what I am, you see, Your Lordship,

I'm not in the business of ripping people off, and I confess I need you too, because in my view, the good Lord created us for each other—and with that he broke off, or rather paused in his great monologue, as he sensed that silence was needed now, and it would be enough for him to look, to just look at this person about whom he'd read everything, it was all there in his head, from *Blikk* to *Metro*, and that's why he'd alighted onto a train headed in that direction—because he wanted to be there when the world-famous Baron arrived in his hometown—and just look at that, he'd gotten onto the train where the Baron was, and he'd sat down exactly in that compartment where the Baron was sitting, and it was all just too good to be true, and he had to tell him, he now told the Baron, that his entire life could be characterized by this oscillation between good luck and misfortune, and by this he meant that he never hid away, never cowered in the corner, but that living riskily was in his blood, he was no wimp on whom the Lord would spit, but a hero, because he was prepared to take anything on while everyone else just sat around, but not him, oh never, never him, he always stood out into the wind, if you could put it that way, let it blow; that's how he began after he'd at first asked everybody in the compartment who they were, to know with whom he was traveling, and he got to the Baron, who didn't answer him for a long time, he just kept looking out the window, and it was plain to see that he was not really interested in what was going on, because this view outside completely held his attention, and this was clearly vexing to the one sitting across from him, and he just wouldn't stop, he just kept saying and saying: well now, but it's as if the gentleman by the window isn't aware that he's being spoken to, and with that he got up for a moment from his seat, reached across, and poked the old gentleman's shoulder a bit, which made the old gentleman shrink toward the window in alarm and look at him in fright, but he didn't say anything, after which he could hardly get him to calm down, and the others just sneered at this little bit of theater, because she had to admit—the schoolgirl told the story on the bus going home toward Mezőtúr—that the fat little man who got on the train at Szolnok was laying it on so thick that that you could split your sides from laughter, he asked everybody who they were, and when he got to the old Spanish guy, it was as if he'd gotten 220 volts, he jumped up, or how shall I put it, he leapt up to the heights, then threw himself down on the floor like an acrobat, you understand? and there he knelt, and the siege began, because there's no other way of putting it, it was a siege, he laid on every idiocy imaginable, and we were almost pissing in our pants with laughter, because it was *so* funny, I've never heard so much hot air in my whole life, it was just a whole lot of hot air, well, and he wanted this Spanish guy to hire him, I don't know what for, and the old grandpa was really frightened, it's also possible that he didn't understand what this clown on the floor was babbling about, maybe he didn't even know Hungarian too well, but that fat guy just kept on talking and talking, and he just didn't run out of words, but thank God after a while, as the old guy was looking around, and he saw that no one else was too bothered, he didn't look so frightened by this figure kneeling in front of him, he just listened, but somehow as if he was taking what he heard seriously, as if he was thinking about it, and I think, said the girl—and she began to grip the strap more firmly, because just at that point the bus had gone round the big turn at Puskin and Bajcsy-Zsilinszky Streets—I think he was still afraid, because at the end he said to him that he'd think it over, I'm telling you seriously, the old guy told him that he would consider it! but unfortunately I have no idea what happened in the end, because I had to get off, still I think that that joker never gave up, and I'm certain that he got what he wanted, because he just swept that old guy away like a storm.

Almost everyone got off at the county seat station; only one water- and central-heating installer wanted to stay on the train, saying that he, too, was traveling farther, but the secretary—as he had begun to call himself—very decisively requested that he find another compartment to sit in, because here, as he could see, serious negotiations were going on, and as his presence wasn't strictly required (even if only temporarily), he shoved him out the door, and winking at him, softly whispered in his ear that he didn't consider it to be inconceivable that he himself might be in need of a water- and central-heating installer at some point, so he should certainly give him his cell phone number, which the installer did, then he disappeared back in the corridor, so they were alone at last, just the two of them, the gentleman and the secretary, the latter noted, crossing his stocky legs and comfortably leaning back; and now, changing the topic, he noted that he didn't know if it was appropriate, but for him the salutation of Lord Baron seemed quite natural, but concerning the issue of how the Baron should address him, he wished to draw the Baron's attention to the manner in which all his business connections had called him up 'til now, because nobody called him by his civilian name—he was simply known as Dante, really, that was no exaggeration, every last one of his friends, his enemies, his business associates, and his employees—from the Carpathians to the snow-capped peaks of Zala County—namely because of this enormous skein of yarn on his head here, because supposedly (he smiled modestly) it really resembles Dante's, by whom I mean the famous rear-guard player for Bayern München—as he too has a huge head of black hair—well, and so he became Dante, and if that would be suitable, do address me by this name from now on, and to his great surprise the Baron spoke, albeit very softly, saying that the identity of the person he was referring to—who had been a member of the aforementioned society in Munich—was not clear to him, but in his opinion, the name Dante, in view of the portrayals that had survived of him, didn't really suit the secretary, to wit the name of Dante was already *very* well occupied, as in the distant past, the great Italian poet had borne this name, so that he, the Baron, would prefer to address him by his civilian name, if possible, and he would be curious as to what the civilian name was, because this, as a matter of course, would appear to be more suitable, but the secretary, getting over his surprise in one brief moment at having heard the old man speak, interrupted him, saying that the Baron shouldn't think that he was speaking about a nobody here, Bayern München was one of the world's greatest teams, if not the greatest, certainly he must have heard of them—no, unfortunately not, the Baron sitting across from him shook his head—well, never mind, that's not important, the self-designated secretary interrupted, the main thing was that he proudly bore the name of Dante, because the Dante who played for Bayern München, you could say, had reached his peak, and for him—he pointed at himself—such a comparison could only be advantageous, namely it expressed that within his own realm of endeavor—which currently—but in fact, only until today, was the colorful world of slot machines—he himself was regarded as a recognized authority, and it would never have occurred to him to apply for the proffered position of secretary, but he knew his own worth, which he was now making available to the Baron, and this value had been associated with the name of Dante for more than two decades, so that ... but the Baron just shook his head again and smiled gently, saying that there was some misunderstanding here, because the person who he was talking about was not from Munich, but from Florence, to be precise, he was the great exile of Florence, the author of the *Divina Commedia,* one of the greatest figures of all world literature, if not the greatest—that didn't matter at all, the secretary quickly replied, although slightly indignantly, because according to many, his Dante was the greatest rearguard ever, and to this he could only add: the greatest rearguard *in the entire world,* as he said, according to many; he recognized—he spread apart his arms in apology—that in the past two seasons he had been in somewhat less stellar form, but still nobody doubted his abilities, even if he played badly, or if the opposing forward got inside the penalty area twenty yards before the goal, everyone, but everyone knew, the Baron should understand, that Dante was Dante, and in his humble opinion so he would remain, among the very best, namely, to bear this name was itself a mark of status ... no, no, the Baron shook his head again, he had no desire to cast into doubt the fact that his traveling companion clearly greatly esteemed a certain person who went by this name, and that he wished only to be of assistance by filling in a few details, there was no problem between them, he, in the fullest measure, would comply with his companion's wish, and would address him by the name of Dante, he would use this name, but if he could make a suggestion—if only for the sake of accuracy—then it would be that Dante had not been a sports figure—to his knowledge he had only been involved with sports as a young man, but that too was more likely to have been hunting with dogs and falcons, and he would add that he had nothing to do with Germany, you know, the Baron now related to his traveling companion readily, we don't know too much about this—but fine, let's stick with your proposal, he smiled: they would agree that inasmuch as here was a Dante, then he would be the Dante of Szolnok, if that would be suitable, because he, the Baron, had come to know his dear traveling companion because of the city of Szolnok, if there had been no Szolnok, then, so to speak, there would be no Dante of Szolnok either, thus the name suggested itself, if the other would consent to it, well, and this was the point where the newly appointed secretary had no desire to push the matter any further, because he had decided that this hadn'tand not been a misunderstanding, but something else was going on, which he'd accounted for by noting that the Baron was a little uninformed when it came to sports, so what was the point of cramming him full of the correct information if he didn't want to know, fine, he nodded, they should stay with the designation of Dante of

Szolnok, it was all the same to him, and sooner or later it would just end up being plain old Dante anyway, because in the living language nobody ever referred to anyone continuously by their full name—ah, yes, the Baron raised his thick eyebrows in surprise, that's really interesting, you know, he leaned toward him a little more confidentially, I left Hungary a very long time ago, and I'm not really acquainted with the recent customs, particularly when it comes to language; Dante's eyes shone, he would help, he said, for why had he become his secretary if not to help the Baron in any matter whatsoever, including this one, at which point the Baron, maybe now for the first time since the ingenious battle of his traveling companion to gain the title of secretary had commenced, noted that for his own part he didn't really understand this secretary matter too well, as he really had no need for a secretary, on the other hand he felt extraordinarily grateful to receive assistance in orienting himself in these local matters, at which point his secretary sprang up, this was joyful news, and he conveyed to the Baron in flowery words that yes, that was exactly it, that was why he was here—and by that he meant that was why he was here on this Earth, for his entire life had consisted of one goal, to be of assistance to his fellow human beings: either by making gasoline available to them at affordable prices (although this wasn't exactly a risk-free endeavor), assisting those who wished to realize the dream of home ownership, or through the creation of leisure-time activities—he had helped, he had fostered all these areas of life, so what else could his task be now but to offer all this to the Baron, and yes, yes—he became completely enthused in the neighboring seat and he began to strike his armrests—to orient him amid the new conditions, that was what he'd been waiting for, although not idly, for two decades now, because God had created him for this task, so that the Baron had nothing to worry about, from this point on his fate was in trustworthy hands, because from this point on Dante would examine every step, and well, he smiled indulgently, he was a multitalented individual going by the name of the Dante of Szolnok, if he wasn't being too immodest in saying that openly, but then again, why shouldn't they speak openly now, in fact it would be necessary for the two of them to open up to each other, because he—Dante pointed to himself—could only truly help if he knew everything that had to be known.

Recently everything around him had become mixed up, the Baron acknowledged in the train compartment, somehow after a period of time he realized he couldn't completely understand what was happening with him and why, people appeared around him whom he didn't recognize, they were odd, and perhaps they were even slightly too "original," as he put it, they always wanted something from him, but he wasn't able to be of assistance to them in anything, because, he confessed—the Baron now confessed to Dante, who was listening tensely—nothing had interested him for a while other than coming home, he sensed that his time had come, and he desired, for the sake of a personal affair of particular importance, to see once again that place whence he had come; that country, which he had been obliged to leave almost as a child, almost forty-six years ago, almost forty-six years, he looked out the window but it had long since grown dark outside, and nothing could be seen, only his own likeness reflected back in the window, and he didn't want to see that, so he turned around; it's like a jewel box—he looked, deeply touched, at his traveling companion—I've been given back a jewel box, because everything here is so, but so wondrous; you know, my dear friend, for many hours now I have only been traveling, and I've been watching the landscape, this enchanting country of yours, and I can't get enough of looking at the earth, the horizon, and the light, I don't know if you can understand, but all of this means so much to an old man like me, and if due to my illness I haven't been able, in every moment, to completely give myself over to this astonishment—because among so many original individuals, and due to so many unfamiliar situations, as a matter of course, I have frequently been somewhat, how should I put it in Hungarian, confused, and well, because of the language, I don't understand everything completely—still I see that Hungary is my ancient homeland, a land of fables, exactly as I had imagined it, so that now I await with extraordinary excitement to see the city of my birth, and in particular an old familiar face there, and you know this is very customary for people of my age—I long to once again walk along the embankment of the River Körös beneath the branches of the weeping willow trees, then to walk along Jókai Street, to cut across, for one last time, the beautiful park on Maróti Square, and over to the Almásy Chateau, and the Snail Garden, you know my dear sir, and the Castle ... I know, I know, Dante nodded a little impatiently, in other words you're planning one of these pensioner outings—and in reality he did understand, he just wasn't interested, because by that point he could already largely tell that this Baron was a pile of misfortune, he'd perceived this within a moment, and it flashed across his brain that possibly he wasn't betting on the right horse by adhering to his plan of meddling in this, but then he chased the thought away, because all the same he sensed the enigmatic taste of a murky affair, and he loved this taste very much, in any event he didn't bother with the Baron's ever more sentimental turns of phrase, moreover some of them were making his blood run cold, because it was very difficult for him to bear aimless banalities and foolish sentimentality, and these were just pouring out of the Baron, and he, Dante, wanted to know how much cash there was in his account and where it was kept, he was curious about bank names and account numbers, concrete plans, namely what this old sack of bones was really doing in this trash heap of a country, and the main reason was because before any business transaction, he always determined the theoretical profit, namely, as he put it: contact details and access, but the Baron didn't betray any of these, in this regard he was either very reclusive or mistrusting, or he didn't know anything about it, and somebody else was standing in the background—Dante speculated nervously—so that for the time being it wasn't looking too good, he decided, with the exception that he was now holding a royal flush: excuse me, ladies and gentlemen, who was on the train now with the Baron?—himself; with whom was the Baron traveling in this compartment?—himself; and whom had the famous Argentinian, now returning home, made his secretary, somewhere in between Szolnok and Békécsaba?—himself: he, who didn't really recall his own name too much anymore, as he went by his real pseudonym, taken from the Romanian national team's famous soccer player, Cosmin Contra, and in all other respects, he was known for his expertise in the arts of squalid wheeling and dealing, an artist, accordingly, for what else could he consider himself to be than an artist whom fate constantly wished to crush, but who was continually able to spring back, was able to take another deep breath of air in order to jump into the thick of things again. We have arrived, Lord Baron, the Dante of Szolnok stood up from his seat, and he pointed outside through the train window. I see they are waiting for us.

# *DUM*

# HE WROTE TO ME

I'm a romantic, I don't deny it, said Marika to the new employee in the tourist agency, I love candlelit dinners, long walks in the Chateau gardens, and refined feelings, and everything, I would never deny it, but I was still surprised that he addressed me as Marietta, I was never Marietta, I don't recall anyone ever calling me that, and really it doesn't seem as if there'd be any reason for him to call me that, and although he can call me Marietta, in any event the fact that he addressed me in this way was so unexpected that at first I didn't even think that the letter was for me, it's just that I don't know anyone else who goes by this name, so I kept on reading, and I realized that it *was* addressed to me, and, well, it was to me—it became ever more obvious, as I kept on reading—and you know he wrote with such beautifully formed letters, his handwriting was always wonderful, and if for no other reason, it was because of that that I should have realized that it was definitely he, my own little one-time beau, because suddenly I recalled that he'd had such beautiful handwriting, my God, she sighed, pulling herself up a little more on the desk that she was sitting on, girlishly crossing one leg over the other, she straightened the pleats of her skirt with her left hand, which also meant that she began to pull down the skirt, which had slid up a bit, I was sixteen or seventeen at the time, and as a matter of fact I didn't even notice that I'd I had attracted his interest, because at that time I had a rather complicated relationship with Ádám Dobos, yes, with Dobos, don't look so surprised, with him, yes, we were still practically children, I was about seventeen, and he—namely Béla—well he certainly was a bit younger, maybe fifteen, or maybe sixteen already, I don't know, I really don't remember, but what is certain was that he was an interesting boy, such an awfully refined soul, I, however, was really surprised when he came over to me at one point, but you know he was so embarrassed he could hardly talk, and he said he'd like to meet up with me, and I just smiled to myself, because he was so sweet, but still a little boy, I could see that, and I still had that complicated relationship with Ádám, you know, I can still see that lanky young lad standing in front of me with his big red ears, although his eyes were wonderful, they were such a bright green that they nearly shone, and maybe that's why I said to him, fine, let's meet up, and with that, if I remember well, our conversation ended, he was certainly happy that he was freed from what was clearly such an awfully painful situation to him; as for myself, to tell the truth, I forgot about the whole thing until that dreadful letter came in the post, I'll tell you in a minute, wait, because it frightened me so, but so much, I'm telling you seriously, because just imagine, it came in an envelope with a black border, and it was a long letter about how he was so much in love with me, and he couldn't bear any longer how I hardly noticed him, and of course I was really frightened, and I immediately got dressed and ran into the city, because at that time, as you know, already it was ten years after the Revolution and we lived in Csókos Road, quite a distance from the Baron and his family, they lived in the center here, by the park on the main square, and I rang the bell, and I said, very frightened, to his mother that I'd like to speak with him, and his mother, who didn't know me, also became somewhat frightened, because she didn't understand what was going on, but by then I had already realized that there was no problem, and he hadn't done anything crazy as I had feared, and well of course he hadn't done anything crazy, he just came out, and he was a little different there in the doorway of his own house, somehow he gave the impression of a somewhat more serious boy, but once again he stood there so awfully confused, and he could hardly even utter the words for me to come in, and I didn't want to go in, because I'm telling you seriously that I was really annoyed that he had misled me with that black-bordered envelope, because you know he had just made up the whole thing, well I don't even know why, but what's certain is that he was *very much* in love with me, whereas I—well, what should I say, she said to the new employee in the travel agency, and her words broke off, she laughed conspiratorially at her colleague whom she herself had recommended for this position a few months ago, she'd left citing family reasons, what should she say now, she said, and she shrugged her shoulder a little bit, all the while looking deeply into her colleague's eyes, there was my complicated relationship with Ádám and everything, I didn't know my own feelings, I was seventeen years old, full of desire and yearning, I saw everything through rose-colored glasses, you know what it's like, you too were once seventeen, and I was a seventeen-year-old girl here, in our own little enchanted city, I dreamt even when awake, dreaming that this would happen or that would happen, well, never mind, so the whole thing was so awfully complicated, and for a while nothing happened, I didn't hear from Béla, but you know he was so skinny, and dreadfully tall, and hunched over, and he had long hair, and the way he dressed was so unfortunate, because I was absolutely certain that his mother still picked out his clothes for him, despite the fact that in those days the sharper boys were able to get hold of a pair of jeans or a nice little pair of Italian boots, but not him, he always wore cardigans, and he always had on some kind of awfully impossible cuffed woven trousers which weren't long enough for him, the ends just dangled around his ankles, and I don't understand why his mother dressed him like that, or why he himself allowed this, because this was already a modern age, you know, at home we crooned the songs of Rita Pavone or Adamo, I did as well, I remember well, I sewed all my things for myself with my mother and my little sister, and I tried to sew the kinds of clothes ... well you know, we saw the San Remo Music Festival and everything ... and my sister was especially good at this, but as you know, she had her own boutique here by the Petőfi statue, yes, she was the one who owned that boutique, yes, yes, so that—where was I?—well, so I didn't hear from him for a while, yet later on I did, and I could see nothing had changed, I still meant something to him, so that I said, fine, no problem, let's meet up, and so we met, which of course Ádám didn't like, and that led (as you can imagine) to a huge fight, and by then the connection between me and Ádám wasn't what it had been before; but that wasn't the only reason I went for a stroll with Béla in the Snail Garden, it was also because I was somewhat pleased that this boy with beautiful eyes was so, but so ... well, you understand what I'm trying to say, don't laugh, when something like this happens to a woman, and she's only only seventeen years old—even then somehow—and we went for a stroll in the Snail Garden, he walked beside me, but he never even touched me, and he talked about such strange things, I didn't understand it too well, because he read some pretty strange books, books which—look, it was so long ago that I've long since forgotten what kind they were—I do know, however, that they were those kinds of philosophical books, because when he saw that I didn't understand what he was talking about, we turned to Russian literature, and with that he crept into my heart, because at that time I had discovered Turgenev, I simply had a passion for him, and this boy knew a lot about Turgenev, moreover when we met for the second time on the banks of the River Körös, and I walked with him all the way from the town center up to the Castle, I realized that he already knew *everything* about Turgenev, and he just kept on speaking, and he spoke about so much, the words just poured out of him, I remember it well, and somehow, you know, I liked him, I'm not saying that I took to him as a man, but

I liked him, his green eyes and everything, and well, I stuck it good to Ádám with these little walks, because up to that point he had been acting as if it was all over for him, but then when these strolls started, then suddenly I became interesting to him, so that he began to lay siege to me again, and of course I—because I was head over heels in love with him—immediately went running back to Ádám, because for me Ádám, that Ádám, he was a man already, he was one year older than me, and he cut such a good figure you know, so that I forgot all about Béla, but it didn't go so well with Ádám, so that finally we broke up for good—by then it was the fourth or fifth time already—don't laugh, because we were children, at least I was, and full of dreams that things would be like this and that, I can dare to tell you because you're my relative and you'll understand, but Ádám was interested in other women too, mainly that busty Zsazsa, you know the one that got married to Dr. Ikos, well, I couldn't stop that, and I knew everything about her maneuvers, because that woman was a major schemer, you know, maybe she was twenty-three or twenty-four years old, and *then* she wrapped Ádám around her little finger, but no mind, because he wrote himself off for me once and for all, if he wanted a busty bimbo, then fine, he could go right ahead, it was over, and then one Sunday afternoon he, namely Béla, showed up again coming from the station, and I just happened to be going somewhere in the opposite direction, and we walked together, and it was so free and easy, how he just greeted me, like someone who had gotten beyond the whole thing, and I suddenly just realized that yes, I was in love with him, he was also a year older now, and there was something in him, something, I don't know what it was, but I felt it, I felt this Béla was no longer that little boy he'd been one year ago, so I invited him for a date, I wrote him a letter, and I tossed it in their mailbox, of course in secret, I just wrote his name on the envelope, and that was it, well, no mind, and there was Béla sitting across from me in an espresso bar, you know on the corner of Jókai Street there was that tiny sweet little espresso bar, well, we met there, and I told him, and I think he was really surprised, and he said he'd never stopped loving me, but he'd resigned himself to Ádám, and I told him there was no more Ádám, there was only him, and of course that was a bit of an exaggeration, I really didn't know what was going on with me, but I said this, or something like it, because from that point on we were going out together; but you know, this boy still never even dared to touch me, not even my hand, yes, he wouldn't even hold my hand, and then it emerged on one of our dates that he had never kissed anyone, we were sitting together above the River Körös, you know, in the Casino, as they called it back then, and it was just a simple sweetshop, and the balcony looked out over the river, and we were all alone on the terrace, and the devil sneaked into me and I started to tell him to kiss me, oh, what a magic afternoon that was, as the weeping willows bent down toward the water so sadly, and he kissed me, but he didn't know how, and so I—don't start laughing now—I began to teach him how to kiss, and we sat there kissing, but it wasn't really proper kissing, because all the same this Béla was still a little boy, in other words he didn't know anything, and I'm not just talking about kissing, but he didn't even have any idea of what love was, just the feelings were there in him somehow, and then suddenly *the One*—Lajos from the gas station—burst into my life, and so that was the end, we met up no more, he still chased me for a while, he sent me his poems, and those stranger than strange letters about Turgenev, but then he stopped, and as a matter of fact I almost forgot about him, just as a person forgets all of those dreams and reveries—she shook her head—a person forgets how many evenings she gazed longingly toward the town, because—she explained her colleague—at the time she was still living at home, and it took at least half an hour to get to the city center along Peace Boulevard; and she just dreamed and yearned, but really, she was the kind of young girl who didn't even know what she was yearning for or whom she was yearning for, Ádám was her youth, she continued dreamily, she could confess this to her, she could tell her about all this because they were relatives, and among her younger nieces, she was always the one—she pointed at the new employee—with whom she was happy to confide her most intimate secrets, and now she was sharing these secrets only with her, and that's why she was so happy that a year ago her niece had moved back to the city with her Papa, because somebody in the city had to know that from all those rumors nothing was true, it revolted her so much—she pointed to herself—all this malicious gossip, because it was all nothing but a pack of lies, and her niece should believe her, because for her, Ádám was really the first one, and Béla, that little boy, had just faded away more and more as the years went by, then came the difficult years of becoming an adult, or how should she put it, she—and once again she pointed at herself—she left the Italian high school, and took up her place next to Lajos at the gas station, of course they always had plans, *big plans*—she drew out the vowels of these words—and once there was even a newspaper article about her, although speaking among themselves, the person who wrote it was the lowest scoundrel who just took advantage of her naivete, because he promised everything, but he only wanted *that* and nothing else, then he threw her away like a rag, so that she held out—she said to her niece—she held out until the very end, next to Lajos; she shouldn't have, however, but at that time he was already a serious soccer player, and he even got into the county's Second Division, then came the weekend matches, and she always had to sit there in the bleachers, it's true that she always had a good seat, Lajos always made sure of that as well as of other things, but it wasn't exactly what she had been dreaming of, and sometimes when she was all alone, she took out the old boxes in which she kept her letters, and she came across those letters that Béla had formerly written to her, and she confessed that she even wept as she read them, she related now, sitting on the desk in the travel agency, because there were no customers, they could talk at length, there was nothing to do, the times when people would just walk in off the street into a travel agency were gone, unfortunately—the new employee said at home that evening at dinner—there was nobody there, tourists don't come here anymore, not even anyone from here wants to be a tourist here, so she didn't understand—she turned to her father accusingly—why he had forced this job with the travel agency on her, because everyone knows that the time when people came from Serbia, Croatia, or Romania in the hundreds to see this town was long gone, because the only thing coming from there now were these waves of refugees, well, they were coming good and thick—and she would note parenthetically that no, of course they didn't want to stay here, of course, not here, but no mind—she shook her head bitterly—those were the good old days, the golden age, but her father should realize that tourism here had only a past, and no future—and all the same she had to talk to that old bag Marika, who was now calling herself Marietta, or as she says it, Mah-ri-et-tah, it was pure vaudeville, well, but, if he could believe her, she went on for a whole hour how it was with Béla, because that's what she calls him, Béla, no joke, you could split your sides from laughter over this Marika and the Baron, everyone here has utterly lost their minds; and she was talking about how the Baron wrote to her, and about how when they were both teenagers there was something between them, and then there was something about how—she vented her rage—when Marika was a teenager and Aunt Julika and her family still lived on Csókos Road, and Marika lived with them, there was the Baron and Marika, and the Wenckheims—communism or no communism—wouldn't let her get anywhere near the Baron, everyone knew that, so when she had finally listened to this entire litany from Marika, she seriously believed she was going to lose it already, but really, father, well what exactly did Marika take her for, that she would believe something like this, and of course she told her this whole pack of lies so she would tell somebody else, well, she would be crazy to spread gossip like that, especially when not a word of it was true, well, never mind, she leaned over her plate, and poked at the food with her fork, *as far she was concerned* it didn't matter, the main thing was that nothing at all would come from this job, she said that now to her father right off the bat, nothing, do you understand, Papa, not only did no tourist, but not even a person step into that office the entire blessed day, she could predict, even after one day there, the good times weren't coming back, it was a waste of time to believe that and drive yourself crazy, instead—and this was her unaltered opinion—she would be much better off trying for a job at the Slaughterhouse, don't you know anyone there, she raised her eyebrows, the position of the Director's secretary was vacant now, well, there was a hope in that, her father couldn't deny it, and she dug into her plate once more with her fork, like someone who wasn't very hungry, at least she hoped so.

He didn't have to shut himself in, because as a matter of fact they only tried to disturb him at lunch and dinnertime, and even then they came up the stairs so loudly that he already knew they were approaching and he had time to prepare for the knock at the door, so he just spoke to them through the closed door, saying: no thank you, then saying: yes, he'd rather have his meal in his room, then the sound of steps grew distant, and he could turn back to that escritoire where he wrote his letters, as the staff informed the family downstairs, he just sits at that writing desk, and he just writes and writes letters, one after the other, or it might have seemed that was the case, but for maybe one week now the Baron had been writing one and the same letter over and over again so he could give it to the valet to post it, but instead he wrote a second letter, in which he attempted to rectify everything that he hadn't, he felt, been able to precisely formulate in the first—my memory is leaving me, as he formulated the sad situation, namely, it was more than likely that with the passage of time, something had occurred with his facility of memory, in other words it was getting rusty, yes, that's what was happening, there were many things he didn't remember, many things now that he could no longer evoke, names fell away, so it seemed, forever, from his head, he searched for street names, but without success, he tried to recall what the name was of that artesian well near the old greater Romanian quarter, and the name of that bridge on the street heading toward the Hospital, but both that artesian well and that bridge were no more, they were clearly lost, just as, he wrote to Hungary, there was hardly anything left of him either, for not only was there a problem with his memory, but as a result of the natural process of aging his legs were weak, and he always walked now with a slight totter, not to speak of his bad sight, his delicate stomach, his creaking joints, the back pain, and his lungs, but then he didn't wish to continue, because it would all come to a wretched end, and that's what he was afraid of—she, Marietta, would be obliged to compose a more dreadful picture of him than existed in reality, *but believe me,* he continued, after crumpling up the previous version of the letter and tossing it into the paper bin next to the escritoire, because he had written "believe" with an "ei"—there is only one ability of mine which shall remain forever "unbroken," to be precise, it is thinking back upon this city with that pain, and within this city, you, Marietta, now, that I am over sixty-five years old, I perhaps may now confess that there are two facts, two things that sustained my life: the fact that I knew a city, and in that city I came to know you, and I can betray as well: for me this means only one thing, *there is nothing I love better in this life than this city—and within it, you*—for surely you know I'm not betraying any great secret here, because I still remember that no matter how cowardly I was, I finally did confess to you that I loved you, I know it's the end now, and I know I'm not what I was, I know I'm nothing but a mere wreck, but you know, Marietta, in my most difficult moments it always helped me to think of this city—and you within it—and in point of fact I would like to seek you out one last time so that I might tell you so in person, I would like to see you, my dear Marietta, because your being—he wrote, but now the paper almost slid slowly by itself on the surface of the escritoire toward the paper bin—your face, your smile, and in that smile those two little dimples in those dear little cheeks have always been more important to me than anything, more important than anything else.

He had been delivering the mail for ten long years now in the second postal zone, so that it wasn't difficult for him to recognize that this was a peculiar letter, and it wasn't just the stamp, it wasn't just the seal, nor was it the address, written out with an elaborate hand, but the shape of the envelope itself diverged from what the common person used these days—if that person used an envelope at all—he related to the journalists, the proportions were different, you know, the length and the height originated from a different kind of envelope system than what a person was accustomed to, and it wasn't that the envelope was too long or too high, because the whole envelope was, to be exact, smaller, indeed, a good deal smaller than the average envelope—but its proportions were unfamiliar, as he picked up the envelope and palpated it when he began sorting letters at dawn in the postal distribution center, because that was how it worked: after the letters had been sorted by machine, they always quickly spun through them to double-check the sorting, they really spun through those letters, and everyone had his own way of doing it, but he would sort them in the order of his usual postal route; thus, if he always went from point A to point B, well, then, these letters had to be sorted in the same order so when he was out there on location he could just hop over there, because he always nearly hopped from the sidewalk toward the mailbox to toss that letter in, so there was no time for reading the address, he always took it in with one glance, like a kind of living computer, he saw it in one flash, and he took one hop from the sidewalk and the letter was already in the mailbox, well, that's how it went more or less, *if they could follow him*, and that was actually meant as a joke, because there was nobody who could follow him, he was the fastest among all his colleagues, some of them even called him—just don't tell anyone else—Speedy Tóni, and in that he saw no mockery whatsoever, because that was just a way of trying to express how fast he was, and well, he really was that fast, like the wind, that's why ... well, do you see now, and the journalists nodded, but they all seemed to be slightly impatient, so he decided not to try their patience any further and he picked up from where he had left off on this little detour, well, so the envelope, well, yes, it was smaller, and its length wasn't that of the general envelope, nor was its height, and that's why he noticed it already at dawn, when the letters were being sorted according to streets and houses and—if the building had them—stories, and that's why he looked to see who the sender was, in normal circumstances he would never do this, not because he wasn't interested, he was interested, but there was never time for that kind of thing, because it was also in the nature of this work, you know—he explained to the journalists—for him to interconnect himself with these letters like a kind of living machine, in a word, the addressee wasn't really the interesting part of the envelope, but the sender was, well, and it was because of that elaborate handwriting that his gaze crept—if he could put it that way—to the upper-left-hand corner of the envelope, but there wasn't anything there in the upper left-hand corner of the envelope where the return address should have been, there was *nothing at all*, it should have been there though, so he was awestruck, and just like any person, when he is awestruck, he turned the envelope over in his hand, and he saw that there was a return address written the old-fashioned way on the back of the envelope, along the upper edge of the flap, and there it said Baron Béla Wenckheim, he wouldn't say that he could read every kind of handwriting out there, but he could more so than the average person who doesn't have to be able to read every kind of script—if he had to, he could read almost every kind of handwriting—and then he already knew what he was holding in his hands as he had read about it in *Blikk*, he'd read already a few days previous that the Baron was coming, and that his wealth was unheard of, and that he was going to distribute it—in all probability—because why else would he be coming here if not for that, this wasn't his opinion, this is what he'd read in *Blikk*, and he already was pulling his iPhone out of his pocket, he was holding the envelope at a good angle up to the light, and he was already clicking the camera, and already, if you please, the picture was in his iPhoto gallery, here it is, just have a look, he wasn't asking anything for it for the time being—although that too was just a joke—and then again, who knew, it was still possible that he'd be able to get some money for it, if things worked out that way, and perhaps this here, this lousy little snapshot of the famous envelope—well, you can see for yourselves—it might be of some value after all.

I don't even know how I should address you, young lady, said the Mayor, looking around the office to see where he could sit down, in a word, my dear . . . what was that again? . . . yes, of course, my dear *Dóra*, but you've now reached a day of the utmost importance, of course you must have a thousand things to take care of, but from this point on you must put all this aside, do you understand, and forget about these other tasks, you must simply forget about them—he finally sat down nervously in a yellow, plastic, modern-looking armchair, while adjusting his bow tie, and he continued: whatever work this office has been involved with up 'til this moment, all other business must be halted immediately, as before this workplace there now stands a task of enormous magnitude, really, I don't even know where to begin, I hardly even know where my own head is; well, never mind, he sighed, and in the meantime he unbuttoned his jacket while his gaze—the morose gaze of a civil servant tormented by worry and care—swept across the face of the woman standing before him, who clearly had no idea what the Mayor was doing here, she was waiting in the greatest of confusion to find out—because the task at hand, said the Mayor, is of enormous magnitude, my dear Nóra—Dóra, she interrupted him—yes, of course, of course, the Mayor corrected himself, Miss Dóra, excuse me, but even this is of no importance, because such a task awaits you now for which I don't know if you are truly ready, I know you fulfill your daily duties here with great assurance and responsibility, what is to come, however, will lift you from the heap of daily toil, you see—he bent toward her—from this point onward you are relieved of all responsibilities having to do with tourism, from this point onward, there will be no more responsibilities having to do with tourism in this office, do you understand? you'll be working for me now; but what am I saying—he broke out in a sharp voice nervously—and he began once again to loosen his bow tie, because it was new, and he was wearing it for the first time, and he hadn't at all gotten used to it, and he wasn't even certain if his wife had tied it around his neck the right way—what I am saying here, he struck the sides of the modern plastic armchair with both his hands at the same time so as to add greater emphasis to his words—from now on you won't be working for me, but for the city, Miss Dóra, and I'm sorry if I'm not pronouncing your name right but I've got a lot on my mind right now, the office of Mayor requires me to do everything at once, and my work in this affair must be beyond all reproach, for my own sake as well, do you understand, for this work demands the greatest possible powers of concentration, because hear me well, Miss Nóra, from now on you will be the one in charge of coordinating the entire operation, do you understand? you will be in charge of ensuring that the celebrations will take place with the least amount of disturbance and to the greatest liking of our esteemed guest, you see—he drew closer to her, and his voice became subdued—the celebrations will have to be as successful as possible, do you understand? but they must also be as cheerful as possible, try to come up with some cheerful entertainments—what am I supposed to be doing? the new employee asked in a completely subdued voice, and by now she was thoroughly nervous because she understood nothing here, and already in this nervousness she was wringing her hands; you will be Acting Coordination Director, the Mayor answered her, and for a moment he had the same expression on his face as when he was awarding a decoration to someone, but it was only really for a moment, because immediately that arsenal of the signs of morose concentration had crept back onto his face, it would be best if you begin to think about this, Miss Nóra, try to come up with some competitive events you could imagine taking place here, and—how should I put it—you'll have to be lightning quick, because don't forget, we have no time; Jesus, no time, just a single day to organize everything, well, what's come to your mind? he asked expectantly and he paused, but the employee who stood across from him couldn't even blurt out that she didn't understand a word of what he had said, so the Mayor once again slightly loosened his bow tie, and he scratched his bald head on that spot he always scratched when he was thinking about something, and he tried to look at her with a countenance that would suggest that he understood her difficulties, and he was trying to help, because then he said to her: look, Miss Nóra, to begin with there's the Budrió Housing Estate, perhaps there you could imagine some kind of cheerful competition, at which suggestion the woman nodded at him very cautiously, well, so—the Mayor released a sigh—this will work, you see, Miss Dóra, because just imagine that at the Budrió Housing Estate, you can get together five or six young people who will then take part in a so-called "who can sneeze the loudest competition," you understand, which at one point last year—before you and your father moved back here—went so well during the inauguration of the kindergarten next to the Castle, everyone loved it, well now, isn't that an original idea? the Mayor asked, not even waiting for an answer, so you see, have a seat already, and he pointed at the desk next to him—and the employee, like a sleepwalker, slowly walked around it, and sat down behind the desk—there's a piece of paper, take that pen, and write this down: "who can sneeze the loudest competition," there you go, and now on the other side, write down this: Budrió Housing Estate, do you follow me, and below on the second row, write the number two—she wrote it down—and well, what do I know, what else is there? you can also suggest something; but the person he was addressing was visibly incapable of doing that, at least not in this way, she just looked at the Mayor as if he had lost his mind, but there was also fear in her gaze, because it was, after all, the Mayor, and he'd been the Mayor for twelve years now, and she still had to—the woman thought to herself, horrified—she still had to try to understand what the hell he wanted from her, what was this insanity all about, in any event she wrote down on the designated left side of the page: Competition: Who Can Sneeze The Loudest? and on the right side of the page she wrote Budrió Housing Estate, then she went one line below and she wrote down the number two, and she waited for the Mayor to say something, but he just looked at her now reprovingly, and for too long, so that she didn't even know where she could disappear to, she related that evening at home, because the Mayor has gone mad, of that there's no longer any doubt, I'm seriously telling you, she told her father at the dinner table, he's completely gone out of his mind, he was spewing nonsense back and forth, saying this and that, that I've been designated as some kind of coordinator, and I have to do this and let everything else go to hell, and I'm asking you—she looked at the old man deeply bent over his plate sitting across from her—Papa, please pay attention, she asked him, what the hell is it that I'm supposed to stop doing if I never even started anything, it was pure insanity, I'm telling you seriously, and then when he saw that I wasn't saying anything, the Mayor just started dictating, and after I wrote the number two in the second column, I had to write down "Chicken Backs Tossing Competition" with the participation of the pensioners' club, then to the side of that, I wrote "Pensioners Club," then came the third line, and there I had to write down the number three, then I had to write "Target Practice: Hitting Pizza Delivery Boys Riding On Motorcycles With Jellybeans From The Third Floor," then on the right-hand side I had to write "Lennon's Ditch"—but by then the Mayor had had enough and he looked at his employee with more than a questioning look, and he said, well, but you haven't thought of anything, no, not very much, the employee answered, and in the space for the fourth line she wrote the number four, but after that she didn't write anything because she was waiting for the Mayor to continue, the Mayor, however, did not continue, but suddenly he looked at his watch, jumped up from the modern plastic armchair, tugged at his bow tie, and then loosened it again, smoothed down and then buttoned up his jacket, and finally he tossed out to her: well, now you finish up, and the plans should be on my desk tomorrow by noon, just show up at City Hall and tell them you're the new person in charge for special matters, and the secretaries will let you in—in brief, the Mayor opened up the door of the travel agency, by noon tomorrow, Miss Nóra, he made a warning movement with this finger humorously, but anxiously, and already he was gone—she related all this that night at the dinner table—and she just sat there like someone frozen in place, it was brutally idiotic, she said, there was this sheet of paper before me with these dictated words, and I just stared at it, I just looked at it, thinking: what?! and then my first thought was—Papa, pay attention!—was for me to call the ambulance, as our Mayor—I decided I'd say this when I called on the telephone—was suffering from some serious psychotic problem.

She read it once, she read it twice, but she didn't know who this Baron Béla Wenckheim was, she looked at the address, and it really was her address, there was no mistake, she said to herself, and she held the letter a little distance away from herself, finding it odd, then she read the letter again, but now she only read every third line, then it suddenly began to dawn on her who this was, a boy vaguely emerged in her memories, but—she shook her head—she didn't remember this being his name, somehow his name was something else, but what was it, and it wasn't coming to mind, she could see it all clearly, yes, it was when she had that complicated relationship with Ádám Dobos while she was attending high school, back then she had met up a few times with another boy whose name she didn't recall at all, my God, she thought, how old could I have been, eighteen, seventeen? or something like that, and he was still like a little boy, that is to say he was big, oh yes—she suddenly remembered—he was very tall, very skinny, he walked around so awfully hunched over, and he was so strange, he wore impossible clothes, moreover he had a bit of bad breath too, but his name, she turned over the unusually shaped envelope yet again, the name here, somehow it's not coming to me . . . and that was it, she couldn't remember anything else, only that he was dreadfully tall and skinny and hunched over, and that slight bad breath, and of course there wasn't anything between them, because if there had been she would have remembered it, but no, so she slipped the letter back into the envelope, she put the envelope onto the cocktail table, and she leaned back in her sofa bed, closed her eyes, my God, these sixty-seven years, my bones are tired even though I don't ever do anything, why do I have to get old, she thought with closed eyes, and why didn't she think of herself as *really* being old; Wenckheim, Wenckheim, she searched in her memory, but because of her dreadful memory with names, nothing was coming, then suddenly a scene from the past leaped up, oh, but that boy was so crazy, and there appeared before her the house on the town's central square, and the boy's mother, an elegant woman in a silk dressing gown who came to open the door after she'd rung the bell, who looked at her so coldly and asked her what she wanted so rudely—I'd just like to speak with him, she'd said, or rather she'd stammered it out, because she was fairly overwhelmed to speak with this elegant lady, with her own cried-out eyes, and it was certainly obvious how upset she was, so that the lady in the door became even colder and asked what she wanted, so she said, startled: well, is he at home?—and by that she meant to ask: was he still alive? then the boy came out, and somehow the anger within her was stronger than the relief—why did he have to send her that envelope and that letter—she'd really thought that he'd done something completely crazy because of her, and now here he stood before her, I just wanted to know, she said to him, if you did something, but I see that you didn't, that you were just playing with me, and you shouldn't have; and with that she turned on her heel and was gone—Wenckheim Wenckheim, she tried to remember something else as well, but she couldn't, because the name and the boy in this sievelike head of hers didn't match up somehow, my God, I have to talk with someone, the thought formed within her, and she'd already picked up the remote control and turned down the volume on the TV, she was calling her one single girlfriend, well, you know I have such a terrible memory for names, but maybe you can help me, listen, tell me if the name Wenckheim says something to you, and at first her friend said it didn't mean anything to her either, but then her voice grew high and sharp, and she said *but of course* I know, I read about him, why, why do you need to know this name—oh you don't want to know, I'll tell you later, just tell me what you know, and then a story was laid out for her, and she sat on the sofa bed as if numbed, she felt her palm sweating as it held the receiver, and she certainly turned bright red as well, she felt she was warm, then she was chilled, then once again she felt warm, and she was certain that her face was still burning, well, of course, she nodded, she listened to her girlfriend's chatty voice, which just kept repeating over and over what she had conveyed at the beginning, I'll call you later on, she said, and put down the receiver in silence, she picked up the envelope again, and she looked at the name again, yes, it's him, she thought, and somehow her whole body began to tremble, oh my God, it was always like this when some fateful event came to pass, her heart beat once, and *something* flashed across her entire body like lightning, my God, if only I weren't so old, because what if he really comes here, ah, no, she shook her head, and, leaning against the backrest of the sofa bed once again, she closed her eyes, then from her sitting position slowly turned onto her side, her head on the pillow, she slipped her feet out of her slippers, and put up her legs too, of course not stretching them out, but just folding them a little, because a sofa bed like this wasn't long enough to stretch out on, especially when it wasn't pulled out all the way, and she lay there motionlessly, on her side, with her head on the pillow, her two hands clasped in front of her chest as if she were praying, but she wasn't praying, she just lay there motionlessly, and she still didn't open her eyes, and she said to herself, oh, no, never, Marika, don't start dreaming again, because it's not going to happen, this will never, but never come to be. She reached for the remote control and turned on the television, right then her favorite program was on: "A Poem for Everyone." But she couldn't pay attention.

The plan is good, the Mayor announced at the 9:30 a.m. meeting, comprised of all the civic leaders of the town judged by him to be useful, as members of the expanded Civic Committee, we will not take rank into consideration with regard to assignments and working groups, they can be amateurs, they can be professionals, it doesn't matter, the main thing is to be able to entrust each of them with a subtask—and so I summarize—one: he grabbed his left thumb with his right hand holding it up, I must now announce that the light entertainment presented in his honor will be taking place across the entire city; and two—he grabbed his index finger and held that up—everything will begin at the train station; and three: the Orphanage is being moved out of the Almásy Chateau this afternoon with immediate effect; and four—he now grabbed, because he'd forgotten to do so before, the middle finger, there will be a moratorium on traffic in the entire city center, because what is it that we know?—he posed the question in a shrill voice, and once again raised his thumb in the air—we know that one, the Baron is inclined to negative moods, therefore during the entire time of his sojourn in our city, only and exclusively events of a cheerful tenor may be permitted; and two, that of course his reception at the train station must be as grand in scope as possible, because don't forget that we're not just speaking of a count here, but frankly of a baron; and three—he once again raised his middle finger into the air—a baron can't just live anywhere, people, we can't just toss him into a hotel, think about it, really, think about the state of the Komló Hotel or the former Trade Union National Council Resort, gentlemen—and he cast a fairly reproachful gaze on the people assembled around the long table, as if they were responsible for the state of the Komló Hotel or the one-time Trade Union National Council Resort—we need the Almásy Chateau, this isn't up for debate, and now—he suddenly leaned back in his chair—I ask for your recommendations, your observations, your thoughts, your ideas, let them scintillate, gentlemen, for the sacred love of God, let them scintillate, because our town is at stake here—at which point silence descended upon the gathering for a minute that seemed unbearably long, until it was finally broken by the Deputy Mayor (a member of the opposition), who sat to the right of the Mayor; he said he agreed with the great majority of the proposed recommendations, such that he could only endorse them, but—he raised his voice—it was necessary to consider what would happen with the horrendous piles of garbage, the homeless, and mainly with the child beggars that continually overran the streets, at which point the Mayor snapped at him, saying, really, Mr. Deputy Mayor, I asked for scintillating ideas, and I have no wish to hear about these obvious matters, gentlemen, well, if there's nobody here with a sound idea ... and then the chief secretary, sitting across from the Mayor, with her meek gaze and making use of the benefit of her opulent bosom, said that of course the Deputy Mayor was correct, and somehow the garbage and the homeless and the child beggars had to be urgently gathered up and removed, and she only dared to hope that the representative of Municipal Utility Services, present here as well at this meeting, was taking note of the task at hand, at which point the representative of Municipal Utility Services, who was present at the meeting (and who was, otherwise, the brother-in-law of the Deputy Mayor), got up from his seat, but he was sitting so far away—at the other end of the table—that he was barely audible, so the Mayor and the Deputy Mayor thundered at him as one to speak up, well—he raised his voice a little angrily—I only wanted to say that for such a high-volume operation an operational plan is strictly necessary, noooo, the chief secretary cried out, and that meek smile suddenly began to throw out sparks; it's not a plan we need here, but action, namely immediate action, I'm asking you, a short squat little person, sitting to her left, said approvingly, while he began to drum with his fingers on the desk—and that's how things continued in the hastily assembled emergency meeting in the large conference room of City Hall, where those present either spoke about how, given their guest's "serious and so-called" propensity to games of hazard, it would be necessary, during his sojourn here in their city, to put under lock and key any such devices upon which online betting—if it could be put that way—could be said to flourish, in other words, they enumerated: computers, smart phones—and then from somewhere in the middle of the left side of the room a woman's voice shrieked out: and what about all the slot machines, to which a concurrent, yet perplexed grumbling was heard in response: but of course, that's right, the only question is how? the Headmaster of the high school put the question, because how are we going to remove them, you know very well that in every single bar in this city, but every single one—and now he was only speaking about bars—there is at least one slot machine, but there are also bars where two slot machines are stationed, and you all know very well, he stated now in a lofty tone (here he was building upon his well-known rhetorical skills), just how many bars there are in this town, at which point someone—and it never emerged who, at least not for him, he only had his suspicions as to whom it might have been afterward—someone noted in a very subdued tone: well, if somebody would know, then it would be you, Headmaster; altogether there are seventy-nine operational bars in the city, the Headmaster's voice trumpeted over the cheerful murmuring that had arisen in response to this underhanded comment, seventy-nine, by all counts, if you please, and I ask you, he asked, how many trucks will be needed to take care of this, well, how many?—the Mayor looked at a nearby point on the table, and the individual who would be responsible for such matters, an older councilman, just cleared his throat for a while as the Mayor looked at him even more fixedly, and then the Mayor said: he would be most pleased if everyone here could end up being able to express their gratitude to the councilman more than they did during the time of the Great Transition, when all the city streets had to be renamed, and they couldn't find any alternative for "Lenin's Ditch" (as you all know, that was where the statue of Lenin once stood next to a ditch, before it was filled in with concrete), and you, councilman, completely hit the bull's-eye by suggesting it should be changed to "Lennon's Ditch," in other words—and the Mayor continued to look at the councilman in an inquiring manner, at which point the person whom he had addressed only said in a soft tone: well, at least twenty trucks—what do you mean "at least," screeched the Mayor, yes, yes, the councilman stammered, or to be more exact I would say fifteen—so we have at our disposal fifteen trucks? the Mayor asked him with glittering eyes, yes, Mr. Mayor, the only thing is, not all of them are operational—well, and how many of them are operational? for the love of God, don't get so nervous, Mr. Hruznyik—four are in working order, he answered, but then he quickly added there was, however, no gasoline in them, gasoline, the Mayor thundered, and he looked across to the other side of the table, who here is responsible for gasoline; there will be gasoline, somebody from over there noted, as long as there's a truck—there will be trucks, the Mayor shouted, isn't that so, Mr. Hruznyik, they'll be as many trucks are as needed—well, we'll have a look and see what we can do, said Mr. Hruznyik, and so it went on in the big conference room for about another three hours, during which time everyone came to realize that there was no time, that they had to act quickly if they didn't want the chief secretary with that meek smile of hers to make the barbed comment every ten minutes that they were "ignominiously failing" the Baron, and we don't want that, do we now, gentlemen, the Mayor asked of those assembled toward the end of the conference, then he sighed wearily, and informed them that whoever hadn't yet done so should immediately pick up the obligatory bow tie from the secretary's office, then he got up from his seat, and he dashed out of the conference room with its stale air.

It could only have been that Irén, she determined, as she passed by the fabric store, and she could feel the gazes of the shop girls on herself from inside, because as soon as she stepped foot outside of the house in the morning, that's how it went, everybody looked at her, and why was she surprised, she asked herself, well let them look if they need to, it didn't bother her, the only thing that did bother her was that she didn't know how to begin to deal with this situation, this changed situation, it must've been that Irén, she must have said something with her gossipy mouth, she couldn't bear to keep something to herself for even a minute; and she was vexed, because really, why was everyone staring at her now, now they were looking at her either because they were jealous or because they were mocking her, or who knew why, and she went on, but the weather just then wasn't good, indeed the weather was decidedly lousy, this icy cold wind and this drizzling rain, but she went on, from one street to the other, from the Göndöcs Garden along Peace Boulevard up to Hétvezér Street, there she turned, and she went up to the main street, and went as far as the large bridge, then at the Golden Cross pharmacy she turned back to the bank of the River Körös, and there she walked along for a while beneath the weeping willows, and finally she turned out again from a little street onto the main road up to the Catholic church, and from there to the park on the main square, but she didn't go as far as the Castle, she turned back, here no one would see that she just turned around and hurried back in the opposite direction, no one could deduce from her movements that she was *just walking around,* not walking somewhere, but because of something, it's always like this with me, she related frequently to Irén, if something is really on my mind, then that little devil within makes me walk—that was how she referred to her state when she had to think about something, well, then I always have to walk it out of myself, you know, my dear, I just can't bear to remain in one place, to go, just to go, at such times that's what I really need, and in the end *I have it,* and by that she meant that in the end, she'd have her decision, that for example yes, she would buy those little black lacquered shoes that had been put out in the window of the Style Boutique not too long ago, or whatever, you understand, my dear, it doesn't matter what's eating me up inside, if I move around outside, after a while I calm down, and the little devil disappears, and I already know what I should or shouldn't do, and that's what should have happened this time too: she would just walk and walk until she calmed down, but right now, when she had to gain clarity around such an important matter, it wasn't happening, she was already completely out of breath, because not only did she usually walk at such times, but she stepped up her pace, walking more quickly than usual, although her usual tempo was quick, it was easy to recognize her from afar, even when she was a little girl her mother could recognize her by this quick pace if she was coming home from school—I should stop somewhere for an espresso, she thought, so she walked back along the main street and went into the first espresso bar that she saw, I'd like an espresso please, she said, then slipped out of her coat and unwound the long knit scarf from around her neck, phooey, she said to the woman behind the counter, who was standing at that moment with her back to her, what rotten weather—well, for those who like that sort of thing, it's a good day, came the answer, as the woman behind the counter knocked out the grounds from the filter of the espresso machine—there was no amiability in her voice, so she didn't force the conversation, and the situation wasn't exactly pleasant, as the espresso bar was extremely tiny, altogether four small tables pressed up against each other, and immediately next to them there was the counter, and the woman behind the counter was right there at arm's length; she knocked back a sip from the espresso and shuddered in the warmth after the cold outside, she looked over here, she looked over there, then feeling the silence to be somewhat painful—as there was no newspaper, fashion magazine, or anything of the sort anywhere in sight in which she could defensively immerse herself, she nonetheless gathered up her courage and spoke again, saying that the forecast this year was for a long winter, at which point the woman responded with a morose expression, only saying "yeah," making any further attempts at conversation impossible, and yet she was really surprised when suddenly this morose espresso-preparing woman suddenly came out from behind the counter, came over to her, and without further ado sat down at her table, and said to her: you certainly don't remember me, do you, Marika, we went to the kindergarten by the Castle together, then in the silence that followed—as she had become deeply confused, and had no idea what to say, the other continued: well, I remember you very well, at that time you still had blonde hair, and you never wanted to eat your stewed cabbage, what, me? I didn't want to eat my stewed cabbage? Marika asked, quickly gulping down her coffee, yes, yes, the espresso-lady nodded, and a kind of sound came out of her which theoretically should have been laughter, you were always such a drama queen, Marika, she said in a presumably cheerful manner, Marika—and then she grabbed her hand, it was the hand that was holding the coffee cup, above her wrist—I don't forget, I never forget anything, because I know everything, everything, my dear Marika, she continued, and she looked out the window at the street, so that she too looked out, and maybe both of them were waiting for the same thing, namely for somebody else to come into the espresso bar, but nobody came, well, enough of this, she thought to herself, and she freed her hand, indicating that she would like another sip of her coffee, but there was nothing left in her cup, just one or two drops, and even those were cold, but never mind, she held the cup up to the edge of her mouth until these one or two drops had rolled out of it, then she said quickly that she would pay, of course, the espresso-lady nodded once, but she didn't move, she just looked at her, which made her extremely uncomfortable, if it hadn't happened here, in our own little enchanted city, she related later on to her girlfriend, I'd have said that I was afraid, namely afraid of this woman, as she suddenly sat down next to me, without a word, without any conversation, just imagine, in this completely empty espresso bar, with that ice-cold wind and the rain outside, and there inside was this horrible woman, well, I'm seriously telling you, she told her, by the time I was able to get out of there, as soon as I could force her to tell me the price of the coffee—she said that I didn't have to pay because we went to the kindergarten next to the Castle together—in a word, by the time it was all over and I was out on the street, seriously, Irénke, the blood was running cold in my veins, well, of course, Irén said, I can just imagine it, my dear, that espresso bar, that woman, your veins, and the blood—and they both laughed out loud, relieved.

If I may permit myself to do so, said the Mayor, then please allow me to address you as . . . of course you may, because for everyone now, I'm just their little Marietta, and there was a kind of acrimonious tone to this, the Mayor could sense it, so that after about a half hour of attempting to persuade her in vain to hand over the letter, inasmuch was possible in the shell chair, he completely turned toward her, and taking her hands into his, he looked deeply into her eyes—look, Marietta, the future of this city is depending on this, and I know—he explained to her, as he let her slowly pull her hands away from his—that you love this town—oh yes, I love it very much, but what does that have to do with anything? she remarked—look here, my dear lady, the Mayor interrupted her, there's no time for this now, I'm asking you, I'm really asking you: please pay attention to what I'm saying, because here every word is important, important to us, important to every single one of us, please understand me, and here I'm—the Mayor pointed at himself—I'm really thinking of all of us, I'm thinking of everyone for whom this town is an affair of the heart, in brief, right now there are 1001 things to take care of in a matter of hours, just think it over, Marietta, this town has never been in a situation like this, as on the one hand—and here he raised his left thumb, grabbing it with his right hand, one: we have to resurrect that women's chorus that's been rotting away for the past few years, and in general we have to organize the entire program taking place at the train station; two: and he raised his index finger as well into the heights, we will have to move the entire—my dear Marietta—the entire Orphanage, out of the Almásy Chateau, the name of which, in addition, from this point on shall be the Wenckheim Chateau—oh dammit, I almost forgot—and that means that thirty-seven or however many whelps have to be removed from there with lightning speed, and the Chateau has to be furnished, do you understand, furn-ished, the Mayor emphasized both syllables, a Chateau, which hasn't been one for sixty years, and here's the third point, the middle finger pointed upward, and the Mayor began to wag this middle finger with passion, a welcoming festival will have to be launched across the entire town, because of, you understand, he leaned toward her confidentially, the Baron's moods, I don't know if you know, but according to the reports they aren't the most buoyant, so this entire town must transmit only merriment, a storehouse of colorful and abundant cultural offerings, Marietta, and he leaned in even closer to her on the shell chair so he was already perched on the edge of it, pay attention to every word I'm saying now, I'm going have to get the garbage and the beggars taken out of here, let them all go to hell, because I've no idea where I'll put them, but they've got to go, and I have to get every single last slot machine out of this town, because as you clearly know, your renowned friend supposedly suffers from a little passion for gambling, look, I'll be frank, the Mayor said, now in a deeper voice, what's going on here is that I have to transform an entire town within a matter of hours, do you understand, this is impossible, he shrieked, and he slid back in the shell chair, and leaning back, glancing, however, at the ceiling, he said, this is much more—he suddenly spoke in a hushed tone—than one Mayor is capable of, and yet there has never been a better Mayor in this town than myself, and there never will be, everyone knows this, and I hope you agree with me—of course I do, she nodded, but she resisted, as what he wanted was sheer absurdity, she related later on to Irén, because just imagine, he wanted me to give him the letters, to him, to the Mayor, so that he—just imagine!—would have them printed up, as he said, and in an edition of one thousand, to be distributed among the citizens of the town—he's gone mad, her girlfriend noted, and she just shook her head in disbelief—well, yes, it's as if some kind of plague has broken out, Marietta continued, I hardly even dare to go out, really—well, fine, Irén gestured, let's not talk about that, because she'd already heard all about that; instead she wanted to know how she finally got rid of him, well, yes, she replied, we decided that I'd just talk about the letter on the four o'clock news, and that's why I'm here, my dear, help me, Marika squeezed her hands together, I have no makeup, and my hair, I haven't even a rag, nothing, I'm asking you, Irénke, she looked at her girlfriend in despair, do something, I can't stand in front of the cameras like this, but she didn't have to say anything else, because among the two of them Irén was the more quick-witted, she was the one who always came to the assistance of her sweet, romantic, melancholy girlfriend with her own practical sense, they had complemented each other ever since that time when they had divorced their respective husbands—their husbands with whom they had both been fated to experience enormous disappointment, and it was at almost exactly the same time that they experienced this enormous disappointment and got divorced and they were on their own—two orphaned cornflowers, as Marika once described it with her own feminine sensitivity, two swaying, orphaned cornflowers who never left each other's side, you'll help me, won't you, Irénke, she looked at her with her big blue eyes, and Irén looked at the wall clock, sprung up, and began to move around the chairs so that her friend, who wasn't exactly in the best state right now, would have a place to sit, and all the while she kept saying: don't be afraid, my dear, everything will be fine, you'll shine like a star.

The question is—they stood in front of him like some kind of delegation—is what you would recommend, as this stable's authorized supervisor, we were thinking of a carriage with four or six horses, at which the person they were addressing just shifted his weight from one foot to another, because he didn't know what to say, so that finally he came up with the idea of saying that he wasn't any kind of authorized supervisor here—he pointed backward toward the stables—he was the chief groom, with three stable hands, but it would be better if these stable hands weren't there, because all they ever did was get in the way, they couldn't even brush out a mare's mane properly, although—he explained—it wasn't even that they didn't know how, it was that they *didn't want* to do the work, because these ne'er-do-wells simply don't want to work, I'll tell you, when we were lads ... we entreat you, sir—one of the more experienced members of the delegation, namely, a physician from the doctor's office then interrupted, let's not lose precious time on the details here, but please tell us directly if you can prepare for us a carriage with four or respectively six horses or not, but don't play with our nerves because we need a straight reply, well, then I'll give you a straight reply, my dear sir, the groom was suddenly overcome with annoyance, because this was all the same too much, it wasn't enough for them to come stand here and order him around, but they came and stood here and they ordered him around as if they were the bosses here, they, however, weren't the bosses here, he didn't even know who these guys were, they just came and stood here, and discussed these things with him like that from *their high horses,* as if he wasn't the one here who was sitting on a horse, well, so much for that, he turned red with anger, and he said to them, visibly upset, because this conversation had already gone on too long, this was no way to approach him, they hadn't struck the right tone, and he didn't understand what was going on, the gentleman shouldn't be talking to him that way, because nobody should talk to him like that from any kind of *high horse,* and it would be better if they literally engraved that into their brains, but then an older person from the delegation motioned to the family physician that he would take charge of the negotiations, and he said to the groom that they'd be very curious to know if he'd be able to give them some advice, because, at the Mayor's request, they were looking for a four-horse carriage—well now, advice, the groom interrupted him, that he could naturally give, if they would not talk to him *from that high horse of theirs,* and ask him about it nicely; for if he understood well what they were saying—he pursed his lips a little, as he appeared to be thinking for a moment—the Mayor would be in need of the most ornate *horse trap* that he had—and not a brougham, please! there are no broughams here, there are only horse traps, in brief, you would need an appropriate horse trap for the occasion, is that right, in that case I would be able to tell you, thinking about it good and hard, and my brief reply would be that we do have one—my dear God, the words came out of the family doctor's mouth, and in his vexation he looked up at the sky—yes, there is such a trap here in the cooperative stables, he repeated more loudly in order to drown out the "my dear God" issuing from the mouth of the family doctor, whom he visibly already detested greatly, and so—he continued at a leisurely pace to the delegation standing in front of him, who were at the extreme limit of their patience—so, what would be needed for a trap like this? well, that's a good question, and from his own point of view . . . here he stopped in the middle of his sentence and started to push around a pebble on the muddy ground with the tip of his boot . . . well, for my own part I think that for a trap like this you'd need four horses—my dear God, at last, the family physician said aside, his eyes still turned up to the heavens; and please tell us, the more experienced of the group now continued, smiling—it was clear he was convinced that he was the only one who understood how to speak to the groom in his own language—please tell us, so there'll be the four horses, can you fit them out nicely? because this is going to be a big celebration, you know, yep, the groom cut the conversation short with one brief word, and to the surprise of everyone present he turned on his heel and went into the stable behind him, so that they were obliged to follow, walking in the soil made muddy by the rain, although they only went as far as the threshold, because the groom yelled at them, saying what were they thinking, they couldn't go in there, so they immediately stopped in their tracks and said to him: fine, fine, we're not coming in, just tell us if you can bring the trap with four horses to the station by four o'clock, why? the groom asked, not even turning toward them, because just then he had set about fixing the bedding for a mare, all the while cursing the stable hands in a hissing voice, where the hell were they—why exactly at four o'clock, he grumbled, and he forcefully stabbed an iron pitchfork into the manure-splattered hay, but the delegation didn't hear this, because they had left the stable, they went back through the mud to the service car, they brushed off, inasmuch as they could, the mud from their shoes, then they scurried away from the grounds of the equestrian cooperative, and he just stayed there alone with the shit-covered hay, and he kept saying and saying: so they leave them here, they're able to leave these poor animals here in this shit, well, they don't even have a drop of feeling, because at least they should have some respect for these poor nags, but these types don't have any respect for anyone or anything, and I'll wring their necks, these spoiled good-for-nothings, I'm going to wring their necks one by one, you think that I'm joking, but I'm not.

It don't work, it just don't, e'en though we give it our all, but we aren't used to it, we know songs like "That Little Lass, That Brown Little Lass," or "Let The Mornin' Star Go Down," or "The Black Kite Laid Three Eggs," well, we always know 'ow to sing these very well, but this new song, it's too much for us, and somehow it just don't want to go into our ears, then there wasn't enough of us, 'cause Jucika didn't show up, or Mrs. Horgos, or Rózsika, or Auntie Káti, or—well, really, Auntie Mariska or not even her neighbor, well, what's her name again, it's not coming to mind, well, never mind, but the choir director just forced us, the poor man just turned on the tape recorder ten or twenty thousand times so's the melody would go into our ears, but it wouldn't go, it didn't want to go in any way at all, I'm not saying, though, that we didn't want to learn it, we wanted to, and so at the end there we were, all in a circle aroun' that tape recorder or whatever it was, like it was the manger of Our Lord Jesus Christ, and we tried, and we tried, we would've hummed "Don't Cry for Me, Arne," after him, well again already, and that was a real difficult word, it just wouldn't go into our heads, that word Arginta, well, what is it, I forgot again . . . Ar, Ar, upon my soul, I'm saying it wrong, Ar-gen-ti-na, well, that's it, that's just one word though, but it was so strange for us, like it was written on the moon, we were supposed to sing it after him, but we just tried an' tried, 'cause then the Mayor came there too, well, he got real nervous once he heard how much it wasn't working, and so he says to us, well ladies, it's just five words, or what, well, five or so lines, and there's just this little melody, well, that can't be too much for you, ladies, but Mr. Mayor, it is too much, we said to 'im, here we are floggin' and flailin' for an hour already, but isn't there anything else, we could sing something real nice for the great gentleman, Mrs. Horgos says to him, because she has a long tongue, and that mischief falls out of her all day long, so she says, now what would Mr. Mayor say to the song "Thirteen Ruffles on My Petticoat," but he just shook his head, sayin' this and that, no excuses, this's what he needed, this . . . Arnin, well, no mind, you see for yourself I can't say it, although at the end we finally could, because our own choir director, by the end he jus' somehow beat it into us, and we just whistled "Don't Cry for Me Armengita," we finally somehow learned it by afternoon, the others slowly showed up, and we got ready today to set off for the station, when up came someone from City Hall, and he says that someone had counted wrong over there at City Hall, because that train wasn't coming now, but t'morrow, the day after t'morrow, you understand, so we have time, well, and so we said to the choir director, that was indeed a shame, because by tomorrow we're certainly going to forget this gobbledygook like a waft of air, we could begin right from the beginning, but that choirmaster, he's a one, he's really such a dear gentle man, that all he says is ladies, now you go on home, and everyone just hum it themselves, but for real start humming, so it wouldn't fall out of our ears, just the melody, said the choirmaster, and he hummed it and hummed it to us again and again, until everyone really knew it, and so that's how we went home, we went home a-hummin' and we were humming so it wouldn't fall out of our ears today, and I, my dear girl, I hummed it at home when I started off on a nice bit of thing, a little Linzer torte, what I learned from Auntie Ibolyka, you know, who used to do the cleaning for the Professor until he went crazy, she could make such a Linzer torte that no one else ever could, certainly not me, to be sure, but it was grand, they ate it up, the family is always happy if I bake something like that, but I always say that it's just a wee nothing, because only Auntie Ibolyka knows how to bake a real Linzer torte, no one else, only that Auntie Ibolyka, for the real thing you have to go to her.

Still, what could she say, she said before the camera, she was just her girlfriend, it's true, she added, that for fifteen years now they been completely inseparable from each other, you know, that Marika, she's always in the skies somewhere above the clouds, I'm more of the type with my feet on the ground, as they say; in other words, she wouldn't deny that they were as thick as thieves, but she didn't know anything, so Marika was the one they should be asking about this, she'll be here in a moment, she vaguely pointed somewhere behind herself, but then the female reporter began to gesture vehemently for her to stop pointing like that, there's no need for that—never mind, she said to the cameraman behind her, we'll edit it out later—in a word, she turned toward her again, just keep on talking about what you know, not what you don't know, at which point she became a little offended, and not even stepping out of her role, said to the little lass, that she really wasn't used to being addressed in such a manner because television or no television, she—to say frankly what she was thinking—couldn't give a damn if this was being recorded, it wasn't her they needed here, but Marika, and they could now leave her alone in peace, and she stepped out of the glare of the reflector light that somebody was holding above her, and there she left the entire crew, as she said to her girlfriend later on, that's all she needed, for these pompous little busybodies to order me around even though I'm an old lady, well you know, that kind of thing doesn't interest me, and so maybe it'll happen, she said, that I'll be on TV, well, and then so what, and so what if I'm not, my hair was completely a mess, and this TV station was just a big piece of crap anyway, if she were to put it frankly, she put it that evening, when they got together at her place for a cup of tea to discuss what had happened, because we have to talk, Marika said breathlessly into the telephone, so much as happened in the past few days, it is simply necessary, my dear Irénke, I have to talk to somebody, well, if it's necessary, then come on over, then don't dawdle around, dear, get dressed, and I'll fix you some nice tea. Marika really loved a nice cup of tea.

He was in a horrific state of mind, and he was so troubled by the thought that he had mailed the letter, and there was nothing he could do about it now, he asked the valet if he was certain that it had been sent off, but already by the second time he had asked, the valet just nodded once mutely with a sympathetic gaze and held his hands apart; he walked around in circles in his room, and for an entire day again he couldn't even touch the meals that were brought to him, no, because the mistake he had made weighed upon him so much, because why did he have to write that letter so thoughtlessly, and then if he had written it already, then why did he have to send it off with the post with such frantic speed, well, couldn't he have waited a bit for things to settle down within him and to read it over one more time, and in tranquility, because then he would have immediately realized that it was a mistake, it was a grave mistake to write it like this, and it was certain that he'd only alarm her, for surely she was so sensitive, it's certain that the whole thing would just frighten her, even the mere fact that he'd written her a letter, that in and of itself was so thoughtless, but the fact that he'd simply laid siege to her, that was unforgivable, she would certainly never forgive him, he had to do something, and after he had cast aside the idea that he would inform her by telegram that the letter which she was to receive from him must remain unread (as it emerged that telegrams as such had not been used for a very long time), he sat down at his escritoire, and he took another piece of writing paper, and he just sat there, he looked at the paper, wondering how to begin, because he couldn't just pen a simple apology, this had to be exclusively an apology from which Marietta could decipher his sincere contrition, so he began by saying how much he regretted that first letter, and how he had laid siege to her, and that he could imagine just what emotional agitation he had caused, and she should trust him when he said that so vexed by his own thoughtlessness was he, that if he could, he would conjure up a wizardly magic from afar and have that dreadful letter burned, he wished he could go back in time and erase his actions, but well, this wasn't possible, so that now, with this new letter he could only be so bold as to seek her out again in order to ask her to forget him, to regard the previous letter as the confession of an idiotic, perfidious, selfish, indelicate man who in general never should have been permitted to speak, for that confession had clearly only disturbed her, and truly if there was one thing that he would never wish to do, it was that: not only would he never want to disturb her, but he wouldn't even wish to go see her again, only to think about her, so that she could forget him; he asked her, he begged her, moreover he pleaded with Marietta to burn that previous letter, to obliterate it, he supplicated her truly to expunge it from her head, he asked, he begged, moreover he pleaded with Marietta to regard that rude confession as something that had never been articulated, and no, to never forgive him, because to brutally trample on somebody's soul like that, somebody with such a refined soul as hers, was a crime, and he felt this crime with all its dreadful strength, and he knew that he could never repair what he'd done, because it was already unforgivable that he was bothering her again, it wasn't enough that he came rushing at her with all of his feelings that burned within him with a flame that was in no way smaller than when he had been a teenager, because those feelings have been burning in him ever since, because they had sustained him, but enough, the Baron wrote, after he had used up maybe twenty sheets of paper—because if he was dissatisfied with the shape of a single letter, that was already enough for him to be pulling out another piece of paper, and he would copy everything that he had written down so far and correct that misshapen letter, but then the same thing happened again, if he felt uncertain in the question of spelling, or if—and this was happening with every other line—he did not find this or the other word to be sufficiently apt, or if that word was not sufficiently compassionate, then he was already pulling out the next piece of paper, and copying down again what he had written, and he corrected it and he kept on correcting it until one evening, he had finally finished the letter, and although he would have been very happy to ring for the valet immediately, to send it off by registered personal mail—because he wished his one-time love to read it immediately—he was still capable of composing himself, he didn't call for the valet, he did not ring the bell, but he lay down on the bed, looked at the ceiling, and he waited for morning to come, and then it was morning, and then he quickly skimmed through the letter again, then he skimmed through it a second time, then he said to himself that he shouldn't just be skimming through it, but he should really be scrutinizing it word by word, with the greatest concentration, and so he did, and after he had done so three times, he reached out to ring the bell, he finally dared to ring it, he put the letter on the tray, and he let them take it away to be sent by post, but from that point on, his hours and days were spent in even more hellish torture, because he had absolutely no idea if he had been able to set right what he had so ruined so much. Two weeks later, the valet knocked at the door, and on the tray being extended to him there was an ordinary envelope, which, as the valet softly noted, had just arrived. In the envelope he found a postcard, on the postcard was a castle with a lake and willow trees, and on the other side there were three words altogether: Waiting for You.

I want all of you to listen carefully to every word, he said from the counter of the Biker Bar, to the troop of men gathered there, Totó, count up how many of us are here, because I hope that in these times when the star has dawned, if I may express myself in such a poetic fashion ... so, twenty-seven, Totó, are you sure about that, in a word, are you sure; that's good, he said—he buttoned up his long leather coat, which of late he had been wearing almost exclusively, and not his leather jacket, like the others, he sat on one of the barstools, and he began to turn around his pint glass on the counter, like someone who is concentrating strongly on how to begin, then he looked around, and he said, we're in good shape, we have as many of you ready as we need, so the task now is for everybody to stop off at Uncle Laci's, not in the front courtyard, but in the back, do you understand? in the back, don't forget, and don't worry about the dog, well, and then, he said, Uncle Laci will set you up nicely one at a time, because Uncle Laci is one of us, and he was working on this yesterday the entire afternoon and the entire evening, he is going to replace your existing motorcycle horns, because he's put together thirty compressor air horns with eight chords, he got the melody in a WAV file from me, and this person is a real Hungarian master, a genius, a terror, that Uncle Laci, you can even clap for him from here into the distance, and the men gathered here dutifully began to clap, Totó raised his pint glass into the air, and he cried out: long live Uncle Laci, but they didn't all cry out after him, so that somehow his voice quickly fell away, just like Totó's hand with the pint glass—go to the back courtyard, I'm telling you, he told them, because if we can't take care of that other matter before the Baron's arrival, then at least this can be taken care of, so everyone should get a new horn nicely installed, one at a time, at Uncle Laci's, on their machine, on every single machine, and no objections, because if we're brothers, then we stick together, right?! that's right, the others growled back at him, well, he continued, and he took a sip of his beer, get the old horn removed and the new one put on, that's the whole thing, and we're not going to bend Uncle Laci's ear about test cables, cutoff relays, contact points, batteries, transformers, connectors, MOSFET regulators, and combustion, nobody is going to get into an argument with Uncle Laci about how many decibels or how many hertz, everyone is going to keep nice and quiet, and just let Uncle Laci roll the vehicle into his workshop, and wait outside, or head off to the Metal Bar, and come back to see how it's going every hour or so, because we can't expect him to be calling us, so in a word, go have a look in on him every hour or so to see if your vehicle is ready yet, and then everyone can take his vehicle home, but—and here he raised up his left index finger—but everyone who is a brother here must be at the train station at exactly five p.m. and zero minutes, as we have only this one chance, because there are a few of us, aren't there, and that's it—we have to line up—in rows of three as usual— next to the station building on the right-hand side, between the ramp and the platform, that's how it's been arranged with City Hall, so we'll meet up there, and one last thing, he raised his index finger once again in the long leather coat sleeve —then he lowered this index finger, pointing at himself—when I raise this hand—do you follow?—and he pointed to show which hand it would be, and when I call loudly to the back "one-two-three," then when I get to four, brothers—and he suddenly leaned forward, showing that when he said "four," everyone should press down on the horn button on their handlebars, because the switch will be there, but we have to do it all at once, because it won't work if you don't all press down on it at the exact same time, so we'll press down on the horn button all at once, and keep your hand on it, and only take it off when you've blown the horn three times, because three are the truths of Hungary, and Madonna sang the song in *Evita* three times, I hope everything is clear, and now no more beer, everyone should get over to Uncle Laci's, and patiently, I'm telling you, patiently wait your turn until Uncle Laci takes your machine into his shop and then brings it out, as we discussed, and beyond that I would only like to tell you: that the sacrifice of Little Star was huge, we all know this, but we will repay this sacrifice, and I'm telling you, we won't be blowing our horns just for anything at all, brothers, believe me, things are going to flourish here, there will be a new Hungarian life, which until now we've only been able to dream about, but now here it is, or namely, it will be, all we have to do is properly press down on that damned melody horn button, everyone at the same time, like one body, one soul, just press down on the button and keep pressing, and then the great flourishing will come, a new life in Hungary, and I hope that everyone has understood what has to be done here.

He raised his pint glass to drain the last drop from it, but then suddenly he stopped halfway through the movement, and the others stopped as well, from Totó to J.T., all twenty-seven of them, they all froze the middle of whatever they happened to be doing, and on the television that was installed up there in the corner, the program stopped, the picture stopped and the sound stopped, and for one moment, the entire Biker Bar and the picture on the television screen came to a standstill, the hand of the barman behind the counter came to a standstill, as it was just approaching the opened drawer of the cash register holding a one-thousand-forint note, and in all the pint glasses the beer foam came to a standstill, and in the beer foam the bubbles that were just then trying to make their way upward so they could burst on the surface, they all came to a standstill, and on the counter, all of the points of light in the beer rings froze, because everything stopped, everything came to a dead halt, everything froze, for a moment, life stopped in the Biker Bar, because this moment somehow had become shattered—as if some kind of weighty, dark, horrific fear had broken out, disturbing everything that existed, and everyone looked up, they looked up, awry, at the television screen, as if there would be some explanation on that screen for the existence of this weighty, dark, horrific fear within them, but there was nothing up there, because on the television screen the picture had also come to a stop, and yet they still just looked up awry, and no one and nothing knew what to do next. And at the same time, something also happened with Marika, with Irén, with the Mayor and the Deputy Mayor, with the chief secretary, with the director of Municipal Utility Services, with the family physician, and with Miss Dóra, and with the woman behind the counter in the espresso bar, the entire women's chorus along with the choirmaster, the entire television crew with their reporters, with the sales girls in the fabric shop, and with Auntie Ibolyka, and with the chief groom and the four horses, now harnessed, and with the stable boys, who were still slacking off, and moreover with the fleeing Professor, and even with the Linzer torte, something had happened, and it all happened exactly in that same moment, because that moment, everywhere in the town, had somehow shattered apart, everything came to a halt, from fear, to a dead stop because of the fear which had swept across the city, although nobody had lost their common sense; this fear which came upon them was overpowering, and everybody gazed up, awry, seeking for an explanation as to what this was, but there was no explanation, there was only fear, pure fear of something unknown, and nobody and no one knew what to do next.

Whoever saw anything of this didn't comprehend anything, because that person wouldn't be able to understand, because a pause had arisen in elementary knowledge and in basic interpretation, so no one could understand who they were or what they were doing here, because there were those who had seen the beginning of the convoy when it arrived from the direction of Békéscsaba and crossed the town limits, and there were those who saw the convoy by Lennon's Ditch, and of course there were those who, despite the cold, were there when he alighted —

from among this horde of men—on the main square and quickly looked around; and there were those who glimpsed the convoy by the Hospital fence, and there were those who saw them when they drove by the Cemetery of the Holy Spirit, then as they passed the sign designating the southeastern city limits, they proceeded to the border crossing, in short there were more than a few who met up with this stupefying automobile convoy, more than a few who saw them, all these hordes of men, and maybe they really saw him too, but no one was able to understand anything about this whole thing, because nobody had any idea of what this was, where they had come from from, where they were going, and most of all why, such was this spectral line of cars—they glided across the city, past all the stories taking place here as if they weren't even gliding past anything—although nobody would have thought they weren't here, but at the same time they wouldn't have thought, yes, they were here, because they weren't able to think, and, especially, they weren't able to say that they saw what they saw, because perhaps they hadn't even seen anything, and yet it was impossible not to see this thing that perhaps didn't even exist, in any event whoever was out there on the streets wouldn't have recognized even a single one of these cars if they had dared to try—if they caught a glimpse of them at all—because these cars were impossible to identify: it was impossible to say that they weren't Mercedes and they weren't BMWs, that they weren't Rolls-Royces and they weren't Bentleys, at the same time no one could say that they were Mercedes or they were BMWs, or Rolls-Royces or Bentleys, because it would have only been possible to say that, without exception, this infinite number of vehicles, glimpsed from a closer perspective, seemed to belong to some kind of otherworldly army than any actual procession of cars, and they moved across the city with extraordinary speed, but nobody said this, everyone kept it to themselves, even those who saw him get out, this person around whom—even before he got out of the car—huge numbers of men began to arrange something, and they were circling around him, doing something around *him*, and he didn't even move while he stood there, everyone was doing something with deathly precision, their faces stiff and severe, but there was no *meaning* to the entire thing, neither in the details nor as a whole, more precisely it was clear that it was something that needed to happen, but nobody was capable of understanding what the point was or what this matter was in which the first and then the second and then the third automobile—and so forth until the one hundredth—was just now proceeding, he, however, the one around whom this great movement had formed, was motionless; those who saw him—and they weren't very many—only saw that his face was unflinching, and very *serious*, and very *severe*, and … very *impatient*; for those, who afterword denied forever having seen him on the main square, their sense was that he was traveling with this formidable army in some kind of monumentally important affair, because yes, the whole thing seemed so colossally huge, as if at the beginning of one moment an entire army had driven through the city, and then, at the end of that moment, completely disappeared—and all because of this matter, which was perfectly concealed from them, and yet of such monumental importance; that's what anyone who saw anything of this at all might have thought; but they never spoke about it afterward, moreover the luckier among them truly forgot about it forever, and it was possible to forget, because when it was over, it was as if it had never happened, as if the whole thing had been just some hallucination, a hallucination, hysteria, a split-second interruption in the brain, that's how they would have explained it if they hadn't forgotten about it, but nearly everyone forgot, because this dreadful procession surpassed their ability to make any sense of it, because they didn't even believe their own eyes, because who would have believed that there really had been that shattered moment, when life came to a stop, but in such a way that there was really nothing, and nothing, no kind of explanation whatsoever of how, for example, if the water faucet was just then turned on in the kitchen, then the water simply stopped as it was flowing, if just at that moment somebody was ripping up a water utility bill in rage because it was outrageously high, that bill just stopped in midair as it was being ripped in two; and the people who were outside at that moment were stunned the most by the drizzling rain, because that too stopped, the rain simply stopped while it was falling, and the drops remained suspended where they were in the air, either higher or lower, it didn't matter, a thousand and ten thousand and one hundred thousand drops just stopped at that moment poised between heaven and earth, and they fell no more, and that's how it was, because the wind also stopped, it didn't just die down, but it stopped at one point and didn't go on any further where it was supposed to go, it was maddening, and of course nobody wanted to believe his eyes, and if somehow something remained in them *afterward* from everything that had happened, it was only fear, a fear that was the mere recollection of that fear a moment ago, fear and the memory of fear, and one just as appalling as the other, but that first fear was something that no one had ever lived through—because it wasn't something that could be lived through—because the strength of this fear was unspeakably deep, primal, and overwhelming, and it didn't resemble any other earlier fear, not any single fear previously bearable or imaginable, because this wasn't even any kind of deathly horror with a nameable or unnameable cause, here there was no cause, there wasn't even a word to name it, and it wasn't any mere evil projecting itself, but instead a kind of horror in which beings and objects under the effect of this horror were instead seized by wonder, a kind of ecstatic but degrading amazement toward *him* standing in the center of everything, because whoever saw him there on the main square, or whoever was able to sense that he was there, could do nothing else but be amazed and be amazed by him, because it was inexpressibly frightening, but it was as if people and things were only too happy to throw themselves down before him, and they groveled before him in their wonder and their amazement, because every being and every object, every process, and everything that was still preparing to enter existence was utterly swept up by the greatness, the unbelievable, incomprehensible, monumental grandiosity that emanated from him, because in that moment—and this is what they mainly wanted to erase from their memories, and as it turned out, they were able to do so to the utmost extent—anyone and anything would have given themselves up to him, but this surrender was the most unbearable to both people and things alike, because the object of this wonder, the object of this amazement, of this surrender, this enchantment, the center of this object, namely its midpoint, its depth, its essence—when he got out of the car in the main square, with his own deadened gaze and with glacial boredom, he looked around in the end like someone who was in a hurry, and got back into the car quickly, because he wasn't interested in this town and in these stories, he was evil—evil, sick, and omnipotent.

Then another moment began, and Marika stepped into the television studio, then she left there, and from that point on there was nothing she could do to stop the curiosity-seekers, as she called them, and how awfully rude they were—for, well, she couldn't deny, she sighed, she had become famous at one blow, and now even people who didn't know about her before knew who she was—she was complaining to her younger relative in the travel agency, where she had dropped in again, because just imagine, she said to her, not even being able to walk around in this town without people staring at you, without them coming over to ask you something you don't know the answer to, because what do they ask me about?—Marika asked her niece in the empty office—of course they're asking me *about that,* but she knew nothing, nothing more than what she'd already said on TV, and which she'd repeated a good few times afterward as well, if her acquaintances stopped her on the street, they asked the same questions—just try to imagine, she explained, all the while making lively gestures, you go into the store to get a bit of bread and some cold cuts, and already the person behind the counter is asking you, then the stock clerk, and finally the cashier, of course, Marika shook her head to and fro, why should the cashier be left out of it, and as for the store next to the small Protestant Church, where she usually shopped, there were two cashiers, both of them awfully unpleasant and sometimes they were capable of speaking to her so rudely that a person just lost her taste for everything, well, never mind, she slid off the table she'd perched herself on so as to exchange a few words with the new employee and to find out if she was adjusting well to the new environment, and if in general there'd been any change in things, i.e., were there any customers, because she certainly hadn't left this pensioned position due to family reasons or anything like that, no, she'd simply gotten exhausted from just waiting and waiting and nobody ever came in whom you could possibly designate, even with the best of intentions, a tourist, so were there any? do any ever come in here? she repeated the question—of course not, her relative turned down her mouth, and she too slipped down from her own desk, no one ever sets foot in here, there aren't any tourists anymore, and well, why would there even be anything like that—her voice became more plaintive as she accompanied her visitor out the door—you can never know if any trains are departing, and then if a train actually does depart, you can never find out if it will be stopping anywhere, and then if it does stop somewhere, you never know when; the buses only run when there's gas, and in general there's no gas, so who's going to travel under such conditions, or come here on an excursion as a tourist or whatever, Auntie Marika, this entire country has gone to the dogs, she said bitterly, because look, Auntie Marika, how could we show anyone anything here, because please tell me what has become of this city, everywhere there are these horrible piles of garbage, the streets are all dark because all the light bulbs have been stolen from the streetlamps, then there are those hundreds and hundreds of plastic bags constantly being blown everywhere by the wind, and all those Albanian vagrants, then the beggar children who work for the mafia, everyone knows about it, but nobody does anything about it, there's the Mayor, then there's the Chief of Police, but those two, she turned down the corners of her mouth, what are they busy with, just this and that for the Baron, everything for the Baron, that's why I'm telling you, Auntie Marika, I no longer hope for anything anymore, because the Baron can come here, even a king can come here, but there'll never be anything here, that's my opinion—my dear little Dórika, her aunt interrupted for the first time, I've told you already, don't call me Auntie Marika, feel free to call me Marietta, because everyone calls me that now, in other words, no formalities here, we have that between us, don't you think? briefly put, in my view you're looking at things with glasses a bit too dark-colored, such a young lady like you can't talk like that—why couldn't she talk that way? well, isn't it true, Auntie Marika? and sorry if I can't switch over suddenly to Marietta, because somehow it's not coming to my mouth, these informalities, it's gratifying when you say I'm young and everything, but in the meantime—she shook her head sadly—I'm not so young as that anymore, I'm forty-one years old, and single, I have no illusions, I don't have a proper job, because in vain I tell Papa that I should have tried to get something in the food industry, he just swears up and down that things will be much better here in your old job—and she did admit, she now admitted, that Auntie Marika certainly had managed everything wonderfully here, but there was nothing left to do, there was no work, the whole day, ever since she started her old job, she just sat there staring at her own ass, and the day before yesterday the Mayor came in and he completely snapped, and was talking all kinds of gibberish because he also thinks that the Baron is going to do this or that for the city, but as for me—she pointed at herself in the doorway of the travel agency—I'll tell you, Auntie Marika, that inasmuch as I see it, that Baron just came here because of you, and he hasn't the slightest intention of doing anything here, and I hear such idiocies that you can't even imagine, Auntie Marika, but it's better if you don't even think about it, then she said goodbye, and she watched her as she left, only to continue her thoughts that evening at the dinner table as she said: just imagine, Papa, she actually came in to see me again, but I know why, she's no idiot, this was no family visit, as she said—she simply wanted to see if something was going on, if I was doing any better than she had done, for example if I'd managed to get a whole busload of Chinese tourists to come here, which was something she could only dream of, and in addition to that she just goes all around town telling everyone how famous she is now that she's been on television, and that's why she decided to drop in on me—she banged on the table with her spoon as she pronounced every word—she had some nerve, she came in to show off and talk more nonsense to me, it boggles my mind, still, Papa, you're so easily misled, and maybe even you believe that the Baron is really going to bestow all his innumerable riches on us, because screw that, he's coming here only because of Marika, and I said this to her too, and only I would know this, because everyone thinks it's certain that the Baron is really going to do something, because, whether you believe it or not, they're already spending, I'm telling you seriously, people are already spending that huge pile of cash of his, and she began laughing bitterly, but she couldn't really laugh, and not only because just at that moment her mouth was full of food, you understand, Papa, they're already spending the Baron's money and he hasn't even gotten here yet, well, who is capable of such idiocy, if not us, they're already planning this, that, and the other thing, well, to hell with it, I say, because they're dreaming that he'll fix up the Chateau again, well, I think that's possible, but they're also saying he's going to build twelve new swimming pools and four new hotels, but I ask you, what do we need even one new swimming pool for, because who even goes to the baths, no one, only the staff and that's it, and now four hotels, would somebody please tell me—and she looked at her father, bent deeply over his plate, but he just kept poking at his food and he couldn't eat any of it—why exactly four, why not three or five, or why not twelve already, that's a nice number, the woman once again lowered her spoon into her food, as it happened that night they were having vegetarian goulash—because neither of them was really hungry—because then, she continued in a sneering tone, there would be as many hotels as there would be new swimming pools, no?—she shook her head, and lowered her voice—tell me now, Papa, but sincerely, if this place isn't just one big lunatic asylum.

She kept the two letters right above her heart; if she went outside, she slipped them into her inner coat pocket; if she was at home and wearing her dressing gown, then she placed them in the side pocket, where, it's true, they weren't above her heart, but to the side of her heart, but that didn't matter, she thought, it was the feelings that mattered: in her thoughts those two letters were above her heart, and forever, and she would never part from them, although she had been wandering around with these two letters for days, indeed even for weeks, and she tried to share this infinite happiness that she felt, to share it with her relatives and her acquaintances, but it wasn't possible, because she couldn't find anyone to share it with, not with Dóra, even though she tried twice; and even Irén wasn't someone with whom she could bare this, her soul's one secret, because this Irén—Irén, who was really her best friend, they'd been together through thick and thin—she couldn't even talk with her about the most important thing in her life, because Irén was so practical-minded, she had such a chilling effect on everything, every feeling and every elation—all this, however, had always been within her—and now, with these two letters held so closely to her heart, Irén would in the end just deride them, just making a sweet little romantic fool of her, which was how she'd always seen her, but in doing so her heart would be smashed to pieces, because she felt that this heart—her heart—underneath these two letters, was so fragile, that it would really fall apart not only at some coarse remark, but even at the sobriety of someone like Irén, so that not only did she move through the city here and there with extreme caution, taking the two letters with her everywhere, she also took this frail heart of hers along, and there was no one, absolutely no one to whom she could reveal either one of them, because there was no one with whom she could speak about how she felt: that once again she felt happy, her happiness could fit into such simple words, she thought happily, because it wasn't that she was weaving plans or anything like that, but simply there were two such letters from which such awfully refined feelings floated in her direction—feelings for which she could never have hoped for anymore, no, because she no longer had had any hope anymore for such infinitely refined words, and she could never have believed that this would happen to her yet one more time in this life, when her life had been so, but so disappointing, she never could have believed that the miracle would happen yet again, the miracle for which she had always waited, but in which she must always be disappointed, because on the one hand—she thought now, as she stepped into the little store next to the small Protestant Church in order to get something for dinner because there was no food at home—on the one hand there was that continual disappointment in people, by whom Marika meant to designate the male species, namely they came, they made promises, they did beautiful things, but then—and always for the most base reasons and in the most base fashion—they tossed her away, and on the other hand there she was, a romantic woman, as she thought of herself, possessed of a heart that was so, but so frail, and in this way she had spent her entire life; on the one hand there was this enormous disappointment, and on the other, this heart within her, and she easily could have thought that it was the end, no more, when one day the postman brought a letter, and the miracle had occurred, and if anyone anywhere had ever thought of her that way—she was trying to choose between the cold cuts, as she looked at the sell-by dates, and tried to decide, by peering through the plastic wrap, which dates she should believe and which ones not—then it was only when she was still a young girl, when she still had such dreams, that there would be somebody far away who was thinking of her, thinking of her with such pure love—she picked out a package of so-so-looking baloney, threw it into her basket, and headed toward the cash register.

Everyone is busy writing the speeches, they reported to him that morning, at which he didn't bat an eyelash, he just nodded and dismissed the subordinate with a movement of his head, then he took off his cap, he wiped his forehead, and adjusted the part on the crown of his head, then once again pulled out the drawer of his writing desk, and he took the materials he used for writing his own things, but it wasn't working, it wasn't going well, and he could have even said it wasn't going anywhere at all, because every time he wrote down one expression or another he was seized by doubt—was this good or not?—not even to mention spelling, because that had to be right too, because he couldn't exclude the possibility that it might be published somewhere or quoted in a newspaper article—how could he know?—if it came off, then yes, it might well be, it's just that he was so uncertain about it—what to do?—he was not a practiced speaker, until now he had always read his speeches from a piece of paper, he wasn't the Mayor, from whom polished and even more polished sentences emanated, in a word, he was going to read this from a piece of paper as well, but this time he didn't want to let anyone in on it, not even the file clerk, who however always had a look over what he wrote, namely, well, why deny it, the file clerk always wrote these things for him, as up 'til now it had almost always been like that—in other words, not almost always, but always—the cadet who worked in the archives (he'd just graduated from high school) always helped him with his speeches, but what should he do now, because this wasn't just any old task at hand, this wasn't a visit to a grade school to give a talk about traffic lights, or a talk at the end-of-year meeting at the Police Station, no, this time a grand gesture was called for, he couldn't entrust this to anyone else, but it was already past ten, and he wasn't getting anywhere, and no and no, so that he finally just called for the cadet, a long-legged lad who'd passed his graduation exams and had eyeglasses like those of Chinese politicians, two thick lenses in thick, black Trade Union Social Insurance frames, and now the cadet stared at him through those lenses, like someone who didn't understand what was wanted of him; he had, however, spoken quite clearly—I'm speaking clearly enough, aren't I, he said to him severely, and of course what could he have said in reply but that of course, everything was perfectly clear, and that he understood, the speech would be ready at two p.m., well, good, he said to him in a now gentler voice, come a little closer, cadet, and the cadet came closer, look, he said to him now not in an official voice at all, but almost confidentially, you have to whip something up here to make them all want to cower behind me, from the Mayor, to the Headmaster, because it is certain, he said, that all of them will be giving speeches as well, and he—he said this now very sincerely—he wanted to outshine them, do you understand, cadet, outshine them, because here is the great moment itself in which you have the opportunity to put such a speech into my hand that will make everybody at the station burst into applause, and then you, standing behind me, will know that part of that applause pertains to you, because you will have taken my thoughts and put them into concrete form, because all the thoughts are coming from me, isn't that so, you know me as your Police Chief, your superior and your boss, but also as a human being, I'm an open book to all of you, so that you have something to work on now until two o'clock, because everything is in that open book, and now you only have to find the form, I'll take care of everything else, as I know there will be no mistakes in terms of how it will sound, because I hope that you too will agree that if there's someone who knows how to give a speech, then that person is myself—yes, Chief, the cadet bowed, which was not at all in keeping with the regulations, it was as if the weight of his eyeglasses were pulling down his head—and still there was something the cadet wanted to mention, because he had just one tiny request in the matter of some unpaid leave, but there was no time for that, because the Police Chief motioned with his head, and that meant that he had to leave his office and go down into the penetrating mustiness of the basement which he hated more than anything else in this world, he had to go down there every morning, for him this was like going down into the underworld, he couldn't stand the mustiness that emanated from all the papers down there and the fluorescent lights, all those florescent lights as they were arranged in rows above his head on the ceiling, and they looked down on him below, alone hunched over his desk, and the hours seemed like days, the days seemed like weeks, the weeks seemed like months, and the months seemed like years, and finally even the minutes seemed like years to him sometimes, and it didn't matter that he had plenty of time to bring out his old Latin favorites from the desk drawer, Cicero, Tacitus and Caesar were with him there; but to no avail—all his graduation exam topics, all eleven of them . . . formerly, in his year of glory—as he confessed once to his friend who was captivated by the fact that he simply *knew* Latin and at the same time was a policeman—he was the only student who, in the fourth year of high school, picked Latin as an elective subject, so that when it was time for the graduation exams he had so few assignments and knew everything by heart he dazzled the exam committee; and if he wanted to, he could also dazzle anyone today who might turn up in his path, because he hadn't forgotten anything from those eleven exam topics, it's just that he wasn't in the mood to dazzle anyone now, he was never in the mood for it, because he was no circus acrobat, he thought to himself, but the victim of a serious mistake, who shouldn't have to sit here as a cadet in this cold storeroom in the basement and it wasn't the boss's speeches that he should be writing in secret, but something worthy of all those great deeds—from Cicero to Tacitus and Caesar—that were so thrilling to him even today, he looked up at the fluorescent lights, and he knew that the lights were watching him, so, well, he sighed, thinking how he shouldn't have to be here, no, and he took out a piece of paper, he threaded it into the Continental typewriter, which he insisted on using, as opposed to any one of those piddling computers, and began by typing: Highly Esteemed Lord Baron, then there was that musty smell coming from all the papers and documents, he was shut in here from eight o'clock in the morning until five in the afternoon, with one hour for lunch, but shut in here, with those lights up there, and that musty smell behind his back, and to no end whatsoever, he just couldn't stand it.

In the library there was such "a movement of people," that's what he called it—very wittily, he thought—a movement of people the likes of which had never been seen in the past decades, ever since the City Library had finally moved from its location in the Göndöcs Garden to a more worthy destination, namely ever since this library had been able to relocate into the enormous building of the former City Hall, and he, for his part, had been able to take up a dignified place in the director's chair, next to the city dignitaries—never had there been so much movement in the library, of people "big and small," as Eszter from the front desk, almost soaring from happiness, had just informed him; they want to know everything, Mr. Director—she shook her head in disbelief from the joy of it—and "if possible, immediately" about Buenos Aires, and just imagine, Mr. Director— said this Eszter from behind her desk, to her boss, watching in satisfaction—already they had gotten to a point where they want to know everything about Argentina, everything, Mr. Director, all of the guidebooks, travel memoirs, recollections, Gilbert Adair, Angelika Taschen, the story of Argentinean soccer, László Kurucz, just everything that we have, all the books, after they have been returned, in the reading room have been placed, because I hope that the Director will agree with me, that in this situation we really can't consider lending these books out again, we can only keep them in the reading room ... I understand, Eszter, and I'm very happy about all this, but please, I ask you, don't use such expressions—at least not here in the library—as "all the books in the reading room have been placed," you're an educated woman, Eszter, and you know that we don't use Germanisms when we're speaking correct Hungarian, you understand that, don't you, so I don't want to hurt your feelings—the director said, hurting her feelings for an entire lifetime, but I already told you once that you're inclined to express yourself in a non-Hungarian way, and I ask you, do not use these kinds of expressions, because we Hungarians have a nice way of putting this, if you agree with me—of course, Mr. Director, she faltered—we have our own syntax, don't we, so the next time, please say that *all the books have been placed in the reading room*, and that's it, the language at once shines, Eszter, yes, she lowered her eyes, and if on the way here it was as if she were floating a little above the ground in her joy, now, on the way back, she was already dragging her slippers which she always wore here in the library, dragging them, namely she shuffled back like a beaten dog, because by what right, she muttered to herself, as she struggled through the crowd and once again stood behind the reception desk, had he taken it upon himself to give me grammar lessons, when I taught Hungarian for twenty-three years in School No. 2, this hurts, she commented to the female colleague standing next to her, but that colleague didn't even hear what she said, because she had just handed out another book, as she'd come across a copy of *Butterfly on my Shoul-*

*der* by Anikó Sándor, describing her adventures in Buenos Aires, the colleague had no idea what to do with that line snaking behind the reader in front of her, and what to give to all these people, where could she find anything, she brooded, while she wrote out the reader's card, something, anything, anything at all about this damned Argentina, and she couldn't ask her colleague Eszter just now, because she knew she'd gone in to see the boss, and she always came out of there completely beaten down, everyone here in the library knew that she was incurably in love with him, fifty-eight years or not, the thought flashed across her, like a smile across a face, when she glanced at her quickly and saw that "yes, he's hurt her feelings yet again," everyone knew about it, it was the director she was in love with, this overweight character, who in addition to those soda-bottle eyeglasses looked exactly like a hippopotamus, and who was preoccupied with only one thing, his own greatness, although—she continued her account already at home, after they had finally closed up the library and she returned home to her family, and they sat down in the living room in front of the TV—just between us, our boss is really such a conceited dud, the likes of which this town has only produced once during the past two decades, ever since—she pointed at herself—I've known this town.

Marietta, my dear, we really only have an hour now, and you're going to give a speech, said the Mayor peremptorily, oh no, not me, Marika resisted, sitting on the sofa bed, I promised I'd be there but I'm not going to speak, she shook her head decisively—oh, so you'll be there! the Mayor cried out in his despair, you're the main event! I ask you, this whole thing is for you, if you're not there it's possible the Baron won't even come—I beg you to understand, Marika resisted as decisively as she could, I'm not going to speak, this is your affair, I'll be there if you want, but I'm certainly not going to say anything, please understand already and stop torturing me, hasn't this been enough already, I've done everything that you wished: I spoke on TV, I talked about the letters and my replies, I talked about the old stories too, down to the smallest details, and yet this is the most personal of topics for me, I ask you—completely agitated, she picked up her cup from the cocktail table and took a sip of tea—but well, it's not even about that, the Mayor tried to convince her, it's not that we don't want the whole thing to be personal, let it be personal, and that's exactly why you need to stand before us and be the very first to greet the great man, and he tried to win her over, he still tried for some minutes, but when he saw that he wasn't getting anywhere, he grimaced with resignation, then he nodded—who knew at what—and finally he suggested to Marika that they leave together, because the time had come, and the people were probably waiting already at the station, he noted with excitement, they're waiting—for you and for me—so that we can all wait for the train together, I only hope, my dear God, that it won't be very late, he jumped up from the upholstered shell-backed chair and began to button his coat, then he quickly unbuttoned it when he saw that Marika was headed for the coat rack to retrieve her own coat; he quickly jumped over there, took down her coat, cordially helped put it on, even gently tapping Marika on the back, which made her shudder a little, so that he soon stopped, and already he was opening the door, opening it for the lady, and they left together, down the steps, out the front entrance into the icy wind, although right now it wasn't raining, but still, within a few moments they were freezing as the wind beat against them, although they only had to walk about fifty steps to the car, then everything went easily, they sped along in the government car along Peace Boulevard, they flew—because I'm flying to you, Marika was thinking in the back seat—and there was nothing else, just these four words, they resounded like a gentle bell ringing in her soul, and all the while she only saw that the Mayor kept on talking and talking, but she couldn't follow a word of what he was saying, because what he was saying had no interest for her, because her attention was preoccupied by the two windshield wipers in front as they tenaciously tried to struggle with the filthy plastic bags that kept being blown underneath the wipers by the wind, she only heard the squeaking sound of the windshield wipers as the plastic bags slid back and forth on the windshield, and in the meantime she flew, and everything flew with her, and there were only these four words, these four words that sang within her, and nothing else.

In her hurry she only found two ballpoint pens and a bunch of markers, but she was looking for a fountain pen, she remembered that she had a fountain pen of some kind of blue or greenish color, she thought, it had to be here, she began to dig around in her woven yarn basket, in which she kept not only balls of yarn, but all sorts of trifling objects she didn't want to throw out but could no longer use, she dug and she dug, but she didn't find it, then she placed her index finger on her lips and tried to think calmly, she looked around the living room, ah, the lower desk drawer, maybe it was in there, she stepped over to it, and she pulled out the drawer, and in the course of time all kinds of things had really collected in that drawer, because there was everything from an India-rubber eraser to a glass globe with the inevitable snowflakes falling down inside onto a manger, to a paper-cutting knife, she picked up a photograph which it somehow ended up here, it was a little creased, and she smoothed it out, there, if you please, she was with her mother, maybe, she thought, musing, she could have been fifteen years old, or maybe even fourteen, my God, what a long time ago it was, she sighed, and for a while she just looked at herself; what a beautiful young girl she'd once been, she liked the picture, because she was smiling and those two little dimples in her face, which always appeared when she smiled, were clearly visible—even then she already knew what affect those dimples had on men, ha, those old days, she sighed, and she carefully put the picture back in the drawer and kept on looking, but she didn't find it there, then she took a step back, and again put her index finger to her lips, and she looked around, where could it be, wasn't it just in the kitchen, she suddenly had a newer idea—but that could be it, she replied to herself, and went into the kitchen to one of the cupboards, she might come upon it anywhere there, she pulled out the drawers and opened the cupboard doors, but nothing, when suddenly it occurred to her where it was, and she quickly went back into the living room, and she opened up the large cupboard, the wardrobe, the one in which she kept her reticule on the bottom shelf, and she was looking for the one made out of fine, light, beige-colored fabric, with golden clasps, which she only used in springtime, and there it was, well, at last, she thought contentedly, but then suddenly she realized that she would also need ink, this, however, wasn't so difficult, as she immediately came across some ink in the writing desk, in the second drawer from the bottom, well, of course, and finally she sat down at the writing desk, and she nicely put everything that she didn't need away, she adjusted the two vases with the cotton branches in them, then she placed the folio of paper in the middle of the desk, she leaned over it, well, but what should she write, once again she pulled out Béla's first letter from one of those strange envelopes, on which she had otherwise already written in hardly visible lead pencil the number one, just as she had written on the other envelope in the same fashion, number two, and she read the first letter again from the beginning to the end, then she read the second letter as well, also from the beginning to the very end, but she became none the wiser, her hand trembled—what should she write now—and finally she put everything aside, and from the upper right-hand drawer she took out her collection of postcards, she picked out three, then she picked out one from those, and so it happened that finally, holding the fountain pen, which in the meantime she had filled with ink, she leaned above the table, her head tilted slightly to the left, and after some thought wrote down three words, then she just sat there looking at the postcard, her back stooped over, and she felt, too, how she was sitting there stooped over, but for a while she didn't do anything about it, although she permitted herself this only very rarely, namely to let herself go like this—as she put it—as she always kept her back, her torso perfectly straight, but now everything was difficult somehow, suddenly everything had become difficult, she looked at the three words on the back of the postcard, and she felt that she was old, I'm old, well, what do I even want from this, and she shook her head a little, as if she'd found herself in the midst of some imprudence, because all the same what was she hoping for, Béla was a graybeard, she was an old lady, there was no embellishing that, so that what could they expect, she just sat there bent over the postcard, she looked at the three words, and tears came to her eyes, and somehow her back became even more hunched, her two shoulders fell forward, this was the back of an old lady, a bad back whose lower part often ached, but then suddenly she pulled herself up, and very quickly she slipped the postcard into the envelope that she'd prepared, sealed it, and after reading the lines, letter by letter, from those two wondrous envelopes she set about addressing her own. Then she jumped up, hurried to the door, quickly put on her coat, her scarf, her hat, and already she was outside in the icy wind and rain, and when she arrived at the post office, and pushed open the door, she was already smiling as she stepped in, because inside her a voice was singing, as if somebody were playing along on the cello—I'm ready, yes, I'm ready for love.

The crowd surpassed all expectations—not only the Mayor was astonished, but even the people standing there just kept looking around for a while, stunned that they were so many in number—not as if the townspeople had been expecting anything else—but now that they were all assembled on the platform, to the right of it, to the left, inside the station building, behind and in front of it, up to the second platform, they were dumbstruck, and in the meantime noted with some pride just how many they were, and how good it was that they too had come out and hadn't remained at home, although of course staying at home never could have seriously occurred to anyone, it's just that the news reports were confused, and some were looking around, wondering if it was really today that the Baron was arriving, because his arrival had been announced yesterday with great fanfare, and then nothing had happened; this was, however, the only doubt expressed by a mere fraction of the participants, because everyone else—namely, the majority—were in agreement, even if they weren't aware of that: namely, if the train was really going to arrive here at some point, if that railway carriage was at one point going to arrive from Békéscsaba, and if at one point he finally was going to disembark from that train—he, whose photograph they'd already seen so, but so many times, and about whom they'd heard so, but so much—as far as they were concerned, there was no other task at hand but to commemorate him, then wait and see what would happen next—because that was the big question which all of the residents of the city took for granted in its broader outlines, only the details, quite naturally, remained obscure—as nobody really knew what the Baron would start with first, if it would be the reconstruction of the Almásy Chateau, or of the Castle, or would he begin with the long dreamed-of small fountains on the banks of the River Körös, or the construction of the seven hotels, and that list, which had been swirling around the town ever since this story had burst upon them, was continually being expanded and revised, the residents of the city proving themselves capable of debating the most diverse eventualities, from the bedrooms to the barbershops, from the shops to the offices, and even the children were discussing it in the kindergartens, simply everywhere and in every moment everyone was only talking about what would happen, and how it would happen, and now, as they conceived it, they no longer had to worry about the most essential thing, because that was already happening—namely the Baron's arrival—as the train was approaching, that wasn't in doubt, namely the train was arriving, namely that at that moment, in this axis of events, there now appeared the stationmaster, who of course hadn't permitted either of the two traffic managers (who were very deeply offended) to man the station during today's shift, every third minute he appeared in the crowd, pushing his way through the throng of waiting people, and went out to the third platform, and he looked to the left, in the direction of Békéscsaba and of the wide world—and in general, the wide world lay in that direction, because in the eyes of the locals, the world of inexhaustible possibilities was to the left of the station building, although toward there you could only see the watchman's house and the level-crossing gates, then a bit farther on the gigantic concrete monstrosity known as the Water Tower, and nothing else, and even the stationmaster himself could only see those things, although he acted as if he were capable of seeing something completely different, as if he were capable of seeing where the train could be found right now, his signal sign, something that undoubtedly commanded respect, was still there in his hand, his uniform was very visibly immaculate, without even the slightest speck of dust upon it, the buttons were polished, and the stitching on the insignias had been reinforced, but even so, the crowd thought to themselves, he couldn't see anything more, just the same things as they did—in other words, nothing—yet despite this, from the severe and searching gaze of the stationmaster, they waited for the great announcement, and he didn't conceal that he was aware of this expectancy, he stayed out there by the third track for as long as he could, not even indicating "not yet," or anything like that with just one nod of the head, and with precisely the same expression on his face he went back through the crowd, back into the stationmaster's office just as he had stepped out of there a moment ago, and immediately, after three minutes, he appeared again, and the whole thing played out once again, only that this time his performance had come to an end, the stationmaster came back from that third platform with a *different* expression on his face, it would have been hard to say how this expression was different, but it was, anyone who had gotten a good enough vantage point for themselves could easily see that, and in general there could hardly be any doubt that something had changed, something was going to happen now, because the stationmaster went back into the office with a completely different kind of step then when he had emerged from there, he was hurrying, it could be stated that he was now hurrying back, and in addition he didn't wait another three minutes because almost as soon as he had gone inside he came out again, and everyone who saw him looked at his hand signal, because now, as he went out among them, he began to tap it against his leg gently, but unequivocally, and this continued as well when he remained out there, the excitement palpably grew, suddenly the crowd had a voice, although no one was talking, but some kind of murmuring had begun, then the stationmaster adjusted his uniform, and from that everyone—who could see him—knew that the train was coming, and then it all began—although this hadn't been agreed on at all beforehand, it just involuntarily occurred to the Mayor, because he was the one who began waving, he turned to his left, toward where the train was expected, and suddenly he just began to wave, he waved with wide enthusiastic movements, and at first just the people standing right around him began to wave as well, and this waving began to immediately spread like a contagion, and hardly one minute had gone by and already everyone, almost without exception was waving—*nearly* everyone, because, for example, the bikers of the Local Force—who had gotten a place around the loading ramp to the right of the platform—didn't wave, they sat there with extremely resolute and valiant expressions on their faces, and in their ears were the studs they wore only for the most solemn of ceremonies, and they held on to the handlebars of their bikes with both hands, so they couldn't wave, but in the same way the stationmaster also didn't take part in the general waving, just as the four horses hitched to the trap of course didn't, but almost everyone else did, only in different ways, everyone raised his hand according to his own frame of mind and temperament, and the women's chorus, too, at first they started waving just haphazardly, but then some of them said something to the others, and they decided upon a certain procedure, so that everyone's hands waved to the right and then to the left, everyone all together nicely in unison, that's showy, thought the Mayor, completely turning red in his elation and nervousness; he himself was gesturing wildly in this spontaneous eruption of mass greeting; but that wasn't the case for Irén, who'd just come here for appearance's sake, a forced grimace on her face, which communicated that fine, she wasn't evading anything here, but she found it all to be a little too rushed, because nobody could see anything yet; but as for the postal delivery man—the reputation of whom had just grown and grown ever since it had emerged that he was the one who placed the two renowned letters into Marietta's hand—he waved so enthusiastically, like someone who saw the train coming, but it wasn't coming, the crowd, though, didn't give up, their hands didn't droop, for somebody already heard something, and then more and more people heard it too, yes, people thought, here and there, some kind of rattling sound, yes, a rattling sound, and they kept on waving, some were waving even more enthusiastically them before, whereas others were tenaciously maintaining their original impetus, and all the alcoholics emerged from the station buffet, but in them, possibly, some kind of switch had been permanently thrown, because they were waving, not as if the train were approaching, but as if it were *leaving* the station, but on their faces was an expression of happiness, just like on the face of the new employee in the travel agency, who had also joined the crowd with extreme joy, because even though originally she had decided that she was only coming because of her father, namely only to push her father there in his wheelchair, lest he too should miss out on the big circus everyone was expecting here, by degrees she somehow became infected by the general mood of expectancy, and she'd hardly even glanced over there, and already her arms were up in the air, and already she was waving them with the others, and even the chief groom from the cooperative stable (although he, being next to the station, couldn't be seen by anyone from the train) kept flourishing his whip, and Auntie Ibolyka was there, too, only she kept shaking her basket in the air, in which, according to the opinion of those standing around her, there could only be concealed one of her famous Linzer tortes, so that it was hardly even noticeable that a few people weren't doing anything at all, just standing there with their hands dug deeply into their pockets, among whom the former love—as they referred to her—of the long-awaited guest, the Baron's former love Marietta, was the most surprising; they didn't understand what was going on with her, why she wasn't waving, because it didn't seem—although she betrayed nothing—that there was any way she could be untouched by this spontaneous eruption of excitement, but in fact everything was taking place inside of her, in those two coat pockets of hers with her hands dug in deep, because those two small hands of hers in general couldn't bear to stop, and both of them kept moving just a little bit, right on rhythm with the crowd, only that these two hands were palpating just a bit there within the warmth of her pockets, while the heart, a little further up from these two rattling hands, there under the coat, was just beating, beating more and more, throbbing ever and ever more loudly, it just pounded and pounded, because this heart felt that the train was getting closer, it was clattering, it was braking already, and slowly, it was coming to a stop.

# *RUM*

# HE WILL ARRIVE, BECAUSE HE SAID SO

The locomotive bearing the route number of M41 2115 and known otherwise as the "Rattler" wasn't too sure: where was that line where it was supposed to stop, and as if it wanted to be extremely precise when it first came to a stop, the train still jolted itself forward about a meter, namely it readjusted itself a bit, which resulted in one big jolting movement, and then the pneumatic brakes blew out the air in a long sigh, in such a way as if the entire journey up until now had been much too wearying, as if the train were breathing out its last—just this far and no more, the locomotive, with all the carriages attached behind it, seemed to indicate with its fatigued moans; the engine driver, though, seemed satisfied as he opened the window next to him, leaning out, even when the engine was idling—as everyone always commented—his facial expression was fairly cheerful, and on the other hand, here, from the locomotive window, he saw everything *from above*; and if the others said, well, fuck that, he's got it good, always seeing everything from above, but still, he's shut in there for an entire lifetime, and well, isn't it boring to always be looking at everything from that locomotive window, because even if you see everything from above, you're always seeing the same thing, because what is there, it's always the same thing over and over—although their attempts to convince him were in vain, he just laughed and kept looking around cheerfully if he happened to stop somewhere, like this time, too, and he now looked out the window with a more cheerful expression on his face than usual, because the crowd was as big as that last time he'd seen such a crowd, in the old days in the summertime when he would pull up to the train station in the capital city, and the summer travelers would rush to the train doors; at first his cheerful gaze passed over the entire crowd, then he himself began to observe the train-car doors, just like everyone down there around the station building—they were all watching the train doors to see when they would open, mainly to see when he would emerge, he for whom everyone was waiting so much—the train driver, namely, didn't read *Blikk*, nor did he watch TV, because he was usually either on his shift, or had collapsed onto his bed at home, no, he didn't have time for things like that; this view, however, he was most visibly enjoying, and he straightened his arms a little bit on the window ledge, so as to be able to more comfortably have a look around, leaning out even more so he could see better, because there were things to see, as he related later on, when he had returned to the Békéscsaba station (for a long time now he hadn't had not stuck to the regulations and he'd handed the locomotive over to the other driver), and somehow for a while the train doors didn't want to open, however there was much to see all the same in the crowd, because everything was here, he related, smirking at his shift-mate, because just imagine, fuck, there was a carriage with four decorated horses, I'm telling you seriously, that a decorated carriage with those four horses was there in the crowd, then on the other side there were about fifty bikers, you know, all fitted out in leather gear, with tattoos, and World-War-II crash helmets, and between the two, up there on the top floor of the station there was a sign that read WELCOME! and Hungarian flags were strung up everywhere, I'm not kidding you, it really was like that, he insisted to his shift-mate—and then the door opened, but he couldn't see which passenger it was for whom everyone was waiting so, but so much, and then something came across on the radio and there was a second priority call he had to deal with for a while, and by the time he came back the chaos was complete, and he, from the locomotive window, couldn't make out what was going on at all, but something unexpected had happened, that was for sure, because people had begun to rush around here and there; he looked at the other driver on the shift, but the other driver didn't say anything, he wasn't really interested in any of this, because what was on his mind was clearing that spot next to "position A" in the drivers' cab, that spot down below to the right, namely he wanted to clean it and put it in order, because he—as opposed to this so-called colleague of his—always placed his briefcase with his vittles *exactly in the same place,* so that he began to shove aside all the things piled up there—because he couldn't stand how no one ever took into consideration that he never just tossed his briefcase anywhere, but always placed the briefcase with his vittles in its proper place, which meant that spot should always be kept free, if he had a shift everybody knew this, except of course for Mr. Chipper here, he just grinned all the time like a crabapple, and was always shooting the breeze, and who the hell cared, maybe for once in his life he could think about when to hand over the route, then things would really be in order, because this was a locomotive, an M41 2115, fuck this cunt—he pursed his mouth in rage, and the jaw muscles in front of his earlobes began to twitch—but he didn't say anything, order had to be maintained here, this was a question of human lives, of schedules, and equipment worth millions, of regard for the railway company and its passengers, this was his view, and this became glaringly evident now too from his expression as he stared at his colleague, who continued to chat idly on, fucking quit it already, but this briefcase—he turned away from him, his eyes glittering with rage—a briefcase is something that should always have its place, and he meticulously adjusted it next to himself, comfortably seating himself in the driver's cab, then he put his hand onto the steering bar, thoroughly looking over the signal lights, the automatic brakes, the emergency brakes, the reversing switches, the speed regulator, the control panel, and so on, one after the other, and then he looked out the side at the mirrors, to make sure that everything was in order, and he found everything to be in order there, and he no longer paid any attention to what to this so-called colleague was blathering on about, his colleague was just ever more cheerfully going on and on, and finally he lost his patience and grumbled at him to shut up already for God's sake, then he just grumbled to himself that's why everything is like that here, because they dare to entrust characters like this with an entire train, he however—as he made a quick test of the brakes—would never even put a toy train into the hands of a clown like that, he was speaking seriously now, not even a toy train.

She could see quite well, because she'd been able to get a place close to the platform railing, although of course there was the danger that she'd be crushed by the crowd, but she trusted herself to hold out, because the main thing was that she wanted to see everything, even if she couldn't be standing next to her girlfriend, because they hadn't been able to come here together, Marika had come in a separate car with the Mayor, like one of the crown jewels, Irén smiled to herself by the railing, well, that was good, though, she said to herself, that dear girl deserves to stay up there in the clouds, because that's where she resides, and that's why she loved her so much, even if that sort of thing was pretty strange to her, she never would have been able to put up with this in anyone else, but Marika was an exception, she was a saint, a real romantic, always living in her dreams, and in the meantime she was already sixty-seven years old, and still up there in the clouds, dreaming, it was no wonder she'd always been so entranced by her, no wonder at all, she thought, and now for the first time she also felt proud, because right at that moment she saw where her girlfriend was standing, she really couldn't complain, the Mayor was hardly letting go of her hand, holding her there behind the main microphone, and she noticed that the organizers had set up quite a few microphones, there was one here right in front of the platform exit, then there was one to the left, next to the first track, not too far away from the horse-drawn carriage, then there was another one, well, where was that one, oh, of course, further off to the right, on a platform, and it was clear that someone in addition to the Mayor was going to speak, but she didn't know who that might be, never mind, the main thing (and she had to frankly confess this) was that the whole thing pleased her, even if she found it to be a bit exaggerated—and she couldn't emphasize this enough: because what was the point of such a huge, but such a huge ado, as she kept repeating to her acquaintances, wouldn't it be enough for just Marika and the Mayor to come welcome him, then they could go back together, show him the town in the horse-drawn carriage, if they felt the need to parade him around in a carriage, but then again why not, after all he's a count, I mean a baron—and she'd wink at those whom she'd been regaling the past few days with this commentary, followed by a scornful smile, as if she were trying to insinuate something with this "count, I meant to say baron" (her interlocutors of course didn't understand what there was to be scornful about in him not being a count but a baron, that's what he was), but this didn't matter to her, and she tried to explain it several times to Marika too: his title didn't matter, it only mattered that he was a good person, because that's all that counts, my dear Marika, she said to her, don't you worry about that, because a title—what is it worth? but if he's forthright, if he's honorable, if he doesn't deceive you like everyone else up until now, my dear Marika, then my blessing is upon you both, and then Marika burst out in a bashful laugh, and Irén—why deny it—frankly admired this little-girl laughter of hers, because she loved her girlfriend, as she had loved no one else among her earlier acquaintances, because she was so naive, so sweet, and so good-hearted, she'd found her place right next to her at the beginning of their friendship, when she became firmly convinced that such a refined, but such a refined soul, such a little ingenue needed a common-sense girlfriend who would always stand by her, who would be there when she was needed, who would protect her—she sighed, truly proud and happy herself, and now one of the train doors was starting to open—what would have become of Marika without her, what (could anyone say), without her?

The door opened, and they saw a man holding a wide-brimmed hat in one hand, and hunched over, because the doorway was too low for him, at first he just poked out his head to have a look around, but then those who were standing closer—namely the members of the Local Force waiting tensely in the first row to start pressing down on their motorcycle horns—they saw that on the face of the older man, an expression appeared which more than anything else could be likened to dread, but the others also perceived that something wasn't proceeding as it should have, because they too saw the door opening in the first train car, and it looked as if he were going to get off the train, because they saw the head and the renowned hat in his hands, then how he was clutching on to the train steps' railing, but then, seeing the crowd and the flag-festooned station, like someone who was shrinking from everything in front of him, he retreated back into the doorway with his hat, moreover, amid the crowd's incomprehensible murmurings, he even shut the train door after himself, well, nobody was counting on that, there they all stood: the horse-drawn carriage, the women's chorus, the Mayor and the microphones, and everything festooned with flags, and WELCOME! and well, such a gigantic flop as this—the few residents of the city who weren't able to come out to the station all heard the story later on—you can't even imagine it, because just imagine, there's this huge crowd, the train pulls up, the door opens, they can see the Baron already as he pokes his head out, and then what happens?!, he pulls his head back in and shuts the train door—well, everyone was struck dumb, they related afterward, almost beyond themselves with malicious delight, which was directed mainly toward the organizers, in particular the Mayor, who had practically turned to stone, he was struck dumb as well, while the whole scene of course was the most disturbing for the stationmaster, because he just stood there with his heels tightly closed together, his hand raised toward his cap in a salute: he saw as the door opened and the passenger appeared, he saw that he was the only one who seemed to be intending to get off the train, but then none of this happened, because the person in question didn't get off the train, he just stayed there in the railway carriage, he pulled the door shut after himself, and now what should he do—he stood there at attention and saluting—and from the locomotive window the driver just smirked at him from those distant heights, and he just stood there and had no idea what to do, because what was going to happen now, was the passenger going to get off the train or not, and in general what was he, the stationmaster, supposed to do in a case like this, because he was the one who—after the passengers finished getting on and off the train—he had received the direction by radio to send the train straight back to Békéscsaba, because there were only a few locomotives left, and especially—they told him on the radio—there weren't too many "Rattlers," because hardly even two of them were even operational by now, the other ones were too dilapidated to even run routes anymore to Gyoma, or Kétegyházas, or Oros, and not even to Battonya, well—but still, wasn't that why he was the stationmaster, so that in a situation like this he would always have a plan B? . . . because that's what he always said: he was never without that plan B up his sleeve, just as he had one now too, because suddenly, as he stood there at attention and saluting, he got tired of this, and he put plan B into operation: he went over to the railway carriage in question, he went up the steps and opened the door, and he said to the man once again appearing in the doorway: last stop, please exit the train, you have arrived, sir—at which the Baron readily bent down, suitcase in hand, and holding it out in front of himself he stepped down onto the top step, but then the crowd began to make such a clamor that the passenger, frightened, came to a dead halt on that step, and the stationmaster sensed that he was going to turn back again, this, however, he no longer permitted, although he was aware of who the arriving guest was, for the time being he had to deal with him as a passenger, and so he spoke to him courteously but decisively, saying: sir, please make up your mind if you would like to disembark from the train or remain on the train, to which the traveler replied that *as a matter of course* he wished to disembark from the train, and so he once again reached forward with his suitcase, which this time the stationmaster took from him, helpfully, but in a manner that brooked no contradiction, so as to make things easier for him, because there was some difficulty with the hat, then he helped him down the steps, but by then the crowd had already begun its cheers, and there was such unrest, that the passenger once again looked around in alarm, because he suddenly heard the sound of several horns blowing at once, but at the same time he heard a chorus somewhere breaking into song, and at the same time the official loudspeakers began to reverberate with truly horrendous volume, and a voice was bawling—exactly three times, for some reason—WELCOME! and it was obvious that despair and not joy was keeping him from moving any further on with his suitcase, but right then, the stationmaster, once again rising to the challenges of his role, extended his arm to him, and the Mayor also came to himself and was next to the Baron in a flash, and he said: this way please, Lord Baron, I'll show you the way, and he took the suitcase from the stationmaster, whose face was drawn, and he jumped between the railway ties, and he hopped forward, the suitcase in one hand, while he balanced on the stones and rocks of the track bed, and with the other he showed the Baron where "this way" was, because the Baron was being shepherded somewhere, he had completely lost his own free will, and was following in the direction being shown to him, he went, with that short, fat person in front of him, he went on uncertainly, and he came closer and closer to the crowd in front of the building, and all the while he would have liked nothing better than to be going farther away from them, but he couldn't get away from this crowd, he could only keep going toward it, moreover suddenly he was standing there in the thick of it, and then suddenly out from behind his back jumped the stationmaster, and before anyone could stop him from doing so, he once again raised his hand in a salute, and he said: Aladár Rabitz, Stationmaster, and the Baron just looked at him and didn't know what to say to this, because what should he say to someone who had jumped out in front of him in such a difficult situation as this and said: Aladár Rabitz, Stationmaster, he didn't know what to say, he just looked at him and smiled constrainedly, and then the short, fat person shoved aside the stationmaster, he gently pushed him to the right so as to position them both closer to the microphone, and he started to speak about how he never could have thought in his wildest dreams . . . because this is not at all how he had imagined the arrival would be, oh, dear God, this was not how he imagined it.

All the flawless organizing had been in vain, the Mayor shook his head, in vain were the flawless sequence of events, the flawless distribution of tasks, in vain every effort they had expended in order to avoid things getting all muddled, things *had* gotten muddled, because—and the Mayor had been saying this ever since the Baron's arrival maybe a hundred times in various places and to the most various constituents—when the train stopped, people suddenly went crazy, and everything got mixed up, because it wasn't that the arrival of the great guest, even in those first moments—well what should I say, he said—was rather disorderly—he preferred not to discuss that, and the train didn't even stop properly, and for some reason he didn't even want to get out of the train at first, well, never mind—what is certain is that when he finally started walking with him from the train to the main microphone, he suddenly heard the bikers blowing that Madonna tune randomly on their motorcycle horns, and then the women's chorus—as if this had been their sign—started in on the same song, at which point the crowd began to yell all kinds of things, but not what he'd instructed them beforehand to call out from his megaphone, instead some were yelling: long live the Baron, some were yelling: welcome, others were screaming: bravo, yet others were yelling: well hail!; can somebody tell me—he had been posing the question for days now—what is "well hail" supposed to mean, well, is that the right way to receive such an important guest? he asked, no, he answered his own question, that's not how it should be done, but none of this should have happened, and everyone sensed—even the women's chorus—that because the commotion was so great, they were screaming to no avail at the top of their lungs, just as loudly as they could:

*Don't cry for me Argentina*
*The truth is I never left you*
*All through my wild days*
*My mad existence*
*I kept my promise*
*Don't keep your distance —*

and every sound that came out of the chorus was nearly lost in the commotion, in vain were they amplified, they just tried harder and harder to see if they could somehow improve the situation, but they couldn't improve anything, because those accursed motorcyclists, those bikers on the other side of the station—the women's chorus had detested them for a long time now, because how many, but how many times had one of their rehearsals been ruined by those bikers revving their engines right below the windows of the Cultural Hall in the Göndöcs Garden—may the crows pick out the eyes of all of 'em—well, those bikers on the other side (and this hadn't been agreed in advance, at least nobody had said anything about this) well, but they were capable of this, with their motorcycle melody horns they all began to blare out *the same thing,* the chorus members could hardly believe their ears, but well, it was that song, that Argemia or whatever the hell it was, well, those accursed bikers were blaring out that song on their horns, and the women's chorus became completely confused, because if somebody were to tell them now that they should be holding the right pitch and a clean melody while singing "Don't Cry for Me, Argentina," and yet at the same time hearing exactly the same tune as if from a herd of bellowing cows—this had not been agreed upon in advance, no one had informed them about this—it was a provocation, they repeatedly said to each other when it was finally all over—and well, why deny it, they'd come short, and they sought the offenders only in *them,* because the bikers were the offenders, everyone, from Julcsi to Auntie Ibolyka, was convinced that the blame for everything should be laid at the feet of that vile crew; in fact, though, it wasn't them who should be blamed, as this was only what the Local Force had agreed upon with the organizers, that was true, but something else had disturbed them, and completely understandably, namely the bikers couldn't decide when it could be said that the great guest had disembarked from the train, because when he opened the door and poked out his head, then a few among them felt—and it must be acknowledged, not without reason—given the pressure of events that this was the sign they should be waiting for, and not the Leader's hand signal, and so they began to press down on their horns at that moment; others still waited, however—partially because in the ensuing commotion they weren't sure if they'd actually seen the hand signal of the Leader, and partially because they judged that the starting signal in this case should be the moment the guest actually got off from the train, but then he went back into the train, therefore—they reasoned according to their own fashion, namely, in the Biker Bar they slammed their pint glasses down on the counter or the table, depending on whether they were standing or sitting, as they truly felt that the "condemnation of the public" was unjust, accordingly it couldn't be considered that the Baron had gotten off the train, because he hadn't, they kept repeating, he only got off the train later; and by getting off the train, they meant—they explained, flourishing their pint glasses—that someone's feet would be touching the ground, namely, when he got down from the last step and started off, next to the Mayor, toward the microphone, then they began pressing down on their horns when that occurred; but of course from that ended up a huge commotion, they acknowledged, as all of them began to press on their horns at different times, and because of that they also reached the end of the melody separately, they just kept pressing and pressing on their horns, and Madonna's great hymn, meant to "coax tears of joy" from the guest—as the Leader had prophesied after his discussion with the Mayor and the Police Chief— the "great Argentinian masterpiece" turned into a completely muddled cavalcade; it was a montage—Totó tried to mitigate things, but without great effect—and it was to no avail that they themselves finally heard what they were doing and realized too late this wasn't going to lead to anything good, they didn't dare stop though, they just kept on pressing and pressing until the Mayor spoke into the microphone, emphatically thanking the participants for their role in the ceremony, and he began to utter his own words of greeting, which finally brought some semblance of order to the festivities.

Of course, when the crowd began to whoop and holler, the four horses startled, then they startled at the sound of the motorcycle horns, then the women began to screech from the loudspeakers, so it was a miracle, I say, said the chief groom, a miracle that they didn't bolt altogether, because they still tried to bolt, but somehow he managed to get hold of them, well, but anyone can imagine, he said later, to the three stable boys—because they were his only audience over there at the stables—this whole thing was pretty unusual for the four harnessed horses, because when was the last time all four of them were together like that, and especially surrounded by such a huge crowd, and with so much commotion, well, never, it was already enough of an ordeal just to hold them together with the reins, but what could he do, could he explain to City Hall that things really didn't work this way—to harness up four horses who can't stand each other—just harness them up, they'd told him—and it would all be ready, of course, the chief groom had said, offended by the abrupt order he'd been given, it's easy for them to say to me: harness up four horses, and if these four horses have never been harnessed up together?—if Fancy can't stand Magus?! and if Mistletoe has never stood next to Aida? then what was supposed to happen here, then what the hell was he supposed to do—he posed the question, and he began hitting the corral fence with a strap, but there was no reply from the three stable boys, and there had been no reply from anyone else either, because no one had even so much as said hello to him, because nobody was paying any attention to the brougham, as everyone was preoccupied with the Mayor's speech, in which, according to the great majority, the Mayor laid it on too thick, clearly he was trying to outdo himself, and it just ended up being a huge blather, in which he enumerated everything, talking about how the Harruckers this, and the Almásys that, but mainly those Wenckheims, well, he praised them to the skies, but he got the counts and the barons all mixed up, he mixed up Krisztina with Jean-Marie, and Frigyes with József, and the people just gawked, not to mention the man he was addressing, because he stood there next to the Mayor with such a face, turning his eyes here and there, like someone who was about to flee, but that was no surprise, because the Mayor was really laying it on way too thick in that welcoming speech of his, and that was the general opinion, because what was the good of immediately assailing that poor Baron, saying how the city needed that money like a suffocating man needed oxygen, well, what kind of vulgar style is that, is that what a citizen expects from an educated person?, no, that's not what he would expect, not that kind of frontal assault, and this wasn't the end of it—those who'd been at the ceremony told the ones who'd remained at home that evening—because after that the squabbling began, because after him, not far from where the Local Force was, the Police Chief began to speak, he too had set up a podium for himself, and he was reading—because he could never recite anything from memory—a speech which simply roused every decent person to indignation, he didn't beat around the bush but immediately advised the Baron to donate all his wealth to the cause of public security, and this Police Chief even went so far, in his speech, as to thank him in advance, and tell him what the money would be spent on—SWAT teams, emergency preparedness, equipment and vehicles, at least two helicopters, four amphibious vehicles, then he enumerated a list of weapons, no one could even follow what he was saying, we stood there freezing, the woman who worked at the espresso bar related to one of her regular customers, who pulled up his left trouser leg, displaying his prosthetic limb, by way of explanation as to why he hadn't been present at the great event, and the woman behind the counter didn't understand why he kept hiking up his pant leg, because she'd known about his prosthetic limb for at least ten years now, as he had already told everyone who stepped in here for an espresso or a Unicum—or the two together—about it at least a thousand times, in any event she just kept telling him: I'm telling you, seriously, we were freezing because of that Police Chief, and he just kept talking and talking, the Mayor had to tap him on the shoulder, because he was brave enough to put a stop to this insolence, because everything has its limits, really, what was that supposed to mean, all his money going for so-called public security, well, it's completely ridiculous to ask for money for something that doesn't even exist, because tell me now—the woman glanced for some reason with rage at her one-legged customer—what about the sidewalks, because just look out the window, here, well, look out, and she went to the entrance of the espresso bar and pointed out the door, a person could break his leg here, that's how big the cracks and holes are on this sidewalk, but everywhere, so one fine day someone comes along and he breaks his neck, because could he just imagine what happened to her even today as she was hurrying out to the station?, well, she almost broke her neck on the sidewalk on one of those holes, but why was she talking about holes here—she came back and stood behind the counter, leaning on her elbows—right there, in the middle of the sidewalk, was a big old ditch, she said, and then that Police Chief has the nerve to keep shooting his mouth off about how everything will go to him, because listen here, and she motioned to her one-legged customer to come closer, and he, of course, did not move, because he took this gesture as he should have, namely in a figurative manner, of course only figuratively—he wants everything for himself, because there's no way he wants any kind of rifle, helicopter, or whatever the hell it is, he just wants to stick all that money into his own pocket, and then this town can suck it up, because that's what this whole game is about, they're going to steal that money, you'll see, she finally noted bitterly, it doesn't matter whether it's the Police Chief or the Mayor or the Milk Powder Factory, I'm telling you, she told him, they're going to pocket it all in the end.

Scandal at the station, you all write that down, said the Chief Editor to the journalists standing in front of him; the real scandal isn't this, that, or the other, although of course write a few column inches on that as well, you understand, it won't hurt the Mayor to finally realize what the opposition thinks about him, but listen here, he said to them, the real scandal is that poor Marika, because what happened—and he spread his hands apart—what happened is that the Baron didn't even notice his supposed one-time great love; I—he pointed himself—I was standing right near him, and I saw everything, because they kept that poor woman waiting until the end, when all the speeches were over already, the Mayor was addressing the Baron, speaking into the microphone—but why, great God in heaven, why did he have to address the Baron through the microphone when the Baron was standing right next to him? well, never mind—he was telling him they were going to take him in the horse-drawn carriage to the Almásy Chateau, but it was only then that he realized —by then everything was over already—it was only then that he remembered about Marika, he remembered that Marika was there, and he hadn't even introduced her, it was only then he said—and I noted this precisely, you all write this down —that he said, Lord Baron, here is Marika, at which point the Baron—the Chief Editor raised his index finger warningly, then he made a movement with it, as if he were indifferently brushing away some speck of dirt—the Baron just nodded once, but not only did he not deign to glance at that poor woman, he just went beside her like a sleepwalker, and then the Mayor jumped in front of him and brushed the people aside until they got into the carriage, you understand, my boys, it's a scandal ... although to tell the truth she didn't really think of it that way, when she was able to think again and sit down alone on one of the shell chairs, she had sent Irén home this time, because she couldn't formulate anything, because she was utterly unable to, she could only feel, and she felt: could there be a more torturous sadness then her own right now, because it hurt, it really really hurt that all of this could have happened there in front of the entire town, she held her face in her hands, and her face was still burning, but what flashed across her was that this situation was still nothing compared to what she was compelled to suffer inwardly, and there, in the view of the entire town, she had to suffer that comedy, she now said to herself, that humiliating situation, because that was what this entire so-called ceremony had meant to her, and not only to her, but to anyone in whom there was even a drop of decency, because did everything really have to happen like this? she asked with infinite sorrow, because really, was all of that dreadful honking necessary, and then that horrible song from *Evita* that those wretched peasant women were screeching into their microphones, were all those speeches necessary, all of those demands so unworthy of him, because who did they take him to be, storming him like that, he, who was only accustomed to the most refined sentiments, for she realized as soon as she glimpsed him in the door of the train, she immediately saw that Béla deserved only the most refined of welcomes, not this atrocious spectacle, because is this really what they wanted?—that horrible Mayor and that horrible Police Captain, and all that came after?—because there, too, was the Headmaster with that speech, my dear God—Marika, leaning forward in the shell chair, buried her face in her hands, what did he say again, good God, that he was deeply ashamed that as a young man he'd given lectures on Marx's *Economic and Philosophic Manuscripts of 1844* in the Party Academy, while in reality he had always been a member of the minor nobility who'd kept his certificate of title hidden away, my Lord, but she was ashamed to have even had to hear this, especially when he kept repeating at the end that he was a down-at-the-heels noble, that he'd always been a down-at-the-heels noble, and so always would remain one, she was ashamed, so, to put it frankly, although everything was so awfully dreadful, she wasn't even surprised when at the end the Baron didn't even want to talk to her, she wouldn't say that her feelings were hurt, they were hurt, but at the same time she understood the why and wherefore of it, because in his position she would have done the same thing, she too would have quickly gotten into the carriage and hurried away from this place with its atrocious welcome, because after all, this was what he would think about this city to which he had longed so much to return, and in general, what was going to happen now, and this was the point where Marika had to stand up and stop herself from thinking anymore, because this was a very delicate point, because now she would have to continue her train of thought in one direction or another, but she didn't dare to continue it in any direction at all, because she couldn't bear to think in terms of "no," nor could she bear to think in terms of "yes," and so that was how the evening found her, it had grown completely dark outside, but she hadn't even noticed, she just sat there in the dark, staring into the space in front of her, trying hard not to think about what she'd just been thinking about, and then came the point when, with the darkness settling down on her, she could no longer bear to say "no," and she let the tears come flooding down her face, they just poured down on her worn-out face, but she didn't even take out a handkerchief, she just let the tears flow down and down, because she didn't even have enough strength to reach for a handkerchief, not even for a handkerchief, she didn't even have that much strength.

He sat in the horse-drawn carriage like someone who was afraid that in the next moment it might explode, or as if it would accidentally crash into something, for it had grown dark, and he was not at all reassured by the little person sitting next to him, who kept gesturing so vehemently in the dark to the right and then to the left while the words just poured out of him, the elastic band on his bow tie had, in the meantime, broken off, but he didn't even notice, and he hadn't even noticed that his tuxedo—if that's what it was—had gotten smudged all over on one side, maybe he'd bumped into a wall somewhere, thought the Baron, if it was indeed a tuxedo, but from a tailor's workshop that he'd never heard of, because the wide lapel hadn't been sewn from the usual lustrous fabric, but— in all likelihood, and however unbelievable—from some kind of plastic material, never mind, the Baron said to himself, as long as we get to wherever we're going as soon as possible, and he continued to clutch the side of the carriage with both hands; and, moreover, it was only in this moment that it occurred to him: that individual who'd designated himself as his secretary while still on the train, that Dante, had completely disappeared, the Baron recalled that this Dante had been looking out of the train window quite intensely, then it was as if he'd seen something that made him nervous, because as the train began to slow down he began looking out of the compartment door as well, but when the train began to brake, and after some hesitation he got off the train, this young man by the name of Dante was simply nowhere to be seen—the Baron hadn't even noticed when he'd disappeared, and there was no explanation as to why, because the Baron, after their acquaintance, had expected his newfound friend to lead him through the practical tasks associated with his arrival, because truthfully speaking he was decidedly unskillful in such practical matters—this fat little person on the other hand . . . in any event, he had viewed the Dante of Szolnok as an individual well-suited to these practical tasks, accordingly on the train he had resigned himself, saying fine, he would accept his acquaintance, and inasmuch as he could, take advantage of the proffered opportunity—let Dante arrange what was necessary—and instead of that, he'd simply vanished into thin air, as the expression presumably went in modern Hungarian, and there he was now sitting next to a visibly deeply agitated little man, and truly, the Baron had judged this correctly: the Mayor was truly beside himself, like someone who senses he is in the midst of a catastrophe, but also that it's much too late to get out of it, and so he just keeps on digging himself in ever deeper, namely he just kept on talking and talking, and he pointed over here and over there, and it was clear that he hadn't yet realized that he was continually pointing here and there in a completely darkened city, saying: here are the famous villas of Peace Boulevard, and this main street is none other than the one formerly named after one of your ancestors, alongside which, in his (the Mayor's) childhood, there still ran a charming narrow-gauge railway, because just imagine, Lord Baron, that this narrow-gauge railway connected Simonyifalva with who-the-hell-knows-what-village, he gesticulated vehemently, but look over there, and he pointed to the other side, that was the Meatpacking Plant, unfortunately today we're no longer able to keep it in operation, because, well, how should I put it, the management made a few accounting errors, well now, have a look over there—and he grabbed the arm of the important guest, who shuddered so much that his provisional guide was forced to let go of his arm immediately—those two buildings there comprise the Police Station, if you please, and next to it is one of our lovely elementary schools, and here—he once again directed the Baron's attention to the other side—is nothing else then the house of the formerly renowned director of our music school, who—just imagine, Lord Baron—was even the chief protagonist in a feature film, well, that's our little city now, he leaned back for a moment in the seat, but then, as he was struck by the fairly moldy smell of the carpet covering the seat, he leaned forward again, and in his joy cried out, pointing to the left-hand side, that there was Strébers, appending no explanation to this whatsoever, as if the very mention of the name and the building would speak for itself, but neither the name nor the building meant anything to the Baron, because he couldn't even see anything, the little man next to him, however, took no notice of this—it was true though, that by now the little man perceived nothing of reality, so shattered were his nerves, he was simply in a trance, continuously tossing himself to one side or the other in the seat next to his guest, and he just kept on talking unceasingly, because he felt that if he stopped he would immediately collapse, and so he didn't stop, he couldn't even register if his words were somehow reaching the Baron, and he didn't even notice that his guest was continually clutching at the side of the carriage that moved ahead at just a very leisurely pace along the street, which accordingly no longer bore the name of one of his ancestors, and where there were hardly any passersby, but the few who were there, as they saw the carriage in the scanty illumination of one of the rarely functioning streetlights, stopped immediately and watched, their mouths gaping open, until it had disappeared from sight—well, there goes the carriage, and look, there's the Baron, so that's him, and so great was their amazement, because they'd heard a lot of things so far, they had heard this, that, and the other about him, but what they saw now—inasmuch as they could see anything in the faint illumination of the haphazardly functioning streetlights—far surpassed all their suppositions, because they all unanimously asserted that the Baron was, beyond doubt, an extraordinary phenomenon—it had to be owned, they later related, that you could tell right away he was a baron—well, and they tried, via the most varied means, to pin down that baronial quality, but they couldn't, so in the end a rather confused picture emerged; everyone, though, hung onto their words with bated breath as they listened to those who'd been lucky enough—although their luck was undeserved, because they hadn't gone to the ceremonial welcome, and yet they still got to see the Baron close up—and, well, at the same time, it had to be acknowledged: it was difficult to nail down that baronial quality, inasmuch as they could define it at all, because it started already with the horse-drawn carriage itself, as it was, they said, like something from another world for a carriage to appear just like that on Peace Boulevard, and for it to appear in the darkness in any event, all polished up, drawn by four horses, well, isn't that something out of a fairy tale? the narrators cried out, and then they described how the Baron was so tall, with his head and that famous wide-brimmed hat swaying back and forth high above, as that creaking horse-drawn carriage rocked him back and forth, because the carriage did creak, the whole thing continually creaked and squeaked as it went along, obviously because the driver hadn't lubricated the wheels properly, or even that couldn't help those old wheels anymore and it was a waste of time to lubricate them, and they winked knowingly at their audience, they knew, however, nothing about the wheels, and they knew nothing about lubrication, they just winked as they went on saying this, that, and the other thing, lengthening their narrative with the most absurd observations, until their audience grew weary of hearing about how skinny he was, or how pale his face was, or what his hat or his coat or the lapel of his coat was like, because they were only interested in one thing and one thing only—in vain did their interlocutors try to describe the Baron's particular elegance, no, everyone was uniformly opposed to hearing about this during the various retellings; tell us *how tall he is,* well yes, came the answer, he's very tall, with a kind of completely particular elegance flowing out of him, well, okay, you can leave that out, they shouted the speaker down, tell us how tall he was, well as for that, they allowed, he's A-1—what do you mean by that? they asked, well what I mean, said the various narrators, is that we could mention many characteristics of the Baron, but there's only one that will make him come to life before your eyes, if we were to mention it, and that is his height—well, at this everyone squealed in satisfaction: so in a word you're saying that he's tall, they looked at that speaker, yes, that's what I'm saying, are you deaf, how many times do I have to tell you that he must be at least six feet tall, that would be my guess, and at this point all inquiries ceased, and everyone began to speak of him simply as the Six-Foot-High Baron, right up to the point until Auntie Ibolyka came up with her own version, because with her own unaffected simplicity, and yet always grabbing the bull by the horns, she compressed the essence of the Baron into one single word, saying well, people, no need to beat around the bush here, no need for measurements of this much and that much, I am telling you, you can put away that measuring tape, because what I have to say here is that this person is a beanpole, and may the Lord high in Heaven fling the skies down upon me—and the others just laughed—if this isn't the whole truth.

The city was so small and dark, the streets were so narrow, the houses were so low-built and run-down, and the sky above them was also so low, that he would be fully inclined to state that *this was not the same town*, and yet he was compelled to acknowledge that it was exactly the same, but it was as if somehow it had become a copy, as if he could only remember—but with hair's breadth accuracy—the original, this, however, was just a copy, not the real town, and he could only hope the real one would be coming along soon, he sat in a chilly, enormous room, in a huge and extremely uncomfortable armchair, and he tried to collect his thoughts as he had been instructed, but it wasn't working, because he just kept ending up at the same point—it wasn't the same, and yet it was—and then he got stuck, as he would have been able to formulate the difference between the two only with extreme difficulty, or namely, not at all, because it wasn't just the task itself that was difficult, but that his brain just wouldn't function anymore beyond this point, he looked at the sputtering fire in the hearth, he tried not to notice the dreadful odor of whitewash, disturbingly mixed with a moldy smell, and he only wished that that young man were here with him now, and at the same time he was relieved that he wasn't here, while another voice within him kept repeating that he had arrived, and so here was a task that appeared to be insoluble, and he really didn't know how to solve it, because how could he make a distinction between the fact that he had to get away from here at once, and yet here he was, the place he'd longed to return to for so many years, and where he had wanted to see everything again, everything that history and his own personal misfortune had stolen from him—what should he do, he stared into the fire, and he couldn't look anywhere else, because the springs of the armchair he was sitting in were completely broken, and pressed into his buttocks, making him sit in such a way that he could only look into the fire and at nothing else, which—as it soon emerged—proved to be an advantage, because being in that enormous room with its own peculiar smell was nothing compared to what he had yet to experience when he finally stood up in order to wash off his limbs a little bit after these extraordinary trials, because he looked around to see where he should go, should his little stroll commence to the left or the right, but he couldn't set off in either direction, because the room was decorated, but in such a way that when he was first led into it he had to catch his breath, he was so beside himself that he couldn't see anything of it, but now, he saw that the entire space was decorated through and through with colorful wreaths, or maybe they weren't even wreaths, he wrinkled his forehead as he tried to figure out just what it was up there festooned high up on the walls, no, they weren't wreaths, but most likely gold and silver garlands used to decorate Christmas trees, but was it actually so close to Christmas now, the Baron began to feel uncertain, no, no, Christmas wasn't that close, and he lowered his gaze, but still not moving away from the armchair, because he had glimpsed a long table, one of those roughly cut pieces with column-like legs, and grown over with cobwebs, and this table was covered with Miska jugs of various sizes, all with folksy reliefs of the faces of mustachioed grandfathers, all originating from the same workshop, arrayed there in complete disorder, when, however, he turned away from there, he noticed on the other side that on the wall, where the whitewash smell was coming from, there'd been placed innumerable carpets with folk motifs, but he really only got scared when he discovered that these folk-motif carpets had been affixed to the wall with enormous nails, they had simply been beaten into the wall, and the heads of the nails were still jutting out, well, those won't be falling down, what a peculiar custom, the Baron gaped at the wall, and he started off toward the left side and he walked around the room once, then he walked around the room another time, and then he felt just how much, but how much there was no strength left in his legs, and there was no strength in his body either, nowhere, so, he thought, it would be much better to lie down, but he didn't even see a bed anywhere, and so he went out from the room into the corridor to summon the staff, but there was no staff anywhere, there was no one there that all, and so he set off by himself in order to find a place where he could lie down, and every door that he tried to open was locked, and moreover with a padlock, so that there was nothing else to do, but to explore further, when he heard, in the distance, a very faint drilling sound, so he set off in that direction, turning to the right at an intersecting corridor, the drilling sound grew louder, and then he pressed down on another door handle, and that door handle let him in, he stepped in through the doorway, and some kind of worker-type person jumped up from the floor where he had been kneeling, and, holding a small electric drill in front of himself, as if he were protecting himself from something, he said, welcome, Your Excellency, but that was all he said, they looked at each other, and both of them kept looking at each other fairly confusedly, then the Baron solved the dilemma—because he hardly had the strength to stand up anymore—by asking this person if he might know where his bedroom could be located, at which the other—with a drill in one hand, a bunch of screws in the other, and a leather tool kit hanging from his belt—began to make excuses and throw out accusations, but the Baron couldn't understand why he was making all these excuses, and who he was so enraged at, in any event the worker just kept on saying and saying: they told him that he had to be finished by that evening at ten, and he was working here peacefully, but they didn't tell him that it wasn't by ten o'clock they needed it finished, but some kind of for-god's-sake-we-need-it-yesterday, this was all their fault, although he didn't say who "they" were, but he gestured in the air with his drill in "their" direction several times, it's their fault, he repeated a few more times, waving the drill around threateningly, and the Baron just stood there in the doorway, feeling that he couldn't bear this standing around too much longer, he had to lie down, he muttered, and he must have created a fairly unfortunate impression, because this laborer type at one point just began talking about how otherwise he'd come to the right place, as this was his bedroom, namely, he added, turning red, it *will be*—at which the Baron weakly asked if he could just point out which bed was his, the reply to which again made him uncertain, because this person just kept repeating that this *would be* his bedroom, then he took one step to the side and pointed at a bed behind himself, but it isn't ready yet, he added, and he swallowed once, and the Baron stepped over there, and only asked if he would permit him to lie down now for a little bit, well, lie down, the laborer type shifted his weight from one foot to the next, you can in fact lie down on this bed; well in that case, you know, I would just like to have a little rest, the Baron answered, and with one hand he pressed down on the bed several times to see if it would hold, or something like that, because it was true, the bed really wasn't ready yet, because this person had actually been working on it right at that moment, the Baron, however, had no more strength left to expend on speech or to worry about what was going on with this bed here, he just sat down on it, and he bent down, and while that laborer type just stared at what the Baron was doing as he slowly untied his shoelaces—then he took off his jacket, and after he had tapped at his inner pocket and taken out an envelope, he placed it at the end of the bed, well, but would the gentleman please wait a moment—and the laborer type jumped over there, he brushed off the head of the bed, and he tried to straighten out the mattress that had just been thrown there provisionally, but the Baron was already lying on this mattress, and the worker-type person was already completely enraged, because there had been no discussion about something like this happening, for this Baron just to show up in the middle of his work, they told him that he had until ten that evening to finish up, they'd only just now brought him over from the Castle to work here, and he needed until ten o'clock to finish up, so the worker sat down at the edge of the bed and started to tell him that he still had to reinforce the pegs, because he had promised to fix the bed, and it still wasn't fixed, the worker sat on the edge of the bed, hunched over in his dirty overalls, and he lowered the drill onto his lap—he never took on a job he couldn't finish, and than the onehe couldn't finish his work if the Baron was lying there on the bed, and what's more, he added angrily, he didn't at all recommend that the gentleman lie on the bed in this way, with the bed in this state, because—he was speaking to the gentleman bluntly now—until now, only field mice and gypsies had slept on this bed, because until today, this bed had been rotting away in a filthy corner in the Castle, it had been dragged over here just this afternoon when it was entrusted to him; he'd been told to work on it 'til ten o'clock this evening, but now it was only seven thirty, and he still had to fix the pegs if the gentleman would permit him, but—he looked into the closed eyes of the Baron—with ever more bitterness, he was realizing more and more that this fine gentleman wasn't going to rise from this bed, he had lain down here, and he didn't and didn't want to get up; he, however, had to finish by ten o'clock, he sat hunched over on the edge of the bed, the Baron lying next to him motionless on his back with his eyes closed, and what was he supposed to say now, it was always like this, working people had no future here, everyone always thought he was up to his neck in money and that the orders were just flooding in, what orders?! the carpenter cried out wildly, sitting on the edge of the bed, what are they talking about?! it's good if I get even eight or ten calls in one month, and even those are just these piddling little jobs, and he gestured with his free hand to show just how much they were piddling, because did this gentleman know how much I was actually earning by doing this?—you don't know, but I will tell you, I asked for five thousand forints, we'll give you thirty-five hundred, they said, and just imagine, that also includes my gas money, and I have to get here from the Krinolin district if I want to work, just now I came from Krinolin, and that's at least six hundred forints' worth of gas, assuming, that is, that I can even get hold of some, he continued to relate sorrowfully to the motionless Baron, for days now there hasn't been any at all, I go over there to the gas pump, over there, behind the Castle, and, if you please, they've got a sign up saying "no gas," I ask you, what does that mean, because more than once I've really felt like hanging another sign out there: so what is there? if there's no gas what's the point in having a gas pump, and you know, those up there—he pointed at the ceiling—it's all the same to them if the little guy has gas or not, because they do have it—and he leaned forward even more, placing his elbows on his knees, holding his head in his hands, and they're not interested in anything else, he went on, because here he was, he had his trade license, but just imagine, sir, that we live in a world now where we all must be multifunctional, so that, for example, he said, he also had his water and central heating licenses, he had his electrician's license, and even then on Sundays—but of course in winter, only in winter—he went to carve up swine with a pig sticker, because he learned how to do that, too, and he had the right paper for it, and even so—the gentleman might wish to know—how much this comes to in one month, one big nothing, because then there are taxes and fees, levies, but never mind, he had no wish to bore the gentleman, you just have a nice rest, he said resignedly, and he got up from the bed—the Baron still hadn't moved an inch, and his eyes remained just as closed as before—well, so now what should he do, here's the Baron sleeping on this . . . piece of wood or something, should he leave him by himself now, should he go? and what if there were some problem, who would get the blame, well, of course he would, but what the hell should he do, there was so much chaos here ever since they had moved all the orphans out yesterday, he couldn't even find one living person, they'd left the Baron there for him, he shook his head helplessly, well, but really, what the hell was he supposed to do, because there wasn't even a blanket or a pillow to put under his head, nothing anywhere, he was a carpenter, not a nurse or hotel employee, where were the people who were responsible for this, he put his drill down next to the bed, and he tiptoed over to the door and looked out into the corridor, but it was just as dead as he imagined it would be, and now he was filled with rage, and in his anger he hit the doorframe and he said to himself: well, is this person my relative, no, so why should I bother with him, I'm going the hell home, and he'd already turned back for his drill, and he was already about to unbuckle his tool belt to pack everything back into his toolbox when, to his own misfortune, he glanced back at the Baron, and only now he noticed that he was lying there with his legs completely hanging off the edge of the bed, but hanging off in such a way that as a matter of fact he was completely stretched out on the bed which was only long enough to reach to the back of his knees, and from his knees, the rest of his legs dangled down, he looked at these two legs hanging down, and he simply couldn't bring himself to just leave him lying there, he simply didn't have the heart—as he related later on at home, when he'd gone back to his house in Krinolin—he couldn't leave him there by himself; that was the truth, because really, how could he leave that old man there with nothing, no blanket, no pillow, nothing, and so he set off along the corridor, and he tried to find something, but upstairs every door was securely padlocked, but when he went down the staircase to the ground floor, he found plenty of "ammunition," as one of the rooms was stocked full with bed linens, clearly they had been thrown in here after the orphans had left—as yesterday they'd all been transported from here in trucks—well, he got hold of some bedclothes, he related, and he went back upstairs, back to the old gentleman, and he covered him with a quilt, and he slipped a pillow beneath his head, and a pillow beneath the legs hanging down—he wasn't called master of all trades for nothing!—he quickly cobbled together a kind of leg support from a chair and some blankets, well, and he nicely lifted those beanpole legs onto it, because he had such spindly legs, he explained to his wife, afterward he had lifted them onto the improvised trundle bed, and then he decided it was time to scram—he finished his account of the events and sniffed at the air to see what was cooking for dinner—so he closed the door nice and quiet, let the poor guy sleep, because if already they didn't care about him so much that they left him all alone . . . and by "him," he meant to say himself, because he'd been left to himself to figure out things as best he could, while they were off somewhere slapping their knees in joy because they didn't have to deal with all this, there was always that nutcase, Markevic, with a *c*, if you please, in other words, yours truly—the carpenter pointed at himself—because they can't even write my name properly, somebody even came up with Markovitz once, with a *t* and a *z*, clearly they all were saying in some little nice bar somewhere: all we have to do is call him, call that Markovic, and he'll take care of everything for us, he's a jack-of-all-trades.

It didn't come off too brilliantly, he said in the Biker Bar, and he was silent for a good long moment so they could all feel just how much he wasn't satisfied with how things had turned out; I'm not—he raised his balding thick head, which of course made his pigtail at the back of it move as well—I'm not satisfied with how things turned out; and again there was a long pause, during which the others just scratched their tattoos, as they had no idea what he was trying to get at here—did we not go over everything, he continued, not even reaching for his beer, which had been slapped down on the counter in front of him a while ago now, and the foam had already begun to sink down, you, for example, J.T., what the fuck did I tell you about when to press on the horn, answer me, because I'll beat your face in, but he didn't even wait for J.T. to say something, even if he did have anything to say, because just as he picked up the pint of beer, he smashed it hard into his face, so that J.T.'s face was immediately covered with blood, and he dropped back like a piece of wood—the one who had just done this, however, only grimaced, and turned back toward the counter, looking at the bartender—what was he waiting for—the bartender already jumped up and was drawing him the next pint—because what we did here, he continued—and nobody dared to make a move to help J.T. or to see how he was, he just lay on the ground like a man who'd had his brains properly knocked out of his head—what we did here has brought shame down on me and on all of you, but also on Uncle Laci, because what can he be thinking now, well, what do you think, isn't it enough that he got everyone their own copy of *Mein Kampf*, and then he worked a miracle with those clunkers of yours in one afternoon and one evening, so what do you imagine Uncle Laci is thinking about us now, because he was there, too, unfortunately he was there, I saw him, standing next to the Police Chief, and he saw, or rather he heard this whole fucked up horn-blowing, or what should I call it, you stop that smirking—he turned around slowly in his seat, and he looked at Totó—don't you start tittering here, my little Totó, and like lightning he was already standing next to him, and he picked up the pint glass that had rolled on the floor next to J.T. and he threw it at him with as much strength as he had thrust it down on J.T.'s face a moment ago, so Totó dropped backward as well, even though he was almost as big and bulky as Little Star, and he didn't even get up, well by then they were all sufficiently convinced that it was necessary to take what they were hearing seriously—as from this point on, he said gravely, there can be no further mistakes, whoever wants to belong to us can no longer make any mistakes, because now it's up to us to wipe out—with blood if we have to, with sweat, if we have to—that shame which we brought upon ourselves at the station; I don't want, he said, and he nodded at the bartender who in the meantime had brought him another pint of beer, I'm not willing for us, in this town—which is sacred for us, because this is our center, this is where we were born, and this is where we want to die, to die for the nation, for the path, for the ideal, and for whoever needs us—I'm not willing to tolerate people laughing at us if they see us in this town, because that's what's going to happen now, he was yelling and everyone trembled, they're going to laugh if they see us, so we have to put things in order here, my brothers, and we must complete the tasks we have undertaken, this town has to be cleaned up, because you all remember what our old slogan used to be: A TIDY YARD, AN ORDERLY HOUSE, and they all began to yell the phrase, because this had been their rallying cry in the old days, and they hadn't forgotten what they had to shout out in reply, namely THERE WILL BE ORDER, well, he said, standing next to the counter, as if everything— thanks to the harmony with which they all yelled out as one person THERE WILL BE ORDER—as if everything were beginning to return to the old routine, and the Leader—because ever since yesterday, they had decided among themselves that they preferred to call him not their boss, but their Leader—he sipped his beer, scratched his beard, and didn't say anything else; they all just stood around for a while with their pint glasses in their hands, then they began to talk a bit, but only softly, because they didn't know if the storm had abated yet, or if it would still rage on, but it had abated, because the Leader said nothing else, he only motioned for Joe Child to come over, he had something to talk over with him, and then he just quietly drank his beer and looked up at the TV in the corner of the room, just then the second season of *The Real World* was on, he just sipped at his beer, but you could tell that he wasn't really interested in the second season of *The Real World,* but rather that he was thinking about something, and it was as if in the meantime something was gnawing at him; his face betrayed nothing, so everything remained unchanged, the men spoke in undertones to those next to them, and the Leader just sipped his beer, taking it in small sips, and up there, mounted on the iron frame, was the second season of *The Real World*. Everyone was waiting for the next command.

He was planning to take a taxi and immediately drive to that address so dear to his heart, and as, while still in Austria, the manservant had been so efficient when he was entrusted with finding the Hungarian postal address for a certain name and barely half an hour later, that address lay before him, placed on a little silver platter on the escritoire, of course he'd thought that no matter the time of his arrival, his first order of business would be to go immediately to that address, because he could go for a walk in the town later on, he could find a hotel later on, everything else could wait 'til later on, the only thing that couldn't wait until later was for him to find her—which not only hadn't come to pass by a long shot, but he ended up being so far away from her, that now, as he lay in this strange, desolate building, in this strange, desolate room, in a horribly uncomfortable though "original" bed beneath the putrid bedclothes, he held in his hand and squeezed, through the thin paper of the envelope, the only remaining photograph he had of her, and he felt like someone whose dream had come true, but who while dreaming had failed to consider that this dream could become a nightmare, for if somebody were to ask him if he hadn't anticipated being received by such a huge crowd, with strangers talking all kinds of mumbo-jumbo, and himself deposited in a horse carriage and brought here to this oppressive, abandoned building and left all on his own, then he would answer that that person still hadn't said enough, because not only hadn't he anticipated such a reception as this, he hadn't anticipated any welcome whatsoever, as he didn't even suspect how anyone could have known when and how he was going to arrive here, how could they have found out? he asked now with his despairing face beneath the stinking pillow, from where? who informed them? and why didn't he at least have enough strength within himself to push aside all these celebratory crowds, to silence the speechmakers, and instead of this circus-like horse carriage, to ask for a regular taxi instead, going instead by his own plans, if he was already obliged to take care of everything himself—because that fellow who had volunteered his services so eagerly on the train, that Dante of Szolnok, was nowhere to be seen—and to pay a visit to that person for whose sake, namely, he had traveled to this place—why hadn't he done that, why had he once again behaved like a genuine idiot; and so he tortured himself like this, he was chilled to the bone, and he just kept squeezing the envelope in his hand, then he took out the photograph, and he looked at it again—who knows how many times he had gazed at this photograph in his long life—because this photograph had always been with him, he never parted from it, it was with him everywhere he went and at all times, no matter what happened, he never left it behind, and during these more than forty years it hadn't gotten bent even once—he turned down the quilt and sat up in the bed, he put the envelope on his knee, and he put the photograph back inside it, he reached for his jacket, but in this moment he heard the sound of steps again, then he heard a few people loudly calling out, and then they were inside his room, suddenly there was an entire troop of people standing in front of his bed, like people who didn't want to believe their eyes, these eyes just stared at him, and only after did one of them ask something—it was that fat little man again—saying, well, Lord Baron? what are you doing here, and how was he supposed to reply to that, was he supposed to say that ominous happenstance had thrown off all of his calculations, and nothing was turning out as he had imagined it, but rather that he had gotten tangled up in some kind of horrific celebration and that people were speaking nonsense to him? was that what he was supposed to say? he gazed at them mutely, because he couldn't speak, because he was considerably dumbfounded, as they had burst into his room as if *they* were taking *him* to task, but then it came to an end, because the little man—perhaps he was some kind of supervisor in this town—who'd been next to him for the entirety of this unhappy day, and whom he had to thank for his lodgings in this deserted building, helped him get his jacket on, and quickly led him out of the room, then in the corridor somebody helped him on with his jacket, his scarf, and his hat—he hadn't even noticed where he'd put them—and with that he was led out of the building, and it was as if the whole thing was starting again from the beginning, because this little man was jumping all around him, asking him if he insisted on a horse carriage, or if an automobile would be sufficient to drive over to the ceremonial dinner, well, then the Baron motioned for this person to stop, to calm down, he pulled him aside, and he informed him that there were many things that he did not understand, or rather that he did not understand what was happening to him here today, but one thing was quite certain, that there could be no question of any kind of ceremonial banquet, he was very exhausted after the long journey, he said, and then he saw that this person just kept leaning in closer to him, maybe because he couldn't hear what he was saying properly, so he repeated it again, saying no, there could be no question of it, he was very honored to be the subject of such attention, but he requested them to please be so considerate as to release him from any further obligations, at which the small man clasped his hands together, and he answered: Your Excellency's words are our command, and the Baron should never consider that they would ever wish to force him to go to any kind of ceremonial banquet against his will, indeed, just between the two of them—this person leaned in closer to the Baron—he had to reveal to him confidentially that the At Home Restaurant, for all of its historical significance, and although excellent in every respect, would be perfectly suitable for a ceremonial banquet, but *they don't cook well,* and then for some reason he began laughing, and with every muscle in his face he was trying to encourage the Baron to start laughing too, but well, the Baron couldn't bring himself to start laughing with this person, it was difficult to muster even a polite smile, because he felt now that really everything, even a conversation like this one, was depleting him, so he requested the little person, if he really wished him well, to take him to the closest hotel, because he desired to rest, that was his one wish, which—this person enthusiastically finished the thought for him—he would fulfill "within minutes," and after that things really occurred as he wished, because this little person motioned for a car, and they took him to a place where amid civilized conditions he was shown into a "suite," and once there he was no longer capable of listening to the hotel manager's speech concerning the renown of his hotel, and how particularly the walls of this suite would be able to "tell such stories," he simply thanked him for his eminently fine service, simply closed the door on the bowing hotel manager and, in the background, the little person who was similarly bowing; he took off his hat, his coat, his suit, shirt, his underclothes, and finally everything, and after a shower he was able to slip into the bed, which was seriously sunken in, but still essentially more comfortable then what he'd been sleeping on before, he lay on his back, he closed his eyes, and immediately fell into a deep sleep.

He knew very well—there was no need to call attention to this fact, he was well aware—a few things that happened shouldn't have happened, well, but still, he announced to the journalists gathered in the hall of the hotel, no one could deny that the welcome at the train station could be termed monumental, all of you write that down, he looked at the journalists, and, if he might make this request, he said, write down that exact word, "monumental," because who would have thought that it'd be possible to bring out such a huge crowd in this day and age, among present conditions, and that was also something that no one could dispute with him—and by this he also meant by his colleagues—namely, *he* was the one who had moved these huge crowds, he was the one who got all these people to come to the station—as well as *to hope*—because he, too, happily acknowledged this, indeed he emphasized it: to hope that things would be different now, and better now than they'd been before, and he kindly requested them, in their news reports, to not cut down the woman's chorus, before whom he could only stand with his hat lowered in respect—but you don't wear a hat, somebody called out, it was impossible to tell who—and so the Mayor continued unperturbed: because they put their heart and soul into it, no one could deny that, nor could anyone deny, for example—as they too were worthy of the same recognition, namely the outstanding speakers, first and foremost the Police Chief and the Headmaster, who both lent to the celebration its own exalted character—feel free to write that down, too, in exactly those words, the Mayor admonished the journalists—and as for the arrival of the train, well, the efforts of the superb boys of the Motorcycle Enthusiasts' Club, ensuring that the Baron would be greeted by a joyful atmosphere right at the beginning, I'm really asking you, he really asked them, please don't mock them any more than is necessary, try to be objective—he looked deeply into the eyes of each individual journalist—and focus on the main point: the fact that he's here, he arrived, it's not just a bunch of hearsay and fabrication or hot air, but it's the truth that Baron Béla Wenckheim has come home, and since that's the crucial thing here, I'm really asking you, inasmuch as you can, so really now—so what if the horn-blowing was a little chaotic, and the folk chorus was a bit unusual, well, and I could go on, but does it matter?—he raised his voice questioningly—or is what counts the fact that they gave it their all, and that the Baron saw that that beloved town where he was born—he wasn't born here, piped up one unruly journalist—okay, fine, then you all write down that the town he loved so much could hardly wait for this hour to arrive, and indeed today that hour finally did arrive, today in the afternoon at 5:40 p.m.—it was ten minutes after six, a voice was heard again from the group—or whenever it was that the local train from Békéscsaba came to a halt, and Baron Béla Wenckheim disembarked from that train, and now he's having a rest, yes, in this hotel, so I truly ask you—he truly asked them—not to disturb his rest, because just imagine his constitution, to the best of our knowledge the Baron is now sixty-four years old and he's been traveling since this morning, well, you can imagine just what a toll a journey like that could take on his body, so what I simply request of all of you, gentlemen, is humanity, the human sympathy, he repeated, to leave him undisturbed until at least tomorrow at noon, and do not trouble him with either questions or with your presence, which means—the Mayor pronounced, somewhat more severely now—that until tomorrow at noon, in the name of this city, I expect to see not a single journalist tramping around here, so then, tomorrow afternoon—you said noon, somebody interrupted—then tomorrow in the afternoon, the Mayor corrected his own statement, we'll see, everything depends on the Baron and what he'd like to do first, if, for example, he'd like to see the ancient castle—which one are you thinking of, somebody spoke out with a bit of an edge in his voice—or perhaps, the Mayor continued unperturbed, we'll drive out with him to the Gyíkos Estate, I don't know, maybe he'd like to see the city, he'll decide, because he decides everything, and please make a note of this: from this point on he will not be restrained by anyone in any way, shape, or form, because—and it's possible that this will sound a little unusual to you, as you're all used to this so-called "democracy"—but be aware that from today onward he is the lord and master here, inasmuch as he is capable, the Mayor lowered his voice, and he wiped his bald head with his palm—it doesn't matter what you think about it all, it doesn't matter what you end up scribbling, because inasmuch as you *don't report the truth*—in other words, what you've just heard right here—then you'll be in plenty of trouble, and your papers as well, because this here (thanks be to high heaven!) is no "democracy" anymore, from now on—and he described wide movements with his hands, which practically embraced the entire surrounding world, then he leaned forward—this is a *dominion* to which, after so many decades (he wiped the sweaty crown of his head once again with the palm of his hand) the lord and master has once again returned.

How did I get in here? well, that's a whole novel, Irén said, I don't want to tire you out with that, because even to find out where you were and then pay—she said to the Baron—because I did pay: the hotel manager, the doorman, I even had to pay two cleaning ladies, because otherwise, believe me, I wouldn't be able to be here, it's like a novel, a bad novel, Lord Baron, please don't be angry and call the staff, I had to meet with you, because it was necessary for someone to say stop! to this ill-fated turn of events, because someone had to come to clear away the obstacles standing in the way of this momentous encounter between the two of you, and if I'd ever met you before, I could certainly say that you know me, and you'd know I'd never do anything like this, only if there were a big problem, and now there is a very big problem, Lord Baron, Marika is sitting at home, not going anywhere, not picking up the phone, and I'm not the type to get scared easily, but I confess I'm scared now, Lord Baron, please hear me out, I'm only asking for one minute of your time and then I'll disappear forever, because even though I have no place in this wondrous fairy tale that concerns you both, I'm asking you, I'm really asking you—but what is this all about, my dear lady, the Baron looked at her from the bed from the midst of all the piled-up pillows, and he didn't dare move from beneath the quilt, he was very ashamed that his two legs were hanging down from beneath the quilt, but he didn't know what to do except to pull them up again very slowly, but the quilt got stubbornly stuck and bunched up, the whole quilt was dragged up with his legs, so that as he pulled up his legs, he tried to quickly manipulate the edge of the quilt with one foot from underneath, while quickly tucking the other leg underneath him so he ended up underneath the quilt in a curled-up position, at least that, he thought, looking up at the ceiling, somewhat relieved, at least he was able to do that, because when he turned his head back toward the lady, it was evident that he would not be able to be free of her for at least a good few minutes—because it isn't right to keep the both of you waiting anymore, the woman continued, everything has conspired against the two of you, I know that, but if we remove the obstacles, if we clear everything away, then nothing can stand in your way, and I—Irén pointed at herself as she stood in the doorway—I'm completely convinced of that, if you will only permit me to get to the heart of the matter, if I may say quite frankly what's going on, because what's going on is that that dear soul, my good friend of more than nineteen years, *was there*, Lord Baron, don't think that she didn't come out to see you, you are her everything, and I know, because I lived these last few weeks with her, I was there when she got your first letter—right then there was a sudden flash of light in the Baron's eyes, and in one moment he comprehended what this lady was talking about, but his heart began pounding so hard from this recognition, although this heart no longer had the strength to order him to act; he certainly wasn't going to jump out of bed in front of this lady, although he would've been happy to, so he listened to her for another minute as she stood in the doorway still talking, but she was talking to him superfluously, it was enough for him to understand that she was talking about Marietta and he became deaf, Saint Pantaleon, help me, take this woman away from me, take her away somehow, but Saint Pantaleon had no effect on this woman—maybe she'd never heard of him and that was why Saint Pantaleon had no effect on her—because she just kept going on and on about Marika this and Marika that, and he was just waiting for her to finally stop, but it didn't seem as if she was going to finish up anytime soon, because she'd been counting on much more resistance, and she had wanted to be certain when she had made her decision this morning, as she hung up the receiver, after it had become clear that her Marika didn't want to talk to her: I'll find out where they've hidden him—she got up, battle-ready, next to the telephone table—because nobody can keep him from me, I'll find him, and she had already put on her coat, and she was already out on the street, and she was already running toward City Hall to leap into battle, a battle which now, she thought, standing here in the doorway, had most likely not yet come to an end, because the Baron just lay there prostrate on the bed, not even moving, and not even giving her any sign that he understood, what should I tell him, how long should I talk to him? she asked herself, when will the old gentleman finally understand what I'm trying to say? she needn't have worried about it though, because there between the pillows, his body tautened, the Baron was gathering up all of his courage, and he finally said, my dear lady, please allow me to get dressed, that was it, that was all he said, and from that Irén understood that he understood, and that she didn't have to go on speechifying, so she just nodded, opened the door, and said, as she left: no doubt the gentleman knew the address, and with that she closed the door behind her, and it was only on the staircase—she ran downstairs—that all the tension that had been building up within her since the celebration yesterday broke out, the tension that had become unbearable because of what happened there between Marika and the Baron, namely, because of what hadn't happened there, in a word, only now, as she ran down the steps of the hotel, did a triumphal yell break out of her, that yes—within her this voice yelled out more and more, ever happier—and she kept repeating it until she got home, saying: he understood, he understood, he understood!

There was some kind of noise from the direction of the door, and she only realized what it was when she came into the foyer, she approached and listened to the soft knocking, it's Irén again, she sighed, and she stood by the door, she put her hands on the key in the lock, but she didn't turn it, well, why couldn't she understand that I can't talk to anyone now, why is she forcing things so much, can't she see that I have no strength for this, that it won't work, I need some time to pull myself together again, and especially—she leaned with her back against the door—how could Irén be of help to me now, I'm not saying that she doesn't mean well, she does, it's just that she means well in such an overbearing way . . . then Marika heard the knocking again, and she answered with some irritation in her voice: I'm not in a position to receive anyone, please understand, but then somebody standing in the hallway answered—most likely a man standing very close to the door—he said: "no . . . it's me," and suddenly she knew who it was, but this was impossible, but it was possible, no, it was impossible, but yes, it flashed through her, and she stepped away from the door as if it were on fire, because suddenly it had become red-hot, but this is absurd, she thought, and she rubbed her face as if that would help her judge the situation more soberly, and then for a while nothing happened, there was no more knocking, but then it wasn't even necessary anymore, because she was *almost* certain, she quickly ran back into the living room, and at first she threw on her dressing gown, she looked into the mirror and just as quickly threw it off, she ran to the closet and began rummaging among the clothes on the hangers, then once again the knocking came, so softly, just as softly as could be, but still she heard it from inside the apartment, and already this wasn't just some random noise, but it was *he*, she was certain, so she slipped into a scarlet-red jumpsuit, looked into the mirror again, but a single glance was enough and she also threw that off, she took out a kind of autumn-brown neat little suit, and with lightning speed she put it on with a pale, lilac-colored blouse, but she didn't put her slippers back on, and she didn't put on her shoes, because after all I'm at home, she thought, and the thoughts fell to pieces in her head, she looked into the mirror, and she thought, that's good, but of course the whole thing was just in fragments inside her, because in that head now there were no more sentences, only words, but even those were no longer intact, and in addition, something just kept jumping around here and there in that head of hers, and her heart had begun pumping so loudly that she was obliged to press down hard with both of her hands onto this heart, and then somehow she just did everything by instinct, at the same time though with the constant sensation that she was taking too long, and taking so long that perhaps he would leave, or maybe—she listened attentively—he had already left, no, she shook her head, he hasn't left, then one last glance in the mirror, and she went out from the living room, but then she glanced back one time, thanks be to God, because she noticed the dressing gown, as well as the other pieces of clothing she'd judged as inappropriate, which she'd flung down on the edge of the armchair and the sofa bed, she ran back and grabbed them up, with one movement tossing the whole pile of clothes into the closet, then she quickly shut the door on them, and then there was just a last, but really just a last glance in the mirror, and then there she was already in the vestibule, and she said in a soft trembling voice: who is it? and the same voice as before answered her, answered slowly, and this slowness was like an eternity, she turned the key in the lock, she pushed down the handle, and without undoing the safety chain, she opened the door just a crack. He stood there outside, his hat in his hands, completely hunched forward so his head would be the same height as hers, and he said: "Good morning, Madame, I'm looking for Marietta."

I can't take it, said the Mayor, I simply can't take it anymore, and then he groaned loudly, because what his wife was doing to him was so good, her hands were like that of a magician, he always said to her, you, my little Erzsike, you're a sorceress, because no one else can do what you can do with your hands, only you, you, you magician, there, yes, he directed her hands as she massaged his back, a little higher up, oh, that's so good, groaned the Mayor, and he turned his head to the other side on the sofa he was lying on, because his head was completely pressed down already to one side, lying on his stomach wasn't a problem with these massages, but what to do with his head, because he started off like anyone else, lying on his stomach on the sofa, and he pressed his face into the fabric, which he could stand for a while, but not forever, his wife, though, launched into these massages as if it would last forever, at least he always hoped that it would, although of course they didn't last forever, but the period of time that he could bear to have his face pushed down into the sofa was shorter than that, so that at first he turned his head to one side, and then to other, but in reality neither side was good, how do the others do it, he asked his wife sometimes, but she didn't understand the question, how could she understand it when she was preoccupied with his fatigued muscles, because she used both of her hands, of course, and this demanded all of her attention, and all the while her husband just groaned, and it was so good to hear that, there wasn't even so much joy in it for her, only that they were together like this, her husband lying on the sofa and moaning, and she sitting on his behind, with her hands she started off at first from the vertebrae above the shoulders, she always said to him that he shouldn't expect her to do the massage like a professional, because she actually had no idea of how professionals do this, she just knew what she knew, she expressed it in her own fashion, and she pressed down on his muscles, she kneaded them, sliding on both sides down to the shoulder joints, and then down to his arms all the way to the elbows, because she only continued on from there *sometimes*, down to the forearms, down to the wrists, and all the way to the knuckles, because usually she only went as far as his elbows and then she jumped back up to the shoulders—and she only knew how to do this in her own impromptu fashion, she always said this to her husband when he began to plead with her to massage him, she would say fine, but I only know how to do it in my own impromptu fashion—and then from the shoulders she started in toward the neck, going along the trapezius muscles, and from there she would work her way upward to the nape of the neck, although, as a matter of fact, she really didn't like this part, she had just gotten used to it from necessity, because she didn't like this part of her husband's body, and of course she never admitted this to him, but in all honesty: she didn't like the nape of his neck, as well as the whole back part of his head, and all the while her husband wanted her to massage this part of his body upward from the neck to the crown of his head, of course, it was possible that it was because of his bald skull that she felt this way, but it would've been better if his whole head were bald, she wouldn't have minded, but like this, with his head bare in front over the crown of his head, but in back, below, from the lower part of his skull down to the neck there was still a little bit of hair, and going down from that it turned into bristles—well, this wasn't her cup of tea, she wouldn't exactly say she hadn't gotten used to it, you can get used to anything in thirty years, but as for loving it, she didn't love it, and now—they were on the sofa again, namely her husband lay on his stomach, and she sat enthroned atop his buttocks, because she had a good reach from here—there was another huge subject of debate between them: in what position should she massage him, usually they ended up in this position, but sometimes her husband wanted her to sit on the chair behind his back, and he, her husband, would sit in front of her on a chair, with his back turned to her, but—she told him frankly—she didn't have good reach in this position, so that usually they used the sofa, just as they were doing now, but then came the point when her husband began to sense that she was tired, and he began to praise more and more just how magical, but just how amazingly magical her hands were, which used to revive her flagging enthusiasm and keep her going for a while, but now he just muttered this praise in vain, in vain did he utter these wheedling words, those two hands of hers were just tired, and she couldn't just replenish them with strength, so she began to press down on him with less force, and she began to just caress his back, and she was caressing it more and more lightly, and finally she thumped him once on the back, and she said well, that's enough for now, I can't do it anymore, don't be mad, I can't do it anymore.

He would have taken the steps two at a time if he could have, but of course he was happy that he could even get out of this building, he wanted to fly, but he was only able to trudge along, he knew this all too well, but he trudged along and in the meantime, he adjusted the scarf on his neck, the hat on his head, and finally he began to button up his coat, but when he got to the front hall of the hotel, he was greeted by a rather surprising sight, as the receptionist behind the counter just happened at that moment to be leafing through *Blikk*, and when he saw the Baron, he jumped up so much that he ended up jamming his shin into one of the sharp corners of the shelves jutting out beneath the counter, bumping his leg into the corner of the shelf so hard that it made him squint from pain, and he didn't know if he should try to bend down in his pain when he wasn't supposed to be hiding but instead be of service to his guest, it's just that the pain in his shin was so sharp that he couldn't bring himself to obey the signal from his brain telling him to stay up, he could only obey his own instinct to dive under the counter so that this tall guest would in no way see his squinting face distorted in pain, well, that ended up creating a rather unusual situation at the receptionist's desk, because to the Baron it looked as if suddenly the receptionist only had a head, which was somehow bobbing up above the counter with a rather unusual countenance, and this lasted a moment until he could request this countenance to please order him a taxi, yes, at once, this face groaned from behind the counter, then the pain began to slowly fade from his shin, and with that he was also able to grab the phone at the top of the counter and pull it toward himself, and then the taxi driver was just dumbfounded, because when was the last time someone had ordered a taxi with a voice like that—a very long time ago, he noted to himself, and he answered into the phone: three minutes, and started up the motor; the Baron, however, was thinking again about that helpful traveling companion of his, wondering where he could be and what could have happened to him, because there could have been some kind of connection between his rather strange disappearance and the trials that had awaited him at the train station, but how could he possibly know what this was, so he accordingly pushed it out of his head, and he thought of it again only when he was compelled to, because the taxi arrived, he told him the address, and they drove off along Peace Boulevard toward the old German Quarter, then as they turned into Jókai Street—and it seemed they would have driven further, alongside the low houses of Scherer Ferenc Street—suddenly just there, where Jókai Street intersected Scherer Ferenc Street, there stood his traveling companion who'd vanished from the train, and the taxi driver—as if this had all been arranged in advance—drove over to the sidewalk and stopped in front of the aforementioned traveling companion—without his even having waved to them, or not even as if he'd seen the Baron in the back seat—they simply stopped, Dante opened the car door next to the passenger seat in front and simply got into in the taxi, and he only said: keep going, and for a while he didn't even utter a sound, as if he were waiting for the Baron to say something first, and the Baron was so surprised by this scene that for a moment he couldn't even bear to speak, but then Dante took control of things—and maybe he'd never even relinquished it, a thought to that effect crossed the Baron's brain – because he turned around, leaning on his elbows on the back of the seat, and smirking at the Baron, he said: well, I really was beginning to think that you were never going to call for a cab.

They sat across from each other, and the confusion in the living room just grew and grew, Marika simply couldn't believe what had happened; all of her attention was directed toward the kitchen so that she could hear when the coffee would be ready, the Baron, for his part, understood less and less why this lady wouldn't answer his queries in a straightforward fashion, as he had immediately begun to tell her, when she had let him through the door and invited him into the living room, what had brought him here: that he'd come from Buenos Aires, and he then confessed to the distinguished gentlelady his heart's desire: to see Marietta as quickly as he possibly could, because—the Baron said in his own subdued voice—his first port of call must be with Marietta; then the two of them just sat there wordlessly, until they heard the gurgling sound of the coffee brewing in the kitchen, Marika gently excused herself, left, and poured the espresso into the porcelain cups, she carried the coffee back in, and she wasn't trembling, although she knew that soon she would be, but for the time being she was still in that state in which a person simultaneously grasps and refutes what has just happened, the lovely coffee fragrance drifted upward, now one of them, now the other sipped their coffee, the Baron was quiet now, then he just cleared his throat, and he tried to puzzle out who this lady could be to Marietta, and no matter from what direction he tried to approach the matter, he kept coming to the same conclusion: most likely she was her mother, or at the very least her great-aunt, anyway, here he sat—the Baron emitted a sigh in the shell chair—and there in front of him sat Marietta's mother, or at the very least her great-aunt; he'd never seen either of them, but this is just how he'd always imagined they would be, with such dear faces, so gentle, so timid, and as he'd never seen them in their own time, he, in his imagination, was able to freely play with their resemblances and behavioral attributes, yes, he thought there is a resemblance there, he wouldn't say that Marietta had completely inherited the traits of this lady, still, though, there were in her face and in her bearing a few minor characteristics that connected them, and in the meantime Marika sipped her coffee with the tiniest possible sips that she could possibly manage, because she was escaping into these tiny sips, as she felt that only these tiny sips could save her, my God, now for the first time her hand—the one that was holding the coffee cup—began to tremble, and it trembled strongly: here, sitting across from her was Béla, that world-famous personage on the front page of every newspaper, he had traveled across the entire world for her, and here he was sitting right across from her, and now the light fixture above their heads was different, and the armchair she was sitting in was different, the entire living room, indeed the entire apartment was no longer what it had been up to that point—Béla, the youthful features of whom she could clearly discern in that aged face, Béla, who had written her those infinitely dear lines from beyond the ocean, that Béla was now sitting across from her, and he was telling her what he felt toward her, because after a while, the Baron really saw no other way out of this confusion—occasioned by the fact that this lady clearly did not wish to talk right now—he saw no other way than to speak to her, in the most sincere way possible, of his most sacred feelings; at first he just said: she must be very surprised that he, the Baron, seemed capable of speaking of such a sensitive and indeed personal affair as the love for a human being, but here somehow—and he cast a glance around the entire living room—he felt at home somehow, for which statement *as a matter of course* he must beg her forgiveness, as it had only been a few minutes since his arrival, and the kind lady had been so, but so gracious, allowing a stranger like this into her home, and now he sat across from her in her salon, because never —my words are true, dear Madame— never, not for a moment, could I ever forget that time, at the age of nineteen years old that I was compelled to leave this city, and this country too, there remained one single point in my life to which I could cling, and that was Marietta—my family traveled, crisscrossing the entire world, until finally we settled in Argentina, but I have never forgotten her face, the contours of her dear face have always been there in front of me, I could evoke them at any time, and there was no day when I didn't evoke them, and in the meantime my family began to die off, or then ended up dispersing to distant locations, I was the only one to remain in Buenos Aires, he said, but there was no day that I didn't see her as she smiled at me, because that was the only thing—and you will certainly laugh at me now, my dear Madame—really, that was the only thing that kept me alive, that smile, because apart from my love for Marietta I had nothing, and I didn't even want to have anything, I wasn't interested in business, I wasn't interested in any kind of erudition, and I especially wasn't interested in art, because that was always what reminded me of her the most, of course I was very careful to make sure that I would never hear the name of Dostoevsky, or Tolstoy, and especially not the name of Turgenev, I read the *Divina Commedia* and I couldn't bear it after the first twenty pages, I read Catullus, and I threw away the book, I picked up a volume of János Vajda, and I wept, and I didn't want to weep, because you know, my dear Madame, weeping is one of the symptoms of my illness, which has obliged me—already as a young man, but particularly starting from the second half of my life—to continually spend time in various institutes and sanatoria, you simply wouldn't believe it—the Baron turned the empty cup around in his hand—but altogether, I have one single picture of Marietta, it's true, that I've kept ever since I fell in love with her, look, here it is, I still have it with me, because I always have it with me, and he reached into the inner pocket of his jacket and pulled out the photograph from an envelope, he handed it to her saying, please have a look, Madame, and see how beautiful she is, and Marika bowed her head and she looked at the photograph, she looked and she looked, then she couldn't bear to look anymore, and she ran into the kitchen, and she only had the strength to call back, my dear God, I forgot the sugar, forgive me, then she leaned against the sideboard, and she tried to control her tumultuous feelings, and really, she couldn't tell if the Baron had lost hold of his senses, because she'd heard so much about him already, she'd heard this, that, and the other about his illness, but to really believe that he didn't recognize her—well, she simply couldn't believe it, but still, was it true?—and she clutched even more strongly at the sideboard, was it possible that something had really happened with the Baron's mind?! because it just wasn't possible for him to come here, to sit down in front of her, look at her, and not remember who she was, that simply wasn't possible, she pushed herself away from the sideboard, and went back into the living room, oh, she said, and struck her own forehead, I forgot the sugar again, then she went back into the kitchen, she opened the upper-cabinet door of the sideboard, took out the sugar bowl, and went back into the living room, she sat down on the sofa bed, but the Baron didn't reach for the sugar bowl when she extended it to him, he didn't reach for it because he was looking at her, and this made Marika start trembling again, and really now she couldn't resist, she couldn't stop herself from trembling, she leaned back in the sofa bed and her entire body was seized by trembling, the Baron continued to look at her uninterruptedly, and he looked at her so intensely, that Marika simply couldn't stand him looking at her, she slowly bowed her head and silently began to cry, but the Baron just kept looking at her with that horrified gaze, he just looked and looked, and there they sat across from each other, long minutes went by, and neither of them spoke—there was nothing to say—when the Baron slowly put the coffee cup down on the cocktail table in front of him, then he got up, he picked up the photograph from the sofa bed, and like a sleepwalker, went into the foyer, opened the door and stepped out of the apartment into the corridor.

The world of slot machines—Dante turned around to the back from the front seat—is one of the most colorful that could ever be imagined, the Lord Baron should picture before himself a kind of mesh, the cords of which extend everywhere, these are tiny, minuscule threads, if you like I can even refer to them as gossamer threads, and everything, but everything can be ensnared with these tiny threads, so that people—and I'm referring here to the broadest possible spectrum of humanity—accordingly the individual human being can, at any time, in any place, for any specific duration, in any form, and for any small or large amount of winnings, engage in this diversionary activity, do you see my point, Lord Baron—he turned around again from the front seat, but the Baron was in a ghastly state, so that Dante turned around again, and while he looked at the road, he felt the need to continue: because you can take many things away from people, he said, and many things have been taken away from them, but their dignity is something you can never take away, and one of the basic components of human dignity is for a person to feel free at times—and freedom is exactly what I offer them, that freedom is offered by anyone who facilitates involvement in the world of slot and gaming machines, because gaming is the natural configuration of freedom, if I may put it like that, and that's why a few years ago I decided to create my own empire of slot machines, so that anyone who wishes to can feel at home there, but you know—and I already mentioned this to you on the train—my own free capacity extends far beyond that, because the situation with my empire of slot machines is somehow similar to that of Our Lord in Heaven, because He set about creating His own world, am I right, then He set the whole thing in motion, and that was good—this functions by itself, He said, when He looked at all the things He'd created, and yet He still had all this free capacity—that's just how things are with me somehow, because the first thing was to create and set in motion my slot-machine empire, now it's enough to just have a look now and then to say well, things are coming along, and they're coming along well, although I have to say . . . and with this I would turn to the fully justified query of the Baron, a query which hasn't been posed yet, but I know it will be, because I know the Lord Baron is expecting an explanation as to why at the train station suddenly I had to deal with an urgent matter, regrettably preventing me from taking part in the great celebration, although I know all about it, he reassured the Baron from the front seat, I heard all about the speeches, from the outstanding to the adequate, I also know that they surprised you with a humorous cultural program, well, I hope you had a good time, but really I sincerely hope so, because I—

who have been active in so many different fields—have, among other things, a thorough overview of the complexity of these organizational matters, and I know just what a complicated task it is, Lord Baron, to bring together such a welcome reception of such volume, so that if possible, I would truly tip my hat to them—but even so I can tip my ushanka—but it emerged that unfortunately, just at that moment, I was obliged to see to some urgent matters, because, I confess, even my little empire is at times battered by certain storms, and this is exactly what happened, I got a text message while still on the train, but in no way did I wish to disturb you with any of this, I wished in no way to ruin the sacred moments of your welcome by boring you with my own petty concerns, which you, on that exalted spiritual level where you reside, could not perceive in any other way than with justified boredom; this is understandable, and in particular I judged (because as your secretary, it was my obligation to consider this as thoroughly as possible) that you were in the best of hands, so I ran around here and I ran around there, I took care of whatever I could, I must, however, also confess to you that I do have enemies—and again he turned around so as to look the Baron straight in the eyes, but he looked into those eyes in vain, because there was no depth in the Baron's eyes to look into, so he turned around again—and once again surveying the scene in front of him, he continued: yes, enemies, because such is my calling: on the one hand there's my one-hundred-percent commitment to the enjoyment of the ordinary man, and on the other, there are the adversaries, the rivals, the self-appointed experts, the turncoats—about which of course you don't have to know anything, but of course if you wished to, I could reveal it all to you in the greatest detail, for the time being though, let it be enough for me to say that in these towns and villages of this region known as the "Stormland," there are a few such people whom I wouldn't exactly designate as my well-wishers, to put it delicately, and thanks to them I can't always be present where I might wish to—and that's what happened yesterday, as well as this morning—thanks to them I must remain incognito, and if you will forgive this minor flaw on the part of your new secretary—because, Lord Baron, this is but a minor flaw—for the time being I'm incognito and so I must remain, but all the while I can assure you that I'm behind you always and in everything, you will always feel my presence, even if in the immediate physical sense I won't be there directly right next to you—watch it already, he said to the driver, don't drive so dangerously, we're going to break our necks because of you, and he could well say this, because the taxi driver was slapping his palm against the steering wheel in a silent laughter that had been making his shoulders shake for a while, but it also broke out from him, and he just kept slapping the steering wheel, as the taxi swerved from side to side in the not too dense traffic, because he was incapable of regaining his self-control, so much was he shaken by this silent laughter, because—he shook his head, like someone who just couldn't believe it—he'd never in his life heard so much hot air, well this ... the driver gasped for breath, and he ha-ha'd and hee-hee'd, for someone to be so full of air ... he gasped for breath and leaned forward in the driver's seat, there's no such thing, what a swindler you are, Contra, but not even that, he looked at him, panting now, so he could laugh himself out properly, you are directly the king of grifters, I've known you already—like bad money— for twenty years, but sometimes I have to ask myself, how the hell did you end up here, you king? Then he added—but he intended his words for both of them—that it would be good if somebody would tell him where they were supposed to go, because they couldn't drive around in circles the entire day, and I don't know if you noticed, he asked Dante, but we've already been driving around and around in circles for almost an hour now, and you just keep gesturing for me to keep going on and on, which is fine, but now I'd like to know, my friend, what is the goal of this journey, where do you want to go?

They say that we're orphans, but an orphan can also be someone who wasn't even abandoned, in our case nobody cared about us to begin with, somehow we got booted out, and that's that, we've got no mom, we've got no dad, just this thing called the Orphanage, so no one gives a shit, said one of the two, who had just one strip of hair on his head, the other one was shaved completely bald, on the necks of both of them, however, there bloomed the tip of a dragon's tail, as both of them were big Yakuza fans, and the rest of the dragon was there properly on their backs—because ever since I can remember, it's only Yakuza, now one repeated it, now the other, as they sat in the back courtyard of the kindergarten next to the Castle, because they didn't want to stay inside in the designated room, you can rot away in there, they said to their caretakers, who couldn't care less anyway, ever since the orphans had been suddenly piled onto trucks and moved out to the Castle kindergarten, into this building that had been padlocked shut for years, and which was even more dilapidated than the Orphanage—*clearly they're running out of children,* said one of them in an exaggerated drawl, and he jumped down, motioning for the other to follow him, and have a round of boxing—in a flash they were gone—*where did they go, the children are screwed,* they took swings at each other from a regular fighting stance, *are the mothers running out of children?* asked one sarcastically, and he swung from the left, the other ducked to one side, and sent a blow to the other's stomach, well, so we're in nursery school again, no? he asked, and he took up a defensive pose, he jumped back and forth on the concrete slab which kept tipping back and forth, the main thing is that we're not orphans but bandits, fuck it, fine, answered the other, then he raised both of his hands, signaling: enough, and once again they chased away the Idiot Child, who as always, if he saw them, came over to box with them, but he didn't know how to speak, he just stammered, which was kind of fun if nothing else was going on, but not now, so they chased him away before he could even make his way over to them, and they trudged back to the concrete slabs on the perimeter, and for a while the two of them just kept nodding their heads and clearing their noses as if there were music playing somewhere, and as if they were moving their heads in rhythm with the bass drum, but there was no music, only the memories, of the "happy hardcore" tracks, which from time to time they could play on the Institute's intercom system, because for them there was only Hixxy, noooo, only Gammer, well, fine, they agreed on that, but the best was Scotty Brown, they said now, like a kind of ritual anthem, which, in a way, this was to them, sometimes they just pronounced the names, and their legs kept the beat, as they did now too, namely if they were sitting down they kept swinging their legs; now, there was nothing to do, because there was no cash, there wasn't anything that could solve their problem, so both of them were a little nervous, and they just hung their legs down and shook them, sometimes the one, then the other one would jump down onto the concrete slabs and begin to run, without a ball, across the courtyard, covered with the concrete slabs, toward a imaginary basketball hoop, then they ran back, silently, without a ball, just like that to stir things up a bit, they dribbled the invisible ball, and that's how it went until the evening, when, if they didn't want any commotion or trouble, they had to return to their comrades, as they called the ones who were much younger than they, because they were the "Chiefs of Staff," apart from them there was no one—among the others, not a single one—who had reached his thirteenth year, whereas they had, both of them, and so they got back just in time, because dinner was being dispensed, and they dashed over to a table just in time to avoid getting docked, they knew that it was worthwhile this time: there was sure to be some serious grub tonight because of all the upheaval, although they normally couldn't care less, least of all about where they were being taken, because it was only a couple of days now and they'd be out of here, they said to each other almost every evening after compulsory lights out, and after one of the cow-brained attendants screamed at them again, finally something like real life could begin in the dark: either playing cards, wanking, their phones or music with some dope, and there was Scotty Brown or DJ Dougal (it didn't matter what it was, as long as it was happy hardcore, because that's what was cool here), and of course the dope, of course, although in all the chaos there wasn't even a gram; so that evening they were just shooting the breeze, as they turned off the lights, and they talked and talked, at least the two of them, about when they would clear out, because they would, and both of their faces grew serious in the dark, that was for sure, like Yakuza death.

He'd picked out the Police Chief immediately in the crowd, that's why he'd gone over to the train door and looked out, there was no doubt that it was him, and in addition this enormous crowd, he had no idea who else would recognize him, but he took it for certain that there'd be at least a few who would know him well, not to mention the Police Chief himself, that traitor, as he was inclined to refer to him when among certain companions, because for a while, in the beginning, "the cooperation"—as they called it among themselves—had gone so well, a phrase to which he, Dante, always added the words, if the atmosphere was a little more relaxed, "mutually beneficial," but where had that time gone; he looked out through the glass of the train-door window, all the while working out a solution to a very complex task; now that he had hit the jackpot, he couldn't let it go just like that, so he simultaneously had to be here, and not here, a dilemma which nonetheless became relatively simplified; thus, while waiting for the Baron to disembark from the train (which took him forever), Dante opened the door on the other side of the train and jumped onto the tracks, he pulled down his ushanka onto his skein-like head, and he ran just as much as he could, which meant that he hobbled alongside the tracks hidden by the train, and finally he was able, although it wasn't easy, to get away from the station, because well, he wasn't too much of a runner, because apart from his short legs and rather indolent nature—as one of his temporary girlfriends always said to him—he'd also put on a lot of weight recently: you, Contra, she said to him giggling, pretty soon you're going to be rolling along if you don't do something about this, at which point he would always make a so-called immediate vow no, it really couldn't go on like this, he really had to lose some weight, but he didn't, he just grew more stout, and this—at a time like this when he had to run—did not make things any easier for him, there was, however, no other escape from the trap he'd found himself in, he couldn't let the Police Chief and his cronies see him, they mustn't know that he was back here in town again, but where the hell was he supposed to go, he reflected, while he turned off from the tracks going to Sarkad onto Csókos Road, then he chose the middling-safe decision, namely the only one, and turned into No. 47, where he ordered a St. Hubertus herbal liquor with a pint of beer, he turned his back to the bartender, and he stared at the dirty window, from which nothing could be seen, because in the meantime it had grown completely dark, he stared at the filthy windowpane and he tried to think about where to spend the night, as he certainly couldn't go to the usual place, his mind ran through all of his people, but he couldn't really trust any of them, so he tried to go over to the counter and pay his bill while hiding his face, he resigned himself once again, and acknowledging the truth to himself, which wasn't even particularly difficult, within a matter of minutes there he was at the head of Nagyváradi Road, clattering on the door until someone finally opened up, and there was Jennifer, with her own ponderous contours, but so sleepy, he could hardly breathe any life into her, so that finally he rolled down on top of her, and they slept next to each other, embracing each other like an old married couple.

He's a real big shot ever since he became the Baron's secretary, said the taxi driver in the taxi drivers' warming stand, how he told him in his haughty way to keep driving, and mainly don't ask any questions, but that didn't change anything, he said, he's just as much of a crook as always, just a little more nervous—he grimaced at the others—of course, when they took away all his slot machines, he didn't even know where to go look for them, or even if he should bother looking for them or not, so we just kept driving around in circles; and the Baron—if he really is a baron, I didn't particularly see him as being one, because apart from his clothing, I could imagine him as being anything else but our Baron—he was like someone who'd just been clobbered on the head, he just sat there with this idiotic expression on his face, not even blinking, and his face was so white, as if it had been smeared with whitewash, he didn't even say a single word, seriously now, not even one blessed word, just at the end when it occurred to me: maybe this sleazy Contra drugged him with something just to make him sit there so quietly, he would do anything so as to be able to think in peace and quiet, because you could see that Contra was really racking his brains underneath that bushy head of his, and well, he had something to rack his brains over, because in my opinion he was a real idiot to come back here—because of that Police Chief, he's not going to last even two seconds, I'm telling you, not even two seconds, because in just one second they're going to nab him and they're going to throw him into the slammer, and then we won't see our Contra again for a good five years, because it's not possible, everyone knows that the Police Chief has a mind of his own and you can't con him with those cheap little tricks that Contra tried, how he tried to steal half, or who even knows how much, of that money, well, he's an idiot, the taxi driver spread apart his hands, then he got up, went over to the teakettle, and poured himself a cup, how could he even imagine, that he, Contra, could come over here from those Romanian bloodsucker friends of his and try to pull a con job on the Police Captain, I just don't get it, but I think that he got a little too arrogant, and that's why he thought he could get away with it, but he shouldn't have, because the Police Chief eats little swindlers like that for breakfast, because just look what happens to us now if we don't fork over to him on the fifth of every month, am I right, is that the case? yes, that's right, then we can just put away the keys, put the car back in the garage, because it'll be game over for us; and this turkey comes here and wants to be pushy, when he knows very well that everything and everyone here is in the Police Chief's hands—and what? the bars, the gas pumps, the border checkpoints, the roads, the electrical utilities, the Milk Powder Factory, the Slaughterhouse, do I have to continue, he asked, and he sipped his steaming tea, because I won't even mention something like the entire City Hall, because he makes them shit their pants in fear just like squirrels—he grimaced at the others again, who just sat there with the infinite patience of taxi drivers, they just listened to him and nodded their heads, but not because what he was expounding on was so interesting for them, but rather from gratitude that somebody was talking about anything at all, because although they weren't in the mood to listen to him, still, time passed more quickly if somebody was talking about something, it didn't matter what, just keep on talking, they looked at the others, sinking down further into their chairs, just keep on talking, Alika, don't stop, time goes by faster when you're talking.

I know a good place in the Krinolin district — he turned around to the Baron—they make such a good pork stew there that you'll be licking all ten of your fingers, because he knew— and he tried somehow to direct the Baron's dead gaze to his own self—he knew what somebody who came home was wishing for, and you, Lord Baron, have come home, isn't that so, and at times like that what's the most important thing, well it's the tastes of home, am I right, he asked, fidgeting back and forth in the seat, but the Baron couldn't be awakened, the Baron, ever since he had staggered back into the taxi, just sat in the back seat like someone who was unconscious, namely, every sign of life had drained from his bloodless face, his eyes were open, but you could see that they weren't looking at anything, and Dante saw that too and tried to bring him back to life—because those fragrances of home, as someone senses them for the first time, in a nice little eatery, he said to the Baron, and he clicked his tongue, well, these are still the most important things, am I not right, because we can put it like this and we can put it like that, but when a person crosses that border, things get simplified, and it turns out that the base of a great love for one's homeland coincides perfectly with that of a good stew, and I—he pointed with his two hands at himself, grabbing at his own jacket, beginning to tug at it—I've wept over a genuine chicken stew, Lord Baron, because I know what a person feels at times like that, the tastes of home, it's something that can't be paid for with money—although of course, as far as that goes, you'll have to pay something later on, indeed, it wouldn't hurt if you would hand me a sum right now, so as not to have to sully your own hands with these matters—and this was the point where Dante held a brief pause, not bothering with the taxi driver, who began to smother his hiccups again, so much was he enjoying the performance; this was the point where Dante was "testing the waters," to use one of his well-known technical terms—just like an experienced fisherman on the banks of the River Körös, who tosses a bit of bread into the water before casting his line, to see if anything is biting—but the Baron showed no interest in this topic, so that Dante decided he should leave it for later for when they got out of the taxi, and he spoke to the taxi driver, saying, so it's clear, right, Alika? you know where we're going, don't you? and there was something in his voice that made the taxi driver stop laughing, and they turned off at Saint László Street, because just then they were coming back from the Castle along the main road, they drove up until the bridge, then out toward Semmelweis Road, then to the left, then straight along King Mátyás Street toward the Krinolin district, because he knew this Contra well already, and he knew his clowning around was a way to waste time, even though he pretended he was just the world's most innocent entertainment artist, with Contra you had to be careful when his voice sounded like this, and the taxi driver really perceived this well, because at exactly that moment, Dante pulled out his phone and vehemently began to tap out a series of text messages, for a while nobody in the car spoke, there was only the sound of the phone bleeping, as Dante tapped out one message after the other with lightning speed and waited until the telephone buzzed, an answer had come, then there was the tapping sound again, then a pause, then the tapping, and it was really at this point that Dante had understood that he couldn't go on like this, he had looked the matter straight in the face, and he volunteered the information that he was ready to meet up at any time, because he recognized—he wrote—that he'd made a mistake, but mistakes were only there so they could be corrected, and that's why he had come back, that's why he had *dared* to come back here again, so he could set things right, and he asked for a chance for this to occur, because right now—he tapped out another text with his own lightning-quick technique—the Baron was with him, and the Baron desired a good pork stew, he, as the Baron's secretary, could do nothing else than take him to the very best place where this desire of the Baron's could be fulfilled, then he waited a bit, then the telephone buzzed, signaling the arrival of another text, then Dante slammed the cover of the phone shut, leaned back in satisfaction, and for a while said nothing, the taxi driver didn't feel like talking too much either, so that a silent vehicle arrived at 23 Sinka István Street, where, when the three of them got out of the car, they could already sense the enticing aromas, and they headed toward the door of the restaurant.

But Police Chief—the Mayor raised his eyebrows—for hours now the entire city has been looking for him, and now you're saying that your latest information about the Baron is that he left the At Home

Hotel in a vehicle early this morning?—well, this is madness, if you'll forgive me, but in this city he was the Mayor, and he was the one who should have been notified immediately, because how could the Police Chief have thought—with the chaos that this sudden disappearance had caused, the worry that it created for everyone, but especially him, the Mayor, who felt a special responsibility toward their guest—that the Baron could just—poof!— wander off without any outside help; where has he gone, he asked his colleagues one after the other, but no one had any idea—and then the Police Chief told him just like that, in a such an offhand way, that *he* knew where to look for him, was that not approaching the very border of insolence already?—no, the Police Chief answered, leaning back in his chair as he placed the office telephone against his other ear—and his voice was something like a blade: maybe you're Mayor around here, baldy, but I'm the Police Chief, whatever information you get is because *I decided you should get it*, is that clear, because I'm the one who decided you should get this job, and you'll only be there for as long as I want you to be, but this isn't the first time that I'm telling you to you start acting with a little respect, Mr. Mayor, because it's no skin off my back and you'll be out on your butt before you can blink, got it, Tibike? and cutting off all possible further comment, he said—although talking into the receiver—you'll get that Baron of yours back right away, no need to shit your pants, and lay off with the hot air already, and he slammed down the phone, and on the other phone he spoke to the record office, telling them to send the cadet to his office immediately.

Unfortunately, they were here just two days ago, they grabbed the two machines in the corner and took them away, without a word, the restaurant owner said sorrowfully, he was infinitely sorry, but he had no machines which could be at the Baron's disposal right now, he knew—he lowered his head guiltily, as he had read about it, he'd heard everything—how much the Baron liked to play the slot machines, but to his greatest regret he could not be of service in that respect today, they were such simple machines, however, jingling and twinkling, and his voice nearly became lachrymose as he kept twisting a checkered dish towel around in his hands, who were those machines hurting, why did they have to be torn away from their natural environment—because just imagine them here, Lord Baron, said the restaurant owner in this weepy, trembling voice, just picture it, there used to be a Fanki Manki and an Ultra-Hot Deluxe, you know, he looked over at Dante, who hadn't as much as glanced over at him, as he was immersed in studying the grease-covered menu, they were over here in the corner like two potted trees or two bouquets of flowers, this was their natural environment, if it could be expressed that way—don't express anything, Dante said softly to him, then he asked: how fresh are the gnocchi for the pork stew? well, we'll make a new batch, came the ready reply, fine, so that will be three servings of pork stew, and bring some homemade pickled vegetables, not from a jar, you see who's here, yes, yes, the restaurant owner stuttered with a brightened face, I see him, I really do, I just don't want to believe it, well, fine then, Dante cut the conversation short, handed him the three menus, then he leaned a little closer to the Baron, who was still sitting just as he'd been sitting in the car, only in a different location now, it didn't matter to him, he took no notice of any of them; he's just as unconscious as before, Dante established, and he warned the taxi driver—but only with his eyes—not to try any antics, jokes, or fooling around here, because the driver wasn't sitting there next to them to fulfill any specific role, but only so that there would be some kind of company, and Dante simply couldn't decide how to get the Baron out of this catatonic state, he wasn't interested in what had brought this on or what had taken place in that apartment, he only wanted to know how he could get back the Baron, that Baron who, on the train coming here, had agreed to take him on as his secretary, to get him back and to talk certain essential matters with him, for example, account management and other administrative affairs, tasks which—it went without saying—he would be more than happy to take off the Baron's shoulders before anybody else turned up here looking for him, and while he still had some time for that, because in his last text message he had given them the farthest possible address from both the center and from this place as well, but how much time did he have left, he brooded, at least a quarter of an hour, or, if they were really clueless, at least a half hour; he looked into the Baron's eyes, but he still didn't see anything there which he could have used as a starting point, three Diet Cokes were brought to the table in champagne glasses, and suddenly he was just out of ideas as to how to get the Baron out of that state, then he began to say that the restaurant owner of course had nooo idea what kind of slot machines were here, because these as well had formed a part of his own little empire, he said now to the Baron that in fact there had been two of them, two slot machines exactly right for this neighborhood, because this neighborhood was up-and-coming, he knew this from certain sources, well, so there had been two pieces, two amusement machines that he'd set up here years ago which perfectly suited the needs of the residents of this neighborhood that was coming up in the world, and on one of them—Dante looked deeply into the lifeless eyes of the Baron—you could play poker; he was completely certain by mentioning poker that he wasn't necessarily proceeding in the right direction, so he was genuinely surprised when there was a sudden spark of life in the Baron's eyes, and the Baron spoke, saying that what had occurred is that sometimes in the Casino they wouldn't let him sit at the gaming tables anymore, and he could only play the slot machines, but he couldn't care less about the tables or the machines, he said in a colorless voice, so softly, that both of them, Dante and the taxi driver, kept leaning more and more toward him so they could hear what he was saying—because at that time he had just started going over there because the place bore the name of Casino, but they never let him just sit there to drink a coffee or a maté, they told him that he had to gamble, and so he gambled, and he wouldn't say that it wasn't enjoyable at times, because he liked the rules, and it was a good feeling to adhere to those rules, but whenever he wanted to stop, they wouldn't let him, and so he always had to play, well of course he lost money, but he wasn't interested in that, for him the most important thing was that they let him in, as the name of that building was the Casino, on the Avenida Elvira Rawson de Dellepiane, and that's how it went on for years, no, of course, not years, he was speaking of decades—he picked up the champagne glass, and sipped some of the Diet Coke, and probably only now did he realize how thirsty he was, because he quickly drank up the entire glass—bravo, cried out Dante, and he poured out the rest of the Diet Coke, he silently motioned to the restaurant owner, who had never taken his eyes off them, to quickly bring another, and the Baron gently nodded at the restaurant owner when he arrived with another bottle of Diet Coke and poured it into the champagne glass, and the Baron drank that in one go as well, so they brought yet another one, and he said that he didn't want anything else now, only the Casino, which, for him, was deeply connected with such fateful events, and he always hoped, at the end of his life, that fate would grant him the possibility to step through the doors of the Casino yet once again, he would like—he said, waiting for the pork stew in the restaurant at 23 Sinka István Street—to go out onto the terrace which overlooked the River Körös, and he would like, if possible, to remain there for a half hour by himself, and that was all, he looked at Dante, whose face had suddenly cleared up, because as for understanding, he really didn't have a clue as to what the hell the Baron was talking about, but he knew that he was on the best possible track right now, because they were in that territory where he was at home—machines, poker, casinos—something will come of this, it flashed through him, the light shone in his eyes, and he said to the Baron that this was possible, indeed, if he insisted on it, he could drive him over there right after lunch, and he pinched the taxi driver's leg underneath the tablecloth, and asked him with his eyes only where the hell was there a place here called the Casino, I have no goddamned idea, the taxi driver also wordlessly conveyed to him, there's nothing like that here, he shook his head, but Dante just kept pinching and pinching him, until finally the taxi driver said, now speaking out loud, that whenever he encountered problems like this, he always called the dispatcher—and he looked at the Baron as if he were seeking his assent—the dispatcher was a very quick-witted woman—so they should call her, but he couldn't say any more, because Dante kicked him under the table—but, come to think of it, he did have some idea about where this Casino could be . . . but well, the Baron looked at him, although he had no idea who was sitting there next to him, he said: there's no need to go looking for the Casino, it's right there by the bridge, you know by the large bridge, ah, yes, Dante began to nod energetically, well, of course it's there, and he once again kicked the taxi driver to make sure he wouldn't say anything, because if the Baron said it was there, then it was, no point in debating this, and now the only problem was how to get over there before the Police Chief's men or whoever else had been mobilized swooped down on them, therefore he recommended that inasmuch as no one seemed to be very hungry—he, for example always had lunch at about two o'clock—this pork stew could wait—he looked at the Baron, who didn't know what the young man was speaking about, nor did he have any idea where were they now, but hearing that he could once again sit in the car and that he would be taken to the Casino rendered any other information superfluous, as in fact he wasn't interested in anything else, only the Casino, which—as it emerged in a quarter of an hour—was none other than a Chinese-owned Billiard Salon located by the large bridge on the embankment of the River Körös, the taxi driver just grumbled, why couldn't he have called the dispatcher, because she would have known in less than a second where the real Casino was, but he didn't force the issue because of Dante, he just muttered behind the wheel, and by now he was only interested in when he would be able to settle the bill, because the only thing he'd been able to make out from this whole story was that he was on pretty shaky territory with these two sitting in his car, well, now, too, had they paid him yet? no, they hadn't, they just drove to this Chinese-owned Billiard Salon, and who knew when this would be over, he just counted up, in his head, how many kilometers they had traveled since that morning, then he began to multiply back and forth, vehicle depreciation, the gas, the taxes, so-called administrative costs, then the fees, and finally he came up with a sum which surprised even him a bit.

She only let me in that evening, I tried three times, though, I was there at ten o'clock, and there were no sounds at all coming out of there, I was there after two o'clock, also nothing, then I tried again at about five o'clock, but it was only in the evening, when I not only rang the doorbell but began to pound on the door as well, at last I heard the chain being unlatched, the key slowly turning in the lock, well, but she looked like she'd aged ten years, she was so broken down that for a second I was so in shock that I couldn't even speak, I stood in the doorway and she didn't say anything either, she just went back into the living room, so that when I went in after her and sat down next to her on the sofa bed, I really wasn't too surprised that when I reached out my hand for hers, she pushed it away—I wasn't upset, because I didn't know was going on, I could only tell that some kind of dreadful thing had happened, and so for a while we just sat next to each other, and I started talking about something, but I didn't dare to talk about *that*, or about what had happened, I didn't even know what I started talking about, I just kept on talking and talking so there would be no silence, and I was seriously afraid; I'm not, as you know very well, the type to get easily scared, but if you could see this wretched woman, well, I'm not going to go into the details—she was relating what happened to her children, with whom she had dropped in quickly before heading home, because she felt she had to discuss what had happened, and she started with this; she had sat down at the kitchen table, she was on the best terms with her daughter-in-law, Zsuzsánka, but her son was home too, indeed even the older grandchild wanted to be there and hear the great story that had made grandma drop in at such an unusual time, it was almost late evening already, but the grown-ups didn't let her, and Zsuzsánka led the grandchild back to her own room and gave her permission to read for another half hour but then lights out, she would come and check, and she tucked the child into bed, came back into the kitchen, and sat down next to her mother-in-law—she always said to her acquaintances at the Slaughterhouse that everyone would love to have a mother-in-law like that, because Irén was the world's best mother-in-law, she was everything you could ever want both in heart and mind, so she and her husband sat down together and they listened to what had happened with Marika, the only problem was that they didn't understand, because Irén herself hardly understood, and it was impossible to figure out, as only one thing was clear: the Baron had been at her place, but then what could have happened—the daughter-in-law clapped her hands together in the office of the Slaughterhouse—a tragedy, that much was certain, because that woman, that Marika, her mother-in-law had said, was neither living nor dead, simply, Irén said to the children, she couldn't imagine what had happened to crush that poor woman so, but so much, she didn't dare ask anything, because as the two of them sat there, and she just kept on babbling about whatever came into her mind, that Marika was like someone who had suddenly lost twenty pounds, her face had fallen in, her eyes were weepy, and Irén's heart was aching so, but so much for her, there was nothing she could do, and she couldn't even find out what had happened between them; because when she had arranged for all the obstacles and misunderstandings to be cleared away—she told the children how she herself had broken into the At Home Hotel where the Baron was being lodged, how she'd literally routed him out of his bed, and things didn't seem at all like they were going to turn out badly, and certainly not at all as if there was going to be so much sorrow from this at the end, on the contrary, she was convinced that the great meeting, which her dear Marika had been waiting for for so long, was finally going to happen, and it seemed the Baron was waiting for this too—but I'll tell you something (she leaned in closer to her son and daughter-in-law at the kitchen table)—there's something not quite right about this Baron, she didn't want to talk of the devil to make it appear, but she had a bad feeling in connection with this Baron already when that whole circus was going on at the train station, because she wouldn't say that he didn't look like a baron, no, that's exactly how you would imagine a baron to look like, but there was something about him—maybe the other barons were quite all right—because he just wasn't all there, she could only keep repeating that she had this feeling, but even just with this feeling—she shook her head—to think that there would be such a huge drama from the great meeting, well, she never would have imagined that in her wildest dreams—well, she wasn't going to meddle, no, she wasn't going to beat the Baron out of here with a broom handle, but whoever could cause her Marika so much pain, she said, is a bad person: I'm telling you, she told the children, this whole thing isn't clear to me, there's something going on here that's being kept secret from people, but especially from Marika, who obviously collapsed when she found this out—how could she not have collapsed—because this person was everything to her, she'd thought of him so many times, she had imagined what and how he would be like, and then at the end for it to be so horrific, and if only I could know why, why it had to end like this, because what in the world has happened? what am I supposed to say to her now, what?!

I have everything, an old Chinese merchant said to them in the Billiard Salon as they stepped in, although when he had first come out to see who was there, he'd vehemently gestured that he wasn't open yet, not open, he said, but Dante said to him, no, you're open, and he asked where the terrace was; oh, said the old Chinese man, and he swayed his head back and forth, no terrace, nothing—but you have a terrace, Dante answered him, at which point the expression on the Baron's face became completely reassured, and life began to return to his face, he just kept repeating yes, this is it, this is the Casino, and he went forward—inasmuch as it was possible among the chaotic columns of piled-up clothing—young man, he called back to Dante, who immediately ran over to him, just imagine, a piano stood here, for the most part playing bar music, but sometimes the Lélu Orchestra played here as well, at that time they were the big fashion, as we say in modern Hungarian, at which point the old Chinese man looked terrified and ran after them: I'll clean up, still not open, not open, I'll clean up, so that they had to reassure him and explain to him that they weren't from the tax office, nor were they policemen, they weren't there in any official function at all, but on a private matter, which the Chinese man didn't understand at all, then Dante motioned him over to himself and he pressed a thousand-forint note into his hand, and he said to him confidentially that this was a family affair, at which the merchant's face lit up, and he said: family, that's good, and the money disappeared as if it had never even been there, he ran forward, overtaking the Baron as well, and at the end of the room, on the right-hand side, he began to energetically pack up a column of jeans, which cleared the way for a door, and the old Chinese man now laughed, he smiled at the Baron, who just nodded, and he invited him over: terrace, good, little, but good, he opened the door, and it really opened up onto a terrace, Dante realized with some surprise, because he'd believed almost nothing from the Baron's earlier tales, but now that there was really a terrace here, he began to think that maybe some of what he was saying was true, and this really was that Casino of which the Baron had spoken, although at first neither he nor the Baron stepped out onto the terrace, in part because it was completely packed with bales of clothing and shoelaces and mountains of T-shirts and men's boxer shorts and teakettles and every kind of bric-a-brac, but packed together so tightly that it was impossible to find a path between the bales, and in part they didn't go out because the old man was blocking the door, he was saying: terrace, family, good, but pay money—your mother, Dante snapped at him, and pulled him away, then Dante set to pushing the bales over to one side, and finally he was able to form a kind of L-shaped path between them; he spoke to the Chinese merchant, who was blinking now a little in fright, saying we need a chair and a table, and he pressed a five-hundred-forint into his hand, but the old Chinese man didn't move, he just looked at the note and shook his head, as if he didn't understand what it was, then Dante laughed, and he pressed another five hundred into his hand, and there appeared a table and a few chairs as well, two chairs are enough, said the Baron to Dante, so that they somehow placed the table and these two chairs on the terrace, then Dante motioned to the elderly Chinese man to leave the Baron alone now for a while, he went back with him to the front of the store, and the old man sat him down in the corner and kindly offered him some tea, so they both sipped away at their tea, while outside on the terrace the Baron sat down on one of the chairs, and turned up the collar of his coat, because he felt chilled, in addition he could sense, on the terrace looking over the River Körös, that it had started to drizzle, but he sat imperturbably in the chair, and next to him was the empty chair, which he now pulled a little closer to himself, and he felt chilled and he shivered, but he didn't move, he just sat next to the empty chair, and he looked down from the heights of the terrace at the willow trees that had all lost their foliage on the banks of the River Körös, then after a while he only watched the wind and how it made the long, dense, bare branches of the willow trees sway, sway back and forth, making them sweep coldly again and again above the river's icy waters.

*ROM*

# INFINITE DIFFICULTIES

You could start from anywhere—from the inconceivability of the essence of the water's surface, through the meaning, forever hidden from us, of vegetable and animal life, right up to the weighty error storm deriving from the cult of measurements, the main thing, thought the Professor—because right at that moment it was 3:41 p.m., even in his current circumstances he couldn't leave off his thought-immunization exercises—the main thing is that I can attack these questions from any direction whatsoever, because I attack gravity, I attack the entire absurdity of the observation of time, and if I want to, I can also attack the trashy flea market of our ideas and throw these useless—albeit valuable-seeming—objects every which way in this flea market, they stand there in bales, he thought, on the disused grounds of the City Waterworks—the tens of thousands of misapprehensions stand there in enormous bales, and not all of them are so interesting, only the ones that sprawl out along the base of our cognition, and they smirk at us—after they're certain that we've built them up so well that we've literally no chance of liberation—away with those bales! —it's time now to go down to the fundament, to examine what has remained there of the essential, and in that way not just to attain, in this catastrophic world history of misapprehensions, the meaning of these misapprehensions, but to get to their use as well; the meaning of misapprehensions, thought the Professor, and their use, that could be a good title for his final book, which—before the one person worthy of reading it would chuck it straight into the garbage—would finally include the proposition of the one single valid thought, according to which there is no such thing as a valid thought: as our thoughts can be interpreted solely as manifestations of the human pan-organism and its functions, and only in terms of revolutionary biochemistry determined by a strongly genetic background, to think is the same as to act from instinct, it can either be good or bad, namely it's all just ones and zeros, in other words: useful when perceived from the momentary desired result, and ruined when seen from the same viewpoint, and so forth, because to act from instinct is the same as not acting at all, but to leave off an activity in a given moment, to dare to go so far as to do that in a certain moment is the same as shutting down cognition in any given moment, by which I mean to say—thought the Professor—the question can be attacked from many points of view simultaneously, and by that we're referring to intuition, well, of course—he cut a rather sour face—it all depends on whose intuition we're talking about, are we talking about the intuition of Auntie Ibolyka or the intuition of the Buddha, because it's not the same, not at all—if, on the one hand we feel like having a piece of Linzer torte, or, on the other, we want to step off the edge of the precipice straight into a freefall—it's not all the same, and in this realm it's not just being playful or clever to state that having Linzer torte (or at least the kind of Linzer torte that Auntie Ibolyka bakes) and stepping out toward that freefall can both be conceived as facts of equal consequence, but in general there is a problem, a huge problem, with significance itself, he thought, because if we're going to pull the rug out from under the feet of our concepts to such an extent, then what you will have is a person who won't be able to say anything anymore, at the very most he'll just puke up words, he'll puke and puke up some more words, this is, nonetheless, a result which we may attain with minimal exertion, but, for example, to reach a state where we don't even begin to start thinking about thinking, but we simply allow ourselves to be woven into existence, allowing ourselves to while away our appointed time like a piece of worn-down stone on the banks of a brook, as it allows, let's say, moss—the Professor's grimace was understandable—to settle down upon it: if we really wish to be free of thought and endeavor, with such a method, to reach a state in which we essay to liquidate thinking through thinking itself, then, in all likelihood, the correct path will not be to destroy the means at our disposal by commencing a thorough carpet bombing of the questions, because it's crucial that we get somehow to the base of this problem-field, and we can only do so with extraordinary circumspection, danger lurks on all sides—the Professor sniffed loudly on the disused grounds of the Waterworks—the big problem is with this attack, presumably with this attack there's the possibility, namely the high probability that in our great hurry we'll end up burning that Linzer torte, namely, we won't pay heed to something that's crucial for the completion of all subsequent steps, therefore: these questions shouldn't be attacked, but instead they should be *deaccelerated* to the greatest possible degree of which the thinking mind is capable, indeed, to put the brakes on these questions to such an extent that the best thing for us is to not even budge an inch, and in this way we won't make the mistake of missing a step, or of failing, in the meantime, to take notice of something; the proper method of liquidating thought is, therefore, the standing position, this is our basic stance, in motionless observation, because only from here, only from this stance, do we have a chance, perhaps—he screwed up his mouth—I repeat, only from here do we have a chance of not losing from sight what is vitally important to take into consideration, and this doesn't mean that we must take everything into consideration, I don't mean to say that everything is equally essential, for if there exists, in this performative liquidation of thought by means of thought itself a certain operational tendency (if there can't be a goal), then there really are certain events in the universe (seen from our viewpoint, of course) that we don't need to take consideration, and this course isn't identical with us not knowing about these events, because everything has to be there in our visual field somewhere, on the edge of our visual field, or whether in our blind fields, as those play an extraordinarily important role in this entire process, that is our one single confirmation, that we can reach over and whip out a fact—a fact of appearance, or an appearance of a fact—of which we still might possibly have a need, and don't forget the blind fields, the Professor reminded himself; then he returned to the question of how it was that human existence—compared to plant and animal existence—proceeded with hair's breadth precision in the same way if it was enriched with cognition or not, as we can state this with an intact mind: namely our mind is sound, for no matter what we do it remains sound, and if it doesn't, then we fall away, we fall away from the line, and someone else comes along and takes our place, and in this universe who cares if it's you or someone else, it doesn't matter, in a word, how can we intelligently discuss this difficult matter: human existence is the same, with thought, or without it, namely, we can state this as being the case, for surely we would say if we were to take a look at the great actors of history and select one—let it be Augustus, but only because in his era a world empire could still be identified with a single person, which today, for obvious reasons, is no longer possible—accordingly, let's say, said the professor to himself, there's Augustus—as the saying goes, what he brought about was no trifle—from the antecedents, of course from the antecedents—but there he is, and there's the great Roman Empire, and now if we take a deep look into this putrid great Roman Empire, we can see that there was indeed such an empire, but no more than that—to put it frankly, this forenote is very important here, frankly speaking, because the most dangerous traps lurk here; now as we approach the question from a certain discretionary angle: was there any Roman Empire at all—because as for the other questions, such as why there was a Roman Empire (this is an idiotic question is it not? as are the questions of how long did it last, what kept it going, to what should it thank its emergence, and here, at the word "thank," our amusement should be strident, but let's not talk about this)—we clutch, like someone who's shipwrecked, at our tree stump in the ocean of these dangers, in other words how can it be inferred that the Roman Empire came into being, well, this here is a problem, he thought, because now we're calling into doubt the existence of the great Roman Empire, for this is what we must actually do if we wish to remain consistent, but to do this, in order to adhere to the spirit of sober reckoning, if we are convinced that the great Roman Empire really existed, well, then we have to say once again we're dealing with a neat discretionary shift of an abstraction of reality, or more precisely the dislocation of an abstraction as it approaches reality, as if this were all a great human geometry, because that's what it should be called, this field of erroneous judgments: a great human geometry, or a great human shiftology, yes, the Professor nodded in the hut on the unused grounds of the Waterworks, it sounds funny, but that's exactly how it is, this is what we have to create within ourselves, within every thinking brain of any person who dares to do so and isn't at the same time an idiotic dilettante in the, in order to confront the real problem with all of human history, namely, why don't we understand it, because whoever doesn't confront this, namely the investigating mind, who doesn't pronounce with conviction that here on one side we have human history, whereas on the other side we have the fact that we don't understand it, and to comprehend why this is the case—well, that person can just put away all those concepts of his very nicely, and he can just run up and down in his room like the Person of Silicon Valley, like a Dostoevsky who ended up somehow in San Francisco with his insane teas and his insane nights, he can just run from one wall to the other or around in circles, and he can classify, he can observe, he can verify, and he can repute what was verified before him, it doesn't matter, he'll never get anywhere, he just builds something up only to immediately knock it down again, or others will knock it down, and he hates them for this, or he loves them, that also doesn't matter, the most important thing is that we must never lose sight—and the Professor stood up from his improvised sleeping place in the dark corner of the hut, on the unused grounds of the Waterworks, in order to stretch his limbs—we must never lose sight of that gaze with which we look at things. 4:59. That was the exact time.

What's your name, he asked, when he noticed that the dog was here again, just then he was pulling shut the door to the hut, he hung up the lock on it, adjusting it so that no one would see that something was amiss here, and he was just about to close it shut when he saw the dog again in front of the door; ever since yesterday, since he had come upon this refuge—whether the Professor was going out or coming in—this little mutt was always wandering around here, its fur bristling in confusion like a coarse brush, it was thoroughly drenched, and shivering as only a dog who is looking for an owner knows how to do, it was a tiny, scrawny, dark-furred mongrel, obviously, thought the Professor, it must belong to the person who comes out here from the Waterworks, only for sure the problem now was that the dog's owner wasn't going to come; even though it was raining, flood season was still a long way off, when, most likely, this small hut would be put to use, but not now, it was left empty, there was only one padlock on the door, which he had been able to knock off with a larger stone so he could—as he proceeded here from the city going along the road to Sarkad—huddle here in some security, not too far away from the city, so he wouldn't get lost, but not too close either for someone to notice him, so that for the most part these conditions corresponded sufficiently to those of a refuge, this came to mind when he had reached the River Fehér-Körös, where the bridge crosses the river and then disappears as it heads toward Sarkad, he went up along the left side of the dike—because above the dike it was very muddy, he went in and down, next to the river, and that was how he came across the hut, because it was a hut fashioned of corrugated metal, and, for the moment, it was left to itself, as clearly such structures were built here only to be used during the flood season, so it looked to be a pretty good refuge, at least for a while, assuming that this little mutt wouldn't bring him any trouble, and that was why he didn't wish to enter into any closer association with it, although already yesterday, and again right now, when he opened and then closed the door to the hut and found the dog there, he always gave it a kick, just to let it know that it wasn't needed here, to step aside and leave him in peace, because he wanted to be alone, but it was just that the dog didn't change its mind; and he'd never been good at this, he never really was able to peel those mutts off himself—he didn't like dogs, and generally they sensed this: they usually growled at him, but not this one, a pox on you, he said in rage and he kicked it again, but the dog was obviously too smart from its many trials which it might have experienced here in the open, and it knew very well that a person would only make a kind of kicking motion in its general direction, but not necessarily hit it, so when the Professor headed back toward the bridge alongside the levee in order to search for some food, and mainly drinking water, he noticed that the dog was following him, it was no longer a question of whether he was going to kick the dog or not, he tried to hit it, but he missed, then he tried again, and he missed the mark again, the dog was very smart, it didn't jump to the side in a showy manner or in fright, but just enough as was absolutely necessary so that the leg wouldn't hit the mark, moreover as the Professor tried again and again, sometimes the dog even let his leg graze his fur a little, aren't you a clever little mutt, said the Professor, and so they went along in the breaking dawn, the rain was drizzling down, and the wind was pretty strong, and he couldn't even decide what was worse, the wind or the rain, what an idiotic question, said the Professor to himself, enraged, both of them together are the fucking worst, fuck this, I'm going to get completely soaked, he wiped the water off his face; because in vain had he found a windbreaker in the hut, which he'd spread over his coat, originally because the weapon fit under it better, but now he used it to protect himself from the rain, only he was beginning to get soaked, or at the very least it was becoming a burden, and all he needed was to get frozen here, when only a few days remained to find some kind of final solution; he had to keep on moving though, and that's how it went, with the dog right behind him, it was a wee little creature, and it was still young, almost still a puppy, so it could move its legs quickly to keep pace with the person who was walking in front of it and occasionally losing his footing on the side of the levee, because the ground was quite damp, if not completely soaked through, there was still only a bit of grass left, so that the Professor decided to walk where the grass was, or above on the levee, when he should have been trudging through the mud in the two usual lines of tire tracks, well, what now, he came to a stop sometimes, and gave a kick in a backward direction, and in that way they got to the bridge, and they penetrated more deeply into the City Forest, because he remembered that not far away from the bridge there was the forester's house, and if the dogs hadn't been let out, and he was careful, maybe he could get hold of some grub and water, but especially water, because he needed that, it doesn't work without water, he'd muttered to himself in the hut, he absolutely had to get hold of some water.

And what's your name, Joe Child asked the second boy, the one with the mohawk, me? the boy asked, shifting his weight from one leg to the other, while his two hands nervously jumped around on his sides, his fingers moving as if quickly counting something, whatever, it doesn't matter, said Joe Child, let's skip that, but just tell me how old you are, how old am I? fourteen, said the boy with the mohawk reluctantly, well, good, Joe Child grimaced at him, no lies allowed here, I'll be ...

the boy with the mohawk added, that is, I'm thirteen; so, both of you are thirteen, I'm surprised, but the thing is I don't know what you want, do you at least have an old Bérva or something like that, he posed the question, but he already knew the answer: these two had nothing at all, you could see by looking at them how down and out they were, they'd clearly just run away from the Institute, which moreover didn't even exist anymore, they'd escaped in the chaos of the move, thought Joe Child, and that's how they were able to bail, well, but what should I do with you, said Joe Child, with us? asked the balder one, with us?—nothing; then what the hell are you looking for here, this is a bar, can't you see that, it's the kind of place, or venue, where there wouldn't be anything for the likes of you; we want to join, the bald one blurted out, and he quickly lowered his head, well, you can go straight to hell, fuck, because you can't join up with us here, there's nothing to join, boys, and as if he'd just heard something completely absurd, he half turned toward the barman, all the while not taking his eyes off them, do you hear that, fuck, they say they want to join, I'm telling you seriously, I have to laugh, they ran away, they have nothing, and what are we? tell them already, what are we, a kindergarten? here no one will wipe your ass, here everyone wipes his own ass, understood? okay fine, forget it, said the boy with the mohawk, then he motioned with his head to the other one, let's go, but then Joe Child shifted his buttocks on the chair, he sighed and said: maybe your feelings are hurt, my little angels, but it's no game around here, fuck it, and on top of that you don't even know what you want, I bet—he spoke again to the bartender in the empty Biker Bar—I bet you just took off like that into the big bad world; okay, the boy with the mohawk muttered, and he again gestured to the other, and hissed to him: we're outta here, and they headed toward the door, but Joe Child called after them, saying stop, kids, come back, the two boys stopped, as if they were thinking about it, then they turned around and began to walk back toward Joe Child, loosely, slackly, as if they didn't care, we're in, no matter what it is, said the balder one, and he lowered his head again, no matter what? asked Joe Child, uh-huh, the two boys nodded once, well, if you're really in, no matter what, then have a seat there in the back, there's the laptop, you know how to use something like that, right?—at which point the two boys grimaced unpleasantly, meaning they knew—well, then type PURE IDEALS dot hu into the browser and read what's there, do you know how to read, we can read, good, so then read the introduction three times over, am I making myself clear, three times, fuck, and if you agree with every word, come back over here to me, and we'll see, but then he didn't have time to deal with them, because suddenly the doors were flung open, and the others came in, but only for a quick beer, because, they said there was a maneuver, then when everyone had been served and had quickly downed a beer, they motioned only with their heads toward them: who was that halfwit standing in front of the door, and then those two kids over there; reinforcements, Joe Child winked at them, then they glanced toward the back of the room, where the two boys were in front of the laptop reading every single word on the PURE IDEALS dot hu website, the men downed their beer from the pint glasses, then they left as they'd come in, like a herd, they pulled out of the Biker Bar, and Joe Child only had enough time to motion to them that that was enough, storytime was over, they could continue later, now there was a maneuver, and if they wanted to so much and they wouldn't be in the way, the best thing would be if they came along. Outside the boys still had to chase away the Idiot Child, because he was following them again, then they followed Joe Child. You sit in the back, he said to them, and hold on, just like in kindergarten.

There was one dog, and there were even two dogs, two enormous Dobermans, but they were in a part of the yard that was fenced off, so that after he had closely observed the house, he went round to the back, and there he slipped through the fence, although as far as that went, he almost certainly could have entered through the front as well, as there were no vehicles in front of the house or in the yard, namely no one was at home, he determined; the children, if there were children, were clearly in school, the wife, if there was one, had clearly gone shopping, and the forest ranger obviously was somewhere in the forest, in any event no one was home, he took this as nearly certain, but still, for caution's sake, because that rotten little mutt was still following him, he thought it better to slip in from the back, and already he was inside with no obstacles, of course the two Dobermans saw them, and they began to run back and forth restlessly in their kennel, and when they saw that he and the little mutt were trying to get in through the back entrance, they began barking, the question was how far the owner of the house might have gone, and he calculated—if there wasn't going to be any goddamned bad luck in this thing—as the dogs hadn't been let off their leashes, someone couldn't be too far away—still though, he assumed he had some ten or fifteen minutes, although he couldn't really be too sure, he had opened the door in the wall at the back of the house in order to get to the well he'd seen before in the courtyard, but the door to the house wasn't locked, which surprised him so much that he closed and opened it again—and when he tried it a second time it still opened, so he, very cautiously—now holding the weapon in a different position underneath his windbreaker—slipped into the house, and he wasn't even in there ten or fifteen minutes—actually not even five minutes—and he was already out again in the yard, then it took him another minute by the well to fill a bucket that he found next to it, so not only was he out of the house again in under ten minutes, but he had already left the forester's house altogether, and he hurried along the path toward the bridge, carrying the bucket as fast as he could, stopping every once in a while in his tracks to see if he could hear the sound of a motor, so as to quickly jump in among the bushes.

He divided them up into three posses, as he always did when there was a manhunt, because a hunt is what he liked to call it, and he felt a particular joy, because he felt how strong they were, and how weak the one was they hunted, and this weakness caused him to feel endless happiness, and it made all the drudgery that was a part of life with this posse worthwhile—to sit on his motorcycle, to put on his helmet, to pull on and do up his gloves, then to start up the motor, and drive out in the direction they'd planned, this always caused him particular enjoyment, and so it did now as well, as he divided up the others and he designated the leaders of each individual group, the Tetra phones were operational, a final check for everyone, and already they turned out from the yard of the Biker Bar, and he loved, he really loved how the motors growled, almost thirty vehicles at once, he thought, that wasn't nothing, as they say, and he was the last to turn out of the yard; he could think with the mind of the one they were hunting, and that's how he had come to be their Leader: for when it came to seeing into the mind of their prey, his brain functioned the best, he could sense how their prey was thinking—he always intuited that, flawlessly, because it had never happened that they had gone after someone and hadn't caught him, and well, such a pompous, rootless cosmopolitan as this, such a rotten traitor, such a piece of garbage, a scrap of filth who had abused their most noble feelings in such a base fashion—he drove on, leading his own posse and really stepped on the gas, because suddenly he was filled again with murderous rage at how a rat like this could debase him on his own turf so, but so much, and as he made a turn out toward Nagyváradi Road, suddenly Little Star's face swam before his eyes, and it hurt him so much to see that face again that he was obliged to stop; he raised his hand for the others to come to a halt as well, and they halted behind him, waiting for him to calm down, because they saw he was very upset, nobody said anything to him over the Tetra, they just waited for him, their legs resting on the sides of the motorcycles, for him to pull himself together, they knew what he was probably feeling, because they felt the same way themselves, and within them was the same rage toward that piece of scum, of course, what did they know of what he was truly feeling, thought the Leader in front, because for them Little Star was just a companion, but for him he was a brother, the only one, his true brother, maybe not from the same father, but still, and it hurt so much that he wasn't among them anymore, and he never would be again, he closed his eyes, cleared his throat, then once again he raised his hand, pointing forward, and with that once again there they were—just where God had created them—they were on the road, divided into three posses, ready to carry out what only they could carry out, because these machines— everyone had their own, which meant more to them than their own mothers—these Kawasakis and Hondas and Yamahas and Hondas and Kawasakis weren't fueled by gas—they often repeated this after the Leader—but by Honor, that's what drove the pistons in them, and with that they drove along Sarkadi Road toward the bridges of the River Körös. They had no doubt whatsoever that they would find him.

From the outset he had to exclude the possibility that he'd stuck around the Thorn Bush, because he was well aware that he now confronted an enemy who had his wits about him, so he had to sense for himself what escape routes this enemy might contemplate: clearly this would only include such directions where he would see himself as having a chance of escape, thought the Leader: obviously, then, he would be avoiding the main roads, so that already excluded the roads leading to Sarkad, Csaba, Elek, Gyíkos, and even Doboz—he sat in the Biker Bar, and as they knew what he was thinking about over there at the counter, they spoke softly only among themselves, and the TV was on up there in the corner with the volume turned down, but it bothered him that they were watching him so much, everyone was on pins and needles, because they were waiting for him to give them the lowdown, so he went out to the yard, took out his Tetra, and he telephoned that one person from whom he always sought confirmation before any larger maneuver, and that person told him he understood the lowdown, and he gave him his blessing, moreover, for his part, he didn't see it as a completely useless idea for his own people to take up some kind of initiative as well—I'd rather you didn't, the Leader interrupted him, and he said: do you get me, Police Chief? this is a personal matter—fine, all right, I'll give you three days, he heard the stern voice, meaning, the Police Chief said, that he wanted results at the very latest within three days, the "causes and effects" could be discussed afterward; understood?—and with that the line broke off, and he went back into the Biker Bar, sat down in his usual place, and opened up the web page hiszi-map.hu on his laptop, and he began to look at maps of the surrounding area; as he scanned these locations, he decided on the directions their manhunt should take, and he designated the routes, choosing for himself the one that seemed the least likely, the Sarkadi Road, primarily because of the City Forest, and if this filthy beast was such a lair-dweller, then it was highly likely that he couldn't exist without it anymore, and from the outset he'd thought this piece of scum might be looking for another lair in some weedy patch somewhere, so—the Leader scrutinized the map—he looked for where there were weeds—unfortunately they were everywhere surrounding the city, and the one possibility seemed to be the City Forest, but still he didn't believe it —in his view, this was the least likely possibility—but he wanted to at least exclude it, and so he chose this route for himself right off the bat, because nobody else could strike these dead ends off the list as lightning quick as he, he was the best at that, so as they headed out toward the City Forest, they surveyed the area around the bridge, but saw nothing, they drove to the forester's house, but he wasn't at home, so they began to look for the forester, and they even found him on the other side of the train tracks leading toward the sanatorium—he was clearing away bracken, or whatever it was, in order to release a fox trap and get at the spoils, because something had been caught in the trap last night; they explained what the great situation was, and that if he came across anything, even the most trifling unusual thing, then he should call this number, said the Leader, and he took out a piece of paper and pen, and he wrote something down and gave it to him, fine, said the forester, who was fairly frightened of these men, so that he could only manage to say: fine, he put the slip of paper in his vest, and he didn't say anything, he just watched as they drove off toward the tracks, he heard as they throttled the gas, tumbling across the tracks, and he was only able to return to his work with the pruning saw in the thicket when he no longer heard the motors of that criminal scum. The fox was still alive; he shot it from close range.

Where is the place where they'd think I'd be the least likely to go, he asked himself in the hut, and he made a movement as if to stand up, he even swung his leg two or three times, but the little mutt just moved over a little, as if it knew full well this whole thing wasn't serious, what a little mutt, it just won't give up, what can it expect from me, though, nothing, the Professor shook his head, and he could only realize—although he wasn't too happy to realize—that he had allowed the dog to stay inside, or more precisely, he'd resigned himself to the dog being inside here, as the door couldn't really be closed properly from within, he'd already had more than enough of the whining, night after night, and the little runt had pushed in the door, come into the hut, and lain down next to the doorway, he'd had enough of this, so he was obliged to leave the dog in peace and instead try to sleep, because he had to rest, these exhausting journeys on foot had really worn him out, first from the Thorn Bush to here—he hadn't even recovered properly from that—and then yesterday, to the forester's house and back, with that bucket full of water, it was so heavy that both of his arms felt like they were about to break off by the time he got back, although hardly any water had dripped out, it was also true that his arms ached all night from the strain, or at least when he was woken up by the dog and he sensed the pain in his arms and how they ached, they were aching in the morning too, and now as well, and it was already afternoon, 2:51 p.m.; he looked at the little mutt lying next to the doorway, and he had to acknowledge that the damned little mutt had two wonderful eyes that were blinking at him right now, but it just lay there, not moving even a centimeter closer, when it saw the Professor take a box of biscuits—which he had succeeded in plundering from the forester's house—and open it up, and the Professor began to chew on one, well, that's all I need, he grumbled from his makeshift bed, which he had cobbled together for himself from an old mattress he'd found here, he chewed, he chewed, and he didn't look at the dog, but after a couple of minutes he flew into a rage, and he took a biscuit out of its plastic wrapper, and from the bed he tossed one over to the little mutt, who just slightly shifted away from it, sniffed it, and then began to chew on the biscuit as well, and the whole time those two eyes were looking at him, this can't be true, what a cheeky little mutt you are, and he threw him another biscuit, the dog began to wag its tail, and he began to gnaw on that biscuit too, at which point the Professor angrily turned around on his bed in rage, his back to the dog, and he said loudly: Little Mutt, that's your name from now on, and you'd better listen to me or I'll throw you into the River Körös.

Everything is just a kind of conceptual round in a boxing match that leads only to nonexistence, and this is, in all likelihood, the greatest *error* of existence—what I mean to say, therefore, he said to himself, is that it isn't even worthwhile dealing with such nonsensical argumentations such as these, what *is* worthwhile to deal with, and in an extraordinarily thorough manner, is this: the *yes*es, with the demonstrables, with positive declarations, designations, expansions, displacement, reflection, meaning amplification, and transference, *this* is our thematic field, this is the ground through which the mere positing of these questions, whether correct or incorrect, can be annihilated; if we are to do anything at all, then it must be this: to exclude the *nos*, denial, the false taken as affirmation, destruction, the formerly recognized arrogance of destruction, as well as the relief of exoneration, itself suspect, at having repudiated all these; accordingly, we must only deal with the *yes*es, if it is even worthwhile to deal with the *yes*es and the *nos*, because the one-time wise and wise-sounding declaration, to the effect that nothing exists without its opposite, can't lead us astray—namely, it would be a sheer blunder to handle anything without also handling this anything's contradictory little sibling with just as much attention, well: even this mere philosophical approach must be scrapped, in other words, there's no point in dealing with this and squandering our precious time when these philosophers and dialecticians come along with this, that, and the other, it boggles my mind; are the notions of consubstantiality or polysubstantiality terms that we may employ in approaching the equation to be solved?—no, all such propositions are primitive, a child feels more than an adult knows, and a child knows more than it feels, and so on; such factors, while observing things—meaning, do I see one essence, or two, or more—indicates that the virus of the quantitative approach has once again gone unidentified and undetected, for this virus is worthy only of scorn and not of precious circulation in the world of ideas—and our work now must be comprised of a permanent and continuous purge, a kind of cleansing operation which never reaches an end, as it never can reach an end, because every last observation, every last pronouncement must be scoured away from our brains, every presupposition must be cleared away, and I cannot emphasize this enough—if there were anyone to emphasize it to, said the Professor, sitting in the depths of his hut among the petals of crumpled coats and various scraps of fabric he'd scavenged from that place—presupposition as such is itself the lethal dose of the bacteria of ignorance; and it boggles my mind when I discover—for example, in myself, because at such times a so-called thinking person sentences his own self to annihilation, because it isn't enough that the entire path that he too started out on is wrong—that, well, that field from where all this emerged: the preliminaries, the preparations, the presuppositions, the preconceptions, all this is merely an inferno from where no road leads anywhere, only in incorrect directions, this much is certain: these tidying and purging operations must be thoroughgoing, not even that, not just thoroughgoing, of course, but continuous, and this continuous purge means that—unceasingly—not a single moment can be left to the brain to find some pretext in order to escape from the questioning gaze, namely, the brain is looking at itself, and this looking must be comprised of sheer mistrust; and all the while even this can't lead to a complete or partial inability to act, because this isn't any kind of counsel on how to act in this or that situation—we always end up doing what we have to anyway, there aren't any other choices, and it's superfluous, boundlessly and profoundly superfluous, if, at some point, we attempt (and we still think it's us!) to make any kind of decision at all, we don't decide anything, which still is, quite simply, I mean the whole thing is simply *not interesting*, it doesn't matter, its significance is zero because it only has a meaning and a mood, and we just keeping doing our little maneuvers on this modulation scale, but only for our own amusement, because we always end up completing the essential, namely we do whatever we have to, and so on, which is the same thing as saying that this purge-continuum exists in a kind of formula where the other factors aren't even factors, but are, in fact, nonexistent, not disregarding the fact that this isn't the same nonexistence we were talking about at the beginning; this is not denial, but rather the affirmation of this equation, namely, there is an equation, not, of course, in a quantitative sense, but in a geometrical one—but no, better to say that it unfolds in a completely extraordinary configuration, a configuration of the dimensional divine, where nothing else is given to us than to singularly perceive this purge-continuum—if we're paying close attention, and we *are* paying close attention—this purge-continuum shines, it doesn't care if it's day or night, it illuminates, it glimmers, it phosphoresces, namely, it's visible, and there's only this, and nothing else from this equation, so that's where we stand now in terms of all these various approaches; and the content of these approaches doesn't matter, no matter how correct they may appear to be, because their so-called correctness is incorrect, namely, their unsatisfactory character is hidden from us; a crystal formation must be imagined, one which is not comprised of a structure—quantities again, quantities!—but instead, any one of its postulated grids, axes, planes of symmetry, basal cleavages, shells, subshells, cells, energy fields, including the black hole it originated from, all surge across our brain without hindrance—or, at the very least, this is what *should* be happening to us, because this brain, our brain, must altogether concentrate on one thing, it must concentrate on immediately purging whatever might be passing through it, namely *this cleansing* should annihilate, and what do we mean here by the word "cleansing," respectively what else could be meant by "clean" other than that something is only clean if it no longer exists, as the perfectamente Pure is the dimension of Not-There, that's where it should be, but it isn't there, and again, this isn't some kind of transition into the realm of denial, we never proceed there, because we can only begin to deal with the question here, where everything is illuminated in the light of assent, affirmation, positive postulation, the strength of Being, and in the last instance, accordingly, here we are, because yes, we have gotten this far, to the strength of the Yes sweeping all before it, and quod erat demonstratum, because it shines, I will say that again and again, the Professor finally thought, this Yes shines forth with horrific intensity into the universe, which is never complete. Well, and if it doesn't—it's five p.m.

The forester hung up the fox in the backyard and skinned it before his wife came home with the children, then he buried the carrion behind the backyard among the oak trees, when he came back, he saw that most likely that same wild boar that had caused him some difficulties in the past few weeks had broken through the fence again while he'd gone to look at the traps, it had paid him a visit again, he quickly had a look around in the chicken coop, but all the chicks were there, so then he went back to where the wire fence had been pried open and repaired it with a thicker piece of wire, and he decided next week, if he went into the city, he would definitely speak with that person who usually took care of such things for him and hire a stonemason, an expense which had already factored into the family budget, but then been postponed, as it seemed too expensive, but things couldn't stay like this, a properly constructed cement fence was needed, although then he wouldn't be able to always let the dogs run free, especially during the day, and how clever to notice that there was no movement in the house, and to choose that moment to break through the fence, and with that he went back into the house and sat down in the kitchen to eat the breakfast his wife had prepared for him, when he noticed that the spice jars and the soup mixes were all jumbled up on the shelves above the stove, and when he stood up in order to see better, he noticed that the door of the lower cupboard, which held the more long-lasting foodstuffs, such as rice, flour, and such items, was open, my wife never leaves that cupboard door open, the forester thought, and so he got up from the table, went over to the cupboard, and without really touching the cupboard at all, pushed open the door and he looked inside; there could be no doubt that somebody had been here in the kitchen in the past two hours, his first thought was to call the police and make a report, because this hadn't been the first time that some errant gypsy or some other kind of vagrant had come into the house, but it never seemed really important to him, so that just as before, he gave up on the idea of calling the police, but then he remembered what that monkey-headed ringleader had said to him just now by the trap, and whom they had said they were looking for, so that he took the scrap of paper with the phone number from his vest and with a few decisive movements he ripped it into shreds, because whomever those people were looking for, that person needed protection, not betrayal, if it was really him, that famous scientist from the city—what was his name again?, he began to rack his brains, because that gang hadn't said the name of the person they were looking for, they'd just given a description of what he looked like, he didn't know him personally, only from sight, but he knew, when the ringleader described him, who it was in all likelihood, although he could hardly imagine why this Nazi horde was after him, so he quickly went up to the first floor and had a quick look around the rooms up there, and then at the rooms on the ground floor, but whoever had been here hadn't taken anything, maybe he was looking for something and didn't find it, who knows, thought the forester, in any event, he decided if he happened to come upon him, he'd tell him that he could certainly count on him.

He had informed him that he was getting three days and not a single day more, the Police Chief looked straight ahead when he came back from the morgue, where he had viewed the corpse, and this was already the second day, already slowly coming to an end, that's all they were getting and not a second more, because it wasn't even that he was shot in the chest or in the leg, or that he was shot in the stomach, or in the heart, but that he was full of bullets, and what gave him the greatest cause for concern was that the corpse's face was shot up as well, which made the head burst apart, it was a pretty grim sight, he didn't like things like that, so they were getting three days and nothing more, because—he sighed as he leaned back in the chair behind his desk—he was going to have to file a report about this at the very latest on the fourth day, and that's all he needed, for one of these journalists or—

God forbid—one of these television reporters to start getting in the way here, because then he would have to explain himself, and if there's one thing he didn't like it was explaining himself, and what he didn't like, he didn't do, on the contrary, he did everything possible so that he would never have to explain himself, so that after a brief period of reflection—which in his case meant no longer than one minute, but usually less than that—he called one of his sergeants and asked him who was out now on patrol, and when he heard the names, he grimaced, dissatisfied, and gave the command to send for such and such and such an officer, and that these officers should designate further officers, put together a reconnaissance mission of twenty officers, and head out to the scene of the crime yes, to the Thorn Bush, and have another look around—he wasn't asking what had happened so far, he immediately interrupted the sergeant, but was telling him what was supposed to be happening now, this was an order, the sergeant saluted, and he set about his task, staying in the building, waiting for news on the police radio, and in general he wasn't too concerned if the Motorcycle Enthusiasts' Club might happen to hear what was being said . . . and in fact they did hear it, the Leader's Tetra receiver wasn't turned off, it flashed, he heard all the main points, so, he thought, he and his men would have to be even more effective, he just didn't understand why the Police Chief couldn't understand that a personal affair was a personal affair, hadn't this been established between them? he asked himself, and he was filled with rage at the thought that he couldn't even trust the Police Chief's word now, although before he'd more or less been able to, although as far as that was concerned he'd never really completely trusted him, partially because he wore reading glasses, partially because, in relation to his so-called military bearing, he always recalled that, as was well known, the Police Chief had never served in the military, so that he was confronted here with someone who was an ally, but who just played at being a soldier, so he didn't particularly feel that the Police Chief really stood by him in this matter of the responsibility assumed for this city, and he particularly didn't feel that he should be subordinate to the Chief's orders, let him go to hell, he muttered in rage; once again he motioned for them to go with him across the bridge and for the time being to drive in the direction of the Sarkad Road, but then after a few kilometers, he waved again, we're turning off here, and they went all the way back to the Reform School, but he didn't think that this filthy piece of scum would be hiding here, so he just sent in one brother to have a quick look around, and then they drove on, the Leader clenching his teeth, and they were going to keep on going until he turned up somewhere, he was going to turn up somewhere, the Leader had mobilized so many of his people at this moment across the entire county, so that he would immediately get any and all information concerning the aggregate means of transport, all buildings standing empty at this moment, as well as the filthy pig's former residence, the Hospital, the City Hall, the Courthouse, the Water Tower, in a word every and all buildings that could be at issue here, and everywhere there were other similarly-minded groups who themselves could alert every relevant person in the county, every person and persons, who would report—if that was needed—what they had to report, and now this was needed, because he saw that this time his prey wouldn't necessarily be as easy to bring down as was usually the case, because this one had a brain, and he had an idea of how to attempt escape, but he wasn't going to, because if they had decided they were going after someone, that person never escaped, it wasn't even a real hunt, because they always bagged the game, there were no maybes and no buts here, no possibility of someone scurrying away, slipping into another territory over which they had no purview, partially because they had purview over everything, because without that the whole thing wasn't operational, and partially because everybody knew—at least in this county—that it was never a good idea to cross them, so that any moment now, the reports would be coming in and coming in, he was sure of that, and he pulled on the accelerator, and within a few moments they were at the town's periphery . . . and he looked at the empty bucket, which had emptied out much too quickly, the problem was he'd been too thirsty, clearly his organism wasn't accustomed to going without water for long periods of time, and now he had to do something, he had to think of how to make himself scarce, which, however, contradicted the fact that this location felt fairly safe, it was far away from everything, and this hut was just one among many such structures: due to the regular flooding, innumerable such small utility buildings had been built up here in the old times, when the Waterworks was still in operation, so the chances of them discovering precisely this exact hut were very small, so as a matter of fact, it'd be better for him to stay here, he reflected, the only problems were certain hard-to-manage short-term difficulties—for example water and food—and beyond that there was the strategic question, which he hadn't yet decided, namely what was the right overall solution to this dilemma—because were they looking for him now as a murderer, looking for him as an armed attacker, looking for him as the murderer of that hulking idiot, as the person who also happened to know everything about the secret weapon stash on the peasant's farmstead, and who was, therefore, life-threatening for them, so that he could easily count on the involvement— if they weren't involved already —of the police, he could count on the involvement—if they weren't involved already—of the army, and possibly also the border-guard patrol officers, but of course the most dangerous of all was this fascist scum and his motorcycle mob, they were the ones he had to get the farthest away from, well, and that was the hard part, because so far he didn't have any ideas how to solve this, and where to find a place where he could just sink into the background so there'd be no trace of him left—because he knew any attempt to escape from them was in vain: if it could be presumed that he, the person they were hunting for, might *still be around anywhere,* no matter how good a plan he came up with, it would still end in disaster, because they'd never give up the search—at least not this gang—they'd keep pursuing him until they found him, and he had no useful ideas, just a few crumbs, which he immediately cast aside, either because they weren't any good, or because . . . well, to take just one of these ideas, there was the Water Tower next to Dobozi Road, he'd considered it once at the very beginning, since the former Observatory, standing empty for years now, was located on the roof, but he also cast it aside, because in addition to the fact that there were too many steps, he knew that the physics teacher from the local high school often took girls there for a so-called "game of chess," in a word no, the main thing was that he still had to strain his brain, he sat up on the bed, because he had to come up with a perfect plan, and he was going to, he kept repeating to himself, and he just watched as Little Mutt turned over the bucket and licked the last drops out of it, well, did you even see such a thing, he muttered in rage, it even knows what I'm thinking, look here, Little Mutt, are you paying attention, and the dog raised his head and looked at the Professor, do you really know what's going through my head? if you do then help me—he leaned back on his improvised piled-up pillow, and tell me what I should do, he looked into that pair of expressive eyes which watched him continuously, tell me, if you want to say something so much, what the hell should I do to save my life. Do you hear me, Little Mutt? I'm talking to you.

It was midnight and by that time I'm already closed, said Lajos, the gas station attendant, to his buddy in the bar known only by its old registration number, 47, because this is where they always bumped into each other, it wasn't a friendship—he didn't have any friends to speak of—they were just drinking buddies, because so many years had gone by, and they had bumped into each other here so many times before, and so once it had started, there was no stopping it, because it was nothing else than just talking: what had happened to one of them, what had happened to the other, was there anything interesting going on, of course there was never anything interesting going on, because nothing interesting ever happened to either of them, but still they kept talking about this, that, and the other thing, and so the years—no, the decades—went by, because so much time had passed already, one of them said one day: do you get this, he asked, and he stared into his wine-spritzer glass, why does time go by so fast, I'm forty-three years old already, but I feel like the last ten years, at least the last ten years—whoosh!—they just went by so fast, fuck, they're about to shove us into the oven, and then for real nothing will happen; it's true, nothing's happened, at least until now, the gas station attendant said—until now, he repeated, and he tried to catch the other's gaze, but this gaze was far away, it was only just now preparing to emerge, preparing in those depths below, where gazes are born, only that even for the love of God it didn't want to emerge, they both waited for it, but no and no, they waited together, he with his empty wine-spritzer glass, and Lajos too, but what should they do now, that gaze didn't want to be born, it didn't matter to Lajos now anyway, just as long as he could tell someone, and now, well, he would tell him, because he couldn't bear not telling anyone any longer before he split for good, that's why he'd dropped in for a wine spritzer at the 47, which was just a stone's throw away, and of course his buddy was already standing around by the counter in that gloomy gaze-seeking state, he was alone, the early crowd had already left, the late crowd hadn't shown up yet, so they were alone, and Lajos said: maybe it was after midnight, I didn't look at the exact time, but it was sometime around then, when suddenly I heard somebody rattling the automatic door, which of course was locked already, because nobody comes in at that hour, and it was some kind of old hooligan type, unshaven, scruffy, even his face was scruffy, I told him and I motioned that we were closed already, but he just kept on rattling the door, and he had such strange light-blue eyes, I had seen these eyes somewhere before but I didn't remember from where, but I had definitely seen him before, so I opened the door with the key and asked him: what do you want, so this sucker says to me that he needs diesel and some regular gas, and so I said, because I wasn't in the mood for a joke—I was so tired that I was almost falling asleep, only the TV was keeping me up—if you want diesel, my man, then you'll have to go across the border, because, as you've no doubt heard, there hasn't been any diesel in this country for years now, and even if there were, I wouldn't be selling it to you—but you will, this sucker says, and then he says: let me in, I'll explain, and he was wearing such a fucking huge yellow windbreaker, and standing next to him was this little mongrel or whatever it was, I tell him: you can come in, but not the dog, but of course the little mutt was already inside by the time I said that, and I didn't bother trying to chase it out because I wanted to get this over with quickly, and so I ask him, well, what do you want, because I thought there would be a little transaction here or whatever, I could tell this guy had some business to conduct, I can tell from a distance who has that intention and who doesn't, and this guy had that intention, it was just that—hey, buddy, pay attention, and the other man jerked his head up, because he was starting to doze off into his wine-spritzer glass—it was just, I'm telling you, that this was no small transaction, but a big one, because he said he needed a larger quantity of diesel, and I need it now, he said, and a small amount of gas, and somehow from his speech I could sense that he wasn't one of those vagrants, this was someone else, but for the love of God I couldn't remember where I'd seen him already, only his eyes were familiar, but I still couldn't tell from that; well, I say to him, what kind of amounts are we talking here, and he says, I need about three thousand liters of diesel—my man, I say to him, this gas station hasn't seen three thousand liters of diesel since the nineties, my man, what country do you think you're living in?—and he just says: ready cash, but he didn't show me anything, his coat was completely buttoned up, and one of his hands was in the pocket of his coat, and I thought fuck, did you just rob a bank or what, and then I look at him, and I asked: did you bring your own canisters, and I meant it as a joke, because I was getting interested now, and I thought why not lighten things up before the negotiations got serious, but this was no joke to him, with his free hand he started to unbutton his coat, and then I see that he had a fucking huge weapon beneath it, well, so this sucker puts it down nicely on the counter, because while we were talking he kept moving in closer to me, over to where I was, at which point I pressed the safety switch and immediately closed the automatic doors from my counter, you know, using the switch underneath the counter, and I reached for the phone, and the guy says: don't do that, why, do you want to rob me, then he shakes his head, and he pulls out a huge bundle of euros, not forints—hey, pay attention, buddy, euros, do you get it? I get it, his companion nodded tiredly—actually he had no intention of robbing me, but he wanted diesel for cash, you know, and he starts slowing down his words like he's talking to some idiot, and I say to him, don't talk to me that way, I'm not an idiot, then I ask him, so where are your canisters, I didn't hear you coming with a truck, and, well—the guy leans in closer into me—besides the three thousand liters of diesel, I need fifteen or twenty canisters of gas delivered, he says, and I ask him, and where to now, and he says, to the Thorn Bush, and I immediately realized who it was, that big jerk-off and celeb, there was a lot about him on TV, you know who I'm talking about—I know, his buddy nodded unconvincingly, could you order me another one, he asked, no, answered Lajos—and so we went to the back, to the depot, you know, where the secret reserve is, that's what we call it, me and my shift-mate, namely, the reserve we put away that no one knows about because it's in the—how should I put it—"shadow" of the officially sequestered reserves, which, thank God, no one ever thinks about, but, well, we all have to make a living somehow, well, do you remember—but there was no answer—well, whatever, he continued, and so the guy says: three thousand liters, you know how much that is? I ask, I know, he says, and he's starting to get impatient, so I say to him: one thing at a time, I can arrange this for you by next week, sir—I was already calling him sir, because by now I knew who the guy was—I need it now, he says, and he was really beginning to get impatient, I could tell he needed it now, that night, so I said to him: look, I don't know with whom I have the honor, but there are set prices for things like this, okay, he says, how much, and I give him a rough estimate, and he says fine, it's yours, and he came in and sat down in the warmth, because I let him in, by then I could tell that I didn't have to be afraid of him, and outside in the back I began to take care of the three thousand liters, I filled up the tanks of the ZiL truck one by one, packed up fifteen canisters of gas, then he paid, sat down next to me in the truck, and we set off, fuck yes, in the pitch dark—hey, you, listen—but it was so dark that when I looked behind me, and I saw there wasn't even one light on in the city, and on top of that he tells me to turn off the headlights, what do you want me to do? I ask, turn off the headlights already, and again he gave me a huge pile of cash, and, well just imagine, fuck, there you are driving along in a ZiL truck with a trailer—that's all I've got—it's pitch dark outside, and suddenly the guy just tells me to stop, and I'm supposed to unload the gas canisters off to the side, then he wants me to open up the spigots on the tanks, and start moving again, but slowly—in plain Hungarian he says he wants me to let all the diesel trickle out of the tanks, so I unload the canisters and open the spigots, and I let the diesel trickle out, fuck it, all of it, and we go nice and slow all along the edge of the Thorn Bush, somewhere behind Csókos Road, and he has me discharge all the material that he bought, and the whole time he keeps saying, keep an eye out and stop immediately if you see someone in the back or the front, so we can turn off the road, and I'm racking my brains already, because this is a big transaction, fine, but how am I going to get out of this, because with this guy sitting there with a fucking huge rifle in his lap, and that mongrel at his feet, as the diesel is trickling out both from the truck bed and the trailer, well, I'm thinking, if they get me for this, then it's game over—me, my gas station, everything—I understand, said his buddy sorrowfully—so then Lajos went over to the counter and ordered two wine spritzers, he sipped at his own, and pushed the other one over to his buddy—so things can be good for you, too, fuck, and you're getting this to keep your mouth shut, get it? because you're a good kid, and because today's a holiday, really—the other slowly raised his head in surprise and looked at Lajos with an oily gaze, what holiday is it today, Easter?—no, fuck it, it's not Easter, answered Lajos, and he took a gulp of his wine spritzer, then said nothing more, because he saw it was no use, his buddy had gone deep into the night, and it was still nighttime for him, so he didn't force things, Lajos sipped his wine spritzer, then he looked at his watch, drank up the rest, patted down both of his coat pockets, and said to his buddy as he left: well, I've quit this job for good now, and as for you, my little fucker, just keep that chin up—no point in moping around here, it's not worth it.

They searched the Professsor's house from the cellar to the attic, and found nothing, they fanned out in every direction along every possible path through the fields, they visited every single village and farmstead: there was Máriafalva, Gyulafalva, Farkashalom, and Szentbenedekpuszta, there was Lencsési Street, Bicere, the area surrounding Veszelycsárda and the ruined castle of Póstelek, then from Doboz they also went to Szanazug, and they had pinned serious hopes on Szanazug, because this was, according to the Leader, the most promising location, as the weekend cottages had been standing empty there for years now, and the individual they were pursuing might well have seen them as an excellent hideout—but nothing, then came the forests, the clearings, any kind of weed-grown area where he could have hidden, there were the abandoned farmsteads of Remete, Pikó, Ebédleső Plain, and Vígtánya; there was Fövenyes, the Makkoshát Forest, followed by Gyíkos, Törökhalom, and Julipusztа—but nothing and nothing anywhere, nowhere could a trace be found, not even the tiniest sign from which they could have drawn some conclusion, he sent J.T. back to the original hut in the Thorn Bush where the piece of scum had been living, nothing, J.T. returned, he had left a few of his personal things there, but nothing that we can use, the Leader sat in the Biker Bar, and by now he wasn't even going out with the other posses, he kept in touch with them on the Tetra and sat in his usual seat, staring into the space in front of him, and he scratched away at his beard for a long time, because he hadn't thought this would be easy, but still he really hadn't thought this piece of filth could vanish without a trace like this, I'm going to crush him to pieces, his arms and legs, his eyes bulged with rage in his clouded-over face, so that the bartender didn't even dare—not even wordlessly—to put down a new pint in front of him, the sound on the TV was already turned down, it had been ever since this brouhaha started, and he had a good mind to turn off the picture too, only he didn't dare reach for the remote control, in case this might disturb the Leader in his thinking, because the Leader was thinking, and from that he could tell—at least the bartender could—that thinking wasn't going so well for the Leader right now, because he heard the reports coming in over the Tetra, the reports saying that he wasn't here, he wasn't there, he wasn't anywhere, so the Leader didn't even wait for the Tetra to give the report again, he'd already turned it off, and he went out, alone, to the train station, and sat down with the stationmaster, he looked deeply into his eyes and questioned him so thoroughly that afterward the stationmaster had to lie down—from exhaustion, and perhaps from the red wine he'd downed to combat his fear—for the rest of the day, then the Leader went on, and he questioned the dispatcher at the bus station, he questioned the taxi dispatcher, he went around to all the public buildings, starting with the portly library director, who was the most obliging, to the supplies purchaser at the Fishermen's Csárda restaurant, to the physics teacher at the high school, whose favorite secret meeting place was the former Observatory on the roof of the Water Tower, everyone, he simply subjected everyone to an interrogation —with the exception of the gas station attendant, because he'd supposedly gone to visit relatives in Sarkadkeresztúr, so he had to wait until he came back ... but he really interrogated me, there's no other word to describe what he was doing, it was an interrogation, he wanted to know everything, the library director related to Eszter at the reception desk, and he also wanted to know how long this readers' craze was expected to last, and when it would be over, and he wanted to know if we have separate buildings for book storage, and if we have any branches, and were there any that were closed right now, Eszter—said the library director, who also seemed fairly fatigued by the interrogation—and he also wanted to know—get ready now—if any librarians are related, however distantly, if any of us are distantly related to the Professor, because just imagine, that's who they're looking for, for some reason or another, and at this point he looked at Eszter insinuatingly, they're looking for the Professor, but why, the library director shook his head as if suspecting something, and he just smiled at Eszter with that all-knowing smile of his, that smile that always made Eszter feel so weak, and so it went on, because the Leader wasn't giving up: he calculated every probability and its opposite too, this was by no means his first manhunt—as they formerly called it—but now he didn't call it anything, because he didn't even say anything to his people when returning from one sortie or another, he just pursed his mouth, he pursed it very seriously, from which the others knew that this piece of scum was going to end up as no one had ended up before, because their Leader was going very slowly to smash his head to bits, because this was his specialty when faced with these pieces of scum, because he never used a weapon, and he didn't beat them like that poor fellow Little Star used to—no, he flung them down on the ground and he trampled upon them, he trampled apart the faces of those pieces of filth, completely apart, as if they were cigarette stubs.

Reporting, sir, that we really found a lot, said the corporal, at which point the Police Chief pulled himself up in his chair, because he was inclined, during the course of the day, to sink down into it ever lower and lower, so immersed was he in his work—yes? he took off his eyeglasses, placing them meticulously in their case, signaling that he was prepared for a detailed account—because, the corporal began: he took nothing with himself, we found his clothes, his personal effects, and on the table, if you could call it that, were his notes—continue, the Police Chief urged him on with an impatient gesture—and he also left his personal ID there, his passport, his birth certificate, his residence card, and all of his assorted cards indicating membership in this or that organization, how do you know that was everything, the Police Chief interrupted, well I can tell, sir, because all these IDs were in his wallet, and there was no empty slot in that wallet which would permit us to conclude that something had been removed from that empty place or slot, but I also report, sir, that the first impression all of us had was that nothing was missing from that hovel, moreover, the impression, that is the first impression, of everyone in our unit was: not only did the wanted individual not take anything with him, but he didn't even go away from there, we believe he's still residing in that location—well, what makes you think that, asked the Police Chief severely, because *that was our first impression*, sir, the commander of the special unit repeated—because he knew, as he'd heard often enough that the Police Chief really liked it when, in the course of an investigation, emphasis was given to these first impressions, because the Police Chief always explained it like this: the first impression was the essence, and the rest was workmanship; this had been repeated to them, during some case or another, every morning for almost an entire month: the first impression this and the first impression that, so that ever since then, he, like everyone else in the Police Station, blurted out these words whenever he could, it always worked, and in this way, in general, they'd all learned to deal pretty well with this Police Chief, it was enough to note what he was saying, and then in their reports—whether verbally or in writing—to repeat and employ these phrases, emphasizing them as if they were their own, so that now, as always, the corporal expected nothing more than a nod of recognition, because that was the most they could expect if the Police Chief was satisfied, and he got it too, the Chief was staring straight ahead across his desk—not at him—and just nodded, while adjusting the part in the middle of his head, signaling that he understood, yes, okay, so, in a word, you're saying that in your view the wanted man never left this crap house, or whatever it is out there, yes, sir, that's it, the corporal replied, snapping to attention; not bad—the Captain pursed his lips—and although the corporal understood this as meaning this wasn't a bad supposition on his part, the Police Chief actually meant this wasn't a bad idea on the part of the wanted man: he saw the corporal had misunderstood him, but he didn't feel like explaining himself, let him be happy, he thought, because in addition maybe they'd finally put their fingers on "the pulse of the matter"—and he tapped a cigarette out of its pack and lit it up; care for one? he asked the corporal, yes indeed, thank you, sir, and he lit up too, this was a special favor, because it was very rare to see the Police Chief offer anyone a cigarette: in addition to his daily Marlboros, he also smoked the Egyptian brand Cleopatra, which had become so legendary at the Police Station, everyone wanted to get hold of these, but no one had any luck, only the Police Chief, he himself got them, of course (as the others did with other items), from Romania, more precisely from the guards at the border crossing; they blew out the smoke—the corporal was standing, the Chief was sitting, because this had to remain unchanged—they were silent for a while, and then the Police Chief suddenly got up and stormed out of the office, he waved at the three guards on duty behind him, they got into his jeep, and they started driving toward the train station, and, as the corporal postulated—when he was asked later about where he'd gone—he said that the Police Chief probably wanted to see the location for himself, and in his opinion, he'd gone to Csókos Road, out to the Thorn Bush.

The ditch, as he recalled, wasn't wide enough, long enough, and it also wasn't deep enough, he couldn't, however, call anyone for help, at least at first he discarded this idea with a dismissive gesture, but then he realized that he really couldn't handle this alone; he decided to set out before sunrise and look for someone adequate to the task, someone, yes, but at the same time he must proceed with the greatest caution, he warned himself, and he did proceed with caution, and that was why his choice fell to the bar the peasant had once mentioned, thinking that he could find somebody there; namely, on the basis of the peasant's description, this bar was fairly distant from the city, as well as seeming abandoned and visited only by a few, so he wouldn't seem too conspicuous; he started out before sunrise, and although he believed it wouldn't be too easy—because the peasant had only referred to it as "the 47 out on Csókos Road" and had spoken fairly confusedly about where it was exactly—it turned out to be fairly easy to find as luck played heavily into his hands, because even before he reached the intersection at Sarkadi Road, next to the former mill on Csókos Road, the first thing he saw was a kind of bar-like structure that exactly conformed to the peasant's description: time had caused the signboard to fall off, so the place had no name whatsoever, the iron security gates in front of the doorway could only be pulled half way up, so that no one ever tried, in all likelihood, to pull them all the way down, and finally, on the door itself, the smudged outlines of that famous sign could be made out—on one side depicting a Unicum bottle with the famously happy drowning man, and on the other side three words in a row, formerly causing many a heart to stir: DRINKS REFRESHMENTS COFFEE, namely there was nothing that indicated there was a functioning bar inside, as those for whom it functioned as one already knew what was in there, they weren't expecting anything else—as they weren't expecting him, so that, well, when he went up to the glazed door and glanced inside, he saw that he hadn't been mistaken, there really was a bar in there, perhaps really under the name of "47"; the bartender on duty, a pimply, adolescent girl, quickly got up from the chair in which she had been sitting and leafing through a copy of *Star* magazine, but it was an old issue, so she really was bored, and she'd just been turning the pages over and over until she saw him—namely, a completely new customer coming through the door at such an early hour—she leapt up immediately, and her face showed that she was happy that she could finally put down the copy of *Star*, because something was happening and her face also showed her fright: maybe the customer wasn't even a customer, but there on some kind of official business, which in such a place as this was in no way desirable—but he gave no time for the girl to address him, he spoke immediately: he needed someone who would be able to dig for a few hours in his garden, but he needed someone now, not later, not tomorrow, and so on, well, there's nothing like that here, the girl gestured around the nearly completely empty bar, and she looked at the newcomer with an icy gaze, as it was already obvious that, unfortunately, he had not come here to drink, well, he asked, pointing to one of the figures standing around shakily at the counter, can that one manage it?—and the girl shook her head and said, well, he won't be what you want, at which point he inquired if he could ask himself, meaning the figure at the counter, the girl shrugged her shoulders, sat down in the chair behind the counter, she picked up the copy of *Star* magazine again—ask him whatever you want, she grumbled, and turned to the page where there was an article about Claudia Schiffer—what did she look like when she was wearing no makeup—and so he went over to the swaying person and asked him if he could do the job, to which this person not too enthusiastically, but decidedly said yes, and when the swaying person saw that this individual had, within moments, purchased an entire bottle of Riesling, he was already outside with him on the street, it was still early, but it wasn't early enough for the Professor, because the sky had already brightened considerably, and he, for obvious reasons, was not too happy about the brightness, so he tried to get this person, who went by the name of Feri, to hurry up, and then somehow, inconceivably, everything proceeded with incredible clumsiness—because to proceed with this person who could barely walk, go with him to his friend's house at 3 Ernyő Road, wait for him until he came out with a spade and shovel, then to take this Feri to the Thorn Bush and persuade him to follow after him through the prickly bushes was torture itself, but finally there they were, about a kilometer from his former hut, more or less in the middle of the Thorn Bush, next to the ditch, and the Professor said to this Feri: well, listen here, Feri, if you can dig this pit properly within an hour, here deepen it two meters, and here—he pointed to a spot on the sodden ground—widen it at least up until here, and extend the length up to here, and he stabbed a branch into the ground to show how far, then this bottle of wine will be yours—an hour won't be enough time, said Feri, and the Professor looked at him in surprise, because now, perhaps because of the fresh air, who knew, Feri's voice was nearly sober, and Feri, realizing himself to be in a kind of purposeful negotiating position, for some reason began to shake his head, and then he shook it again, indicating that one hour wasn't enough, and that in addition to this bottle of wine, he had something else coming to him as well, as he believed this would be a much bigger job, because when he dug in the New Reform Cemetery, that took up to a half day, because lately he'd been getting work there, as due to some property-dispute issues, it was being completely liquidated, and the graves were being dug up: whoever had a relative there could have the bones taken to the Holy Spirit Cemetery, the bones without relatives, though, were just scattered for now behind the mortuary, the skeletons were piled up on top of each other, if the gentleman could just imagine that, well, whatever, he didn't want to waste time chatting, he only wanted the gentleman to understand that he had a certain overview of things, and overview of what the soil was like in the New Reform Cemetery, namely, that it was the same as here, because it was right nearby, not too far away at all, and with his own overview of the matter, he would say—well, how marvelous that you have such an overview of things, the Professor bellowed at him severely, because right now there's a view of this ditch, because this right here is almost dug out, and in addition I'm here as well, you can't mess around with me, Feri, so get going and don't give me all this crap as if you're not interested in making this bit of extra cash, get going on that damned ditch already, and start digging, and he moved a little over to the side of the ditch, he scooped away a bunch of old leaves, retrieved something from beneath one or two planks, and that something was a weapon, so Feri started working fairly quickly, and he only spoke once from the pit, saying: well, of course this ground soil is much better than in the New Reform Cemetery, but after that he didn't speak, because he didn't dare stop, he just dug and dug, no matter how damp the earth was, he didn't say a word, he just panted and groaned, but he dug and he shoveled, and he didn't stop, because the person who had consigned him to this work remained next to the ditch, watching his every move; he sat on a tree stump thinking about something intensely, all the while with the weapon resting in his lap, and he never stopped looking at him, and he placed the wine bottle, as if it were a bouquet of flowers, on a stone exactly opposite from Feri, so that every time Feri threw out a shovelful of earth from the ditch—and he was about to say something about the ever worsening difficulties that confronted him in the midst of his work with this ground soil, which, although it wasn't exactly like that of the New Reform Cemetery, nonetheless was still fairly pebbly—he saw the wine bottle, not to speak of the weapon in the lap, and then he bit his own tongue, bent down again for the spade, and he shoveled and he dug, so that after not an hour had passed, but after three, he got his bottle of wine, and this strange person with his rifle gave him an extra two thousand forints, so that in the end this person proved to be completely humane, and he even chatted with him about what the work was like over there in the New Reform Cemetery, about the work conditions, and what would be the fate of those bones scattered behind the mortuary, as well as other such matters, and finally he was dismissed, but this strange person warned him to watch out for that girl in the pub, because I didn't see anything good in that girl's eyes, believe you me, there was nothing good in those eyes, so keep your wits about you, Feri, when you're ordering there.

Everything's burning—the announcement came from the radio when they were circling around the location in the commander's jeep—something has made the entire Thorn Bush go up in flames, it's smoking like a thunderbolt, and there's a huge stench, the flames are huge, we need four vehicles right away, and ask for help from Békéscsaba, because those four vehicles won't be enough, although make sure there's enough water, because these flames are as big as —for Christ's sake, he yelled at the driver, get back!, the driver immediately shifted into reverse, and, stepping on the gas, backed up about twenty meters, because the flames were bursting above them, nearly touching the jeep and the people inside, listen here, the Police Chief shouted at the driver, if you want to cook, go get yourself a grill, yes sir, answered the driver, but the others didn't even really hear what they were saying, because they were so struck dumb by the fire, because first of all, there was the fact that any fire had started at all when just a few days ago it had been properly drizzling, and two, what could have made the weeds here light up like this, because everybody knew there was nothing and no one here, and the person who had been here—the wanted man, well, if anyone was going to be coming back here, then it certainly wouldn't be him, just to be rounded up by them—mainly he wouldn't be lighting up this whole place, because why, and third—and this point was raised now by the Police Chief, only to himself, but aloud, so everyone heard him—namely that there was some kind of oil stench, but for fuck's sake, it couldn't be oil, as—according to his knowledge—there was no oil to be found anywhere in town, and so what could be making it burn so much, what was this material that could create such huge flames?—well, Captain, sir, the driver, a lance corporal from the special unit, began cautiously—go on, the Police Chief nodded—well, I'm thinking that it's not burning like the fire in that German-owned house four years ago, which burned up quite regularly, this fire is different; well, what are you thinking of, the Police Chief asked—well, said the corporal, the flames keep flaring up again and again—yes, yelled out the Police Chief, you're right: that's the problem—I was trying to remember where I had seen such flames before, but well, I recalled those documentaries on the Discovery Channel about the great firebombing of Dresden or the carpet bombing in Vietnam, well, that's when I saw something like this, the way these flames are leaping up here; *this is no fire,* the Captain pronounced, and at that point there was silence in the jeep, because they understood more or less what he was trying to say, but what the hell else could this be other than a fire, they asked themselves, namely *a fucking huge fire,* here in the Thorn Bush, but then they heard the sirens, and the first fire truck appeared at last, proceeding at a much slower pace than was mandated in their regulations, then the second, the third, and finally the fourth showed up as well, and it was clear the vehicles were struggling tortuously in the muddy ground —well, but that's their job, the Police Chief noted dispassionately in the jeep, they have to be able to get everywhere, am I not right—but Captain, sir, they said to him in the jeep, they're coming already, they reassured him, and really, there they were, the fire trucks all nicely lined up one after the other, as they approached the "Weeds"—that's what they called the Thorn Bush—about seventy or eighty meters away, and they would have started trying to put out the fire, but at first the Fire Chief—or rather, the most senior fireman, who'd taken up the command for the Fire Chief, the Police Chief didn't recognize him in the chaos—surveyed the location, he tried to cautiously approach to see what kind of fire they were dealing with, but then suddenly an enormous flame burst close to him, he started back, and he examined a small bough on which tiny flames were jumping back and forth; he looked at this carefully, attentively, moreover he even sniffed it, then he tossed it away, he went back to the first truck, and gave the order to *not* start disassembling and pulling out the fire hoses, but to request reinforcements and as many sand sprayers and foam extinguishers as possible—he gave the order for the water tankers to return to the station, and the Impulse Storm fire extinguishers to get here right away, and only the dry-powder extinguishers should remain, that truck however, should get ready to start performing "peripheral maneuvers"—finally he returned to the jeep, motioned for them to roll down the window, and he uttered only these words: it's diesel fuel, Captain, it's dirty fuel, but it's diesel, and apart from that it may be mixed with some kind of gas—and the Captain just looked at him, he didn't say anything, then he just gave the order for them to survey the entire area so as to assess the range of the fire, and if the flames might, in any sort of unfavorable scenario, endanger the city, namely, could the fire reach as far as Csókos Road; but no, the fire wouldn't reach this far, he said to his subordinates, they had driven to Csókos Road, he got out of the car, put both his hands on his hips, put one of his legs on a stone, and leaned on his elbows, and he watched as the entire area burned down; the corporal went over and stood behind him, waiting for a command, he waited for a while but no command came, they just watched the flames and how they jumped back and forth—they were tiny, as seen from here—then the Captain said, at first just to himself, but aloud: clever, in its own way, very clever, to set himself on fire along with the forest, namely, he knew what was waiting for him, so he got hold of some diesel, or something like that, from somewhere in Romania, and he just lit himself up, then they were silent again, because the corporal really didn't know what to say to this, they watched the flames, as the fire exploded again and again in this or that location, and they saw how it was spreading more and more, and how the entire region was now in flames, when the Captain finally took his leg off the stone and pulled himself up; turning the vehicle around and casting a final glance at the catastrophe, he said to the corporal: you can call the journalists now, you can alert the TV stations too, because this is a story for them, look here, corporal, said the Police Chief, here will be tomorrow's front-page headline: BURNING THORN BUSH.

We're not selling good luck charms here, and between us, my friend, this could get you eight years in solitary, the Police Chief said to him in the interrogation room, which they referred to—but only in the department—as the "Incubator," it doesn't matter to me whether you talk or you don't talk, but you'll be in big trouble, my friend, and Feri just sat there at the other end of the table, he was literally trembling, his entire body was shaking with cold, especially his hands and his head, because the thought of what he'd gotten himself mixed up with made him shudder with cold, as did the thought that his punishment would be completely lawful—he'd given himself up already quite a while ago, he'd given himself up when they grabbed him from both sides in the

"47" bar, and pushed him into the police car, he'd given himself up already when he heard that what that fish-eyed bartender was saying on the telephone to the police, he'd given himself up lock, stock, and barrel, that's what those rheumy, reddened eyes said, but he couldn't bring himself to speak, he simply became mute, so terrified was he, so the Police Chief personally took over and continued the interrogation, because the others had tried one after the other, and they spread their hands out helplessly and shrugged their shoulders, indicating that even their more "colorful" methods were futile, any kind of threats were futile, they had all ended in failure, so there was nothing left to do, he had to deal with this minor barfly himself, all right, he said, he stubbed out his cigarette, got up, and went into the "Incubator," he sat down across from the suspect, and he said to him: eight, but it could be more if you don't talk, but if you do talk, maybe you won't get anything at all, namely he gave a turn of the screw, because he somehow instinctively realized that this wretch wasn't speaking because he was terrified, he'd never been in a position like this in his entire life, this was no criminal, just some kind of two-bit worm, the Police Chief looked indifferently at Feri, who wasn't even trying anymore to stop the trembling in his hands or head, well, never mind; this Feri then lifted up his right arm—what are you doing, the Police Chief said sternly, because he didn't understand—there's something I'd like to say, Feri finally stammered out—and that's why you put your arm up?—yes, nodded Feri, as best he could, and he quickly lowered his hand—on the holy Blessed Virgin, listen here, you better start talking and tell me everything you know, then I'll let you go home, don't be afraid, just start already, because we don't have much time, and Feri began to talk, and he just talked and talked, and he warmed up to the subject more and more, so in the end the words were just pouring out of him, and he wrung his hands, and he trembled more and more, because he had understood this much: if he kept on talking for a long time they would let him go home, so if they'd asked him to lick clean the premises, or to drink his own urine, he would do so, and he even told the big commander: I'll do whatever you want, just let me go, and not even one quarter of an hour had gone by, and the big commander got up, and he said well, that's good, that will be enough, we understand, and now my colleagues will take you to the location, and you'll explain everything to them, then you can go home and godspeed, and with that Feri jumped up, ran over to the Police Chief, grabbed his hands, and kissed his hand once, then he kissed his hand twice, and finally the big commander was able to free himself, and he said to him that's fine, there's no need for gratitude, but watch out for yourself, boy, because if it happens again, do you understand, if we find you mixed up in something like this again, we'll lock you up and throw away the key—oh, stammered out Feri, but the great commander would never hear of him again, because he was going to lead a quiet life, indeed even up until now he'd led a quiet life, never even hurting a fly, and he was speaking seriously now, throughout his whole life not even one little fly, and well, it was another matter altogether that his life had been difficult and full of many tragedies—well, no mind, said the great commander, and Feri clammed up, as he saw now that he didn't want him to talk, the main thing was for there to be a good ending to this whole horror story, and that's how it concluded: they put him in a car and whisked him over to the Thorn Bush, and it was easy for him to find the spot because the whole area was charred, and it was easy to see where it was, he pointed to the exact location of the ditch, and then they didn't ask him anything else after that, they just sent him on his way, telling him to leave already, and not be in the way, so he took a few steps backward, but he somehow still didn't dare completely leave, and they had to snarl at him: beat it!, only then did he understand that he was free to go, my dear Lord, what did I get involved with for a bottle of wine, I should have known better than to start talking to such strange miscreants, how could I have been so stupid, and he went along, and still for a while he kept trying to listen into the air, to check if he heard the sound of a motor, because he still didn't dare take anything for granted, but then he came out onto Nagyváradi Road, and he quickly headed toward his own street, in through the door, and then he slid in the bolt, because the lock hadn't been working properly for a long time, he quickly plopped down in the chair and didn't move, he sat there motionlessly for about a half hour, and he listened to his heart, because it was pounding so hard, he thought for sure he was going to get a heart attack, but he didn't luckily, because after a half hour the throbbing calmed down somewhat, at last he was able to breathe normally too, then he went over to the hot plate, and from the shelf above he took down a can of sausage and beans, put on some water to boil, put the can in the pot, then, tossing the boiling hot can from one hand to the other, he somehow opened it and sat back down in his chair, he put it in his lap, holding the tin can with both hands to warm them up and devoured the entire thing—without bread, although he didn't like it without bread, but there was no bread here at home—he didn't even leave one bean uneaten in that tin can; it had been there on his shelf, he always had four or five tin cans towering up there, boiled beans with sausage, that's what he liked, he could always eat two of these at once, and sometimes he ate three, but he also had to ration it so he could only eat one for each meal, because his invalid pension wasn't enough, sometimes, like now, to even have a crust of bread, so that it was just the can of beans, because he always feasted well with that, well, and then a drop of wine, but this of course was his weakness, he acknowledged that, and he didn't need any prompting to recognize that, and he really didn't need very much anyway, one can of beans with sausage, and a little bit of wine, every day, that was enough.

The official investigation is closed, the Police Chief said to him over the Tetra—the timbre of his voice made it impossible not to understand: no more, the case was closed—and what this means, as far as your group is concerned, said the Police Chief, is stop, have I made myself clear, the Police Chief asked—but he didn't reply, up there his brain was charging, it was overcharged, more precisely, it was so overcharged that now, when he was being informed of the so-called good news, this good news was instead just another blow to him, and, in his view, to everyone who stood with him, a blow, a fiasco—that wasn't even the right word, but now he didn't even know what the right word would be—because that charging, that strain, that readiness, that thirst, if he could put it so poetically, for vengeance to be fulfilled—he related the events in the Biker Bar—had only grown in him, and he would sincerely say, he said, that somehow he didn't believe it, because fine, he accepted what happened, looking at things from the official point of view—and now he really emphasized the word "official"—in other words, from their perspective, the case really could be seen as closed, but still there was something in it that he just didn't like, and, he said it wasn't because he hadn't been counting on this kind of outcome or something similar—because he'd only been counting on some unexpected outcome, knowing this piece of filth for who he was—but this, that he would set the Thorn Bush on fire, with himself inside that filthy pit, where he'd hidden away from them, this somehow seemed a little too easy to him, but it could be that this brain-charging was still working in him and hadn't yet calmed down, because he sincerely would say, he said again, that he could never resign himself to Little Star's villainous murderer getting off so easily, because that was what this piece of scum was up against here, he was up against all of them, a brotherhood where revenge was a central category, and what kind of revenge was it that wasn't executed by them on their prey but by the prey upon himself, the whole thing just seemed a little too smooth, said the Leader again, although in many respects it did fit with how he recalled the Professor, because I imagined—he explained, half to the others, half to himself—that he would come up with a solution that even we wouldn't be expecting, and this really is such a solution; there's just this one little hitch—he looked at the two new recruits, who visibly didn't understand too much of the matter, but were listening intensely—the hitch was that this piece of filth had figured out exactly something that he, the Leader, was expecting—namely something unexpected, something that would surprise him—something that would make him say: Lord Almighty, he really outsmarted me, because I didn't think of this; but I did think—and he looked at Totó, and Totó nodded once, indicating that he understood, he was following the line of argument, drinking up his every word—I have thought about it, and this is exactly what bothers me; anyway, my brothers, he raised his voice, I hope everyone can hear me properly, this case—even if we can do nothing else and have to accept that this piece of filth is no longer—this case is still by no means closed, because no matter how it turned out, we must do this for Little Star, to do nothing is not an option for me, I have to at least liquidate the remains of this piece of filth, do you understand—we understand, the others murmured their approval, especially J.T., who was inflamed like embers, because he was enraged that they hadn't found him and he hadn't been able to complete the task assigned to him, namely to return to the hut, to look over everything thoroughly once more, because he hadn't found the key, the clue to the whole thing, what was the point of this whole game, and now that label—that he was no good at reconnaissance—would remain on him, nobody said this to him openly, not even the Leader himself, but J.T. knew that the judgment was still there, and that is why he was the one who most vehemently approved when the Leader said: we're heading out now, everyone have a weapon on him, understood? and until they reached the scene, the Leader just kept turning it over and over again in his head—did everything in this story really fit? —he led with a slow pace in front, because he wanted to grant the thing its dignity, but at the same time he really wanted to go over in his mind the details of that version once more, according to which: the piece of filth could have returned to his hut after J.T. and the others had left there and taken his belongings and placed them in the ditch, which, in the end, made a lot of sense too—after his escape, he could have built that ditch—because at that point they weren't looking for him, so he could have built that ditch with his insulation panels, he could have brought over the table and the bed, who knows what else—reflected the Leader at the head of the procession, as they turned, in three columns, by the Hospital into Szent László Street—he could have easily set up the whole thing within one or two hours, and of course he was waiting for nighttime, so how many nights had he been there?—two, maybe three, if he was already so brazen as to spend the first night there, but he didn't lose too much time, that's for sure, because to build up that dump of his, and have that drunken tool dig the pit for him, he'll get in trouble for that ... and that worried the Leader, too, the Captain had promised that he wouldn't touch him, but a little lesson never hurt anyone—the procession reached the edge of Maróti Square, they turned to the right, going toward the road that led to the Castle—so at the very most three nights, fine, that's possible, he thought, I can buy that: he had the pit dug, he brought his stuff over, fine, I can accept that, because besides the bones the cops found a few things in that dump, and they were able to determine that they were his personal things—his birth certificate and things like that, and these were the same things that J.T. had seen in the first hut he built, fine—but I just want to ask, he asked himself: doesn't it seem as if he deliberately left these things in the hut so that afterward, after he'd set everything on fire, these same objects would be found again in that ditch and identified as his personal items, after he blew himself up with the Thorn Bush?, because why did he leave money there in a plastic purse, was it in there because he knew that it wouldn't burn so much and they'd be able to identify it; namely if somebody leaves so much money somewhere, then everyone is going to automatically assume that he did burn up in this pit, well, fine, he proceeded with a measured pace all along the edge of the park, the others following behind, maybe this is a slightly convoluted line of reasoning, I admit that, but I'm just asking, he said to himself, I'm just posing the questions, and well, what am I supposed to do, I'm just throwing out questions, like this one, for example: because the whole thing seems somehow a little too clever, a little too elaborate, because it's hard to imagine, nobody who is chased by a posse backed up by a team of cops really thinks like that, they don't even think, even if a person has as much wits about him as this rat did; he recognized that this rat did have his wits about him, he sincerely admitted that if everything really did happen as the Police Chief thought it did (that he had concealed himself, hardly a stone's throw away, during the entire manhunt), then that attests to a pretty good mind, the Leader acknowledged that, because he hadn't really taken into consideration, or rather he didn't think it possible that this rat would go back to the sealed-off crime scene, dig himself a little pit a short ways off, and hide out there; it was just that there was something else, a minor detail—they turned onto the road to the Castle at the Prekup Well—it was really just a minor detail, but still: if this two-bit rat imagined having that pit dug for himself and hiding out there, then exactly how long would he imagine holding out there, how long, and if he couldn't hide out there anymore, then what would he do, what then? and again this was just a question, he wasn't insinuating anything—he continued his inner monologue—he was just posing questions and waiting for his brain to answer, because then what came afterward, and this afterward, how did this rat envision it? because he couldn't have thought that everything would go so nice and smooth, that they'd just forget about the whole thing and he could just stroll away nicely from that spot with no problem, there's no way he could have seriously thought that; he still had to have some idea of who he was facing here, what they were capable of, and so when did he realize there was no escape from that rathole, when would he have decided the best solution would be for him to dispose of himself, because the Leader wasn't concerned about what he had used to ignite the fire, it was obvious that no matter what it was, he only could have gotten hold of it in Romania, he could have easily made the journey in one night with a truck if he'd had enough money to pay off the border guards, and let's say, he said, that he did have enough money, well, never mind; and yet the Leader continued, because he couldn't stop this speculation, even if he couldn't do anything else for the time being than wait for the gas station attendant to return from Sarkadkeresztúr where he'd supposedly gone to visit some relatives, he'll come back—he dug into his beard—he'll come back, and I'll turn him over a bit, because if there's someone who knows where that rat got a hold of that diesel, then it is the gas station attendant, he'd know where he had got the diesel from, and how he got it here, but what was he saying, how?—because where did he get the truck from, if not from the gas station attendant, of course he got it from him, and of course the fuel was from some Romanian source—but this wasn't the main question now, he thought, this also didn't matter; but somehow he couldn't bear to think beyond this—beyond "this also didn't matter": because what was it exactly that did matter, because he could no longer hold up under this discipline that he had to force on himself in order to be able to think, because suddenly before him there appeared the face of Little Star, and a few scenes from their childhood: the very first time they took aim at some frogs with their slingshots by the floodgates of the River Körös—he was a brother, for him he was family, of course he wasn't even speaking of his biker brothers, but Little Star, he was different, he really belonged to him, he was always right there next to him, always supporting him, procuring the hard stuff if he had to; the Leader had given him a goal, he'd introduced him to ideals, he'd provided him with that refurbished Honda, and he started to nicely solve the life of Little Star, and then came along this piece of filth, this garbage, this traitor, this rat, because someone like that really was just a rat, he stepped into the picture and murdered the person whom he loved the most; and he was filled with rage, and drove along, the others driving after him, so when they went along the houses on Nagyváradi Road, and the residents cautiously pulled back their curtains to look and see what that awful commotion was outside, well, they could see that the Local Force was on the move again, because they were watching over the night, because tranquility lay in their hands, they'd made that pledge—the Leader thought now, as he led the posse past the cemetery on Sarkadi Road to the small path leading into the Thorn Bush, and he led the others among the charred trees, the back wheel of his motorcycle skidding at times, to where this rat had dug out his pit, but he didn't find it, because he wasn't exactly sure where it was, as he could only remember that original hut the piece of filth had built for himself, so he motioned for J.T to come to the fore and lead them further on, and then there was nothing left to do but stand all around that rotten pit, all of them stood around it in a circle, and they pointed their weapons down at it, and they looked at the Leader, who in the first minutes motioned for them to be silent, then he gave them the sign with his eyes, but he was the first to pull the trigger, the others fired only after he did, and then they began, and they didn't take their fingers off the triggers, they just shot into that putrid ditch, and they shot and they shot until there was no ammunition left in their magazines, because they wanted to shoot that piece of filth to bits, and they did shoot it to bits, because everybody was thinking how even after the cop investigation, at least a handful of ashes still had to be there, and so they shot it to bits, horrifically, and he just looked at the remains in the ditch, imagining him as he lay there, curled like an embryo, he lay there, and he aimed accurately, accurately at his head, and he just shot out all the bullets, he shot and he shot, until all of his ammunition was used up.

I begin with this—he said to someone in the tiny waiting booth of the train stop at Bicere—namely, I have to think for two hours a day so that I won't have to think during the entire day, because thinking for the entire day depletes my organism, as well as being a kind of passion which never leads anywhere, because a passion can never lead anywhere, as that ensues inevitably from the nature of the thing; so I won't abandon this practice, which is good, as those things that I require for my brain functioning happen to coincide with those things that I tend to be rather good at, so I mustn't permit these extraordinary circumstances to impede me in the continuation of my thought-immunization exercises, and as the compression of this exercise into two hours daily has proven useful—namely it's been going splendidly, as for months now it hasn't even occurred to me to engage in the activity of thinking at any other time than between the hours of three and five p.m., and in ten seconds it will be three p.m.—this undeniably powerful exhaustion from which I suffer is no excuse, for I must complete my exercises today as well, because I can talk about Georg Cantor, and I must talk about him, because he is a central figure to the entire problem—how should I express it, he expressed to someone in the empty waiting area of the train stop—he's a central figure, just as he was at an earlier time, because, in vain, he has been forgotten, what has emerged with Cantor, and to which Cantor gave his own answers, means the whole thing is going round again in circles, as with Cantor, this unfortunate comet of St. Petersburg and Halle, we return to that point from which we started out so many times, and to which we have returned so many times as well; but he was the first to provide these answers, as he was deeply infected with that well-known messianism, and it can't be doubted for a moment: he believed intently in a monotheistic Being, such as could only spring forth from that deep shared passion for the Tanakh, and this Being did spring forth, because Georg Cantor—he tasted the name in his mouth—where did he go astray: well, of course he went astray with his roots in the Tanakh, of course, because the problem always emerges from the roots, or at least most probably it emerges from there, and diffuses outward haphazardly, as Cantor didn't even hypothesize that there is no infinity, he knew *ab ovo* that there is, and altogether he felt this to be his vocation—or perhaps he felt himself summoned to create a so-called scholarly foundation, in his own way, based on his own belief, entrenched particularly deeply in him, because he hadn't been satisfied with the developments hitherto in that regard, poor Cantor, this strange genius, whose sheer brilliance and charlatanry can both be traced back to the same point, namely he was made ill by faith, because it's always like this, we always get to this point, because it isn't true that In The Beginning There Was This and There Was That, because actually what should have been written was: In The Beginning, there was FAITH, and CHECKMATE!—he explained to that someone, and there was no heating in the tiny train booth at Bicere, because nobody was here waiting for any kind of train, although the local train service had been reinstated a few years ago, at least on paper, and trains supposedly stopped now again at Bicere, namely, the route had been reinstated after about two decades, during which time no trains whatsoever had stopped here, so there was no heating, there wasn't even a railway employee here, nor was there a switch controller, nor a track watchman, and well, as for passengers, there were none, as if no one were even interested in the idea that a train might come along, and what would happen then if it did, or maybe everyone already knew that no train was going to come, or they knew when it was going to come, and that's why they weren't here right now—in any event the station was unheated, yet there was an iron stove in the waiting booth; what would happen—the Professor threw out the question to that someone in the empty waiting booth—what would happen if I were to look for a little kindling, and he rubbed his frozen limbs, he exited the tiny booth-like structure, and to his great surprise, he found everything he needed by a back wall: namely there was a pile of wood, chopped nicely and neatly, as well as some dry newspapers—he still had matches, obviously—so he was able to create some warmth in the tiny waiting area fairly quickly, only that stove was smoking a lot, although just temporarily, because as the heat finally dislodged the backed-up smoke or whatever had been blocking it—maybe dead leaves or who even knew what had been in there—but at last it wasn't so smoky inside anymore, and finally he began to shiver—he shivered, because the cold was finally leaving his limbs, and he thought: the mere appearance of a thought hauntingly reminds us that the way a person thinks is but one concept of infinity, and of course it's just one among many, but this is what truly should give rise to suspicion, and sure enough, there were always those who had their suspicions, but no one ever took them seriously, and frankly speaking, it wasn't even possible to take them seriously, because the main intellectual current—ever since Aristotle—was far too strong, sweeping all those reticent doubters out from the shore, and there they floated with all the other tossed-out branches; there, in the history of the great mainstream of intellectual inundations, they got all stuck together along the crenellating shoreline—so it's precisely the infinite that casts light upon how the brain thinks, and how clever it is in showing us something that seems real when it's merely an abstraction, namely that brain introduced or employed to great effect those methods of distortion, that dislocation—how should I put it, he said and he moved a little farther away from the stove, turning a little, because one side of his body was almost singed already, whereas the other side was still numb with cold—because what did people say before Cantor (well of course only in the scientific fields, in particular after the end of the so-called ancient philosophical school of thought in our Western culture, but not in philosophy or in poetry, because those people kept coming up with all these bad infinities and things like that, no, we're only speaking of the history of thought in the natural sciences), and what do I mean by that? well, to echo the most primitive of formulations: the infinite is a part of reality, the infinite is real, and what is this based on, of course on the unacknowledged view—they should, however, have perceived this and they could have perceived it—that the infinite is just one axiom of the problem; there is, however, another dictum, and that is the inability of the human being to accept the view, occurring with real weight, that there are *quantities*, only that the mind simply would have to "believe" that things presenting themselves to the mind as an entity—even that word, en-ti-ty! it boggles my mind—present themselves in exclusively finite quantities, but no, ah, no, that's not what happened, what happened was that this human mind always treated measurements—and we are thinking in this case of both very enormous measurements, as well as very tiny ones, do you understand—this human mind treated these measurements as reality even though they formed no part of tangible reality, for Cantorian set theory also says something about this, and in addition it's pretty ingenious, but still we have to concede that not only is there an infinite, but there are innumerable infinities, well of course because of this he immediately got in trouble with Berlin, with those Kronecker types and the rest, and the takedowns were precisely as logical and confirmable as they possibly could be, marinated in a little Hilbert to help it along, they had to be, and here exactly was the blunder, because this "demonstrability," namely what can be examined as empirical evidence is precisely that which is sacred in so-called scientific thought, and by these means—there's no point in denying it—we can go far, but at the same time, by following this method, we greatly distance ourselves from the problem, because it's so, but so manifest that empirical proof itself is something that no one has ever heretofore truly dealt with, namely, no one has ever wished genuinely to confront the deeply problematic nature of empirical verification as such, because whoever did this went mad, or appeared to be a pure dilettante, or—what's even worse—*became* a pure dilettante, as, for example, the greatly promising Whitehead, who could not be accused of not proceeding from logic, and where did he end up, well, the Professor would prefer not to respond to this, he noted resignedly, because the time spent on all these philosophical worldviews wasn't worth it, not even on a single one, the only thing that was worth dealing with was a brain capable of rising above its own cleverness, in order to understand how it understands something, namely, as in our case, to deal with the problem of how it believes that reality—and now think of this in whatever terms you see fit—takes place in an infinity, when the human being is a creature capable of comprehending *only* the finite, and now what would I say to that, would I say anything at all? he asked, then he turned his other side to the stove, well, I would say that now we are returning to the question of quantity, and let's say that only finite quantities exist, as infinite quantities do not exist, well, so there are finite qualities, as surely the idea of an infinite quality is nonsense; every process, event, and instance is exclusively finite, everything that takes place in the so-called universe is finite: it has a beginning and an end—or at least it appears that way to the brain of a human being, that's how it appears to be, and it doesn't matter at all where we are positioned on one of the various observational stages, there's only that which takes place, there's no other way to express it, this wording is, of course, arbitrary, but every wording is always arbitrary in the fullest measure; if anything exists at all, and we subsequently term this as the Great Flow of Being—then that is truly what takes place... the mere word "nothing"—or not even that, I'll express it better—simply the sentence "there is nothing" is in and of itself unintelligible, because only that which exists can be named, that which exists, however, is never extant, because nothing is extant, only that which takes place, and in this Great Flow there is nothing outside of itself, and—and this is the essential point—there is nothing within itself, either!!!—so we will not prove fruitful in grasping for results in these exploratory examinations, that's why we ran into a dead end, and it wasn't because we discarded the correct direction in our researches, because there is no correct direction, but we've spoken of this already, and this is why we can state—more precisely this is why we can *only* state—that yes, the only thing that exists is a YES; that, however, can't be expanded, expansion is a process in our brain, I would mention this again, because I never cease repeating it yet again and again and again, in general, because as it may have occurred to you, I am fond of repetition, because repetition stupefies, and this stupefaction is greatly needed for the emergence or the birth of intuition—call it what you want, well, never mind, let's leave this, he motioned to that someone—so we're merely facing a process here, by means of which, if we proceed along the route confirmed as correct, we shall immediately reach a result, only that this result is woeful, and from the beginning of the beginning what did it lead to, the Great Hypothesis, the Great Tribal Idea, that there is, there exists, a component part of reality, whereby it is excluded that it would not exist, a component part of reality which is *outside* of reality, existing beyond it, as it were above it—now this again, this spatiality, along with all these quantitative errors, namely in the Beginning of the Beginning there appeared God and that which is godly, and the whole KIT AND CABOODLE, and this is the only virus, the only fatal and actual virus, the only virus that genuinely prods all of humanity into an incurable disease, from which really—but really and truly—we will never be able to free ourselves; in vain is the endeavor to annihilate thought, the consistent, dreadful, awful, the rigorous attention with which we must continuously prevent ourselves from arriving at some result in thinking, the mind will never be able to free itself from this, not even for a moment, because it's not even worthwhile talking about those epochs in which these Hypotheses first emerged, but chiefly there's no point in talking about so-called modernity, which according to some is founded upon knowledge without belief, the self-evidence of the absence of God, and so on; and this age—while it is triumphant, while it is devastating, while it is victorious—in its depths, this age is a mere chronicle of shame, and not liberation, once again the atheists have gotten somewhere, and this is lamentable, because they actually got nowhere, because they were afraid of courage, because this is what they always lacked, the courage to take that one extra step, and take the measure of what they really had *come up with* in their idea that there is no God, they were accused, and perhaps even today are accused, of lacking consistency, well, no, I'll tell you what it was, because it was courage they lacked: they were cowardly, and cowardly they remain, even up until this day, no true atheist has ever come along (of course, they still could), in any case, those pitiful panhandlers—the atheists of yesterday and today—they pronounced the big sentence and immediately shit their pants because of what they'd just said, they shouldn't have, however, because they themselves didn't even realize the significance, the astonishing importance of what they'd just stumbled on, so that it isn't worthwhile dealing with them—he waved them aside in the waiting booth—because the problem with them was that even the more intelligent ones among them didn't know what to do with that basic sense, when it's there, when you've come upon something and you still don't have any words for it, and concepts aren't any use, but it's there, it's right there in your hands, you grasp at it compulsively, fearful it will slip away, and of course it does slip away once you open your palm, you try to track it down but it's nowhere—and that's how it goes, if they hadn't opened up their hands, then they could have realized the kernel of the problem, right there in their hands, because if you can forgive me the mixed metaphor, they would have realized, they would have been able to grasp it in its entirety, he added, but no, they never did that, but let's leave it—the denial of God is merely the cell of the condemned, stemming from rage, arrogance, from the glimpse of greatness, and behind it lurks the envy of greatness: it's ridiculous, and yet clear-sighted, because even the fact that we see clearly, this desire gathers its ammunition completely from a misunderstanding, because what should we do with our desire to see clearly, what?, well, I say, that we should realize what an interesting mistake, what an inordinately interesting mistake it is to want clear-sightedness, and for us to think we can see clearly in any sort of matter, whichever it may be, whether in the matter of the infinite, or of transcendence, because these are not mere topics, these are authentic unrealities, best dealt with by psychology or neo-psychology, although it would also be best for both of these disciplines immediately to be eradicated as the withered and puny fruits of human stupidity, nonetheless, what we must deal with here is, namely, Cantor and his god—because if we're dealing with this, then at least we're dealing with *something*, namely we're dealing with fear, and we have to deal with that if Cantor and his god are interesting—and they are interesting—and that's why, at this point, we must refocus our attention on this, as fear is what defines human existence, because you can say that it's only a mere feeling, easily gotten rid of, well, no, we don't get rid of it with ease or with difficulty, because fear is so much at the center of our question—of Cantor and his god—that it becomes unavoidable for us to find out what it is, that's not so difficult, though, as our one task here is for our gaze to take in fear's entire domain, and what does this mean? well, of course it means that we must examine fear with all of its consequences, and by this I mean: just take a look at the human being—but no, I'll put it another way: look at all the aggregate living beings on the earth, no, that's not good either, I'll put it this way: look at everything existing on the earth—all of the card-bearing Party members of the organic and inorganic worlds—and you will see that fear is the deepest element that can be grasped in this organic and inorganic world, and there's nothing else other than fear, because nothing else bears within it such dreadful strength, because apart from fear, nothing else defines anything in the organic and inorganic world to such an enormous degree, everything can be inferred from it, to say that you can't trace this or that back to fear is ridiculous, so that we're not going to bother with this anymore, but we're going to say enough of these wily excuses, and we will turn our attention to fear, and then we reach the point where fear becomes the essence of existence—but I almost rushed ahead too much, and I told you that we can't say anything else about existence, only that it is driven by fear, because Attila József (and it would be best if you were to engrave his name into your consciousness right now) came upon, in a completely interesting way, an expression: "like a pile of hewn timber / the world lies heaped upon itself," and it doesn't matter whether he really thought it through or not, because he illuminated such a huge territory with this formula, in any event, his genius blundered upon this expression, because in reality the fear that existence will cease, and that always in a given case it will cease, is the most elemental force that we know—and if we can't really enclose this fact in a nice, little box, if we were to nonetheless place all our most significant knowledge in a capsule, and shoot it off to Mars—if we could finally make up our minds and leave behind this earth, which in general we don't deserve (although who knows who's in charge here)—well, and so here we are again, back with fear, because gigantic tomes should be written about that, a new Bible, new Testaments, but nobody has written these, there were incidental murmurs here and there, as is customary with epoch-making thinkers, but I feel strongly the absence of the great fundamental works—the new *Principia*, the new *Divina Commedia*, and so on—and everyone should feel their absence, because not only is it a terrible irresponsibility to leave this concept to the psychologists—whom, as you already must have clearly perceived from my words, I greatly detest—but doing this is simply an error, which in reality is careless, because it diverts us from the essence, because just think about what that means: fear, if we regard it as a creationary force, a general power center, from where the gods evaporate, and finally God emerges, and yes, the God of Cantor too, because the fear of the cessation of existence is a force field which we can't even measure, because we have never had and never will have an instrument which will allow us to measure such a horrifying strength—this, the fear of nonexistence, impedes the possibility of the existence of nonexistence; fear helps everything striving for nonexistence to remain within existence; you ask why would it be that the gods and God appear in every culture, even in those cultures that never could have encountered each other, given the contingencies of time or space, well, what do you think, well, of course, it is this common factor of fear that takes hold of people in every culture and doesn't let them go, but I will say something else, not just people but animals too, you've seen an animal in a state of fear, no? indeed I'd say—and I hope that in doing so I won't fall prey to the charge of muddled esoterism—this fear is also present in the inorganic world, I wouldn't of course designate it by the same name, I'd name it something else if I could—although I can't—but never mind, because this isn't the interesting thing now, the main point is that fear is the Fundamental Law, fear is the basis of the Constitution of Being, namely let's look at the whole thing again, I'd recommend that: what we say now is even more essential than what we think, what we sense with thinking requires newer reinforcements to what we've already said about fear, more precisely, what we thought about fear, and even more precisely, what we sensed about it—and what would that be? you ask, and your question is justified, because first and foremost we have to make it clear when it comes to such auxiliary concepts as reality or existence, the only thing we should perceive are the events through which it can easily be seen that the world is nothing more than an event-lunacy, a lunacy of billions and billions of events, and nothing is fixed, nothing is confined, nothing graspable, everything slips away if we want to clutch onto it, because there isn't any time, and by that I mean that there isn't any time for us to grasp at something, because it always slips away, because that's its function, as it is nothing more or less than the Great Flow—these billions and billions of events—they are extant, and yet nonexistent: let us thus presume that so-called horizon, and on this horizon, as we have already said, there are merely these events, vanishing from sight in that very same moment (which itself is also not real) in which they appear, events on the event horizon, this exists and is no abstraction—at last something which isn't an abstraction—and so much so that it's the one thing we may presume as extant before tossing it aside—I ask you now though, I really ask you now to think deeply about the universe, and then you will see what this universe is like, these events occurring in insane succession and overlapping with each other, events, namely, take place, and this is the correct expression, and one event is the cause of another event, well, but what kind of cause can this be, the internal nature of which does not elicit the next event, but since *it is the case* that the question of what event is solicited by another event is so dependent, and to such a horrific degree, on the contingent, that we need to deal with this question much more thoroughly, namely the contingent is nothing more or less than the necessary nature which allows for the contingent to exist as a condition; well now, to get back to the event horizon, and to that inconceivably huge conglomeration—but not infinite, for the sacred love of God, but a merely inconceivably *huge* conglomeration, where we must also say that we too are part of the universe, in order to make a huge jump here toward our own selves, as we ourselves are part of the mesh of events, where our own gently shifting consolidation or temporary sustainability cannot be attributed to anything else than to the fact that events are capable of originating other events, moreover, even a kind of genetic replication, and in exactly the same manner, namely contingently, as these events must of necessity subsist, I hope you haven't misunderstood this "of necessity," I really hope so, because the hard part is coming now, namely that inasmuch as we think of ourselves as human monads, then we can express our uncertain conviction in this question as well: the fear that is within us and the joy of life that is within us, well, these two things are *one and the same*, two sides of one fact, because we are a web of events that seeks to sustain one thing and one thing only, namely continuity, about which we can say, for the moment—if there would be a moment, but there isn't, because nothing unfolds in time, time is once again just one of these auxiliary concepts which we live as if it were a reality—well, never mind, so accordingly events are just one gigantic heap, really a gigantic heap, if we look at things from our own direction, and we do look at things from here, because from where the hell else could we look at things—a heap in which similitude loves similitude, it wishes for it, goes out of its mind for it, is crazy in love with it, this is not contradiction, but it is similitude, that which we long for in this event resemblance, and what comes next is that we must once again connect back to that discussion where fear is the lord, but not even the lord, here it's about something much more fundamental, much more earth-shattering, and this is where I want to get with you now, so you can comprehend fear in this system, which of course is not a system, but instead is chaos—it contains elements which we have termed as events, horizon, and other such things, but in reality, accordingly, fear is horrifically strong, residing within our most profound depths, and these depths are far too deep for us to ever really understand how truly deep they are, well, never mind, because what I want to say to you is that it is precisely fear and its dreadful strength that gave birth to culture, and perhaps this—in light of my previous statements—is no surprise to you, and what you should understand is that the cradle of human culture isn't the valley of the Yellow River, nor Egypt, and it isn't Mesopotamia, nor is it Crete, nor the city-states of ancient Greece, nor is it the Holy Land, and so on, but it is fear itself; and this is so important that I'm inclined to repeat this—I'm joking now, because of course I'm always repeating something—in a word, every human culture is created by fear, and from this grows the order of conceptions, if you understand what I'm saying, but permit me now to join this up for you, back to our idea of the joy of life, because I hope that what I'm about to say won't come as a surprise to you, that this is really one and the same thing—if you say: fear, or if you say: the joy of life—but of course then what would be that one word that expresses the two sides of fear and of the joy of life, I don't know, and I'm not planning to set my sights on that, because—and here I'm joking again—I prefer not to express myself in exact terms, because I sense when I'm getting close to it; accordingly, I ask you, let's go back to the theme of why Cantor is worth it, because it's also worth taking a closer look at Cantor's God, because then, as we said, at least we'll be dealing with something—and with what?, well, we deny, namely we affirm the denial of the existence of God, and we annihilate the questions, or rather we endeavor to attempt the impossible, and we liquidate the questions themselves, because questions as a rule only permit a limited set of answers, namely in this sense we have no need of questions in order to proceed in this great liquidation, which is nothing else, of course, than the fruit of continual attention, we must accept this—he noted in the tiny structure of the Bicere train stop— because we are convinced that in a finite universe there is no kind of god or God, so that if I say that we live in a world without God, then I myself am heading out on thin ice, but I can't set off in any other way, where all the same I crouch for a long time on the ice, but nonetheless I can finally say that there is no kind of God *whatsoever* in reality, no matter what we mean by the term reality—which of course for us, for the thinking mind, is the most horrific if we understand that this also means that everything, including the entire culture of humans has been built upon a false basis, it based itself upon a belief, indeed it nourished itself from that belief, and it brought forth masterpieces, from the *Principia* to the Homeric epics, through the *Divina Commedia,* from Pheidias of Athens to the angels of Fra Angelico, to the *Die Grundlage der allgemeinen Relativitätstheorie,* from the Pali Canon through the Bible to the Created World appearing to us, and I won't go on, because I'm leaving out Bach, and I'm leaving out Zeami, and I'm leaving out Heraclitus, I'm leaving out the nameless geniuses of architecture, and what kind of list is that in which they do not figure, but this isn't even the most essential thing, because just what kind of collapse would it be —my heavens— he shook his head, smiling, next to the stove, when we understand, when we really grasp that the basis of all human culture is false, but how bleak everything will be then, he bowed his head, because then it is necessary to admit that everything that aroused our enthusiasm—all of the inimitable works of the human creating mind—rests on an illusion, and emerged from that illusion, namely an acknowledgment such as this will certainly have considerable destructive strength, the same as the knowledge that that God who was given to us with complete certainty does not exist, that, too, is a similarly unpleasant recognition, indeed perhaps immediately annihilating, when we are programmed to believe He exists, whether we deny His existence or not, namely, we affirm the denial of His existence, we therefore at once affirm and deny, it's a sad, sad world that knows certainly that there is no God, there never was a God, and now it seems *there never will be a God,* it's really tremendously sad, he put another piece of wood or two onto the fire, and once again he sat down onto the bench in the tiny waiting booth at the Bicere train stop, and he looked into the eyes, moist from love, of that someone—a pair of eyes which were concealed by a thicket of fur, and at the end of that thicket there was a tail too, and that tail was now cheerfully wagging; maybe for us, there's nothing more sad than that—that's what I think, Little Mutt. He looked at his watch. 5:01. Maybe the train wasn't even going to show up here.

# WATCH OUT FOR —

It's not that I don't understand why a person has to die, but rather, I don't understand why a person has to live, Baron Béla Wenckheim pondered, and he turned his head toward the window, but he didn't want to look outside, he didn't want to see anything, this was his way; although he wouldn't have been able to see very much of the town anyway, as everything outside was gray, and on his side, the window was fogged up; he'd been asked if he wanted to see the high school with Lennon's Ditch in front of it, he shook his head; did he wish to see his parents' house, he shook his head; did he want to be taken to the Krisztina Castle in Szabadgyíkos, now home to a vocational school, which had been fixed up to a certain degree—no, the Baron motioned from his seat in the back—or the cheerful celebrations, for example, at the Budrió Housing Estate, or in the Seniors' Club, but the Baron motioned again, indicating no, he didn't want to see anything, well, but Lord Baron, the Mayor urged him on gently, certainly you don't wish to cancel the meeting with the county Lord Lieutenant, to which the Baron wordlessly nodded, yes, he did wish to cancel it, well, but—the Mayor looked at him flabbergasted —there are the discussions, for surely you know that the Lord Lieutenant will be conducting those negotiations, the essence of which is that the government, Lord Baron, the Hungarian government itself! wishes to create a strategic partnership with you, the exploratory talks have already begun, no, no, motioned the Baron, and he just sat in the car with his head drooping down, while the Mayor just kept saying what he had to say, but ever more despairingly, and even more disconnectedly, talking about these things as they came into his head, because he simply could not understand, he didn't understand what was going on here, or what it was that swept the Baron into "such a profound" depression, and why the Baron was so dissatisfied, he didn't understand anything anymore; he'd put his heart and soul into this, though, and he didn't want to give up, he couldn't bear to, he couldn't resign himself to everything being destroyed by this "unexpected relapse in mood" of the Baron's, while all of the celebrations arranged in his honor were still going on, and the two local television stations were broadcasting *Evita* every evening; please—the Baron suddenly spoke, but he was speaking so softly that he had to lean across the gap between the two seats dividing them—please, murmured the town's noble benefactor (as every newspaper and radio and television station called him now), please take me back to the hotel, and so what could he do, he told the driver to take them back to the hotel, and they were driven back, and the Baron went up wordlessly to his suite on the first floor and closed the door behind him, and he didn't even say anything to Dante, who was waiting for him, dozing off in one of the armchairs, to finally come back so he could begin the negotiations with him which could no longer be postponed, although as a matter of fact he couldn't even be certain if the Baron had noticed he was also in the room, so he rubbed his eyes, stretched his limbs, then he went out of the living room and into the bathroom to "take a leak," the Baron went into the bedroom, sat down on the bed, but he didn't at all look like someone who hadn't noticed that Dante was there, or like someone who earlier hadn't heard the Mayor's questions— his gaze was clear, he sat on the bed with a straight back, but with his head lowered, because he was looking at his shoes; Dante decided to try once more, and he peeked in through the door to ask if the Baron was going to start crying again, no, answered the Baron readily, he didn't think so, indeed he was of the opinion that he was never going to cry again, so there was no reason for Dante to be worried, and he motioned to him with his head, in which there was both at once a request and a command for Dante really to leave him alone, because he had something he had to attend to—Dante disappeared from the doorway, and the Baron once again lowered his head, he liked to sit like that, when he was still in Buenos Aires he would often sit like that for hours, just sitting on the edge of the bed, and these were his momentary retreats into tranquility, when he could sit on the bed, and the light was already turned off, or he would have turned the light off himself, it depended on whether he was out free or if he had been confined in El Bordo again, at times like that he felt himself to be released from all obligations, he felt himself to be free not only from worry, but even from thought itself, and the current instance, taking place this late afternoon, was only different from the previous in that there were thoughts in his head now, there were no memories though, not even from the past few days, and especially nothing, but really nothing from yesterday morning, these had somehow been erased from his brain, and yet still something remained there, and he wanted to be alone with this—something about death, or more precisely, about life, namely, he understood that the end had come—this farewell from the world, from the place of his origins hadn't worked out, as this world wasn't in its place, it looked like it was, but it wasn't, it only gave the appearance of being that way, namely—he added, and sensed ever more decisively that his thoughts were headed in the right direction—nothing remained from the world that had been here, he could even have found it to be humorous if he had been capable of finding anything to be humorous: where the train station used to be, there still stood a train station; where the main street, named after his ancestors, used to be, there was still a main street, named after his ancestors; where the Hospital used to be, there was a hospital; where the Castle used to be, there was a castle, where the Chateau used to be, there was a chateau, and he could go on—it's just that these were not the same train stations, main roads, hospitals, castles, or chateaus, they just happened to stand in exactly the same spot where the old ones used to be; they weren't the old ones, they were new, they were different, they were strange, and they—now that the scales had fallen from his eyes—they left him completely cold, and this was completely to be expected, he determined without any particular emotion, because what did he have in common with these train stations, these main roads, these hospitals, these castles and chateaus, if they weren't the same ones that had once stood in their place, so they were no concern of his any longer, there was a wasteland here in place of the city he'd once left, fine, and he really had nothing to to do with this wasteland, and that too was perfectly fine, so that in the last few hours when this nervous-seeming little person was taking him all over the city, offering to show him this or that, he couldn't even see what this person was pointing out, because he only saw the vanished traces of everything that had once been *there,* but were no longer *there,* whether it was the train station or the main street or the Hospital or the Castle or the Chateau, it didn't matter, he thought, and he saw in this exclusively the sign of a kind of heavenly benefaction, not a deprivation, because when, when could he have been deprived—as people put it, the Baron smiled to himself as he sat on the bed—of that which maybe never had been true, maybe never even had been true, he leaned down to his left shoe and tied up the shoelace because it had come undone, he tied it up again, and now he gazed at how the knot had been really cleverly tied so that one of the loops fell to one side and the other loop fell to the other side, he found it to be beautiful when his laces were tied this way, so he also tied his shoelace on the other shoe so it would look the same, and on that shoe as well it worked out quite nicely, so that with a sensation of tranquility, previously unknown to him, he sat looking at the two wonderful shoes with their nicely tied shoelaces and completely symmetrical loops, then he called out into the living area, and he summoned Dante and asked him, if his other obligations didn't prevent him, to do him the kindness of taking him out incognito to the City Forest, and because it was only a journey of fifteen or twenty minutes, it wouldn't be too demanding, he reassured Dante, who, for his part, finally seeing something move on that dead track, displayed intense enthusiasm, he smirked at the Baron, and only said to him, while he slipped into his coat in the foyer, that he would take him "with tremendous pleasure" wherever he should wish to go, and perhaps on the way there they could talk, he said to him as they went down the back stairs of the hotel and as they slipped out, perhaps they could talk about those matters which could no longer be delayed.

You've been drinking, said the track boss on the phone, and the foreman whose job it was to supervise the crew mustered up his strength, well, I would have been drinking, boss, but—you've been drinking, his boss repeated on the other side of the line in a tone meant to convey his deep disappointment over this occurrence, he'd really expected more of him—no, it's not like that, the foreman continued to protest, I'm on duty now, and when I'm on duty I don't even touch a drop—but I can hear in your voice how you're pronouncing every word distinctly, I know very well that you do this when you've been drinking, you always try to pronounce every word, and you're doing that now, so I don't have to see you, it's enough for me to hear how you try to clearly formulate every single one of your words, in short, I can hear you forcing it, I don't need all this crap, the boss lowered his voice sadly—but if I tell you that when I'm on duty, never, not even one drop, not now, not ever, the foreman said, trying to turn the situation around, because it wasn't promising anything good, and he held the receiver away from himself, covered the phone's receiver for a moment, and spoke to the other men, telling them to quiet down, because there would be big problems if he heard all this whooping and hollering going on, although the others couldn't care less, they just continued to whoop and holler in the repairmen's shop, because old Halics Junior, as the colleagues called him, was even drunker than them, and he'd informed them that if they wished, he'd show them who he really was, and in the sudden cacophony that had arisen he'd already made a place for himself in the center of the group, yes, it wasn't so easy at the beginning, because the others were already pretty wasted from the Riesling, and it took some time until everybody could keep their balance, and in addition all together, but they kept on clutching onto each other, and they kept their balance, so the circus with old Halics began, and somehow the circle formed, and Halics Junior stepped into the center and he just stood there, swaying, he didn't move, he raised and then he spread apart his two hands, like someone who was going to fly from a peak, like someone who stood at the edge of a horrific, breathtaking precipice, he spread his arms apart, and in a moment he was going to push himself off, he was going to fly, but he didn't even move, like someone who demands rapt attention, because he was willing to show who the real Halics was only when he'd received the others' complete and total attention—his pause signaled this—the others slowly comprehended that if they wanted something to emerge from this mayhem, then they really had to calm down, and so they began to hiss at each other, saying quiet people, quiet, because old Halics is going to show us who he really is, and so they quieted down nice and slowly, and Halics Junior, to the great surprise of the others, didn't fly off from that mountain peak, but instead closed his eyes, and then from his hitherto motionless state, to the rhythm of a tempestuous music heard only by him, suddenly took four lightning-fast steps forward, then came to a dead stop, still holding up his hands in that position of flying motionlessness, and his colleagues reacted with the greatest of appreciation, but then suddenly he made a quick half turn and threw back his head, like someone who gazes with closed eyes into the heights and yet not at all into the heights but deeply into his own self, and he began to take four steps back without even turning around, but this was already too much for him, the Riesling had extinguished his ability to rise to this nearly acrobatic challenge which was so, but so risky: to complete the same four steps going backward, as he had just completed going forward, this was already impossible, already by the second step he was tipping over, namely he fell out of rhythm, and under this ominous influence he took a step to the side, in order to support this body already falling into a lurch, but it unfortunately just lurched all the more, and so he had to support it with yet another step, and his eyes remained closed all the while, he wasn't inclined to open them, because he was trying desperately to make sure he wouldn't topple over, because there was still within him a pure desire to maintain his balance with more of these small, propping-up steps, which, unfortunately, wasn't possible, he therefore began to break it up, namely these small propping-up steps began to multiply with an ever-increasing tempo, in a sequence of precipitous velocity, but every effort was to no avail, to no avail were those hurried steps, that body had given up, because it just lurched and lurched all the more, and then old Halics lay sprawled on the ground like an old, fatally exhausted, tottering tango dancer, lacking the energy for even one last breath, and so the moment had come when he couldn't go on anymore, the end, and he collapsed onto himself, and here in the Sarkad track worker's repairmen's shop, that was the moment when of course his colleagues simply began to holler for him to get up, and keep going, because they really wanted to know who the real Halics was, although of course all their shouting with red faces above the body of Halics Junior lying motionless on the ground was fruitless, the only thing they accomplished was that the foreman once again began to hiss at them to be quiet, as he tried more and more to convince the boss on the other end of the line: what me, drinking on the job, never!—and his boss didn't even reply, because he was disappointed, almost embittered, and putting aside his disappointment and bitterness, he said sternly that he didn't care what kind of state they were in over there in Sarkad, they were on duty, and they had to go out now, take the Lencse crane railcar and go to track number 1041, because last night it was reported that track number 1041 had started to wobble a bit, so they had to go out, this was no joke, the boss repeated dispassionately on the telephone, he didn't care how much they'd drunk, they all had to go out now, because this was their job, they were at work now, they were on duty, and take note: track number 1041, and when they got back he wanted a report, and in writing, because there were going of course to be consequences to all this, because he was initiating an investigation, he wasn't just going to leave it at this because he knew the foreman had been drinking, the boss said to him—but the foreman could hardly hear what his boss was saying, unfortunately he had to ask again several times exactly what piece of track they had to go to, where was it, and why did he have to take the Lencse, because the other workers were so noisy, it certainly could be heard on the other end of the line, because they hadn't given up in trying to rouse the old man to come to life again, but it was all in vain, because old Halics Junior didn't even move, instead he began pulling his knees up on the floor and curled up in that embryonic position in which he always slept the best, and in vain did the other men shriek for him to get up, on that evening they weren't able to find out who the real Halics really was, because this Halics kept the secret all to himself and fell into the deepest of slumbers, let them go to hell with their Lencse, let them rot, the men cursed the track bosses for sending them out in such foul weather, always them, it was always the repair shop at Sarkad that got sent out—and what about the one at Békéscsaba, wasn't that the central repair shop? why did it always have to be them in Sarkad, why not Csaba? let the whole thing go to hell, and of course it just had to be that piece of track 1041, they hated that section of track the most, there were always problems with it, it was impossible to repair. The entire group lurched outside to the Lencse, they dragged themselves along, and started up the motor, and as they left the station they quickly turned off the Lencse's lights. Because we're going deer hunting, my boys, the foreman clutched at the steering mechanism in the locomotive, because if they're sending us out in this rotten weather, then it's deer that we're after, that's all, and he told them to hold on tight, because he was going to drive that railcar just as fast as he could.

There was a bridge where the old bridge used to stand, and he had the car stop at the foot of it, finally explaining to his escort why he'd wanted to come here, namely that as it hadn't been raining at all for a while now, he desired to go for a nice long walk, namely in this place, in the City Forest, because this was the singular and central location of his youthful outings; he begged him, namely Dante, to make his way back to the city with no worries, and to wait for him in the hotel, because the Sarkad train almost certainly still ran through the forest, and there was the so-called Sanatorium stop where he could easily get on the train coming back to town, and from there take a taxi to the hotel, and then—he gazed reassuringly into the other's eyes—they could discuss that matter which, according to his companion, could no longer be postponed, but Dante, although he was pleased by this last formulation, tried to force the matter a bit, that he had, at the moment, no other pressing tasks, and the Baron should just go for his walk in peace and refresh himself in his memories, he'd be more than happy to wait for him here—no, the Baron insisted, there was no point to that, because the train ran right through the middle of the forest, so why would he head back this way anyway, especially after the exertion of a walk, only just to go back with Dante's car—oh, no, said the Baron, you are a very kind young man, and I deeply honor your proposal, but no, and he said goodbye, then when Dante, after some hesitation, sat down next to the taxi driver, the Baron motioned back to him again, he pulled out his wallet, and he extended it to him through the car window, saying that he had some small change for the ticket back, but for Dante, please, to place this securely somewhere in the hotel suite, because he was continually forgetting to do so himself when he left the hotel, and now he was afraid that he would lose it somewhere, and he certainly didn't need any bad luck from that sort of inattentiveness, so the Baron's wallet ended up in Dante's inner pocket, the taxi turned around, and headed back toward the town; and the Baron—like someone not proceeding from memory, but from habit—turned without hesitation from the road, came down from the dike, then purposefully, albeit with his own usual irregular manner of walking, at times slightly losing his balance, set off on the path which led into the depths of the forest.

It's not that it was superfluous, he thought, because how could he be the judge of that, but rather, he didn't know why it had to be, because certainly there had to be some kind of meaning even to that life which was his, but he kept asking the question—what would've happened if ... in vain, the trees did not reply, the shrubs didn't reply, neither did the path reply to him, so that he just kept following this path, slipping now and then on the sodden ground—it wasn't a good place to have come in regular walking shoes, that much was clear, but well, that's what had happened: it was only when he'd tied up his shoelaces that he had decided what to do—and this was the kind of decision where it couldn't matter less if a person was wearing regular shoes or a different kind of shoe—the main thing was that he'd decided in that hotel room, and exactly in that moment when he had completed the tying of his shoelaces, that if he could no longer wait for death, then he had to overtake it, because he had to, because he could no longer allow himself to be exposed to another fiasco, could no longer allow yet another incongruity to impede him in the inevitable endgame of his life—namely in this city, perched upon a barren plain, with these assorted exceedingly strange figures, there was the possibility of his mood clouding over, and this had to be avoided by all means—namely he had to overtake death before this came to pass, because a baron with a clouded-over mood is no longer the master of himself, namely he wished to remain the master of his own self, he'd already decided this when the Viennese relatives, whose kindness he could never return, had decided to throw him a lifeline at the very last moment, and he'd already decided that he would bid farewell —namely, wait for death—of his own free will, and here, in this very place whence he'd come, because now the time had come for that, to wait here, this had been his plan, but somehow exactly during that certain moment of shoelace-tying, the scales had suddenly fallen from his eyes, because this new world in place of the old was so "original" that whenever he encountered a surprise—and he had encountered surprises, ever since his arrival here, he had only been encountering them—these surprises were not really helpful in terms of things working out as he had planned, because there was nothing for him to take leave of anymore, because he had somehow arrived in a counterfeit space where he'd ended up the foolish victim of a "phenomenal deception," the victim of a deception for which, as a matter of course, nobody in particular was responsible, in any event the moment had come, and he was ready—he smiled to himself again—he was ready for this moment to the greatest possible extent, because here he was, if you please, walking along that very same path, in that place where he had spent so many hours alone in his youthful days, because here there had "indeed" been a forest where he could daydream, weave plans for the future, and feel himself to be audacious, because he never felt audacious enough to go anywhere else alone, only to the City Forest, they let him come here under the pretext that bike riding would be good for his weak muscles and nervous system and his frail bones, no one questioned—there at home among the family—that his outings to the City Forest could have anything but the best possible effect on the young child, so that he, in exchange for this misapprehension, got an entire forest to himself where he could be alone, and where he could take pleasure in the sweet taste of solitude, and now here he was again, once again he could stroll along this path in the last hours of his life, this was a gift, thought the Baron with gratitude in his heart, but sadly he noted that unfortunately his eyes had once again filled with tears, although this was not the same symptom from which he had suffered his entire adult life, and for which there was no explanation, because these tears truly fell because of his gratitude, and not *just because*, of this he was certain, so he didn't fall into despair at the possible return of his symptoms, they weren't coming back, he shook his head, and for a moment he stopped in his tracks, because he'd glimpsed the forest ranger's house, where the forest ranger's house had once stood, there was the house of the forest ranger, and as he didn't wish to be seen, he cautiously avoided it, looking for another path circumventing the house in a great arc, then he returned to his own path, because it was only on that path that he could safely reach the train tracks, it was staggering, he noted to himself, how much everything was in the same place, as if it was the same, although nothing was the same, yet this path meandered exactly like the one that meandered here fifty or sixty years ago, it was staggering, he thought, and he felt an even deeper gratitude toward the fate that had brought him here, which had allowed him to reach this point, to conclude what he had begun on this same path, and once again, alone, he was grateful in his walking shoes as he skidded slightly here and there, but essentially still he walked on and on, and now the forest ranger's house was a good way behind him, so that he expected to be coming to the tracks any moment now, and he did reach them in a moment, then he turned to the left, and set off, walking in the middle of the tracks, toward the József Sanatorium stop, respectively toward Sarkad.

Someone called out to him suddenly from behind, he heard the voice clearly, but when he turned around he didn't see anyone behind him, and well, of course he didn't see anyone, the reason was that nobody was there, nobody could even have been there, in any event, this incident, which he immediately put out of his mind, called forth a memory within him, because very many years ago somebody had called out to him with the same voice, it had been a heavily built man, only about a head shorter than him, but with wide bones, broad shoulders, a strong chest, and so on, he too was making his way home from the Casino in the empty city, it could have been sometime between four and five a.m., well, and from behind, this strong, cheerful, dear, and simple person had caught up with him, at first he was afraid of him, he recalled that now sharply, as he walked along amid the railway ties, and now he saw this person on his left side, but just for a moment, and then he stopped sharply and held out his arms, and he asked himself: well, what's going on with me, have I grown confused again, because what in the world is this, why should I be thinking about this now, when I finally need to really take care of a really serious matter and not piddle around with these memories, and this was the voice of sobriety in him, and he knew that it would lead him back in the right direction, but this memory—and within the memory, this heavily built man with broad shoulders and a broad chest—wouldn't leave him alone, so when he started off again amid the railway ties, this man came along too, and what could he say to that but: well, you come along too, the Baron said this to him, and if he had already been surprised by this sievelike brain of his, then let the picture emerge fully, he thought, and so it did emerge, and everything became clear: how this heavily built man caught up with him and spoke to him, and he was really so dear and so simple, and the fear he'd felt when he'd been surprised in the sinking light of the evening by the voice from behind and this person had suddenly stepped up beside him, his fear was almost immediately dissipated by the gentleness of his manners, and he didn't even need a minute to see that his anxiety in connection with this man had been completely baseless, because he wished him no harm, he wasn't a robber or a swindler: he too was going home, just as he said, namely, he said, it seemed that the whole city was asleep already, there was no one out on the streets, no transportation running, and he'd already been thinking that he'd have to tramp home by himself, and then he'd seen him walking along, so that if he wouldn't mind, he'd join him for as long as their routes took them in the same direction, and he did join him, and they chatted as they walked, and this conversation essentially wasn't really about anything at all, although later on, this sudden companion betrayed that he'd turned up in his path because he unconditionally felt the need to speak to somebody with whom he could discuss a thought that had been torturing him considerably, a thought that was, between the two of them, "fairly heretical," namely: how was it possible—putting the essence of the matter succinctly—that "if *one* good isn't enough for good to prevail, how is it possible that *one* evil is enough for evil to prevail," but, he added by way of explanation—and now they were walking together in this lovely, silent, enormous city—he didn't feel like discussing this torturous problem with him anymore, indeed it didn't even seem so important, he added, laughing, so he began to talk about trifles, and from this point on their conversation remained there, with these trifles, and yet he, the Baron, felt this man was talking to him about the most essential things of all, and it wasn't because of the subject matter of this conversation, of this friendly and frank chitchat, but because of the fact of it, the tone, the easy, everyday themes following one upon the other—accordingly memories, the Baron thought now, well, there were memories that still yet emerged, as if they were trying to caution him not to torture himself with weighty questions, or to examine what might have happened if that conversation, that light chitchat had not been so inessential; but then it occurred to him that well, no, it actually hadn't been, the next day he couldn't even remember what these everyday themes had been, only that the whole thing caused him great joy, if he thought back on it, maybe it was the blades of grass next to the sidewalk, or the meadows with their wildflowers, which, as it turned out, both of them greatly loved, it could have been that, but he didn't remember exactly, or maybe their discussion of what was the secret to a good parrillada, or why the sidewalks were so bad in the darkness of who knew what streets, it could have been that, one thing was sure, though, they were talking about very simple things, but at the same time very important things in relation to weeds or parrillada or the bad sidewalks; as a matter of fact he could hardly remember now—the Baron walked on, now stumbling over the railway ties—where, or along what streets, they had walked together, maybe first it was along the Avenida Brasil? and then the Avenida 9 de Julio? and then Calle Venezuela?—maybe, but it didn't matter now, the main thing was that he had remained walking beside him for a while, indeed, as he thought back on it now, it was as if they had walked together the entire night and had parted only at dawn, which of course was impossible—he shook his head again—still, it was strange, and he still had a feeling that it was dawn when the other one had said that it had been a joy to tramp home with him, and he truly thanked him and said: don't be afraid, my name is Jorge Mario Bergoglio, I am the Archbishop of Buenos Aires, and he pulled his coat apart a bit, and you could see that in fact he was some kind of personage of the church, but all of this didn't say much to him, to the Baron, indeed, it was many years later, more precisely when he'd been in prison, only a few months ago, that he had discovered that his Archbishop of that evening had become the Roman Catholic Pope, well, he thought then, and he thought again now, but it's really a shame that I didn't know who I was walking with, because then I could have asked him why I have to live, because back then I didn't know, just as I don't know now, because death is simple—he now returned to his original train of thought—my life, however—why it had to be, why I have to exist—for that, there is no explanation.

He couldn't allow his thoughts to become dispersed like this, he rebuked himself, and he was happy when he glanced to his left side, and he saw this Bergoglio was already nowhere to be seen, so he could now turn back to that one thing which, he felt, was the one thing he should be clinging to, he must cling to this, he exhorted himself, because he didn't have much time left, and in this short period of time he somehow had to get to the end of what he had started, to the end of, accordingly—he concentrated intensely—that question why it had to be that he had to be, because this was the question that was worthy of his last hour, and to which he sincerely would wish to receive an answer; here—he looked at the two tracks in front of him—things were coming to a close, namely, if everyone carried something, then, in this great existence, what had he carried, what was it that had made it necessary for him to be born and live this life out to its last days, namely why had it been necessary for this whole thing to take place, he stopped, as he had done so already a few times, because it was as if he had heard a train coming from the other direction, but no, he was just imagining it, so he kept on walking, not only did he not feel fear, he felt not even a drop of fear, on the contrary, he knew himself to be decisively liberated, not even as if he were strolling toward death, but really as if he were just simply going along, lost in thought, walking along the middle of the lonely train tracks through the now completely darkened forest, and he just walked and walked, and no train came either from the direction of József Sanatorium or from Sarkad, and he was at the point of really calling upon the Good Lord, something to which he had become greatly unaccustomed in the last decades, somehow he didn't perceive this Good Lord above everything down here, he felt awkward and incompetent as he'd tried to occasionally address Him, so he'd ceased—and this really had been a few good decades ago—now, however, the idea didn't seem so out of place, the idea that he would address Him again, and once again ask: if it had been necessary for him to exist, then could He enlighten his mind in these last few minutes—he pleaded—to explain what had been the use of bringing him into this life and keeping him alive, if his life had been so, but so utterly useless, because well, what kind of life had been his—he posed the question within himself, but nice and loudly so that the Good Lord could hear him clearly up there—well, what kind of life is that in which nothing, and to such a degree, had happened beyond the fact that there is a world, and within it, there is a love, a love in the world, the illusory character of which only emerged at the end of his life, because that's what it was, illusory, it didn't exist, and perhaps it never existed, because it wasn't real, because its object could never be real, because what had been, and what there was now in its place, was bleak and desolate and empty and fraudulent, what had been the point of all this, the Baron posed the question to the Good Lord as he strolled toward death, which, he thought, marching on between the railway ties, could *still* come any moment now, but it didn't want to come; taking off his hat, he knelt again and again to one or the other side of the tracks and touched his ear to the ground to see if he heard the train coming from the József Sanatorium or the local train from Sarkad, but he heard nothing, and so he went on, how many kilometers have I walked already, he turned around and looked back, and of course because of the innumerable bends in his path he could hardly use that to measure how far he had come, because of course he had no idea whatsoever—it was no use that he had his watch with him when he'd set off from the bridge (in any event, he wasn't that interested in time, it could have been a few minutes or even an hour ago when he'd set off on his stroll)—the main thing (he shook his head again) was that no train was coming; he'd made inquiries, however, with the hotel doorman (making him swear on his soul not to tell anyone), who subsequently sneaked him the information when no one was looking, and the Sarkad-Békéscsaba schedule had turned up, and from that he had read the times of the trains that could have an impact on him: the 5:32, the 6:32, the 7:32, the 8:26—this latter being the last train—these were the trains, with never more than an hour between each, and that meant that either the schedule wasn't good, or there was a delay, a delay—the Baron shook his head again—and he stood still for a bit in order to gather his strength, and, leaning on his knees, he breathed the sharp forest air in and out deeply, then he set off again, and he tried from another angle to get into the good graces of the Good Lord there above, saying that he was more than willing to patiently await His reply, because it seemed that some obstacle had emerged and the train was delayed, so he had a bit more time now, but the fact that he was patiently waiting down here didn't mean that he didn't trust that there would be a reply to his question, a reply in the spirit of which he could throw himself tranquilly into the arms of death; of death he had no particular notions, he thought, he was simply strolling along the tracks toward the delayed local train, and he would keep on strolling until this delayed train—arriving from the József Sanatorium stop, but basically from the direction of Sarkad—emerged at one of the bends here, and so there really wasn't much else for him to do but to remain, remain between these two train tracks, because if we can presume, he presumed, that such a train wasn't going to stop before turning a bend, and of course it wasn't going to, the Baron said to himself, and if we presume that the order of things is such that a person suddenly emerging out of nowhere at one of these bends is much too close for the train to be able to brake, in other words the train will hit that person, and it is possible that person will be smashed *to bits*, but why was that interesting to him now, he thought, the important thing was for him to hurry and overtake that which he had come here to wait for, although until that point he was really waiting for an answer, in order to know what this whole thing had been for.

It was so dark already, especially here in the middle of the forest, that if he looked behind him, he saw exactly the same as if he looked in front, and if he looked in front of himself, he saw exactly the same thing as if he looked behind: he saw the railway ties beneath his feet, then he saw about fifteen or twenty meters of track and nothing else, so it often happened that he stumbled on one thing or another, either a larger pebble in the ballast, or the tip of a railway tie which was sticking out more than he thought it would, and he was tired, he was really tired, and in addition it seemed more and more that the train wasn't coming, he looked at his watch, which showed the time as 7:37, and he was waiting for the answer to two questions now: one answer had to come from the Good Lord up there, and the other, from Sarkad: why wasn't what was supposed to come not coming already, but of course, despite his extreme fatigue, he kept turning those two questions over in his mind, wondering if perhaps the problem was that he hadn't posed them well, perhaps the Almighty only answered questions that were well posed, and even before, he'd been thinking perhaps he could have tried to supplicate Him, but sadly, it had been so long since he had prayed, not a single word was coming to mind, no sort of formulation at all with which he might present himself before the Good Lord, so that he might express himself in a somewhat more courteous manner to Him whose reply he awaited, as he thought really for the first time that there had really been no tactfulness in his question; I'm just attacking the Good Lord with these questions, and He has more than enough problems, I think, because how many, but how many are walking like this, walking here or there, but exactly now and exactly for the same reasons, as they wait for their own trains, everyone is asking Him, and no doubt everybody is asking Him *all at once*, it's no wonder—the Baron made excuses for the Good Lord to himself—that he can't say anything, maybe you just have to get in line, he thought, and once again he knelt down to the tracks, but nothing, there was just a flock of deer about ten or fifteen meters in front of him, standing on the tracks, he noticed them suddenly, because of the darkness he only noticed them suddenly, and what was strange about the deer was that they didn't want to cross the tracks and then go in, farther into the forest—no, that had certainly been the original idea, but once they got to the tracks, it was if they somehow didn't want to go on, he stopped so as not to frighten them away, then it crossed his mind that perhaps they were standing here with the same intent as he, which of course was nonsense, because clearly they had just stopped on the tracks, maybe this was their habit, maybe they liked train tracks, who knew; finally, the Baron thought, watching them, they're at home here, he just watched them in the looming dark, as they lowered, then raised their heads, they didn't bother with him at all, although they clearly saw him, but he didn't matter to them as long as he wasn't moving, he thought, everything stayed like that, and because he was already very exhausted, this small pause during his long walk felt good to him, so that he just stood there with his wheezing lungs, he watched the flock of deer, and he thought again about his question, and it was exactly at that moment—when the deer suddenly tensed their muscles, took impetus, and in a moment jumped away from the tracks into the forest—the thought came to him: namely what was he asking here when he himself already knew the answer, he had to come back down to earth with these questions of his, and not pester the Good Lord up there, because this sudden *whoosh* from the deer, as they suddenly slipped across the tracks, and were already swallowed up by the forest, was enough, as if they were trying to awaken him, or as if they wanted to rescue him from the weight of his own question, but it wasn't even that, what was he talking about, he shook his head, and he still didn't move from there, it wasn't the weight—because what kind of weight could a question like this have before the Good Lord, who was so, but so pestered by other questions—but that there wasn't even any question, or that his question was completely meaningless, because his question—why did he have to live, and so forth—simply wasn't a question, *but was itself the answer*, this was the answer to his question, thought the Baron, his question was the answer, but then—he looked around in the darkness—what the hell was he doing here, because how did his wants count for anything, they didn't count for anything at all, oh, Saint Pantaleon, what a fool am I, well, I'm really an idiot, because it's not the train I should be waiting for, or wondering when it will be coming from the József Sanatorium stop or from Sarkad, but instead I must go back to the city as soon as possible, as a matter of course, and find her, and I must ask her forgiveness, this is what I have to do, not throw myself in front of trains which moreover don't even arrive, the Baron turned around, I must beg her forgiveness, he thought resolutely, and he already clearly saw why, because he had hurt somebody who had wanted nothing else from him, only tact, for surely they were both trapped in the same illusion—he had run away, and he hadn't said a word, he'd only snatched that photograph up from the sofa bed and run away, oh my God, he sighed, and suddenly he could see clearly in the darkness, and he turned around, and overcoming his fatigue he began to hurry in the other direction, he would ask for help at the forest ranger's house, to get back to the city, somehow it'll work out, he thought, more cheerfully now, and he went, now in the opposite direction, namely backward, because what kind of question was that, well of course, he himself already knew the answer, there was no need to pester the Good Lord with all these questions, those deer, with their sudden leaping away from the tracks, had told him that he still had to live so that at the end he could ask forgiveness from Marietta, poor Marietta, because he had humiliated her, and he tapped that inner pocket in his coat, and the envelope was there in its place, and he went backward, in the other direction, because he didn't even really feel the fatigue anymore, because the true path had opened up before him, the true path which would lead where he now had to be, he went, he went, and he thought: questions, and answers, and killing myself with a train, my God, what a fool am I! And in his great fervor, it would have been better if he had been paying attention. He should have come down from the ballast, and not kept on walking between the tracks, back in the other direction.

# *RA DI DA*

# LOSERS (ARREPENTIDA)

Papa, you were saying—considering how much the whole thing wasn't to my taste, how enthusiastically I was waving and everything, but Papa ... said Dóra from the travel agency, and the resentment could be read fairly clearly on her face—but still, sometimes you are unfair and maybe a bit too harsh with me, Papa, because the reason why I was enthusiastic at the train station was because I was so happy to be able to push you over there, and I could see how happy you were, and I'll tell you this: I wasn't the one who wanted to go out there, said Dóra, shaking her head, emphasizing her words—surely, Papa, you must remember, it wasn't so long ago, because you said how much you'd like to be there when he arrived and everything, but I won't say anything about this right now, because I don't think it's worthwhile to keep discussing this, indeed, the way things are shaping up here, it's not worth arguing about, do you think so, too, Papa? on the one hand, when such a horrific tragedy has occurred, and on the other, if we look at it from another angle—because we can also look at it from another angle, at least I think so —now that the entire circus has been exposed—and I'm happy about that, I'll say that sincerely—because to go into this whole thing scatterbrained, without thinking, just because of a couple of journalists ... and no one even checked what they said, they just parroted the news reports from Pest about this property of the Baron's and that property of the Baron's, and how big his bequest was going to be, like diligent little schoolchildren, well,

I'll show you, Papa, how big that bequest was—fine, I'm not yelling, Dóra lowered her voice a bit, because her father, from the wheelchair, motioned to her with his hand that he was finding not only her voice, but also her tone to be a bit too intense—fine, yes, I know I don't have to be so loud, I realize that, fine, all right, but still, the fact that the whole thing ended up like this puts me out a little, because when the Mayor came into my office and said that I had to drop everything and start helping him organize all the welcoming events in honor of the Baron, I still had some faint hope that something from all of this would somehow trickle down to the tourist industry, but no, I was wrong, truly I was—although actually maybe I wasn't that wrong, maybe it really was reasonable to think that a little life would be breathed into local tourism from the money bequeathed to the city, and what do we have now, absolutely nothing, Papa, you can't even imagine what I go through every single day, I sit there in an empty office, nobody opens the door to come in, the telephone never rings, because tourism in this city has shut down completely, it's dead, over and out, but I told you this already—Papa, please eat your dinner—that there was no point in starting work in this office, I even said at that time that we should ask about the director's secretary's job at the Slaughterhouse, but you just insisted on this, that, and the other, Papa, telling me there's a future in tourism, well, I would say there's also a future at the Slaughterhouse, but that doesn't matter anymore, because I heard that supposedly they found somebody for the job, that skin-and-bones Cincike Kráner got it, supposedly, I'm telling you, I don't know for certain, I just heard it, well, never mind, now I really have to stay there if I don't want to end up in the street, because that will be the end of all of this—please try to understand, Papa—the end of this will be that I'll go in every morning not to work, but to the Job Center, and there I'll stand in line for hours, and there won't be anything, but the only thing that will cheer me up will be that Marika won't be doing any better than me, moreover if I think about it, she's ended up the worst of anyone, because she turned herself into a laughingstock with all that stuff about how she's Má-ri-ét-tá now, well, how do you like that, Má-ri-ét-tá, that knight of yours is finished now, as well as all of your pretentiousness, I'm never one to take delight in other people's problems, you know how much I don't, Papa, but still, the fact that she was so humiliated was just a wee bit gratifying, because there's no point in you saying, Papa, that we can thank her for this job, well, that's not what I say, but rather, the fact is that tourism in this city is dead, she knew that, and that's why she offered me the job, that's my opinion, and I'm guided by the facts, Papa, the facts—so that now with the Slaughterhouse also out of the question, as I've heard, here we are, so poor our butts are sticking out from our trouser seats, and there's nothing on the horizon, because we've gone properly belly-up with this tourist office, Papa, please eat your dinner, how many times must I tell Papa that he has to eat.

Is that what you call straight? he shrieked at the corporal standing in front of him, stand at attention properly, that's why things are like this here, because none of you even know how to stand up properly, where were you trained, tell me, where, at a pig farm?, there a person has to hunch over so he won't bump his head on top of the sty—back pulled up, stomach in, chest out, well, I can't believe this, why do I have to be giving basic instructions to my corporal, and exactly now, when I'm waiting for his report; why am I smitten by such a fate that my own men don't even know how to stand at attention properly—don't salute me, I didn't say to do that, he shrieked again at the flustered corporal, I told you to stand at attention because I thought you knew how to stand up straight, but you don't understand—he lowered his voice—because nobody taught you, and I, well, I'm not inclined to do so, start over from the beginning, but properly this time, and now his face was tired, and he raised that face, and with a despairing expression he addressed the corporal: what are you doing? well, I've been given the command, said the corporal—and he once again stood at attention, but completely flustered—to go out and come back in again, and the Police Chief pushed back his cap on his head, buried his face in his two hands, and said to him: don't get so nervous, corporal, because that's obviously not what I was thinking, well, I can't even expect my own men to understand what I want, how long have you been with me here—three years, came the answer—well, so don't make plans too far in advance, then; the Police Chief leaned back in his chair, adjusted his part beneath the cap, adjusted the cap on his head, and then no longer looking at the person standing in front of him, he only said: stand at ease, and give me the report already, for the love of God ... well, began the corporal, they still have no idea what he was trying to do there, and they don't even know if he planned the whole thing, or if it was an accident, namely was it an accident or a suicide attempt, because everyone they interrogated gave completely contradictory facts, thus rendering impossible an unequivocal answer to this question, in any event he was struck by a local train that was running off schedule, namely a train that was delayed, namely, well, it could be described that way, but in reality the train hadn't even started its route, because nobody was there, in other words, the corporal explained, there were no travelers in the evening hours, and really there were none, because there usually aren't until you get to Békéscsaba, so the 8:19 never began its route, which moreover no longer originates in Vésztő, because that's where the train is actually supposed to originate from, not Sarkad ... that's enough with the details, the Police Chief motioned to him urgently—in brief, the train that hit and dismembered him wasn't one of the local trains running according to the regular schedule, but a so-called—he glanced into a small notebook that he held in his palm—a Lencse universal crane car which had been sent out by the stationmaster at Békéscsaba for track maintenance work, the time was 8:30 in the evening, accordingly the aforementioned vehicle could have reached the fatal bend in the tracks approximately between 8:48 and 8:50, and although the driver of the vehicle denies it and claims he was only traveling at twenty or twenty-five kilometers per hour, the inspection of the tracks' brake-mark distance (as the JRU data-storage recorder was damaged in the accident) demonstrates that the driver took the bend at a speed of at least thirty-five km/h, although it is more likely that he took the bend at a maximal speed of forty km/h, which, moreover, is thoroughly against the regulations; the engine driver's blood alcohol concentration was 1.826/1,000, so of course this explains everything, namely that he was not driving the Lencse, but rather the Lencse was driving him, and the work team was drunk, and then they had turned off the headlights on this Lencse crane car, because, as one of them confessed, they were hoping to "go hunting" for deer with the vehicle, so this is one side of it, the other is that we don't know why, but, on the basis of the confessions given, the victim didn't hear the railcar approaching from behind, on the other hand, sir, there was yet another fatal circumstance, said the corporal—well, I'm listening, the Captain urged him on dryly, but even then he didn't look at him, he just fidgeted with the fake gold penholder set he'd once gotten as a gift from his Romanian counterpart, the police commander from the town across the border—well, so the victim might have been too close to the bend, and perhaps right at that moment he'd left the bend—this isn't possible to determine fully, but this is probably what happened—the railcar came round the bend, namely, it had already made the turn, and the victim in question was there on the tracks, and according to the confession of one track worker on the railcar, he stumbled as he tried to get down from the track bed, because all the witnesses decisively claim that he was trying to run away from the tracks, he stumbled, and he fell headlong across the tracks, namely they were already so close that the engine driver tried to brake immediately but it was too late, if we can even speak of "immediately" in his state, or of braking distance with that kind of speed, the speed could have been forty kilometers per hour or even more—go on, the Chief motioned wearily—well, it struck him down, and it was really unlucky how he was lying sprawled across the tracks like that, because the railcar cut him up into exactly three pieces, it cut off his head and cut off both his legs right in the middle of his shins, so from his body only the middle part was left—in a word, four pieces? asked the Chief without even looking up—indeed, sir, I report that he was sliced up into four pieces, and the middle piece was dragged forward by the train for approximately eighty, possibly one hundred meters, until they were able to stop—in a word, eighty, possibly one hundred meters, the Chief repeated resignedly, he looked at the window, mumbled something to himself a bit, then he turned back to the corporal, he sighed, and he was no longer yelling, but when he finally spoke to the corporal, it was somehow even more threatening: try for at least a minute to stand like a soldier, in a word, pull yourself together, is that how you stand around at home? I don't even want to think about it, but at home you can do what you want, this here, however, is the Police Station, and here you can't just stand around like a bookkeeper with his cooked accounts, please give me the whole thing in writing, and append all of the investigative reports, you may go, the Captain said to him now almost sadly, he looked at him, as the corporal stood at attention and saluted again, then turned around, and before he had left the office and closed the door—something which he by now greatly desired to do—he was told to send up the cadet from the archives—he should get here within five minutes, if he didn't want all hell to break loose.

He picked up the receiver, but he didn't speak into it, he just listened as somebody spoke to him, and for a while he didn't even say a single word, he just said, at the end: well, listen here, it's time to lay off this case, I've already made it very clear, the matter is finished, case closed—his voice was severe—there were no more clues worth following up, no more evidence from Bicere, everything else was just "facts" pulled out from a hat, because there were no facts here, only what he accepted as such, and he didn't accept these theories, because they were theories, and theories should be entrusted to the experts, whereas he—he told the person at the other end of the line—should stick with diesel propulsion, the latest brands of motorcycle helmets, ignition starters, and the newest Kawasakis, get off this case, and get your people off it too, I want peace on the streets, is that clear—the Police Chief raised his voice—that's all I want, and nothing else, then he was silent for a while as he listened to what the other had to say, but he was visibly losing his patience as he listened, because then he said: enough already, listen here, the matter is *ad acta*, and that means no more of this "personal matter" crap, got it, he asked his interlocutor threateningly, then: what the hell kind of cooperation are you talking about, but by now he was yelling, and he jumped up from his chair and yelled: how dare you speak about cooperation with me, if you don't shut your trap I'll lock you up with your whole band of thugs right away, do you get it, and he waited for the answer, which came quickly, and it seemed he was satisfied with what he heard—okay, now you see, he said this several times ... of course it's just a theory, and as such that's what it's worth ... you just do what you have to do with your people ... yes, he said, calming down now, you're taking care of that very well, and that's why you always get the praise of the Police Station ... well, fine now, we've had enough shooting the breeze and all that, and he was about to put down the receiver, but he suddenly clapped it back on his ear, are you still there, give my greetings to Uncle Laci, and tell him that I'll stop by for a beer at his place if I've got time.

He put down the receiver, but they saw that he used all of his self-discipline not to slam it down, so that a minute went by until he more or less calmed down, he didn't say anything, he reached for his beer, he took a sip—he was thinking about something—then Totó stepped in to the Biker Bar, and mutely motioned to him—everything was ready—he too nodded, and that expression of pious dignity returned to his face, the same expression that had been on everyone's face ever since the morning, because they weren't preparing for just any maneuver, because the essence of what they were preparing for—he had told them yesterday evening—was dignity, because it was with dignity that they had to pay their final respects, and it wasn't as if just any old person had left them, because Little Star was not only a person, not only his little brother, but a member of this brotherhood consecrated in blood and honor, he was, more precisely, a true brother whom they had lost, who had sacrificed for them, and to whom they must now bid farewell with the most sacrosanct of feelings, and that is why tomorrow—more precisely, today—the members of this fraternity looked at each other in the Biker Bar, deeply moved—the key was for everyone to make their final farewells in a dignified fashion; everything is ready, said Totó, expressing himself without words, and so they made their way outside, and everyone was different than they usually were, everyone was wearing a black suit, but even those who weren't—because a few were like that—tried to dress fully in black garb (black trousers, a black sweater, black boots or shoes), only the motorcycles remained colorful: yellow, red, blue, depending on the owner, but they had thought of that too, because now a black ribbon was tied to the handlebars of each one, and that's how they set off, full of dignity, they slowly turned out from the back courtyard of the Biker Bar, slowly they made their way toward the Holy Trinity Cemetery, where a reverential-looking person in a black suit was waiting for them at the gate, and he showed Totó the way, because he thought that he was the boss with whom all official matters had to be conducted, so that Totó was obliged to point to the Leader, indicating that it was he who deserved the attention, that he was the one who should lead the procession into the mortuary where the coffin of Little Star had already been placed atop an iron frame, the surprise was visible on a few faces because they weren't used to seeing something like that in a mortuary, but clearly customs were different here, here they used iron frames, maybe it was just Totó's idea for the catafalque to be made of iron, because in other respects it was quite nicely set up, as at the head of the coffin there were enormous arched handlebars made of flowers, on which two handles, created with dark-petaled meadow blooms of some kind, were visible, and on top of the coffin—because they had clearly tried, truly tastefully, to place it in the area where his head would be—there was a black silk pillow with Little Star's yellow helmet resting on it, and whoever could squeeze in went into the mortuary, and those who couldn't remained outside, and there they stood around in a group, then someone—it must have been Totó again—pressed on a horn, as clearly this had been arranged in advance, and when the horn blew the priest entered from the right-hand side, and then the incense burning and the prayer chanting started up, because although Totó had tried to explain to the priest—as it later emerged—that they didn't need any prayers, because they had their own, the priest insisted on it, and wanted to stick to tradition, as he put it, well, whatever, his great wailing commenced and nobody puckered up his mouth, namely no one showed how much he didn't like it, everyone remained dignified and pious, and the priest just wailed and shook his censer, and they thought he would never stop, they stood there shifting their weight from one leg to the other, when finally the four gravediggers came in, they too were more or less in black, although they were all wearing tracksuits, but special formal track suits, so they didn't stick out too much from the others, and in the blink of an eye they had put the helmet into the coffin, but so quickly that hardly anyone even noticed them lifting up the coffin's lid and placing the helmet inside, they just saw them nailing down the coffin's lid, then they lifted up the whole thing, along with the helmet, and they, the bikers, drifted out nicely behind them, and they set off, in the mud, beneath the cemetery's gray sky, the priest still wailing now and then, the hearse slowly moving ahead in front, this was unusual for all of them, and it could be seen from the expressions of some that they were starting to get a bit bored, but of course everyone held up well, and they trudged along nicely, next to each other and behind each other, in the mud, that is, as many as there were, but only them, the members of this brotherhood—because although they had spoken of inviting people who were important to them from the city, nobody had come, but it was enough even like this, thought the troop of mourners to themselves—because this is how it was and how it would always remain: they were real family to each other, this was real togetherness, as the Leader always expressed it so nicely, and so they reached the gravesite, where the first unpleasant surprise awaited them, as it was only when the four gravediggers put down the coffin about two meters away from the edge of the pit, and they stood around the pit, when they saw that it had not been properly dug out, but nobody showed any surprise, not even the Leader—just those two muscles on his jaw, beneath his ears, where his beard started to thin out, began to twitch again, as he looked at the four gravediggers—and this went on for a while, they watched them as they jumped into the pit and dug and shoveled out the muddy earth, but they weren't making too much progress, this had to be stated, as the ground was truly muddy, and somehow so dreadfully full of loam, so the whole thing was agonizing, they stood and watched the four gravediggers in the ditch, they watched as they kept scraping off the mud from their spades and shovels, and they only finished about twenty minutes later, the men in the ditch—and not only them—were fairly worn out from this, because the sweat was rolling down their faces, and it was clear how exhausted they were, they hardly were able to pick up the coffin so that they could shove the two planks beneath it, they didn't even do that right, because—as the ones standing close to them were thinking—first they should have placed the two planks across the grave, and then placed the coffin on top of that, but no, instead, two of them were holding the coffin above the ditch while the other two were trying to somehow shove the planks underneath the coffin, well, never mind, they thought, and their faces didn't flinch even a bit, finally the coffin was placed there on the two planks, and the four gravediggers, their strength utterly depleted, stood aside to make room for the priest, because somehow they hadn't been able to get rid of him yet, oh no, him again, a few of them thought, he has some nerve sticking his nose in here again, and once again he began to wave his hands around and wail his prayers, and it seemed like everything was going according to plan, because neither Totó nor the Leader indicated that anything should have been any different, so they just kept standing there looking at the coffin, the priest just wailed and wailed, but by now everyone was pretty tired, only the Leader wasn't, because at one point he just shoved the priest to one side and said: we will now sing the anthem, which created a bit of a problem because they didn't know which anthem he was thinking of, the Hungarian one or their own, and so one part of the group began to sing the Hungarian national anthem, and the other began to sing their own, but after a few beats they stopped, and the Leader hissed at them—but so everyone could hear—*their own anthem*, and they started again, and now it was easy to follow it, and from that point on there were no more mishaps, everything went fine, they all threw a clump of mud onto the lid of the coffin when the four gravediggers finally lowered it into the ditch, then the Leader waited while the gravediggers pressed the muddy earth back into the ditch—inasmuch as they could—but as soon as they had reached ground level, they immediately stopped, and they didn't begin to form the earth into a mound, so exhausted were they, the sweat pouring down off of them, so Totó slipped an envelope into one of their pockets, and they all cleared out of there, but first they shoved a wooden cross into the head of Little Star's grave, and then the Leader stepped over there, placed his left hand onto the cross, sighed, bowed his head, then he raised his head again and gave a speech—which was so, but so byootyful, more beautiful than he'd ever given—they came to that conclusion later on in the Biker Bar, as in addition to the usual themes of brotherhood and ideals and the honorable person and loss, he also brought in the theme of the Hungarian homeland, and what he said about the homeland was so, but so beautiful, I'm telling you seriously, said J.T. in the Biker Bar, I really thought I was gonna start bawling my eyes out right then and there, and all the others nodded and murmured their approval, and they grabbed their pint glasses, because that part about the homeland was beautiful, it was so much more beautiful than anything they'd ever heard before, they nodded, but then they ran out of things to say about it, so sooner or later everyone began looking up at the corner of the room above the entrance, because on the TV the second season of *The Real World* was playing, it's true they were just repeating an earlier program, but still it somehow captured everyone's attention, although they'd already seen this part, and some of them more than once.

They usually didn't meet up personally, because usually it wasn't necessary, speaking on the telephone had always been good enough, but this wasn't a matter or a situation that could be handled on the telephone, so, well, there they sat in the Police Chief's office, because he'd come here personally with the Deputy Mayor, as the latter had declared that in such a delicate affair, it was his immediate obligation to make sure the opposition's viewpoint would be represented as well, so they sat in the Chief's office, and the meeting got off to a fairly tense start, because the Police Chief began in his usual way, conspicuously holding his reading glasses in one hand, signifying that he had important work to attend to here, and no matter what they had to say, it wouldn't be worth his time, because he didn't even see what there was to talk about, as everything was perfectly clear, at least to him—but then the Mayor began speaking, and with his own well-known "captivating rhetorical skills," informed the Police Chief that he found himself obliged to disagree, this wasn't indeed the case, namely, he must immediately be informed as to whether or not what he had come here to inquire about existed or not, this—as he expressed it—was the cardinal question, and the Deputy Mayor visibly agreed with him; because despite the fact that everyone knew, despite the fact that City Hall, as well as the assembled leading figures of this city, knew that the estate was of course bequeathed to the city—for the soul of everything is order—he, the Mayor, nonetheless would not like to see a shambles emerging later from this situation; if—he held his hands apart, what did he know—if, for example, some relative would show up (the family was fairly dispersed, you never know) . . . but the Police Chief really had had enough already of the Mayor's deluge of words, and he didn't want to listen anymore, because if there was one voice he *could* bear listening to, it was his own, and he mentioned this frequently to his employees as a kind of witticism, but there was one thing that he really couldn't stand, and that one thing was the Mayor—and more than anything else, his voice, his orations, all of his officiousness as he came in here and slammed that fat ass of his down on the chair and didn't want to get up—the Chief had a thousand and one things to attend to, so he said: there wasn't anything to discuss here, that's what he wanted to make clear right at the beginning, because nothing had been found, they'd gone over everything, because, do bear in mind, he raised his voice a little, this was a criminal investigation, here things had to be put in the hands of experts, and these experts had determined that nothing remained: they inspected the hotel, they inspected all his items of clothing, and he—he pointed himself—even after all that, he personally went to the morgue when his colleagues had finished their work, so that he could once again put the thing—i.e., the dead man—back together, to see if there remained even the tiniest sign which could lead them to the sought-after last will and testament, but no, he'd put the things and the victim back together one more time in the morgue and in the end he had to put the file on ice, because he hadn't found anything, and he was someone with twenty years of experience, so that if there had been anything, he would have sniffed it out immediately, they should believe him, there was nothing, the victim had simply left no last will and testament, this is what he now declared, and if the criminal investigation was still going on for a while—given the blood alcohol level of the engine driver, the only thing he could have been capable of driving was a herd of cows from the barnyard to the stable, accordingly there were still a few details to clear up in the case, but the main thing is that there was no last will and testament—but, the Mayor broke in, and he was now really on pins and needles, as it was hard for him to tolerate other people speaking for so long—but, he raised his voice, there is the question of his last *wish*, that does exist, am I not right, nobody can have any doubts that on the one hand there is the last *will*—and according to what you've told me, there is none—and on the other hand there is the last *wish*, which clearly did exist, and does exist, because it is real, and according to this last *wish* his estate would, of course, be bequeathed to the city—he, rebutted the Police Chief, really couldn't care less, because he generally didn't like the Mayor's tone of voice and somehow today he really didn't like it, so that he had to interrupt here—he couldn't care less what the Mayor called it, last will or last wish, the main thing is that neither existed—well, if the Police Chief would be so kind as to excuse him, the Mayor interrupted again, but he himself had never heard of there not being a last wish, and he wondered where exactly the Police Chief was getting his information from, for surely everyone knew that there had been a last wish, and surely he also knew what this last wish was, namely that his estate, as such—the Mayor drew a large circle with his squat little hands—belonged to the city, this was not a matter for debate; but it was, said the Chief, now slightly enraged, or rather it wasn't, there doesn't seem to be any point in my telling you, but I repeat myself, as that seems to be necessary —we didn't find anything, do you understand me, Mr. Mayor? nothing, not a single measly *fillér*, not even one measly *forint* or *pezo* or whatever that currency is called: nothing, just nothing, and I have a man, the best I could ask for in a matter like this, educated in Latin, who, as soon as this matter cropped up—he emphasized the first syllable of the word "matter" strongly— began researching the relatives (and he knows where this estate that you mentioned is), he knows the account numbers, he knows which bank, and so on, and he knows how to get to all this, but his investigations led to the sad result—which for me personally is also rather dispiriting, and so there is nothing more to blather on about in this regard—that there is NO ESTATE, listen to me now, because this baron—and he gestured with his reading glasses—left nothing behind, not even one measly *fillér*, and I'll tell you something—and the Police Chief paused for effect, and his two guests leaned closer toward him in excitement so they could hear what he had to say, even if with serious indications of skepticism and incredulity on their faces—I'll tell you something, that there was NEVER any kind of estate, the whole thing is one huge capital scam, this baron, our Baron, Mr. Mayor, was nothing but a fraud who came here literally without a single *fillér*, because we couldn't even find that trifling sum in euros that his family in Vienna had given to him for travel expenses, do you understand, we didn't even find his wallet, he said, not at the scene of the accident, nor in his hotel, and we turned everything over there, you can trust what I'm saying, because it isn't a matter of indifference for us to get at the ... the ... truth ... and suddenly he stopped talking, it was clear this wasn't how he originally intended to conclude, and he stopped talking as if something had suddenly flashed across his brain, a fleeting idea, one that he wished, however, to keep to himself, in any event he no longer said anything, and just looked at the Mayor thoughtfully, who now again flooded the office with one of his never-ending tirades, the Police Chief just looked at him though, but he didn't hear what he was saying, not only because he wasn't interested, but because he was preoccupied with this fleeting idea, so he let him go on speaking, but just for a bit though—let the Mayor get what he had to say out of his system—but then, making reference to urgent matters, he kicked them both out, and when the Mayor did not show an inclination to leave, because in his view this matter was still not fully resolved, then the Police Chief resorted to one of his more severe techniques—as he was compelled to use from time to time with this fat little blister of a person—he ordered him to leave, not only his office, but the entire building, as work was going on here, and there was no point in any further deliberations on this closed matter, especially after all deliberations on such a matter had been declared concluded, and of course in the end he was successful in getting rid of them, because he began shoving them toward the exit, the Mayor, completely flabbergasted, just kept backing up toward the door, as did the Deputy Mayor, who looked fairly alarmed, but while the latter remained quiet, the Mayor couldn't bring himself to stop, he just kept on talking and talking, informing the Police Chief that he did not consider this kind of treatment to be acceptable, so don't fucking accept it then, the Police Chief finally said, indifferently, and with that he shut the door on both of them.

I didn't recognize her, said Irén still devastated as she sat there in the kitchen, the family across from her, they were looking at her just as she was looking at them, with drawn faces, because just think what I was expecting when I finally decided that if she'd fallen apart, if she had broken, I wouldn't let her stew in her juices alone and if necessary—I thought—I would break down her door, because it really wasn't okay that three whole days had gone by, and already it was the fourth, and she just wasn't coming out of her apartment, this was somehow unnatural, because no matter what had happened, no matter how great a tragedy had occurred, and no matter what had happened between them, it wasn't all right: not only was she not letting her best girlfriend in, but she was pretending not to be at home, but well, where the hell else could she be than at home—Irén related to them at the kitchen table—so I began to knock at her door, and I just kept on knocking, loudly, until she opened the door, but then came the surprise, because you know what I was expecting—someone who was broken, unhappy, plunged into mourning—and what did I see there standing in front of me but a completely transformed Marika, her mouth thin like a blade, she hadn't even put on lipstick—I mean, without it she's just . . . well, she only looks good with lipstick on somehow—anyway, not even lipstick, just that thin mouth, and then, children, she said with an ice-cold gaze, still standing in the door, she says to me, to her very best friend: well, what are you doing here—I was so shocked I couldn't even speak, do you understand, I just stood there looking at her, wondering what her problem was, you know, I thought that she was confused, because that sweet little dear of mine is so sensitive, just like a mimosa, and then there was her need to mourn; you know, when people are in shock and they don't know how to deal with the loss, well, you understand, that's what I was thinking, and I didn't suspect anything about what was going on here, and what this talk of hers was, well, but I found out soon enough, because all the same she let me in through the door, because I wouldn't give up, and I just pushed her aside, I went into the living room and sat down in the armchair, but she didn't sit down, she just came in after me and stood in the door of the living room, as if she were waiting to see when I would get up and leave, but I just said to her, Marika, my dear girl, you can't do this, and by that I meant that she couldn't just stay there in between those four walls, that she had to come out, moreover, that she was going to come out with me, well, but what I got in response to this—from Marika—well, I can't even bear to think about it now, because it was as if she weren't even the same person, like when a veil falls away from someone and her true face is shown, she stood there in the living room in front of me, and she said: what's past is past, it's my own private affair, and not public property, so I now kindly request you—but she said it like this, Irén told the children, and acted out for them just how cynical it had sounded—"to leave my apartment, but at once," and she just kept on standing there in the living room, and really she was waiting for me to get up and go, but I just sat there as if I'd been struck by lightning, you understand, I didn't want to believe my eyes or my ears, because Marika had changed so much, that I'm telling you seriously, I barely recognized her, because her face had grown so hard, like a cliff was looking at me, cruel, but so cruel, really, it wasn't the same person anymore, and this is what she did to me, this is how she spoke to me, and really I'm not that kind of mimosa-soul like her, or rather as she used to be—but then it occurred to me to get up, I made a beeline for the door, and let her go to hell, because to do this with your best friend, how many times did she cry her heart out on my shoulder, how many times did she break down, how many times did she come to me to be consoled, and I never breathed a single bad word to her, and well, really, she was also my best ... somehow ... and Irén began to search for the words, and her family at the table just looked at her, because they'd never seen anything like this before, and they didn't want to believe their eyes either, because they saw that Irén was about to cry.

The foot race for the new mothers with baby strollers on the obstacle course is still going on, I've just come from the Budrió Housing Estate, and it's still going on, so I would like, please, to ask you—gently, for the time being, gently—who is responsible for this, namely who is responsible for putting an end to this, because whoever it is, they haven't put an end to it, she said, looking at everyone seated around the table, and there was something to look at, because almost everyone who'd been urgently summoned was seated around the table in the large conference room, as quite literally they'd been threatened with grave consequences if anyone who received the personal invitation didn't show up—threatened with unforeseeable consequences, moreover, in certain individual cases—and this last phrase had really frightened them, because somehow everyone took it to mean him or herself, sensing this clause to be aimed explicitly at his or her person, so that it wasn't even ten o'clock yet, and they were all was sitting around the table in the large conference room—and all were watching the luxuriant bosom of the chief secretary, who wasn't looking at anyone, and she didn't even say anything else, but she seemed to smile enigmatically as she arranged the pile of folders she'd lugged to the meeting, first to her right, then to her left, and she smiled enigmatically, those sitting around her determined, and the reason why she was smiling this way was because she knew something—although as a matter of fact she didn't know anything more than the others, she knew only one thing, but she knew that precisely, just how hard it was to get these people to sit down at one table, everyone was always finding some pretext (and there are those who didn't even seek a pretext, they just didn't show up, and that was it); now, though, everyone was here, the chief secretary smiled enigmatically, and she knew why: it was because of the phrase "moreover, in certain individual cases," which had been her own personal handiwork; so, displaying her bosom in her décolletage, now to the left and now to the right —it had become slightly more rounded in her moment of pride—she waited patiently for the Mayor to arrive and take his place at the table, but when that occurred she wasn't too interested in what he had to say, because what interested her was always the same thing: order, organization, for things to come together, as she liked to say, so that even now questions of content didn't engage her, but what held her interest was if everything was going in the right direction, because everyone had shown up today, and so there was already a chance that they would find a solution to the items on the agenda—especially one item, and that was: after the sudden and dramatic turn of events, what will become of us.

Because what were these people thinking—she posed the question and directed it to the world at large, because it wasn't Irén and her crowd that she was addressing now but the great whole, and by that she meant the city—what were they thinking and how long could she endure this; she had been forced to endure it her entire life, because just what had she been a part of here—she curled her lips sarcastically—in this so-called "enchanted little city of hers," what had this "enchanted city" given her during her lifetime besides torture, mockery, scorn, besides contempt, so that in the end she would just be kicked around like a dog, that's what she had gotten from her beloved city, here she stood, sixty-seven years old, and in quite good repair, she had that experience of being a woman looking daily into the mirror and noticing this and that with hair's breadth accuracy—she shook her head as if chasing away an objection—and what's more every single morning . . . well, she had lived a modest and quiet life, and it was good like that, she'd long ago renounced her great dreams, or if she hadn't quite renounced them, she had at least stifled them within herself—until this worthless wretch had come along out of the blue and thrown himself at her, because what else would you call such a person who trifles with the feelings of others as if they were some kind of plaything, she didn't care if he had psychological problems or whatever, she could become awfully enervated when people made excuses for someone, saying this, that, and the other, saying that you have to take this or that into consideration, and in the end that person is let off the hook—well, not her, and she stamped her foot a little in the slippers that she wore inside the apartment—she was not only incapable of that, but after everything that had happened, she would frankly throw anyone like this man to the dogs, or whatever, because this man, who had swept her off her feet, had done something he never should have done, because how many, but how many men had there been already in her life, she'd been forced to experience disappointment with all of them whether for this reason or that, the end was always the same—they always cast her away like a used object of pleasure, because to tell the truth, these men simply strung her along, wheedled and flattered her, swept her off her feet, and really, with every single man, she had been forced to experience disappointment; and yet not a single one of them had done to her what this one had done, because none of them had ever debased her in her own womanliness, because this person—why even call him a person—had assaulted her in her own womanly nature, and then—she jumped up nervously from the armchair —even that wasn't enough for him, then he had to go running away to the great wide world, leaving everything behind, because the Baron had to run away in his great "sorrow," and Marika drawled out the "oh" in the word "sorrow" very sarcastically, standing in the middle of the living room, and no, *he* hadn't run to the world—she pointed at herself—the world, in its hypocrisy, had come running to *her*, because what had she been just a few days ago but a queen, that's how they'd been parading her around, and now, if she were to set foot out of the house, everywhere there would be *those looks*, and at that word "looks," she trembled, as if she could have done something about it, still it was good that they hadn't yet said to her that she was the one who'd shoved him in front of the train, that's all she needed now, to be accused of that, because that would come up too, she was certain of it, she knew this "enchanted city" of hers all too well, she knew precisely what she could count on if she were to go outside, because they were going to accuse her, they wouldn't say it directly to her—oh, straight to her face, never—but she would still hear it behind her back, even here in her building at home, as they whispered behind her back, she couldn't even go out for a piece of bread, it was good that a few days ago she had done some substantial grocery shopping, and she still had a bit of bread, milk, butter, a few tomatoes, she didn't need much, at her age and with her pension what could a person eat anyway, especially if she was still watching her figure, because of course she had grown old and all that, but that didn't mean that she'd let herself go, not her, nobody was ever going to see her sitting in the living room in front of the TV with a bit of something to munch on, just a little snack, and there you are, already the scales go up, well no, not that, nobody could ever say about her that she lacked discipline—but they could say whatever they wanted to now, it was just the jealousy speaking in people, because this time too that's what it was, because why else would people be gossiping about her if not from jealousy, because of course they were shocked when it turned out that the "great Baron"— and she was incapable of pronouncing these words other than with the greatest contempt—that he, whom half the world was talking about, had named precisely her, the resident of this "enchanted city," as someone for whom he could travel and did travel halfway across the world—the truth that had emerged was something else altogether—she could well imagine what people were feeling in the city, because frankly—she sat back in the shell chair but didn't turn on the TV—was there anyone at all here for whom somebody would travel from the neighboring town, let alone the other side of the globe, of course they envied her, of course they whispered behind her back, of course there was this gossip and that hearsay, and all that, she could imagine it all too well, she didn't need to hear it with her own ears, she had always known very well—just as she knew now—just what kind of schadenfreude was burning in this little "enchanted city" of hers, she knew how thrilled everyone would be here now, seeing her misfortune, how after the great soaring emotions, the great hopes and the great dreams, here she was empty-handed—but she hated this expression, "empty-handed"—my God, she thought, what should she do, because she didn't even have anyone to talk this whole thing out with, with who, a girlfriend? maybe Irén, with her thick legs and her practicality—but she hated that word also, "practicality"—in short, with her earthy principles, and that searching gaze of hers, Irén always just saw a fool in her, a little naïf, always requiring her protection, no, most decidedly no, and she even told her this when she—almost literally—broke the door down, she wasn't going to come here and break in again and demand explanations, because who was she, who was Irén to demand explanations from her, and why, because she didn't even know what happened nor would she, moreover—Marika decided now, sitting in the shell chair—she would never tell anyone, no one here; what was that sound, though, my dear God, is it that woman again, why doesn't she leave me in peace, but whoever it was just kept knocking and wouldn't stop, so that she knew it was Irén again, well, no mind, she said to herself and got up, but only "to impart the necessary information," and I'll tell her it's over for once and for all, no more friendship, what need did she have for friends like that, and she reached for the key, she turned it in the lock, and of course she never unlatched the chain unless she knew for certain—as this time too—the identity of her visitor.

It really wasn't very friendly of him, but what else could I have expected—he divulged the matter in the restaurant in Krinolin to the restaurant owner—a person chooses his friends properly, but he didn't even wait for me to finish my words of greeting, we hadn't seen each other in years, and already he was hollering at me, I'm telling you seriously, you won't believe it, but that's what happened, in vain did I try to talk to my friend, but he interrupted me and started yelling at me as if I were his vassal, I even told him, hey you, don't talk to me that way, I'm not your subordinate, I'm just your friend, and the restaurant owner couldn't let that go without a comment, he warily asked his guest, half incredulous, half amazed: did he ... I mean, did you ... did you really dare to speak to him that way, do you have that kind of relationship with him, but seriously now—he looked at him seriously—the reply, however, didn't convince him, because Dante uttered no more than a curt yes, and he continued where he left off: he threatened me with this, that, and the other, said he was going to chuck me straight into jail in this place or that place, but before that he was going to have me beaten up properly, he promised that first, since no one could swindle him just like that without consequences, but I ask you—and he looked at the restaurant owner with the most innocent and despairing of expressions—when have I conned anyone, tell me, you're my real friend, when did I ever do anything bad to you, and he looked at him, and as the restaurant owner looked back at him, he suddenly realized just how much of a thrashing Dante must have gotten, he had no desire now to mention it again but he wanted to say: of course you've swindled me, you never pay your bill, but you always collect the money from those two slot machines right as rain; well, never mind, he thought now, and he looked aghast at Dante's smashed-in face, the time for that was not now, so he just said: I don't understand, if you were such good friends, why did he have you beaten up so much, it's not that way with me: if someone is my friend, not only would I not beat him up or have him beaten up, it would never even occur to me, even if the guy owed me money, because —as you know well, because you know me —for me the greatest sin a friend can commit against another is when that friend doesn't pay up in time, because friendship is a matter of trust, and it's all about . . . well, never mind, Dante interrupted him, and he motioned toward the counter for him to get him something to drink—just because of his wounds, and the restaurant owner, who had such a good heart, brought him a shot glass of *pálinka,* the best plum brandy he had, he put the glass in front of him, and Dante tossed it back in one shot, then he began to search with his tongue for something in his mouth, but maybe he didn't find it, because then he asked the restaurant owner if he had any Unicum, because on the label all the medicinal herbs and everything that it contained was listed, he was in need—as anyone could see—of some serious medicine, so the restaurant owner brought him a shot glass of Unicum, and Dante threw it back without even swallowing, he just opened up the "sluice gates," as he used to say, and poured down the whole thing, well, that was good, I hope it helps, muttered the restaurant owner, he went back behind the counter and made a note of the two drinks in some grimy notebook behind the washed-out glasses, well, but now you could tell me already—he looked up from the notebook—why was the Police Chief so unhappy with you—well, how the hell should I know, snapped Dante, he didn't say anything, he just threw me into an empty cell, then two thickset brutes came in and they started in, you can imagine how I felt, I go over to pay a visit to a friend who I haven't seen in such a long time, and I get thumped on the neck, then on my head, and then they left me lying on the floor, it was damn cold, and they only took me to him an hour later, I don't even know how long I was lying there, I said to him: hey you, listen here, my good friend, I get the feeling you're mad at me about something, but maybe after all this you could tell me what the problem is—and he was filled with rage, and he yelled at me so much that the veins in his neck were popping out, this much—he showed how much they had popped out on his neck—so that I didn't try to force things, I just laid low, because I saw that I hadn't caught him on a good day, and what's more he just kept asking me if I knew something about a certain sum of euros, but I didn't know anything about that, I just looked at him, and I said: listen here, if I knew about it I'd tell you, after all you're my friend, at least you were my friend, and at that he just started yelling again, threatening me with this, that, and the other, telling me to hand over those euros, but not only had I never seen those euros anywhere or at any time, I never even heard anything about them; the restaurant owner shook his head sympathetically—I don't follow you, what was he after, what was it?—never mind, answered Dante, and for a second, in that smashed-in face, there was a flash of life, and he asked: would you be able to give something to a disillusioned friend, so that he might have a bite to eat, because I can sense—he pointed toward the kitchen—that lunch will be ready in a minute; and what would a true friend do in a situation like this, but sigh, go into the kitchen, and bring his friend a plate of goulash—and then Dante just tilted his head to one side, and he poured in the soup, he had to spoon the liquid in so carefully, and as for what there was to chew on, he chewed so carefully, but only on the left side, which left no doubt: he'd been properly thrashed within an inch of his life—don't get yourself worked up, the restaurant owner said to him, and as the regular lunch customers hadn't yet shown up, he said: just a moment, and he sat down across from Dante at the table, and he only asked in a low voice: were you by any chance able to find out when I'll be getting the slot machines back?

They locked the doors to the two newspaper editorial offices, not even to speak of the two television studios—the television studios had closed up shop immediately, if only temporarily—and from home, the Chief Editor began arranging the most essential matters on the phone, first he spoke with the other Chief Editor, then with his secretary, then he began to call various individuals, all of whom shared one thing in common: namely they had either given a speech at the train station or at one of the other locations where there had been a welcoming celebration for the Baron; and in addition, he, or more precisely one of his colleagues, had written a speech for these individuals, and now he was volunteering to completely erase the speeches in question from the offices' computers and destroy every such trace of any one of these speeches; he could assure them, he told them one after the other, of his own commitment to excellence in this work—perhaps this had been their experience with his paper—and this was vivid proof that he wasn't just bleating into the air when he said: no one would ever lay his hands on any of those speeches ever again, and if anyone began flourishing copies of the printed newspaper, he gave his solemn guarantee that in such an unlikely and undesirable case as that, he would claim that any quotations accidentally figuring from these speeches had simply been snatched out of thin air, moreover, he would state under oath that to his knowledge no such speeches had been uttered, and if still somehow one or two sentences managed to show up in this or that article about the card-playing Baron, then he would unequivocally state that they had been the fabrication of such colleagues no longer in the newspapers' employ, and so forth, because, as he said to them, he always thought of everything, and his interlocutors, from the Headmaster to the Mayor, were really touched, the Headmaster even went so far as to say that the Chief Editor could ask him for anything—anything, just not his certificate proving his minor nobility, well, fine, the Chief Editor replied, but he really shouldn't think that he'd wish to extort any kind of financial provision from such local luminaries as himself, the Headmaster, or the Mayor, and so forth, because this was the first reaction of everyone to his offer: how much did he want, how much?—you mean money?! don't even think about that, what was he?! the Chief Editor asked indignantly, a doctor who takes money under the table from vulnerable people?—there was no question of that, he said, it would be more than enough for him if they'd simply take note of the instance in their memories, a simple "thank you" on the phone was more than enough for now, because we can always end up in a situation where we too will have some need of human sympathy, and he was only doing this because this city was important to him, he wished for nothing else than for their city to be uplifted, even in mundane matters, that's what he was working for, and that's what he would always work for, inasmuch as in the upcoming City Hall vote, he would gain their backing, and continue his work as their Chief Editor for four more years, that was enough for him, because he only needed trust, for trust to be extended to him from both the government and the opposition, without that there was no free press, of which he—ever since he could remember—had been an unconditional believer, surely everybody knew this about him. He put down the receiver, and called the next person.

He was the town's official photographer, and if the legs of an official photographer can get worn down—being on one's feet all day—then he wasn't even walking on his feet anymore, but just on stumps, I'm telling you, he said to the woman behind the counter at the espresso bar, as he sat in front of a steaming cup of espresso, she wouldn't even believe him—but I believe you, the woman at the espresso bar muttered to herself, as she knew this character all too well, and she was truly sick of him and the others like him too, because these types never drank anything, just one rotten espresso, and that was it, you can't make a living from that, just listening to their idiotic meanderings, including this one here, who hadn't yet finished his sentence, but he just kept on saying: the young lady would never believe what was going on now, because business had suddenly really picked up, albeit—and this was his favorite word, "albeit"—he'd never really thought that at one point he would make such a bundle, and not by taking photographs, but rather by deleting them, because this is what they want now, young lady, for days I haven't been doing anything else besides making a living off those memory cards, they come asking for me, suddenly everyone knows my cell number, I'm telling you, before, no one ever called me—and now they ask me: please, would you be so kind as to ... not even that, they say: I'm begging you ... and everything that the young lady could possibly imagine, I've heard it all, just so that I'll delete those photos, and I'll tell you exactly what this entails: for the naive ones, I just delete the pictures they want me to, the pics from the train station or the entertainment events, I do it in front of them, I look for the memory card, put in the camera, and together we look for the pictures they want me to erase, and I delete the pictures in front of them; then they ask me, and I tell them that no one will ever see these pictures again, well of course, no one ever will see them, never again, rest assured, and this is all so much work that I can't keep up with it—and in addition, it's pretty difficult to get hold of these memory cards for my own camera in this town—I use a Canon EOS, the most professional version—and the memory cards for this, surely the young lady knows, cost a pretty penny, so that's the situation with the naive ones, but then the big boys come along, and of course for them it's not enough to see that the data is gone, they already know the deal, they want to keep the memory cards themselves, well of course there's a price for that too, of course there's the question of copyright and the labor charge, and altogether it ends up being a nice little sum, and they pay me, young lady, they pay like little angels, my dear God—the photographer sipped away at his coffee—if I had just known this earlier, I wouldn't have had to live my whole life under a frog's ass, never even having enough to come into an espresso bar and drink a cup of coffee in peace, and you see, here I am, sitting in your espresso bar, and I'm drinking an espresso, and you know what—he leaned in a little closer to her in his great happiness—I'm at peace, for the first time in my life I'm not all nervous that I suddenly have to be here or there, just because here the Deputy Mayor is inaugurating a new row of toilets in the kindergarten in the German Quarter, or there the deputy chair of the Milk Powder Factory is cutting the ribbon for the opening of a new soccer field, and I won't go on, you can't even imagine how I had to hustle every single day, my legs are really worn out, I've got such flat feet that I might as well be a goose, and nothing, my income was nil, just this rat race, and the stress of whether I would get there, was I late or not, because it was always like that, I had to be here right away, or be there right away, they were always pestering me to go here, there, or to some other place, and everybody was always ordering me around, but now—and you know what, young lady, I'll have another espresso—now it's as if I were the one giving orders.

They could have been only about one hundred or one hundred and fifty meters away from the train station, but they were able to conceal themselves so well among the columns of stacked-up railway ties that nobody could see them there, and of course they'd already chased away the Idiot Child, because he was capable of following them even here, that Idiot Child was a real snoop, they noted with a certain recognition, but to get him out of this habit, they had said to him that if he came after them one more time, then they'd rip off his dick and burn it in front of him, or vice versa, and this he understood, so he cleared off in the direction of the Water Tower as if he'd been shot from a pistol, well, and finally they lit up, and they only spoke occasionally, because each one always knew what the other was thinking, and usually there wasn't that much to say anyway, but well, now, when they did have something to say, and when a person really was thinking about what he would say, they still said nothing, they just blew out smoke and they looked to see if the train was coming from Sarkad, but no, then the bald one trampled down the butt with one end of his foot, and even if the train wasn't coming, he started into a monologue, saying: no reason for panic, we were never going to get in with those motorcycle dudes anyway, and for sure they would have ratted on us, the coolest thing is to seek out a more serious crowd, because around here there were only these pretentious countryboy cocksuckers getting into brawls, these losers are all just the same, just a worthless pile of crap, they needed to swing their axes at a bigger tree, start a bigger enterprise, said the bald one, and he smirked at the boy with the mohawk—our own business, not standing nicely in line somewhere, *entrepreneurs*—the other one tasted the word, I think that's cool—that's what I say, listen up, said the bald one again, if I say we should go to Pest, what do you say to that—cool, that'd be wicked, answered the one with the mohawk… wait, Pest, fuck, how do we get to Pest, they'll kick us off the train in less than a minute, because they'll be looking for us, that's for sure—I wouldn't be so sure of that, announced the bald one, why would they look for us, is anyone even interested in us, do you think they'll even notice that we're not there, everything's so chaotic, fuck, they won't even notice we're not there, and we can make use of that, do you get it—got it, said the other one, then they were quiet for a bit, they both lit up another cigarette, well, the bald one said, but we still need cash, this pack of smokes is running out, and it won't work without cash, why wouldn't it work, the one with the mohawk said, you want to pay? where? we don't have to pay anywhere, I'll show you—of course you'll show me, sure, the bald one answered—yes, I'll show you, the boy with the mohawk cut in, follow me and you'll learn how, fuck, because I need a cigarette, there'll be a cigarette, and we gotta get on a train, we'll get on that train, because we need some grub, we'll get some grub, and if we need some dope, we need some snow, we need some dough, we'll get everything we need, just listen, fuck, and watch how I do it, *'cos we don't need no loot, don't need no drugs, if I got my girl, then that's enuf,* he recited the rhyming tag, and he began to move amid the pallets of wood, because he'd always been really good at this, even as a small kid, everyone realized that he should have been a rapper, but for that you need real gear, and there wasn't too much of that in the Orphanage, so he rapped for free, without any gear, just rapped whatever came into his mind, but now, he said, he would try his luck in Pest, and—he blew out the smoke in a long trail in front of him, and his gaze became dreamy, like someone who clearly sees what he is talking about—the first place I'll walk into, got it? and I'll go up to the stage just like Eminem, and then everyone will realize just who this sucker is, no one's gonna call me a country hick without even a mom, you get it, they'll just listen to my every word and wait for me, because their jaws will drop, I'll get so rich, got it? and he said to the bald one I'll take you there too, don't be afraid, you hold the microphone for me, don't be afraid; fuck, if only that fucking train would come already, but I don't hear anything, and when that train comes, we're going to Csaba, then to Pest, fuck it, and if we get to Pest—he slapped his companion, hard on the back, reassuringly—then Canaan is here.

It had been announced in the rolling news reports on the Körös 1 station right away; so since clearly everyone had heard about it *then*, it wasn't perhaps necessary to enter into a detailed explanation *now*—the Mayor began to speak, when at last he, too, sat down in the large conference room—but before he began this meeting, for which he had, in fact, summoned the expanded Civic Committee here today, the Mayor said, he would be very gratified if everyone here were to assess the situation accurately, because there was also a personal dimension to all of this, and this personal dimension was, in fact, himself—for people had been saying about him, just a few days ago, that he was the soul of the city, its soul, this is the word our fellow citizens uttered on the streets, stopping him everywhere and squeezing his hand; and now everyone turned away when they saw him, and why, the Mayor asked wrathfully, was he possibly a chameleon, or something like that, had he, within the space of a few days, turned into a completely different man?—nooo, he shook his head decisively; he was the same person he'd always been, he hadn't changed; he was, if they wished—and here he really requested his colleagues from the opposition, just this once, to not interrupt him—he was still the soul of the city, because without him (he dared, without undue modesty, to declare this) the city would fall apart—but that's happened already, one of the wittier opposition delegates piped up—and here he was, right with them, to make sure that never happened, and here they were too, the Mayor said, now turning to the individuals assembled, and slowly looking around at everyone—because only together, gathered as one, could they master this situation which had come about, because there was a situation—I think that's the expression the Police Chief would use—and he looked at the policeman, sitting intensely bored next to him, but he didn't make any statement—so I now await your observations, the Mayor said; but before anyone could do so, he added that he wished to summarize his previous train of thought about that personal dimension he'd alluded to, he now wished to announce in the most decisive manner possible that there was no proof whatsoever that he had given any kind of speech at the train station, and he'd told the Körös 1 reporter this as well (when it was still on air, that is)—but even if he had given a speech anywhere comprised of a few words, even then no one could ever claim that he'd uttered any words that he would not back "now and forever," although by that he didn't mean to imply that any speech at all had issued from his mouth, because—tell me honestly now, he said—was he not right when he claimed that in that chaos it was impossible to hear a single sound, let alone with such vocal cords as his, and he didn't wish now to make jokes at his own expense, as he wasn't particularly in a joking kind of mood, but with this mouthpiece of his, a speech coming from him would be completely inaudible in the chaos that broke out there when the Baron arrived on the train, and a situation did develop which could not be characterized by any other word then anarchy, yes, he repeated, anarchy, chaos, and he would immediately add, in order to further illuminate the situation, that there arose a cacophony, and in this cacophony a person really had to be on their toes to hear anything at all from the speeches, his closest colleagues had told him this immediately—here he looked at the chief secretary with a meaningful glance—they'd heard nothing, nothing at all, and yet they had been standing right next to him, for example, Jucika here, she wasn't even a meter away—he looked again at the chief secretary, who at this gifted her boss with a full view of her bosom, namely she turned toward him and nodded in assent, and Jucika here said that she hadn't heard anything at all from his speech, although—and the chief secretary began to now turn her luxurious bosom toward the row of people sitting to her right—although I am absolutely convinced that the Mayor's speech was truly outstanding—well, you see, continued the Mayor with a rather chagrined face, because he did not consider the secretary's intervention to be particularly fortunate, and it always threw him off balance when Jucika offered him this "view" of her breasts—still, even she didn't hear anything, namely people could only get information about what had and hadn't been said from our press, and this is the main thing, only from there, only from the newspapers and the news bulletins, namely from those colleagues who likewise hadn't heard anything whatsoever from his speech, the quality of which naturally he didn't care to dwell on right now, let that be the privilege of others, and the consequence of this was that what they had written and reported was sheer tomfoolery, he'd read one account, and he'd listened to the news, and to be perfectly honest he was completely dumbstruck when he heard what idiocies they had put in his mouth, according to which he was so grateful to the Baron for bequeathing so much of this and that to the city and other such gibberish, well, he had to laugh, and he would even smile now if he were in the mood for jokes, it was all such a load of nonsense, of course he'd never said such things, and his speech had contained nothing other than a greeting for the guest, who after long decades was once again returning to the city, and that was all, the Mayor bowed, and anyone could look into this, if those newspapers and those recordings of the news reports were actually still available—he too had tried to get hold of some in order to present them to the expanded Civic Committee here today, but just imagine, he said—and it was as if from the surprise that his features had suddenly dispersed—there was not a single one to be found anywhere, so that the esteemed community members gathered here would simply have to believe what he was telling them, because his word, as had always been the case, contained only the truth, and so he concluded his remarks concerning that personal dimension of the matter—and now he would kindly make room for the next speaker, if he pleased, and he pushed the microphone away from himself to the Police Chief, but the latter just gestured that he had nothing to say, and he pushed the microphone further on, and so it went until the microphone had circled all the way around the long conference-room table, because then the Mayor grabbed it again, and he said to those gathered there: our task here, after the horrific incident, is to clearly state: what happened has truly shaken the sympathetic inhabitants of our city, but we cannot regard it as anything else than the personal accident of an unlucky old man, after which the city must still confront its own fate, its own momentous tasks, such as employment, development, pensions, raising the birth rate, the unresolved problems of public hygiene, the maintenance of public order, the constant monitoring of the hygienic conditions of food distribution, and—should he say it?— for the time being, in connection with these questions, he had only one announcement to make, and this really was rather dispiriting, he confessed, indeed he experienced it as his own personal failure, but he had to announce that a decision had been made concerning the most enchanting of ideas (originating from one of the city's oldest and most ardently treasured urban beautification plans), namely it had long been planned that along the River Körös, between the two great bridges, fountains would be placed at intervals of every fifty, or possibly even every twenty-five meters, which on summer evenings would gladden the mood of the commendable working citizens of this city with their refreshing spray—well, this had been the dream, and unfortunately, due to unresolved matters in the overall budget, this plan could not be realized anytime in the near future.

She walked across the circulation room almost on tiptoe, then turned into the corridor, where she already sensed the nervousness in her stomach, then she knocked very softly on the director's door, she felt as always, when she had to go to him because of a matter which could no longer be postponed, that she was hardly able to stammer out a single word, and from within she heard his vigorous bass voice, she pushed down the handle and took a step, but she just poked her head in, and in the meantime she held on to the door, actually she clutched at it, and she said that she didn't know if this would be of interest to the director, but today it was as if the entire library, the entire lending library, and the entire reference room had gone mad—come in, Eszter, the director spoke to her in that energetic bass voice of his, yes, sir, she stepped into his office, but she only dared to go a few steps in, and she closed the door so softly after herself so it wouldn't be heard, because that's what's going on, sir, I'm telling you, they're returning . . . no, that's not the right way to put it . . . they're carting back the books, usually we mail them notices for months on end, and no reaction, and now they're returning all the books without even a notice, and the lending period isn't even over, they're just carting back all the books, and there they stand, sir, piled up on my desk in columns, and I can hardly manage all the work, sir, but that's not why I'm disturbing you, because if this is how it is, then that's how it is, but—tell me, Eszter, the director again lowered his serious gaze onto the document, which he had just been studying in front of him on his writing desk, signifying that he was either not interested or he already knew all about it, probably he already knew, it flashed through Eszter's brain, but she just continued because now she had to say it to the end: and in the meantime they're cursing—here she lowered her voice—what are they cursing, the director asked without raising that serious gaze of his—well, the Baron, sir, the enthusiasm had been so great, surely you remember what was going on here for an entire week, well, now they're talking about it so rudely, saying this, that, and the other, and one of them said he hadn't checked out that travel guide to Argentina for himself, but for his grandmother, and the other one said that he took the book out by mistake, because it wasn't that one he wanted, but another, only I can't think of what it was now, one of those good long ones, that's what he said, sir, it's an absolute circus—well, yes, said the director, is there anything else?—but he didn't look up, and Esther knew that their conversation would be short, so she quickly mentioned that there was even someone who said—bringing back *Don Segundo Sombra,* he said: *those rotten gauchos,* can you imagine that, director, sir, for somebody to just say like that, about this amazing novel, rotten gauchos, I don't understand people—but I understand, Eszter, the director now raised his head, and he adjusted his glasses, which because of the strong prescription made his eyes look twice as big, because, he said, it was clear to him—and he was already smiling insinuatingly—because what has to be our starting point here in the City Library, Eszter, remember what I told you, I'm not fond of quoting myself, but do you remember—yes, sir—well now, what was it that I called your attention to, he asked, and he pursed his mouth, and he looked at his subordinate, waiting for her to reply, but she knew that he wasn't waiting for her to, but rather pausing so that he could then provide the most precise formulation possible for the question that he had just posed, for this *briefing,* as it were—Esther from the lending library always stored up within herself these pronouncements from the director—I was talking about how, if you remember—yes, I remember, sir—about how we here in the City Library must make human nature our starting point, human nature, which certainly is formed by current events, hearsay, fashions, namely manipulations, and this human nature is weak, Eszter—the director now took off his glasses, beginning to massage the bridge of his nose where a small red indentation was visible, and as Eszter particularly venerated this part of his face, from this point on she could hardly even pay attention to what he was saying—because what are we talking about here, the director continued, we're talking about the fact that our readers just a few days ago heard that their redeemer was coming, an event about which, here in the chilly sobriety of the library, we had a slightly different opinion, do you remember—Eszter didn't remember, but she nodded willingly and she didn't interrupt so as not to impede the flow of his words, because she wanted to hear everything in one go—that our readers (with all respect to the exceptions) at times, and particularly in such intense situations, behave like children, is that not so, Eszter, he asked her, and she once again nodded in agreement—because now they would wish to deny that they had anything at all to do with this particular situation, and we could even say that they didn't, perhaps we may permit ourselves such an admission in the chilly sobriety of this library, can't we, Eszter—of course we can, Eszter faltered—moreover, if somebody would wish to know what happened with our readers, well, I'll tell you: it has emerged that they have unmasked their own selves in *knowing nothing about Argentina,* and that is what we (as adults working here in this library and not children) have to filter out; thus, if their enthusiasm has waned, what we need to do is to initiate a special program, let's say with the title of "The South American Continent as the Mirror of the Contemporary World," or something like that—what a brilliant idea, murmured Eszter in front of the door, still clutching the door handle behind her—because our single task, here in the City Library, is the dissemination of erudition, learning, elevating the general level of knowledge, and it isn't our concern—the director took an eyeglass cloth from his side pocket, and he began to wipe the thick lenses of his eyeglasses, first the left side, then the right, he liked to do it in this order, or he was used to that order, Eszter could never decide—in other words, what has made people go mad (because they do go mad here sometimes) is not our concern; and our application for the Erkel Competition has already been handed in, so we can be calm, because I'm convinced that we stand a great chance of winning that grant, and among other things, we'll be able to expand our musicological materials, won't we, Eszter, and won't that be wonderful, and personally I'm truly happy, because I am the one who is singly and alone responsible for this institution, and I don't get mixed up in politics, not even the local kind, we simply don't meddle in that sort of thing, do you understand me, Eszter—only the pursuit of knowledge, or to put it in other words: to see, but not be seen, this has always been my ars poetica, and so it shall remain, the director placed his glasses back on the bridge of his nose, and with this gesture he judged this incidental conversation with this excellent employee of the lending service as more or less settled, because of course he hadn't the faintest notion of how Eszter felt for him—and she took this as certain—because "he was so, but so utterly naive, and so completely caught up with his work," so she pressed down on the door handle behind her as far as it would go— even though she had been pressing down on it this whole time anyway, and with the remark "yes, director, I completely agree with you," she backed out through the door, in the meantime she let go of the inner door handle, stepped out of the office as quietly as possible, gently closed the door, and, holding her breath for a few moments, let the outer door handle move back into place without a sound.

Well, so life is beginning to settle back into its old routine, that's what I say, said the director of Municipal Utility Services, just another couple of days, and everyone will be completely beyond it, and certainly after a week, and after a month, nothing will remain at all from the whole hullabaloo, just like a memory from a bad dream; the two of them stood at the corner of Lennon's Ditch, observing one of their trucks, from which two robust workers were, just at that moment, lowering a slot machine; he'd personally decided himself to have them returned, in other words, following the phone call from the Police Chief, who'd talked to him confidentially (namely it should remain between the two of them), which, why deny it, was quite gratifying for him, because it wasn't every day that somebody asked him anything at all "in such a way," but now this had happened, and moreover it had sounded very convincing, the argument being that if, *for example,* the slot machines were all returned nicely to their usual places, then the mood of the public would calm down, so why wouldn't anyone who could do something like that not do it, because the truth was, as the Police Chief had mentioned to him, that life always returned back to its usual channels, and that's exactly how all the troublesome things quiet down, because life—the Police Chief concluded his remarks—must go on, and the bad events must be brought to a conclusion—so of course this had been his decision, and the Utility Services Director began the work, because one had to work, he said that morning to the employees blinking sleepily and morosely in the chill wind at the Municipal Utility Services depot, they too were obligated to work, and so they began: they went to the dressing room of the soccer field, where just a few days ago they had stored all the slot machines they'd taken away from restaurants and other establishments, and they began to transport them back, and now the director of Municipal Utility Services wanted to see how the work was progressing, so he had been driven out to this location in the service car, and now he stood in front of Lennon's Ditch with his assistant, and they watched as the two workers just at that moment let a machine drop to the ground, fortunately from not too high, the workers just motioned to the boss not to worry, no damage, they lifted one of the machines from its corners, then rolled a hand truck beneath it, they took it back into the nearby Pinball Arcade, then came the second slot machine, and with that they were done, they nodded to the boss, climbed back into the truck, and already they were gone, the boss and his assistant got back into the service car, and the assistant asked, where to now, well, let's take a turn around the city, said the director, to which the assistant just nodded, and he stepped on the gas, then they started off from Lennon's Ditch along the main street, up to the former building of the Water Works, then the director said, let's turn to the left toward the statue of Petőfi, and he watched as really life was beginning to return to the old routine, because on the streets the homeless were already beginning to appear, although you couldn't see the Albanian child beggars yet, the homeless had been let out again though, the assistant pointed out to his boss, here's one, you see there's another one too, everywhere, they're really swarming over the streets again, clearly the Mayor has let them out, thought the director, as obviously it would have been impossible to keep this filthy mob forever in the Old People's Home, cooped up there with our elder citizens, this obviously couldn't last for too long, but at the time nobody had any other ideas of what to do with them, and then the complaints had to be addressed, because right after they were moved in, the old people began to complain—they stank, and they stole, and the old people wailed about it, but there was no one around to deal with these complaints, because there was so much to arrange with all the welcome celebrations and everything, the director now recalled; well, but now it's over, he sighed, as they turned at the statue of Petőfi in front of the hardware store onto the main street, then the assistant looked at him with a questioning expression—where should they go from here?—but his boss was a little uncertain at this point, because as a matter of fact they had nothing to do, things were proceeding along just fine by themselves, they could go back to the depot, no, or they could go have a look and see how it was going with the slot machine redeliveries, no, what time is it, he asked the assistant, ten minutes to noon, well in that case, the director answered, the church bells will start ringing in a minute, let's go, he said to the assistant, to the Komló Restaurant, by the time we get there, we can park and go in, it'll already be noon, and we can get the menu for lunch, the bells are ringing out for lunch time, he gazed cheerfully at his assistant—what do you think?

If they don't pay up, then they shouldn't expect anything from me, the carpenter unscrewed the screws from the bed in the room of the Chateau, and they still owed him his fee, still owed him his travel expenses, and for the synthetic resin—and how do I get that out, and all of these damn screws as well?—he hit one in rage on the edge of the enormous bed with his electric drill, I can pull them out, but they're not the same screws anymore, they're used screws, no matter how I unscrew them, you can see they're not what they were when they were first screwed in, here's one, just look at it, he held up yet another to the light, this one too is already kind of bent, well, what am I, a magician? no, I'm not a magician, and you can't unscrew a screw in such a way that on that screw there won't be any mark anywhere indicating that screw was once screwed in somewhere, and once again he was flooded with rage, and he kicked his tool chest so hard that it ended up in one of the corners of the room in the Chateau, and moreover it got knocked over, which made him even more enraged, because then he had to go over there and start putting everything back in the tool chest, and not just the screws, one by one—let them all go to hell—but all the tools that had been in there, and he was so enraged that at the end he didn't even put back the tools back, but just threw them at the tool chest, so of course they went flying everywhere, he picked them up again; but it's no surprise—he said to himself aloud, as in the course of the years he had begun to talk to himself—for he had no assistant, how could he have permitted himself one in these circumstances—and now an assistant, he muttered—and he tried somehow to regain his composure, so at last he could pack up everything, he had to toil and drudge alone, and, if you please, for nothing, and now he would pull out these screws because he wasn't leaving them here for them, those motherfuckers: they had summoned him here and here he came, they promised him the world, telling him he'd get a bonus and everything, and then, if you please, at the very end they told him, as if he were some kind of good-for-nothing, that his services weren't needed, he'd been called there by mistake, and the city coffers were so empty that for the time being they requested his patience—his patience!—the carpenter yelled at the bare walls in the chateau room, and now I'm supposed to be patient, well do they really think I was born yesterday or what, and now patience, they're never going to pay my wages, but I, if you please, I'm going to pull out every single last screw, I'm not even going to leave one rotten screw here, let all of those shitheads go to hell, because that'll be the end of it, I'll pull out all my screws, pack up, and that's it, but first I'm going to kick apart this whole piece of crap, because when am I going to see my pay? do they think I'm working for free? no, I work for my livelihood, not for frauds or swindlers—and now patience! and he gave a good kick again to his tool chest, which this time was not knocked over, but still slid over to the corner, but he didn't go over to it, he just kept extracting the screws from the bed, and he was enraged, and he kept talking to himself but to no avail, because nobody heard him, although there was a fair bit of ruckus, as they were bringing back those orphan kids now and the kids were yelling like Indians, and it made him even feel more enraged that someone was in a good mood, because well, this chateau was for them, because no one ever wanted to spend the money to renovate it, and it had gotten into such a state that it couldn't even be fixed up, and then some wise guy comes along—because it's always these wise guys—and he decides it's perfect, even in this state, for the orphans, who until then had been stuck in the reform school out there by Sarkadi Road, and they were even capable of bringing them here, to this chateau, and now that all this hysteria with the Baron is over, they brought this gang of bandits back here, why? why even bother with them if their own mothers can't be bothered, why give them money, work, and what else, for what, what was the point of having these guttersnipes around—he was almost finished pulling out all the screws—because what are they going to turn into, they'll all be criminals as soon as they're kicked out of here, they already run around stealing and cheating, fighting and robbing, well, do they need to have a chateau, a motherfucking chateau, they should all be chucked into jail right away, they should have been chucked into jail even as little brats, that would solve everything, because then there wouldn't be so many hooligans, homeless, and beggars, because just look at these beggars, well, where do they come from, I'm telling you—and he pulled out the last screw and slammed the lid down on his tool chest—they come from here, because we're the ones who raise them so they can end up robbing and stealing, and in the meantime a guy just toils and drudges from morning 'til night, and for what, no one pays him, because that's what happens, what does he get for his good work, not even a fig, that's what he gets—he grabbed up the tool chest and left through the door—and these no-good guttersnipes get a fucking chateau, well, this is where we've gotten to in this country of ours, but we don't even deserve anything else—he slammed the door so forcibly behind him that it opened again—just this. And he stormed out of the Orphanage.

There was only the large gray suitcase left, but she couldn't reach it, so she had to get the ladder from the bathroom and stand on the ladder to take it down, all the other suitcases were already open on the bed, as well as the clothes and anything else she might need, everything nicely folded, now only this large suitcase remained, because everything was ready—as she had come to the point of realizing the only possibility was for her to leave: first she had taken all her undergarments out of the cupboard, because she always had to take those along, her undergarments, at least the ones of good quality, and as far as undergarments were concerned, she always selected only the best, that was a fundamental principle of hers, in short, the undergarments were expensive, so she wouldn't leave even a single one here at home; accordingly she began with the undergarments, and then she folded them up again, because when she'd taken them out of the cupboard drawers they'd slid out of shape, although she tried to be careful, then she packed them tidily into the smaller suitcases, arranging everything nicely, then came the blouses, the shirts, and smaller accessories such as scarves, stockings, socks, and lingerie, these didn't take up too much space—of course she was a little worried about the rest fitting in—then there were the skirts and suits and jumpsuits, but here she hesitated a bit, because it occurred to her: should she pack only for the winter, or should she plan on staying away for the following spring as well, this was very hard to decide; the simplest, of course, would be to also pack her spring things, but at the same time she knew she didn't have enough room for that, so she decided not to place the spring items into the suitcase, but to stack them up on the bed, with the thought that she would look them over and then, when the most essential pieces were in the suitcase, she could determine how much space she had left, or rather if she had any space left at all, because if she didn't, then the whole thing was pointless and these lighter items could simply be put back into the cupboard, well, never mind, she licked the side of her mouth as she stood, thinking, above the large suitcase, let's just concentrate on the most urgent for now, and one after the other, into the large suitcase went her woolen things, and a few knit pullovers, then once again with the coats she was forced to stop and think, because who knew what the winter would be like, if it would be bitterly cold or mild like last year, when she almost didn't even have to wear a warm fur coat, but the fur coat—she sighed in worry—she could only see taking if she wore it, and it wasn't cold enough for a fur coat yet, well then, what should she do, she could hardly set out for the great wide world without one, and with winter on the way, so that for the time being she also put that on the bed, she'd think it over later and figure it out, and she just packed and packed, and unfortunately her large suitcase also became full quite quickly, and there she stood between the closets and the large suitcase, looking at first in one direction, then in the other, and now what should she do, my God, she sighed, I have no one with me who can give me any advice, I had to live to see this as well, and the corners of her mouth turned down as she began to cry: I'm standing here all alone in the middle of the living room, on the bed are five small suitcases and one big one, and they're all full, and I'm looking at them, and the cupboard is still half full, what am I to do, what—and she just stood there between the cupboards and the suitcases, and she couldn't decide, this was too much for her all at once, and there was the question of the fur coat, there was the question of the spring things, and there was the half-full cupboard, all the things on the shelves, well, would somebody tell her now, and she looked up at the living room's low ceiling, and on her face, on her tortured, elderly face there was real despair—well, was this what she deserved after living out her entire life, this?

He was out by the train stop at Bicere and trying to dissect what he was seeing down to the minutest elements, because while he thought the bikers' suspicions were exaggerated, he still couldn't completely let the matter rest, because that's how he was—he'd explained this once to the corporal: he always saw everything down to the minutest details, but never lacking the sweeping overview as well, and he put things together from that, that's why the Police Station was so effective, and now he was doing the same—he went into the tiny building of the station and looked to see what was there: an iron stove with cold ashes in it, no matches in sight, a paper handkerchief—namely, two used paper tissues on the floor—and apart from that there was nothing, nothing but a few dog hairs, and then some kind of dirt on the walls and on the floors, well and so—he asked himself—what do we have here, what do these ashes signify, this means that somebody lit up the stove here at one point, well, but who and when, it could have been even a year ago, nothing can be determined from these cold ashes, or there's the question of these used tissues—and that old crone who was always baking those pastries knew nothing at all, she was so frightened she could hardly talk and said that she had no idea if those paper tissues could be traced back to there, so that wasn't going to get him anywhere—but should he really be trying to deal with these dog hairs now, no, the Police Chief turned his head away, a bunch of dog hairs like that could have turned up here any time and from any dog, in addition whom could this dog have belonged to, some completely untrustworthy boozer, some little scared shitless worm, whose word he wouldn't be able to trust anyway, well, so here he was standing in this train stop, which itself stood in the middle of the great plain, people used to board the train here from the former farming settlements, but those were long gone, that was true, Biker Joe was right about that; still it was there, precisely in the middle of the plain, and anyone could come in, the door was never locked; but there were no traces anywhere, even the pile of wood hadn't been knocked over, it just seemed that somebody had taken a few pieces from it, and well—the Police Chief held apart his hands—this is not evidence, this is shit, and with that he stepped out of the tiny building at the Bicere stop, and he repeated to the corporal standing next to him, who had come out here with him: this is not evidence, this is just a pile of shit, nothing, let's go, we can forget it already; they got into the jeep, and already they were headed back to the city, back to the Police Station, where a piece of news awaited them: something had happened, which was surprising, because it was at the hotel, which hotel, the Police Chief yelled at the reporting officer, a courier had arrived at the At Home Hotel, something they didn't see there too often—yes, I mean, no, the Chief of Police groaned and threw himself behind his desk—it was some foreign delivery service making a personal shipment, and since the address wasn't completely correct they first took it to the wrong place, and it seems they tried as hard as they could to find the real address and they found it out, and now here they were, well, but what did they bring, and to whom, the Police Chief snapped at the officer on duty, nine valuable suitcases, and for the Baron, what, the Police Chief jumped up, and already he was in his jeep again, already he was at the hotel, and already somebody stood before him who said he was the manager, he didn't know him, and from the expression on his face it was clear that he had no wish to know him, tell me, the Police Chief said, and he heard the same report, almost word for word, which had just been given at the Police Station—let me see the items, the Police Chief interrupted the account of the hotel manager already at the beginning, and they led him into the booth next to the hotel delivery room where there really were nine suitcases, well, and what's interesting about this, the officer on duty standing behind him said, is that these were delivered to the Baron, and maybe there's something in them, which ... but the Police Chief already interrupted him: what would be in them?—well, maybe some document, the officer on duty stammered out—a document, but about what? about the Baron's plans, or—or what?! and once again the Police Chief had to muster all of his self-control, because when his subordinates got to this point—because they always got to this point, this far and no more—they reported something but they never thought about what they were reporting, why didn't his subordinates know how to think, why weren't they capable of offering even one conclusion, or anything, but the Police Chief didn't say anything, and the officer on duty didn't know if he should say something, so instead he said nothing, he just stood at attention behind the Police Chief and looked at the suitcases from behind his boss's shoulder—Prada, said the Police Chief, not even turning around, yes, the officer on duty clicked his heels together, I'm saying, said the Chief of Police again, Prada, the suitcases are Prada, and for a while he didn't say anything else, he just looked at them, you didn't move them, did you, he asked the hotel manager, who was standing farther back, and he didn't understand what the question was, what it was supposed to be about—well, sir, we brought them in, and since then, we haven't . . . fine, do you have a room where we can open them up?—the Police Chief now turned his gaze to him—do you understand, I want to unpack them next to each other, all of these nine suitcases here, do you understand, one after the other, I want to open them up, is that possible here, at which the hotel manager readily replied yes, he was a little afraid of the police officer, so he just motioned with his eyebrows to some of his staff standing around behind him to arrange this, and so they did, they opened up a room on the ground floor, where in a matter of minutes all nine suitcases to be inspected by the Police Chief had been carried in; he stood in front of them as they lay on the ground, he marched up and down in front of them, first from left to right, then from right to left, he looked them over thoroughly, and at last he motioned to the officer on duty indicating that he should open the locks, and he himself rummaged through all nine suitcases, but he saw that beyond items of clothing there was nothing in them, nothing in the entire heaven-sent world, then he looked up at the officer on duty indicating for him to step forward, and he too looked over the nine suitcases, and while this was occurring, he never took his eyes off the officer on duty, he just waited for him to speak, looking at him with a questioning gaze, he waited, he waited with his hands clasped behind his back, but it wasn't clear to the officer on duty what was expected of him, so he just cleared his throat, he went over to one of the suitcases, he rummaged through it, then he stepped away, I would like to know—the Police Chief said—what you see in that suitcase, do you get it? his eyes flashed threateningly, I don't want you to tell me what you think, but my humble request is for you to tell me what you *see*—clothes, garments, well, that's it; the Police Chief rose on his heels, you have good eyesight, what is special about these nine suitcases—well, and this was already a trick question—I mean, there's nothing personal in them, the officer on duty replied nervously, at which the Police Chief looked entirely surprised, he looked at the officer on duty, and motioned him to step closer to him: Sergeant, how long have you been under my command, he asked—almost the entire hotel staff had swarmed around the open door to get a glimpse of what was going on in there—seven years, I report, sir, answered the officer on duty, so now is the time, the Police Chief said, for me to start paying a little more attention to you, because you can see things, and in my Police Station that is a great treasure, you know how to draw conclusions—at this, the frightened face of the officer on duty became even more frightened, because he believed the customary dressing-down, a frequent occurrence at the Police Station, was about to come—but it didn't, rather the Police Chief said to him: that's exactly the point, namely, there is nothing in these suitcases that could connect them personally to the Baron, therefore they were sent to him by someone, which, leaving aside the dispatch note, clearly only could have been a family member in Vienna, that we already know—yes, yes, the officer on duty nodded in a soldierlike fashion—which accordingly tells us that these nine suitcases mean nothing, for us they are irrelevant, yes, that's it exactly, said the officer on duty again, namely, as for what we should do now, I don't know what that is, the officer on duty continued, but the Police Chief had already stormed out of the room and out of the hotel, the officer on duty could hardly catch up with him—start the car, the Police Chief said to him, then he just looked out through the window at the gray, gloomy houses on Peace Boulevard, and he noted: well, that's how it is, sergeant, that's all our work is now, we go out after every possible trace, and how many of them are even worth something, he asked sorrowfully, but he answered the question himself, saying: not even one, sergeant, and we could just throw these nine suitcases into a stinking cunt.

She didn't unlatch the chain, and she'd done well not to, she thought, when she saw the two unfamiliar faces, she asked who they were looking for and what they wanted, but just out of habit, because she wasn't expecting a reply, as one of these two faces had been frighteningly disfigured by some recent injury, and she wanted to close the door immediately; the person with the injured face, however, started in, saying that he had arrived with a final explanation, a message which he must unconditionally pass on to her from the Baron, who had perished amid such tragic circumstances, and the man pointed to his own wounded face, as if confirming his own statement, as if he too had been a part of this tragedy—and because she heard the name of the Baron, as well as the word "tragedy," she was thrown off her balance for a moment, and she didn't close the door immediately, although of course the chain remained in place—she only asked this man, through the crack of the open door, if he could kindly tell her what the message was, and could he pass it on to her even like this—by which she meant: without her opening the door even one more centimeter—and at this, the words began to flow out of this man, and the problem was that in his speech something reverberated, a few words that moved her to consideration—she, who was packing on the eve of her departure—so the door remained as it had been, opened just a crack, and she listened to the words of this short, fat, mushroom-headed person with thick curly hair and a wounded face, namely that he had accompanied someone—no, not accompanied!—he had *brought* the Baron to this very location just the other day, and while the well-known events that concluded so woefully had transpired in Marika's presence—events which he, the mushroom-headed person, considered to be "of immeasurable regret"—he was also certain that there'd been a misunderstanding, and the message spoke of this, the message which—now that the Baron was no more—he must transmit, unconditionally, to its addressee, namely to this fine lady, in comparison to whom the Dulcinea del Tobozó, from the well-known novel, was a mere pale imitation, unconditionally, because—the man said through the crack in the door—perhaps the lady could consider: that message, which a mere few days ago had been a mere "sentimental missive" was now one expressing the last wish of its author, a last wish for him; now, he pointed at himself, although Marika could only deduce his gesture, she couldn't see it fully through the crack in the door, in any event, he said, this was something he "must transmit," and he couldn't just leave the city—because this was going to happen given the way things had ended up for him, namely he was leaving the city—but he couldn't take even one step in that direction without transmitting this final "expression of volition" to the one for whom it was intended, so therefore he greatly asked the lady if she would excuse an unknown person showing up at her door and in such a state, and once again he pointed his face, he greatly requested if she could overcome her natural—and, these days, completely justified—mistrust, and allow him in, so that he might really convey the message entrusted to him by the Baron amid more dignified circumstances, namely would she let him in, and after some hesitation, Marika unlatched the security chain and let the two men in, although she added that she was "on the eve of departure," so she requested that the gentleman—as she called her uninvited guest, leading him and his companion in to the apartment and sitting them down in the living room—that he show her the consideration of sparing her any longer discussions and to transmit "what he had brought," namely the essence of the matter, the essence of that certain final wish, if he would be so kind, then, to allow her, as she was indeed running out of time, to call a taxi as soon as possible, and to commence her journey, as, in this moment—whatever the contents of the gift or the message—she desired nothing more than that.

He was certain that the money was there somewhere, and even if he wouldn't be able to say exactly what he meant by "money," he was convinced that it was nowhere else, only with this woman, whom that swindler, that old nutcase with his unhinged mind, had sought out here in this apartment only a few days ago, it couldn't be anywhere else, and no matter how he looked at the matter, he kept finding more and more good reasons to think that he wasn't mistaken, that he was on the right track, and that there could be no delay, because the situation here was growing ever more tense, he explained to his newly appointed business associate, who at first had designated himself as Mr. Leslie Bolton and wore an old-fashioned bowler hat, but who, as it turned out, knew not even a word of English, and so he proposed the name of László Olteanu, and finally when he saw on Dante's face even that didn't suit him, he finally admitted that his friends just called him Lenyó, and so Lenyó he remained—accordingly things here were headed in an increasingly lousy direction; Dante looked at his new companion, perhaps they should relocate their firm's headquarters back to Szolnok—and he, namely Lenyó, was the best choice in Dante's estimation, because Lenyó had an excellent sense of how to operate a slot-machine business, and because, according to his best knowledge, Szolnok had extraordinary development potential, so Dante could only recommend the following: Szolnok, he said to him, and he was just making a recommendation, he didn't ask, he didn't want to force anything, so that from this point on, as they worked out the ownership agreement, and after a small advance had been paid, already he, Lenyó, was the new owner of this empire with its vast financial and cultural reserves, but reliably operational as well from a business perspective—and here Dante always raised his index finger above his wavy crown of hair into the heights, every time he repeated this statement—it was profit-yielding *from a business perspective as well*, this empire of slot machines, because with this agreement, a profit-yielding gaming-business empire had simply fallen into the other's lap, this he could guarantee, because it had brought uninterrupted and indeed marvelous results to him in every regard, only that now, he—and now Dante was explaining this to the woman as he sat on her sofa bed, where she had motioned for them to sit down—now, in terms of going forward (and by that he meant in the future), he wished to test his capabilities in the newly expanding field of human development; as for him, innovation was something that applied first and foremost to his own self, because he was the kind of person who wasn't motivated by mere profit, but primarily by the felt needs of his fellow human beings, and it was precisely on the basis of these that he deployed ever newer organizational structures, in other words, he was now transitioning into the field of communications: if, until now, his first priority had been the creation of games—with their pledge of freedom— and making them available to the wider public, now, however, his current endeavor consisted of the facilitation of interpersonal communications; namely he was planning, within the forthcoming hours, to invest in a mobile phone concern, headquartered in Arad, Romania, although due to the regular and never-ending flood of refugees, the news concerning rail transportation wasn't too reassuring, nonetheless from time to time it was still possible to get on the Budapest-Bucharest line at the Békéscsaba station, and if he could make it that far, from there it was just a hop and a skip to Arad, this, therefore, was his plan, and with this information he considered that the introductions had been taken care of, after which—he shifted his weight above the springs of the sofa bed—nothing else remained but for him to convey the message, the transmission of which he had been entrusted, at which point the lady of the house began to fidget, because she was looking at the hands of the wall clock above her uninvited guest very impatiently, and once again she mentioned that perhaps her guest could put things a little more succinctly, if she might so request, well, but of course, my dear lady, I shall immediately tell you the message corresponding to the Baron's last wish, but please allow me to beg your forgiveness in advance, he said, because I am merely a minor character in this whole affair, a true, honest-to-goodness minor character with no wish whatsoever to push himself to the forefront of this story, and fine, that's enough about me, so yes, well, the message, namely, the message is composed of two parts: the first part—and here Dante, adopting a more confidential tone of voice, leaned in closer to Marika—was that *something* which the Baron had entrusted to her, Marika, should now be given to him, as the Baron clearly must have left some kind of piece of paper here, an envelope, or an envelope with a card, or some kind of little coffer, or a so-called belt pouch, he didn't know what it was, but whatever it was, he was now supposed to take possession of it, as the decisive wish of the Baron was that this piece of paper, envelope, package, little coffer, or belt pouch be given to him, Dante, because he had been entrusted to act upon the contents of this envelope, package, little coffer or belt pouch, in accordance with the last wishes of the Baron; so that the person who rang your doorbell today, my dear lady, is a kind of estate handler—Dante, sitting on the sofa bed, nodded, confirming his own words—and he would repeat that he didn't know exactly what was in this little bundle or box, but the Baron had only told him that he should ask for it at Marika's, because Marika would immediately know what he was talking about; he hoped, he said, she hadn't progressed too far in her packing—he glanced at the suitcases, visible from where they sat, strewn on and around the bed in the bedroom—no, no, she hadn't packed too much yet, Marika finally managed to speak, not too much, but she had no idea of what the gentleman was speaking, as the Baron had left nothing with her, discounting that immeasurable affront, which not a single female person could bear, but still, she was bearing it—not here though, in this city, she said bitterly, where, after everything that the Baron had done to her, there was no longer any place for her, that's why—she involuntarily motioned toward the bedroom—she'd resolved in that very hour to leave that place where she had lived out her long life, so that really could he cut to the chase, she added, with a sterner face now, and as she had understood that there would be no kind of "gift" forthcoming from him here, but rather that he wanted something from her, which was really more than outrageous, she stood up, as it were obliging her uninvited guests to bring this visit to an end, but then Dante—although he leapt up, grabbing Lenyó and yanking him up too, Lenyó, who'd been sitting there with a fairly dim-witted expression on his face, seemingly understanding nothing of what was going on here—he said: my dear Madame, if you say that the Baron left nothing here in trust for me, namely that he left nothing for a person coming here especially at his request, then I will accept that, and I certainly don't want to trouble you in any respect before the commotion of your travel; I am, however, obliged to entrust you with the second part of the message, according to which the Baron, in his solicitude for you, requests that whatever he may have left behind here, if you prefer not to give it to me, then let it be in your possession, and put it to that good purpose which the Baron presumed to find in you through his entire life, and to which—Dante slowly moved after Marika, who had already made a few steps toward the front door, signifying again that she was ready to see them out, because as far she was concerned, this conversation was over—he, Dante, would only wish to add: by this solicitude, the Baron also meant that he should help her in whatever matter was at hand, and if now—he motioned back toward the suitcases—she was now planning to leave this city, and if her destination was Budapest, would she permit him (similarly in accordance with the Baron's wishes) to recommend the assistance of this gentleman right here beside him, who would be more than happy to help her with her suitcases, as it turned out that his itinerary led him in the same direction, although originally he'd planned to travel for only half of her journey, he had now reconsidered the matter—Dante looked at Lenyó, who had no idea what he was talking about and tried to conceal the fact that he was somewhat surprised—and he would be more than happy to accompany her until her final destination and would be at her service after their arrival as well—to which Marika, who had already placed her hand on the door handle, after a bit of visible reflection, answered that she would accept this last gift—at the word "gift," she pursed her lips sarcastically—because she truly needed assistance with her suitcases, whether here or in her final destination of Budapest, and this assistance *might as well* come from the circle of the Baron's former acquaintances, because in vain had she lived her entire life in the city—but it was already now on the train that she was relating this to her newly fledged acquaintance—and now she had been compelled to renounce that life, she didn't wish to divulge too much about this, because every word in relation to this matter caused her great pain, but she would say this much: that it was sorrowful, endlessly sorrowful, that an old lady of sixty-seven years was obliged to start a new life in the capital city, to which Lenyó really didn't know what to say, as usually he didn't have much of an idea what to say anyhow, because it wasn't really clear to him who was who in this whole scenario; and if, on the basis of a small down payment, he'd just acquired a share in a slot-machine empire, making him the boss of an enterprise headquartered in Szolnok, but with operations from the Tisza all the way to the border, as Dante had formulated it between the two of them at the train station as he took his leave, then why did he have to keep tailing this lady all the way to Budapest and not leave her alone until he could get out of her where she was keeping the money, the amount of which Dante had conveyed to him with just one grimace, as he also conveyed that inasmuch as he could manage this, he'd get half the amount—he, the new-hatched director of the slot-machine empire headquartered in Szolnok—but as far as he was concerned it wasn't clear why Dante had gotten mixed up in this, maybe Lenyó was troubled by that grimace, although it could mean a few million, he speculated, and he thought of these millions while looking at this woman's face in the train that set off with a series of jolts, after waiting for almost an hour; Lenyó kept turning over in his head if he should go or not go, were those few little millions really waiting for him, or had Dante just made the whole thing up, it was difficult, he pondered the matter intently in the train compartment, really difficult, but he couldn't make up his mind, so that transferring at the Békéscsaba station, he was already lugging the woman's innumerable suitcases—turning back for them several times—onto the local train to Budapest, where once again he sat down across from her, after the conductor, in exchange for a friendly amount, had extended the validity of his ticket to Budapest, and so it went on, at Szolnok he only saw the huge station building with the countless train tracks, and already they were rumbling on to Budapest; and even when he had brought the woman, according to her wishes, to a hotel on Blaha Lujza Square, to which they'd made their way only with great difficulty among the refugees lying everywhere, finally he'd sat down with her for coffee to try to get out of her what he hadn't been able to yet, and she claimed she didn't know anything about these millions, she didn't even have the faintest idea, and because he had been spending so much time with her, he took it as more and more of a given that this woman had something, he pledged to be at her service henceforth as well, and Marika accepted this, although she wasn't in the habit of striking up acquaintances such as these, with complete strangers, well, times have changed, she sighed, on Blaha Lujza Square, and she looked out at the restive traffic through the rather smudged window of her room with a single bed, and she cried a little, that she had to be so alone, then crumpling up her handkerchief into her handbag, she got dressed and called the number she'd been given, and a half hour later Lenyó was there, and they set off to look at a rental apartment, which Marika had copied out for herself from the want ads in *Blikk*, in the fifth district, close to Parliament, it couldn't be too bad, she thought, and she had even circled it three times on her copy of *Blikk*, then they started off and got as far as Nyugati Station in a taxi, but the taxi driver said it would be better for them to get out, they'd get to their destination quicker on foot, as from here, everything was "fairly chaotic" due to some demonstration, the streets were all closed, the taxi driver explained, then he thanked them for the fare, and they were fairly nervous, because for them, coming from the provinces, the idea of demonstrations was decidedly frightening—and now they'd bumped right into one—but they had to reach their goal and so they set off on foot, but they didn't take the detour the taxi driver had recommended, as being from the provinces, both of them trusted only one single route, and this route led across Kossuth Square, so there they were already on this certain Kossuth Square, wishing to cut across it, but unfortunately they had to make their way across a really enormous crowd, which wouldn't have been "completely smooth," so they tried to go along the side where the crowd wasn't so dense, but even there, along this more sparsely populated edge, it was difficult to move forward, especially for Marika—because here she was in the capital city and she had decided that her rarely worn red high heels would be the most appropriate footwear, which, however, already after one hundred meters, caused her heels to ache so much that they could only proceed slowly, and she hobbled along and tried here and there to avoid the protesters who were shouting about something very loudly—they proceeded slowly along the edge of the square toward the other side, so from there they could finally reach Kálmán Imre Street, which was their goal, but then, somewhere roughly in the middle of the square, where the crowd was really a bit more sparse, Marika stopped dead in her tracks, because she noticed something familiar in this crowd, it wasn't a familiar person, but a coat, because this coat—Marika was struck dumb—was familiar to her, indeed very familiar, because this coat was none other than that of the Professor from home, and she was so flabbergasted that she stopped in her tracks, well, but how did the coat of that famous Professor end up here, maybe she was mistaken? she asked herself, no, she answered immediately, there was no mistake here, that was his coat, she knew it out of a hundred, because no one made coats like that anymore: the material, the velvet collar, the cut, the belt sewn from the same material, the length, the finishing, there was no mistake, she determined, because in matters of clothing she was never mistaken, and so she just looked and tried to make out who was wearing this renowned coat, and by what kind of route this person could have got hold of this coat that had belonged to their own famous Professor who'd had gone mad—according to rumor, he had lost his life in a fire in the Thorn Bush not too long ago, this was still before the dramatic events—she tried to make out who it could be, but his back was turned toward her, and she couldn't circle around in order to look at his face, so she only saw it was a complete stranger, when that person, of his own accord, unexpectedly turned toward her for a moment, someone completely unknown to her, Marika looked at the man, who had no other familiar traits, she looked at his shoes, but he was wearing boots, and on his head, instead of the hat that the Professor had always worn, there was a kind of Russian fur hat, in addition, this man's face was so covered by his beard that she could hardly see it at all, not permitting her to draw any conclusions from his features, not even to mention that Dante some little mutt kept rubbing up against his leg, and it was well known, Marika recalled, that the Professor always hated dogs, but still it was odd, as she stood there in the crowd a few paces behind this man, for some reason she just couldn't take her eyes off his coat, because how could his coat have ended up here, in Budapest, on Kossuth Square, Marika was really absorbed by this problem for a minute, and she didn't even want to admit to herself why: namely on the one hand she was hoping this person might end up being an acquaintance of hers, because she truly didn't really trust Mr. Lenyó, and on the other hand, because the sight of the coat somehow evoked something in her which made her heart quake, namely, there was a place called home, that's where this coat had come from, however, she had no more time for contemplation, because suddenly the crowd began to move, and once again they began to shout loudly, and by now Lenyó didn't bother to conceal from her that he'd come to the end of his patience and he never looked back at her with the kind of pleasant expression, that she, Marika, would have expected from him, but never mind, he could look at her with impatience, because of those shoes it was heavenly just to rest a bit, and all the while she looked at this coat and tried to puzzle out what kind of play of happenstance had been needed for her to drop anchor here on a complete stranger, she looked at this coat and then turned to see what this man was looking at, he was at that moment listening to the speaker in the distance, and it was as if he were smiling a bit, but because of his abundant beard and the sharp angle from which she was looking, she wasn't completely sure, in any event she was quite certain that the man was watching the speaker, who was a young woman, but she couldn't make out any more details because of the distance, just that something was familiar, something—Marika squinted while resting at the edge of the crowd—ah, yes, the scarf around her neck, a thick scarf was wrapped around the neck of the female speaker, she couldn't see anything more than that, but she (who was so good in matters of apparel) was certain that she'd seen the scarf before somewhere, and precisely wrapped around the neck twice in this manner, but she wasn't sure where she'd seen it, she was certain, however, that she had seen it, and she hesitated, but then she decided that she'd spent enough time on matters that were essentially of no relevance to her and so she decided to go onward, because these high-heeled shoes were already torturing her heels so much that it was painful even to stand around in them, not even to speak of Lenyó, who by now no longer concealed the fact that he wasn't merely urging her on, but that he was fed up with this whole thing, he was really fed up, because somehow he had lost all his faith in this woman as they arrived on this square from the hotel, and he'd be happy now to return to Szolnok, not only because he had serious doubts, but frankly he no longer even believed that this hysterical limping old maid was in possession of any kind of serious sums of money, and finally he was convinced that even if she was, he wouldn't be seeing any of it as remuneration for his services—or whatever Dante had had in mind—anyway. He left the woman to totter on by herself, and without a word he disappeared into the crowd, not even looking back. Even though Marika had decided she had to go on, she remained standing there at the crowd's edge, and listened to the young woman, although, because of the reverberations from the loudspeakers, she couldn't understand a single word; but she didn't care, she listened for a while, she looked at that coat, and she was thinking only of home, my dear God, while all this commotion is going on here, what is it like back there: at home. Because nonetheless that was an island of peace, of tranquility, of calm, of everything that she loved so much. And her heart give a leap.

They'd never heard of Savile Row, and they never were going to, they'd never heard of Mr. Darren Beaman, just as they'd never heard of Mr. O'Donoghue, so they didn't even try to guess where these items had come from, and who was responsible for the outrage that had been visited upon these fine fabrics, because to make such a mess of a pair of trousers, to bungle the measurements of a jacket, to ruin a greatcoat of such delicate material—for them this was scandal itself, although they tried not to show what they were thinking as they stood around the pile of clothes that the two volunteers had tossed to them from the van that came round with provisions for the homeless—they'd just tossed the pile of clothes in their direction, as they didn't want to stop the van, because to tell the truth, they weren't really too fond of the homeless, and if they were donating clothes, as opposed to dispensing meals, they proceeded as hastily as they could, just slowing down the van and tossing the bundles in their direction, then they stepped on the gas and were already speeding away, because if they had to mention a single reason (among many) as to why they really didn't like the homeless, they'd frankly state: it was because they stank, but this was a stench, they explained, which you could only imagine if you actually did this kind of work, because it was simply intolerable, impossible to get used to, formed of the stench of urine, shit, and vomit, no feeling person could withstand it, compounded over multiple years, and it wasn't—they defended themselves against the accusation of unconcern—because they were poor, or that they had no roof over their head, or they were out on the streets, and if it froze outside, they too froze, and such things, but if they could at all manage it they avoided breathing in this stench, so that now as they approached the group of people on the small square next to City Hall, where such a group was always to be found, and it was necessary—especially with Christmas drawing near—to "bring some joy into the lives of these homeless," as the head of distribution, a young Catholic charity worker expressed it, the van, as it approached the group, simply deaccelerated, and the charity packages were tossed to "these homeless" on the small square next to City Hall, which didn't really cause them to move or react, one of them slowly turned his head in that direction, then in the other, but they didn't run over there in a stampede, no stampede whatsoever came about, because as one of their number—a woman of uncertain age, but wearing a snow-white fur cap—always remarked, if conversation turned to such matters, "there is still human dignity in this world, and we aren't some starving Syrians lunging at food packages thrown across a border fence," so even now they just glanced over to see, well, what have we got this time, then, at a nice and easy pace, one after the other, like people who aren't particularly intrigued, they walked over, stood around the bundles, and for a while they just looked at the "assembled donations" tied up in a bedsheet, when finally one of them, a man wearing a black fur coat that reached to the ground, crouched and began to undo the bundle, but the others just kept standing around and took no part in the untying, like people who first wanted to see what the hell was being chucked out to them here *yet again*—and only later they would decide if anything was worth their attention—but then there was a surprise, as the man with the black jacket picked up, from the bundle of clothes, a pair of trousers from among many such garments, and he just kept on pulling and pulling, it was as if the trousers would never come to an end, and the faces of everyone he was standing around visibly lengthened in surprise when they realized this long thing was meant to be a pair of trousers, the man in the black jacket grabbed another item of clothing, and he began to pull that out of the pile, and he just pulled and pulled, and that too turned out to be a pair of trousers, and well, was this supposed to be a joke, or what the fuck; one of the people standing around—a tall man with a warty face—made a wry expression, but the others just stood there and observed, with conspicuous indifference for the time being, they just watched because they couldn't believe the absurd things emerging from this bundle, and yet this was supposed to be some kind of gift parcel for Christmas after all, or whatever the hell, so they just waited and watched the man in the black jacket diligently continue to rummage in the pile of clothes, and he wasn't even looking at them, but then he looked up at the woman in the snow-white fur cap while he was grasping another item, and he began to pull that out too, but by now the entire group was standing around dumbstruck, because this was a jacket, but cut with such long arms and torso, and the shoulders had been tailored to such a narrow measure, that when this man in the black jacket held it up—like some kind of corpus delicti—someone just blurted out: there's no human being like that, and the entire group moved in closer, and crouching, they began to rummage for what could be worthwhile to pick out for themselves, and they didn't want to believe their eyes when from this bundle there emerged, one after the other, these overelongated items, so the indignation grew and suddenly turned to rage when they saw that the shoes were of such dimensions as to be good for no purpose whatsoever, and that the various items of clothing which they had picked out for themselves were completely worthless, then first one, then another began to get up from their crouching positions, they didn't immediately walk away, but remained standing around the edge of the bed sheet and watched the others who were still looking at this or that shirt or jacket or pair of trousers, but finally nobody was crouching anymore, they were just standing around the edge of the bed sheet in the small square next to City Hall, and they tried to find the words: they didn't find them though, as it was quite hard to decide what was going on here, who had dared to ridicule them in the midst of their bad luck, in general who dared to deride them and to trample down their self-respect, for there was no doubt as to the intention of this package: it was meant to ridicule them, it was meant to trample down their self-regard, and they couldn't leave matters like this; the man in the black coat looked around to see if anyone was watching them, but of course the van had long ago disappeared, the windows of the City Hall were bolted down, nailed shut, so that the windowpanes couldn't be smashed from below, as often occurred, and they could have been in the mood for that now, if there had been a point to it, but there was no point, because they wouldn't have been able to get at even one windowpane, because they all were bolted, boarded up, covered with planks, so their rage grew in vain, and for the time being it couldn't really break out, because in vain did the fur-capped woman grunt, "well, fuck this," or the wart-faced man mutter, "they'll regret this," and other such statements, there was no strength in it, nothing which could have incited the others, although sometimes it occurred that a well-timed and well-chosen word would get them worked up and they'd go on a rampage for a while, and that was good, because then they could "let off steam," as they put it to the policemen who rounded them up on such occasions and then let them go again, because sometimes they had to let off steam, they explained, because they noted that they just couldn't stand it any longer; now, though, for the time being, they didn't know what to do, each waited for a solution to come from one of the others as to "well, what the hell should we do with all of this," and exactly at that point a young fellow among them whom (because of his age) they called "the Lad"—no one had any idea how he had turned up among their midst—once again crouched down, and taking one of the coats in his hands, began to caress the fabric, and he looked up at the others and said, "there's no material like this," and by that he meant that he was enchanted, because this material was so uncommonly fine, and he expressed this by saying that "it's noble, this fabric here is extremely noble, that's what I say," at which point the woman on the other side of the bed sheet crouched down as well, and she too began to assess the situation similarly, and she too began to caress what was in her hand at that moment, then she held up a jacket and said, "I think this could be worth at least a few thousand forints," and the man in the black jacket crouched next to her, and then each and every one of them began to caress the trousers, jackets, coats, and the shirts, moreover, even the shoes, as if somehow the whole thing had become worthwhile now, they began not only to caress this or that piece of clothing, but they began to snatch yet another piece and yet another and another from the pile, to hold it up, and now nobody was speaking, they discontinued their conjectures and appraisals of how many forints this or that piece could fetch at the Chinese market behind the soccer field, and a general fever of acquisition swept over them as it emerged that this one, that one, and the other had come here precisely for this reason—to remove whatever he could from the heap and take it away, only that this intention immediately met with the resistance of that person standing next to him, and skirmishes broke out, and now already they were snatching the trousers, the coats, the shirts, and so on, out of each other's hands, and the fact that these trousers and coats and shirts hadn't been sewn from just any kind of material was amply shown, for example, by how when a fight broke out over a shirt, and two people were trying to wrench it out of each other's hands from two different directions, it took a good long time for the fabric to rip, good material, they muttered at each other, but as a matter of fact only to themselves, and the struggle continued, they ripped the clothes out of each other's hands, and people shoved each other so they would lose their balance, so the fabric would end up in the hands of this or that person, and it would have gone on in this way until fistfights broke out—until the final victory—if the man with the black coat hadn't, in a given moment, stopped, and stood up, and said loudly, "people, stop it, this whole thing isn't even worth a piece of shit," as these pieces of clothing could neither be retailored, nor worn, nor sold, he said, because what kind of idiots will they take us for, trying to foist these circus costumes on people, we already have enough blankets, he said, with a dismissive final gesture, and turning away, he added: these things aren't good for anything ... so before the man with the warty face had left off his struggle for another pair of shoes, the Lad got up, and threw back what he'd been holding in his hands onto the pile, and finally they all stood up, and they all threw back onto the pile what they'd just come to blows over a moment ago, and they stood around for a while and looked at the pile: it was really a shame it was like this, and yes, the whole thing wasn't even worth a piece of shit, and only then did they go back to the benches on the square behind City Hall, their constant abode for the day and perhaps tonight as well, when the man in the black coat took out a lighter, picked up from the pile of clothes one of the shirts with peculiar tailoring, lit it, and threw it back, and suddenly the whole thing caught fire, because when the pile of clothes burst into flames it was good to stand close by, because at least it gave off some warmth, but then, just as quickly as the pile of rags burst into flames, it died down, and the interlude came to an end, and once again they sat on the benches, lighting up cigarettes—whoever had them, that is—while others pulled out bottles of alcohol, they were quiet, and finally shrieks of laughter were heard as they reacted to the outburst of the woman in the white fur cap, who looked back at the charity gift bundle burnt to ashes, and yelled out—like a wolf to the skies—"take your Christmas and shove it, you scumbags!"

And the shrieks of laughter would have died out, when suddenly all of them, on the little square behind City Hall became rigid, because something had happened, only they didn't know what, all told they only sensed their stomachs contracting, as well as an inundation of intense heat across their entire bodies—and fear, an ever deeper fear, the content, cause and explanation of which remained obscure, but the hand of whoever was smoking and just about to raise the cigarette to his lips came to a halt, and the smoke, as it drifted upward, came to a halt as well; the glass of the person who was about to drink came to a halt in his hand, it came to a halt in the air, and the wine in the glass stood still; they all froze, became motionless, their eyes bulging outward, as if they'd suddenly seen something appalling, but they didn't see anything at all, because they couldn't see anything, because what was happening now wasn't visible to them, just as it wasn't visible to anyone from the train station all the way to the Milk Powder Factory, from the kindergarten next to the Castle to the orthodox church in the Lesser Romanian Quarter, from Krinolin to Csókos Road—everything that until that moment had been flowing unimpeded was now shut down, everything that had been free was no longer free, because it was exactly the free course of things and beings, the possibility of free initiations and free impulses that had suddenly become impossible; the possible and the real were possible and real no longer, the Great Flow was over, finished—because that infinite-seeming convoy had appeared, and once again, he was in this convoy, and before him were innumerable black Mercedes and BMWs and Rolls-Royces and Bentleys, and behind him were innumerable Mercedes and BMWs and

Rolls-Royces and Bentleys, and they practically glided across the city, so speedily—this time gliding *back,* exactly in the opposite direction as before, because this time they were arriving from the direction of the Romanian border, and if there'd been anyone to see them, they would have lost sight of them at the Csabai Road exit—that is, if there had been anyone strolling there in that shattered moment, right there, where Highway 44 meets Csabai Road—but at that moment there was nobody *outside,* because, with the exception of those sitting on the benches on the small square behind City Hall, all of the city's residents were at that moment *inside* somewhere, so that not even a car, a motorcycle, a bicycle, or horse carriage, or anything or anyone—not a single soul—was outside, not a single eyewitness, passerby, driver, bicyclist, or drayman was out on the streets, as they swept through the city without a sound, as if the tires on their cars weren't even touching the asphalt all along Highway 44, as this time they chose not to go along Temesvári Road, nor Szent István Street, not turning at Eszperantó Square onto the Street of Martyrs and then on to Csabai Road, but instead they used the detour, Highway 44, they glided through the city on that road, and this time they didn't even stop, and no one even got out anywhere to slowly have a look around this place, and then, bored, get back into the car and drive on farther, no, not this time, because now they were visibly following a more frantic tempo, attending to some kind of tremendously significant piece of business, as if the stakes had become much higher now; this would have been the realization of anyone who saw them (but no one did): they now had to proceed in some matter that was exceptional, gigantic, monumentally important, and this was underscored by the dignified manner with which the convoy swept through the city soundlessly, and yet, if there had been anyone to see them, that person would have realized this matter that was exceptional, gigantic, and monumentally important had no meaning—it bore no meaning within itself, no, meaning was excluded from this procedure, just as it contained no motive, because this matter propelling him on—he in the midst of that convoy—was purged of motive, just as it contained no goal; this matter, then, had no meaning, cause, or goal, and this in fact might have been the essence of that matter, if words themselves hadn't given up the ghost in the mind of an eyewitness (one, moreover, not even present at the scene), because words would have come to a dead halt in this brain, they wouldn't have been able to circle around anymore, because the manifestation of that horrific strength rendered all extant things null and void, rendered even the precept of becoming null and void null and void, because anything and everything that ever was or ever could be was nullified, as the manifestation of his presence required no object, only *it* abided in existence; and while he himself, in the middle of that convoy with all these innumerable Mercedes, BMWs, Rolls-Royces, and Bentleys, in this shattered moment, was nonetheless moored—to nearly a laughable degree—to human life, he wasn't at the mercy of existence, the manifestation of his horrific strength, having no object, appeared, then vanished, because it didn't say what it was referring to, because it wasn't referring to anything, because it was nothing more or less than a horrific warning: I shall come again, because I can, and then the manifestation contained within the shattered moment *will* have an object, even if there will still be no meaning, cause, or goal—as if, through a car window tinted black, that dead face that had appeared in that city once before now spoke: *it is a mistake to split me asunder, because I am one, and apart from me there is no other Lord, because I am neither creator nor destroyer, because the place where I abide in existence is far, far deeper, it is within the inconceivable, forever and ever— to which you may no longer say: Amen.*

The surface of the wine in the bottle at first trembled a little, just once, but as if giving the signal: now everything else could once again reconnect, and the hand completed its movement, the sip of wine appeared in the mouth and in the throat, and there was another sip and another until the person sitting next to him took the bottle, and had a few quaffs himself, but by then everything had already come back to life, the cigarette smoke snaked upward in the air, another sip of wine went down, and the smoke went on its way, it could drift upward once again; and the flying ashes also came to life amid the pile of garbage and the died-out flames that were the Christian social worker's charity bundle given in vain; and to the left of the benches, suspecting nothing of what had just occurred, the Lad got up from where he'd been sitting and, to the applause of the others, pissed on the heap of ashes; and everything else, too, flowed back imperceptibly into the continuum of existence, deemed to have been uninterrupted by all; an old married couple came out of the entrance of the house next to Stréber's—taking advantage of the lull in the rain—to go for a "constitutional" along the barren chestnut trees of Peace Boulevard; while Tóni appeared in the door of the post office, with that enormous postal bag on his shoulder, much too big for him, so he could toss this or that pretty postcard, arrived here only by accident, into this or that mail slot according to his fancy; and only the two orphans weren't too happy, because although they'd gotten as far as the Békéscsaba train station, having jumped unseen from the train, now, however, they were coming back in the other direction, and across from them sat two taciturn policemen: exhausted, starving, sober, and due to that fairly enraged; the cops kept staring at them to see what they could find objectionable in the behavior of these two wanted individuals, so they could give them a good whack, as they particularly couldn't stand to look at the boy with the mohawk—so that life, including that imperceptible pause, began both here, on the way back to the city, and over there, in the city itself: in the bar in the

Krinolin district, the owner began to serve up today's menu, which was—unfortunately, as the pensioners who came here for lunch quietly noted to themselves—once again potato soup with a plate of groats and fruit preserves, even though "they'd served the same thing just three days ago"; and in the cemetery of the Orthodox church in the Lesser Romanian Quarter, the priest waited in vain—for decades now, the Romanian residents had been quietly moving back to Romania, so now, following the tradition this church had established, they buried those unfortunates for whom no one else would pay—the priest waited in vain, the hour announced for the funeral had long since passed; he looked through the windows of the cemetery attendant's office ever more despondently, along with the four taciturn gravediggers who'd been told to show up only at the end of the service by the catafalque; he looked to see if anybody was coming, but no one arrived to take final leave of the deceased—there will be no official representation from our end, he had been told at City Hall, when he'd inquired as to the denomination of the deceased—no one had any idea—and that's why we're entrusting this to you, they'd told him, because you are of such an "*ecunomical* constitution," and they didn't explain exactly what they meant by that, but only added that he should invoice City Hall for the usual expenses, but they urgently requested him, as per his usual practice, to keep the funeral service as simple as possible, because they would have been all too happy to put him in a common grave, but still, they wouldn't do that ... they gazed fixedly into the priest's eyes at City Hall, where they'd summoned him a couple of days before, precisely indicating, as they always did, that this would be a "poor burial," because neither the Holy Trinity nor the New Reform Church ever took these on—and for this amount!—only they did, because, as the priest repeated to himself, they never let a single soul be placed in the earth without "final funeral rites and all the rest," but now he kept looking at his watch intensely, certainly it was already a quarter to two, so there was nothing else to do, he thought, he got up and put on his cloak, took up the censer with one hand, and with the other he took the Book of Books, and he went from the lovely warmth into the freezing cold, as it wasn't possible to heat the mortuary, he was really sensitive to cold: as usual, when the Lord summoned him to service, he'd put on his warm underclothes, but somehow he was never able to manage this properly, or—how should he put it—fundamentally enough, namely, to wear a sufficient enough number of layers underneath, somehow it always happened that he wasn't wearing enough layers and he froze—he didn't deny that the reasons could be at least partially psychological (as he himself at times acknowledged to an older lady in the congregation when the subject came up, namely, he brought up this topic whenever humanly possible), that is, *the mere thought* that a person would freeze was already enough to make that person freeze, well, but still, a funeral, that's something else, in a season like this, and if the season is just like this current one, and it just rains and rains, and the wind is icy cold—and for sure he'd have to stand behind the coffin even in the dripping rain and the blowing wind to perform the final rights on behalf of the church for anyone at all, even for this hapless wretch, for whom not a single soul had shown up to say farewell, and yet a mere few days ago they'd all come out to see him, or maybe it was a week or even two weeks ago already, and what a huge brouhaha there'd been … he hadn't been interested in any of this, even now he wasn't interested, because he had dedicated his life to the Lord—still, though, it wasn't so easy to step out of the warm parish house, in short, a funeral was something else, during a funeral—by the time he got to the bier and took his place behind the coffin—he could really sense that he hadn't enough warm layers beneath his robes—and yes, he hadn't—he went into the mortuary, and well, this was really unusual, because he had never been in this position of performing the funeral rites all alone—no one to hear the *bocet*, the *hora mortului*—but, well, what could he do, the Lord had spoken, and he fulfilled the commandments of the Lord, he stood behind the coffin, and if the cold wasn't exactly striking him, he could still feel it, he had all his layers on, though: two pairs of good thick socks (in addition, one pair was knee-highs), then long thermal underwear, thick woolen trousers, two thick undershirts, a checked woolen shirt, a lighter pullover on top, and on top of that a thick knitted sweater, and then he stopped reviewing the entire ensemble, because now he had to think of the Lord and the deceased, but still, as he stood behind the coffin, about to commence the service, he felt the cold sinking into him, what should he do now, he reflected, while—his head lowered—he recited Psalm 119 to himself, should he go back for another layer, but in the meantime what about this funeral service here; since this was meant to be an "ecunomical" service, he should begin by consoling those gathered here whom the deceased had left behind in their sorrow, but there was no one here, not a single person, not one family member, relative, or at least a person from the crowd that had been supposedly so enthusiastic, there was no one in need of solace; he thought about this and tried to chase the devil away, because the devil was unruly and wouldn't let him pray in peace—he'd left, in his bag in the cemetery attendant's office, a long-sleeved white T-shirt, and that too was made of wool, maybe he could go back for it—but then he resisted that impulse and began the service, but inwardly because he'd decided he would conduct the service only within himself and not recite the prayers out loud, because—well, because, to whom?—and he could leave out St. John of Damascus, the Beatitudes, and the sermon, and he did leave them out, because those were only necessary for the vigil, which in this case, wasn't going to occur—the Lord would forgive him—so he spoke within himself about the sorrowful, and yet simultaneously uplifting, last hours the deceased spent in this world, he spoke of this as he always did on such occasions, but then he quickly jumped ahead to the usual portion of the Gospel, because he recalled that the deceased lay in the coffin in four pieces, so, well, better not to drag out his last hour, he thought, and he skipped another passage, because he noticed that the cold was really sinking into his bones, well, that's all he needed now, to get thoroughly chilled so that for days afterward he would have to lie in bed, Lord Almighty, forgive me, he thought, as he recited the Farewell Blessing, and the Eternal Memory, well, this ceremony will be quite short, so short that it was over already, at least the section by the catafalque, and instead of a funeral procession—which obviously made no sense now—he simply exited the mortuary, and motioned toward the cemetery attendant's office windows for the gravediggers to come out, although for a while there was no visible movement from within, it was only when he lost his patience and began to walk over there, as if intending to go and fetch them, that the door opened and those four good-for-nothing boozers appeared, but, well, the servant of the Lord had to cook with the ingredients that were available to him, and so they set off to the gravesite, the priest sang and shook his censer, and those four just moaned as if they had been entrusted with a truly monumental task, three of them, however, only had to pull the handcart, while the fourth simply had to ensure that the coffin stayed put as they hauled it toward the grave; well, as for these ones—the priest looked back at them from time to time with resentment—they couldn't even manage that properly, because the coffin was continually sliding around here and there on the handcart, and either this fourth person was the most incompetent in this whole wide world, or the other three couldn't even be bothered to be just a bit careful, because they just hauled that handcart along like madmen, not bothering at all about the potholes and the small mounds on the path; the coffin slid over to one side, then the other, and the person in back just jumped around as much as he could, trying to stop the coffin from sliding off, but well, it kept sliding around, and sometimes so precipitously that this fourth person was forced to shout to the others, STOP! STOP!, then he would readjust the coffin, then they would set off again, and the whole thing continued, but these three good-for-nothings in front didn't care about anything, only about getting to that gravesite as quickly as possible, while the fourth one just jumped from side to side, and for the last fifty meters the fourth just kept shouting out STOP! STOP!—at the grave, however, everything went as smoothly as could be, because the gravediggers were only interested in finishing as quickly as possible, and that's how the priest was feeling as well, so he just sang one or two prayers, then sprinkled the holy water, with two or three flourishes of the censer, finally a clump of earth, and at last he'd already clasped his fingers around the Book of Books, and he left them there, let them finish their work, he wasn't going to stick around for that, he wasn't so dim-witted as to wait for them to lower the coffin, then torture that loamy, muddy earth, then shove the cross into the ground, oh no, he wasn't sticking around for that, he hurried to the cemetery attendant's small building, quickly went back into the warmth, sat down next to the stove, clasped his hands, closed his eyes, and pleaded for absolution for himself and for the deceased, as well as for every being in creation, particularly those who were in need, who'd been left on their own, who remained alone on the earth—but not in heaven, the priest said to himself, not in heaven, because the Lord is with them there. He put more wood on the fire.

# *RUIN*

# TO THE HUNGARIANS

The free press was everything to him, he said, sitting in the armchair before the Chief Editor's large desk, nothing mattered to him as much as the free press (and this was true ever since he'd been elected), because the freedom of the press was equivalent to the freedom of the citizens of this town, and so therefore to his own as well, namely—he explained, gesticulating vehemently, because he somehow didn't get the sense the Chief Editor, sitting there behind the desk, was really convinced by his words—the free press and him (he pointed to himself) were one and the same, if there was no free press, then he wasn't free either, and vice versa, he hoped that the Chief Editor understood what he was trying to convey, because that so-called tract—what else could you call it—that had turned up at this newspaper was nothing more than an incoherent scribble, a foul invective against everything that was most important to them in this city, in this country; let us declare, he declared, it to be a heap of garbage—its proper place was, therefore, in his opinion, in the garbage pail, and he could only regret—namely he regretted deeply—that the Chief Editor, as well as this news organ, the city's most sober-minded, that kept the citizenry's interests most in mind, didn't share his opinion, this must change, and until that occurred, he greatly requested they put this "composition" where it belonged, in that garbage pail, because he was convinced that's where it should end up, because no—he shook his head, he simply couldn't understand, indeed he couldn't imagine what would happen if that entire pile of garbage were exposed to the public; he truly appreciated that apart from the two TV stations (just closed due to recent developments) and the official government spokesperson, the only press organ still standing—and one never bereft of critical perspective—was this paper, he truly appreciated this, but he didn't understand how it could even occur to them, he didn't and he couldn't understand, because whoever even hastily skimmed through this diatribe—and here, if he weren't taking into account the fact that he was in an editorial office where serious and deliberate work was taking place, he would have raised his voice—because if anyone were to read through it even superficially, even then it was evident: the only thing this shoddy piece of work deserved was destruction, but fine, no problem, he understood that there were opposing views, and he—as an unconditional believer in the free press—also understood that someone might hold an opinion antithetical to his own "with respect to" the fate of that boorish attack against everything that was sacred, but there was no way that he could accept what the Chief Editor had just proposed, and he guaranteed that the entire expanded Civic Committee—if they were capable of making a decision at all—would vote this down, particularly considering that the Catholic vicar himself was, exceptionally, going to honor them with his presence, although in no way should this impede—on this point he bowed his head—the debate involving these so-called opposing opinions; so it was up to the Chief Editor now to designate, well, if not his seconds—heh, heh, the Mayor sniggered—then the day and the hour, but let them come up with a day and an hour for the Civic Committee to render a decision concerning this aforementioned piece of invective as quickly as possible—today, said the Chief Editor, at two o'clock in the afternoon—but well, that's impossible, the Mayor objected, he certainly couldn't bring together the Committee members in such a short time; then three o'clock, but not a moment later, said the Chief Editor, because space was being reserved for this material in the evening edition, and as everyone was aware, this was a serious and deliberate editorial office where things operated according to schedule, every edition had its closing, so three o'clock at the very latest—and the Mayor saw on the Chief Editor's face that he had no hope of delaying the decision until at least the following day, he was forced to agree—fine, he said, pursing his mouth, and he leaned forward in the armchair like someone already leaping into action, or like someone who'd already left, because in this matter every single minute was precious, and he even said: well, every minute is precious here, so he had to go now, because this was his life—he sighed and leapt up from the armchair, while the Chief Editor, sitting with a sarcastic smile on his face in his own chair behind the desk, didn't even move, and ever since he had taken this on, he would like to note, the Mayor said, that in his civic work—the task with which he'd been honored, of representing—no, not representing, *leading, directing,* and indeed *instigating* the momentum of life in this little city that was wondrous in its own way—well, that's how it was, all day long he had to hustle, so that he'd be off now, if they would excuse him; and he headed toward the door, he had already stepped out of the room into the corridor, and the Chief Editor still didn't budge in his chair, not even saying goodbye to the Mayor, in connection with which, the Mayor noted to himself, he had his own opinion, because while they were representatives of differing political viewpoints, there still existed a so-called "gentlemen's agreement," so that he always greeted characters even like this scribbler politely, this scribbler who didn't even appreciate his opponent enough to accept his farewell, that was the last straw, and if he'd been obliged to stifle his anger until now, then here, in the stairwell of the editorial office, he now freely expressed his rage, because anyone who told him that there was a problem allowing these voices, namely these characters, into the political arena at all would be right. Downstairs he closed the door with a good slam. He thought: maybe that pretentious good-for-nothing cosmopolite can hear it up there. And the sound of the slamming door echoed.

She'd just had a bad premonition, and she wouldn't be able to say why and what it was about, but she had a decidedly bad premonition, and the Mayor knew very well that she was always right when it came to this, since they knew each other, well, was it twelve years already?—if at any point she said that she had a bad premonition, then that meant something, of course she couldn't say specifically what this something was, it didn't matter how many times she repeated it, but she was sure of one thing: it was bad, and somehow something was suggesting to her that there was a reason why someone—in this case, she—would have such a bad premonition, she wouldn't even bring up negligible details, as, for example (in contrast to other things), all the vagabonds, beggars, and Gypsies from Albania, or wherever they came from, they'd all disappeared, not a single one of them was out on the streets, they formed, however, practically an integral part of the street scene, and you know how it is, Mr. Mayor—and if until now she'd been standing fairly close to him, behind his chair, now she leaned down from behind toward her boss, and her renowned bosom nearly brushed up against the Mayor's shoulder, and the Mayor could *nearly* feel that renowned bosom through his jacket (although it had proper shoulder pads); well, as for the whens and the whys and the wherefores, she couldn't account for that, even if these were minor details, but even so, wasn't it strange—well, could anyone tell her—there was the Orphanage where all of those poor waifs had been moved back, those motherless and fatherless orphans, those poor things, and what had happened with them? who'd taken them away? and where and why and for what? this is what she would sincerely ask, and her voice began to take on a droning quality, the Mayor, however, was incapable of shrinking more into his chair so he slid over a bit to the left, as far as he could, which was only about a half centimeter—Mr. Mayor, I won't go on with this now, the chief secretary breathed into his ear, she knew very well that these were just minor details, but at the same time how could it be that when she walked along the street, instead of her usual beggars and homeless people and who knew what, she saw complete strangers coming along the sidewalk, Mr. Mayor, the city is full of complete strangers, who are they, why did they come here and for what reason? she sincerely asked, what's going on here, what's happening, she had no wish or desire to make him nervous—that was the last thing she wanted to do—but she said now openly that she had a bad feeling, a premonition: something was going to happen here—she didn't know what would happen, but something was going to happen, something nobody was expecting, some sixth sense was whispering this to her, and as no one ever doubted her sixth sense was just as reliable as when she'd begun her career, this sixth sense was now telling her to get ready for this something, whatever it was, this something—she had no idea what it was going to be—but it will be, this was what her sixth sense, or whatever it was, was telling her as she walked on the sidewalk toward City Hall: because where, for example, were the vehicles on the streets, because there almost weren't any at all, Mr. Mayor, this wasn't normal, why? she asked, was it normal for there not to be a single vehicle on the streets, and after that, it's hardly a surprise if there are hardly any pedestrians or passersby either, not counting, of course, those complete strangers, and there's nothing good coming from them—that's what her presentiment was telling her, and of course, she might be mistaken, well, maybe at other times she'd been, but not now, because there were too many details, Mr. Mayor, said the chief secretary, and she stood up—and the Mayor, freed from his rather uncomfortable situation, took a deep breath like someone who hadn't dared breathe for several minutes, lest those two enormous breasts at the end would really come to rest upon his shoulders, he sucked in the air almost with a rattling sound, so the secretary had to extend a glass of water to him from the side, and he drank it so quickly, like someone who had counted on the fact that he would need a quick glass of water, as soon as possible.

We don't know who wrote it, don't even ask, and now he wasn't speaking—as was the way with journalists—about how the source hadn't been uncovered and other such matters, since this piece of writing—which, in his modest opinion, was the most salient to emerge in recent times, not only in the life of the editorship of this newspaper, but in the life of this city as well—it had arrived in an envelope with no return address, and at the bottom of the text were only the words, written on a typewriter, clearly with ironic intent: "your Baron"; and yet the signer was manifestly not identical with the deceased who perished in such tragic circumstances, whose presence here had so burdened the days of the recent past, and who would certainly receive a distinct chapter in the history of this city, of this, he—the Chief Editor pointed at himself—was completely certain; no, it wasn't him, that was obvious: as on the one hand this piece had been composed on a typewriter, and the deceased, as perhaps wasn't commonly known, always wrote by hand, namely he never used typewriters, but in any event—the Chief Editor shook his head—that would have been completely absurd; no, the author was somebody else, and perhaps one day his identity would come to light, perhaps it will never come to light, I would, however, wish to emphasize to everyone assembled here that in view of the significance of this piece of writing, the question of authorship is completely irrelevant, because what matters here is the writing itself, what matters is that this piece of writing cuts to the quick of what this city has been suffering ever since you and your colleagues came to power—and he didn't even look at the Mayor, he only gestured, disparagingly, in his direction—as this piece of writing gets to the essence, it doesn't beat around the bush, it's sharp like a scalpel; well, that's enough of that, the Mayor got up, but not only did he rise from his chair, he also raised his voice, like someone who's no longer listening to what is being said, for surely they all hadn't assembled at this meeting today (moreover, while being honored by the presence of the vicar) just to hear a campaign speech, which, frankly speaking—because, let's be frank—at least here, in this room, was boring everyone to tears; but rather, my dear Chief Editor, they'd come together in order to debate the fate of what was, in his own opinion (in this he was not alone, the Mayor swung his right index finger sharply upward), a scurrilous sheet, a scrawled invective seeking to drag each and every one of them into the mud, he didn't understand how they could have reached a point where they would even consider discussing an anonymous scrawl such as this, which should immediately—please do understand me—immediately be tossed into the nearest wastebasket, why were they even sitting here, and why were they, the leading citizens of the city, allowing themselves to be brought so low—I ask you, asked the Mayor—and he looked straight into the eyes of the Chief Editor, who looked straight back at him, and since he had been standing since the Mayor interrupted him just a moment ago, he could pick up where he'd left off, the Editor said, namely this was a question of a document of extraordinary significance, ripping the veil away to show who we really are—well, that's all we need, somebody said, and from the Headmaster to the city's captain of industry they all looked at each other while the vicar conspicuously remained silent, it really wasn't possible to tell what he was thinking; we're going to vote this down is what these faces said—only then, the Chief Editor, who understood what the Mayor was counting on, announced, without even finishing his previous sentence: lest there be any misunderstanding, we've all assembled here in order to discuss this extraordinary text, because ours is the one oppositional press organ (he smiled at the Mayor), the one single press organ of all genuinely democratically minded citizens of the city, namely its true citizens with their own highly defined sense of responsibility, in other words: we are the one single press organ of the majority of this town—that, Mr. Mayor, is us, and we have the requisite breadth of vision; and here the Chief Editor paused and added that even though he was personally mentioned in this text, and in a truly painful fashion, even so (and precisely despite that), he couldn't say no to making this text public, and so he was compelled to state that he and the entire editorial board in a far-reaching manner and on several levels were demonstrating a true breadth of vision, namely they weren't deciding this matter based only upon their own narrow interests (which they could easily have done)—and it was precisely this extraordinary acquiescence on their part, this undeniable breadth of vision that indicated the extraordinary importance of this affair—no, what we have agreed upon, if I may respectfully remind you, the Chief Editor respectfully reminded them, isn't for the expanded Civic Committee to discuss *whether or not* this text will be published (as the editorial board won't be considering any suggestions to the contrary), but, if you please, *in what form* it should be published; this is the question at hand, Mr. Mayor, and not your attempts to rile up this Committee, because your suggestion that we vote on whether an article may appear in the free press is the height of absurdity itself, a clear slap in the face to that free press, and he didn't think—the Chief Editor once again sought out the Mayor's gaze—that he, precisely the Mayor, who was such a believer in the free press, would be so inclined, no, he had no wish to slap the free press across the face, Mr. Mayor, and on the Mayor's face every individual feature seemed to be in agony, but he still didn't intervene, he was still trying to think, because sooner or later he would have to intervene in this, because he could hardly allow this here, in this room in City Hall, where after all he was supposed to be boss, somebody else should be doing the ordering around, it was just unfortunate that things were somehow wrong, and as yet he hadn't formulated his reply, he wasn't ready yet with his retort, he was still standing up, because he didn't want to sit down again, and yet he couldn't really speak, he just kept on listening as the Chief Editor spoke about the various permutations they could discuss, which for him, the Mayor, was disaster itself, a disaster, because nothing in this discussion meant that there was no way this article could be published; he just stood there, and the words of the Chief Editor rained down on him like stones upon the condemned, and he sensed that the longer he waited to speak, the more manifest his resignation to this defeat became, and he already felt that in fact defeat had ensued, that with this Committee he wouldn't even be able to prevent the most essential thing, namely to edit out, from this villainous invective, *all* of the so-called denunciations related to specific persons which named names, because as he quickly glanced at everyone assembled there, he didn't see, on a single face, even the faintest sign of the hope of resistance, everyone who was familiar with this text—and they were all familiar with it by now—would have agreed to anything, as long as they could alter the parts of the text that *specifically referred to them*; the Mayor saw they were all caught up in this, so, acknowledging defeat, he sat down and was silent, and he didn't speak until the end, until the discussion turned to what should happen with the "personal remarks," as they now termed the vituperative sections, but even then he wasn't able to speak up with some kind of recommendation to simply destroy the tract altogether, when the Chief Editor, waving the text above everyone's heads, proposed: fine, no problem, all of the real names, as well as any additional specific personal descriptions will be left out, or respectively reformulated, but in this case he insisted that the general section—as he designated this diatribe's "abuse of morality," unacceptable to every true patriot—should remain untouched; the Mayor felt he should do something, but his brain had simply switched off, and he couldn't switch it back on again, or so it seemed, he thought, and he just shook his head, he massaged his eyes, and with the signs of acknowledged failure on his face, he sat ever more hunched over in his chair, and it seemed that he'd been very worn out by this past week, he thought: an organism like mine gets corroded by events such as what has happened here recently, and he felt himself to be very tired, he began not even to be able to understand what they were speaking about around him; the words—as if he were sitting in some bell jar—somehow only reached his ear in a dull drone, then his chest began to feel tight, somewhere in the middle, no, it didn't even feel tight, it hurt, and it was hurting ever more strongly, but by then he was already on the floor, the chair tipped over without a sound, and he only saw how much dust there was next to the walls, there were entire dust mice accumulated there by the wainscoting, all along the walls, and his last thought was that somebody should notify the cleaning staff, because slovenliness like this could not be permitted: dust mice along the baseboards in the large conference room, all along the wall, this was not at all permissible in this large conference room.

For never has this earth carried on its back such a repulsive people as you, and while we certainly can't be overjoyed by what we generally observe to be occurring on this earth, yet never have I met with fouler people than yourselves, and as I'm one of you, accordingly I'm too close to you, so it will be difficult on this first try to find the precise words to describe exactly what comprises this repulsive aspect, that aspect that causes you to sink below every other nation, because it's hard to find words with which we can enumerate the hierarchy of that storehouse of loathsome human qualities with which you repel the world—the world, which has had the great misfortune to have known you—because if I begin by saying that to be Hungarian is not to belong to a people, but instead it's an illness, an incurable, frightening disease, a misfortune of epidemic proportions that could overcome every single observer with nausea, then I wouldn't be starting off on the right path, but no, it's not that it's an illness, rather ... what is this illness comprised of?—that's what's hard to formulate here in this piece of writing which I am addressing to a gene, so I can dissuade it from carrying this nation any further in the midst of life's unintelligible continuum: I'm writing to a gene so it will show itself no more, for it to withdraw its DNA molecules, to rescind its nucleic acid sequences within the nuclei's chromosomes, to retract itself along with its sugar phosphates, base pairs, and amino acids; these Hungarians didn't work out—the gene should state this frankly, and retreat from the insane order of albumins, because no matter where you start here, it's hard to find that most basic characteristic to which all the others can be connected, as if on a string; because if we begin with slovenly malice, that's good, but it doesn't dig deep enough; we can say: hey, you, putrid Hungarian, you're the epitome of envy, petty-mindedness, small-time sluggishness, indolence, shiftiness and sneakiness, impudent shamelessness, ignominy, constantly primed to betray, and at the same time arrogantly flaunting your own ignorance, lack of refinement, and insensitivities; you, Hungarian, are an exceptionally disgusting subject whose breath, now stinking of sausage and *pálinka*, now of salmon and champagne, could strike anyone dead; who, if someone tells him this to his face, either thumps on the table, replying to this clinical report with pretentious loutishness, proud of his uncouthness, aggressive like a blustering moron, or else there arises in him a sly thirst for revenge against anyone who confronts him with his true features, he never forgets that, and at the first possible opportunity, he'll trample this truth-teller into the ground, he'll execute him, dishonor him ... no, no, but that's still not enough, because it still doesn't reach the depths of your nature, because such are these depths that you not only react this way to whoever confronts your worthlessness, but you do it to anyone at all who happens to turn up in your path, anyone whom you can't exploit, make use of, bleed dry, all in order to satisfy your own desires; and you're spineless and two-faced, perfidious and contemptible, lying and rootless, because after you've exploited somebody, you do the same thing, namely you throw them away, you spit into their eyes, if they're not good for anything else, because you're primitive, you worthless Hungarian, you're a primitive chump who will gladly degrade himself at any time if he can reach a position that is favorable to him . . . but no, even that doesn't capture it somehow, to seize the essence of the Hungarian by the roots exceeds my abilities, I could only rip out these roots by seizing them, but I can't, because everything that has thus far come together in this piece of writing all simultaneously forms the basis for the Hungarian character, but I still haven't found the *clue* to the Hungarian, because every human weakness doesn't merely exist in him, but is accumulated in him, these weaknesses don't merely exist in him, but at the same time they make the Magyar what he is; so if you were to say envy, then think of the Hungarians; if you were to say hypocrisy, once again, think of the Hungarians; and if you were to say latent aggression, whether revealing itself through arrogance or sneaky cringing, then you're back with the Hungarians again, because no matter what bad trait you can think of, there you are with the Hungarians, but at least you're there, at least then you can grab the Hungarian by the forelock; and if you were simply to say that the Hungarian is an asshole, that hits the bull's-eye, although—it depends whom you say this to—there's no point telling it to him, because to him it's just another insult in a bar that has to be met with blows, or else he'll sidle out along the wall, waiting for the offender outside in the dark, he'll lie in ambush—there's no point in telling him, because nothing ever really hurts him, and all the while he is capable of crazed self-pity; don't bother telling him what he's like because it's hopeless—he'll never understand, never comprehend, and he'll never recognize it, because in order to understand, conceive, and recognize this, you can't be a Hungarian, but you are one, that's what you are, and that's what you shall remain forever and ever—Hungarian, unbearable, and don't start telling me about all the exceptions, because the exceptions make me sick, because in reality there are no exceptions, whoever is Hungarian is my confrère, because whoever is Hungarian issues from one root, he is a simple, dangerous buffoon who thinks he is a king, but he is not king, he continually rants but immediately slinks away if someone yells at him, believe me ... well, that's enough now! please stop already, I can't stand it! the Headmaster snapped, that voice, so full of abuse, so full of hate, I can't stand it, I can't put up with it, he said, and he even closed his eyes, when—after the unfortunate intermezzo during which the Mayor had to be transferred to the Hospital, and the Committee had returned to their places, continuing where they had left off— no, I hope you understand, Chief Editor, it's completely superfluous to read this aloud, and in addition it's hardly my belief—this was his favorite turn of phrase, "it's hardly my belief"—that there's anyone among us who isn't acquainted with this libelous screed, truly, I don't see the point of reading it aloud, in brief, I respectfully ask you to stop, and with that he sat down, but the Chief Editor didn't stop, instead he informed them that if they'd convinced him this time to allow discussion of this material before publication—which contradicted his deepest ethical imperatives as a journalist—then they certainly had to put up with hearing the entire piece; this is a profession, Headmaster, not just some slapdash operation, that's not how things work around here, so I ask you all to please pay attention, because I'd like to have all your agreement in publishing this following passage without any changes, namely where he writes: well, let's take a look now at how the Hungarian sees himself, because that has to be the most ridiculous aspect of this whole thing, or, if you're Hungarian, as am I, then the most oppressive, because the Hungarian belongs to me, just as I belong to him; because the Hungarian thinks, for example, that he is a Christian, moreover—the Chief Editor looked at the vicar above the piece of paper that he held in his hands—he thinks he is a generous Christian, always ready to help those in trouble, then truly no God or person can stand in his way, he rushes out to the barricades, he rushes out to help, he's always ready to burst into tears in public, so sorry is he for himself, in his readiness to help and sacrifice, and all the while nothing is more alien to him than a readiness to help and a willingness to sacrifice, because it's impossible to even imagine a more indifferent people than the Hungarians; it happened that a squalid war was taking place nearby, and yet where the Hungarians were, only twenty or thirty kilometers away, life gaily went on as if nothing at all was happening on the other side of that border a mere twenty or thirty kilometers distant, they went on, right next to this misfortune, with blithe indifference, and even if one of them were to conquer within himself that indifference stemming from cowardice and went there and tried to help, then he'd be so touched by his own actions that he'd seriously, really seriously, believe that he was a hero, although deep inside he would know precisely that he was no hero, but a rat, a creature play-acting at survival . . . but no, he wasn't going to listen to this anymore, the director of Municipal Utility Services stood up, he too was familiar with this text, but no, it was completely unnecessary to read it aloud, and not only was reading it aloud completely unnecessary, but there was no way it could be published, this was his opinion, this text couldn't even be revised, because this text—no matter what the Chief Editor said—was unrevisable, every line, every word of it was an ignominy, he, for example, held himself to be a Christian, and he was not particularly prideful, but now he was deeply indignant, and namely had they even reached a decision as to whether or not this text should be published?—what do you mean, *whether or not* the text should be published, the Chief Editor yelled at him, his eyes riveted on the director of Municipal Utility Services, what was that supposed to mean, that wasn't the question here, the question, as he had already stated, was in what form, and with what permutations, was that clear? —these were the questions to be discussed and nothing else, because the appearance of this text in print had been decided upon with the unanimous support of the editorial board, because never had there been such a need for critical voices as now, when it seemed that things—well, how could he put it, he said, hesitating—could go wrong; and when, he asked the Municipal Utility Services director, would it finally be time for the free press to raise its own pure voice if not now, as nobody doubted that the author of this text, whomever it might be, was speaking just as much about himself as about others, just as he was speaking about this city, about this entire country, where it was time to finally bring a halt to this ascendancy of inaction, because according to him (and the editorial board was in complete agreement), the time for action had come, this city—let's state it frankly, stated the Chief Editor—stood on the brink of a precipice, and, as articulated by the writer of this text, this was itself the fundamental consequence of complete and total spinelessness, no one here could contradict that, for that is exactly what we have to struggle against, everyone with his own means, because—and I quote: "who can call into question . . . ," and the Chief Editor held up the manuscript before his eyes and continued to read the text aloud, it was as if he himself were the author, as he declared not just once that "despite the fact that he himself was personally affected," he did enjoy its tone and melody—who can call into question, he read, that if we at once regard being Hungarian as an illness, a disease, and an incurable epidemic—that we should try to designate the cause of this illness, disease, and epidemic, which is child's play, because it's obvious the reason is to be found in his moral depravity: Hungarian morals have reached rock bottom, and this is enough, namely even this explanation is sufficient: the Hungarian is equivalent to the lowest degree of moral debasement with no place left to fall, this is the formula; of course, we have to proceed very cautiously here, because we can easily fall into the trap of asserting that there is someplace to fall from; well, no, there's no question of that, there is no past which shows itself more clearly than ours, because without trampling through all the historical details, we can designate the entire history of the Hungarians—the glorious past so eulogized by our fathers—as the history of shame, for in that history there is more betrayal, apostasy, perfidious intrigue, ignominious defeat, well-deserved failure, base vengeance, merciless retaliation, and brutality that no hypocrisy can mask, how should I put it—the Chief Editor read aloud with visible pleasure—more than in a deer full of gunshot, so let's forget about the past and the old glories, namely let's leave it be, let's no longer bring up those shames of the past, and the jumbled mendacities considered worthy of praise, it's more than enough for us to somehow just remain on the surface of that swamp if at all possible, that swamp denoting the state of moral values today—well, what is exactly your problem with that, Mr. Director, Mr. Headmaster, the Chief Editor lowered the manuscript, isn't the author saying something here, he raised his voice and tapped on the manuscript impetuously—and really, it was as if he were defending his own writing—isn't he just saying what we're all thinking of ourselves?—no, the Headmaster jumped up (and at that point the others also began stirring in their seats around the large conference-room table), no, no, I don't agree with any of this, and above all it's not clear to me what's going on here, and what do you want from all this—he looked at the Chief Editor, his face distorted in rage—to besmirch this city, to besmirch everything that is sacred, for here this text is vilifying our past, I tell you, as someone who was originally a history teacher by profession, I cannot allow this to stand, critical voices concerning the present age are one thing, but it's another to go to stomping on the truly glorious centuries of the Hungarian past ... and so it went on, then four o'clock passed, and then five o'clock passed too, and the meeting was still going on, and the Police Chief, whose idea it originally had been to arrange this meeting, when the Chief Editor had solicited his opinion, as he always did before embarking on any kind of risky endeavor, well, he just sat there silently, but he hadn't even been paying attention at all for a while now, because something was telling him that this whole thing was pointless, and the suggestion he'd made to the Chief Editor—namely, it was important to see what kind of reaction an article like this would solicit from the town's civic leaders to gauge the effect it would have on its residents—had been a mistake, as much bigger things were on the horizon now, in comparison to which this entire article and whether or not it would be published or not in tomorrow's morning edition was completely meaningless, some inner voice just kept telling him and telling him, and it also told him that he shouldn't be wasting his time here, listening to this interminable blather, because outside in the streets something had happened or was going to happen, he didn't know what, but something was happening, something about which he had not even the faintest idea, but the essence of which he—and precisely he himself, because he was the one who truly guided the city, and not these halfwits—should know about.

He stood outside in the courtyard, and he didn't care at all about the slanting rain striking him, he hadn't even put on his jacket, and he spoke into his cell phone, saying that he didn't want to disturb him, and he didn't know if he was calling at the right time, but it was important—and here he paused for a moment, to see if there would be any response, but his interlocutor on the other end of the line was silent, so he just continued, saying: *he didn't know what was going on, but something was happening,* and another pause followed, this time because he didn't know what to say next, because that, as a matter of fact, was the one statement he had to make, there were no details, he reported in a military-like manner, so there at least would be some kind of framework to what he was saying, that is, well, there were strange things happening here and there, things that never happened before, he didn't claim that they were important, but he did maintain that none of them had happened here before—how should I put it, he said in a subdued voice—for example, in Snail Garden, on Thursday at dawn, unknown assailants knocked over the bust of Countess Krisztina Wenckheim, but not only that, they completely smashed apart her face with a hatchet, and how do I know it was with a hatchet, well, because we found the hatchet, but we don't understand why they did it, and the main thing is that we didn't even hear anything, even though we've increased the number of patrols across the entire city over the past few days —stop babbling, get to the point, said the person on the other end of the line, fine, well, that's about it, and here he fell silent again, and he waited to see if the other person said anything, but he didn't, and he didn't ask if he was still there on the line because he heard him breathing, meaning he was still there, but then he couldn't take the silence anymore, and he spoke again, saying: all the statues on Maróti Square have been knocked over—so what are you now, the voice at the other end of the line asked, a friend of the arts? why you so interested in these statues; it's not that I'm so interested in them, he answered, and he tried to stand even more underneath the courtyard's fairly narrow eaves, because the rain had started up again—but none of it makes any sense, I can understand pushing over the statues, he explained, but they also smashed apart the faces, although we didn't find any hammers or hatchets or anything like that anywhere, well, and that's it, and again there was a pause, and once again the person on the other end of the line said nothing, he just sighed occasionally, like someone who was engaged in another activity in addition to speaking on the telephone, maybe he was leafing through some book, because the Leader seemed to hear something like paper rustling in the background, and well, that's it, he repeated; fine, anything else, the other asked, well, in the Slaughterhouse, in the large stable where they lock up the livestock at night in order for them to be, you know, slaughtered the next day, well, there, one of my men—he's a night watchman there—on Wednesday at midnight he found two cattle frozen in their own blood, their heads were also smashed apart, and they were evidently held by the head, how should I put it, as they were beaten to death—hmm, noted the voice, as if this were not in the least bit interesting to him, anything else?—well, just things like that and then there aren't any local people on the streets even during the day, just a whole bunch of unknown people, and it's not as if the residents are afraid or anything, although maybe they are by now, but there are no cars, no local people, just this whole bunch of unknown faces, it's impossible to understand, and—go on, encouraged the voice—well, during the night on Wednesday somebody broke off the bell in the Romanian Orthodox church, and almost no one heard it, only the family of the cobbler who cleans up the church . . . what do you mean they broke off the bell, the other asked, well, most likely they did it with one of those huge power hacksaws, or they sawed the whole thing off, and the bell broke off, and of course it tore through everything, and this person found it, this cobbler, I don't know his name, he found it when he went there to clean up, the bell was lying on the ground turned upside down, what can that mean—nothing, answered the person on the other end of the line, and he put the receiver down.

Because all of them, without exception, are servile—Dóra read at the dinner table—as servility is one of the deepest elements of the repulsive Hungarian soul, always coming to heel when faced with might, and it doesn't matter what kind of power we're talking about, it could be, for example, greatness, genius, even grandiosity, it doesn't matter, the Hungarian hangs his head—but, in point of fact, only until he feels that he can bite, like a stray dog, and then he bites, but mainly he attacks that which is great, immeasurably great, that which is, say, colossal, genial, gigantic, that which towers over him, because it is proportions above all that he can't stand, he can never accept proportions, and that's why, if he weren't such a coward, he would turn against them; he skulks in the proximity of the great, the genial, and the gigantic, but only until he can attack, because he can't withstand that which is superior, that which towers above him, that surpasses him, or outstrips his comprehension, his narrow brain and that shrunken expanse of his diseased soul; well, and so this is his servility, which we will now explore in greater detail via the most self-evident examples in this city, and especially in this city, because there is no other single locale in this endlessly withering country of ours where we may gain such a glimpse into the bottomless depths of the Hungarian soul, into this dark and empty abyss ... and then there are all these names, he explained, and the forester showed the newspaper to his wife, hiding it a bit from the children, as if they'd be able to understand anything in the article, and as he and his wife read each name, they looked at each other, and their faces lengthened, as they read the information that was associated with these names, they winced; the forester's wife, at the description of this or that completely scandalous event, looked at her husband with an incredulous expression on her face, an expression that wanted to say WHAT?!, because they were completely stupefied, because not only was the veil ripped away from well-known persons in this article, and for the most part with descriptions of events which they were hearing about for the first time, incidents they couldn't imagine in connection with these people, but there were also descriptions of people they didn't know, who had committed every kind of act from the horrifying to the loathsome and disgraceful, if this article was to be believed, said the forester, and that's exactly what the girl behind the counter at the bar on Nagyváradi Road said as well, and she just kept on reading the article aloud to her audience of one who, according to his wont, was standing propped up against the counter next to the empty wine-spritzer glass while he scratched away at this or that point on his smashed-in, disfigured face (already beginning to heal), because it was itchy; and the three stable hands in the stables emphatically made the same remark, and so did everyone, from the counter of the Biker Bar to the hotel manager, from the train stationmaster all the way to the counterwoman in the espresso bar, from Tóni the postman to Eszter, up to and including every single citizen in the city and the city's vicinity, as the stories were so disgraceful that to imagine they were true seemed just as delectable, just as casting any doubt upon their credibility seemed impossible, because listen to this, the carpenter continued, when, as usual after coming home from work and washing his hands thoroughly, he finally sat down in front of the TV (tuned to RTL) and picked up that day's newspaper—the opposition paper of course, that was the one he took, as he knew very well whom he had to thank for this wretched torture which they called life, and well, of course he was against them ... in brief it's hard to decide what is the most frightening trait—their cowardice or blustering boorishness—are you listening, he said to his wife, who was dozing off in front of the TV, they're writing about the Hungarians ... because it's really hard to decide, if we detect—and we do so—in any quality that characterizes the Hungarians a kind of adhesive, a sort of mucus-like unguent connecting their sneaky foulness to their barbaric self-aggrandizement, their shrieking envy with their inclination to perfidy, and this particularly abominable compound of overfamiliarity is truly known and understood only by those who belong among us: those eternal fetters of mutual bestiality, with their prickling, acidic smell of sweat, that exhalation binding Hungarian to Hungarian, and causing all others to shrink away from us, anyone who is fortunate enough not to be Hungarian; this horrific fraternity acknowledges only the informality of the second person singular, there is nothing more monstrous, I say ... are you listening? the carpenter asked his wife, because she'd fallen asleep, it seemed, while he was reading aloud, so then he didn't bother her anymore, let her snore away to RTL, and he just read on and on, about how the Hungarian is so, but so hideous—and as he himself was of Slovak origin, he was enjoying it for a while—but then he too fell asleep in the chair, the newspaper slowly slid into his lap, and from there onto the floor, where he would have reached for it, but the desire to sleep, after the travails of the entire day, was stronger, so that his hand stopped in mid-journey, and the newspaper finally ended up on the floor next to his foot, and only the RTL station relayed the information that something terrible had happened in Veszprém just an hour ago, unfortunately, the announcer said, in the zoo, the three-day-old baby elephant, the one the children loved so much, had sadly died.

We all know this is going to explode, won't it, he asked, smirking at the three section heads, because my opinion is—and I don't know what you all think about it—apart from some small stylistic adjustments, we can let it run as is, it's fine, and his pronouncement was greeted with silence, as the three section heads had no desire to state their opinion, in part because their boss always made all the decisions anyway, in part because they felt that in this particular matter, as with everything else, everything had been decided in advance, everything would once again be exactly the way the Chief Editor wanted it, he only wanted to hear their opinions so he could use them against them later on, as he always did, so no thanks, not a peep out of me—this was clearly written on the faces of the three section heads in their boss's office a few minutes before eight o'clock in the evening—well, one of the editors finally spoke up, there are a few stylistic things, for example, where he writes (and I quote): "in some things, though, they're good, and that is in mendacity, they know how to tell lies in two directions at once, on the one hand outward, to others, and on the other hand inward, to themselves, and they've cultivated this very well, in this they are true masters"—well, as for this part, said one of the three subeditors, and he quickly gulped up what remained of his espresso, it's not bad, but still I would ... of course I don't know how you feel about it, but I would suggest ... in brief, this is just a recommendation of course, but I wouldn't insist on it, only if you agree ... well, so tell me, the Chief Editor encouraged him, he smiled at him pleasantly, which made the section head not want to say another word, but what could he do, now he had to say something: well, instead of "on the one hand, and on the other hand," I would phrase it a little differently, the section head said, because in general I don't really like this wordage, and you understand, by that I mean when it's used by anyone anywhere, you aren't the anonymous author, but even in general, this "on the one hand—on the other hand," and "in one respect—in the other respect," well, if I see phrases like that creeping in—even in my own work—I always replace it with something else, because sometimes those phrases do creep in, as you know, because you know me, you've even corrected that kind of thing with me sometimes, well, what do I know—the section head stammered on —maybe it really does go in two directions, outward and inward and all that, you understand, I would be inclined to leave out this "on the one hand—and on the other hand," you understand, but I'm not insisting, it's really just meant as a suggestion—fine, replied the editor, not bothering to hide the fact that he didn't like this suggestion, which for some reason touched upon a sore point, but let's hear from the rest, you're all familiar with this text, he encouraged them, and he leaned back nonchalantly in his chair and began to drum his fingers on the surface of his editor's desk; well, the second one spoke—he was in charge of the culture column —because he had to, this is how it was if the three of them were called in to his office, each one had to say something, because that's the kind of profession it was—when he writes: "whoever is Hungarian continually postpones his present, exchanging it for a future which will never arrive, whereas he has neither a present nor future, because he has renounced the present for the sake of the future, a future which is not a true future, but a kind of postponement, a kind of allusion to a postponement, namely if you're looking for one with neither a present nor future, then it's a Hungarian you want, but I would immediately add, referring to my previous statement, that as for the past, the Hungarian doesn't even have that, whereas he has lied so much all over the place that essentially he's annihilated it, whereby there's nothing more frightening for him than to be confronted with what he was in the past, because then he is obligated to be confronted with what he is now, and what he will be tomorrow, thereby this whole thing is so hopeless, and thus frightening, that he'd rather lie through and through to himself and the world as well, just so he can escape from confronting ..." well, it's this part, blurted out the second section head, who was sitting in the middle and finding it difficult to speak, well, in my opinion, a phrase such as "escape from confronting," that phrase doesn't work, that's not how we would say it, we don't use that, this combination of a preposition and "confronting" is incorrect, not to mention—the second section head warmed up to his subject—the gratuitous use of all these innumerable "whereas's" and "wherebys," I think we should just wipe these out like fleas in a pigsty—yes, the Chief Editor raised his eyebrows, and with that he began to rub his forehead, which caused the other two, it would appear, to comprehend what was really going on here: this was no editorial discussion, and the stakes weren't the redacting of the ominous scandal-text, but of they themselves—he wants to give us the boot, these two thought at almost exactly the same moment, while the other one, who was sitting in the middle, said quickly: of course all of these are just minor details, all these "whereas's" and "wherebys," the whole thing is fine as it is, it's excellent, it'll definitely be a bomb, at least in my opinion—it's not too long like this, in this form? the Chief Editor asked, trying to catch the gazes of the section heads, but he didn't find them because those gazes had wandered off somewhere, away from the direction of their boss, anywhere but there, and for that reason silence settled upon them for a little while, a silence which was finally broken by the Chief Editor, who said that in his opinion a few passages could be cut from the beginning, for example, this personally offensive bit, where he says: "not even to mention the director of the Milk Powder Factory, this idiot who doesn't even have as much wit as the powder he manufactures, and who, with his own tepid, lazy, simple being is the embodiment of everything that lies in the mere concept of milk powder, can there be any more horrific idea than that—making milk out of powder—and is there a more horrific figure in the entire milk-powder industry than this so-and-so and the whole 'splendid' gang of ..." well, I would leave out this section, said the Chief Editor, up to and including the Police Chief, what do you think?—very good, the three of them answered from the other side of the desk, that's exactly what I was thinking, said the first one, that this section, the second one added, should be taken out, the third one finished the sentence, well, so we'll cut it, said the Chief Editor, and he laid out the pages in question on the table, took out a ballpoint pen, and drew a line through the sections beginning with "not even to mention the director of the Milk Powder factory" up until "including the Police Chief." But so as not to leave ourselves open to reproach, we'll leave in all the invective about us, because the main thing is authenticity. Namely I couldn't care less what anyone reads about me or about us, because for me, colleagues, there's only one thing that matters, and that's a sensation, I've been waiting for this for years, for us to come out with something like this, because this is sensational, the entire first page is going to go up in flames. Okay with you? The three of them nodded in unison, at the exact same moment. The whole thing will go up in flames.

Anyone might say: what are these absurd and exaggerated generalities, what is this, and why—this person would ask—gather up all of these assembled human weaknesses, and, thus equipped, go charging into a people, an entire nation, this can only be someone with some kind of secret personal wound out for blood revenge, read the chief secretary in the obscurity of the hospital's intensive care ward, holding up the newspaper to the ray of light issued by a small lamp; yes, you could say that no, this is unacceptable, the devil's hooves are showing from beneath his robes, because it's too transparent, because this can't be about anything other than the raging fury of some offended person unable to expend his accursed ill mood on anything but his own nation, that's what this person would say—if this were the case, but it isn't the case, unfortunately—because I'm writing to a gene, it is a gene to whom I'm addressing all of this, because no, there's no question of any personal offense here, nor am I led by any personal affront, there isn't even the faintest shadow of the desire for revenge in me, all that's going on here is that I'm sitting down to have a little chat with a gene, the gene responsible for the Hungarians, and I can state that *sine ira et studio, quorum causus procul habeo*, I have no need for explanations or confirmations, that no, this isn't personal, there's no affront, no desire for revenge, I have no need for that, this is just a little chitchat, believe me, my Hungarian confrères, I'm repelled *sine ira* by everything that promulgates the Hungarian in me, and well, I had a good look around within myself, and it all does promulgate, because I'm Hungarian ... and here, beneath the light of the small lamp, the chief secretary had to turn the page, but only very quietly, because she didn't want to disturb the poor unfortunate bodies lying naked and dying in the intensive care unit with the sound of the rustling newspaper, but she particularly didn't want to disturb that body lying next to her on the bed after she'd sent his wife, who'd been keeping vigil until then, home to sleep, so sticking out her tongue a bit on the left side of her mouth from the effort, and holding her breath, she folded the newspaper, slowly turning to the next page ... and everything that I've given an account of here in the preceding sections I've also located within myself, so if I'm speaking about you I'm also speaking about myself; but this isn't a question of self-hatred, I don't hate myself, not in the least, I just thought I'd sit down and have a little chat with a gene, the gene that is responsible for the Hungarians, and that I'd let it know, taking each thing one at a time, where things stand with these Hungarians, and well, that's where things stand, and everything here—from the first word to the last—is true, and you yourselves know this better than anyone else, and if this piece of writing, against my wishes, somehow turns up in your hands—as what I've put together here was really composed only for a gene—if you end up reading it too, well, I don't really care; however, I wouldn't claim that I'm not seized with bitterness when I think of all those ways in which I've characterized us, well, I wouldn't even necessarily use the word "bitterness," but rather that I'm sad, immeasurably sad—because of all you and because of myself —this is what I am, and this is what you are, because I'm this way, and you're this way, my Hungarian confrères, we, who belong together in our own immeasurable loathsomeness, and now I'm speaking directly to you, bypassing this gene; we, who have promulgated the most repulsive breed on this earth, let's hand over this decision concerning ourselves to the gene—that's my advice— the gene to whom I've written all of this, in brief, let the gene decide, let *it* be entrusted with this matter, let this gene be the arbiter who hands down judgment, and all the while of course I'm hoping it will be not only judge but executioner, and make us disappear, revoke us, there are so many other repulsive ethnicities remaining among humankind anyway, so delete us, the most hateful of all, from evolution, regard us as a mistake, whatever, just do whatever is necessary, strike us off the list—is that so hard for a gene?—and now once again I speak directly to the gene itself, I say: wipe out everything that is Hungarian, you've heard what I've laid out here, you are in possession of the executioner's sword, so I beg you: smite it down upon us, don't hesitate and don't reflect, and most importantly don't delay, because we are an imminent threat to the entire human race—raise, raise, raise that sword, ever higher, and smite it down upon this wretched people. Well, he can never be allowed to read this, thought the chief secretary, folding up the newspaper again cautiously, then, placing it in her lap, she raised her mournful gaze to the patient whose signs of life were betrayed only by a faint fluttering sound and a thin, green, wavy line, spiking as it jumped up and down on the monitor positioned next to his head.

Look, Eszter, said the library director stiffly, you—and I have never denied this—have been for years one of my most faithful and trustworthy librarians, but this I cannot allow, I know that in saying this I am infringing on your personal rights, but forgive me as I can't permit this, just as I had no business being at the meeting of the expanded Civic Committee yesterday at City Hall, where a decision was supposed to be reached in this very matter, you have no business reading this filth; it's one thing for us to have it out on the newspaper shelves, because that is our readers' right, but for our library workers to openly read such a smutty article discredits the library itself in the eyes of our readers, henceforth this is no longer a question of personal rights, but of my library, and I cannot permit this, don't be offended that I'm speaking to you so directly, but perhaps you're used to me speaking my mind—this is, moreover, an exceptional case, because otherwise why wouldn't you read this article, or any article for that matter, if your work happens to make that possible, a library worker on duty in the library, although I would note humorously, the library director noted, that's not what I'm paying you for, but leaving that aside, this is about something else, because I'm talking about this same article that everyone is talking about, Eszter, and he looked deeply into the eyes of the visibly trembling woman, this article is a base provocation, you yourself should have been aware of this, and in reading it publicly you aren't setting a good example, because this article is a deliberate act of intellectual arson, and we—this library—don't want to assist anyone in committing such an open act of arson, namely in the figurative sense, of course; clearly you understand what I'm trying to say, this can't be allowed, so I ask you, please put the newspaper back in its place and reach for it no more, indeed I would counsel you—and this is a piece of advice from one person to another, namely now I'm not speaking as your boss—that in your place I wouldn't even read it at home, because believe me, this is a malicious attack against our city, and I don't just say that because this article dares to mention me, calling me an empty buffoon—my decisions are never influenced by such personal concerns, in a word no, and the question of who committed this isn't even interesting, although I do have my own ideas about this as well—and at this point the library director concealed something that he wished to conceal with his own usual all-knowing smile—but let's leave this for now, the main thing is that the newspaper should be put back in its place, and instead of reading it, you should go back to the reference desk and continue your work, and with this he waited, while the woman, trembling, lest the director still address her on the way out, left his office, then he leaned back in his chair, he took off his glasses, he massaged the bridge of his nose, which was aching, then the muscles around his eyes, and finally, leaving his hands in place, he buried his face in them, as the decision had been extremely difficult, because he hadn't been able to speak, just now, of what was truly weighing on him, because he wasn't concerned with this idiotic, perfidious outburst, but rather something a hundred times more significant, namely that grave changes were taking place in the city, and although—as, in his own estimation, he was someone with a good overall perspective, as well as being a thinking, moreover a fairly clear-thinking, moreover a decidedly logical person—he had not yet arrived at a fully formed opinion as to the essence of these changes; but the reality of these changes wasn't itself a question for him, namely—he summarized it to himself, leaning on his desk, his face buried in his hands—the situation had become dangerous, and he, in his position of responsibility, because he was responsible not only for his work colleagues and the reading public, but for himself as well, and this responsibility preoccupied him the most right now, namely he couldn't expose his colleagues, or the reading public, or especially his own self, to the risk of exposure to any kind of hitherto unforeseeable trouble (including any potential risk to his own person); it had been enough for him to come into the library this morning, because the street upon which he traveled was simply not the same street it had been before, namely the street—upon which he had been commuting for years now in his meticulously cared-for '80s Ford Escort, as he did this morning as well—was different today, and not just because, apart from a few unknown individuals, he hadn't seen even one pedestrian on the sidewalk, and in addition he hadn't seen even one other car on the road until he reached the library gates, no, he wouldn't be able to say exactly what it was that he'd sensed, but it was something, although he had his own ideas as to what the cause of this might be, and perhaps even too many at once, they just swirled around in his head, and this time, to his own surprise, he wasn't able to choose the correct one—even though he judged his own capabilities, in his career hitherto, as being first-rate, they weren't working now, especially because he didn't see any point in those things that could furnish him with an explanation, thus designating the root of the problem, because of course the background to all this could well be the famous Baron and his tragic end, but don't forget (he reminded himself not to forget) equally in the background could be the Professor, who (with all the commotion around the Baron) we have utterly forgotten, the Professor and his completely criminal, insane, and, in fact, inconceivable and inexplicable mysterious deed, the nearly enigmatic character of the whole story with the Professor—he liked that word, enigmatic—in brief, these two extraordinary background stories occurred to him as self-evidently relevant at the very least, and yet he still didn't have a sense this morning when he'd woken up and begun to brood over what was to be done in such a situation, just as he had no idea now, so with his head still supported by his hands, he stared at one point in the office, because that was his usual position when he was thinking, so these two events would lead him to finally understand what he needed to understand, because this was what he wanted—because as far as he could judge, nothing like this had ever happened to him: never before had he—exactly he—amid the chaos of events been unable to come upon a logical coherence when something like this occurred, and thus not be able to arrive at an explanation—this time, he wasn't able to do so and he was surprised, he wasn't used to an explanation taking up so much of his time, you could say he was proud that his mind was just as sharp as his sight, namely in the figurative sense, since in his youth there'd been unfortunate worries with his eyesight, leading him to wear glasses with ever thicker lenses, and because of which, as a matter of fact, he wasn't supposed to drive, so he had to constantly be "arranging" this matter with the relevant authorities, because apart from reading books, he had one passion, and that was driving, this he frankly adored, it was hard to explain why, but driving was one of his deep passions, one that wasn't manifested in other realms of his life, for example he had no interest in women, driving was everything to him, well, of course next to reading, because during his whole life he had read innumerable books, and, of course, this led him to feel that, in his own opinion, he could consider himself to be—all immodesty aside—a fairly clever, informed, intelligent person, only that now this clever, informed, intelligent person kept staring, in a fair amount of puzzlement, at that point in the office, as it were holding his gaze there, as always when he was deeply immersed in thought, he was puzzled, and a little despairing, because he sensed that the problem—the content of which was completely obscure, as were its cause, its essence, and moreover, its symptoms—was only growing larger and larger there outside, namely that in a situation like this he could do only one thing, and that, he decided, he was going to do—not confront this problem, but make preparations for defense, the decision was born in him; and immediately he called out to one of his staff to have all of the City Library employees immediately assemble for an impromptu meeting, then when they had gathered together in his office, he informed them that due to erratic and hitherto unforeseen events, about which he could not provide precise details right at this moment, the library would be closing immediately; he therefore requested, he said with a stern gaze and very seriously, for the rooms to be evacuated without delay, and for him to receive notification as soon as possible of this having occurred, so there arose considerable commotion in the City Library, and those few people who'd come there to borrow a book by Danielle Steel or Magda Szabó or Albert Wass to while away the time during these difficult days were quickly led out of the building—and the staff solved this in a fairly clever fashion, they thought, explaining it away by technical problems, then, quickly grabbing their own coats and umbrellas, they themselves left the building, and only he remained behind, the library director, so he himself would be the one to shut the City Library's heavy doors—because now as ever, in this moment of tribulation, he insisted on this—just like the captain of a ship listing dangerously on a storm-tossed sea, he was the last one to leave the deck. He looked at his watch before getting into his car on the deserted main thoroughfare: it was 11:40.

He had reinforced the patrols on duty throughout the entire city—not because something was happening, but because nothing was happening, and he didn't like this, said the Police Chief to the Leader, when they sat down in the Biker Bar across from each other, while the others respectfully withdrew to the farthest corner they could and raised their eyes to the TV—so the Police Chief would be curious as to whether the other had noticed anything, but he, the Police Chief, wanted details first and foremost, he didn't want to hear again about the knocked-over statues and things like that, the Leader instead should focus on those things that may seem completely meaningless but shared one trait in common: he should tell him about any phenomenon with which he hadn't met before—the Professor has disappeared, the Leader retorted immediately without even thinking, because he'd understood the request to mean that he shouldn't think about it, but say immediately what came to his mind without reflecting; you already mentioned that, the Police Chief said, discarding the first fruit of this thought-free extemporization, and he was already standing up, because he had no time to waste, and this was wasting time, he should drop this theme already, he'd told him a hundred times—fine, no problem, said the Leader, then I would say that all of the motorcycles are leaking oil—yes, the Police Chief raised his head—yes, nodded the Leader, nothing like that ever happened before, for all of them to be leaking at once, because of course something is always dripping from one or another of our engines, this is completely natural, but for all of them to be leaking at once, this never happened before, in addition the cause was the same for every engine, a cracked gasket, I understand, the Police Chief sipped his beer, and he motioned to the Leader not to continue discussing the reasons, but to continue with his enumeration, because he wanted a list, fine, said the Leader, then I would say that the guy behind the counter who's here today, when I got here, he greeted me by telling me today's beer delivery was nowhere in sight, no one was picking up the phone at the the distributor where it had been ordered, and when in the morning they went out to the depot, they found the doors had been broken into, and it was as if before that, they'd been locked up, because a huge lock lay on the ground, knocked out of place, and there wasn't a single soul on the entire premises, but the kegs were in good order, and—go on, the Police Chief motioned, taking another sip of his beer—well, I don't know, for example, there's that large grassy square in front of the Castle, you know what's there, well, one of my men, the one over there, look—he motioned at Totó in the corner—found a sword, which was 100 percent from the exhibit inside the Castle, and it was plunged halfway into the ground, like some kind of sign, halfway into the ground, the Leader repeated, and the Police Chief looked at him, but he didn't say anything; then, the Leader continued—he wasn't reaching for his beer at all, because he was disconcerted by the Police Chief sitting with him here in the Biker Bar, where the Police Chief had never been before, this indicated, he felt, a matter of exceptional importance, only he had no idea of what it could be—then the gas station attendant just completely vanished from the gas station, or he never came back from Sarkadkeresztúr, where maybe he never even arrived, as it turns out, and I don't even think that rotten piece of scum got the diesel from Romania, as we thought, but he was in cahoots somehow with those two swindlers, because the other guy on the gas station night shift also vanished, they'd been working together maybe twenty years, and some assistant has been filling in, just so somebody can be there, although as for gas, there's none, as you know, namely, well, officially there isn't any—go on, said the Police Chief—I don't know any more than that, answered the Leader; but you do know, try to stretch your memory; well, I don't know if this counts or not, the Leader speculated nervously, but, for example, here these unknown people, they just keep loafing around, not doing anything, and they don't seem to me like they have anything to do with anything, we tried to ask them what they were doing here, but no use, they didn't give us any reasonable explanation, they said they came here to go to the thermal baths, or they were looking for some relative, or they just came over here for a brief visit from Sarkad, or Vésztő, or one of them said he'd come from Elek, there was nothing in the gas pumps where he was, and maybe he could get some gas here—yes, yes, I know about them, go on—I can't think of anything else, the Leader shook his head, and he looked at his pint glass as the foam on the top of his beer sank down, he could just pour the whole thing out, oh, he suddenly lifted his head, a woman was raped in the travel agency, when, the Police Chief asked—last night—and why don't I know about it? why wasn't it reported, the Police Chief asked, I only heard about it by chance, said the Leader, through a nurse in our own network; do you know who it was? no, I don't know, but I asked the nurse if she knew who it was, and supposedly the victim said she'd never seen him, she didn't even remember his face, just that he had a beard, and there was a birthmark above the right corner of his mouth, well, that's good, that's what I like, because it means you're paying attention, the Police Chief stood up, because why else do I keep all of you on, if only because you pay attention—only now there's a situation, and everything has to be done differently, do you get what I have in mind, because your efforts will have to be even more focused, or rather, to put it more clearly, I want you to double your attention, and tell your people this: I want them to be constantly rumbling and zooming and revving and foraying and circling around and around this city for me, and no matter what happens don't call, he said, looking back from the door of the Biker Bar, I'll call you if I need to.

The human being is a monstrosity, I hope I am not too late in speaking, he read, reaching the last line in the column, where he had to turn the page—a monstrosity—he raised his head to the first line on the next page and pushed his eyeglasses farther back up his nose—a fact of which you are all undoubtedly well aware, as to no avail are his continual lies flowing unimpeded in every direction; moreover this true monstrosity, while he has his bad moments, at times stumbles across a good intention within himself, but he quickly forgets about that, and it remains a mere memory, but he builds upon it later, as this sort of monstrosity is convinced that fate has selected him for good, or at the very least as the representative of truth, his own truth, or his own truth as vindicated by others, and in this he stands very close to the so-called

Christian, who is exactly the same but even worse, because he continually calls upon a particular alliance with his own Almighty Lord, an alliance through which he exempts himself time and time again from every kind of outrage amongst which he lives, and he lies, because for him, to live and to lie are two sides of one and the same coin, and that's what makes the Christian so repulsive, but the Christian Hungarian, in particular, is truly the most base of all, because the hitherto described Hungarian, if in addition he calls himself a Christian, then to his original defects are added those of the most base and vulgar servility and arrogance, because this is the height of everything, when the Christian Hungarian, let's say, blesses the soldiers' flag before the bloody skirmish, or when the Christian Hungarian slinks away into some protected corner if danger threatens so-called human dignity in his vicinity, or when the Christian Hungarian, this scoundrel in disguise, puts on the most benevolent of faces and goes to obtain his own share of power and privilege; everything that takes place in a church after all this is a desecration, if I may express it that way, more precisely this is true desecration, because no matter how he enters that church—and even the fact that he enters a church at all is the pinnacle of hypocrisy, and then he walks out of there as if nothing had happened—the essence of the relationship between priest and believer in a Hungarian Christian church is that of a band of mafiosi cutting their deals, no matter what is at hand, one legitimizes the other, and the other, after muttering some mumbo jumbo in exchange, lets him loose on the world again, well, this is how it is in Hungary, this is how it is in woeful Hunnia, this is how it goes among these sneaky gangsters beneath the cross, and their faces don't burn in shame, moreover they form an integral part of society; but the most despicable part of the whole thing is that they do all of this in the name of Jesus Christ, designating themselves as the single refuge of the innocent, the excluded, and the defenseless; and already: that their sins don't cry out to the heavens, that with their parlance, all of their church buildings from Körmend to Létavértes, from Drégelypalánk to Hercegszántó, haven't yet collapsed on top of their heads, this shows that they have no God; their belief is a deliberate treachery; that they haven't yet gone astray in the great fear common to all human beings who are nothing more than sneaky yokels ... and he read to the end of the sentence, he got to that point, but then he read no more, but folded the newspaper, slowly lowering it into his lap, and he didn't lift his head, he took off his glasses, and those too he dropped into his lap, and when he looked at the pretty little cross nailed onto the wall above the bookshelves in his room, that cross so dear to his heart, at first he just began to pray mechanically to the Lord, saying forgive me, forgive me, forgive me, and it was as if he himself didn't know whom should be forgiven or why, or was he praying for them, the subjects of this long newspaper article, or for the one who had put all of this down on paper—he looked at the little wooden cross up there on the wall that was facing his velvet armchair in which he said, and he thought, once he finished his prayer, that here it was, that this was His word, and now would come the punishment he'd long feared. He looked at his watch, which showed a quarter past six. It would be better if he started getting ready, it occurred to him, because in a moment he had to go over to the church. He had to begin the 6:30 mass.

Why has everything been forgotten, the chief secretary asked herself, while she was waiting for the Mayor's wife to come back; she glanced at her watch, and really she was thinking that even though only a few days had gone by, all of a sudden everything was topsy-turvy, and not only was everything topsy-turvy, but suddenly and simply it had gone mad, because until now there had always been just this or that little incident, because there was always something—this was her favorite phrase, "there was always something," but there weren't any words for what had happened in the past few days, because if she recalled it, then she thought: what about everything that had happened before, for example, with the Professor, that whole horrific story—even today the wider public knew nothing about it—that had occurred out there, supposedly beyond Csókos Road, in that dreadful Thorn Bush, and then there was that huge fire, *who even remembered that now*, no one, everything that came after simply swept it away, and what came after was more than enough, because who even remembered the Professor's daughter and that whole circus, who, she asked, no one, because it happened before all the commotion around the Baron's arrival, and all the organizing they had to do, then the huge disappointment—I meant to say, she said to herself quickly, *that accident*, that inconceivable catastrophe on the train tracks in the City Forest—had there been any time for anyone to process any of this, she asked herself, no, she immediately answered, and again she looked at her watch, but there was no word of the wife, where was she already; that poor man, even if he was a fraud, she shook her head a little as she thought about it, still he was stylish; and the whole thing was still a catastrophe, but there was no time for a person to understand or grasp what had occurred, because already there was the next catastrophe and the next one, because ever since yesterday there had been no mail delivery, and it was impossible to establish connection with any of the other county districts, as in all likelihood all the relay stations had been switched off in order to shut down both the telephone and the internet, and there was neither bus nor train service to Békéscsaba, in other words, no connection between them and the wider world, in addition none of the central broadcasters were transmitting any longer, and that their own little local TV stations had ceased operations was just the "icing on the cake," not to speak of the press organs, also crucial for them, because if those were suspended, there was nothing left but that smutty opposition rag, but all this was still nothing, because to reflect upon what had happened during and after all these events was frightening: she had a bad premonition about things, but what was so bad wasn't even that people had forgotten the events of the past few days, but that the speed of all these events was like that of some kind of flood when it breaks across a dam, the events occurring and occurring one after the other, the news reports of this happening here, that happening there, and over there something else was happening, a person just clutched his head, and it was no wonder that the boss, that poor man, who always impressed her with his energy, and who clearly always strove to be a true leader of civic values in this city, it was no wonder that here he lay, the poor thing, all stretched out, and, as the doctors had said before they left the Hospital, he had no chance, and that was happening too, all the doctors were decamping back home—she'd found this out completely by chance, when, a little while before, she'd overheard the nurses talking when she had gone out for a moment to the washroom—the doctors were fleeing from the Hospital, and now only they were here; one or two nurses?! and no doctor anywhere in sight?! in the intensive care ward?!, it boggled a person's mind, the chief secretary looked at her watch again, and she didn't understand where the Mayor's wife could be, because it was already 6:30, and they had mentioned six o'clock as the very latest, when they had said goodbye by the sickbed, she, said the wife, would be back here at the very latest at six o'clock, she'd just pop home for about an hour to cook something, because this hospital fare, well, they both knew, his wife looked at Jucika, appreciating her faithfulness now for the first time, how she wished to remain next to her husband, the Mayor, she was genuinely touched, it almost shook her, because until now she'd only felt anger when she had to think again and again about how her husband spent at least eight or ten hours every day with her in that City Hall, and he behaved so provocatively with her at home, behaving more like an adolescent boy than a married man, it boggled her mind and filled her with rage at home, but then the tears practically welled up in her eyes, as they brought in the patient, rolling him into the intensive care ward, and Jucika informed her that she would stay here for as long as she was needed, she was practically in tears, because she wasn't expecting this, and she truly regretted that for years she'd thought of Jucika in that way, because now she only felt the most sincere gratitude, and certainly it was only in these tough moments that a person found out who their true friends were, and Jucika was just such a true friend, thought the wife, so she told her that she'd just dash home for a moment, cook something quickly, then come back and take her place by the patient's bed, at the very latest by six, and she'd be back, and now here it was already 6:45, and nothing, the chief secretary was looking at her watch every minute, she didn't understand, maybe something had happened, but what, maybe the meat burned or something like that, although what would she even cook for herself with her husband in such a state, lying here unconscious with only a sheet covering him, in such a condition as this, so then she gets up to go home and eat steak or whatever, well, she's not in her right mind, thought the chief secretary, and she went out into the hallway to see if she was there already, because she herself was hungry, the boss had lost consciousness at 3:30 in the afternoon, and she hadn't had a bite to eat since, of course, she'd been so frightened that she hadn't even thought of eating, but now, with nothing happening for hours, the machine just kept making that chirping noise above the bed, and those spiky waves just kept running ahead and running ahead, nothing, she only had today's newspaper with her, and she couldn't eat that, although she could really eat almost anything already, she was almost ashamed to think like this sitting next to the sickbed, but her stomach was growling with hunger, the hallway was empty, she didn't see anyone in the nurses' room, and finally, she saw no wife at all, what the hell should she do, she couldn't leave him here, she reflected, as she sat back down in the ward and looked at that ashen face, the motionless body lying on its back with only a little paunch rising beneath the sheet, but even that was hardly visible, only from time to time—she'd go home, she suddenly decided, because well, this woman was going to be back here at any moment now, maybe she'd even bump into her on the staircase or at the Hospital entrance, she'd go home, she decided, and she was already outside, and she stepped lively, hurrying along, I don't even have an umbrella with me, she thought angrily, when she went out onto the street, and the cold wind that had risen beat the icy rain almost straight into her eyes, and she continued home that way, bent forward, her head turned to the side, so the rain wouldn't beat into her eyes, the streets were completely deserted, the doors and the windows of the houses shut, and everything else she came across was shut as well, the gate pulled down on the small greengrocers' shop, the iron shutters were padlocked at the hairdressers', what time could it be for everything to be closed down already like this, but well, it was still only 7:15, well, what's going on here, could this be the Last Judgment?

Irén's horrific death—as they found her on the sidewalk, having to see that beloved human face now smashed into fragments—bore down on the family with a merciless crushing weight, so the son, orphaned amid such tragic circumstances, and his adored bride were among the few who weren't really affected by all the other events that had ensued; the son in any event wasn't very much the talkative type, but from that moment, when they came home from the morgue, where he had to identify his own mother, he spoke no more, he just sat at the kitchen table, and in vain did the two children surround him, in vain did his wife tell him that dinner wasn't ready yet, he wasn't willing to move away from there, then, later on, he watched as his wife Zsuzsánka ate her dinner, and although she urged him to eat something himself, he just sat there to the end of dinner and didn't even take as much as a forkful, but you have to eat, my dear, Zsuzsánka tried to encourage him, now we need strength, because we must endure what has happened, even if we can't resign ourselves, even if we can't accept it, we need strength, because we still must endure it, there is nothing else for us to do, she said to her husband, who sat slumped over in the same chair where his mother would always sit when she came over, she'd sit down there and talk about the events of the day "to the children," as she called them, just like that, always in the plural, and Zsuzsánka tried everything, that day, and the next day too, as they heard reports of newer and newer murders, each one more horrific than the last, but she wasn't able to get him up from the chair and to lie down next to her in bed, he remained in the chair, and he kept staring at one spot on the kitchen table, and when he could no longer remain awake he slumped over there, onto the kitchen table, and woke up in the same place the next morning, when the two children moved around him again but didn't dare wake him up, and Zsuzsánka just patted his face to awaken him gently, and to come lie down at last in the bed, but he didn't, he remained in that chair, he wasn't fully conscious, and in the meantime that spot on the kitchen table had become ever more important to him, he couldn't take his eyes off of it, in any event Zsuzsánka was already thinking of calling a doctor, but then she recalled that according to the rumors she'd heard there were no more doctors in the city, there was no one in this tragic situation who could tell her what to do, and so she remained alone with the manifold burden of her beloved mother-in-law's decease, the collapse of her husband whom she loved more than anything else in the world, and this catastrophe, daily ever more threatening, which had settled into their lives, crushing her; there were moments, hours, when she felt it was all too much for her, here with the two children, from whom she couldn't keep all of this a secret forever, because, well, she wasn't as tough as Irén had been, she was only a weak copy of Irén, she couldn't cope with so many troubles—if only life wouldn't burden her with so many—but in vain did she repeat the supplicating words within herself, her husband's collapse (which otherwise could have been expected) made her head of the family, so now, right in the middle of these continuous gruesome events, what suddenly came to her mind wasn't the question of what would become of them, but rather: what would Irén be thinking of in this situation?—and she knew, immediately she knew what that was, namely, Irén would want to know what was going on with Marika, that frail touch-me-not, as Zsuzsánka always called this "shadow member" of their family in secret, only to herself and never before her mother-in-law, because in her mother-in-law's eyes this Marika was a saint in need of never-ending protection and support, in short, this really came into Zsuzsánka's mind suddenly, while she looked at her husband's motionless back from the doorway of the bedroom: why, amid so much dread and so many horror stories, had they not asked themselves what was happening with her—was she still even alive?—as from one moment to the next, and altogether during just the past few days, the world around Marika as well had been turned upside down, especially around her, as the tragic events in relation to the Baron clearly were far more troubling, distancing Marika from her own earlier self, and Zsuzsánka just looked at and looked at her husband's motionless back, and she already knew what that poor Irén, if she were still alive, would do in this situation: she would immediately go there, despite everything, despite the fact that at their last meeting this Marika had literally shown Irén the door in such an appalling manner, and because that's what she would have done, Zsuzsánka felt this to be a kind of last wish, for them as well—and they must obey this distant last wish, so she said to that motionless back: there was something they had to unconditionally see to, and this was none other than that Marika, she explained, to see what had become of her, as for days now they'd heard nothing about her, namely these days had been exceedingly difficult, and they had been for Marika as well; at first her husband didn't even move, he just continued to stare fixedly at the spot on the kitchen table, and he only raised his head and glanced at his wife when Zsuzsánka began to speak of how they had to think of Irén, and what she expected from them there above, because it was certain that she was up there above, Zsuzsánka said, because only the very best ones ended up there—well, what did she want from them, what? her husband asked, speaking for the first time in days, well, for us to at least have a look in on her, answered his wife, and tell her what happened, because it's also very possible she hasn't heard, and in general we'll ask her how she is, and if she needs anything in these difficult times, fine, answered the husband, they bundled up something to eat in Irénke's old woven basket, they told the children to be good, and not worrying about what awaited them outside, they mutely set off for the city, to have a look in on Marika and ask how she was, and ask her if she needed anything in these difficult times. But they rang the buzzer of her door in vain.

He took off his glasses, and as always he massaged the bridge of his nose, because as he wore them throughout the day, the bridge of the glasses pressed down heavily on his nose, although he always ordered eyeglasses of the finest quality, it was important to him, as he always said, for his eyeglass frames to be of the very best quality, especially if his lenses were of such a strong prescription, he couldn't scrimp on this, and in particular, he liked objects of good quality, he didn't have so many things, apart from his books, a hi-fi system, a huge flat-screen TV, an enormous easy chair measured to his own "corpulent" bodily frame, and a few bottles of fine red wine, an old bachelor as he was didn't need too much, he used to say, it was enough for him to have his own quantity of books, because books were everything to him, books were his obsession, as well as being the source of his self-confidence, he'd almost say that as well, he mentioned to a few close acquaintances—when he still had some, although in recent years he didn't have any, but when he still did have them, he'd say: his self-confidence, it all came from books, and so on; what had enabled him to gain a firm footing in the world, in this troubled world—he raised his index finger—was the thought of his books at home, and, interestingly enough, what he had in mind wasn't the many tens of thousands of volumes in the City Library—that was something else, he always thought, that City Library, although that's my creation, let's not deny that—but at the same time the foundation of my self-confidence is my collection at home, this small private library with its own few thousand volumes, because he had everything that was important, from the ancients to the moderns, from philosophy to the historical sciences, to the field of automotive engineering, and of course, if the subject came up, he emphasized automotive engineering, because the subject of automotive engineering stood closest to his heart, and how could it have been otherwise, because here he found everything worthy —in the profoundest sense of the word —of being read, because he had in his possession every great series and curiosity, from *Driver's License Test Questions, New Technology*, the *Reference Library of Auto-Engineering*, and, of course, the renowned series *Cars-Motors*, to *Electrical Equipment for Motor Vehicles*, by László Hodvogner, *Modern Motor-Vehicle Construction*, by Zoltán Ternai, *Garages, Service Stations, and Repair Shops*, by Béla Haris, László Müller, and Béla Soltész (ed. Dr. Kálmán Ábrahám), up to and including his true favorites, accordingly *Motor-Vehicle Braking Systems*, by Dr. Ferenc Sidó, as well as the 1981–88 editions of *Fix It Like This!* by Dr. Hans-Rüdiger Etzold, and he hadn't even yet mentioned—he said at times, if he was initiating someone into the treasures of his own personal library—the series *Special Automobiles*, by Dr. Imre Hörömpöly and Dr. Károly Kurutz, *Auto Diagnostics*, by Dr. Ottó Flamisch, or such rarities as *Wartburg —What Next?* by Horst Ihling, which could be said to be a truly unique publication, as well as, of course—he lowered his voice if he had gotten this far in his account—all of the collected technical literature he'd been able to locate on the subject of Ford automobiles, of course, in this area, he had everything—or rather, he rectified his statement—because this was one of his favorite words, "rectify"—*almost* all of the important and less important publications, and if he wasn't just then watching TV, then he read, and he watched TV because he watched the local news every evening (that is, when there still was local news being broadcast, he thought now, in his armchair), and he watched the national news, but he didn't really watch movies, he preferred sports, especially Formula One, he never missed that, the only problem was recently not only some of the better sports channels weren't coming in, no channels at all were coming in, so he could only speak in the past tense of how, at the mercy of chance or the whims of the national broadcasters, he'd been able nonetheless to catch a more interesting race now and then, well, then he always sat in front of the TV, watching the race with loud cries, but apart from this he was always reading, mainly in bed after lying down, but also sometimes when he was sitting in the armchair after dinner, a matter about which he was not particularly demanding, and one could even say not at all, because for him, when it came to food, what was important was not quality but quantity, namely he devoured, because he had to devour, he never was fussy about the ingredients; he was ashamed, and so no one knew about this, but every evening, he decimated monstrous quantities of pork-based products with bread and milk; he preferred not to eat in the morning, because he always hurried to get to work in time, or at lunch, when everyone would have seen him; in the evening, however, he gobbled up fantastic quantities of headcheese, sausage, and bacon, eating so fast that he didn't even chew the mouthfuls properly, he just swallowed and swallowed, after the headcheese the sausage, after the sausage the bacon, and milk to go with it, or on holidays red wine, he'd drink maybe two liters of milk or two bottles of wine during these one-man dinners held in secret, always biding his time for when he got home from work, postponing it, because he was ashamed even before himself, but then suddenly he rushed into the kitchen, grabbed the food from the fridge, hauling it on a tray into the living room, and he set to it, but then, when he had finished, and he leaned back in the armchair, and he just sat to calm down a bit, he sat and he farted, because there was no one to hear him, he just looked into nothingness with rounded eyes, and he liked to sit like this and not do anything, and at such times, as a matter of fact, he wasn't even really present, that's how he would have expressed it to himself: he was spending some time in this switched-off state, and really that's what it was, he switched himself off and just sat there, not thinking about what he'd just done with all this food a moment ago, he wasn't thinking about anything, he took off his heavy eyeglasses, he massaged the bridge of his nose, he put his glasses back on, and he'd just sit there motionlessly, sometimes even for half an hour, and nothing—with the exception of today, not today, because today, as soon as he'd gotten home he'd immediately begun to devour, but while still standing in front of the fridge, then he went into the living room, collapsed his colossal body into the easy chair, and he took the newspaper into his lap—which he hadn't done yet, not even in his office, because he'd forbidden his staff from doing so, and so he could hardly permit himself to do the same, but here at home it was different, he wanted to see things clearly, so that while still in the library he'd decided when he got home he would examine the ominous article sentence by sentence, and he would in this manner uncover the author's identity, because in his view this was the main question (in fact the only one), who had written it?—then everything could be understood, and then something could be done, but of course that doing something wasn't his job, his job was to uncover the author's identity, as a person, who by dint of his refinement, erudition, and his innate human intelligence (which he had never forfeited), because if this happened—and he was confident it would—then he would feel calmer, because he was apprehensive, like everyone whom he'd come across either in the library, or even before, when there were people still in the streets; that nervousness—as people reacted to recent events and the ensuing changes—had finally infected him as well; no matter how maliciously he'd taken note, just a few days ago, of such frights, saying that the whole thing was just empty hysteria—namely, he had identified it as such and for his own part he didn't care to join in, if the city would forgive him, as he wasn't inclined to forfeit his own sober intellect, and so on and so on—but by now the situation with him had also changed, and not because he was affected by people's behavior, no, the behavior of other people had never represented any kind of norm for him—he thought about this with pride, when he had occasion to think back on it—but because something was really happening in the city, and what was affecting him precisely was that nothing was happening at all, one could only feel that perhaps something was going to happen, or maybe that something had already happened, and the news hadn't reached them yet, he would have listened to or watched the central broadcasters on the radio or television, but the central radio or television channels had ceased functioning, so today, before deciding he would close the library immediately, and send the people home, he'd also immediately determined that when he got home, he would try to solve what could be solved here, namely he would give to this article, this notorious piece of writing, an in-depth analysis, because he believed in this way that he would find an explanation, more precisely he would come upon the individual who was responsible for this, and he already had two designees, but there were problems with each of them, as with each candidate there were certain characteristics that excluded that one and placed suspicion on the other, but then there were also some things that excluded the second and placed suspicion back on the first one, so that now he read the entire piece from the beginning, executing, sentence by sentence, a stylistic analysis, as he felt that this would lead him to the identity of the writer, but no—he read the article thoroughly in vain from the very first to the very last sentence, he couldn't figure out which of the two it could be: for his first candidate, he couldn't presume such a stylistic quality as was evidenced in the article, and for the second, there were certain extenuating circumstances, so after an hour he was back where he'd been at the beginning, and he realized he kept turning back to that section that discussed him, where the writer of the article characterized him as a puffed-up, empty blubber head, "namely, a real typical Hungarian, a cowardly provincial asshole," he quickly folded the newspaper shut, then he opened it to the same place, and he read what had been written about him again and again and again, and he didn't deny that it was painful, what he read about himself was painful, but not only was it painful, it was offensive, because it took aim at his most sensitive point, and it was, he felt, unfair—exceedingly and savagely unfair—to call precisely him an asshole, he, who during his entire life had been convinced (and rightfully in his view) that if he was unassailable in anything, then it was in his fundamental stance toward life, deliberate, clear, impassively intellectual, built upon reason, experience, knowledge, and a kind of wise sobriety, and now here comes this someone who called him a cowardly asshole, and before the entire city, saying that he was a coward and he was an asshole, exactly him, this was the limit. He slammed the paper shut and threw it onto the floor. Later on he would take it out, he thought, and "fuck it," throw it into the garbage can. Just at that moment, it was as if somebody was rattling his front door from outside.

Right then, Tacitus was telling him: *Noctem minacem et in scelus erupturam fors lenivit: nam luna claro repente caelo visa languescere. Id miles rationis ignarus omen praesentium accepit, suis laboribus defectionem sideris adsimulans, prospereque cessura qua pergerent, si fulgor et claritudo deae redderetur. Igitur aeris sono, tubarum cornuumque concentu strepere; prout splendidior obscuriorve laetari aut maerere; et postquam ortae nubes offecere visui creditumque conditam tenebris, ut sunt mobiles ad superstitionem perculsae semel mentes, sibi aeternum laborem portendi, sua facinora aversari deos lamentantur,* but he couldn't continue reading because he was being summoned again, this was the fourth time today already, so he closed the *Annals* and put the book aside, and he didn't even understand what was wanted of him in the boss's office, because what the hell was he supposed to say when he was asked if he'd come across any instance anywhere in the authors known to him that could explain the connection between the rapes of five women—one in the travel agency the day before yesterday, the second on the banks of the River Körös, at the base of the Dugó Bridge, the third in some espresso bar, the fourth out by Nagyváradi Road in a bar, and the fifth on the street, as the woman hurried home from the Hospital—each case having occurred yesterday in the early evening—and people were disappearing, namely without a trace, and the heads of statues were being smashed apart, and bells were breaking off from bell towers, and cattle were being slaughtered, their heads smashed asunder, and somebody or some persons had released many thousands of gallons of water from the city Water Tower in a single evening, and the water had flooded all of Dobozi Road; and on the wide sections of Jókai Street, Semmelweis Road, Csabai Road, and on Eminescu Street behind the Castle the asphalt had been ripped up with a hydraulic excavator, who even knew how many people were involved, there were no witnesses, and then there were the nine murders that had just occurred—but I won't go on, the Police Chief said to him, because I just want you to think if you've encountered something similar in those famous Roman authors of yours, I'm not interested in the facts, but whether you see, between these aforementioned facts—the Police Chief asked him, visibly nervous—any, do you understand, *any kind* of connection whatsoever—no, he answered briefly, he saluted, and asked for permission to leave, and as he took the steps two at a time as was his wont, briskly making his way downstairs to the basement archives, he wondered why everyone here had lost their minds, why was even the boss asking him things like this now, well, what was he, a seer or something, he was just a simple cadet who knew Latin and who was hoping for a few days leave without pay, but in vain, and he lived among his favorite books, above him were those murderous florescent lights, around him was that unbearable lair-like scent, and mainly there was Tacitus, because mainly there were Caesar, and Cicero, but how did his boss end up getting to them because women were being raped, well, women have been raped at other times too, and because vandals have been smashing up this and that, vandals smashed up this and that at other times too; what does that have to do with these writers here in the basement, he posed the question, but mainly what does this have to do with Tacitus or Caesar or even more so with Cicero, it really boggles my mind, he sat down at his desk, pulled out the *Annals*, adjusted his enormous Trade Union Social Insurance eyeglasses, then he opened the first book at chapter 28, and bending his head deeply over the first line, continued his reading.

Somehow everything here is falling apart, he wrote to the parish bishop, the connections can no longer be perceived, namely, in the sense of how all this has been able to persist until now, although now it truly isn't persisting, one hears of various horrific events, but things are no longer certain, it isn't certain that these events have really occurred, as each of these reports is so horrific, it is difficult to grant them credibility, there is nothing to back them up, as our parish members are not speaking from their own experience, but passing on what they've heard from others, and the ones who really could speak are silent; this morning, for example, a man, a woman, and two children came to mass; their respective mother, mother-in-law, and grandmother was the alleged victim of a rape before she was murdered—and I emphasize the word alleged—but they made no mention of this; when, following the ceremony I talked with them, I knew the rumors people had been spreading about this case, but they only said their respective mother, mother-in-law, and, with regard to their children, their grandmother, had not been a believer, and that's why they were here this morning, but then they said nothing, they just sat down across from me, answering not even one of my questions, they were visibly still in shock, so as you would expect, Your Excellency, I didn't torture them, but let them go with a blessing; but then a similar thing occurred with that poor unfortunate who visits the local adornment of our parish only on the more important holidays, more precisely he was wheeled in among the pews, and now the report is being spread that his daughter as well fell victim to that same violent act, his daughter who until now has taken care of him, and thanks to the good offices of whom this poor soul was able to attend the aforementioned more important ecclesiastic celebrations in our church in his wheelchair; I sought him out as well, because I was afraid the rumor was true, and that I might find him left on his own, and so it was—my daughter is in the Hospital, he yelled through the door when I rang the buzzer, and he wasn't inclined to say more than this, perhaps he didn't understand or realize what had happened, as I myself hardly knew, and he wouldn't let me in, or perhaps he couldn't let me in through the door, so I entrusted him to one of the members of our parish residing close by, who promised that inasmuch as he could, he would take care of him, and so on, Your Excellency, the news reports, each more horrific than the last, reach us here at the parish, and not only are they horrific but they make no sense, and please permit me to explain this in a more adequate manner, as somehow the events serving as the basis of the reports, regardless of whether they are hearsay or actual events, lack any sort of coherence in and of themselves, and what is perhaps a bit less surprising is that there is no kind of intelligible connection whatsoever between them—how shall I explain this, perhaps via an example if you would permit me, because just imagine, Very Reverend Bishop, if we remain for a moment with the hearsay and take only three cases from among the many: in the exquisite Romanian Orthodox Church on Maróti Square, someone, around midnight, sawed off the iron bar holding up the bell, and the bell broke through the tower's ceiling; everything burst asunder as it came crashing down, the baptismal font near the entrance to the church was smashed apart, because the Orthodox church is more or less in the same position as us, Most Rev. Bishop; or to take another case: the day before yesterday, in the morning, state employees found the rail tracks completely torn up on the route leading to Békéscaba—if the news is true—as if some kind of huge machine or (as chatterboxes claim) some kind of enormous monster had simply ripped up these tracks and thrown them all around; or, what is even more frightening, Most Rev. Bishop, is that in the Hospital there are only patients now, because all the doctors and the nurses—with the exception of two nurses who, of course, are faithful believers in our Sacred Mother Church—have departed, and I cannot even conceive of this with a mind that remains intact, but they have left their patients behind, and these patients are now entrusted to these two nurses; all this isn't merely hearsay, because this morning I heard it with my own ears from one of the affected persons himself, who, greatly fearing—as he put it—everything that is occurring here, quickly dashed into our church for a quick prayer to Christ our Lord, and he met up with us and told us about this, but he was so troubled, so distraught, and he trembled so much, that I could hardly doubt that every single one of his words was true; and in a similar fashion, our parish is full of reports that in recent days people have been disappearing, giving news neither to their own families nor anyone else of where they are going and why, and—Your Excellency, forgive me for writing this, I myself tremble at the thought that even one report from these terrifying dispatches may be true, I only pray to the Lord every blessed day, every blessed noon, and every blessed evening before the empty pews of our empty church, and I pray at night as well, incessantly—for the last three days sleep has eluded me, I only keep vigil and I pray for the souls who are entrusted into our care, and I can do nothing else but pray, for how could I do anything else than to state that everything here is plunging unimpeded toward something much worse—I do not give myself over to faintheartedness, Very Rev. Bishop, but I must confess that I too am afraid, as are the other believers and errant souls here, I am afraid, because I don't know what is happening to us, for still my prayer is against the deeds of this thing, even if I don't even know what it is, I beg you to respond to me, Most Rev. Bishop, and tell me what to do, not for my own sake but for the sake of our believers, for the sake of every cherished member of our congregation, what should I do, Your Excellency, so they shall fear no longer, and so that I shall not fear, so that we may offer them consolation, and I too may receive such consolation, my dear Bishop, I ask you to please respond to my letter, as quickly as you can. Dated at such and such a time, at such and such a location.

He was only here at the station temporarily, he explained, terrified; Lajos and his shift-mate had asked him while they were away to pop in and look after things, he had nothing, but really nothing—in the whole God-given world—nothing to do with this gas pump, nothing to do with even the gas at all, this whole domain of gas as it was was completely alien to him, he'd gotten mixed up in this whole thing by chance, like Pontius Pilate in the Credo, and in addition he didn't even know why, because there was no gas here, to his knowledge not even a single liter, well of course they'd told him that if somebody came from the Police Station, or City Hall, or from some public institution, or . . . there was actually a list here somewhere, if they wanted to see it—he could pull it out right away—of the people he was supposed to supply from the so-called security reserves, namely with diesel, but they should understand that he had nothing to do with any of this, he was just a simple hang-gliding school director, and nothing more, and he would immediately add that as for the hang-gliding school, it had long since ceased to exist, it was closed, the doors shut, the hang gliders were in the hangar, namely the two machines he possessed, but those were already completely ruined, he was certain of that, because a delicate machine like that can't take being stuck somewhere in a hangar, it needs to be taken care of, not just dumped there in a hangar like shit that a dog's left behind, he, only he, went out there, when he was able to get hold of some fuel, but he wasn't able to get hold of it anymore because there wasn't any left, and he'd been banned, along with his whole gliding school, from the gas pumps here, as if towing his two lovely little machines demanded so much fuel, but no, he didn't need so much for the gliders, but for his motorbike, because that's how he got to his gliding school beyond Csabai Road below Békéscsaba, and his name definitely wasn't on that list—if they wanted to see it, he would get it right away—just for a few liters for his motorbike, no, they didn't give him permission, so he "closed the shutters," as the expression went, and ever since then, he was telling them sincerely now, he'd been officially on sick leave on the basis of psychological symptoms, because he couldn't go on like this without his hang-gliding school, he'd founded it, he'd scrimped and saved to start it, he'd run it, he'd organized whatever had been needed to create this gliding school, so it was no surprise that when the authorities had made him close the shutters, his life went to pieces, and ever since then he'd been one big bag of ailments and that's certainly why he'd been asked to pop in temporarily to replace the gas station attendant, he lived quite nearby, he could show them if they wanted to see where it was, just one room with a kitchen, that was enough, he didn't need a family, he respected those who had families, but his gliding school had been everything to him, and now he had nothing at all, and he had nothing to do with this gas pump, if they wanted, he would repeat this just as many times as they wished, and he had no idea how much diesel was here in this he-didn't-even-know-what-it-was-called, but he could show them how it worked, if they wanted, because it was outside to the left, there were these two iron discs which had to be opened—here's the key, look, here's both keys, because each has its own key, and there's this cover on it, that opens up with its own key, here it is, look—he could show them how it worked, you just had to pull out, from behind, this kind of thick worm-like hose, he could show them if they wanted, then you had to screw the end to the hole of this oil cistern, or whatever you call that thing on the top, they'd just happened to show him how the whole thing works, then you turned a lever (or whatever it was) and then out flowed the juice, because the pump was built into both of them, it worked automatically, you didn't have to do anything, you just let it do its job, and that was it, that was the whole thing, and if necessary he could explain how it worked in even more detail, if only they would stop hitting him, his nose, his mouth—look—they were covered in blood already, well, what's the use of this, he asked, what was the use, he'd tell them everything himself for just as long as he could keep on talking.

Something's not right here, brothers, he said to them in the Biker Bar, Totó, J.T., Dódi, I can count on you, yes? and the others as well? because the damned situation is that we are retreating, by which I mean—and I hope you understand this—that we're all going to go out nicely to the courtyard, get on our machines, and quietly, three by three, just as quietly as we are able, we're all going home, and at home everyone will seek out the most hidden corner possible, and retreat into that corner and huddle there, because that's the deal, my brothers, because the times will always tell you what you have to do, and now they're telling us this: we must hide, because it isn't clear what's coming along next, and if this is the situation, namely, that it isn't completely clear, then we have to retreat, that's what Sun Tzu writes, my brothers, and that's what my ancient Hungarian Turul instinct within me is saying as well, and that's how it was with our sacred ancestors when they sensed that great danger was approaching, then they acted in wisdom, do you understand, in wisdom, not like cowards, but wisely, because there is a huge, but a really huge difference between a wise decision and a cowardly decision, and now I say that we must decide, wisely and not helter-skelter, namely to not leave the city, not to back down like cowards, but to ride home nicely and quietly, because this is a wise choice, as the need for us might arise at any given moment, but until that happens, we must await the signal at home, do you understand, so let everyone finish up his beer, pay the tab, and then, as I said, in a jiffy, we'll ride home all nice and quiet; and with that he turned away from the others, and tried to catch the gaze of the bartender, he motioned him over, but as he paid, he asked him softly, so the brothers wouldn't hear: well, where do we stand, but the bartender just pursed his mouth and said: we're closing down too, because there's no more beer, what you just drank was the last—he spoke just as quietly as the Leader—I'm not happy with things here either, and I'm also doing what you just said, I'm getting the hell out of here because I don't like what's going on, because nothing at all is going on, or even still, I'm fed up with both these things, I don't like to fight kung fu in the dark, because I'm not as good at it as Bruce Lee, you know that if he shows up, then I'll stand behind him, but without him nothing, you understand, Leader, nothing, I'm closing the register, putting away the proceeds, and that's it, I'm leaving, and pulling down the gate, lock and key, get it, and then I'll be gone, no one's going to see me anymore, this whole place can go to hell; because I don't like it in the dark, I never did, this isn't karate, Leader, this is some kind of phantom game, and I don't like theater, I never liked it—somebody's playing with us here, and something's telling me it's a game where we can only lose, and I'm no black belt, who . . . do you get it, so I'm outta here; well, here's the bill, you pay up, Leader, and then let's get our asses outta this dump, I'm saying the exact same thing as you. That'll be six thousand five hundred even.

How many victims were there, he asked, and he was asking again, and of course, he had the patience, how the hell wouldn't he?—and he began to bang his hat down on the table, that's why he was here, just so he could patiently wait until someone ... did they understand? ... until someone among them would be capable of understanding what they were being asked, so he repeated the question: was anyone able to tell him exactly—he pursed his lips sarcastically, but his mouth still trembled from agitation—exactly how many fresh victims there were; twelve, the corporal repeated, pulling himself up to attention, at which the sergeant on duty immediately interrupted, saying fourteen, well, make up your minds, I've got the patience, I can sit here and listen to you both until the end of time, and the Police Chief's face was red, and the part in his hair was crooked; I'm sitting here at my desk—bring me a coffee—and I'm waiting to hear how many; but neither of them dared to open their mouths, the corporal looked at the sergeant, the sergeant looked at the corporal, so, the Police Chief leaned back in his chair; well, there's the woman from Semmelweis Road, there's the man who was helping out at the gas station, there's the woman in the Hospital who came from the travel agency ... because she died, then there's the Mayor's wife from Damjanich Road, then there's the library director, three doctors from the train station, and that makes—said the corporal, and a bead of sweat began to drip down his forehead—that makes eight so far, then there's Tóni the postman, the two children who escaped from the Orphanage, and then the two foreigners from the Komló Hotel, so there are thirteen victims in all, sir, and there's also—the sergeant now snapped to attention, clasping his two hands together— the stationmaster and his family, namely the two children, and altogether, he said, that makes sixteen, he hadn't heard about the stationmaster, the corporal reported, because he hadn't received a report, that's because I didn't write one yet, the sergeant replied, at ease, said the Police Chief, and he looked at one, then the other—

motives? he asked, but he didn't expect a reply—this was written all over his face—so the two policemen didn't even attempt to answer the question, as the Police Chief had asked mechanically, from habit, because all the same he knew that there were no motives here, these people had been murdered using completely different methods, and there was nothing in common between them, nothing in the whole God-given world, only that these were almost all local people, really, it boggled his mind, the Police Chief explained later on to the cadet, whom he had summoned from the basement, because he was the only one in the entire Police Station whom he thoroughly trusted, and with whom, moreover, he was able to discuss various matters, and the one single reason was because the cadet read, more specifically—as the Police Chief continually repeated to his subordinates—he read in Latin, really, with those huge eyeglasses of his, down there in the basement, when nobody had gone down there with some kind of request, because then he'd to get up, find the relevant data in the computer database, then get up and go over to the relevant shelf, find the file in question, hand it over, handle the paperwork, which of course didn't take too long, and already he was cracking open a book, maybe one of his old favorites, or maybe a new one which he had just gotten from the secondhand bookshop in Békéscsaba, with the exception of the last few months, because in these past few months he'd hardly gone over to Csaba, because the trains were running on completely irregular schedules, a person never knew when he'd be able to get back, and for the past few days there hadn't been any transportation service at all, there was no way out of here, just as there was no way here from outside, as if the outer world had completely disappeared, he established, so he stayed in place and made do with what he had, because, as a matter of fact, he didn't have too much cause for complaint: he had spent everything that he'd been able to save from his paycheck for his entire life up until now on books, that's why he had almost everything that he could ever desire, a nearly complete collection of the Ancient Classics, as he called his little library at home—he'd been collecting the Greeks for a while, but just halfheartedly; instead he'd say (when on certain occasions the Police Chief turned to these private themes with him) that a volume of Homer or a Thucydides or a Xenophon had just crept in there somehow, but his fundamentally three great favorites—Cicero, Caesar, and Tacitus—were the ones he could read endlessly, and he did read them endlessly, but he hadn't found anything, he now reported, as he had once again been summoned to the boss's office, he'd tried to read them from *that* viewpoint as the Police Chief had requested, but nothing, he had found no kind of textual passage that could be interpreted as relevant to the cases at hand—these aren't cases, the Police Chief interrupted in rage, this is an interrelated sequence of events, there must be some connection here, but I just can't see what the hell it could be; in general the Police Chief avoided impolite words, moreover he demanded of his subordinates that they, too, avoid such language at the Police Station, because, as he always explained, he wanted to see a civilian-friendly, or how should he put it, a civic-oriented internal security organization, and there was no room for words like fuck or cock, and so on, so that the usage of these words now permitted one to conclude—and the cadet did conclude—that the Police Chief was starting to lose it, because visibly he didn't know what to do with this sequence of events, as he designated these incidents, the cadet just looked at him with his hair disheveled on the crown of his head, what was he supposed to say now, he just stood there, shifting his weight from one foot to the other, actually not too soldierlike, but the Police Chief overlooked it, because he believed that at such times the cadet was thinking, however, he wasn't thinking, he was flustered because he didn't know what to say, and just then the sergeant on duty stepped into the room, stood at attention, his hand flying up to his cap in a salute, and said: I report the number to be twenty-four, sir.

There's someone here, Uncle Pista, the cobbler from the Greater Romanian Quarter, who cleaned up the church, said to him, alarmed, in the parish house, and then he opened the doors wide, and an older, elegant gentleman stepped into the room, inclined his head toward him slightly, and said: Reverend Father, my name is —, and I'm looking for the grave where supposedly my beloved relative, Baron Béla Wenckheim, was recently interred, and he held a large bouquet of fresh-cut flowers in his hands, and the priest was so confused that his first thought was: where did this person get such a huge bouquet of fresh-cut flowers, to get flowers like that these days, that was simply impossible in their city, and especially roses at this time of year— that's what first came to his mind as he offered the gentleman, clearly very nervous for some reason, a place to sit down; the man, though, brushed his invitation aside, he didn't in any way wish to cause affront, but he was here on a very urgent matter, which meant that he truly had no time to lose, his only wish was to visit the grave and place upon it a missive, namely this bouquet of flowers, from the family, and then he had to travel back to Vienna where he had just come from—Vienna? the priest asked in surprise—yes, he'd just come from Vienna, and he was going straight back there, if someone could be so kind as to show him to the gravesite, but do please sit down for a moment, the priest urged him, like someone who had suddenly regained his senses, wouldn't his visitor sit down for just a moment to hear about the circumstances under which all this had come about—but the man only said, still standing in the doorway: no, no, this truly wasn't necessary, he truly would have appreciated being able to sit down for a moment to hear how everything had happened, but this he couldn't do, as he was truly in a great hurry—so there was nothing else to do, the priest quickly threw on the robes he wore in church, he didn't need his umbrella, because since yesterday, the rain had completely stopped, there was only the wind blowing, a very strong wind, which suddenly had dried out everything; so he got into the black limousine in which the visitor had arrived and he took him to the cemetery, but he could hardly bear the pace, because this pace, at his age, was very great, this pace was now dictated by the visitor while he pointed out the way in the cemetery, among the gravestones, there was no more mud, as it had all been dried out by the wind that had arisen so suddenly, so they could hurry to the grave without obstacle; and well, here it is, he said, a little ashamed, because the earth above the grave had never been formed into a mound, when they reached the gravesite, the visitor —facing the grave-cross, which had already fallen over to one side—stopped, bent his head, and remained there motionless; something suggested to the priest that it would perhaps be best if he left the visitor alone, in case he wished to pray; the man stood there facing the cross, holding the large bouquet of roses, his head was deeply bent, and the priest only said very softly—before he hurried away, back to the cemetery entrance—for the gentleman not to worry, they had done right by the Baron, because they had led him, if he might say so, according to the precepts of the Holy Mother Church, into Heaven, in brief—he cleared his throat, definitively leaving the guest to himself—the Baron's funeral had truly been very beautiful.

He poured tea for them, starting from the left: for the taxi driver, then for the homeless, one after the other, and finally for the countless beggar children who'd also sought refuge with him, because they were seeking refuge, and somehow the news had spread that he was able to keep the bad spirits away, and although none of them really believed any of this, they had nowhere else to go—neither the homeless, naturally, nor the beggar children, who always slept here anyway, paying between fifty and twenty forints for a sleeping place, which altogether meant a meter-wide strip for each between two bales of goods on the balcony, the taxi driver somehow knew that the old Chinese man was supposedly some kind of oracle and knew what was going to happen tomorrow and the day after, and at the same time he offered protection, there were those who believed in such things, although he didn't; as the joke went: he didn't believe in superstition, because it was a bad sign, but he thought that he *might as well* come here tonight, he had his phone with him, in the very unlikely event that the mobile networks suddenly began to work, and if somebody wanted to call for a taxi, they could easily get in touch with him here, but that wasn't going to happen, because for more than a few days now, nobody had dared to go out onto the streets even in a car, but the biggest joke about the whole thing—the taxi driver explained to the old man—was that no one had any idea why precisely someone who hadn't heard anything at all—like himself—didn't dare go outside, just as someone who'd heard about some concrete incident also didn't dare go outside; the taxi driver explained the situation to this old Chinese man, who just nodded after almost every single word, but clearly he didn't understand, or in any event it never really emerged if he understood or not, each time, however, that he filled a cup of tea he charged ten forints, and he collected it too, immediately, extending in front of everyone his money box, which was an empty tin fish can, he winked gaily at whoever was just then tossing in the ten-forint coin, then he sat down among them and listened, and the gaiety didn't leave his face for a moment, or rather it was something that resembled gaiety more than anything else, and it reassured everyone present, just as his entire personality had a reassuring effect on those who regularly slept here, such as the beggar children, or those who slept here only occasionally—like one or two of the homeless, if it was already really freezing outside—

the old man spoke only occasionally, but still he created the impression that he was perpetually about to say something, namely that everything would be fine in just a moment, just patience and patience and patience, this was the cure, and sometimes he explained it too in his own language, namely just a little patience, a little patience, and everything would be okay, like someone who says that one plus one makes two, because his mother tongue was made of numbers, and that was why everything that he tried to say corresponded to a mathematical operation at the end of which he always winked at his interlocutor with his right eye, who, just then standing in front of him in alarm, was thinking: this is all I need, for someone to start talking some nonsense about how everything is going to be fine, when we all know that nothing here is getting better, on the contrary, everything is getting worse, moreover much worse, moreover, there is going to be trouble, big trouble, at any moment now; in this way the little old Chinese man offered a refuge like a temple, the children loved him because they understood that mother tongue, in which counting, and within that, addition, were the most important operations; the homeless trusted him—at least up to a certain point, because they had their limits, even now in these difficult times, so if they slept amid the crowded chaos of the countless bundles, bags, boxes, and bales, they only partially fell asleep, remaining half awake even during their deepest dreams, their eyes opened just a mere crack, never losing sight of the old man and what he was doing—they flew like birds up there in the heights, way above up there in the clouds, their arms outspread, happy, entrusting themselves to the soft currents of the breeze, up here, everything above stopped, and down here, everything below stopped, they floated without obstacle, in a peculiarly heavenly space, each one by himself, and there were only the puffy folds of the eiderdown clouds somewhere beneath their arms, there was only the clear, empty blue above their arms, and all around was silence, because there weren't even any birds chirping, only this infinite silence, they just descended and then ascended again, their arms spread wide, as if they would have wished to embrace this emptiness, this heavenly silence, this enormous blueness, granted to them at last—and it was only through the cracks of their eyelids that they saw the old Chinese man take the tea tin into his lap, and, removing the lid and shaking the box from side to side, examine how much tea had been used up this evening.

There were DAFs and MANs and Tatras and Mercedes-Benzes and Scanias and Kenworths and a huge number of Freightliners, but so many that if anyone had been out on the streets after midnight at 1:15 a.m.—no one was—then that person wouldn't have believed his own eyes, because they came down Csabai Road, and they came down Dobozi Road, and they came from the Romanian border, they came from the direction of Eleki Road, from every single direction they came, rumbling, the pneumatic brakes screeching, then the engines revved, then the pneumatic brakes again, they came in a line, one after the other, and within the space of barely an hour the entire city was full of these gigantically enormous fuel carriers, and the whole thing was as if they'd ended up here by mistake, as if they wanted to go someplace completely different, but because of some mistaken GPS signal these innumerable enormous tankers had all ended up here in the middle of the night, because there was some kind of bewilderment in them, as if at a certain point they weren't able to go on any further, and they braked, and once again the brakes screeched and hissed loudly, and they stopped in a row exactly where they were, and that was how they parked, every single truck stopped exactly at that point where it couldn't go on any farther, and no one got out from the driver's seat, and no one peeked out from anywhere to say anything to anyone to impart some meaning to their mistaken arrival here, no, nothing happened, because there came a moment when all the larger streets—Csabai Road, Eleki Road, Dobozi Road, Nagyváradi Road—every, but every single street became full of them, and it seemed as if even more would be coming along, but they wouldn't fit, because all around Lennon's Ditch all the streets in the city center were full of them, and Peace Boulevard was also packed full from one end to the other, as was Göndöcs Garden, Snail Garden, the main thoroughfare, the area around the Great Catholic Church, and the entire Greater Romanian Quarter, the entire German Quarter, the entire Lesser Romanian Quarter, the entire Hungarian Quarter, all the small streets leading to the Castle, every location was jam-packed with them, and after the last pneumatic brakes wheezed their last gasp and they stopped, they really moved no more, and there stood on all of the city streets and squares these infinitely innumerable transport trucks, and everything within them was mute and everything around them was mute, there was no movement anywhere, their headlights were switched off, and then suddenly—as if the entire thing were dependent on a single switch—the entire city was plunged into total darkness, because in that moment the streetlighting, which in any event was only partial and incidental, went out, and there were no lights in the shop windows, the lit advertising signs switched off, and even the beacon that blinked on a rod set up (somewhat from pride) atop the Castle tower—because once upon a time there had been air traffic here—it blinked no more, only the wind roared across the city, turning over everything it could, just this icy wind, it swept again and again among these innumerable transport trucks, but in such a way that every door in every house, every window in every wall, every lamp on the streets along the way trembled, and only these ghastly tankers did not tremble, no, these—faced with the wind that rose against them—didn't even quiver, they just stood there imperturbably, but also aimlessly, stupidly, and monstrously, like some horrific mistake.

# *DOM*

# WHOEVER HID AWAY

It would have been hard to say what was more shocking for them when they woke up the next morning: was it that the city was full of tankers, down to the very last street wherever they had been able to squeeze in, or was it that when it had grown completely light outside, the tankers just stood next to and behind each other in dense columns, and nothing was happening, namely, not a single one of them moved, the hours went by, and nothing; and for a long time no one dared set foot outside, people just tried to consider—although it was nearly impossible to do so with an intact mind—*what this was* and so on, not daring to step outside, because this was, as it were, the culmination (or so it seemed at first glance) of what had been happening these past days, all of them were already living deep inside the fear that if they went outside they'd be the next to be murdered, raped, harassed, and disappeared without a single trace, so no one, not a single dweller of that town, dared go outside, they just cowered behind their windows, peeking out from between the curtains to see what was going on out there, so it would be difficult to explain why they ended up going outside anyway, it wasn't on the basis of it-doesn't-matter-anymore, that was certain, they weren't yet broken enough for that, but it was precisely because of the fear, when they saw that one of the town residents had appeared out there outside—and the reason was precisely because he was so afraid—then the second one went out too, and because there were already two of them out there, the third one went, prompted by fear as well, and so it continued, the fourth one came out, then the fifth, and so on, and later on, after ten a.m., half the city was out there milling among the tankers, they walked around them; but either they couldn't see anything through the tinted windshields, or, if they climbed up the step next to the driver's seat, which a few of them dared to do, and looked inside, they only saw an unknown person, in whom they found no notable characteristics, sitting at the steering wheel; they waved to him, signaling: so, what's going on here, and the driver in question slowly turned his head, and just looked at them with a questioning gaze, as if he too were asking: so, what's going on here—and at noon everything was exactly the same, and in the afternoon too, the tankers stood there, taking up all the available streets and squares; and toward the end of the afternoon, those residents of the city that had been driven out of their houses by fear wanted to see the tankers from an even closer angle, and to see if perhaps they'd brought something, or what they were doing here, so there was a lot of movement in between the tankers in the unceasingly icy wind lashing back and forth, there were those who went all the way from the Greater Romanian Quarter to the Lesser Old Romanian Quarter, and there were those who went from Csókos Road all the way to the Elek turnoff to see if they could figure out what these trucks were looking for here, what they wanted, and mainly, what they were waiting for here, but they didn't understand, and especially no one understood—because it was really strange—that there were no representatives whatsoever out on the streets from any of the official institutions, or any sort of official person, the Mayor was nowhere to be seen, neither was the Deputy Mayor or the chief secretary, there was no one from Municipal Utility Services, moreover there wasn't even anyone from the Police Station, whoever went along in that direction on Peace Boulevard saw the doors were locked, there was no movement in front of the building or within, it looked completely deserted, there weren't even any fluorescent lights on inside, which usually you could see even by day, nothing, it was silent, as if there wasn't even one policeman left in the building, and in relation to this they also perceived, with slightly less comprehension, that the Local Force was also nowhere to be seen; they just crept around until twilight, but were none the wiser, and nothing moved, so that when it began to really get dark—as not a single citizen wished to greet complete darkness out there on the streets—the very last city resident slowly but surely disappeared, locking the door to his own dwelling securely, and there were those who, once inside, feeling themselves to be now within the security of their own home, immediately stood by the window, and continued to watch the tankers through a gap in the curtains, because not only was it incomprehensible to try to envisage what these countless fuel trucks, as they called them, were looking for here, but it was also as if it would really be best for them not to know why they were here, because it was at that point that they began to really think about how this whole thing was utterly absurd, it was impossible to imagine that so many tankers even existed, let alone that they could trundle in from somewhere in the space of one evening, and, as one could say, occupy the city, and then, after they'd all trundled in, that nothing would happen for an entire day, nothing, but nothing at all—these tankers just stood there next to each other and behind each other in dense columns, and the drivers were doing nothing, weren't saying anything, giving no sign whatsoever that they, the residents of the city, were of any significance at all, that was the general opinion—namely, the opinion of everyone individually, but unanimously, they agreed that these drivers were waiting for something, and that's why they didn't get out of their trucks, they just sat behind the steering wheel, not even eating anything, they just all kept their hands on the steering wheel, as if waiting for some sign that could arrive at any moment, and that was why they never even let go of the steering wheel, they just sat there, looking straight ahead, their hands on the steering wheel, and they waited—and so it was no wonder that fear didn't really leave the residents of the city, as they stared yet for a while from behind their curtains, at the section of the street that their windows overlooked, the fear didn't leave them, it just grew, and now they saw the entire incident as being decisively phantomlike, as if they had somehow ended up in some frightening fairy tale which could only end badly. But everything has its own limits, including physical endurance, so that sometime that evening between nine p.m. and midnight at the very latest, they all succumbed to exhaustion behind the curtains, they weren't used to staying up so late, their lower backs and legs and knees began to ache, their eyelids began to close and their heads began to droop, in brief not a single resident of the city could hold out after a while, and finally, in each and every one of them the decision arose: there was nothing left to do, they had to lie down and go to sleep, because there was nothing else to do anyway, the next morning they would see what this whole thing was, because they all trusted that this was no ghost story—there were no such thing as ghost stories—there was only reality, the real world, in which, namely, they could rightly expect that, however appalling, some kind of explanation would be provided for all this, tomorrow, they thought, completely worn out by their anxiety and by their exhaustion and primed for sleep—there were those who didn't even brush their teeth, they just collapsed into bed as they were, and they slept until the next morning. Tomorrow, they thought, and they fell into dreaming with enormous velocity, tomorrow everything will obviously be explained.

Some of them got up before it grew light outside, awakening as if to an indistinct signal, but there were also those who later confessed that they had not slept so well and deeply for years, without any disturbances, without any interruptions, the drool seeping out of their mouths, but regardless of who woke up when, when they all woke up, of course the first thing that came into their minds was yesterday, and the first path of the day led to their windows, and not only did they try to make out what was going on down there in the streets from between the gap in their curtains, but suddenly they yanked the curtains apart, and there were even those who immediately opened their windows and leaned out, and then they all saw the same thing: the streets were completely empty—and they quickly got dressed, and now, their fear almost gone, they went outside, and they began to wander here and there in the neighborhood, but they were forced to believe their eyes, in vain did they rub them, massage them, as if they didn't want to believe their eyes, but these eyes informed them that all the tankers had completely disappeared, not only from their street, but from every street, no longer were the tankers standing next to each other and behind each other in dense columns, the streets resounded with emptiness all around the Castle and in the Greater Romanian Quarter, they rang with emptiness in Krinolin and from the direction of the border crossings on both sides, they rang with emptiness in the Greater Hungarian Quarter and on Peace Boulevard, and in the old German Quarter and in the Lesser Romanian Quarter and around the train station and on Csókos Road, and beyond Csókos Road, all along Nagyváradi Road, on both sides—they stared, astonished, because if it had been the height of absurdity yesterday to see the city completely jam-packed with these columns of tankers, then today, it was an even greater absurdity to see that these same tankers had—completely unnoticed by them—left the city, they wandered all around, and nothing nowhere, there wasn't a single trace of them, not even one or two had remained behind, moreover there wasn't even a single trace of the fact that they had stood there just yesterday—it was a chimera, said the Headmaster to Auntie Ibolyka, who were the first ones outside among the houses of the city center after waking up early; nightmarish, the carpenter and his neighbors looked at each other, standing on Erdélyi Sándor Street; I just can't believe my own eyes, the families dressed in mourning said to each other in completely subdued tones, they had thought that nothing would dislocate them from their grief for a very long time to come, and yet this had dislocated them yesterday, as well as today, mainly, people gaped at each other, as if waiting for someone else to supply an explanation, they went up, they went down, they went to neighborhoods they hadn't been to for years, but everywhere they just encountered puzzled gazes in the deserted city, so that at around eight a.m., when really many residents were out on the streets, their shock turned to anger, because somebody really should have issued a statement, as the Headmaster formulated it, his gaze darkened, this, if you please, is unacceptable, he said in general to the people standing around him, there are *things happening* here, and we, who nonetheless are the citizens of the city, never received any information, this, I tell you, is a violation of the contract of civic cooperation in the promise of which our elected officials have been chosen, we demand an explanation, he formulated in decisive tones, a thought which was completed by the Chief Editor of the only still-functioning newspaper, who had just stumbled into the group, who said: this is altogether the story of the past two days, but what has to be considered are all the similar events of the past ten or even the past twenty-five years when we were left without any explanation, and because of this, I—he said, drawing closer to the Headmaster—I am of the opinion that the elected officials of the city must resign today and immediately, yes, that's right, the people standing around cried out, and hearing their own voices, but in unison, made them courageous, and they began to look around, at first just decisively, but after a minute they were ever more resolved; this happened in other locations as well, for example in front of Stréber's Butchers, where at first they sought an explanation that would help them to feel in control of the events of yesterday and today, the unfortunate events, said one, moreover, I would add, another person added, the *extraordinarily* unfortunate events, yes, that's right, everyone standing around grumbled in approval, and the first one now spoke again: because if they were to disregard the fact that in yesterday's, but particularly in today's occurrences—he called them "occurrences," a designation which visibly met with everyone's approval in the group—there was, and there is—he truly liked this phrase, "there was, and there is"—something which more than anything else reminded him of the beginning of a horror movie, and yet, he continued, he in no way thought this was going on here, he saw the matter in a much more practical light, by which he didn't mean to deny that he was (and he wasn't afraid to pronounce this word) *frightened* by what had been going on recently, but especially yesterday; and then how those tankers vanished without a single trace, he didn't deny that, he, however, did deny that any one of the town officials had given them precise instructions; I just don't know—another person interrupted—where the people are who are responsible for all of this, because there's no question that someone is responsible; moreover, a third person spoke in front of Stréber's Butchers, I think someone must take direct responsibility for the fact that we were standing here yesterday like stupid cows in the Slaughterhouse, and we waited, but we waited in vain, and today we're standing here too like those stupid cows, and where was the person responsible for all this, he would ask, the first speaker now asked again, why is it that these so-called civic leaders, if he could put it that way, only show up when they have to cut some ribbon, speak at some celebration, could someone tell him why it is that all of these so-called civic leaders have vanished into thin air, well, why, the second one spoke up again, and he was visibly enraged, because they've all gone and shat themselves, if you'll all please forgive me for this perhaps excessively frank formulation, but I—he pointed at himself, and one could see just how much he too was shitting himself— I'm inclined to frankly say that this is an *opprobrium,* and most of the people in the group began to nod as one person, mainly because they weren't exactly sure of the meaning of "opprobrium," however, it seemed that the conviction formed very speedily that they wanted the responsible parties to be held accountable, and they wanted information—accountability and information—and this became the general sentiment across the entire city, because no matter how difficult it was to acknowledge how thoroughly eerie the previous day's events had been, what had happened today—apart from the initial shock of the morning—had (taking everything into account) somehow been the onset of calm, because the empty streets had, so to speak, given them back their own city; the sudden appearance and oozing away of the tankers, along with their drivers, in contrast with the nightmarish apparition they'd presented at first, were now, in the eyes of the city's residents, the emblem of a return to normal life, really as if—and this included their peculiar arrival, their strange occupation of the city, and their sudden evaporation—as if normality had returned, both factually and contingently, and they began to think about the matter along these lines: well, and so what if the tankers and what happened wasn't the announcement of some definitive bad ending, but, what if they came in order to rescue them? it's possible, each one thought to himself, hiding his view before the others, it's possible to think that in fact what they had been faced with here was the first operational phase of a *rescue*, only they didn't know how to interpret it, so they hypothesized the presence of a *higher concern* in the fiendish admixture of unabated fear and the absence of any possible coherence —they all sensed that, even those who, whether in Krinolin, or the immediate vicinity of the Great Catholic Church, demanded the speediest and most exhaustive of explanations.

It had gotten stuck other times too, but Dóra had always been able to fix it, it's true that she always had to struggle for a while if it broke down, but what was he supposed to do with it now that he was alone, he thought despairingly, and although he felt utterly exhausted, he tried again, with his healthy left hand, somehow to disengage the brake handle on the right-hand side, because it had gotten stuck, but he couldn't, and really, it was already an unbelievably long time, and he really had to do something now, it couldn't stay like this, and all this had happened because yesterday morning, he hadn't paid close enough attention when he had rolled his wheelchair down the downward-sloping floor in order to get a jar of apple preserves from the sideboard shelf, but unfortunately he had been thinking of something else, wondering just at that moment—as he was now as well—why Dóra hadn't come home that evening, and while he was wondering about this, his wheelchair had accelerated, and he wasn't able to bring it to a halt before reaching the wall, and of course he ended up pulling on the brake handle too late, and with too much strength, so that it broke and got stuck, it locked into place, and for the love of God he couldn't budge it a single inch, so that he just wondered where she could be, and he began with the fact that she hadn't come home from the office at the usual time, then not even that night, and not even today, for the entire day, she hadn't come home, the second day of her absence was drawing to a close, and in a moment—he squinted sideways up at the clock on the sideboard—it would be six o'clock in the evening, had she by any chance gone to see Auntie Piroska in Kötegyán, that was, after all, a possibility, but no, it wasn't possible that his Dóra, who was so, but so prudent, would have gone off like that, impossible, he shook his head at the idea, that she would leave him alone like this for two days without any provisions, nothing to eat or drink; of course, he brooded, it was possible that she'd thought he would take care of these things himself, because he had always been able to do so if he needed something, and Dóra had reconstructed the entire apartment years ago, when she had insisted on him using a wheelchair: she had had built, into almost every room, a gently yet decisively sloping floor, one half of which inclined upward to the middle of the room, and on the other side, going toward the doorway, the floor sloped downward, so if he happened to be alone—because Dóra, at that time, had finally begun working in the travel agency—he could, with the minimum of exertion, reach everything he needed in the apartment, he practically only had to touch the wheels of his wheelchair and he was already rolling over to where he needed to be, because his daughter, that Dóra, had always been a quick-witted child, remaining so attentive even until today; she'd nearly cleared away all the difficulties for him when he had to start sitting in this wheelchair, with which otherwise there had never been any frequent problems, just a few minor details, the wheel lock or the brakes sometimes, which, concerning this last, caused problems for Dóra as well, but she was always able to fix it, never having to call a repairman, she just got out her tool chest, took something out, and she just tapped away at it, she twisted and tightened that blasted brake-plate or that rotten brake lever, or whatever it was that was broken, until at the end she emerged triumphant, he could never praise enough how, but just how efficient she was, well, but neither of them had ever imagined that one day he'd have to try to figure out all of this himself, and he certainly hadn't been able to figure it out for two days now, so that when it first became clear that it wasn't working, he stopped struggling with it, deciding not to injure his good arm by pulling and pulling at that rotten lever, deciding instead to wait for Dóra, because she'd be getting home any moment now, fine, nothing like this had ever happened before, he had thought to himself yesterday morning, after the first night, but there was surely an explanation for this, it was obvious that she'd had to travel somewhere for some exceptional reason, maybe she had gone to greet a group of Chinese tourists, and there'd been no time to notify him, because he took it as certain that she had had to travel somewhere, just as he took it as certain that he hadn't counted, just as Dóra hadn't, on her not getting home in time, well, even then she couldn't have thought that there would be a problem with him being at home by himself, as there'd never been any problems before, only now, exactly now, this exceptional occurrence had come about with her having to travel, and moreover for two days; he gave a yank at the brake handle again, but nothing, and the side of his body that he was using to keep his upper torso away from the wall grew numb again; he'd bumped straight into the wall when this lousy wheelchair had started rolling too fast down the gently sloping floor that led from the middle of the kitchen, and it led him exactly to the wall, right next to the sideboard—supporting himself with his good hand, he tried to raise the side of his buttocks that had grown numb, as he couldn't bear sitting on it any longer, and he held himself in that position while he could so the blood circulation would return to his muscles, then he lowered himself back down, but he couldn't even turn his head properly, because he had rolled over to a most unfortunate point, right into the wall next to the sideboard, so that his body was completely pressed, or you could almost say smeared against the wall, and no matter how he tried to turn his head, his neck kept jutting out at an uncomfortable angle; he continually had to change the position of his head, so that he was looking either at the edge of the sideboard just a few centimeters away, or at the window frame that gave out onto the staircase a few meters away, I can't even believe it, he said to himself, it was impossible to even imagine that a person could get stuck here in such a hopeless manner, unable to turn either out, or in, to one side, or to the other, with the two turning wheels, the wheelchair had somehow gotten stuck between the sideboard and the wall, so that even for the love of God it didn't want to move out of here, of course it was possible that he was just an exceptionally clumsy fellow, not at all like his Dóra, she was really going to have a good laugh when they sat down together at the table, and he'd get his dinner, and they would really laugh at this event, of course that'll happen, he thought, and he calmed down a bit, it was just that he unceasingly felt himself to be extremely weary, because of course he hadn't been able to sleep, especially not like this, he remained perpetually awake, and it took some time before he was able to grasp fully this place where he was trying to fall asleep, and just what his position here was, imprisoned between the sideboard and the wall, he felt the whole thing to be so absurd that for a long time he didn't even want to believe that the brakes hadn't simply stopped working, but had given up the ghost definitively, so that for hours on end, he would start up again, after a brief resting period, trying to release the brake, he just pulled and pulled at it, but he pulled in vain, because it wasn't just the fact that he was crushed up against the wall in such an unfortunate fashion that had caused the brake on the right-hand side to jump forward and clamp down onto the wheel, but he was really so, but so unlucky that the other wheel couldn't be moved because of the knock against the wall, somehow it had gotten bent, or at least as much as he could judge from his position of being pushed up against the wall, by turning his body halfway around he could appraise the situation, then, of course, the remote-control button for the wheels wasn't working, and he had also gotten pretty knocked up himself, as he had hit this wall, so now it occurred to him: really, he wouldn't even be able to tell her normally, when she finally got home, what had happened, because to relate such a fateful incident wasn't even possible, to relate how it wasn't enough that he was confined to this wheelchair because of his paralyzed legs and one side of his body—because his left arm had become paralyzed five and a half years ago, along with his torso when he had had the brain hemorrhage—no, this whole condition wasn't enough, but then he had to go rolling, with complete velocity, into the kitchen wall, and exactly when he had been left to himself, this was impossible, and Dóra simply wouldn't believe it when she got home, and once again he yanked at the brake handle, but nothing, of course, the brake-plate just clamped onto the wheel so that he couldn't move it in any direction whatsoever, is there anyone as unlucky on this Earth as myself, he thought, he'd tell her all about it when she finally got home, I'm a pure catastrophe, my little daughter, that's what I'm going to tell her, and that's how he would begin, before he got started on how it all began and how the whole thing had progressed, in any event she couldn't be too far away now, and really—he sighed, as his strength completely waned away—it would be so good if she came home, or if that person who knocked on the door three days ago would knock on the door again, or if at least somebody among the neighbors would knock on the door, because that was also pretty strange, he thought to himself a few times yesterday as well, and today too, there seemed to be no movement in the hallway, he didn't hear the footfall of even a single neighbor to whom he could have called out to try to get into his apartment somehow and liberate him, the whole thing was so troublesome, because this wheelchair in the end had two large wheels with two smaller wheels, and that damned brake had gotten stuck only on one of the big wheels, but well, what could he do if he couldn't even turn the other wheel, because it had gotten completely stuck when he'd bumped into the wall, and the sideboard was exactly where he would have been able to turn out with the wheelchair, this is pure madness, he said to himself for the hundredth time, and this was the second day already, and in a moment it would be evening, it wasn't that he was hungry, he was never hungry, or that he was thirsty, even that wouldn't be so tragic now, but well, he really had to admit to himself after these two days that he was completely incapable of helping himself, so now really, it was time for Dóra to get home already, accordingly he left off for a while trying to pull at the brake handle, better for him to rest, because these two days and two nights, crushed up there between the sideboard and the wall, in this completely ungainly—and now truly desperate—situation, when the mobile networks hadn't been functioning for days, at the very least to be able to hear if Dóra was trying to call him, but of course he wouldn't be able to pick his phone up, because he couldn't roll over to where it was, because that remained inside on the bed and not in his pocket, but well, that didn't matter anyway as it wasn't working, there was no signal, the telephone lay completely mute on the bed, this was now much more than he could bear, now she really had to get home, because she certainly wouldn't leave him all alone now, he had nothing to eat, no water, his mouth had dried out, his forehead and half of his face were bruised, all his muscles were numb, he could no longer sit, nor turn around, and couldn't even somehow turn the chair over with himself in it and crawl to the bed, or to the refrigerator, in a word, nothing, here he was in this state of being pressed up against the wall, in a word she had to get home, she could no longer put it off, no matter what had happened to her, and yes, he turned his head toward the front door, yes, he listened to that general numbed silence here inside and there outside, and it was as if somebody, as if somebody were coming along the hallway. Oh no, he then realized, one of the other tenants had just come from the stairwell and latched the large chain onto his door from inside.

At dawn not a single bird appeared in the trees, because they had already flown far away, the cats disappeared from the cold bottomless depths of the city's dwellings, in the courtyards the dogs were troubled, and tearing themselves away from their chains, they escaped somewhere, and in the settlements on the city's periphery, the chickens and pigs ran around crazily in their sties, not to mention the wild animals in the City Forest as well as in the greenbelt surrounding the city, animals which began to trample all over each other in an insane escape, and it wasn't that they were trying to escape in the same direction, say, to the west, or to the north, but in all directions at once, they would rush off in one direction, then come to a dead halt, and immediately set off in another direction, so they continued to frantically rush back and forth, here and there, as if no direction was any good anymore, although nobody even cared, people had much more important things to deal with than to pay attention to them, so that when the city began to swarm with toads no one even attributed any particular importance, beyond the inconvenience, to them—gigantic, pig-swill-brown toads with pockmarked skin, the devil only knew where they had come from, maybe from nothing, and where had they been living until now? one or another resident of the city glanced at them, they nonetheless did notice as they kicked them out of the way on the sidewalk so they could proceed normally—from where?— maybe from beneath the earth, and yes, this must be the situation, they had come from beneath the earth, they had crept forth from there, and if somebody had been able to recognize them, it would have been clear how crazy these toads were, these lunatic toads had come forth from beneath the earth, as there below, in the bountiful darkness, they had all gone mad, and they had wrenched themselves out of the earth and emerged, at first they began to jump back and forth, who the hell would have thought that so many hideous toads existed beneath the earth, those few residents looked at them, the ones who had even taken upon themselves the effort to do so, kicking them out of the way, but then you couldn't even say anymore that they were proceeding in this or that direction, because on the one hand they weren't proceeding as a unit, but jumping upward insanely, up into the air, as if, as a matter of fact, they weren't even trying to find any direction to go in on the earth, but as if they wanted to go up, upward, into the air, toward the heavens, they jumped in ever larger leaps, they tried to jump ever higher, and of course they weren't able to jump as high as they wished, because that height that they wished to reach was in no way high enough, they threw themselves upward, spinning round the axes of their own bodies, their eyes bulged out, and from time to time they released a yellowish fluid from their bodies, the toads were quickly filling up all of the streets and squares, every street and every square from north to south, from east to west, and by then people were really watching them, horrified, most of them watched from inside, again from behind the curtains, but a few audacious ones who were out walking on the street, toward a now completely incomprehensible goal which nonetheless seemed comprehensible to them, sensed, beneath their feet, the repulsive horde, and if they weren't able to kick them out of the way—by now they couldn't, because there were so many on the sidewalk—then they tried to locate, in this slowly forming contiguous mass, a foot-sized spot where they could step and proceed forward without any larger mishap, but needless to say without success, as they were soon stepping on one or the other of the toads, they slipped and nearly fell, but then regained their balance, then once again they fell, because this balance was already impossible to regain, they crushed one or another toad with the hand that was supporting them, and they stood up, feeling disgusted, wiping their hands off on their own coats, cursing all the while, and they continued on toward that incomprehensible goal that nonetheless seemed comprehensible to them, in brief it was no longer possible not to notice that the city was swarming with toads, and it wasn't possible not to attribute any significance to them, so that if the day had begun in fear, by now they really couldn't find the words to express what they felt seeing all this—they looked at the toads down there, or they tried to keep their balance among them, and everyone thought of the future, thinking what will come of this, and in general: what *will happen*, still, it would have been better if they thought only of that moment, the moment that had now begun on their behalf, because it had already drawn them into itself, surrounded them, encircled them, it crushed their bodies—and there was no release anymore.

This was the hardest—to decide to send home the entire staff, but there were no other possibilities, he'd thought about everything, deliberated about everything, he stood in the doorway of his office, which was in point of fact just a glass coop in the hall-like space on that floor, he stood there, and looked at his people, then he thought of the staff who were one floor down, taking them into consideration as well, then he thought of the staff who worked on the floor above him, and he also took them into consideration, then in his thoughts he surveyed the warehouse, the repair shops, the ammunition depot, and the indoor parking lot, and then he made his decision, he immediately gave out the command, and his people immediately fulfilled it too, and to tell the truth, he was even surprised how every individual policeman left the Police Station within minutes, as if they all had been waiting for this command and already gotten everything ready in advance, but what surprised him most of all was that everyone put on their civilian clothes before they left the building, accordingly, he understood: they knew, every single one of his people knew that the game was up for the Central Police Station, and it was up for him too, and now he could sit here like the captain of a sinking ship, and not as the head of the Police Station any longer, because what could he write to the county commanding officers, there was no postal service, the patrol officers on motorcycles who handled deliveries had disappeared without a trace, and he couldn't call the main office, what main office? and on what line? because for days now nothing had been working normally, neither telephone nor internet, nothing, the outside world had disappeared, or rather it was as if because of the same kind of fears, all the neighborhoods, cities, and counties of the country had isolated themselves from the world, he tried sending a text message, he tried email, he tried the Tetra, he tried every possible means of communication, but no reply came from anywhere; sometimes he had the feeling that they heard him, and they knew that somebody was calling, that he was trying to reach them, but they didn't want to know about him—there was just a little crackling noise and the line broke off, the texts weren't received, the emails all came back, so that he was already thinking that he would send another patrol officer, for example to Csaba, and finally he would have gone himself, but, on the one hand, all the patrol officers had disappeared, and on the other, there was no more fuel in the remaining police cars, he didn't even dare to think closely about the reasons why, in brief no matter how he attempted to connect with the world, this attempt ended in failure, and from this point on every kind of absurdity began to seem possible; he had no idea what decision had been made and by which commander, but it seemed conceivable to him that all of the police stations of the entire country, hiding this fact from each other, had, at the very latest today in the afternoon, given the same command as he, this was not a retreat, he determined bitterly, this was an unprecedented defeat, a desertion, but he had to face the fact that it was possible that everyone in the country was in the same position as himself, but what was certain was that his city, this one here—no matter what else was going on—had been left to itself, namely he and the entire community here had "become severed" from the outside world, they were in quarantine, this had become clear to him in the past few hours, and forgetting his earlier train of thought, in which he had considered that the situation might be the same elsewhere, he now determined that the situation elsewhere wasn't of interest to him, what was certain, however, was that here they had been "enclosed," and now he no longer stood by his office door, looking at the empty room, because he couldn't bear that what he had done had been necessary to do, still he couldn't have sent his people out onto the empty streets prepared for military action, what should he tell them, to brandish their revolvers and submachine guns if something came up? but nothing was coming up, he determined, nothing had come up until now, because there was no enemy—he'd realized that this afternoon: something there outside was wreaking havoc or preparing to do so, but he couldn't call it an enemy, because that something was simply nowhere to be found; he'd been raised at home and he'd been trained in the police academy to be prepared, always, in every circumstance, to confront an enemy, but here, if he went outside, and he too began flailing around, he wouldn't find anyone, not a single entity whom he could confront, even on his own, because he *would* have gone after them, even by himself, he wasn't interested in anything else, only battle, and he was good at that, but there was no one to go after, because there was no one, nothing, nowhere—he sat down behind his desk, taking off his cap, adjusting his part on the crown of his head, then he took out a cigarette from the Egyptian pack, and he lit up, and in that moment, as he clicked the flame of the lighter, and he was already about to take a drag on his cigarette, the pressure of a horrific explosion struck down on the room from beyond the doorway, and it lifted up his office, and threw it against the wall of the conference room, but this took no longer than a moment, it didn't allow any recognition of what was going on, because the enormous firestorm caused by the explosion destroyed everything around it while in the middle of that moment, he was consumed, he burned up immediately, as did that charred mass that he'd immediately become, and then, still in the middle of this moment, he wasn't even a charred mass anymore, he was nothing, the fire explosion reached the hallways leading to his office, the stairwells, and the building's floors all at once, as if they'd all ended up in this enormous fiery whirlwind with the entire Police Station building; and this horrific strength lifted up the entire building as if, at the end of that moment, it had wanted to hold it up to the heights, but it was hard to know if this even happened, because the entire thing played out with dreadful speed, and the building had already splayed out, and already it was only incandescent material, something aflame, smitten down by yet another burst of flame creating a whirlwind and storming off above it, so that nothing at all would remain, but nothing, only cinders and flying ashes, then not even smoke, because this fire had no smoke, it only had flames, as its combustion proved to be so, but so flawless.

Stréber's Butcher's burst into flames, the train station building was in flames, as were the Great Catholic Church, the Prekup Well, the Golden Triangle, the City Hall with the City Library and the Slaughterhouse along with the Milk Powder Factory, the Castle, the Thermal Baths, the Orphanage, and the parks and the streets and the gardens, and yet at the same time to describe it like this is misleading, because then you'd think that somebody was saying this, that somebody was narrating, that somebody was putting into words: that at once Stréber's Butcher's burst into flames, the train station building was in flames, as were the Great Catholic Church, the Prekup Well, the Golden Triangle, the City Hall with the City Library and the Slaughterhouse, along with the Milk Powder Factory, the Castle, the Thermal Baths, the Orphanage, and the parks and the streets and the gardens, but no, it wasn't like this, not in this order, because there wasn't any kind of order, because these things didn't burst into flames one after the other, but all exactly in the same moment, because the choice of words creates a problem here, because if there were somebody who could narrate this—as there wasn't—obviously that person would have used such words as "burst into flames," or "caught fire," or "fell prey to the flames," and you could continue with that, only that in this case the predicates of these sentences could in no way suggest any kind of order to these events, whether they wanted to or not, because what happened was that a single, inconceivably huge, a single monumental fire assault smote the city, a fire assault *a great deal larger than the city itself,* so there could be something to talk about, but there was no one left to say what happened, and that would only be the words following mechanically one after the other, as they lined up nicely in space in single file, but there was no one anymore to say them, so let the words just line up, one after the other: the fire swept from the direction of Csabai Road and Csókos Road and Nagyváradi Road, and from the direction of the Romanian border, from the direction of Eleki Road, and within a moment it had consumed the city, and the velocity of this fire assault was so enormous, so immeasurable, that these words—which can no longer be pronounced by anyone—don't even exist, because there isn't even time for them to appear, and to tell a story about destruction—because everything happened just as in a nightmare fairy tale—here, gone, vanished—and so there was no longer any City Hall and there was no Peace Boulevard, and there was no Greater Romanian Quarter, no Lesser Romanian Quarter, no Greater Hungarian Quarter and no Krinolin, no city center, and nothing, and there was no single resident in the city anymore, because with this assault the city had renounced existence, and yet, in a strange fashion, on the city's outskirts, out there going toward Doboz, the enormous cement Water Tower still stood, even if it was seriously burning, but it stood, even if it wobbled, which meant that perhaps it too was going to collapse, and at the very top of it, from one of the empty and gaping windows of the one-time legendary Observatory—the glass had immediately been knocked out by the wave of heat—the Idiot Child dangled his feet out from the window, the Idiot Child from the Orphanage, who had been led here yesterday evening, on a whim and by the demands of his own troubled mind, he dangled his legs, and he didn't reach toward the iron frame, because he found it to be too hot, he therefore balanced his two hands farther in on the cement window ledge, at first he kicked out his left leg, then his right leg, then he got tired, and then he sawed the air with them a little, and he looked at the glowing embers that just a few moments before had been his city, and he sang softly to himself, he crooned:

*The city's burning, the city's burning,*
*Fetch the engines, fetch the engines,*
*Fire, fire, fire, fire,*
*Pour on water, pour on water.*

And he began again:

*The city's burning, the city's burning,*
*Fetch the engines, fetch the engines,*
*Fire, fire, fire, fire,*
*Pour on water, pour on water.*

There was no stopping, and then he wasn't leaning on his two hands any longer, he just sat there, swaying his body back and forth in the empty window, he looked at the smoldering ruins, the place where the city had been, and again, and always from the beginning, as the tune and the text wished it to be:

*The city's burning, the city's burning,*
*Fetch the engines, fetch the engines,*
*Fire, fire, fire, fire,*
*Pour on water, pour on water.*

And at the end he looked up to the sky, the darkening sky, raising both his hands, and as he had clearly seen someone, maybe a conductor, do before, he motioned to the invisible audience, at the same time cheerfully calling out the encouraging summons:

*And now everybody—*

*SHEET MUSIC LIBRARY*

## UTILIZED MATERIALS—MISSING:

the Professor
Little Mutt
Georg Cantor
the brown woolen coat with a black velvet collar
the Professor's daughter
the Scottish plaid scarf
Marika
Dante of Szolnok and a calfskin wallet containing 713 euros
Lenyó
the Idiot Child
Lajos and his fellow night-shift worker
tisztaeszme.hu

## UTILIZED MATERIALS—DESTROYED:

the homeless
the Mayor and the corpse of his wife
the Deputy Mayor and his family
the director of Municipal Utility Services and his employees
the Professor's weapon

the child beggars
the chief stable hand and his three assistants
the horses: Fancy, Magus, Mistletoe, and Aida
the brougham
the Headmaster
the poppy-red lipstick
the hotel manager
the hotel doorman
the employees of the hotel
the nine Prada suitcases made from ostrich leather
the kindergarten near the Castle
the pensioners in the restaurant in Krinolin (subscribers to the meal plan)
the employees of the Komló Hotel and Restaurant
the Castle guards
*The Real World,* second season
the Csepel motorbike
the director's secretary at the Slaughterhouse
the cows in the Slaughterhouse
the City Forest
the squawk box
plastic bags
the bridge on Sarkadi Road
the Reform Institute on Sarkadi Road
the train stop at Bicere with the iron stove
the ashes of Bicere in the iron stove
the matchsticks around the stove
the dog hairs in the train stop at Bicere
the bucket in the temporary flood hut on the banks of River Körös
the cooled-off ashes in the ditch in the Thorn Bush
the slot machines

the Cemetery of the Holy Trinity
the remains of the bundle of donated clothes on the square behind City Hall
the New Reform Cemetery
Turgenev
the Orthodox Cemetery in the Lesser Romanian Quarter
the pile of bones thrown into the back corner of the New Reform Cemetery
the empty wine-spritzer glass in the 47 bar
*Star* magazine with Claudia Schiffer (without makeup)
the physics teacher and the girls from the high school who were interested in chess
the wind
the priest in the Orthodox cemetery in the Lesser Romanian quarter
the gravediggers in the Orthodox cemetery in the Lesser Romanian quarter
the priest and the gravediggers in the Cemetery of the Holy Trinity
the workfare laborers in the New Reform Cemetery (in the process of being liquidated)
the house doctor from the Expanded Civic Committee
the chief secretary
the bosom of the chief secretary
the postcard showing the Castle and the boating lake
two Doberman pinschers
the Fire Chief and his subordinates
four fire trucks
Satantango
the parish priest
the Hungarian sheepdog
the bishop of the synod
Eszter and her family

unwashed pint glasses in the Biker Bar
the willow trees on the banks of the River Körös
the morgue
the Casino (the Billiard Salon)
the corpse of the library director and his glasses (prescription of 11.5)
the librarians
the books in the library (from D. Steel to Albert Wass)
Uncle Laci
the ZiL heavy truck
the Chief of Police
fourteen packs of the Egyptian Cleopatra brand of cigarettes (plus one opened pack)
King Kong, J.T., Totó, Dódi, and the Alliance of the Just
the corpse of Little Star in the grave
the fox skin (untanned)
the fox trap
the stock clerk and cashier in the shop next to the Small Protestant Church
the corpse of the Baron in the grave
Penny Market (continuous discounts)
St. Pantaleon
Kawasakis, Hondas, Yamahas, Suzukis, etc.
the dried-out rings from the pint glasses on the counter and tables of the Biker Bar
the journalists and their coworkers at the television/radio stations
one can of boiled beans with sausage
Newton's *Principia*, the Homeric epics, the Athena of Pheidias, the angels of Fra Angelico, Einstein's *Der Grundlage der allgemeinen Relativitätstheorie*, the Pāli Canon, the Bible, Bach, Zeami, Heraclitus
the corporal, the lieutenant, the constable, the sergeant, and the other coworkers at the Police Station

the track repairmen on Sarkadi Road and their foreman
the Sarkadi track supervisor
Marika's springtime reticule made of fine, light, beige-colored fabric with a golden clasp
Halics Junior
The Lencse crane rail car (invented by József Lencse)
the forest ranger and his family, their farm animals
the wild animals of the City Forest
Irén's corpse
the deer
the Trade Union Social Insurance (reading) glasses
Thucydides, Xenophon
melody motorcycle horns
the Continental typewriter
the restaurant owner in the Krinolin district
the two small envelopes (addressed with beautifully formed letters), with one letter in each
Dante of Szolnok's taxi driver
the old Chinese man and the tea leaves, men's briefs, undershirts, leisure clothes for men and women, bathrobes, socks, women's stockings, women's underwear, shoes for both sexes, children's toys made from plastic, Christmas-tree decorations, candles, lighting fixtures, cooking pots, dinnerware, screwdriver sets, tool chests, small kitchen appliances, ashtrays with the Heavenly Temple, incense, corkscrews, love amulets made of painted plastic
Auntie Ibolyka
The Budrió Housing Estate (prefab)
the house doctor
the film *Evita*, starring Madonna
the score and text to the song "Don't Cry for Me Argentina" (twenty copies)

the entire folk chorus with the choirmaster
the peasant from the farmstead
Feri
the corpse of the hang-gliding school director
the carpenter and his wife
the three members of the delegation from Szabadgyíkos
the new owner of the Professor's house, who came upon some old documents while rummaging in the attic
the Chief Editor, the section heads
the Old People's Home with the pensioners
Irén's son and his family
the former Trade Union National Council Resort
Jennifer
the Biker Bar
groats and fruit preserves
*Economic and Philosophic Manuscripts of 1844*, by Karl Marx
the bartender in the Biker Bar
the two employees who brought provisions to the homeless and the Christian volunteer
the engine driver of the "Rattler" locomotive from Csaba, the other driver on the shift and his bag
the corpses of the stationmaster and his family
the medals and insignia of the stationmaster
the counterwoman at the espresso bar
the barmaid at the 47 bar
the works of Tacitus, Cicero, and Caesar
the one-legged man in the espresso bar
the large-screened TVs across the entire city
the two nurses from the Hospital
the city photographer
*Don Segundo Sombra*

the Ford Escort (well taken care of)
the corpse of Speedy Tóni
the orphans and their caretakers
the corpses of the orphan with the mohawk and the bald orphan (the ones who ran away)
the cashier at the grocery store next to the Protestant Church
the 79th bar
30 bowties
the shop girls in the fabric shop
the TV set in the Biker Bar mounted on the iron bars
the shell chair and the sofa bed, as well as the clothes closets in Marika's apartment
the remains of the Hungarocell panels
the Aladddin with the weapons
Dóra's corpse
Dóra's father
the wheelchair
the broken brake on the wheelchair
Auntie Ibolyka's Linzer torte with two baking dishes and a basket covered by a gingham tea cloth
The Almásy Chateau
the dust mice in the large conference room in the City Hall
the shop window of the Fashion Boutique
the Greater Hungarian Quarter, the Lesser Romanian Quarter, the Greater Romanian Quarter, the German Quarter, the city center, Stréber's, Erdélyi Sándor Street, Main Street, Forget-me-not Street, Highway 44 (detour), Csabai Road, Dobozi Road, Nagyváradi Road, Csókos Road, Jókai Street, Peace Boulevard, the Meatpacking Plant, the Milk Powder Factory, Eleki Road
the intensive care ward in the Hospital
the unknown people

the envelope with a photograph inside (a young girl)
the Central Police Station
the Train Station
the pork stew

and much, much more